THE VIKING CRITICAL LIBRARY

SONS AND LOVERS

THE VIKING CRITICAL LIBRARY

MALCOLM COWLEY, General Editor

Winesburg, Ohio
BY SHERWOOD ANDERSON
EDITED BY JOHN H. FERRES

Death of a Salesman
BY ARTHUR MILLER
EDITED BY GERALD WEALES

A Portrait of the Artist as a Young Man
BY JAMES JOYCE
EDITED BY CHESTER G. ANDERSON

Dubliners
BY JAMES JOYCE
EDITED BY ROBERT SCHOLES AND A. WALTON LITZ

THE VIKING CRITICAL LIBRARY

D. H. LAWRENCE

Sons and Lovers

TEXT, BACKGROUND, AND CRITICISM

EDITED BY JULIAN MOYNAHAN
RUTGERS UNIVERSITY

NEW YORK: THE VIKING PRESS

CONTENTS

Editor's Preface   vii
A Lawrence Chronology   xi

I. *SONS AND LOVERS*: THE TEXT   1

II. *SONS AND LOVERS*: CONTEXTS OF
        RESPONSE   421

EARLY REVIEWS

The Athenæum, June 21, 1913   423
The Saturday Review (London), June 21, 1913   425
The New York Times, September 21, 1913   428

STARTING FROM THE VILLAGE

D. H. Lawrence, Nottingham and the Mining
    Countryside   432
Ada Lawrence Clarke, A Reminiscence   442
William Edward Hopkin, A Personal Memoir   446
Anonymous Eastwood Miner, A View from the Pit   452

POEMS OF A SON AND LOVER

D. H. Lawrence, From Foreword to *Collected Poems*   453
D. H. Lawrence, From Two Letters to Rachel Annand
    Taylor   455

May Chambers Holbrook, "Mother Is Dead"   457
D. H. Lawrence, Poems: 1910–1912   461
D. H. Lawrence, "Spirits Summoned West"   474

TWO WOMEN

Jessie Chambers, The Clarification That Time Brings   478
Frieda Lawrence Ravagli, As I Look Back   486

LAWRENCE AND PSYCHOANALYSIS

D. H. Lawrence, To Edward Garnett   491
Simon O. Lesser, Two Modes of Insight   493
Sigmund Freud, The Most Prevalent Form of
    Degradation in Erotic Life   498
J. Middleton Murry, Genius and a Syndrome   511
Philip Rieff, Two Honest Men   518

LAWRENCE AND LITERARY CRITICISM

Dorothy Van Ghent, On *Sons and Lovers*   527
Mark Spilka, How to Pick Flowers   547
Julian Moynahan, *Sons and Lovers*: The Search for Form   560
G. H. Ford, The "S" Curve: Persephone to Pluto   577
Alfred Kazin, Sons, Lovers and Mothers   597

Topics for Discussion and Papers   611
Bibliography   619

Editor's Preface

Sons and Lovers can be and has been read as the first great novel of English working-class life written from the standpoint of an insider; as a crucial episode in Lawrence's spiritual and psychological autobiography, providing him with opportunities to explore, evaluate, and finally transcend the confining and emotionally damaging circumstances of his early upbringing within a household constantly disturbed by parental strife and economic anxiety; and as a major work of art that enlarges the formal possibilities and greatly extends the affective range of English prose fiction in this century. To slight any of these aspects is to settle for something less than a full appreciation of a modern classic. My chief principle in selecting and arranging the material that follows the text has been simply to provide a basis for the fullest possible appreciation of *Sons and Lovers*. The literature on Lawrence, including Lawrence's own writings on himself, is vast, and the main problem has been to decide what to leave out in order to produce a book of reasonable size. But there are also the questions of where to begin and whence to proceed and where to end.

After the section "Early Reviews," recording the event of publication and indicating the first stirrings of a response in England and America, it seemed right to begin in Lawrence's home village of Eastwood, Nottinghamshire, in the industrial Midlands. Here Lawrence himself, his younger sister, an older friend, and an iconoclastic miner from the mid-1950s define, each in his own way, the specific conditions of impoverishment, physical bleakness, and familial tension in which the author's genius and the pattern of his whole career were rooted.

The next section, called "Poems of a Son and Lover," is rather special. Unlike most great novelists, Lawrence was also a substantial poet. During the years when he was coming to terms with the central emotional problems of his youth and early manhood—by writing his earliest stories and the early drafts of *Sons and Lovers*—he was also writing verses that dealt in a peculiarly naked way with the main themes and personages of *Sons and Lovers*. Included here are poems about the tie to the mother, about Miriam, about the trauma of the mother's lingering mortal illness, and about the poignant aftermath of her death during which the son suffered a self-abandonment to grief and a sense of desolation described in the novel as a *nuit blanche* or "white night." Some of these poems seem insufficiently detached from the painful events in real life that inspired them, but at least two, "End of Another Home Holiday" and the haunting, enigmatic "Spirits Summoned West," are among the finest in the Lawrence canon. All are extraordinarily illuminating with respect to a number of questions—debated by the critics for over fifty years—about *Sons and Lovers* in relation to Lawrence's personal history. More surprising, these poems have never previously been placed in close proximity to the text of the novel for the purpose of appreciative and critical comparison.

When Lawrence's mother died, his closest companion and confidant was Jessie Chambers, the person on whom the character of Miriam is based. A few years later, when Lawrence was writing the final version of *Sons and Lovers* in Italy, he had put Eastwood and "Miriam" behind him and had found the woman he would remain with for the rest of his life, Frieda Weekley, *née* von Richthofen, subsequently Frieda Lawrence. The section called "Two Women" contains the testimony of these two remarkable, sharply contrasted, yet equally appealing women, both of whom contributed to the making of a great book and a great career perhaps more than any other persons in the entire Lawrence story.

Early criticism of *Sons and Lovers* made much of its Oedipal themes, of the crippling effects of a dominant and frustrated mother's fierce love on the emotional development of her two older sons. From the vantage point of the present all this seems fairly obvious. Surely more interesting to the modern reader is the much larger question of the extent to which Lawrence,

both in *Sons and Lovers* and in his later work, parallels, sometimes disputes, yet often extends the significance of Sigmund
Freud's researches into the unconscious and into various dis-
turbances of the instinctive life in modern man. The section
called "Lawrence and Psychoanalysis" is designed to place the
novelist and the analyst in a kind of dialectical relation. Its
principal exhibit is Freud's great essay called "A Prevalent Form
of Degradation in Erotic Life," which was first published just
one year before *Sons and Lovers* and which investigates in the
language of discursive thought precisely the same "syndrome"
the novel interprets in the language of narrative art. According
to the phrase of Philip Rieff, whose subtle comparative assess-
ment of Lawrence and Freud concludes this section, the English miner's son and the Viennese physician were "two honest
men" attacking, for the sake of a renewal of human creativity
and growth, the moral and psychological diseases bred by civilization itself.

The last section contains the literary criticism proper. It is
fitting that it is by far the longest section, since Lawrence is,
after all, first and last a great literary artist. These essays are a
fair sample of the work that has been done on *Sons and Lovers*
by professional critics and scholars, but the serious reader will
no doubt wish to consult the bibliography at the end of the
volume as well and to read through "Topics for Discussion and
Papers" for further leads and further stimuli in his study of
one of the greatest twentieth-century books.

I want to conclude this preface with a personal account of
a paradoxical experience. In 1961, on the last day of February,
I traveled from London to visit Lawrence's Eastwood and spent
several hours walking through the village and out into the
nearby countryside where Paul Morel had gone cycling and
walking and flower-picking with Miriam and Clara. It was a
cold, gray, windy day. The fallow fields were brown and dank-
looking, and the hedgerows between the fields were full of
dead weeds. The brick row-houses of the village looked weather-
beaten and shabby. The air was gritty with coal dust.

At first I thought, "So this is the way it *really* was." Lawrence tried to set it all down exactly as it was, yet because he was a great imaginative writer he couldn't help making everything seem vivid and memorable and important. Paul's life had been hard, but it had also been full of magic and mystery—I thought of him going to the "Wakes" or riding his bicycle without a light down into the gulf of darkness on his way back late from Miriam's house. But I couldn't see any magic and mystery about the actual Eastwood and its neighborhood. It obviously hadn't changed much in fifty years, and it never had been anything to write home about.

A little later, I was walking up a hill in the direction of the Leivers farm, with the village at my back and the steam-plumed headstocks of a colliery off to my left. Up ahead, a farmer and his young helper were coaxing a heifer out of a stubbly pasture. Suddenly, the whole scene sprang into vivid, energetic life and became charged with the most extraordinary significance and magic. Every detail stood out sharply, yet everything fitted and flowed together and made intense, almost joyful sense.

Of course, after a while, things settled back—although not all the way back—into drabness, and I returned to London. I suppose for those few minutes I was seeing things under Lawrence's influence and in the way he habitually saw them—clearly, truly, and with a certain force of revelation.

Great writing—great art generally—redeems the drabness of the world through a visionary perspective that remains true to things as they are. *Sons and Lovers* never falsifies the facts of human failure and misery. At the same time the book shows how all human experience is immeasurably rich, potent, and charged with a mysterious promise of wholeness and joy. Like my own small experience at Eastwood, this last statement creates a paradox. Readers of this novel, after getting acquainted with the harsh and beautiful world of *Sons and Lovers*, can decide for themselves whether such paradoxes make sense.

—J.M.

A LAWRENCE
CHRONOLOGY

1885   Born in Eastwood, Nottinghamshire, England, September 11, the second son of Arthur John Lawrence, a coal miner, and Lydia Lawrence *née* Beardsall.

1898   Wins county-council scholarship and attends Nottingham High School.

1901   Leaves school and works as a clerk for three months at a surgical-appliance factory in Nottingham. Is dangerously ill of pneumonia toward the end of that year.

1903 – Becomes a "pupil-teacher" at Ilkeston, Derbyshire, for two
1906   years, followed by a year as an uncertificated teacher in the British School, Eastwood.

1906 – Attends Nottingham University College in the two-year
1907   normal-school course.

1908   Begins teaching at a boys' elementary school in Croydon, near London.

1909   His early short stories and poems are published in *The English Review*, edited by Ford Madox Ford.

1910   In partial collaboration with Jessie Chambers works on early version of *Sons and Lovers*, called *Paul Morel*. His mother dies of cancer in December, after protracted, painful illness.

1911   His first book, *The White Peacock*, is published in January. His close relationship with Jessie Chambers increasingly attenuated.

1912   Resigns his teaching post and falls in love with Frieda Weekley-Richthofen, wife of one of his former Nottingham University professors. In May he goes to the continent with Frieda. His second novel, *The Trespasser*, is published. Finishes *Sons and Lovers* in November at Gargnano, Italy.

1913   Publishes *Love Poems and Others* in February and *Sons and Lovers* in May. Returns with Frieda to England and associates with Edward Garnett, J. Middleton Murry, and Katherine Mansfield. Back on the continent by August, he begins *The Sisters*, later to become *The Rainbow* and *Women in Love*.

1 9 1 4   The Weekley divorce becomes final, and he marries Frieda in London in July. *The Prussian Officer*, his first short-story collection, published.

1 9 1 5   *The Rainbow* is published in September and is suppressed by magistrate's order within a few weeks. Meets Aldous Huxley, plans an abortive lecture series with Bertrand Russell, and edits, along with J. M. Murry and Katherine Mansfield, a short-lived antiwar magazine, *The Signature*.

1 9 1 6   Resides in Cornwall and completes *Women in Love*. Publishes first travel book, *Twilight in Italy*, and second poetry collection, *Amores*.

1 9 1 7   Expelled from Cornwall as suspected spies by the military authorities, the Lawrences live in Berkshire and London. *Look! We Have Come Through!*, poem sequence, published.

1 9 1 8   Publishes *New Poems* and begins magazine publication of *Studies in Classic American Literature*.

1 9 1 9   Leaves England, never to return except for three brief visits. Resides in Italy and publishes *Bay: A Book of Poems*.

1 9 2 0   *Women in Love* is published in New York and *The Lost Girl* (begun 1913, resumed and completed 1920) in London. Wins the James Tait Black prize for latter.

1 9 2 1   Publishes *Sea and Sardinia* and *Psychoanalysis and the Unconscious*. Resides in Taormina, Sicily.

1 9 2 2   Publishes *Aaron's Rod*, *Fantasia of the Unconscious*, and second short-story collection, *England, My England*. Visits Ceylon and Australia; writes his eighth novel, *Kangaroo*. Moves to ranch at Lobo, New Mexico, near Taos.

1 9 2 3   Visits Mexico and works on *The Plumed Serpent*. Publishes *Studies in Classic American Literature*, *Kangaroo*, and the poetry collection *Birds, Beasts and Flowers*.

1 9 2 5   Completes *The Plumed Serpent* at Oaxaca, Mexico, and suffers near-fatal illness. Returns to Europe in December.

1 9 2 6   Publishes *The Plumed Serpent*. Resides near Florence, Italy, and begins writing *Lady Chatterley's Lover*.

1 9 2 7   Publishes *Mornings in Mexico*, tours the Etruscan cities of Italy.

1 9 2 8   Completes *Lady Chatterley's Lover* and arranges its publication by private subscription. Publishes short-story collec-

tion, *The Woman Who Rode Away*. *The Collected Poems* issued in two volumes.

1 9 2 9   Legal skirmishes with British police over London exhibition of his paintings. Publishes *The Escaped Cock*, subsequently called *The Man Who Died*, and *Pornography and Obscenity*, a pamphlet attacking censorship.

1 9 3 0   Dies of tuberculosis March 2, at Vence in the south of France. *Assorted Articles, Etruscan Places*, and *À Propos of Lady Chatterley's Lover* are published posthumously.

THE LAWRENCE COUNTRY

UNDERWOOD

NEW BRINSLEY

Felley Mill
("STRELLEY MILL")

Willey
Spring
The Hagg's
("MIRIAM'S FARM")

Brinsley Hall

NOTTINGHAM AND EREWASH VALLEY LINE

Moorgreen
Reservoir
("MINTON")

High Park Wood

WILLEY LANE

Brinsley Colliery

Lambclose House

Highpark
Colliery

BRINSLEY

BEGGARLEE BROOK

Plumtree Colliery

Moorgreen
Colliery

TO NOTTINGHAM

Eastwood Hall

Cricket
Ground

Beggarlee Works

Moor Green

LANGLEY MILL

Public House

The Breach
("THE BOTTOMS")

The
Greasley
Fields

GREAT NORTHERN RAILWAY

NOTTINGHAM

THE EREWASH

NOTTINGHAM ROAD

BEGGARLEE

EASTWOOD
("BESTWOOD")

NEWTHORPE

CANAL

CANAL

BROOKHILL LEYS

DERBYSHIRE

NOTTING G HAMSHIRE

NEW EASTWOOD

NEWTHORPE
COMMON

Burkhardt

One Statute Mile

Sons and Lovers:
The Text

CONTENTS

PART I

CHAP.   PAGE

  I   THE EARLY MARRIED LIFE OF THE MORELS   I

  II THE BIRTH OF PAUL, AND ANOTHER BATTLE   26

 III THE CASTING OFF OF MOREL—THE TAKING ON
      OF WILLIAM   45

 IV THE YOUNG LIFE OF PAUL   57

  V PAUL LAUNCHES INTO LIFE   83

 VI DEATH IN THE FAMILY   113

PART II

 VII LAD-AND-GIRL LOVE   142

VIII STRIFE IN LOVE   179

 IX DEFEAT OF MIRIAM   215

  X CLARA   252

 XI THE TEST ON MIRIAM   278

 XII PASSION   301

XIII BAXTER DAWES   341

XIV THE RELEASE   379

 XV DERELICT   409

PART ONE

CHAPTER I

THE EARLY MARRIED LIFE OF THE MORELS

"The Bottoms" succeeded to "Hell Row". Hell Row was a
block of thatched, bulging cottages that stood by the brook-
side on Greenhill Lane. There lived the colliers who worked
in the little gin-pits two fields away. The brook ran under the
alder trees, scarcely soiled by these small mines, whose coal
was drawn to the surface by donkeys that plodded wearily in
a circle round a gin. And all over the countryside were these
same pits, some of which had been worked in the time of
Charles II, the few colliers and the donkeys burrowing down
like ants into the earth, making queer mounds and little black
places among the corn-fields and the meadows. And the
cottages of these coal-miners, in blocks and pairs here and
there, together with odd farms and homes of the stockingers,
straying over the parish, formed the village of Bestwood.

Then, some sixty years ago, a sudden change took place.
The gin-pits were elbowed aside by the large mines of the
financiers. The coal and iron field of Nottinghamshire and
Derbyshire was discovered. Carston, Waite and Co. appeared.
Amid tremendous excitement, Lord Palmerston formally opened
the company's first mine at Spinney Park, on the edge of Sherwood Forest.

About this time the notorious Hell Row, which through
growing old had acquired an evil reputation, was burned down,
and much dirt was cleansed away.

Carston, Waite & Co. found they had struck on a good thing,
so, down the valleys of the brooks from Selby and Nuttall,
new mines were sunk, until soon there were six pits working.
From Nuttall, high up on the sandstone among the woods, the
railway ran, past the ruined priory of the Carthusians and past
Robin Hood's Well, down to Spinney Park, then on to Minton,
a large mine among corn-fields; from Minton across the farm-
lands of the valleyside to Bunker's Hill, branching off there,
and running north to Beggarlee and Selby, that looks over at
Crich and the hills of Derbyshire: six mines like black studs

on the countryside, linked by a loop of fine chain, the railway.

To accommodate the regiments of miners, Carston, Waite and Co. built the Squares, great quadrangles of dwellings on the hillside of Bestwood, and then, in the brook valley, on the site of Hell Row, they erected the Bottoms.

The Bottoms consisted of six blocks of miners' dwellings, two rows of three, like the dots on a blank-six domino, and twelve houses in a block. This double row of dwellings sat at the foot of the rather sharp slope from Bestwood, and looked out, from the attic windows at least, on the slow climb of the valley towards Selby.

The houses themselves were substantial and very decent. One could walk all round, seeing little front gardens with auriculas and saxifrage in the shadow of the bottom block, sweet-williams and pinks in the sunny top block; seeing neat front windows, little porches, little privet hedges, and dormer windows for the attics. But that was outside; that was the view on to the uninhabited parlours of all the colliers' wives. The dwelling-room, the kitchen, was at the back of the house, facing inward between the blocks, looking at a scrubby back garden, and then at the ash-pits. And between the rows, between the long lines of ash-pits, went the alley, where the children played and the women gossiped and the men smoked. So, the actual conditions of living in the Bottoms, that was so well built and that looked so nice, were quite unsavoury because people must live in the kitchen, and the kitchens opened on to that nasty alley of ash-pits.

Mrs. Morel was not anxious to move into the Bottoms, which was already twelve years old and on the downward path, when she descended to it from Bestwood. But it was the best she could do. Moreover, she had an end house in one of the top blocks, and thus had only one neighbour; on the other side an extra strip of garden. And, having an end house, she enjoyed a kind of aristocracy among the other women of the "between" houses, because her rent was five shillings and sixpence instead of five shillings a week. But this superiority in station was not much consolation to Mrs. Morel.

She was thirty-one years old, and had been married eight years. A rather small woman, of delicate mould but resolute bearing, she shrank a little from the first contact with the Bottoms women. She came down in the July, and in the September expected her third baby.

Her husband was a miner. They had only been in their new home three weeks when the wakes, or fair, began. Morel, she knew, was sure to make a holiday of it. He went off early on the Monday morning, the day of the fair. The two children were highly excited. William, a boy of seven, fled off immediately after breakfast, to prowl round the wakes ground, leaving Annie, who was only five, to whine all morning to go also. Mrs. Morel did her work. She scarcely knew her neighbours yet, and knew no one with whom to trust the little girl. So she promised to take her to the wakes after dinner.

William appeared at half-past twelve. He was a very active lad, fair-haired, freckled, with a touch of the Dane or Norwegian about him.

"Can I have my dinner, mother?" he cried, rushing in with his cap on. " 'Cause it begins at half-past one, the man says so."

"You can have your dinner as soon as it's done," replied the mother.

"Isn't it done?" he cried, his blue eyes staring at her in indignation. "Then I'm goin' be-out it."

"You'll do nothing of the sort. It will be done in five minutes. It is only half-past twelve."

"They'll be beginnin'," the boy half cried, half shouted.

"You won't die if they do," said the mother. "Besides, it's only half-past twelve, so you've a full hour."

The lad began hastily to lay the table, and directly the three sat down. They were eating batter-pudding and jam, when the boy jumped off his chair and stood perfectly still. Some distance away could be heard the first small braying of a merry-go-round, and the tooting of a horn. His face quivered as he looked at his mother.

"I told you!" he said, running to the dresser for his cap.

"Take your pudding in your hand—and it's only five past one, so you were wrong—you haven't got your twopence," cried the mother in a breath.

The boy came back, bitterly disappointed, for his twopence, then went off without a word.

"I want to go, I want to go," said Annie, beginning to cry.

"Well, and you shall go, whining, wizzening little stick!" said the mother. And later in the afternoon she trudged up the hill under the tall hedge with her child. The hay was gathered from the fields, and cattle were turned on to the eddish. It was warm, peaceful.

Mrs. Morel did not like the wakes. There were two sets of horses, one going by steam, one pulled round by a pony; three organs were grinding, and there came odd cracks of pistol-shots, fearful screeching of the cocoanut man's rattle, shouts of the Aunt Sally man, screeches from the peep-show lady. The mother perceived her son gazing enraptured outside the Lion Wallace booth, at the pictures of this famous lion that had killed a negro and maimed for life two white men. She left him alone, and went to get Annie a spin of toffee. Presently the lad stood in front of her, wildly excited.

"You never said you was coming—isn't the' a lot of things? —that lion's killed three men—I've spent my tuppence—an' look here."

He pulled from his pocket two egg-cups, with pink moss-roses on them.

"I got these from that stall where y'ave ter get them marbles in them holes. An' I got these two in two goes—'aepenny a go —they've got moss-roses on, look here. I wanted these."

She knew he wanted them for her.

"H'm!" she said, pleased. "They *are* pretty!"

"Shall you carry 'em, 'cause I'm frightened o' breakin' 'em?"

He was tipful of excitement now she had come, led her about the ground, showed her everything. Then, at the peep-show, she explained the pictures, in a sort of story, to which he listened as if spellbound. He would not leave her. All the time he stuck close to her, bristling with a small boy's pride of her. For no other woman looked such a lady as she did, in her little black bonnet and her cloak. She smiled when she saw women she knew. When she was tired she said to her son:

"Well, are you coming now, or later?"

"Are you goin' a'ready?" he cried, his face full of reproach.

"Already? It is past four, *I* know."

"What are you goin' a'ready for?" he lamented.

"You needn't come if you don't want," she said.

And she went slowly away with her little girl, whilst her son stood watching her, cut to the heart to let her go, and yet unable to leave the wakes. As she crossed the open ground in front of the Moon and Stars she heard men shouting, and smelled the beer, and hurried a little, thinking her husband was probably in the bar.

At about half-past six her son came home, tired now, rather pale, and somewhat wretched. He was miserable, though he did not know it, because he had let her go alone. Since she had gone, he had not enjoyed his wakes.

"Has my dad been?" he asked.

"No," said the mother.

"He's helping to wait at the Moon and Stars. I seed him through that black tin stuff wi' holes in, on the window, wi' his sleeves rolled up."

"Ha!" exclaimed the mother shortly. "He's got no money. An' he'll be satisfied if he gets his 'lowance, whether they give him more or not."

When the light was fading, and Mrs. Morel could see no more to sew, she rose and went to the door. Everywhere was the sound of excitement, the restlessness of the holiday, that at last infected her. She went out into the side garden. Women were coming home from the wakes, the children hugging a white lamb with green legs, or a wooden horse. Occasionally a man lurched past, almost as full as he could carry. Sometimes a good husband came along with his family, peacefully. But usually the women and children were alone. The stay-at-home mothers stood gossiping at the corners of the alley, as the twilight sank, folding their arms under their white aprons.

Mrs. Morel was alone, but she was used to it. Her son and her little girl slept upstairs; so, it seemed, her home was there behind her, fixed and stable. But she felt wretched with the coming child. The world seemed a dreary place, where nothing else would happen for her—at least until William grew up. But for herself, nothing but this dreary endurance—till the children grew up. And the children! She could not afford to have this third. She did not want it. The father was serving beer in a public house, swilling himself drunk. She despised him, and was tied to him. This coming child was too much for her. If it were not for William and Annie, she was sick of it, the struggle with poverty and ugliness and meanness.

She went into the front garden, feeling too heavy to take herself out, yet unable to stay indoors. The heat suffocated her. And looking ahead, the prospect of her life made her feel as if she were buried alive.

The front garden was a small square with a privet hedge. There she stood, trying to soothe herself with the scent of flowers and the fading, beautiful evening. Opposite her small gate was the stile that led uphill, under the tall hedge between the burning glow of the cut pastures. The sky overhead throbbed and pulsed with light. The glow sank quickly off the field; the earth and the hedges smoked dusk. As it grew dark, a ruddy glare came out on the hilltop, and out of the glare the diminished commotion of the fair.

Sometimes, down the trough of darkness formed by the path under the hedges, men came lurching home. One young man lapsed into a run down the steep bit that ended the hill, and went with a crash into the stile. Mrs. Morel shuddered. He picked himself up, swearing viciously, rather pathetically, as if he thought the stile had wanted to hurt him.

She went indoors, wondering if things were never going to alter. She was beginning by now to realise that they would not. She seemed so far away from her girlhood, she wondered if it were the same person walking heavily up the back garden at the Bottoms as had run so lightly up the breakwater at Sheerness ten years before.

"What have *I* to do with it?" she said to herself. "What have I to do with all this? Even the child I am going to have! It doesn't seem as if *I* were taken into account."

Sometimes life takes hold of one, carries the body along, accomplishes one's history, and yet is not real, but leaves oneself as it were slurred over.

"I wait," Mrs. Morel said to herself—"I wait, and what I wait for can never come."

Then she straightened the kitchen, lit the lamp, mended the fire, looked out the washing for the next day, and put it to soak. After which she sat down to her sewing. Through the long hours her needle flashed regularly through the stuff. Occasionally she sighed, moving to relieve herself. And all the time she was thinking how to make the most of what she had, for the children's sakes.

At half-past eleven her husband came. His cheeks were very red and very shiny above his black moustache. His head nodded slightly. He was pleased with himself.

"Oh! Oh! waitin' for me, lass? I've bin 'elpin' Anthony, an' what's think he's gen me? Nowt b'r a lousy hae'f-crown, an' that's ivry penny——"

"He thinks you've made the rest up in beer," she said shortly.

"An' I 'aven't—that I 'aven't. You b'lieve me, I've 'ad very little this day, I have an' all." His voice went tender. "Here, an' I browt thee a bit o' brandysnap, an' a cocoanut for th' children." He laid the gingerbread and the cocoanut, a hairy object, on the table. "Nay, tha niver said thankyer for nowt i' thy life, did ter?"

As a compromise, she picked up the cocoanut and shook it, to see if it had any milk.

"It's a good 'un, you may back yer life o' that. I got it fra' Bill Hodgkisson. 'Bill,' I says, 'tha non wants them three nuts, does ter? Arena ter for gi'ein' me one for my bit of a lad an' wench?' 'I ham, Walter, my lad,' 'e says; 'ta'e which on 'em ter's a mind.' An' so I took one, an' thanked 'im. I didn't like ter shake it afore 'is eyes, but 'e says, 'Tha'd better ma'e sure it's a good un, Walt.' An' so, yer see, I knowed it was. He's a nice chap, is Bill Hodgkisson, 'e's a nice chap!"

"A man will part with anything so long as he's drunk, and you're drunk along with him," said Mrs. Morel.

"Eh, tha mucky little 'ussy, who's drunk, I sh'd like ter know?" said Morel. He was extraordinarily pleased with himself, because of his day's helping to wait in the Moon and Stars. He chattered on.

Mrs. Morel, very tired, and sick of his babble, went to bed as quickly as possible, while he raked the fire.

Mrs. Morel came of a good old burgher family, famous independents who had fought with Colonel Hutchinson, and who remained stout Congregationalists. Her grandfather had gone bankrupt in the lace-market at a time when so many lace-manufacturers were ruined in Nottingham. Her father, George Coppard, was an engineer—a large, handsome, haughty man, proud of his fair skin and blue eyes, but more proud still of his integrity. Gertrude resembled her mother in her small build. But her temper, proud and unyielding, she had from the Coppards.

George Coppard was bitterly galled by his own poverty. He became foreman of the engineers in the dockyard at Sheerness. Mrs. Morel—Gertrude—was the second daughter. She favoured her mother, loved her mother best of all; but she had the Coppards' clear, defiant blue eyes and their broad brow. She remembered to have hated her father's overbearing manner towards her gentle, humorous, kindly-souled mother. She remembered running over the breakwater at Sheerness and finding the boat. She remembered to have been petted and flattered by all the men when she had gone to the dockyard, for she was a delicate, rather proud child. She remembered the funny old mistress, whose assistant she had become, whom she had loved to help in the private school. And she still had the Bible that John Field had given her. She used to walk home from chapel with John Field when she was nineteen. He was the son of a well-to-do tradesman, had been to college in London, and was to devote himself to business.

She could always recall in detail a September Sunday afternoon, when they had sat under the vine at the back of her father's house. The sun came through the chinks of the vine-leaves and made beautiful patterns, like a lace scarf, falling on her and on him. Some of the leaves were clean yellow, like yellow flat flowers.

"Now sit still," he had cried. "Now your hair, I don't know what it *is* like! It's a bright as copper and gold, as red as burnt copper, and it has gold threads where the sun shines on it. Fancy their saying it's brown. Your mother calls it mouse-colour."

She had met his brilliant eyes, but her clear face scarcely showed the elation which rose within her.

"But you say you don't like business," she pursued.

"I don't. I hate it!" he cried hotly.

"And you would like to go into the ministry," she half implored.

"I should. I should love it, if I thought I could make a first-rate preacher."

"Then why don't you—why *don't* you?" Her voice rang with defiance. "If *I* were a man, nothing would stop me."

She held her head erect. He was rather timid before her.

"But my father's so stiff-necked. He means to put me into the business, and I know he'll do it."

"But if you're a *man*?" she had cried.

"Being a man isn't everything," he replied, frowning with puzzled helplessness.

Now, as she moved about her work at the Bottoms, with some experience of what being a man meant, she knew that it was *not* everything.

At twenty, owing to her health, she had left Sheerness. Her father had retired home to Nottingham. John Field's father had been ruined; the son had gone as a teacher in Norwood. She did not hear of him until, two years later, she made determined inquiry. He had married his landlady, a woman of forty, a widow with property.

And still Mrs. Morel preserved John Field's Bible. She did not now believe him to be—— Well, she understood pretty well what he might or might not have been. So she preserved his Bible, and kept his memory intact in her heart, for her own sake. To her dying day, for thirty-five years, she did not speak of him.

When she was twenty-three years old, she met, at a Christmas party, a young man from the Erewash Valley. Morel was then twenty-seven years old. He was well set-up, erect, and very smart. He had wavy black hair that shone again, and a vigorous black beard that had never been shaved. His cheeks were ruddy, and his red, moist mouth was noticeable because he laughed so often and so heartily. He had that rare thing, a rich, ringing laugh. Gertrude Coppard had watched him, fascinated. He was so full of colour and animation, his voice ran so easily into comic grotesque, he was so ready and so pleasant with everybody. Her own father had a rich fund of humour, but it was satiric. This man's was different: soft, non-intellectual, warm, a kind of gambolling.

She herself was opposite. She had a curious, receptive mind which found much pleasure and amusement in listening to other folk. She was clever in leading folk to talk. She loved ideas, and was considered very intellectual. What she liked most of all was an argument on religion or philosophy or politics with some educated man. This she did not often enjoy. So she always had people tell her about themselves, finding her pleasure so.

In her person she was rather small and delicate, with a large brow, and dropping bunches of brown silk curls. Her blue eyes were very straight, honest, and searching. She had the beautiful hands of the Coppards. Her dress was always subdued. She wore dark blue silk, with a peculiar silver chain of silver scallops. This, and a heavy brooch of twisted gold, was her only ornament. She was still perfectly intact, deeply religious, and full of beautiful candour.

Walter Morel seemed melted away before her. She was to the miner that thing of mystery and fascination, a lady. When she spoke to him, it was with a southern pronunciation and a purity of English which thrilled him to hear. She watched him. He danced well, as if it were natural and joyous in him to dance. His grandfather was a French refugee who had married an English barmaid—if it had been a marriage. Gertrude Coppard watched the young miner as he danced, a certain

subtle exultation like glamour in his movement, and his face
the flower of his body, ruddy, with tumbled black hair, and
laughing alike whatever partner he bowed above. She thought
him rather wonderful, never having met anyone like him. Her
father was to her the type of all men. And George Coppard,
proud in his bearing, handsome, and rather bitter; who preferred
theology in reading, and who drew near in sympathy only to
one man, the Apostle Paul; who was harsh in government, and
in familiarity ironic; who ignored all sensuous pleasure:—he
was very different from the miner. Gertrude herself was rather
contemptuous of dancing; she had not the slightest inclination
towards that accomplishment, and had never learned even a
Roger de Coverley. She was puritan, like her father, high-
minded, and really stern. Therefore the dusky, golden softness of this man's sensuous flame of life, that flowed off his
flesh like the flame from a candle, not baffled and gripped into
incandescence by thought and spirit as her life was, seemed to
her something wonderful, beyond her.

He came and bowed above her. A warmth radiated through
her as if she had drunk wine.

"Now do come and have this one wi' me," he said caressively.
"It's easy, you know. I'm pining to see you dance."

She had told him before she could not dance. She glanced at
his humility and smiled. Her smile was very beautiful. It
moved the man so that he forgot everything.

"No, I won't dance," she said softly. Her words came clean
and ringing.

Not knowing what he was doing—he often did the right thing
by instinct—he sat beside her, inclining reverentially.

"But you mustn't miss your dance," she reproved.

"Nay, I don't want to dance that—it's not one as I care
about."

"Yet you invited me to it."

He laughed very heartily at this.

"I never thought o' that. Tha'rt not long in taking the curl
out of me."

It was her turn to laugh quickly.

"You don't look as if you'd come much uncurled," she said.

"I'm like a pig's tail, I curl because I canna help it," he
laughed, rather boisterously.

"And you are a miner!" she exclaimed in surprise.

"Yes. I went down when I was ten."

She looked at him in wondering dismay.

"When you were ten! And wasn't it very hard?" she asked.

"You soon get used to it. You live like th' mice, an' you pop out at night to see what's going on."

"It makes me feel blind," she frowned.

"Like a moudiwarp!" he laughed. "Yi, an' there's some chaps as does go round like moudiwarps." He thrust his face forward in the blind, snout-like way of a mole, seeming to sniff and peer for direction. "They dun though!" he protested naïvely. "Tha niver seed such a way they get in. But tha mun let me ta'e thee down some time, an' tha can see for thysen."

She looked at him, startled. This was a new tract of life suddenly opened before her. She realised the life of the miners, hundreds of them toiling below earth and coming up at evening. He seemed to her noble. He risked his life daily, and with gaiety. She looked at him, with a touch of appeal in her pure humility.

"Shouldn't ter like it?" he asked tenderly. " 'Appen not, it 'ud dirty thee."

She had never been "thee'd" and "thou'd" before.

The next Christmas they were married, and for three months she was perfectly happy: for six months she was very happy.

He had signed the pledge, and wore the blue ribbon of a tee-totaller: he was nothing if not showy. They lived, she thought, in his own house. It was small, but convenient enough, and quite nicely furnished, with solid, worthy stuff that suited her honest soul. The women, her neighbours, were rather foreign to her, and Morel's mother and sisters were apt to sneer at her ladylike ways. But she could perfectly well live by herself, so long as she had her husband close.

Sometimes, when she herself wearied of love-talk, she tried to open her heart seriously to him. She saw him listen defer-entially, but without understanding. This killed her efforts at a finer intimacy, and she had flashes of fear. Sometimes he was restless of an evening: it was not enough for him just to be near her, she realised. She was glad when he set himself to little jobs.

He was a remarkably handy man—could make or mend any-thing. So she would say:

"I do like that coal-rake of your mother's—it is small and natty."

"Does ter, my wench? Well, I made that, so I can make thee one!"

"What! why, it's a steel one!"

"An' what if it is! Tha s'lt ha'e one very similar, if not exactly same."

She did not mind the mess, nor the hammering and noise. He was busy and happy.

But in the seventh month, when she was brushing his Sunday coat, she felt papers in the breast pocket, and, seized with a sudden curiosity, took them out to read. He very rarely wore the frock-coat he was married in: and it had not occurred to her before to feel curious concerning the papers. They were the bills of the household furniture, still unpaid.

"Look here," she said at night, after he was washed and had had his dinner. "I found these in the pocket of your wedding-coat. Haven't you settled the bills yet?"

"No. I haven't had a chance."

"But you told me all was paid. I had better go into Nottingham on Saturday and settle them. I don't like sitting on another man's chairs and eating from an unpaid table."

He did not answer.

"I can have your bank-book, can't I?"

"Tha can ha'e it, for what good it'll be to thee."

"I thought——" she began. He had told her had a good bit of money left over. But she realised it was no use asking questions. She sat rigid with bitterness and indignation.

The next day she went down to see his mother.

"Didn't you buy the furniture for Walter?" she asked.

"Yes, I did," tartly retorted the elder woman.

"And how much did he give you to pay for it?"

The elder woman was stung with fine indignation.

"Eighty pound, if you're so keen on knowin'," she replied.

"Eighty pounds! But there are forty-two pounds still owing!"

"I can't help that."

"But where has it all gone?"

"You'll find all the papers, I think, if you look—beside ten pound as he owed me, an' six pound as the wedding cost down here."

"Six pounds!" echoed Gertrude Morel. It seemed to her monstrous that, after her own father had paid so heavily for her wedding, six pounds more should have been squandered in eating and drinking at Walter's parents' house, at his expense.

"And how much has he sunk in his houses?" she asked.

"His houses—which houses?"

Gertrude Morel went white to the lips. He had told her the
house he lived in, and the next one, was his own.

"I thought the house we live in——" she began.

"They're my houses, those two," said the mother-in-law.
"And not clear either. It's as much as I can do to keep the
mortgage interest paid."

Gertrude sat white and silent. She was her father now.

"Then we ought to be paying you rent," she said coldly.

"Walter is paying me rent," replied the mother.

"And what rent?" asked Gertrude.

"Six and six a week," retorted the mother.

It was more than the house was worth. Gertrude held her
head erect, looked straight before her.

"It is lucky to be you," said the elder woman, bitingly, "to
have a husband as takes all the worry of the money, and leaves
you a free hand."

The young wife was silent.

She said very little to her husband, but her manner had
changed towards him. Something in her proud, honourable soul
had crystallised out hard as rock.

When October came in, she thought only of Christmas. Two
years ago, at Christmas, she had met him. Last Christmas
she had married him. This Christmas she would bear him a
child.

"You don't dance yourself, do you, missis?" asked her nearest
neighbour, in October, when there was great talk of opening a
dancing-class over the Brick and Tile Inn at Bestwood.

"No—I never had the least inclination to," Mrs. Morel
replied.

"Fancy! An' how funny as you should ha' married your
Mester. You know he's quite a famous one for dancing."

"I didn't know he was famous," laughed Mrs. Morel.

"Yea, he is though! Why, he ran that dancing-class in the
Miners' Arms club-room for over five year."

"Did he?"

"Yes, he did." The other woman was defiant. "An' it was
thronged every Tuesday, and Thursday, an' Sat'day—an' there
was carryin's-on, accordin' to all accounts."

This kind of thing was gall and bitterness to Mrs. Morel, and
she had a fair share of it. The women did not spare her, at first;
for she was superior, though she could not help it.

He began to be rather late in coming home.

"They're working very late now, aren't they?" she said to her washer-woman.

"No later than they allers do, I don't think. But they stop to have their pint at Ellen's, an' they get talkin', an' there you are! Dinner stone cold—an' it serves 'em right."

"But Mr. Morel does not take any drink."

The woman dropped the clothes, looked at Mrs. Morel, then went on with her work, saying nothing.

Gertrude Morel was very ill when the boy was born. Morel was good to her, as good as gold. But she felt very lonely, miles away from her own people. She felt lonely with him now, and his presence only made it more intense.

The boy was small and frail at first, but he came on quickly. He was a beautiful child, with dark gold ringlets, and dark-blue eyes which changed gradually to a clear grey. His mother loved him passionately. He came just when her own bitterness of disillusion was hardest to bear; when her faith in life was shaken, and her soul felt dreary and lonely. She made much of the child, and the father was jealous.

At last Mrs. Morel despised her husband. She turned to the child; she turned from the father. He had begun to neglect her; the novelty of his own home was gone. He had no grit, she said bitterly to herself. What he felt just at the minute, that was all to him. He could not abide by anything. There was nothing at the back of all his show.

There began a battle between the husband and wife—a fearful, bloody battle that ended only with the death of one. She fought to make him undertake his own responsibilities, to make him fulfil his obligations. But he was too different from her. His nature was purely sensuous, and she strove to make him moral, religious. She tried to force him to face things. He could not endure it—it drove him out of his mind.

While the baby was still tiny, the father's temper had become so irritable that it was not to be trusted. The child had only to give a little trouble when the man began to bully. A little more, and the hard hands of the collier hit the baby. Then Mrs. Morel loathed her husband, loathed him for days; and he went out and drank; and she cared very little what he did. Only, on his return, she scathed him with her satire.

The estrangement between them caused him, knowingly or unknowingly, grossly to offend her where he would not have done.

William was only one year old, and his mother was proud of him, he was so pretty. She was not well off now, but her sisters kept the boy in clothes. Then, with his little white hat curled with an ostrich feather, and his white coat, he was a joy to her, the twining wisps of hair clustering round his head. Mrs. Morel lay listening, one Sunday morning, to the chatter of the father and child downstairs. Then she dozed off. When she came downstairs, a great fire glowed in the grate, the room was hot, the breakfast was roughly laid, and seated in his arm-chair, against the chimney-piece, sat Morel, rather timid; and standing between his legs, the child—cropped like a sheep, with such an odd round poll—looking wondering at her; and on a newspaper spread out upon the hearthrug, a myriad of crescent-shaped curls, like the petals of a marigold scattered in the reddening firelight.

Mrs. Morel stood still. It was her first baby. She went very white, and was unable to speak.

"What dost think o' 'im?" Morel laughed uneasily.

She gripped her two fists, lifted them, and came forward. Morel shrank back.

"I could kill you, I could!" she said. She choked with rage, her two fists uplifted.

"Yer non want ter make a wench on 'im," Morel said, in a frightened tone, bending his head to shield his eyes from hers. His attempt at laughter had vanished.

The mother looked down at the jagged, close-clipped head of her child. She put her hands on his hair, and stroked and fondled his head.

"Oh—my boy!" she faltered. Her lip trembled, her face broke, and, snatching up the child, she buried her face in his shoulder and cried painfully. She was one of those women who cannot cry; whom it hurts as it hurts a man. It was like ripping something out of her, her sobbing.

Morel sat with his elbows on his knees, his hands gripped together till the knuckles were white. He gazed in the fire, feeling almost stunned, as if he could not breathe.

Presently she came to an end, soothed the child and cleared away the breakfast-table. She left the newspaper, littered with curls, spread upon the hearth-rug. At last her husband gathered it up and put it at the back of the fire. She went about her work with closed mouth and very quiet. Morel was subdued. He crept about wretchedly, and his meals were a misery that day. She spoke to him civilly, and never alluded to what he had done. But he felt something final had happened.

Afterwards she said she had been silly, that the boy's hair would have had to be cut, sooner or later. In the end, she even brought herself to say to her husband it was just as well he had played barber when he did. But she knew, and Morel knew, that that act had caused something momentous to take place in her soul. She remembered the scene all her life, as one in which she had suffered the most intensely.

This act of masculine clumsiness was the spear through the side of her love for Morel. Before, while she had striven against him bitterly, she had fretted after him, as if he had gone astray from her. Now she ceased to fret for his love: he was an outsider to her. This made life much more bearable.

Nevertheless, she still continued to strive with him. She still had her high moral sense, inherited from generations of Puritans. It was now a religious instinct, and she was almost a fanatic with him, because she loved him, or had loved him. If he sinned, she tortured him. If he drank, and lied, was often a poltroon, sometimes a knave, she wielded the lash unmercifully.

The pity was, she was too much his opposite. She could not be content with the little he might be; she would have him the much that he ought to be. So, in seeking to make him nobler than he could be, she destroyed him. She injured and hurt and scarred herself, but she lost none of her worth. She also had the children.

He drank rather heavily, though not more than many miners, and always beer, so that whilst his health was affected, it was never injured. The week-end was his chief carouse. He sat in the Miners' Arms until turning-out time every Friday, every Saturday, and every Sunday evening. On Monday and Tuesday he had to get up and reluctantly leave towards ten o'clock. Sometimes he stayed at home on Wednesday and Thursday evenings, or was only out for an hour. He practically never had to miss work owing to his drinking.

But although he was very steady at work, his wages fell off. He was blab-mouthed, a tongue-wagger. Authority was hateful to him, therefore he could only abuse the pit-managers. He would say, in the Palmerston:

"Th' gaffer come down to our stall this morning, an' 'e says, 'You know, Walter, this 'ere'll not do. What about these props?' An' I says to him, 'Why, what art talkin' about? What d'st mean about th' props?' 'It'll never do, this 'ere,' 'e says. 'You'll be havin' th' roof in, one o' these days.' An' I says, 'Tha'd better stan' on a bit o' clunch, then, an' hold it up wi' thy 'ead.' So 'e wor that mad, 'e cossed an' 'e swore, an' t'other chaps they did laugh." Morel was a good mimic. He imitated the manager's fat, squeaky voice, with its attempt at good English.

" 'I shan't have it, Walter. Who knows more about it, me or you?' So I says, 'I've niver fun out how much tha' knows, Alfred. It'll 'appen carry thee ter bed an' back.' "

So Morel would go on to the amusement of his boon companions. And some of this would be true. The pit-manager was not an educated man. He had been a boy along with Morel, so that, while the two disliked each other, they more or less took each other for granted. But Alfred Charlesworth did not forgive the butty these public-house sayings. Consequently, although Morel was a good miner, sometimes earning as much as five pounds a week when he married, he came gradually to have worse and worse stalls, where the coal was thin, and hard to get, and unprofitable.

Also, in summer, the pits are slack. Often, on bright sunny mornings, the men are seen trooping home again at ten, eleven, or twelve o'clock. No empty trucks stand at the pit-mouth. The women on the hillside look across as they shake the hearth-rug against the fence, and count the wagons the engine is taking along the line up the valley. And the children, as they come from school at dinner-time, looking down the fields and seeing the wheels on the headstocks standing, say:

"Minton's knocked off. My dad'll be at home."

And there is a sort of shadow over all, women and children and men, because money will be short at the end of the week.

Morel was supposed to give his wife thirty shillings a week, to provide everything—rent, food, clothes, clubs, insurance, doctors. Occasionally, if he were flush, he gave her thirty-five. But these occasions by no means balanced those when he gave her twenty-five. In winter, with a decent stall, the miner might earn fifty or fifty-five shillings a week. Then he was happy. On Friday night, Saturday, and Sunday, he spent royally, getting rid of his sovereign or thereabouts. And out of so much, he scarcely spared the children an extra penny or bought them a pound of apples. It all went in drink. In the bad times, matters were more worrying, but he was not so often drunk, so that Mrs. Morel used to say:

"I'm not sure I wouldn't rather be short, for when he's flush, there isn't a minute of peace."

If he earned forty shillings he kept ten; from thirty-five he kept five; from thirty-two he kept four; from twenty-eight he kept three; from twenty-four he kept two; from twenty he kept one-and-six; from eighteen he kept a shilling; from sixteen he kept sixpence. He never saved a penny, and he gave his wife no opportunity of saving; instead, she had occasionally to pay his debts; not public-house debts, for those never were passed on to the women, but debts when he had bought a canary, or a fancy walking-stick.

At the wakes time Morel was working badly, and Mrs. Morel was trying to save against her confinement. So it galled her bitterly to think he should be out taking his pleasure and spending money, whilst she remained at home, harassed. There were two days' holiday. On the Tuesday morning Morel rose early. He was in good spirits. Quite early, before six o'clock, she heard him whistling away to himself downstairs. He had a pleasant way of whistling, lively and musical. He nearly always whistled hymns. He had been a choir-boy with a beautiful voice, and had taken solos in Southwell cathedral. His morning whistling alone betrayed it.

His wife lay listening to him tinkering away in the garden, his whistling ringing out as he sawed and hammered away. It always gave her a sense of warmth and peace to hear him thus as she lay in bed, the children not yet awake, in the bright early morning, happy in his man's fashion.

At nine o'clock, while the children with bare legs and feet were sitting playing on the sofa, and the mother was washing up, he came in from his carpentry, his sleeves rolled up, his waistcoat hanging open. He was still a good-looking man, with black, wavy hair, and a large black moustache. His face was perhaps too much inflamed, and there was about him a look almost of peevishness. But now he was jolly. He went straight to the sink where his wife was washing up.

"What, are thee there!" he said boisterously. "Sluthe off an' let me wesh mysen."

"You may wait till I've finished," said his wife.

"Oh, mun I? An' what if I shonna?"

This good-humoured threat amused Mrs. Morel.

"Then you can go and wash yourself in the soft-water tub."

"Ha! I can' an' a', tha mucky little 'ussy."

With which he stood watching her a moment, then went away to wait for her.

When he chose he could still make himself again a real gallant. Usually he preferred to go out with a scarf round his neck. Now, however, he made a toilet. There seemed so much gusto in the way he puffed and swilled as he washed himself, so much alacrity with which he hurried to the mirror in the kitchen, and, bending because it was too low for him, scrupulously parted his wet black hair, that it irritated Mrs. Morel. He put on a turn-down collar, a black bow, and wore his Sunday tail-coat. As such, he looked spruce, and what his clothes would not do, his instinct for making the most of his good looks would.

At half-past nine Jerry Purdy came to call for his pal. Jerry was Morel's bosom friend, and Mrs. Morel disliked him. He was a tall, thin man, with a rather foxy face, the kind of face that seems to lack eyelashes. He walked with a stiff, brittle dignity, as if his head were on a wooden spring. His nature was cold and shrewd. Generous where he intended to be generous, he seemed to be very fond of Morel, and more or less to take charge of him.

Mrs. Morel hated him. She had known his wife, who had died of consumption, and who had, at the end, conceived such a violent dislike of her husband, that if he came into her room it caused her hæmorrhage. None of which Jerry had seemed to mind. And now his eldest daughter, a girl of fifteen, kept a poor house for him, and looked after the two younger children.

"A mean, wizzen-hearted stick!" Mrs. Morel said of him.

"I've never known Jerry mean in *my* life," protested Morel. "A opener-handed and more freer chap you couldn't find anywhere, accordin' to my knowledge."

"Open-handed to you," retorted Mrs. Morel. "But his fist is shut tight enough to his children, poor things."

"Poor things! And what for are they poor things, I should like to know."

But Mrs. Morel would not be appeased on Jerry's score.

The subject of argument was seen, craning his thin neck over the scullery curtain. He caught Mrs. Morel's eye.

"Mornin', missis! Mester in?"

"Yes—he is."

Jerry entered unasked, and stood by the kitchen doorway. He was not invited to sit down, but stood there, coolly asserting the rights of men and husbands.

"A nice day," he said to Mrs. Morel.

"Yes."

"Grand out this morning—grand for a walk."

"Do you mean *you're* going for a walk?" she asked.

"Yes. We mean walkin' to Nottingham," he replied.

"H'm!"

The two men greeted each other, both glad: Jerry, however, full of assurance, Morel rather subdued, afraid to seem too jubilant in presence of his wife. But he laced his boots quickly, with spirit. They were going for a ten-mile walk across the fields to Nottingham. Climbing the hillside from the Bottoms, they mounted gaily into the morning. At the Moon and Stars they had their first drink, then on to the Old Spot. Then a long five miles of drought to carry them into Bulwell to a glorious pint of bitter. But they stayed in a field with some haymakers whose gallon bottle was full, so that, when they came in sight of the city, Morel was sleepy. The town spread upwards before them, smoking vaguely in the midday glare, fridging the crest away to the south with spires and factory bulks and chimneys. In the last field Morel lay down under an oak tree and slept soundly for over an hour. When he rose to go forward he felt queer.

The two had dinner in the Meadows, with Jerry's sister, then repaired to the Punch Bowl, where they mixed in the excitement of pigeon-racing. Morel never in his life played cards, considering them as having some occult, malevolent power— "the devil's pictures," he called them! But he was a master of skittles and of dominoes. He took a challenge from a Newark man, on skittles. All the men in the old, long bar took sides, betting either one way or the other. Morel took off his coat. Jerry held the hat containing the money. The men at the tables watched. Some stood with their mugs in their hands. Morel felt his big wooden ball carefully, then launched it. He played havoc among the nine-pins, and won half a crown, which restored him to solvency.

By seven o'clock the two were in good condition. They caught the 7.30 train home.

In the afternoon the Bottoms was intolerable. Every inhabitant remaining was out of doors. The women, in twos

and threes, bareheaded and in white aprons, gossiped in the
alley between the blocks. Men, having a rest between drinks,
sat on their heels and talked. The place smelled stale; the slate
roofs glistered in the arid heat.

Mrs. Morel took the little girl down to the brook in the
meadows, which were not more than two hundred yards away.
The water ran quickly over stones and broken pots. Mother
and child leaned on the rail of the old sheep-bridge, watching.
Up at the dipping-hole, at the other end of the meadow, Mrs.
Morel could see the naked forms of boys flashing round the
deep yellow water, or an occasional bright figure dart glittering over the blackish stagnant meadow. She knew William
was at the dipping-hole, and it was the dread of her life lest he
should get drowned. Annie played under the tall old hedge,
picking up alder cones, that she called currants. The child
required much attention, and the flies were teasing.

The children were put to bed at seven o'clock. Then she
worked awhile.

When Walter Morel and Jerry arrived at Bestwood they felt
a load off their minds; a railway journey no longer impended,
so they could put the finishing touches to a glorious day. They
entered the Nelson with the satisfaction of returned travellers.

The next day was a work-day, and the thought of it put a
damper on the men's spirits. Most of them, moreover, had
spent their money. Some were already rolling dismally home,
to sleep in preparation for the morrow. Mrs. Morel, listening
to their mournful singing, went indoors. Nine o'clock passed,
and ten, and still "the pair" had not returned. On a door-
step somewhere a man was singing loudly, in a drawl: "Lead,
kindly Light." Mrs. Morel was always indignant with the
drunken men that they must sing that hymn when they got
maudlin.

"As if 'Genevieve' weren't good enough," she said.

The kitchen was full of the scent of boiled herbs and hops.
On the hob a large black saucepan steamed slowly. Mrs. Morel
took a panchion, a great bowl of thick red earth, streamed a
heap of white sugar into the bottom, and then, straining herself
to the weight, was pouring in the liquor.

Just then Morel came in. He had been very jolly in the
Nelson, but coming home had grown irritable. He had not
quite got over the feeling of irritability and pain, after having
slept on the ground when he was so hot; and a bad conscience

afflicted him as he neared the house. He did not know he was angry. But when the garden gate resisted his attempts to open it, he kicked it and broke the latch. He entered just as Mrs. Morel was pouring the infusion of herbs out of the saucepan. Swaying slightly, he lurched against the table. The boiling liquor pitched. Mrs. Morel started back.

"Good gracious," she cried, "coming home in his drunkenness!"

"Comin' home in his what?" he snarled, his hat over his eye.

Suddenly her blood rose in a jet.

"Say you're *not* drunk!" she flashed.

She had put down her saucepan, and was stirring the sugar into the beer. He dropped his two hands heavily on the table, and thrust his face forwards at her.

"'Say you're not drunk,'" he repeated. "Why, nobody but a nasty little bitch like you 'ud 'ave such a thought."

He thrust his face forward at her.

"There's money to bezzle with, if there's money for nothing else."

"I've not spent a two-shillin' bit this day," he said.

"You don't get as drunk as a lord on nothing," she replied. "And," she cried, flashing into sudden fury, "if you've been sponging on your beloved Jerry, why, let him look after his children, for they need it."

"It's a lie, it's a lie. Shut your face, woman."

They were now at battle-pitch. Each forgot everything save the hatred of the other and the battle between them. She was fiery and furious as he. They went on till he called her a liar.

"No," she cried, starting up, scarce able to breathe. "Don't call me that—you, the most despicable liar that ever walked in shoe-leather." She forced the last words out of suffocated lungs.

"You're a liar!" he yelled, banging the table with his fist. "You're a liar, you're a liar."

She stiffened herself, with clenched fists.

"The house is filthy with you," she cried.

"Then get out on it—it's mine. Get out on it!" he shouted. "It's me as brings th' money whoam, not thee. It's my house, not thine. Then ger out on't—ger out on't!"

"And I would," she cried, suddenly shaken into tears of impotence. "Ah, wouldn't I, wouldn't I have gone long ago, but for those children. Ay, haven't I repented not going years ago, when I'd only the one"—suddenly drying into rage. "Do you think it's for *you* I stop—do you think I'd stop one minute for *you*?"

"Go, then," he shouted, beside himself. "Go!"

"No!" She faced round. "No," she cried loudly, "you shan't have it *all* your own way; you shan't do *all* you like. I've got those children to see to. My word," she laughed, "I should look well to leave them to you."

"Go," he cried thickly, lifting his fist. He was afraid of her. "Go!"

"I should be only too glad. I should laugh, laugh, my lord, if I could get away from you," she replied.

He came up to her, his red face, with its bloodshot eyes, thrust forward, and gripped her arms. She cried in fear of him, struggled to be free. Coming slightly to himself, panting, he pushed her roughly to the outer door, and thrust her forth, slotting the bolt behind her with a bang. Then he went back into the kitchen, dropped into his arm-chair, his head, bursting full of blood, sinking between his knees. Thus he dipped gradually into a stupor, from exhaustion and intoxication.

The moon was high and magnificent in the August night. Mrs. Morel, seared with passion, shivered to find herself out there in a great white light, that fell cold on her, and gave a shock to her inflamed soul. She stood for a few moments helplessly staring at the glistening great rhubarb leaves near the door. Then she got the air into her breast. She walked down the garden path, trembling in every limb, while the child boiled within her. For a while she could not control her consciousness; mechanically she went over the last scene, then over it again, certain phrases, certain moments coming each time like a brand red-hot down on her soul; and each time she enacted again the past hour, each time the brand came down at the same points, till the mark was burnt in, and the pain burnt out, and at last she came to herself. She must have been half an hour in this delirious condition. Then the presence of the night came again to her. She glanced round in fear. She had wandered to the side garden, where she was walking up and down the path beside the currant bushes under the long wall. The garden was a narrow strip, bounded from the road, that cut transversely between the blocks, by a thick thorn hedge.

She hurried out of the side garden to the front, where she could stand as if in an immense gulf of white light, the moon streaming high in face of her, the moonlight standing up from the hills in front, and filling the valley where the Bottoms crouched, almost blindingly. There, panting and half weeping in reaction from the stress, she murmured to herself over and over again: "The nuisance! the nuisance!"

She became aware of something about her. With an effort she roused herself to see what it was that penetrated her consciousness. The tall white lilies were reeling in the moonlight, and the air was charged with their perfume, as with a presence. Mrs. Morel gasped slightly in fear. She touched the big, pallid flowers on their petals, then shivered. They seemed to be stretching in the moonlight. She put her hand into one white bin: the gold scarcely showed on her fingers by moonlight. She bent down to look at the binful of yellow pollen; but it only appeared dusky. Then she drank a deep draught of the scent. It almost made her dizzy.

Mrs. Morel leaned on the garden gate, looking out, and she lost herself awhile. She did not know what she thought. Except for a slight feeling of sickness, and her consciousness in the child, herself melted out like scent into the shiny, pale air. After a time the child, too, melted with her in the mixing-pot of moonlight, and she rested with the hills and lilies and houses, all swum together in a kind of swoon.

When she came to herself she was tired for sleep. Languidly she looked about her; the clumps of white phlox seemed like bushes spread with linen; a moth ricochetted over them, and right across the garden. Following it with her eye roused her. A few whiffs of the raw, strong scent of phlox invigorated her. She passed along the path, hesitating at the white rose-bush. It smelled sweet and simple. She touched the white ruffles of the roses. Their fresh scent and cool, soft leaves reminded her of the morning-time and sunshine. She was very fond of them. But she was tired, and wanted to sleep. In the mysterious out-of-doors she felt forlorn.

There was no noise anywhere. Evidently the children had not been wakened, or had gone to sleep again. A train, three miles away, roared across the valley. The night was very large, and very strange, stretching its hoary distances infinitely. And out of the silver-grey fog of darkness came sounds vague and hoarse: a corncrake not far off, sound of a train like a sigh, and distant shouts of men.

Her quietened heart beginning to beat quickly again, she

hurried down the side garden to the back of the house. Softly she lifted the latch; the door was still bolted, and hard against her. She rapped gently, waited, then rapped again. She must not rouse the children, nor the neighbours. He must be asleep, and he would not wake easily. Her heart began to burn to be indoors. She clung to the door-handle. Now it was cold; she would take a chill, and in her present condition!

Putting her apron over her head and her arms, she hurried again to the side garden, to the window of the kitchen. Leaning on the sill, she could just see, under the blind, her husband's arms spread out on the table, and his black head on the board. He was sleeping with his face lying on the table. Something in his attitude made her feel tired of things. The lamp was burning smokily; she could tell by the copper colour of the light. She tapped at the window more and more noisily. Almost it seemed as if the glass would break. Still he did not wake up.

After vain efforts, she began to shiver, partly from contact with the stone, and from exhaustion. Fearful always for the unborn child, she wondered what she could do for warmth. She went down to the coal-house, where there was an old hearth-rug she had carried out for the rag-man the day before. This she wrapped over her shoulders. It was warm, if grimy. Then she walked up and down the garden path, peeping every now and then under the blind, knocking, and telling herself that in the end the very strain of his position must wake him.

At last, after about an hour, she rapped long and low at the window. Gradually the sound penetrated to him. When, in despair, she had ceased to tap, she saw him stir, then lift his face blindly. The labouring of his heart hurt him into consciousness. She rapped imperatively at the window. He started awake. Instantly she saw his fists set and his eyes glare. He had not a grain of physical fear. If it had been twenty burglars, he would have gone blindly for them. He glared round, bewildered, but prepared to fight.

"Open the door, Walter," she said coldly.

His hands relaxed. It dawned on him what he had done. His head dropped, sullen and dogged. She saw him hurry to the door, heard the bolt chock. He tried the latch. It opened—and there stood the silver-grey night, fearful to him, after the tawny light of the lamp. He hurried back.

When Mrs. Morel entered, she saw him almost running through the door to the stairs. He had ripped his collar off his neck in his haste to be gone ere she came in, and there it lay with bursten button-holes. It made her angry.

She warmed and soothed herself. In her weariness forgetting everything, she moved about at the little tasks that remained to be done, set his breakfast, rinsed his pit-bottle, put his pit-clothes on the hearth to warm, set his pit-boots beside them, put him out a clean scarf and snap-bag and two apples, raked the fire, and went to bed. He was already dead asleep. His narrow black eyebrows were drawn up in a sort of peevish misery into his forehead while his cheeks' down-strokes, and his sulky mouth, seemed to be saying: "I don't care who you are nor what you are, I *shall* have my own way."

Mrs. Morel knew him too well to look at him. As she unfastened her brooch at the mirror, she smiled faintly to see her face all smeared with the yellow dust of lilies. She brushed it off, and at last lay down. For some time her mind continued snapping and jetting sparks, but she was asleep before her husband awoke from the first sleep of his drunkenness.

CHAPTER II

THE BIRTH OF PAUL, AND ANOTHER BATTLE

AFTER such a scene as the last, Walter Morel was for some days abashed and ashamed, but he soon regained his old bullying indifference. Yet there was a slight shrinking, a diminishing in his assurance. Physically even, he shrank, and his fine full presence waned. He never grew in the least stout, so that, as he sank from his erect, assertive bearing, his physique seemed to contract along with his pride and moral strength.

But now he realised how hard it was for his wife to drag about at her work, and, his sympathy quickened by penitence, hastened forward with his help. He came straight home from the pit, and stayed in at evening till Friday, and then he could not remain at home. But he was back again by ten o'clock, almost quite sober.

He always made his own breakfast. Being a man who rose early and had plenty of time he did not, as some miners do, drag his wife out of bed at six o'clock. At five, sometimes earlier, he woke, got straight out of bed, and went downstairs. When she could not sleep, his wife lay waiting for this time, as for a period of peace. The only real rest seemed to be when he was out of the house.

He went downstairs in his shirt and then struggled into his pit-trousers, which were left on the hearth to warm all night. There was always a fire, because Mrs. Morel raked. And the first sound in the house was the bang, bang of the poker against the raker, as Morel smashed the remainder of the coal to make the kettle, which was filled and left on the hob, finally boil. His cup and knife and fork, all he wanted except just the food, was laid ready on the table on a newspaper. Then he got his breakfast, made the tea, packed the bottom of the doors with rugs to shut out the draught, piled a big fire, and sat down to an hour of joy. He toasted his bacon on a fork and caught the drops of fat on his bread; then he put the rasher on his thick slice of bread, and cut off chunks with a clasp-knife, poured his tea into his saucer, and was happy. With his family about, meals were never so pleasant. He loathed a fork: it is a modern introduction which has still scarcely reached common people. What Morel preferred was a clasp-knife. Then, in solitude, he ate and drank, often sitting, in cold weather, on a little stool with his back to the warm chimney-piece, his food on the fender, his cup on the hearth. And then he read the last night's newspaper—what of it he could—spelling it over laboriously. He preferred to keep the blinds down and the candle lit even when it was daylight; it was the habit of the mine.

At a quarter to six he rose, cut two thick slices of bread and butter, and put them in the white calico snap-bag. He filled his tin bottle with tea. Cold tea without milk or sugar was the drink he preferred for the pit. Then he pulled off his shirt, and put on his pit-singlet, a vest of thick flannel cut low round the neck, and with short sleeves like a chemise.

Then he went upstairs to his wife with a cup of tea because she was ill, and because it occurred to him.

"I've brought thee a cup o' tea, lass," he said.

"Well, you needn't, for you know I don't like it," she replied.

"Drink it up; it'll pop thee off to sleep again."

She accepted the tea. It pleased him to see her take it and sip it.

"I'll back my life there's no sugar in," she said.

"Yi—there's one big 'un," he replied, injured.

"It's a wonder," she said, sipping again.

She had a winsome face when her hair was loose. He loved

her to grumble at him in this manner. He looked at her again, and went, without any sort of leave-taking. He never took more than two slices of bread and butter to eat in the pit, so an apple or an orange was a treat to him. He always liked it when she put one out for him. He tied a scarf round his neck, put on his great, heavy boots, his coat, with the big pocket, that carried his snap-bag and his bottle of tea, and went forth into the fresh morning air, closing, without locking, the door behind him. He loved the early morning, and the walk across the fields. So he appeared at the pit-top, often with a stalk from the hedge between his teeth, which he chewed all day to keep his mouth moist, down the mine, feeling quite as happy as when he was in the field.

Later, when the time for the baby grew nearer, he would bustle round in his slovenly fashion, poking out the ashes, rubbing the fireplace, sweeping the house before he went to work. Then, feeling very self-righteous, he went upstairs.

"Now I'm cleaned up for thee: tha's no 'casions ter stir a peg all day, but sit and read thy books."

Which made her laugh, in spite of her indignation.

"And the dinner cooks itself?" she answered.

"Eh, I know nowt about th' dinner."

"You'd know if there weren't any."

"Ay, 'appen so," he answered, departing.

When she got downstairs, she would find the house tidy, but dirty. She could not rest until she had thoroughly cleaned; so she went down to the ash-pit with her dust-pan. Mrs. Kirk, spying her, would contrive to have to go to her own coal-place at that minute. Then, across the wooden fence, she would call:

"So you keep wagging on, then?"

"Ay," answered Mrs. Morel deprecatingly. "There's nothing else for it."

"Have you seen Hose?" called a very small woman from across the road. It was Mrs. Anthony, a black-haired, strange little body, who always wore a brown velvet dress, tight fitting.

"I haven't," said Mrs. Morel.

"Eh, I wish he'd come. I've got a copperful of clothes, an' I'm sure I heered his bell."

"Hark! He's at the end."

The two women looked down the alley. At the end of the Bottoms a man stood in a sort of old-fashioned trap, bending over bundles of cream-coloured stuff; while a cluster of women held up their arms to him, some with bundles. Mrs. Anthony herself had a heap of creamy, undyed stockings hanging over her arm.

"I've done ten dozen this week," she said proudly to Mrs. Morel.

"T-t-t!" went the other. "I don't know how you can find time."

"Eh!" said Mrs. Anthony. "You can find time if you make time."

"I don't know how you do it," said Mrs. Morel. "And how much shall you get for those many?"

"Tuppence-ha'penny a dozen," replied the other.

"Well," said Mrs. Morel. "I'd starve before I'd sit down and seam twenty-four stockings for twopence ha'penny."

"Oh, I don't know," said Mrs. Anthony. "You can rip along with 'em."

Hose was coming along, ringing his bell. Women were waiting at the yard-ends with their seamed stockings hanging over their arms. The man, a common fellow, made jokes with them, tried to swindle them, and bullied them. Mrs. Morel went up her yard disdainfully.

It was an understood thing that if one woman wanted her neighbour, she should put the poker in the fire and bang at the back of the fireplace, which, as the fires were back to back, would make a great noise in the adjoining house. One morning Mrs. Kirk, mixing a pudding, nearly started out of her skin as she heard the thud, thud, in her grate. With her hands all floury, she rushed to the fence.

"Did you knock, Mrs. Morel?"

"If you wouldn't mind, Mrs. Kirk."

Mrs. Kirk climbed on to her copper, got over the wall on to Mrs. Morel's copper, and ran in to her neighbour.

"Eh, dear, how are you feeling?" she cried in concern.

"You might fetch Mrs. Bower," said Mrs. Morel.

Mrs. Kirk went into the yard, lifted up her strong, shrill voice, and called:

"Ag-gie—Ag-gie!"

The sound was heard from one end of the Bottoms to the other. At last Aggie came running up, and was sent for Mrs. Bower, whilst Mrs. Kirk left her pudding and stayed with her neighbour.

Mrs. Morel went to bed. Mrs. Kirk had Annie and William for dinner. Mrs. Bower, fat and waddling, bossed the house.

"Hash some cold meat up for the master's dinner, and make him an apple-charlotte pudding," said Mrs. Morel.

"He may go without pudding *this* day," said Mrs. Bower.

Morel was not as a rule one of the first to appear at the bottom of the pit, ready to come up. Some men were there before four o'clock, when the whistle blew loose-all; but Morel, whose stall, a poor one, was at this time about a mile and a half away from the bottom, worked usually till the first mate stopped, then he finished also. This day, however, the miner was sick of the work. At two o'clock he looked at his watch, by the light of the green candle—he was in a safe working— and again at half-past two. He was hewing at a piece of rock that was in the way for the next day's work. As he sat on his heels, or kneeled, giving hard blows with his pick, "Uszza— uszza!" he went.

Animal Sounds

"Shall ter finish, Sorry?" cried Barker, his fellow butty.

"Finish? Niver while the world stands!" growled Morel.

And he went on striking. He was tired.

"It's a heart-breaking job," said Barker.

But Morel was too exasperated, at the end of his tether, to answer. Still he struck and hacked with all his might.

"Tha might as well leave it, Walter," said Barker. "It'll do to-morrow, without thee hackin' thy guts out."

"I'll lay no b—— finger on this to-morrow, Isr'el!" cried Morel.

"Oh, well, if tha wunna, someb'dy else 'll ha'e to," said Israel.

Then Morel continued to strike.

"Hey-up there—*loose-a'!*" cried the men, leaving the next stall.

Morel continued to strike.

"Tha'll happen catch me up," said Barker, departing.

When he had gone, Morel, left alone, felt savage. He had not finished his job. He had overworked himself into a frenzy. Rising, wet with sweat, he threw his tool down, pulled on his coat, blew out his candle, took his lamp, and went. Down the main road the lights of the other men went swinging. There was a hollow sound of many voices. It was a long, heavy tramp underground.

He sat at the bottom of the pit, where the great drops of

water fell plash. Many colliers were waiting their turns to go up, talking noisily. Morel gave his answers short and disagreeable.

"It's rainin', Sorry," said old Giles, who had had the news from the top.

Morel found one comfort. He had his old umbrella, which he loved, in the lamp cabin. At last he took his stand on the chair, and was at the top in a moment. Then he handed in his lamp and got his umbrella, which he had bought at an auction for one-and-six. He stood on the edge of the pit-bank for a moment, looking out over the fields; grey rain was falling. The trucks stood full of wet, bright coal. Water ran down the sides of the waggons, over the white "C.W. and Co.". Colliers, walking indifferent to the rain, were streaming down the line and up the field, a grey, dismal host. Morel put up his umbrella, and took pleasure from the peppering of the drops thereon.

All along the road to Bestwood the miners tramped, wet and grey and dirty, but their red mouths talking with animation. Morel also walked with a gang, but he said nothing. He frowned peevishly as he went. Many men passed into the Prince of Wales or into Ellen's. Morel, feeling sufficiently disagreeable to resist temptation, trudged along under the dripping trees that overhung the park wall, and down the mud of Greenhill Lane.

Mrs. Morel lay in bed, listening to the rain, and the feet of the colliers from Minton, their voices, and the bang, bang of the gates as they went through the stile up the field.

"There's some herb beer behind the pantry door," she said. "Th' master 'll want a drink, if he doesn't stop."

But he was late, so she concluded he had called for a drink, since it was raining. What did he care about the child or her?

She was very ill when her children were born.

"What is it?" she asked, feeling sick to death.

"A boy."

And she took consolation in that. The thought of being the mother of men was warming to her heart. She looked at the child. It had blue eyes, and a lot of fair hair, and was bonny. Her love came up hot, in spite of everything. She had it in bed with her.

Morel, thinking nothing, dragged his way up the garden path, wearily and angrily. He closed his umbrella, and stood it in the sink; then he sluthered his heavy boots into the kitchen. Mrs. Bower appeared in the inner doorway.

"Well," she said, "she's about as bad as she can be. It's a boy childt."

The miner grunted, put his empty snap-bag and his tin bottle on the dresser, went back into the scullery and hung up his coat, then came and dropped into his chair.

"Han yer got a drink?" he asked.

The woman went into the pantry. There was heard the pop of a cork. She set the mug, with a little, disgusted rap, on the table before Morel. He drank, gasped, wiped his big moustache on the end of his scarf, drank, gasped, and lay back in his chair. The woman would not speak to him again. She set his dinner before him, and went upstairs.

"Was that the master?" asked Mrs. Morel.

"I've gave him his dinner," replied Mrs. Bower.

After he had sat with his arms on the table—he resented the fact that Mrs. Bower put no cloth on for him, and gave him a little plate, instead of a full-sized dinner-plate—he began to eat. The fact that his wife was ill, that he had another boy, was nothing to him at that moment. He was too tired; he wanted his dinner; he wanted to sit with his arms lying on the board; he did not like having Mrs. Bower about. The fire was too small to please him.

After he had finished his meal, he sat for twenty minutes; then he stoked up a big fire. Then, in his stockinged feet, he went reluctantly upstairs. It was a struggle to face his wife at this moment, and he was tired. His face was black, and smeared with sweat. His singlet had dried again, soaking the dirt in. He had a dirty woollen scarf round his throat. So he stood at the foot of the bed.

"Well, how are ter, then?" he asked.

"I s'll be all right," she answered.

"H'm!"

He stood at a loss what to say next. He was tired, and this bother was rather a nuisance to him, and he didn't quite know where he was.

"A lad, tha says," he stammered.

She turned down the sheet and showed the child.

"Bless him!" he murmured. Which made her laugh, because he blessed by rote—pretending paternal emotion, which he did not feel just then.

"Go now," she said.

"I will, my lass," he answered, turning away.

Dismissed, he wanted to kiss her, but he dared not. She half wanted him to kiss her, but could not bring herself to give any sign. She only breathed freely when he was gone out of the room again, leaving behind him a faint smell of pit-dirt.

he threatens her in some way

Mrs. Morel had a visit every day from the Congregational clergyman. Mr. Heaton was young, and very poor. His wife had died at the birth of his first baby, so he remained alone in the manse. He was a Bachelor of Arts of Cambridge, very shy, and no preacher. Mrs. Morel was fond of him, and he depended on her. For hours he talked to her, when she was well. He became the god-parent of the child.

preacher

Occasionally the minister stayed to tea with Mrs. Morel. Then she laid the cloth early, got out her best cups, with a little green rim, and hoped Morel would not come too soon; indeed, if he stayed for a pint, she would not mind this day. She had always two dinners to cook, because she believed children should have their chief meal at midday, whereas Morel needed his at five o'clock. So Mr. Heaton would hold the baby, whilst Mrs. Morel beat up a batter-pudding or peeled the potatoes, and he, watching her all the time, would discuss his next sermon. His ideas were quaint and fantastic. She brought him judiciously to earth. It was a discussion of the wedding at Cana.

Lawrence speaks

"When He changed the water into wine at Cana," he said, "that is a symbol that the ordinary life, even the blood, of the married husband and wife, which had before been uninspired, like water, became filled with the Spirit, and was as wine, because, when love enters, the whole spiritual constitution of a man changes, is filled with the Holy Ghost, and almost his form is altered."

Mrs. Morel thought to herself:

"Yes, poor fellow, his young wife is dead; that is why he makes his love into the Holy Ghost."

she has not love

They were halfway down their first cup of tea when they heard the sluther of pit-boots.

"Good gracious!" exclaimed Mrs. Morel, in spite of herself.

The minister looked rather scared. Morel entered. He was feeling rather savage. He nodded a "How d'yer do" to the clergyman, who rose to shake hands with him.

"Nay," said Morel, showing his hand, "look thee at it! Tha

niver wants ter shake hands wi' a hand like that, does ter? There's too much pick-haft and shovel-dirt on it."

The minister flushed with confusion, and sat down again. Mrs. Morel rose, carried out the steaming saucepan. Morel took off his coat, dragged his armchair to table, and sat down heavily.

"Are you tired?" asked the clergyman.

"Tired? I ham that," replied Morel. "*You* don't know what it is to be tired, as *I'm* tired."

"No," replied the clergyman.

"Why, look yer 'ere," said the miner, showing the shoulders of his singlet. "It's a bit dry now, but it's wet as a clout with sweat even yet. Feel it."

"Goodness!" cried Mrs. Morel. "Mr. Heaton doesn't want to feel your nasty singlet."

The clergyman put out his hand gingerly.

"No, perhaps he doesn't," said Morel; "but it's all come out of me, whether or not. An' iv'ry day alike my singlet's wringin' wet. 'Aven't you got a drink, Missis, for a man when he comes home barkled up from the pit."

"You know you drank all the beer," said Mrs. Morel, pouring out his tea.

"An' was there no more to be got?" Turning to the clergyman—"A man gets that caked up wi' th' dust, you know,—that clogged up down a coal-mine, he *needs* a drink when he comes home."

"I am sure he does," said the clergyman.

"But it's ten to one if there's owt for him."

"There's water—and there's tea," said Mrs. Morel.

"Water! It's not water as'll clear his throat."

He poured out a saucerful of tea, blew it, and sucked it up through his great black moustache, sighing afterwards. Then he poured out another saucerful, and stood his cup on the table.

"My cloth!" said Mrs, Morel, putting it on a plate.

"A man as comes home as I do 's too tired to care about cloths," said Morel.

"Pity!" exclaimed his wife, sarcastically.

The room was full of the smell of meat and vegetables and pit-clothes.

He leaned over to the minister, his great moustache thrust forward, his mouth very red in his black face.

"Mr. Heaton," he said, "a man as has been down the black

hole all day, dingin' away at a coal-face, yi, a sight harder
than that wall——"

"Needn't make a moan of it," put in Mrs. Morel.

She hated her husband because, whenever he had an audience,
he whined and played for sympathy. William, sitting nursing
the baby, hated him, with a boy's hatred for false sentiment,
and for the stupid treatment of his mother. Annie had never
liked him; she merely avoided him.

When the minister had gone, Mrs. Morel looked at her cloth.

"A fine mess!" she said.

"Dos't think I'm goin' to sit wi' my arms danglin', cos tha's
got a parson for tea wi' thee?" he bawled.

They were both angry, but she said nothing. The baby began
to cry, and Mrs. Morel, picking up a saucepan from the hearth,
accidentally knocked Annie on the head, whereupon the girl
began to whine, and Morel to shout at her. In the midst of this
pandemonium, William looked up at the big glazed text over
the mantelpiece and read distinctly:

"God Bless Our Home!"

Whereupon Mrs. Morel, trying to soothe the baby, jumped
up, rushed at him, boxed his ears, saying:

"What are *you* putting in for?"

And then she sat down and laughed, till tears ran over her
cheeks, while William kicked the stool he had been sitting on,
and Morel growled:

"I canna see what there is so much to laugh at."

One evening, directly after the parson's visit, feeling unable
to bear herself after another display from her husband, she took
Annie and the baby and went out. Morel had kicked William,
and the mother would never forgive him.

She went over the sheep-bridge and across a corner of the
meadow to the cricket-ground. The meadows seemed one space
of ripe, evening light, whispering with the distant mill-race. She
sat on a seat under the alders in the cricket-ground, and fronted
the evening. Before her, level and solid, spread the big green
cricket-field, like the bed of a sea of light. Children played in
the bluish shadow of the pavilion. Many rooks, high up, came
cawing home across the softly-woven sky. They stooped in a
long curve down into the golden glow, concentrating, cawing,
wheeling, like black flakes on a slow vortex, over a tree clump
that made a dark boss among the pasture.

A few gentlemen were practising, and Mrs. Morel could hear

the chock of the ball, and the voices of men suddenly roused; could see the white forms of men shifting silently over the green, upon which already the under shadows were smouldering. Away at the grange, one side of the haystacks was lit up, the other sides blue-grey. A waggon of sheaves rocked small across the melting yellow light.

The sun was going down. Every open evening, the hills of Derbyshire were blazed over with red sunset. Mrs. Morel watched the sun sink from the glistening sky, leaving a soft flower-blue overhead, while the western space went red, as if all the fire had swum down there, leaving the bell cast flawless blue. The mountain-ash berries across the field stood fierily out from the dark leaves, for a moment. A few shocks of corn in a corner of the fallow stood up as if alive; she imagined them bowing; perhaps her son would be a Joseph. In the east, a mirrored sunset floated pink opposite the west's scarlet. The big haystacks on the hillside, that butted into the glare, went cold.

With Mrs. Morel it was one of those still moments when the small frets vanish, and the beauty of things stands out, and she had the peace and the strength to see herself. Now and again, a swallow cut close to her. Now and again, Annie came up with a handful of alder-currants. The baby was restless on his mother's knee, clambering with his hands at the light.

Mrs. Morel looked down at him. She had dreaded this baby like a catastrophe, because of her feeling for her husband. And now she felt strangely towards the infant. Her heart was heavy because of the child, almost as if it were unhealthy, or malformed. Yet it seemed quite well. But she noticed the peculiar knitting of the baby's brows, and the peculiar heaviness of its eyes, as if it were trying to understand something that was pain. She felt, when she looked at her child's dark, brooding pupils, as if a burden were on her heart.

"He looks as if he was thinking about something—quite sorrowful," said Mrs. Kirk.

Suddenly, looking at him, the heavy feeling at the mother's heart melted into passionate grief. She bowed over him, and a few tears shook swiftly out of her very heart. The baby lifted his fingers.

"My lamb!" she cried softly.

And at that moment she felt, in some far inner place of her soul, that she and her husband were guilty.

The baby was looking up at her. It had blue eyes like her own, but its look was heavy, steady, as if it had realised something that had stunned some point of its soul.

In her arms lay the delicate baby. Its deep blue eyes, always looking up at her unblinking, seemed to draw her innermost thoughts out of her. She no longer loved her husband; she had not wanted this child to come, and there it lay in her arms and pulled at her heart. She felt as if the navel string that had connected its frail little body with hers had not been broken. A wave of hot love went over her to the infant. She held it close to her face and breast. With all her force, with all her soul she would make up to it for having brought it into the world unloved. She would love it all the more now it was here; carry it in her love. Its clear, knowing eyes gave her pain and fear. Did it know all about her? When it lay under her heart, had it been listening then? Was there a reproach in the look? She felt the marrow melt in her bones, with fear and pain.

[handwritten margin note: Paul's fate — born out of guilt.]

Once more she was aware of the sun lying red on the rim of the hill opposite. She suddenly held up the child in her hands.

"Look!" she said. "Look, my pretty!"

She thrust the infant forward to the crimson, throbbing sun, almost with relief. She saw him lift his little fist. Then she put him to her bosom again, ashamed almost of her impulse to give him back again whence he came.

"If he lives," she thought to herself, "what will become of him—what will he be?"

Her heart was anxious.

[handwritten margin note: sub conscious]

"I will call him Paul," she said suddenly; she knew not why.

After a while she went home. A fine shadow was flung over the deep green meadow, darkening all.

As she expected, she found the house empty. But Morel was home by ten o'clock, and that day, at least, ended peacefully.

Walter Morel was, at this time, exceedingly irritable. His work seemed to exhaust him. When he came home he did not speak civilly to anybody. If the fire were rather low he bullied about that; he grumbled about his dinner; if the children made a chatter he shouted at them in a way that made their mother's blood boil, and made them hate him.

On the Friday, he was not home by eleven o'clock. The baby was unwell, and was restless, crying if he were put down. Mrs. Morel, tired to death, and still weak, was scarcely under control.

"I wish the nuisance would come," she said wearily to herself.

The child at last sank down to sleep in her arms. She was too tired to carry him to the cradle.

"But I'll say nothing, whatever time he comes," she said. "It only works me up; I won't say anything. But I know if he does anything it'll make my blood boil," she added to herself.

She sighed, hearing him coming, as if it were something she could not bear. He, taking his revenge, was nearly drunk. She kept her head bent over the child as he entered, not wishing to see him. But it went through her like a flash of hot fire when, in passing, he lurched against the dresser, setting the tins rattling, and clutched at the white pot knobs for support. He hung up his hat and coat, then returned, stood glowering from a distance at her, as she sat bowed over the child.

"Is there nothing to eat in the house?" he asked, insolently, as if to a servant. In certain stages of his intoxication he affected the clipped, mincing speech of the towns. Mrs. Morel hated him most in this condition.

"You know what there is in the house," she said, so coldly, it sounded impersonal.

He stood and glared at her without moving a muscle.

"I asked a civil question, and I expect a civil answer," he said affectedly.

"And you got it," she said, still ignoring him.

He glowered again. Then he came unsteadily forward. He leaned on the table with one hand, and with the other jerked at the table drawer to get a knife to cut bread. The drawer stuck because he pulled sideways. In a temper he dragged it, so that it flew out bodily, and spoons, forks, knives, a hundred metallic things, splashed with a clatter and a clang upon the brick floor. The baby gave a little convulsed start.

"What are you doing, clumsy, drunken fool?" the mother cried.

"Then tha should get the flamin' thing thysen. Tha should get up, like other women have to, an' wait on a man."

"Wait on you—wait on you?" she cried. "Yes, I see myself."

"Yis, an' I'll learn thee tha's got to. Wait on me, yes tha sh'lt wait on me——"

"Never, milord. I'd wait on a dog at the door first."

"What—what?"

He was trying to fit in the drawer. At her last speech he

turned round. His face was crimson, his eyes bloodshot. He
stared at her one silent second in threat.

"P-h!" she went quickly, in contempt.

He jerked at the drawer in his excitement. It fell, cut sharply
on his shin, and on the reflex he flung it at her.

One of the corners caught her brow as the shallow drawer
crashed into the fireplace. She swayed, almost fell stunned from
her chair. To her very soul she was sick; she clasped the child
tightly to her bosom. A few moments elapsed; then, with an
effort, she brought herself to. The baby was crying plaintively.
Her left brow was bleeding rather profusely. As she glanced
down at the child, her brain reeling, some drops of blood soaked
into its white shawl; but the baby was at least not hurt. She
balanced her head to keep equilibrium, so that the blood ran
into her eye.

Walter Morel remained as he had stood, leaning on the table
with one hand, looking blank. When he was sufficiently sure
of his balance, he went across to her, swayed, caught hold of
the back of her rocking-chair, almost tipping her out; then leaning forward over her, and swaying as he spoke, he said, in a
tone of wondering concern :

"Did it catch thee?"

He swayed again, as if he would pitch on to the child. With
the catastrophe he had lost all balance.

"Go away," she said, struggling to keep her presence of mind.

He hiccoughed. "Let's—let's look at it," he said, hiccoughing
again.

"Go away!" she cried.

"Lemme—lemme look at it, lass."

She smelled him of drink, felt the unequal pull of his swaying
grasp on the back of her rocking-chair.

"Go away," she said, and weakly she pushed him off.

He stood, uncertain in balance, gazing upon her. Summoning
all her strength she rose, the baby on one arm. By a cruel effort
of will, moving as if in sleep, she went across to the scullery,
where she bathed her eye for a minute in cold water; but she
was too dizzy. Afraid lest she should swoon, she returned to
her rocking-chair, trembling in every fibre. By instinct, she kept
the baby clasped.

Morel, bothered, had succeeded in pushing the drawer back
into its cavity, and was on his knees, groping, with numb paws,
for the scattered spoons.

Her brow was still bleeding. Presently Morel got up and came craning his neck towards her.

"What has it done to thee, lass?" he asked, in a very wretched, humble tone.

"You can see what it's done," she answered.

He stood, bending forward, supported on his hands, which grasped his legs just above the knee. He peered to look at the wound. She drew away from the thrust of his face with its great moustache, averting her own face as much as possible. As he looked at her, who was cold and impassive as stone, with mouth shut tight, he sickened with feebleness and hopelessness of spirit. He was turning drearily away, when he saw a drop of blood fall from the averted wound into the baby's fragile, glistening hair. Fascinated, he watched the heavy dark drop hang in the glistening cloud, and pull down the gossamer. Another drop fell. It would soak through to the baby's scalp. He watched, fascinated, feeling it soak in; then, finally, his manhood broke.

"What of this child?" was all his wife said to him. But her low, intense tones brought his head lower. She softened: "Get me some wadding out of the middle drawer," she said.

He stumbled away very obediently, presently returning with a pad, which she singed before the fire, then put on her forehead, as she sat with the baby on her lap.

"Now that clean pit-scarf."

Again he rummaged and fumbled in the drawer, returning presently with a red, narrow scarf. She took it, and with trembling fingers proceeded to bind it round her head.

"Let me tie it for thee," he said humbly.

"I can do it myself," she replied. When it was done she went upstairs, telling him to rake the fire and lock the door.

In the morning Mrs. Morel said:

"I knocked against the latch of the coal-place, when I was getting a raker in the dark, because the candle blew out." Her two small children looked up at her with wide, dismayed eyes. They said nothing, but their parted lips seemed to express the unconscious tragedy they felt.

Walter Morel lay in bed next day until nearly dinner-time. He did not think of the previous evening's work. He scarcely thought of anything, but he would not think of that. He lay and suffered like a sulking dog. He had hurt himself most; and he was the more damaged because he would never say a word to her, or express his sorrow. He tried to wriggle out of it. "It was her own fault," he said to himself. Nothing, however, could prevent his inner consciousness inflicting on him the punishment which ate into his spirit like rust, and which he could only alleviate by drinking.

He felt as if he had not the initiative to get up, or to say a word, or to move, but could only lie like a log. Moreover, he had himself violent pains in the head. It was Saturday. Towards noon he rose, cut himself food in the pantry, ate it with his head dropped, then pulled on his boots, and went out, to return at three o'clock slightly tipsy and relieved; then once more straight to bed. He rose again at six in the evening, had tea and went straight out.

Sunday was the same: bed till noon, the Palmerston Arms till 2.30, dinner, and bed; scarcely a word spoken. When Mrs. Morel went upstairs, towards four o'clock, to put on her Sunday dress, he was fast asleep. She would have felt sorry for him, if he had once said, "Wife, I'm sorry." But no; he insisted to himself it was her fault. And so he broke himself. So she merely left him alone. There was this deadlock of passion between them, and she was stronger.

The family began tea. Sunday was the only day when all sat down to meals together.

"Isn't my father going to get up?" asked William.

"Let him lie," the mother replied.

There was a feeling of misery over all the house. The children breathed the air that was poisoned, and they felt dreary. They were rather disconsolate, did not know what to do, what to play at.

Immediately Morel woke he got straight out of bed. That was characteristic of him all his life. He was all for activity. The prostrated inactivity of two mornings was stifling him.

It was near six o'clock when he got down. This time he entered without hesitation, his wincing sensitiveness having hardened again. He did not care any longer what the family thought or felt.

The tea-things were on the table. William was reading aloud from "The Child's Own", Annie listening and asking eternally "why?" Both children hushed into silence as they heard the approaching thud of their father's stockinged feet, and shrank as he entered. Yet he was usually indulgent to them.

Morel made the meal alone, brutally. He ate and drank more

noisily than he had need. No one spoke to him. The family life withdrew, shrank away, and became hushed as he entered. But he cared no longer about his alienation.

Immediately he had finished tea he rose with alacrity to go out. It was this alacrity, this haste to be gone, which so sickened Mrs. Morel. As she heard him sousing heartily in cold water, heard the eager scratch of the steel comb on the side of the bowl, as he wetted his hair, she closed her eyes in disgust. As he bent over, lacing his boots, there was a certain vulgar gusto in his movement that divided him from the reserved, watchful rest of the family. He always ran away from the battle with himself. Even in his own heart's privacy, he excused himself, saying, "If she hadn't said so-and-so, it would never have happened. She asked for what she's got." The children waited in restraint during his preparations. When he had gone, they sighed with relief.

He wasn't wanted at home — true

He closed the door behind him, and was glad. It was a rainy evening. The Palmerston would be the cosier. He hastened forward in anticipation. All the slate roofs of the Bottoms shone black with wet. The roads, always dark with coal-dust, were full of blackish mud. He hastened along. The Palmerston windows were steamed over. The passage was paddled with wet feet. But the air was warm, if foul, and full of the sound of voices and the smell of beer and smoke.

"What shollt ha'e, Walter?" cried a voice, as soon as Morel appeared in the doorway.

"Oh, Jim, my lad, wheriver has thee sprung frae?"

The men made a seat for him, and took him in warmly. He was glad. In a minute or two they had thawed all responsibility out of him, all shame, all trouble, and he was clear as a bell for a jolly night.

On the Wednesday following, Morel was penniless. He dreaded his wife. Having hurt her, he hated her. He did not know what to do with himself that evening, having not even twopence with which to go to the Palmerston, and being already rather deeply in debt. So, while his wife was down the garden with the child, he hunted in the top drawer of the dresser where she kept her purse, found it, and looked inside. It contained a half-crown, two halfpennies, and a sixpence. So he took the sixpence, put the purse carefully back, and went out.

The next day, when she wanted to pay the greengrocer, she looked in the purse for her sixpence, and her heart sank to her shoes. Then she sat down and thought: "*Was* there a sixpence? I hadn't spent it, had I? And I hadn't left it anywhere else?"

She was much put about. She hunted round everywhere for it. And, as she sought, the conviction came into her heart that her husband had taken it. What she had in her purse was all the money she possessed. But that he should sneak it from her thus was unbearable. He had done so twice before. The first time she had not accused him, and at the week-end he had put the shilling again into her purse. So that was how she had known he had taken it. The second time he had not paid back.

This time she felt it was too much. When he had had his dinner—he came home early that day—she said to him coldly:

"Did you take sixpence out of my purse last night?"

"Me!" he said, looking up in an offended way. "No, I didna! I niver clapped eyes on your purse."

But she could detect the lie.

"Why, you know you did," she said quietly.

"I tell you I didna," he shouted. "Yer at me again, are yer? I've had about enough on't."

"So you filch sixpence out of my purse while I'm taking the clothes in."

"I'll may yer pay for this," he said, pushing back his chair in desperation. He bustled and got washed, then went determinedly upstairs. Presently he came down dressed, and with a big bundle in a blue-checked, enormous handkerchief.

"And now," he said, "you'll see me again when you do."

"It'll be before I want to," she replied; and at that he marched out of the house with his bundle. She sat trembling slightly, but her heart brimming with contempt. What would she do if he went to some other pit, obtained work, and got in with another woman? But she knew him too well—he couldn't. She was dead sure of him. Nevertheless her heart was gnawed inside her.

"Where's my dad?" said William, coming in from school.

"He says he's run away," replied the mother.

"Where to?"

"Eh, I don't know. He's taken a bundle in the blue handkerchief, and says he's not coming back."

"What shall we do?" cried the boy.

"Eh, never trouble, he won't go far."

"But if he doesn't come back," wailed Annie.

she doesn't consider the needs of the children

And she and William retired to the sofa and wept. Mrs. Morel sat and laughed.

"You pair of gabeys!" she exclaimed. "You'll see him before the night's out."

But the children were not to be consoled. Twilight came on. Mrs. Morel grew anxious from very weariness. One part of her said it would be a relief to see the last of him; another part fretted because of keeping the children; and inside her, as yet, she could not quite let him go. At the bottom, she knew very well he could *not* go.

will she do anything about it

'layers' of consciousness

When she went down to the coal-place at the end of the garden, however, she felt something behind the door. So she looked. And there in the dark lay the big blue bundle. She sat on a piece of coal and laughed. Every time she saw it, so fat and yet so ignominious, slunk into its corner in the dark, with its ends flopping like dejected ears from the knots, she laughed again. She was relieved.

Mrs. Morel sat waiting. He had not any money, she knew, so if he stopped he was running up a bill. She was very tired of him—tired to death. He had not even the courage to carry his bundle beyond the yard-end.

As she meditated, at about nine o'clock, he opened the door and came in, slinking, and yet sulky. She said not a word. He took off his coat, and slunk to his arm-chair, where he began to take off his boots.

"You'd better fetch your bundle before you take your boots off," she said quietly.

"You may thank your stars I've come back to-night," he said, looking up from under his dropped head, sulkily, trying to be impressive.

"Why, where should you have gone? You daren't even get your parcel through the yard-end," she said.

Assured of her place of dominance

He looked such a fool she was not even angry with him. He continued to take his boots off and prepare for bed.

"I don't know what's in your blue handkerchief," she said. "But if you leave it the children shall fetch it in the morning."

Whereupon he got up and went out of the house, returning presently and crossing the kitchen with averted face, hurrying upstairs. As Mrs. Morel saw him slink quickly through the inner doorway, holding his bundle, she laughed to herself: but her heart was bitter, because she had loved him.

CHAPTER III

THE CASTING OFF OF MOREL—
THE TAKING ON OF WILLIAM

Slow death of Morel

DURING the next week Morel's temper was almost unbearable. Like all miners, he was a great lover of medicines, which, strangely enough, he would often pay for himself.

"You mun get me a drop o' laxy vitral," he said. "It's a winder as we canna ha'e a sup i' th' 'ouse."

So Mrs. Morel bought him elixir of vitriol, his favourite first medicine. And he made himself a jug of wormwood tea. He had hanging in the attic great bunches of dried herbs: wormwood, rue, horehound, elder flowers, parsley-purt, marshmallow, hyssop, dandelion, and centaury. Usually there was a jug of one or other decoction standing on the hob, from which he drank largely.

"Grand!" he said, smacking his lips after wormwood. "Grand!" And he exhorted the children to try.

"It's better than any of your tea or your cocoa stews," he vowed. But they were not to be tempted.

This time, however, neither pills nor vitriol nor all his herbs would shift the "nasty peens in his head". He was sickening for an attack of an inflammation of the brain. He had never been well since his sleeping on the ground when he went with Jerry to Nottingham. Since then he had drunk and stormed. Now he fell seriously ill, and Mrs. Morel had him to nurse. He was one of the worst patients imaginable. But, in spite of all, and putting aside the fact that he was bread-winner, she never quite wanted him to die. Still there was one part of her wanted him for herself.

irony

turning point

The neighbours were very good to her: occasionally some had the children in to meals, occasionally some would do the downstairs work for her, one would mind the baby for a day. But it was a great drag, nevertheless. It was not every day the neighbours helped. Then she had nursing of baby and husband, cleaning and cooking, everything to do. She was quite worn out, but she did what was wanted of her.

And the money was just sufficient. She had seventeen shillings a week from clubs, and every Friday Barker and the other butty put by a portion of the stall's profits for Morel's wife. And the neighbours made broths, and gave eggs, and such invalids' trifles. If they had not helped her so generously in those times, Mrs. Morel would never have pulled through, without incurring debts that would have dragged her down.

The weeks passed. Morel, almost against hope, grew better. He had a fine constitution, so that, once on the mend, he went straight forward to recovery. Soon he was pottering about downstairs. During his illness his wife had spoilt him a little. Now he wanted her to continue. He often put his hand to his head, pulled down the corners of his mouth, and shammed pains he did not feel. But there was no deceiving her. At first she merely smiled to herself. Then she scolded him sharply.

"Goodness, man, don't be so lachrymose."

That wounded him slightly, but still he continued to feign sickness.

"I wouldn't be such a mardy baby," said the wife shortly.

Then he was indignant, and cursed under his breath, like a boy. He was forced to resume a normal tone, and to cease to whine.

Nevertheless, there was a state of peace in the house for some time. Mrs. Morel was more tolerant of him, and he, depending on her almost like a child, was rather happy. Neither knew that she was more tolerant because she loved him less. Up till this time, in spite of all, he had been her husband and her man. She had felt that, more or less, what he did to himself he did to her. Her living depended on him. There were many, many stages in the ebbing of her love for him, but it was always ebbing.

Now, with the birth of this third baby, her self no longer set towards him, helplessly, but was like a tide that scarcely rose, standing off from him. After this she scarcely desired him. And, standing more aloof from him, not feeling him so much part of herself, but merely part of her circumstances, she did not mind so much what he did, could leave him alone.

There was the halt, the wistfulness about the ensuing year, which is like autumn in a man's life. His wife was casting him off, half regretfully, but relentlessly; casting him off and turning now for love and life to the children. Henceforward he was more or less a husk. And he himself acquiesced, as so many men do, yielding their place to their children.

During his recuperation, when it was really over between them, both made an effort to come back somewhat to the old relationship of the first months of their marriage. He sat at home and, when the children were in bed, and she was sewing —she did all her sewing by hand, made all shirts and children's clothing—he would read to her from the newspaper, slowly pronouncing and delivering the words like a man pitching quoits. Often she hurried him on, giving him a phrase in anticipation. And then he took her words humbly.

The silences between them were peculiar. There would be the swift, slight "cluck" of her needle, the sharp "pop" of his lips as he let out the smoke, the warmth, the sizzle on the bars as he spat in the fire. Then her thoughts turned to William. Already he was getting a big boy. Already he was top of the class, and the master said he was the smartest lad in the school. She saw him a man, young, full of vigour, making the world glow again for her.

And Morel sitting there, quite alone, and having nothing to think about, would be feeling vaguely uncomfortable. His soul would reach out in its blind way to her and find her gone. He felt a sort of emptiness, almost like a vacuum in his soul. He was unsettled and restless. Soon he could not live in that atmosphere, and he affected his wife. Both felt an oppression on their breathing when they were left together for some time. Then he went to bed and she settled down to enjoy herself alone, working, thinking, living. — *she must have her way.*

Meanwhile another infant was coming, fruit of this little peace and tenderness between the separating parents. Paul was seventeen months old when the new baby was born. He was then a plump, pale child, quiet, with heavy blue eyes, and still the peculiar slight knitting of the brows. The last child was also a boy, fair and bonny. Mrs. Morel was sorry when she knew she was with child, both for economic reasons and because she did not love her husband; but not for the sake of the infant.

They called the baby Arthur. He was very pretty, with a mop of gold curls, and he loved his father from the first. Mrs. Morel was glad this child loved the father. Hearing the miner's footsteps, the baby would put up his arms and crow. And if Morel were in a good temper, he called back immediately, in his hearty, mellow voice:

"What then, my beauty? I sh'll come to thee in a minute."

And as soon as he had taken off his pit-coat, Mrs. Morel would put an apron round the child, and give him to his father.

"What a sight the lad looks!" she would exclaim sometimes, taking back the baby, that was smutted on the
face from his father's kisses and play. Then Morel laughed
joyfully.

"He's a little collier, bless his bit o' mutton!" he exclaimed.

And these were the happy moments of her life now, when
the children included the father in her heart.

Meanwhile William grew bigger and stronger and more
active, while Paul, always rather delicate and quiet, got
slimmer, and trotted after his mother like her shadow. He
was usually active and interested, but sometimes he would
have fits of depression. Then the mother would find the boy
of three or four crying on the sofa.

"What's the matter?" she asked, and got no answer.

"What's the matter?" she insisted, getting cross.

"I don't know," sobbed the child.

So she tried to reason him out of it, or to amuse him, but
without effect. It made her feel beside herself. Then the father,
always impatient, would jump from his chair and shout:

"If he doesn't stop, I'll smack him till he does."

"You'll do nothing of the sort," said the mother coldly.
And then she carried the child into the yard, plumped him
into his little chair, and said: "Now cry there, Misery!"

And then a butterfly on the rhubarb-leaves perhaps caught
his eye, or at last he cried himself to sleep. These fits were
not often, but they caused a shadow in Mrs. Morel's heart, and
her treatment of Paul was different from that of the other
children.

Suddenly one morning as she was looking down the alley of
the Bottoms for the barm-man, she heard a voice calling her.
It was the thin little Mrs. Anthony in brown velvet.

"Here, Mrs. Morel, I want to tell you about your Willie."

"Oh, do you?" replied Mrs. Morel. "Why, what's the
matter?"

"A lad as gets 'old of another an' rips his clothes off'n 'is
back," Mrs. Anthony said, "wants showing something."

"Your Alfred's as old as my William," said Mrs. Morel.

"'Appen 'e is, but that doesn't give him a right to get hold of
the boy's collar, an' fair rip it clean off his back."

"Well," said Mrs. Morel, "I don't thrash my children, and
even if I did, I should want to hear their side of the tale."

"They'd happen be a bit better if they did get a good hiding,"

retorted Mrs. Anthony. "When it comes ter rippin' a lad's
clean collar off'n 'is back a-purpose——"

"I'm sure he didn't do it on purpose," said Mrs. Morel.

"Make me a liar!" shouted Mrs. Anthony.

Mrs. Morel moved away and closed her gate. Her hand
trembled as she held her mug of barm.

"But I s'll let your mester know," Mrs. Anthony cried after
her.

At dinner-time, when William had finished his meal and
wanted to be off again—he was then eleven years old—his
mother said to him:

"What did you tear Alfred Anthony's collar for?"

"When did I tear his collar?"

"I don't know when, but his mother says you did."

"Why—it was yesterday—an' it was torn a'ready."

"But you tore it more."

"Well, I'd got a cobbler as 'ad licked seventeen—an' Alfy
Ant'ny 'e says:

> 'Adam an' Eve an' pinch-me,
>   Went down to a river to bade.
> Adam an' Eve got drownded,
>   Who do yer think got saved?'

An' so I says: 'Oh, Pinch-*you*,' an' so I pinched 'im, an' 'e was
mad, an' so he snatched my cobbler an' run off with it. An' so
I run after 'im, an' when I was gettin' hold of 'im, 'e dodged,
an' it ripped 'is collar. But I got my cobbler——"

He pulled from his pocket a black old horse-chestnut hanging
on a string. This old cobbler had "cobbled"—hit and smashed
—seventeen other cobblers on similar strings. So the boy was
proud of his veteran.

"Well," said Mrs. Morel, "you know you've got no right to
rip his collar."

"Well, our mother!" he answered. "I never meant tr'a done
it—an' it was on'y an old indirrubber collar as was torn
a'ready."

"Next time," said his mother, "*you* be more careful. I
shouldn't like it if you came home with your collar torn
off."

"I don't care, our mother; I never did it a-purpose."

The boy was rather miserable at being reprimanded.

"No—well, you be more careful."

William fled away, glad to be exonerated. And Mrs. Morel, who hated any bother with the neighbours, thought she would explain to Mrs. Anthony, and the business would be over.

But that evening Morel came in from the pit looking very sour. He stood in the kitchen and glared round, but did not speak for some minutes. Then:

"Wheer's that Willy?" he asked.

"What do you want *him* for?" asked Mrs. Morel, who had guessed.

"I'll let 'im know when I get him," said Morel, banging his pit-bottle on to the dresser.

"I suppose Mrs. Anthony's got hold of you and been yarning to you about Alfy's collar," said Mrs. Morel, rather sneering.

"Niver mind who's got hold of me," said Morel. "When I get hold of *'im* I'll make his bones rattle."

"It's a poor tale," said Mrs. Morel, "that you're so ready to side with any snipey vixen who likes to come telling tales against your own children."

"I'll learn 'im!" said Morel. "It none matters to me whose lad 'e is; 'e's none goin' rippin' an' tearin' about just as he's a mind."

"'Ripping and tearing about!'" repeated Mrs. Morel. "He was running after that Alfy, who'd taken his cobbler, and he accidentally got hold of his collar, because the other dodged—as an Anthony would."

"I know!" shouted Morel threateningly.

"You would, before you're told," replied his wife bitingly.

"Niver you mind," stormed Morel. "I know my business."

"That's more than doubtful," said Mrs. Morel, "supposing some loud-mouthed creature had been getting you to thrash your own children."

"I know," repeated Morel.

And he said no more, but sat and nursed his bad temper. Suddenly William ran in, saying:

"Can I have my tea, mother?"

"Tha can ha'e more than that!" shouted Morel.

"Hold your noise, man," said Mrs. Morel; "and don't look so ridiculous."

"He'll look ridiculous before I've done wi' him!" shouted Morel, rising from his chair and glaring at his son.

William, who was a tall lad for his years, but very sensitive, had gone pale, and was looking in a sort of horror at his father.

"Go out!" Mrs. Morel commanded her son.

William had not the wit to move. Suddenly Morel clenched his fist, and crouched.

"I'll *gi'e* him 'go out'!" he shouted like an insane thing.

"What!" cried Mrs. Morel, panting with rage. "You shall not touch him for *her* telling, you shall not!"

"Shonna I?" shouted Morel. "Shonna I?"

And, glaring at the boy, he ran forward. Mrs. Morel sprang in between them, with her fist lifted.

"Don't you *dare!*" she cried.

"What!" he shouted, baffled for the moment. "What!"

She spun round to her son.

"*Go* out of the house!" she commanded him in fury.

The boy, as if hypnotised by her, turned suddenly and was gone. Morel rushed to the door, but was too late. He returned, pale under his pit-dirt with fury. But now his wife was fully roused.

"Only dare!" she said in a loud, ringing voice. "Only dare, milord, to lay a finger on that child! You'll regret it for ever."

He was afraid of her. In a towering rage, he sat down.

When the children were old enough to be left, Mrs. Morel joined the Women's Guild. It was a little club of women attached to the Co-operative Wholesale Society, which met on Monday night in the long room over the grocery shop of the Bestwood "Co-op". The women were supposed to discuss the benefits to be derived from co-operation, and other social questions. Sometimes Mrs. Morel read a paper. It seemed queer to the children to see their mother, who was always busy about the house, sitting writing in her rapid fashion, thinking, referring to books, and writing again. They felt for her on such occasions the deepest respect.

But they loved the Guild. It was the only thing to which they did not grudge their mother—and that partly because she enjoyed it, partly because of the treats they derived from it. The Guild was called by some hostile husbands, who found their wives getting too independent, the "clat-fart" shop—that is, the gossip-shop. It is true, from off the basis of the Guild, the women could look at their homes, at the conditions of their own lives, and find fault. So the colliers found their women had a new standard of their own, rather disconcerting. And also, Mrs. Morel always had a lot of news on Monday nights,

so that the children liked William to be in when their mother
came home, because she told him things.

Then, when the lad was thirteen, she got him a job in the
"Co-op." office. He was a very clever boy, frank, with rather
rough features and real viking blue eyes.

"What dost want ter ma'e a stool-harsed Jack on 'im for?"
said Morel. "All he'll do is to wear his britches behind out, an'
earn nowt. What's 'e startin' wi'?"

"It doesn't matter what he's starting with," said Mrs. Morel.

"It wouldna! Put 'im i' th' pit we me, an' 'e'll earn a easy
ten shillin' a wik from th' start. But six shillin' wearin' his
truck-end out on a stool's better than ten shillin' i' th' pit wi'
me, I know."

"He is *not* going in the pit," said Mrs. Morel, "and there's an
end of it."

"It wor good enough for me, but it's non good enough for
'im."

"If your mother put you in the pit at twelve, it's no reason
why I should do the same with my lad."

"Twelve! It wor a sight afore that!"

"Whenever it was," said Mrs. Morel.

She was very proud of her son. He went to the night school,
and learned shorthand, so that by the time he was sixteen he
was the best shorthand clerk and book-keeper on the place,
except one. Then he taught in the night schools. But he was
so fiery that only his good-nature and his size protected him.
All the things that men do—the decent things—William did.
He could run like the wind. When he was twelve he won a
first prize in a race; an inkstand of glass, shaped like an anvil.
It stood proudly on the dresser, and gave Mrs. Morel a keen
pleasure. The boy only ran for her. He flew home with his
anvil, breathless, with a "Look, mother!" That was the first
real tribute to herself. She took it like a queen.

"How pretty!" she exclaimed.

Then he began to get ambitious. He gave all his money to
his mother. When he earned fourteen shillings a week, she
gave him back two for himself, and, as he never drank, he felt
himself rich. He went about with the bourgeois of Bestwood.

The townlet contained nothing higher than the clergyman.
Then came the bank manager, then the doctors, then the tradespeople, and after that the hosts of colliers. William began to
consort with the sons of the chemist, the schoolmaster, and the

tradesmen. He played billiards in the Mechanics' Hall. Also
he danced—this in spite of his mother. All the life that Bestwood offered he enjoyed, from the sixpenny-hops down Church
Street, to sports and billiards.

Paul was treated to dazzling descriptions of all kinds of
flower-like ladies, most of whom lived like cut blooms in
William's heart for a brief fortnight.

Occasionally some flame would come in pursuit of her
errant swain. Mrs. Morel would find a strange girl at the door,
and immediately she sniffed the air.

"Is Mr. Morel in?" the damsel would ask appealingly.

"My husband is at home," Mrs. Morel replied.

"I—I mean *young* Mr. Morel," repeated the maiden painfully.

"Which one? There are several."

Whereupon much blushing and stammering from the fair
one.

"I—I met Mr. Morel—at Ripley," she explained.

"Oh—at a dance!"

"Yes."

"I don't approve of the girls my son meets at dances. And
he is *not* at home."

Then he came home angry with his mother for having turned
the girl away so rudely. He was a careless, yet eager-looking
fellow, who walked with long strides, sometimes frowning,
often with his cap pushed jollily to the back of his head. Now
he came in frowning. He threw his cap on to the sofa, and
took his strong jaw in his hand, and glared down at his mother.
She was small, with her hair taken straight back from her forehead. She had a quiet air of authority, and yet of rare warmth.
Knowing her son was angry, she trembled inwardly.

"Did a lady call for me yesterday, mother?" he asked.

"I don't know about a lady. There was a girl came."

"And why didn't you tell me?"

"Because I forgot, simply."

He fumed a little.

"A good-looking girl—seemed a lady?"

"I didn't look at her."

"Big brown eyes?"

"I did *not* look. And tell your girls, my son, that when
they're running after you, they're not to come and ask your
mother for you. Tell them that—brazen baggages you meet
at dancing-classes."

discord

"I'm sure she was a nice girl."

"And I'm sure she wasn't."

There ended the altercation. Over the dancing there was a great strife between the mother and the son. The grievance reached its height when William said he was going to Hucknall Torkard—considered a low town—to a fancy-dress ball. He was to be a Highlander. There was a dress he could hire, which one of his friends had had, and which fitted him perfectly. The Highland suit came home. Mrs. Morel received it coldly and would not unpack it.

"My suit come?" cried William.

"There's a parcel in the front room."

He rushed in and cut the string.

"How do you fancy your son in this!" he said, enraptured, showing her the suit.

"You know I don't want to fancy you in it."

On the evening of the dance, when he had come home to dress, Mrs. Morel put on her coat and bonnet.

"Aren't you going to stop and see me, mother?" he asked.

"No; I don't want to see you," she replied.

She was rather pale, and her face was closed and hard. She was afraid of her son's going the same way as his father. He hesitated a moment, and his heart stood still with anxiety. Then he caught sight of the Highland bonnet with its ribbons. He picked it up gleefully, forgetting her. She went out.

When he was nineteen he suddenly left the Co-op. office and got a situation in Nottingham. In his new place he had thirty shillings a week instead of eighteen. This was indeed a rise. His mother and his father were brimmed up with pride. Everybody praised William. It seemed he was going to get on rapidly. Mrs. Morel hoped, with his aid, to help her younger sons. Annie was now studying to be a teacher. Paul, also very clever, was getting on well, having lessons in French and German from his godfather, the clergyman who was still a friend to Mrs. Morel. Arthur, a spoilt and very good-looking boy, was at the Board school, but there was talk of his trying to get a scholarship for the High School in Nottingham.

William remained a year at his new post in Nottingham. He was studying hard, and growing serious. Something seemed to be fretting him. Still he went out to the dances and the river parties. He did not drink. The children were all rabid tee-totallers. He came home very late at night, and sat yet longer

she doth worry too much

studying. His mother implored him to take more care, to do one thing or another.

"Dance, if you want to dance, my son; but don't think you can work in the office, and then amuse yourself, and *then* study on top of all. You can't; the human frame won't stand it. Do one thing or the other—amuse yourself or learn Latin; but don't try to do both."

Then he got a place in London, at a hundred and twenty a year. This seemed a fabulous sum. His mother doubted almost whether to rejoice or to grieve.

"They want me in Lime Street on Monday week, mother," he cried, his eyes blazing as he read the letter. Mrs. Morel felt everything go silent inside her. He read the letter: " 'And will you reply by Thursday whether you accept. Yours faithfully——' They want me, mother, at a hundred and twenty a year, and don't even ask to see me. Didn't I tell you I could do it! Think of me in London! And I can give you twenty pounds a year, mater. We s'll all be rolling in money."

"We shall, my son," she answered sadly.

It never occurred to him that she might be more hurt at his going away than glad of his success. Indeed, as the days drew near for his departure, her heart began to close and grow dreary with despair. She loved him so much! More than that, she hoped in him so much. Almost she lived by him. She liked to do things for him: she liked to put a cup for his tea and to iron his collars, of which he was so proud. It was a joy to her to have him proud of his collars. There was no laundry. So she used to rub away at them with her little convex iron, to polish them, till they shone from the sheer pressure of her arm. Now she would not do it for him. Now he was going away. She felt almost as if he were going as well out of her heart. He did not seem to leave her inhabited with himself. That was the grief and the pain to her. He took nearly all himself away.

A few days before his departure—he was just twenty—he burned his love-letters. They had hung on a file at the top of the kitchen cupboard. From some of them he had read extracts to his mother. Some of them she had taken the trouble to read herself. But most were too trivial.

Now, on the Saturday morning he said:

"Come on, Postle, let's go through my letters, and you can have the birds and flowers."

Mrs. Morel had done her Saturday's work on the Friday, because he was having a last day's holiday. She was making him a rice cake, which he loved, to take with him. He was scarcely conscious that she was so miserable.

He took the first letter off the file. It was mauve-tinted, and had purple and green thistles. William sniffed the page.

"Nice scent! Smell."

And he thrust the sheet under Paul's nose.

"Um!" said Paul, breathing in. "What d'you call it? Smell, mother."

His mother ducked her small, fine nose down to the paper.

"*I* don't want to smell their rubbish," she said, sniffing.

"This girl's father," said William, "is as rich as Crœsus. He owns property without end. She calls me Lafayette, because I know French. 'You will see, I've forgiven you'—I like *her* forgiving me. 'I told mother about you this morning, and she will have much pleasure if you come to tea on Sunday, but she will have to get father's consent also. I sincerely hope he will agree. I will let you know how it transpires. If, however, you——' "

" 'Let you know how it' what?" interrupted Mrs. Morel.

" 'Transpires'—oh yes!"

" 'Transpires!' " repeated Mrs. Morel mockingly. "I thought she was so well educated!"

William felt slightly uncomfortable, and abandoned this maiden, giving Paul the corner with the thistles. He continued to read extracts from his letters, some of which amused his mother, some of which saddened her and made her anxious for him.

"My lad," she said, "they're very wise. They know they've only got to flatter your vanity, and you press up to them like a dog that has its head scratched."

"Well, they can't go on scratching for ever," he replied. "And when they've done, I trot away."

"But one day you'll find a string round your neck that you can't pull off," she answered.

"Not me! I'm equal to any of 'em, mater, they needn't flatter themselves."

"You flatter *yourself*," she said quietly.

Soon there was a heap of twisted black pages, all that remained of the file of scented letters, except that Paul had thirty or forty pretty tickets from the corners of the notepaper—

swallows and forget-me-nots and ivy sprays. And William
went to London, to start a new life.

CHAPTER IV

THE YOUNG LIFE OF PAUL

PAUL would be built like his mother, slightly and rather small.
His fair hair went reddish, and then dark brown; his eyes were
grey. He was a pale, quiet child, with eyes that seemed to
listen, and with a full, dropping underlip.

As a rule he seemed old for his years. He was so conscious
of what other people felt, particularly his mother. When she
fretted he understood, and could have no peace. His soul
seemed always attentive to her.

As he grew older he became stronger. William was too far
removed from him to accept him as a companion. So the
smaller boy belonged at first almost entirely to Annie. She
was a tomboy and a "flybie-skybie", as her mother called her.
But she was intensely fond of her second brother. So Paul was
towed round at the heels of Annie, sharing her game. She raced
wildly at lerky with the other young wild-cats of the Bottoms.
And always Paul flew beside her, living her share of the game,
having as yet no part of his own. He was quiet and not noticeable. But his sister adored him. He always seemed to care for
things if she wanted him to.

She had a big doll of which she was fearfully proud, though
not so fond. So she laid the doll on the sofa, and covered it
with an antimacassar, to sleep. Then she forgot it. Meantime
Paul must practise jumping off the sofa arm. So he jumped
crash into the face of the hidden doll. Annie rushed up, uttered
a loud wail, and sat down to weep a dirge. Paul remained quite
still.

"You couldn't tell it was there, mother; you couldn't tell it
was there," he repeated over and over. So long as Annie wept
for the doll he sat helpless with misery. Her grief wore itself
out. She forgave her brother—he was so much upset. But a
day or two afterwards she was shocked.

"Let's make a sacrifice of Arabella," he said. "Let's burn her."

She was horrified, yet rather fascinated. She wanted to see
what the boy would do. He made an altar of bricks, pulled

some of the shavings out of Arabella's body, put the waxen fragments into the hollow face, poured on a little paraffin, and set the whole thing alight. He watched with wicked satisfaction the drops of wax melt off the broken forehead of Arabella, and drop like sweat into the flame. So long as the stupid big doll burned he rejoiced in silence. At the end he poked among the embers with a stick, fished out the arms and legs, all blackened, and smashed them under stones.

"That's the sacrifice of Missis Arabella," he said. "An' I'm glad there's nothing left of her."

Which disturbed Annie inwardly, although she could say nothing. He seemed to hate the doll so intensely, because he had broken it.

All the children, but particularly Paul, were peculiarly *against* their father, along with their mother. Morel continued to bully and to drink. He had periods, months at a time, when he made the whole life of the family a misery. Paul never forgot coming home from the Band of Hope one Monday evening and finding his mother with her eye swollen and discoloured, his father standing on the hearth-rug, feet astride, his head down, and William, just home from work, glaring at his father. There was a silence as the young children entered, but none of the elders looked round.

William was white to the lips, and his fists were clenched. He waited until the children were silent, watching with children's rage and hate; then he said:

"You coward, you daren't do it when I was in."

But Morel's blood was up. He swung round on his son. William was bigger, but Morel was hard-muscled, and mad with fury.

"Dossn't I?" he shouted. "Dossn't I? Ha'e much more o' thy chelp, my young jockey, an' I'll rattle my fist about thee. Ay, an' I sholl that, dost see?"

Morel crouched at the knees and showed his fist in an ugly, almost beast-like fashion. William was white with rage.

"Will yer?" he said, quiet and intense. "It 'ud be the last time, though."

Morel danced a little nearer, crouching, drawing back his fist to strike. William put his fists ready. A light came into his blue eyes, almost like a laugh. He watched his father. Another word, and the men would have begun to fight. Paul hoped they would. The three children sat pale on the sofa.

"Stop it, both of you," cried Mrs. Morel in a hard voice. "We've had enough for *one* night. And *you*," she said, turning on to her husband, "look at your children!"

Morel glanced at the sofa.

"Look at the children, you nasty little bitch!" he sneered. "Why, what have *I* done to the children, I should like to know? But they're like yourself; you've put 'em up to your own tricks and nasty ways—you've learned 'em in it, you 'ave."

Morel + Children

She refused to answer him. No one spoke. After a while he threw his boots under the table and went to bed.

"Why didn't you let me have a go at him?" said William, when his father was upstairs. "I could easily have beaten him."

"A nice thing—your own father," she replied.

" '*Father!*' " repeated William. "Call *him* my father!"

"Well, he is—and so——"

"But why don't you let me settle him? I could do, easily."

"The idea!" she cried. "It hasn't come to *that* yet."

"No," he said, "it's come to worse. Look at yourself. *Why* didn't you let me give it him?"

"Because I couldn't bear it, so never think of it," she cried quickly.

And the children went to bed, miserably.

When William was growing up, the family moved from the Bottoms to a house on the brow of the hill, commanding a view of the valley, which spread out like a convex cockle-shell, or a clamp-shell, before it. In front of the house was a huge old ash-tree. The west wind, sweeping from Derbyshire, caught the houses with full force, and the tree shrieked again. Morel liked it.

making of discord

"It's music," he said. "It sends me to sleep."

But Paul and Arthur and Annie hated it. To Paul it became almost a demoniacal noise. The winter of their first year in the new house their father was very bad. The children played in the street, on the brim of the wide, dark valley, until eight o'clock. Then they went to bed. Their mother sat sewing below. Having such a great space in front of the house gave the children a feeling of night, of vastness, and of terror. This terror came in from the shrieking of the tree and the anguish of the home discord. Often Paul would wake up, after he had been asleep a long time, aware of thuds downstairs. Instantly he was wide awake. Then he heard the booming shouts of his father, come home nearly drunk, then the sharp replies of his

especially Paul

mother, then the bang, bang of his father's fist on the table,
and the nasty snarling shout as the man's voice got higher.
And then the whole was drowned in a piercing medley of
shrieks and cries from the great, wind-swept ash-tree. The
children lay silent in suspense, waiting for a lull in the wind
to hear what their father was doing. He might hit their mother
again. There was a feeling of horror, a kind of bristling in the
darkness, and a sense of blood. They lay with their hearts in
the grip of an intense anguish. The wind came through the
tree fiercer and fiercer. All the cords of the great harp hummed,
whistled, and shrieked. And then came the horror of the
sudden silence, silence everywhere, outside and downstairs.
What was it? Was it a silence of blood? What had he done?

The children lay and breathed the darkness. And then, at
last, they heard their father throw down his boots and tramp
upstairs in his stockinged feet. Still they listened. Then at last,
if the wind allowed, they heard the water of the tap drumming
into the kettle, which their mother was filling for morning, and
they could go to sleep in peace.

So they were happy in the morning—happy, very happy
playing, dancing at night round the lonely lamp-post in the
midst of the darkness. But they had one tight place of anxiety
in their hearts, one darkness in their eyes, which showed all
their lives.

Paul hated his father. As a boy he had a fervent private
religion.

"Make him stop drinking," he prayed every night. "Lord,
let my father die," he prayed very often. "Let him not be
killed at pit," he prayed when, after tea, the father did not
come home from work.

That was another time when the family suffered intensely.
The children came from school and had their teas. On the hob
the big black saucepan was simmering, the stew-jar was in the
oven, ready for Morel's dinner. He was expected at five o'clock.
But for months he would stop and drink every night on his way
from work.

In the winter nights, when it was cold, and grew dark early,
Mrs. Morel would put a brass candlestick on the table, light a
tallow candle to save the gas. The children finished their bread-
and-butter, or dripping, and were ready to go out to play. But
if Morel had not come they faltered. The sense of his sitting
in all his pit-dirt, drinking, after a long day's work, not coming

home and eating and washing, but sitting, getting drunk, on an empty stomach, made Mrs. Morel unable to bear herself. From her the feeling was transmitted to the other children. She never suffered alone any more : the children suffered with her.

Paul went out to play with the rest. Down in the great trough of twilight, tiny clusters of lights burned where the pits were. A few last colliers straggled up the dim field path. The lamplighter came along. No more colliers came. Darkness shut down over the valley; work was done. It was night.

Then Paul ran anxiously into the kitchen. The one candle still burned on the table, the big fire glowed red. Mrs. Morel sat alone. On the hob the saucepan steamed; the dinner-plate lay waiting on the table. All the room was full of the sense of waiting, waiting for the man who was sitting in his pit-dirt, dinnerless, some mile away from home, across the darkness, drinking himself drunk. Paul stood in the doorway.

"Has my dad come?" he asked.

"You can see he hasn't," said Mrs. Morel, cross with the futility of the question.

Then the boy dawdled about near his mother. They shared the same anxiety. Presently Mrs. Morel went out and strained the potatoes.

"They're ruined and black," she said; "but what do I care?"

Not many words were spoken. Paul almost hated his mother for suffering because his father did not come home from work.

"What do you bother yourself for?" he said. "If he wants to stop and get drunk, why don't you let him?"

"Let him!" flashed Mrs. Morel. "You may well say 'let him'."

She knew that the man who stops on the way home from work is on a quick way to ruining himself and his home. The children were yet young, and depended on the breadwinner. William gave her the sense of relief, providing her at last with someone to turn to if Morel failed. But the tense atmosphere of the room on these waiting evenings was the same.

The minutes ticked away. At six o'clock still the cloth lay on the table, still the dinner stood waiting, still the same sense of anxiety and expectation in the room. The boy could not stand it any longer. He could not go out and play. So he ran in to Mrs. Inger, next door but one, for her to talk to him. She had no children. Her husband was good to her but was in a shop, and came home late. So, when she saw the lad at the door, she called:

"Come in, Paul."

The two sat talking for some time, when suddenly the boy rose, saying:

"Well, I'll be going and seeing if my mother wants an errand doing."

He pretended to be perfectly cheerful, and did not tell his friend what ailed him. Then he ran indoors.

Morel at these times came in churlish and hateful.

"This is a nice time to come home," said Mrs. Morel.

"Wha's it matter to yo' what time I come whoam?" he shouted.

And everybody in the house was still, because he was dangerous. He ate his food in the most brutal manner possible, and, when he had done, pushed all the pots in a heap away from him, to lay his arms on the table. Then he went to sleep. Paul hated his father so. The collier's small, mean head, with its black hair slightly soiled with grey, lay on the bare arms, and the face, dirty and inflamed, with a fleshy nose and thin, paltry brows, was turned sideways, asleep with beer and weariness and nasty temper. If anyone entered suddenly, or a noise were made, the man looked up and shouted:

"I'll lay my fist about thy y'ead, I'm tellin' thee, if tha doesna stop that clatter! Dost hear?"

And the two last words, shouted in a bullying fashion, usually at Annie, made the family writhe with hate of the man.

He was shut out from all family affairs. No one told him anything. The children, alone with their mother, told her all about the day's happenings, everything. Nothing had really taken place in them until it was told to their mother. But as soon as the father came in, everything stopped. He was like the scotch in the smooth, happy machinery of the home. And he was always aware of this fall of silence on his entry, the shutting off of life, the unwelcome. But now it was gone too far to alter.

He would dearly have liked the children to talk to him, but they could not. Sometimes Mrs. Morel would say:

"You ought to tell your father."

Paul won a prize in a competition in a child's paper. Everybody was highly jubilant.

"Now you'd better tell your father when he comes in," said Mrs. Morel. "You know how he carries on and says he's never told anything."

"All right," said Paul. But he would almost rather have forfeited the prize than have to tell his father.

"I've won a prize in a competition, dad," he said.

Morel turned round to him.

"Have you, my boy? What sort of a competition?"

"Oh, nothing—about famous women."

"And how much is the prize, then, as you've got?"

"It's a book."

"Oh, indeed!"

"About birds."

"Hm—hm!"

And that was all. Conversation was impossible between the father and any other member of the family. He was an outsider. He had denied the God in him.

The only times when he entered again into the life of his own people was when he worked, and was happy at work. Sometimes, in the evening, he cobbled the boots or mended the kettle or his pit-bottle. Then he always wanted several attendants, and the children enjoyed it. They united with him in the work, in the actual doing of something, when he was his real self again.

He was a good workman, dexterous, and one who, when he was in a good humour, always sang. He had whole periods, months, almost years, of friction and nasty temper. Then sometimes he was jolly again. It was nice to see him run with a piece of red-hot iron into the scullery, crying:

"Out of my road—out of my road!"

Then he hammered the soft, red-glowing stuff on his iron goose, and made the shape he wanted. Or he sat absorbed for a moment, soldering. Then the children watched with joy as the metal sank suddenly molten, and was shoved about against the nose of the soldering-iron, while the room was full of a scent of burnt resin and hot tin, and Morel was silent and intent for a minute. He always sang when he mended boots because of the jolly sound of hammering. And he was rather happy when he sat putting great patches on his moleskin pit trousers, which he would often do, considering them too dirty, and the stuff too hard, for his wife to mend.

But the best time for the young children was when he made

fuses. Morel fetched a sheaf of long sound wheat-straws from the attic. These he cleaned with his hand, till each one gleamed like a stalk of gold, after which he cut the straws into lengths of about six inches, leaving, if he could, a notch at the bottom of each piece. He always had a beautifully sharp knife that could cut a straw clean without hurting it. Then he set in the middle of the table a heap of gunpowder, a little pile of black grains upon the white-scrubbed board. He made and trimmed the straws while Paul and Annie filled and plugged them. Paul loved to see the black grains trickle down a crack in his palm into the mouth of the straw, peppering jollily downwards till the straw was full. Then he bunged up the mouth with a bit of soap—which he got on his thumb-nail from a pat in a saucer —and the straw was finished.

"Look, dad!" he said.

"That's right, my beauty," replied Morel, who was peculiarly lavish of endearments to his second son. Paul popped the fuse into the powder-tin, ready for the morning, when Morel would take it to the pit, and use it to fire a shot that would blast the coal down.

Meantime Arthur, still fond of his father, would lean on the arm of Morel's chair and say:

"Tell us about down pit, daddy."

This Morel loved to do.

"Well, there's one little 'oss—we call 'im Taffy," he would begin. "An' he's a fawce 'un!"

Morel had a warm way of telling a story. He made one feel Taffy's cunning.

"He's a brown 'un," he would answer, "an' not very high. Well, he comes i' th' stall wi' a rattle, an' then yo' 'ear 'im sneeze.

"'Ello, Taff,' you say, 'what art sneezin' for? Bin ta'ein' some snuff?'

"An' 'e sneezes again. Then he slives up an' shoves 'is 'ead on yer, that cadin'.

"'What's want, Taff?' yo' say."

"And what does he?" Arthur always asked.

"He wants a bit o' bacca, my duckie."

This story of Taffy would go on interminably, and everybody loved it.

Or sometimes it was a new tale.

"An' what dost think, my darlin'? When I went to put my

coat on at snap-time, what should go runnin' up my arm but a mouse.

" 'Hey up, theer!' I shouts.

"An' I wor just in time ter get 'im by th' tail."

"And did you kill it?"

"I did, for they're a nuisance. The place is fair snied wi' 'em."

"An' what do they live on?"

"The corn as the 'osses drops—an' they'll get in your pocket an' eat your snap, if you'll let 'em—no matter where yo' hing your coat—the slivin', nibblin' little nuisances, for they are."

These happy evenings could not take place unless Morel had some job to do. And then he always went to bed very early, often before the children. There was nothing remaining for him to stay up for, when he had finished tinkering, and had skimmed the headlines of the newspaper.

And the children felt secure when their father was in bed. They lay and talked softly a while. Then they started as the lights went suddenly sprawling over the ceiling from the lamps that swung in the hands of the colliers tramping by outside, going to take the nine o'clock shift. They listened to the voices of the men, imagined them dipping down into the dark valley. Sometimes they went to the window and watched the three or four lamps growing tinier and tinier, swaying down the fields in the darkness. Then it was a joy to rush back to bed and cuddle closely in the warmth.

Paul was rather a delicate boy, subject to bronchitis. The others were all quite strong; so this was another reason for his mother's difference in feeling for him. One day he came home at dinner-time feeling ill. But it was not a family to make any fuss.

"What's the matter with *you*?" his mother asked sharply.

"Nothing," he replied.

But he ate no dinner.

"If you eat no dinner, you're not going to school," she said.

"Why?" he asked.

"That's why."

So after dinner he lay down on the sofa, on the warm chintz cushions the children loved. Then he fell into a kind of doze. That afternoon Mrs. Morel was ironing. She listened to the small, restless noise the boy made in his throat as she worked. Again rose in her heart the old, almost weary feeling towards him. She had never expected him to live. And yet he had a great vitality in his young body. Perhaps it would have been a little relief to her if he had died. She always felt a mixture of anguish in her love for him.

He, in his semi-conscious sleep, was vaguely aware of the clatter of the iron on the iron-stand, of the faint thud, thud on the ironing-board. Once roused, he opened his eyes to see his mother standing on the hearth-rug with the hot iron near her cheek, listening, as it were, to the heat. Her still face, with the mouth closed tight from suffering and disillusion and self-denial, and her nose the smallest bit on one side, and her blue eyes so young, quick, and warm, made his heart contract with love. When she was quiet, so, she looked brave and rich with life, but as if she had been done out of her rights. It hurt the boy keenly, this feeling about her that she had never had her life's fulfilment: and his own incapability to make up to her hurt him with a sense of impotence, yet made him patiently dogged inside. It was his childish aim.

She spat on the iron, and a little ball of spit bounded, raced off the dark, glossy surface. Then, kneeling, she rubbed the iron on the sack lining of the hearth-rug vigorously. She was warm in the ruddy firelight. Paul loved the way she crouched and put her head on one side. Her movements were light and quick. It was always a pleasure to watch her. Nothing she ever did, no movement she ever made, could have been found fault with by her children. The room was warm and full of the scent of hot linen. Later on the clergyman came and talked softly with her.

Paul was laid up with an attack of bronchitis. He did not mind much. What happened happened, and it was no good kicking against the pricks. He loved the evenings, after eight o'clock, when the light was put out, and he could watch the fire-flames spring over the darkness of the walls and ceiling; could watch huge shadows waving and tossing, till the room seemed full of men who battled silently.

On retiring to bed, the father would come into the sick-room. He was always very gentle if anyone were ill. But he disturbed the atmosphere for the boy.

"Are ter asleep, my darlin'?" Morel asked softly.

"No; is my mother comin'?"

"She's just finishin' foldin' the clothes. Do you want anything?" Morel rarely "thee'd" his son.

"I don't want nothing. But how long will she be?"

"Not long, my duckie."

The father waited undecidedly on the hearth-rug for a moment or two. He felt his son did not want him. Then he went to the top of the stairs and said to his wife:

"This childt's axin' for thee; how long art goin' to be?"

"Until I've finished, good gracious! Tell him to go to sleep."

"She says you're to go to sleep," the father repeated gently to Paul.

"Well, I want *her* to come," insisted the boy.

"He says he can't go off till you come," Morel called downstairs.

"Eh, dear! I shan't be long. And do stop shouting downstairs. There's the other children——"

Then Morel came again and crouched before the bedroom fire. He loved a fire dearly.

"She says she won't be long," he said.

He loitered about indefinitely. The boy began to get feverish with irritation. His father's presence seemed to aggravate all his sick impatience. At last Morel, after having stood looking at his son awhile, said softly:

"Good-night, my darling."

"Good-night," Paul replied, turning round in relief to be alone.

Paul loved to sleep with his mother. Sleep is still most perfect, in spite of hygienists, when it is shared with a beloved. The warmth, the security and peace of soul, the utter comfort from the touch of the other, knits the sleep, so that it takes the body and soul completely in its healing. Paul lay against her and slept, and got better; whilst she, always a bad sleeper, fell later on into a profound sleep that seemed to give her faith.

In convalescence he would sit up in bed, see the fluffy horses feeding at the troughs in the field, scattering their hay on the trodden yellow snow; watch the miners troop home—small, black figures trailing slowly in gangs across the white field. Then the night came up in dark blue vapour from the snow.

In convalescence everything was wonderful. The snowflakes, suddenly arriving on the window-pane, clung there a moment like swallows, then were gone, and a drop of water was crawling down the glass. The snowflakes whirled round the corner of the house, like pigeons dashing by. Away across the valley the little black train crawled doubtfully over the great whiteness.

While they were so poor, the children were delighted if they could do anything to help economically. Annie and Paul and Arthur went out early in the morning, in summer, looking for mushrooms, hunting through the wet grass, from which the larks were rising, for the white-skinned, wonderful naked bodies crouched secretly in the green. And if they got half a pound they felt exceedingly happy: there was the joy of finding something, the joy of accepting something straight from the hand of Nature, and the joy of contributing to the family exchequer.

But the most important harvest, after gleaning for frumenty, was the blackberries. Mrs. Morel must buy fruit for puddings on the Saturdays; also she liked blackberries. So Paul and Arthur scoured the coppices and woods and old quarries, so long as a blackberry was to be found, every week-end going on their search. In that region of mining villages blackberries became a comparative rarity. But Paul hunted far and wide. He loved being out in the country, among the bushes. But he also could not bear to go home to his mother empty. That, he felt, would disappoint her, and he would have died rather.

"Good gracious!" she would exclaim as the lads came in, late, and tired to death, and hungry, "wherever have you been?"

"Well," replied Paul, "there wasn't any, so we went over Misk Hills. And look here, our mother!"

She peeped into the basket.

"Now, those are fine ones!" she exclaimed.

"And there's over two pounds—isn't there over two pounds?" She tried the basket.

"Yes," she answered doubtfully.

Then Paul fished out a little spray. He always brought her one spray, the best he could find.

"Pretty!" she said, in a curious tone, of a woman accepting a love-token.

The boy walked all day, went miles and miles, rather than own himself beaten and come home to her empty-handed. She never realised this, whilst he was young. She was a woman who waited for her children to grow up. And William occupied her chiefly.

sub
~~~~~~
conscious

But when William went to Nottingham, and was not so much at home, the mother made a companion of Paul. The latter was unconsciously jealous of his brother, and William was jealous of him. At the same time, they were good friends.

Mrs. Morel's intimacy with her second son was more subtle and fine, perhaps not so passionate as with her eldest. It was the rule that Paul should fetch the money on Friday afternoons. The colliers of the five pits were paid on Fridays, but not individually. All the earnings of each stall were put down to the chief butty, as contractor, and he divided the wages again, either in the public-house or in his own home. So that the children could fetch the money, school closed early on Friday afternoons. Each of the Morel children—William, then Annie, then Paul—had fetched the money on Friday afternoons, until they went themselves to work. Paul used to set off at half-past three, with a little calico bag in his pocket. Down all the paths, women, girls, children, and men were seen trooping to the offices.

These offices were quite handsome: a new, red-brick building, almost like a mansion, standing in its own grounds at the end of Greenhill Lane. The waiting-room was the hall, a long, bare room paved with blue brick, and having a seat all round, against the wall. Here sat the colliers in their pit-dirt. They had come up early. The women and children usually loitered about on the red gravel paths. Paul always examined the grass border, and the big grass bank, because in it grew tiny pansies and tiny forget-me-nots. There was a sound of many voices. The women had on their Sunday hats. The girls chattered loudly. Little dogs ran here and there. The green shrubs were silent all around.

Then from inside came the cry "Spinney Park—Spinney Park." All the folk for Spinney Park trooped inside. When it was time for Bretty to be paid, Paul went in among the crowd. The pay-room was quite small. A counter went across, dividing it into half. Behind the counter stood two men—Mr. Braithwaite and his clerk, Mr. Winterbottom. Mr. Braithwaite was large, somewhat of the stern patriarch in appearance, having a rather thin white beard. He was usually muffled in an enormous silk neckerchief, and right up to the hot summer a huge fire burned in the open grate. No window was open. Sometimes in winter the air scorched the throats of the people, coming in from the freshness. Mr. Winterbottom was rather small and fat, and very bald. He made remarks that were not witty, whilst his chief launched forth patriarchal admonitions against the colliers.

The room was crowded with miners in their pit-dirt, men who had been home and changed, and women, and one or two children, and usually a dog. Paul was quite small, so it was often his fate to be jammed behind the legs of the men, near the fire which scorched him. He knew the order of the names —they went according to stall number.

"Holliday," came the ringing voice of Mr. Braithwaite. Then Mrs. Holliday stepped silently forward, was paid, drew aside.

"Bower—John Bower."

A boy stepped to the counter. Mr. Braithwaite, large and irascible, glowered at him over his spectacles.

"John Bower!" he repeated.

"It's me," said the boy.

"Why, you used to 'ave a different nose than that," said glossy Mr. Winterbottom, peering over the counter. The people tittered, thinking of John Bower senior.

"How is it your father's not come!" said Mr. Braithwaite, in a large and magisterial voice.

"He's badly," piped the boy.

"You should tell him to keep off the drink," pronounced the great cashier.

"An' niver mind if he puts his foot through yer," said a mocking voice from behind.

All the men laughed. The large and important cashier looked down at his next sheet.

"Fred Pilkington!" he called, quite indifferent.

Mr. Braithwaite was an important shareholder in the firm.

Paul knew his turn was next but one, and his heart began to beat. He was pushed against the chimney-piece. His calves were burning. But he did not hope to get through the wall of men.

"Walter Morel!" came the ringing voice.

"Here!" piped Paul, small and inadequate.

"Morel—Walter Morel!" the cashier repeated, his finger and thumb on the invoice, ready to pass on.

Paul was suffering convulsions of self-consciousness, and could not or would not shout. The backs of the men obliterated him. Then Mr. Winterbottom came to the rescue.

"He's here. Where is he? Morel's lad?"

The fat, red, bald little man peered round with keen eyes.

He pointed at the fireplace. The colliers looked round, moved aside, and disclosed the boy.

"Here he is!" said Mr. Winterbottom.

Paul went to the counter.

"Seventeen pounds eleven and fivepence. Why don't you shout up when you're called?" said Mr. Braithwaite. He banged on to the invoice a five-pound bag of silver, then in a delicate and pretty movement, picked up a little ten-pound column of gold, and plumped it beside the silver. The gold slid in a bright stream over the paper. The cashier finished counting off the money; the boy dragged the whole down the counter to Mr. Winterbottom, to whom the stoppages for rent and tools must be paid. Here he suffered again.

"Sixteen an' six," said Mr. Winterbottom.

The lad was too much upset to count. He pushed forward some loose silver and half a sovereign.

"How much do you think you've given me?" asked Mr. Winterbottom.

The boy looked at him, but said nothing. He had not the faintest notion.

"Haven't you got a tongue in your head?"

Paul bit his lip, and pushed forward some more silver.

"Don't they teach you to count at the Board-school?" he asked.

"Nowt but algibbra an' French," said a collier.

"An' cheek an' impidence," said another.

Paul was keeping someone waiting. With trembling fingers he got his money into the bag and slid out. He suffered the tortures of the damned on these occasions.

His relief, when he got outside, and was walking along the Mansfield Road, was infinite. On the park wall the mosses were green. There were some gold and some white fowls pecking under the apple trees of an orchard. The colliers were walking home in a stream. The boy went near the wall, self-consciously. He knew many of the men, but could not recognise them in their dirt. And this was a new torture to him.

When he got down to the New Inn, at Bretty, his father was not yet come. Mrs. Wharmby, the landlady, knew him. His grandmother, Morel's mother, had been Mrs. Wharmby's friend.

"Your father's not come yet," said the landlady, in the peculiar half-scornful, half-patronising voice of a woman who talks chiefly to grown men. "Sit you down."

Paul sat down on the edge of the bench in the bar. Some colliers were "reckoning"—sharing out their money—in a corner; others came in. They all glanced at the boy without speaking. At last Morel came; brisk, and with something of an air, even in his blackness.

"Hello!" he said rather tenderly to his son. "Have you bested me? Shall you have a drink of something?"

Paul and all the children were bred up fierce anti-alcoholists, and he would have suffered more in drinking a lemonade before all the men than in having a tooth drawn.

The landlady looked at him *de haut en bas*, rather pitying, and at the same time, resenting his clear, fierce morality. Paul went home, glowering. He entered the house silently. Friday was baking day, and there was usually a hot bun. His mother put it before him.

Suddenly he turned on her in a fury, his eyes flashing:

"I'm *not* going to the office any more," he said.

"Why, what's the matter?" his mother asked in surprise. His sudden rages rather amused her.

"I'm *not* going any more," he declared.

"Oh, very well, tell your father so."

He chewed his bun as if he hated it.

"I'm not—I'm not going to fetch the money."

"Then one of Carlin's children can go; they'd be glad enough of the sixpence," said Mrs. Morel.

This sixpence was Paul's only income. It mostly went in buying birthday presents; but it *was* an income, and he treasured it. But——

"They can have it, then!" he said. "I don't want it."

"Oh, very well," said his mother. "But you needn't bully *me* about it."

"They're hateful, and common, and hateful, they are, and I'm not going any more. Mr. Braithwaite drops his 'h's', an' Mr. Winterbottom says 'You was'."

"And is that why you won't go any more?" smiled Mrs. Morel.

The boy was silent for some time. His face was pale, his eyes dark and furious. His mother moved about at her work, taking no notice of him.

"They always stan' in front of me, so's I can't get out," he said.

"Well, my lad, you've only to *ask* them," she replied.

"An' then Alfred Winterbottom says, 'What do they teach you at the Board-school?' "

"They never taught *him* much," said Mrs. Morel, "that is a fact—neither manners nor wit—and his cunning he was born with."

So, in her own way, she soothed him. His ridiculous hypersensitiveness made her heart ache. And sometimes the fury in his eyes roused her, made her sleeping soul lift up its head a moment, surprised.

"What was the cheque?" she asked.

"Seventeen pounds eleven and fivepence, and sixteen and six stoppages," replied the boy. "It's a good week; and only five shillings stoppages for my father."

So she was able to calculate how much her husband had earned, and could call him to account if he gave her short money. Morel always kept to himself the secret of the week's amount.

Friday was the baking night and market night. It was the rule that Paul should stay at home and bake. He loved to stop in and draw or read; he was very fond of drawing. Annie always "gallivanted" on Friday nights; Arthur was enjoying himself as usual. So the boy remained alone.

Mrs. Morel loved her marketing. In the tiny market-place on the top of the hill, where four roads, from Nottingham and Derby, Ilkeston and Mansfield, meet, many stalls were erected. Brakes ran in from surrounding villages. The market-place was full of women, the streets packed with men. It was amazing to see so many men everywhere in the streets. Mrs. Morel usually quarrelled with her lace woman, sympathised with her fruit man—who was a gabey, but his wife was a bad 'un—laughed with the fish man—who was a scamp but so droll—put the linoleum man in his place, was cold with the odd-wares man, and only went to the crockery man when she was driven—or drawn by the cornflowers on a little dish; then she was coldly polite.

"I wondered how much that little dish was," she said.

"Sevenpence to you."

"Thank you."

She put the dish down and walked away; but she could not leave the market-place without it. Again she went by where the pots lay coldly on the floor, and she glanced at the dish furtively, pretending not to.

She was a little woman, in a bonnet and a black costume. Her bonnet was in its third year; it was a great grievance to Annie.

"Mother!" the girl implored, "don't wear that nubbly little bonnet."

"Then what else shall I wear," replied the mother tartly. "And I'm sure it's right enough."

It had started with a tip; then had had flowers; now was reduced to black lace and a bit of jet.

"It looks rather come down," said Paul. "Couldn't you give it a pick-me-up?"

"I'll jowl your head for impudence," said Mrs. Morel, and she tied the strings of the black bonnet valiantly under her chin.

She glanced at the dish again. Both she and her enemy, the pot man, had an uncomfortable feeling, as if there were something between them. Suddenly he shouted:

"Do you want it for fivepence?"

She started. Her heart hardened; but then she stooped and took up her dish.

"I'll have it," she said.

"Yer'll do me the favour, like?" he said. "Yer'd better spit in it, like yer do when y'ave something give yer."

Mrs. Morel paid him the fivepence in a cold manner.

"I don't see you give it me," she said. "You wouldn't let me have it for fivepence if you didn't want to."

"In this flamin', scrattlin' place you may count yerself lucky if you can give your things away," he growled.

"Yes; there are bad times, and good," said Mrs. Morel.

But she had forgiven the pot man. They were friends. She dare now finger his pots. So she was happy.

Paul was waiting for her. He loved her home-coming. She was always her best so—triumphant, tired, laden with parcels, feeling rich in spirit. He heard her quick, light step in the entry and looked up from his drawing.

"Oh!" she sighed, smiling at him from the doorway.

"My word, you *are* loaded!" he exclaimed, putting down his brush.

"I am!" she gasped. "That brazen Annie said she'd meet me. *Such* a weight!"

She dropped her string bag and her packages on the table.

"Is the bread done?" she asked, going to the oven.

"The last one is soaking," he replied. "You needn't look, I've not forgotten it."

"Oh, that pot man!" she said, closing the oven door. "You know what a wretch I've said he was? Well, I don't think he's quite so bad."

"Don't you?"

The boy was attentive to her. She took off her little black bonnet.

"No. I think he can't make any money—well, it's everybody's cry alike nowadays—and it makes him disagreeable."

"It would *me*," said Paul.

"Well, one can't wonder at it. And he let me have—how much do you think he let me have *this* for?"

She took the dish out of its rag of newspaper, and stood looking on it with joy.

"Show me!" said Paul.

The two stood together gloating over the dish.

"I *love* cornflowers on things," said Paul.

"Yes, and I thought of the teapot you bought me——"

"One and three," said Paul.

"Fivepence!"

"It's not enough, mother."

"No. Do you know, I fairly sneaked off with it. But I'd been extravagant, I couldn't afford any more. And he needn't have let me have it if he hadn't wanted to."

"No, he needn't, need he," said Paul, and the two comforted each other from the fear of having robbed the pot man.

"We c'n have stewed fruit in it," said Paul.

"Or custard, or a jelly," said his mother.

"Or radishes and lettuce," said he.

"Don't forget that bread," she said, her voice bright with glee.

Paul looked in the oven; tapped the loaf on the base.

"It's done," he said, giving it to her.

She tapped it also.

"Yes," she replied, going to unpack her bag. "Oh, and I'm a wicked, extravagant woman. I know I s'll come to want."

He hopped to her side eagerly, to see her latest extravagance. She unfolded another lump of newspaper and disclosed some roots of pansies and of crimson daisies.

"Four penn'orth!" she moaned.

"How *cheap*!" he cried.

"Yes, but I couldn't afford it *this* week of all weeks."

"But lovely!" he cried.

"Aren't they!" she exclaimed, giving way to pure joy. "Paul, look at this yellow one, isn't it—and a face just like an old man!"

"Just!" cried Paul, stooping to sniff. "And smells that nice! But he's a bit splashed."

He ran in the scullery, came back with the flannel, and carefully washed the pansy.

"*Now* look at him now he's wet!" he said.

"Yes!" she exclaimed, brimful of satisfaction.

Tht children of Scargill Street felt quite select. At the end where the Morels lived there were not many young things. So the few were more united. Boys and girls played together, the girls joining in the fights and the rough games, the boys taking part in the dancing games and rings and make-believe of the girls.

Annie and Paul and Arthur loved the winter evenings, when it was not wet. They stayed indoors till the colliers were all gone home, till it was thick dark, and the street would be deserted. Then they tied their scarves round their necks, for they scorned overcoats, as all the colliers' children did, and went out. The entry was very dark, and at the end the whole great night opened out, in a hollow, with a little tangle of lights below where Minton pit lay, and another far away opposite for Selby. The farthest tiny lights seemed to stretch out the darkness for ever. The children looked anxiously down the road at the one lamp-post, which stood at the end of the field path. If the little, luminous space were deserted, the two boys felt genuine desolation. They stood with their hands in their pockets under the lamp, turning their backs on the night, quite miserable, watching the dark houses. Suddenly a pinafore under a short coat was seen, and a long-legged girl came flying up.

"Where's Billy Pillins an' your Annie an' Eddie Dakin?"

"I don't know."

But it did not matter so much—there were three now. They set up a game round the lamp-post, till the others rushed up, yelling. Then the play went fast and furious.

There was only this one lamp-post. Behind was the great scoop of darkness, as if all the night were there. In front, another wide, dark way opened over the hill brow. Occasionally somebody came out of this way and went into the field down the path. In a dozen yards the night had swallowed them. The children played on.

They were brought exceedingly close together owing to their isolation. If a quarrel took place, the whole play was spoilt. Arthur was very touchy, and Billy Pillins—really Philips—was worse. Then Paul had to side with Arthur, and on Paul's side went Alice, while Billy Pillins always had Emmie Limb and Eddie Dakin to back him up. Then the six would fight, hate with a fury of hatred, and flee home in terror. Paul never forgot, after one of these fierce internecine fights, seeing a big red moon lift itself up, slowly, between the waste road over the hill-top, steadily, like a great bird. And he thought of the Bible, that the moon should be turned to blood. And the next day he made haste to be friends with Billy Pillins. And then the wild, intense games went on again under the lamp-post, surrounded by so much darkness. Mrs. Morel, going into her parlour, would hear the children singing away:

> "My shoes are made of Spanish leather,
> My socks are made of silk;
> I wear a ring on every finger,
> I wash myself in milk."

They sounded so perfectly absorbed in the game as their voices came out of the night, that they had the feel of wild creatures singing. It stirred the mother; and she understood when they came in at eight o'clock, ruddy, with brilliant eyes, and quick, passionate speech.

They all loved the Scargill Street house for its openness, for the great scallop of the world it had in view. On summer evenings the women would stand against the field fence, gossiping, facing the west, watching the sunsets flare quickly out, till the Derbyshire hills ridged across the crimson far away, like the black crest of a newt.

In this summer season the pits never turned full time, particularly the soft coal. Mrs. Dakin, who lived next door to Mrs. Morel, going to the field fence to shake her hearth-rug, would spy men coming slowly up the hill. She saw at once they were colliers. Then she waited, a tall, thin, shrew-faced woman, standing on the hill brow, almost like a menace to the poor colliers who were toiling up. It was only eleven o'clock.

From the far-off wooded hills the haze that hangs like fine black crape at the back of a summer morning had not yet dissipated. The first man came to the stile. "Chock-chock!" went the gate under his thrust.

"What, han' yer knocked off?" cried Mrs. Dakin.

"We han, missis."

"It's a pity as they letn yer goo," she said sarcastically.

"It is that," replied the man.

"Nay, you know you're flig to come up again," she said.

And the man went on. Mrs. Dakin, going up her yard, spied Mrs. Morel taking the ashes to the ash-pit.

"I reckon Minton's knocked off, missis," she cried.

"Isn't it sickenin!" exclaimed Mrs. Morel in wrath.

"Ha! But I'n just seed Jont Hutchby."

"They might as well have saved their shoe-leather," said Mrs. Morel. And both women went indoors disgusted.

The colliers, their faces scarcely blackened, were trooping home again. Morel hated to go back. He loved the sunny morning. But he had gone to pit to work, and to be sent home again spoilt his temper.

"Good gracious, at this time!" exclaimed his wife, as he entered.

"Can I help it, woman?" he shouted.

"And I've not done half enough dinner."

"Then I'll eat my bit o' snap as I took with me," he bawled pathetically. He felt ignominious and sore.

And the children, coming home from school, would wonder to see their father eating with his dinner the two thick slices of rather dry and dirty bread-and-butter that had been to pit and back.

"What's my dad eating his snap for now?" asked Arthur.

"I should ha'e it holled at me if I didna," snorted Morel.

"What a story!" exclaimed his wife.

"An' is it goin' to be wasted?" said Morel. "I'm not such a extravagant mortal as you lot, with your waste. If I drop a bit of bread at pit, in all the dust an' dirt, I pick it up an' eat it."

"The mice would eat it," said Paul. "It wouldn't be wasted."

"Good bread-an'-butter's not for mice, either," said Morel. "Dirty or not dirty, I'd eat it rather than it should be wasted."

"You might leave it for the mice and pay for it out of your next pint," said Mrs. Morel.

"Oh, might I?" he exclaimed.

They were very poor that autumn. William had just gone away to London, and his mother missed his money. He sent ten shillings once or twice, but he had many things to pay for at first. His letters came regularly once a week. He wrote a good deal to his mother, telling her all his life, how he made friends, and was exchanging lessons with a Frenchman, how he enjoyed London. His mother felt again he was remaining to her just as when he was at home. She wrote to him every week her direct, rather witty letters. All day long, as she cleaned the house, she thought of him. He was in London: he would do well. Almost, he was like her knight who wore *her* favour in the battle.

He was coming at Christmas for five days. There had never been such preparations. Paul and Arthur scoured the land for holly and evergreens. Annie made the pretty paper hoops in the old-fashioned way. And there was unheard-of extravagance in the larder. Mrs. Morel made a big and magnificent cake. Then, feeling queenly, she showed Paul how to blanch almonds. He skinned the long nuts reverently, counting them all, to see not one was lost. It was said that eggs whisked better in a cold place. So the boy stood in the scullery, where the temperature was nearly at freezing-point, and whisked and whisked, and flew in excitement to his mother as the white of egg grew stiffer and more snowy.

"Just look, mother! Isn't it lovely?"

And he balanced a bit on his nose, then blew it in the air.

"Now, don't waste it," said the mother.

Everybody was mad with excitement. William was coming on Christmas Eve. Mrs. Morel surveyed her pantry. There was a big plum cake, and a rice cake, jam tarts, lemon tarts, and mince-pies—two enormous dishes. She was finishing cooking— Spanish tarts and cheese-cakes. Everywhere was decorated. The kissing bunch of berried holly hung with bright and glittering things, spun slowly over Mrs. Morel's head as she trimmed her little tarts in the kitchen. A great fire roared. There was a scent of cooked pastry. He was due at seven o'clock, but he would be late. The three children had gone to meet him. She was alone. But at a quarter to seven Morel came in again. Neither wife nor husband spoke. He sat in his arm-chair, quite awkward with excitement, and she quietly went on with her baking. Only by the careful way in which

she did things could it be told how much moved she was. The
clock ticked on.

"What time dost say he's coming?" Morel asked for the fifth
time.

"The train gets in at half-past six," she replied emphatically.

"Then he'll be here at ten past seven."

"Eh, bless you, it'll be hours late on the Midland," she said
indifferently. But she hoped, by expecting him late, to bring
him early. Morel went down the entry to look for him. Then
he came back.

"Goodness, man!" she said. "You're like an ill-sitting hen."

"Hadna you better be gettin' him summat t' eat ready?"
asked the father.

"There's plenty of time," she answered.

"There's not so much as *I* can see on," he answered, turning crossly in his chair. She began to clear her table. The kettle
was singing. They waited and waited.

Meantime the three children were on the platform at Sethley
Bridge, on the Midland main line, two miles from home. They
waited one hour. A train came—he was not there. Down the
line the red and green lights shone. It was very dark and very
cold.

"Ask him if the London train's come," said Paul to Annie,
when they saw a man in a tip cap.

"I'm not," said Annie. "You be quiet—he might send us off."

But Paul was dying for the man to know they were expecting someone by the London train: it sounded so grand. Yet
he was much too much scared of broaching any man, let alone
one in a peaked cap, to dare to ask. The three children could
scarcely go into the waiting-room for fear of being sent away,
and for fear something should happen whilst they were off the
platform. Still they waited in the dark and cold.

"It's an hour an' a half late," said Arthur pathetically.

"Well," said Annie, "it's Christmas Eve."

They all grew silent. He wasn't coming. They looked down
the darkness of the railway. There was London! It seemed
the uttermost of distance. They thought anything might
happen if one came from London. They were all too troubled
to talk. Cold, and unhappy, and silent, they huddled together
on the platform.

At last, after more than two hours, they saw the lights of an
engine peering round, away down the darkness. A porter ran

out. The children drew back with beating hearts. A great train,
bound for Manchester, drew up. Two doors opened, and from
one of them, William. They flew to him. He handed parcels
to them cheerily, and immediately began to explain that this
great train had stopped for *his* sake at such a small station as
Sethley Bridge: it was not booked to stop.

Meanwhile the parents were getting anxious. The table was
set, the chop was cooked, everything was ready. Mrs. Morel
put on her black apron. She was wearing her best dress. Then
she sat, pretending to read. The minutes were a torture to
her.

"H'm!" said Morel. "It's an hour an' a ha'ef."

"And those children waiting!" she said.

"Th' train canna ha' come in yet," he said.

"I tell you, on Christmas Eve they're *hours* wrong."

They were both a bit cross with each other, so gnawed with
anxiety. The ash tree moaned outside in a cold, raw wind.
And all that space of night from London home! Mrs. Morel
suffered. The slight click of the works inside the clock irritated
her. It was getting so late; it was getting unbearable.

At last there was a sound of voices, and a footstep in the
entry.

"Ha's here!" cried Morel, jumping up.

Then he stood back. The mother ran a few steps towards
the door and waited. There was a rush and a patter of feet, the
door burst open. William was there. He dropped his Gladstone
bag and took his mother in his arms.

"Mater!" he said.

"My boy!" she cried.

And for two seconds, no longer, she clasped him and kissed
him. Then she withdrew and said, trying to be quite normal:

"But how late you are!"

"Aren't I!" he cried, turning to his father. "Well, dad!"

The two men shook hands.

"Well, my lad!"

Morel's eyes were wet.

"We thought tha'd niver be commin'," he said.

"Oh, I'd come!" exclaimed William.

Then the son turned round to his mother.

"But you look well," she said proudly, laughing.

"Well!" he exclaimed. "I should think so—coming home!"

He was a fine fellow, big, straight, and fearless-looking. He looked round at the evergreens and the kissing bunch, and the little tarts that lay in their tins on the hearth.

"By jove! mother, it's not different!" he said, as if in relief.

Everybody was still for a second. Then he suddenly sprang forward, picked a tart from the hearth, and pushed it whole into his mouth.

"Well, did iver you see such a parish oven!" the father exclaimed.

He had brought them endless presents. Every penny he had he had spent on them. There was a sense of luxury overflowing in the house. For his mother there was an umbrella with gold on the pale handle. She kept it to her dying day, and would have lost anything rather than that. Everybody had something gorgeous, and besides, there were pounds of unknown sweets: Turkish delight, crystallised pineapple, and such-like things which, the children thought, only the splendour of London could provide. And Paul boasted of these sweets among his friends.

"Real pineapple, cut off in slices, and then turned into crystal—fair grand!"

Everybody was mad with happiness in the family. Home was home, and they loved it with a passion of love, whatever the suffering had been. There were parties, there were rejoicings. People came in to see William, to see what difference London had made to him. And they all found him "such a gentleman, and *such* a fine fellow, my word"!

When he went away again the children retired to various places to weep alone. Morel went to bed in misery, and Mrs. Morel felt as if she were numbed by some drug, as if her feelings were paralysed. She loved him passionately.

He was in the office of a lawyer connected with a large shipping firm, and at the midsummer his chief offered him a trip in the Mediterranean on one of the boats, for quite a small cost. Mrs. Morel wrote: "Go, go, my boy. You may never have a chance again, and I should love to think of you cruising there in the Mediterranean almost better than to have you at home." But William came home for his fortnight's holiday. Not even the Mediterranean, which pulled at all his young man's desire to travel, and at his poor man's wonder at the glamorous south, could take him away when he might come home. That compensated his mother for much.

CHAPTER V

PAUL LAUNCHES INTO LIFE

MOREL was rather a heedless man, careless of danger. So he had endless accidents. Now, when Mrs. Morel heard the rattle of an empty coal-cart cease at her entry-end, she ran into the parlour to look, expecting almost to see her husband seated in the wagon, his face grey under his dirt, his body limp and sick with some hurt or other. If it were he, she would run out to help.

About a year after William went to London, and just after Paul had left school, before he got work, Mrs. Morel was upstairs and her son was painting in the kitchen—he was very clever with his brush—when there came a knock at the door. Crossly he put down his brush to go. At the same moment his mother opened a window upstairs and looked down.

A pit-lad in his dirt stood on the threshold.

"Is this Walter Morel's?" he asked.

"Yes," said Mrs. Morel. "What is it?"

But she had guessed already.

"Your mester's got hurt," he said.

"Eh, dear me!" she exclaimed. "It's a wonder if he hadn't, lad. And what's he done this time?"

"I don't know for sure, but it's 'is leg somewhere. They ta'ein' 'im ter th' 'ospital."

"Good gracious me!" she exclaimed. "Eh, dear, what a one he is! There's not five minutes of peace, I'll be hanged if there is! His thumb's nearly better, and now—— Did you see him?"

"I seed him at th' bottom. An' I seed 'em bring 'im up in a tub, an' 'e wor in a dead faint. But he shouted like anythink when Doctor Fraser examined him i' th' lamp cabin—an' cossed an' swore, an' said as 'e wor goin' to be ta'en whoam—'e worn't goin' ter th' 'ospital."

The boy faltered to an end.

"He *would* want to come home, so that I can have all the bother. Thank you, my lad. Eh, dear, if I'm not sick—sick and surfeited, I am!"

She came downstairs. Paul had mechanically resumed his painting.

"And it must be pretty bad if they've taken him to the

hospital," she went on. "But what a *careless* creature he is! *Other* men don't have all these accidents. Yes, he *would* want to put all the burden on me. Eh, dear, just as we *were* getting easy a bit at last. Put those things away, there's no time to be painting now. What time is there a train? I know I s'll have to go trailing to Keston. I s'll have to leave that bedroom."

"I can finish it," said Paul.

"You needn't. I shall catch the seven o'clock back, I should think. Oh, my blessed heart, the fuss and commotion he'll make! And those granite setts at Tinder Hill—he might well call them kidney pebbles—they'll jolt him almost to bits. I wonder why they can't mend them, the state they're in, an' all the men as go across in that ambulance. You'd think they'd have a hospital here. The men bought the ground, and, my sirs, there'd be accidents enough to keep it going. But no, they must trail them ten miles in a slow ambulance to Nottingham. It's a crying shame! Oh, and the fuss he'll make! I know he will! I wonder who's with him. Barker, I s'd think. Poor beggar, he'll wish himself anywhere rather. But he'll look after him, I know. Now there's no telling how long he'll be stuck in that hospital—and *won't* he hate it! But if it's only his leg it's not so bad."

All the time she was getting ready. Hurriedly taking off her bodice, she crouched at the boiler while the water ran slowly into her lading-can.

"I wish this boiler was at the bottom of the sea!" she exclaimed, wriggling the handle impatiently. She had very handsome, strong arms, rather surprising on a smallish woman.

Paul cleared away, put on the kettle, and set the table.

"There isn't a train till four-twenty," he said. "You've time enough."

"Oh no, I haven't!" she cried, blinking at him over the towel as she wiped her face.

"Yes, you have. You must drink a cup of tea at any rate. Should I come with you to Keston?"

"Come with me? What for, I should like to know? Now, what have I to take him? Eh, dear! His clean shirt—and it's a blessing it *is* clean. But it had better be aired. And stockings —he won't want them—and a towel, I suppose; and handkerchiefs. Now what else?"

"A comb, a knife and fork and spoon," said Paul. His father had been in the hospital before.

"Goodness knows what sort of state his feet were in," continued Mrs. Morel, as she combed her long brown hair, that was fine as silk, and was touched now with grey. "He's very particular to wash himself to the waist, but below he thinks doesn't matter. But there, I suppose they see plenty like it."

Paul had laid the table. He cut his mother one or two pieces of very thin bread and butter.

"Here you are," he said, putting her cup of tea in her place.

"I can't be bothered!" she exclaimed crossly.

"Well, you've got to, so there, now it's put out ready," he insisted.

So she sat down and sipped her tea, and ate a little, in silence. She was thinking.

In a few minutes she was gone, to walk the two and a half miles to Keston Station. All the things she was taking him she had in her bulging string bag. Paul watched her go up the road between the hedges—a little, quick-stepping figure, and his heart ached for her, that she was thrust forward again into pain and trouble. And she, tripping so quickly in her anxiety, felt at the back of her her son's heart waiting on her, felt him bearing what part of the burden he could, even supporting her. And when she was at the hospital, she thought: "It *will* upset that lad when I tell him how bad it is. I'd better be careful." And when she was trudging home again, she felt he was coming to share her burden.

"Is it bad?" asked Paul, as soon as she entered the house.

"It's bad enough," she replied.

"What?"

She sighed and sat down, undoing her bonnet-strings. Her son watched her face as it was lifted, and her small, work-hardened hands fingering at the bow under her chin.

"Well," she answered, "it's not really dangerous, but the nurse says it's a dreadful smash. You see, a great piece of rock fell on his leg—here—and it's a compound fracture. There are pieces of bone sticking through——"

"Ugh—how horrid!" exclaimed the children.

"And," she continued, "of course he says he's going to die—it wouldn't be him if he didn't. 'I'm done for, my lass!' he said, looking at me. 'Don't be so silly,' I said to him. 'You're not going to die of a broken leg, however badly it's smashed.' 'I s'll niver come out of 'ere but in a wooden box,' he groaned. 'Well,' I said, 'if you want them to carry you into the garden

in a wooden box, when you're better, I've no doubt they will.'
'If we think it's good for him,' said the Sister. She's an awfully
nice Sister, but rather strict."

Mrs. Morel took off her bonnet. The children waited in
silence.

"Of course, he *is* bad," she continued, "and he will be. It's
a great shock, and he's lost a lot of blood; and, of course, it *is*
a very dangerous smash. It's not at all sure that it will mend
so easily. And then there's the fever and the mortification—if
it took bad ways he'd quickly be gone. But there, he's a clean-
blooded man, with wonderful healing flesh, and so I see no
reason why it *should* take bad ways. Of course there's a
wound——"

She was pale now with emotion and anxiety. The three
children realised that it was very bad for their father, and the
house was silent, anxious.

"But he always gets better," said Paul after a while.

"That's what I tell him," said the mother.

Everybody moved about in silence.

"And he really looked nearly done for," she said. "But the
Sister says that is the pain."

Annie took away her mother's coat and bonnet.

"And he looked at me when I came away! I said: 'I s'll
have to go now, Walter, because of the train—and the children.'
And he looked at me. It seems hard."

Paul took up his brush again and went on painting. Arthur
went outside for some coal. Annie sat looking dismal. And
Mrs. Morel, in her little rocking-chair that her husband had
made for her when the first baby was coming, remained
motionless, brooding. She was grieved, and bitterly sorry
for the man who was hurt so much. But still, in her heart of
hearts, where the love should have burned, there was a blank.
Now, when all her woman's pity was roused to its full extent,
when she would have slaved herself to death to nurse him and
to save him, when she would have taken the pain herself, if
she could, somewhere far away inside her, she felt indifferent
to him and to his suffering. It hurt her most of all, this failure
to love him, even when he roused her strong emotions. She
brooded a while.

"And there," she said suddenly, "when I'd got half-way to
Keston, I found I'd come out in my working boots—and *look*
at them " They were an old pair of Paul's, brown and rubbed

through at the toes. "I didn't know what to do with myself, for shame," she added.

In the morning, when, Annie and Arthur were at school, Mrs. Morel talked again to her son, who was helping her with her housework.

"I found Barker at the hospital. He did look bad, poor little fellow! 'Well,' I said to him, 'what sort of a journey did you have with him?' 'Dunna ax me, missis!' he said. 'Ay,' I said, 'I know what he'd be.' 'But it *wor* bad for him, Mrs. Morel, it *wor* that!' he said. 'I know,' I said. 'At ivry jolt I thought my 'eart would ha' flown clean out o' my mouth,' he said. 'An' the scream 'e gives sometimes! Missis, not for a fortune would I go through wi' it again.' 'I can quite understand it,' I said. 'It's a nasty job, though,' he said, 'an' one as'll be a long while afore it's right again.' 'I'm afraid it will,' I said. I like Mr. Barker—I *do* like him. There's something so manly about him."

Paul resumed his task silently.

"And of course," Mrs. Morel continued, "for a man like your father, the hospital *is* hard. He *can't* understand rules and regulations. And he won't let anybody else touch him, not if he can help it. When he smashed the muscles of his thigh, and it had to be dressed four times a day, *would* he let anybody but me or his mother do it? He wouldn't. So, of course, he'll suffer in there with the nurses. And I didn't like leaving him. I'm sure, when I kissed him an' came away, it seemed a shame."

So she talked to her son, almost as if she were thinking aloud to him, and he took it in as best he could, by sharing her trouble to lighten it. And in the end she shared almost everything with him without knowing.

Morel had a very bad time. For a week he was in a critical condition. Then he began to mend. And then, knowing he was going to get better, the whole family sighed with relief, and proceeded to live happily.

They were not badly off whilst Morel was in the hospital. There were fourteen shillings a week from the pit, ten shillings from the sick club, and five shillings from the Disability Fund; and then every week the butties had something for Mrs. Morel —five or seven shillings—so that she was quite well to do. And whilst Morel was progressing favourably in the hospital, the family was extraordinarily happy and peaceful. On Saturdays and Wednesdays Mrs. Morel went to Nottingham to see her husband. Then she always brought back some little thing: a small tube of paints for Paul, or some thick paper; a couple of postcards for Annie, that the whole family rejoiced over for days before the girl was allowed to send them away; or a fret-saw for Arthur, or a bit of pretty wood. She described her adventures into the big shops with joy. Soon the folk in the picture-shop knew her, and knew about Paul. The girl in the book-shop took a keen interest in her. Mrs. Morel was full of information when she got home from Nottingham. The three sat round till bed-time, listening, putting in, arguing. Then Paul often raked the fire.

"I'm the man in the house now," he used to say to his mother with joy. They learned how perfectly peaceful the home could be. And they almost regretted—though none of them would have owned to such callousness—that their father was soon coming back.

Paul was now fourteen, and was looking for work. He was a rather small and rather finely-made boy, with dark brown hair and light blue eyes. His face had already lost its youth-ful chubbiness, and was becoming somewhat like William's— rough-featured, almost rugged—and it was extraordinarily mobile. Usually he looked as if he saw things, was full of life, and warm; then his smile, like his mother's, came suddenly and was very lovable; and then, when there was any clog in his soul's quick running, his face went stupid and ugly. He was the sort of boy that becomes a clown and a lout as soon as he is not understood, or feels himself held cheap; and, again, is adorable at the first touch of warmth.

He suffered very much from the first contact with anything. When he was seven, the starting school had been a nightmare and a torture to him. But afterwards he liked it. And now that he felt he had to go out into life, he went through agonies of shrinking self-consciousness. He was quite a clever painter for a boy of his years, and he knew some French and German and mathematics that Mr. Heaton had taught him. But nothing he had was of any commercial value. He was not strong enough for heavy manual work, his mother said. He did not care for making things with his hands, preferred racing about, or making excursions into the country, or reading, or painting.

"What do you want to be?" his mother asked.

"Anything."

"That is no answer," said Mrs. Morel.

But it was quite truthfully the only answer he could give. His ambition, as far as this world's gear went, was quietly to earn his thirty or thirty-five shillings a week somewhere near home, and then, when his father died, have a cottage with his mother, paint and go out as he liked, and live happy ever after. That was his programme as far as doing things went. But he was proud within himself, measuring people against himself, and placing them, inexorably. And he thought that *perhaps* he might also make a painter, the real thing. But that he left alone.

"Then," said his mother, "you must look in the paper for the advertisements."

He looked at her. It seemed to him a bitter humiliation and an anguish to go through. But he said nothing. When he got up in the morning, his whole being was knotted up over this one thought:

"I've got to go and look for advertisements for a job."

It stood in front of the morning, that thought, killing all joy and even life, for him. His heart felt like a tight knot.

And then, at ten o'clock, he set off. He was supposed to be a queer, quiet child. Going up the sunny street of the little town, he felt as if all the folk he met said to themselves: "He's going to the Co-op. reading-room to look in the papers for a place. He can't get a job. I suppose he's living on his mother." Then he crept up the stone stairs behind the drapery shop at the Co-op., and peeped in the reading-room. Usually one or two men were there, either old, useless fellows, or colliers "on the club". So he entered, full of shrinking and suffering when they looked up, seated himself at the table, and pretended to scan the news. He knew they would think: "What does a lad of thirteen want in a reading-room with a newspaper?" and he suffered.

Then he looked wistfully out of the window. Already he was a prisoner of industrialism. Large sunflowers stared over the old red wall of the garden opposite, looking in their jolly way down on the women who were hurrying with something for dinner. The valley was full of corn, brightening in the sun. Two collieries, among the fields, waved their small white plumes of steam. Far off on the hills were the woods of Annesley, dark and fascinating. Already his heart went down. He was being taken into bondage. His freedom in the beloved home valley was going now.

The brewers' waggons came rolling up from Keston with enormous barrels, four a side, like beans in a burst bean-pod. The waggoner, throned aloft, rolling massively in his seat, was not so much below Paul's eye. The man's hair, on his small, bullet head, was bleached almost white by the sun, and on his thick red arms, rocking idly on his sack apron, the white hairs glistened. His red face shone and was almost asleep with sunshine. The horses, handsome and brown, went on by themselves, looking by far the masters of the show.

Paul wished he were stupid. "I wish," he thought to himself, "I was fat like him, and like a dog in the sun. I wish I was a pig and a brewer's waggoner."

Then, the room being at last empty, he would hastily copy an advertisement on a scrap of paper, then another, and slip out in immense relief. His mother would scan over his copies.

"Yes," she said, "you may try."

William had written out a letter of application, couched in admirable business language, which Paul copied, with variations. The boy's handwriting was execrable, so that William, who did all things well, got into a fever of impatience.

The elder brother was becoming quite swanky. In London he found that he could associate with men far above his Bestwood friends in station. Some of the clerks in the office had studied for the law, and were more or less going through a kind of apprenticeship. William always made friends among men wherever he went, he was so jolly. Therefore he was soon visiting and staying in houses of men who, in Bestwood, would have looked down on the unapproachable bank manager, and would merely have called indifferently on the Rector. So he began to fancy himself as a great gun. He was, indeed, rather surprised at the ease with which he became a gentleman.

His mother was glad, he seemed so pleased. And his lodging in Walthamstow was so dreary. But now there seemed to come a kind of fever into the young man's letters. He was unsettled by all the change, he did not stand firm on his own feet, but seemed to spin rather giddily on the quick current of the new life. His mother was anxious for him. She could feel him losing himself. He had danced and gone to the theatre, boated on the river, been out with friends; and she knew he sat up afterwards in his cold bedroom grinding away at Latin, because he intended to get on in his office, and in the law as much as he could. He never sent his mother any money now. It was *extravigant*

all taken, the little he had, for his own life. And she did not want any, except sometimes, when she was in a tight corner, and when ten shillings would have saved her much worry. She still dreamed of William, and of what he would do, with herself behind him. Never for a minute would she admit to herself how heavy and anxious her heart was because of him.

Also he talked a good deal now of a girl he had met at a dance, a handsome brunette, quite young, and a lady, after whom the men were running thick and fast.

"I wonder if you would run, my boy," his mother wrote to him, "unless you saw all the other men chasing her too. You feel safe enough and vain enough in a crowd. But take care, and see how you feel when you find yourself alone, and in triumph."

William resented these things, and continued the chase. He had taken the girl on the river. "If you saw her, mother, you would know how I feel. Tall and elegant, with the clearest of clear, transparent olive complexions, hair as black as jet, and such grey eyes—bright, mocking, like lights on water at night. It is all very well to be a bit satirical till you see her. And she dresses as well as any woman in London. I tell you, your son doesn't half put his head up when she goes walking down Piccadilly with him."

Mrs. Morel wondered, in her heart, if her son did not go walking down Piccadilly with an elegant figure and fine clothes, rather than with a woman who was near to him. But she congratulated him in her doubtful fashion. And, as she stood over the washing-tub, the mother brooded over her son. She saw him saddled with an elegant and expensive wife, earning little money, dragging along and getting draggled in some small, ugly house in a suburb. "But there," she told herself, "I am very likely a silly—meeting trouble half-way." Nevertheless, the load of anxiety scarcely ever left her heart, lest William should do the wrong thing by himself.

Presently, Paul was bidden call upon Thomas Jordan, Manufacturer of Surgical Appliances, at 21, Spaniel Row, Nottingham. Mrs. Morel was all joy.

"There, you see!" she cried, her eyes shining. "You've only written four letters, and the third is answered. You're lucky, my boy, as I always said you were."

Paul looked at the picture of a wooden leg, adorned with

elastic stockings and other appliances, that figured on Mr.
Jordan's notepaper, and he felt alarmed. He had not known
that elastic stockings existed. And he seemed to feel the business world, with its regulated system of values, and its impersonality, and he dreaded it. It seemed monstrous also that a
business could be run on wooden legs.

Mother and son set off together one Tuesday morning. It was
August and blazing hot. Paul walked with something screwed
up tight inside him. He would have suffered much physical
pain rather than this unreasonable suffering at being exposed
to strangers, to be accepted or rejected. Yet he chattered away
with his mother. He would never have confessed to her how
he suffered over these things, and she only partly guessed. She
was gay, like a sweetheart. She stood in front of the ticket-
office at Bestwood, and Paul watched her take from her purse
the money for the tickets. As he saw her hands in their old
black kid gloves getting the silver out of the worn purse, his
heart contracted with pain of love of her.

She was quite excited, and quite gay. He suffered because
she *would* talk aloud in presence of the other travellers.

"Now look at that silly cow!" she said, "careering round as
if it thought it was a circus."

"It's most likely a bottfly," he said very low.

"A what?" she asked brightly and unashamed.

They thought a while. He was sensible all the time of having
her opposite him. Suddenly their eyes met, and she smiled to
him—a rare, intimate smile, beautiful with brightness and love.
Then each looked out of the window.

The sixteen slow miles of railway journey passed. The
mother and son walked down Station Street, feeling the excitement of lovers having an adventure together. In Carrington
Street they stopped to hang over the parapet and look at the
barges on the canal below.

"It's just like Venice," he said, seeing the sunshine on the
water that lay between high factory walls.

"Perhaps," she answered, smiling.

They enjoyed the shops immensely.

"Now you see that blouse," she would say, "wouldn't that
just suit our Annie? And for one-and-eleven-three. Isn't that
cheap?"

"And made of needlework as well," he said.

"Yes."

They had plenty of time, so they did not hurry. The town was strange and delightful to them. But the boy was tied up inside in a knot of apprehension. He dreaded the interview with Thomas Jordan.

It was nearly eleven o'clock by St. Peter's Church. They turned up a narrow street that led to the Castle. It was gloomy and old-fashioned, having low dark shops and dark green house doors with brass knockers, and yellow-ochred doorsteps projecting on to the pavement; then another old shop whose small window looked like a cunning, half-shut eye. Mother and son went cautiously, looking everywhere for "Thomas Jordan and Son". It was like hunting in some wild place. They were on tiptoe of excitement.

Suddenly they spied a big, dark archway, in which were names of various firms, Thomas Jordan among them.

"Here it is!" said Mrs. Morel. "But now *where* is it?"

They looked round. On one side was a queer, dark, cardboard factory, on the other a Commercial Hotel.

"It's up the entry," said Paul.

And they ventured under the archway, as into the jaws of the dragon. They emerged into a wide yard, like a well, with buildings all round. It was littered with straw and boxes, and cardboard. The sunshine actually caught one crate whose straw was streaming on to the yard like gold. But elsewhere the place was like a pit. There were several doors, and two flights of steps. Straight in front, on a dirty glass door at the top of a staircase, loomed the ominous words "Thomas Jordan and Son—Surgical Appliances." Mrs. Morel went first, her son followed her. Charles I mounted his scaffold with a lighter heart than had Paul Morel as he followed his mother up the dirty steps to the dirty door.

She pushed open the door, and stood in pleased surprise. In front of her was a big warehouse, with creamy paper parcels everywhere, and clerks, with their shirt-sleeves rolled back, were going about in an at-home sort of way. The light was subdued, the glossy cream parcels seemed luminous, the counters were of dark brown wood. All was quiet and very homely. Mrs. Morel took two steps forward, then waited. Paul stood behind her. She had on her Sunday bonnet and a black veil; he wore a boy's broad white collar and a Norfolk suit.

One of the clerks looked up. He was thin and tall, with a

small face. His way of looking was alert. Then he glanced round to the other end of the room, where was a glass office. And then he came forward. He did not say anything, but leaned in a gentle, inquiring fashion towards Mrs. Morel.

"Can I see Mr. Jordan?" she asked.

"I'll fetch him," answered the young man.

He went down to the glass office. A red-faced, white-whiskered old man looked up. He reminded Paul of a pomeranian dog. Then the same little man came up the room. He had short legs, was rather stout, and wore an alpaca jacket. So, with one ear up, as it were, he came stoutly and inquiringly down the room.

"Good-morning!" he said, hesitating before Mrs. Morel, in doubt as to whether she were a customer or not.

"Good-morning. I came with my son, Paul Morel. You asked him to call this morning."

"Come this way," said Mr. Jordan, in a rather snappy little manner intended to be business-like.

They followed the manufacturer into a grubby little room, upholstered in black American leather, glossy with the rubbing of many customers. On the table was a pile of trusses, yellow wash-leather hoops tangled together. They looked new and living. Paul sniffed the odour of new wash-leather. He wondered what the things were. By this time he was so much stunned that he only noticed the outside things.

"Sit down!" said Mr. Jordan, irritably pointing Mrs. Morel to a horse-hair chair. She sat on the edge in an uncertain fashion. Then the little old man fidgeted and found a paper.

"Did you write this letter?" he snapped, thrusting what Paul recognised as his own notepaper in front of him.

"Yes," he answered.

At that moment he was occupied in two ways: first, in feeling guilty for telling a lie, since William had composed the letter; second, in wondering why his letter seemed so strange and different, in the fat, red hand of the man, from what it had been when it lay on the kitchen table. It was like part of himself, gone astray. He resented the way the man held it.

"Where did you learn to write?" said the old man crossly.

Paul merely looked at him shamedly, and did not answer.

"He *is* a bad writer," put in Mrs. Morel apologetically. Then she pushed up her veil. Paul hated her for not being prouder with this common little man, and he loved her face clear of the veil.

"And you say you know French?" inquired the little man, still sharply.

"Yes," said Paul.

"What school did you go to?"

"The Board-school."

"And did you learn it there?"

"No—I——" The boy went crimson and got no farther.

"His godfather gave him lessons," said Mrs. Morel, half pleading and rather distant.

Mr. Jordan hesitated. Then, in his irritable manner—he always seemed to keep his hands ready for action—he pulled another sheet of paper from his pocket, unfolded it. The paper made a crackling noise. He handed it to Paul.

"Read that," he said.

It was a note in French, in thin, flimsy foreign handwriting that the boy could not decipher. He stared blankly at the paper.

" 'Monsieur,' " he began; then he looked in great confusion at Mr. Jordan. "It's the—it's the——"

He wanted to say "handwriting", but his wits would no longer work even sufficiently to supply him with the word. Feeling an utter fool, and hating Mr. Jordan, he turned desperately to the paper again.

" 'Sir,—Please send me'—er—er—I can't tell the—er—'two pairs—*gris fil bas*—grey thread stockings'—er—er—'sans—without'—er—I can't tell the words—er—'doigts—fingers'—er—I can't tell the——"

He wanted to say "handwriting", but the word still refused to come. Seeing him stuck, Mr. Jordan snatched the paper from him.

" 'Please send by return two pairs grey thread stockings without *toes*.' "

"Well," flashed Paul, " '*doigts*' means 'fingers'—as well—as a rule——"

The little man looked at him. He did not know whether "*doigts*" meant "fingers"; he knew that for all *his* purposes it meant "toes".

"Fingers to stockings!" he snapped.

"Well, it *does* mean fingers," the boy persisted.

He hated the little man, who made such a clod of him. Mr.

Jordan looked at the pale, stupid, defiant boy, then at the mother, who sat quiet and with that peculiar shut-off look of the poor who have to depend on the favour of others.

"And when could he come?" he asked.

"Well," said Mrs. Morel, "as soon as you wish. He has finished school now."

"He would live in Bestwood?"

"Yes; but he could be in—at the station—at quarter to eight."

"H'm!"

It ended by Paul's being engaged as junior spiral clerk at eight shillings a week. The boy did not open his mouth to say another word, after having insisted that *"doigts"* meant "fingers". He followed his mother down the stairs. She looked at him with her bright blue eyes full of love and joy.

"I think you'll like it," she said.

" 'Doigts' does mean 'fingers', mother, and it was the writing. I couldn't read the writing."

"Never mind, my boy. I'm sure he'll be all right, and you won't see much of him. Wasn't that first young fellow nice? I'm sure you'll like them."

"But wasn't Mr. Jordan common, mother? Does he own it all?"

"I suppose he was a workman who has got on," she said. "You mustn't mind people so much. They're not being disagreeable to *you*—it's their way. You always think people are meaning things for you. But they don't."

It was very sunny. Over the big desolate space of the market-place the blue sky shimmered, and the granite cobbles of the paving glistened. Shops down the Long Row were deep in obscurity, and the shadow was full of colour. Just where the horse trams trundled across the market was a row of fruit stalls, with fruit blazing in the sun—apples and piles of reddish oranges, small greengage plums and bananas. There was a warm scent of fruit as mother and son passed. Gradually his feeling of ignominy and of rage sank.

"Where should we go for dinner?" asked the mother.

It was felt to be a reckless extravagance. Paul had only been in an eating-house once or twice in his life, and then only to have a cup of tea and a bun. Most of the people of Bestwood considered that tea and bread-and-butter, and perhaps potted beef, was all they could afford to eat in Nottingham. Real

cooked dinner was considered great extravagance. Paul felt
rather guilty.

They found a place that looked quite cheap. But when Mrs.
Morel scanned the bill of fare, her heart was heavy, things
were so dear. So she ordered kidney-pies and potatoes as the
cheapest available dish.

"We oughtn't to have come here, mother," said Paul.

"Never mind," she said. "We won't come again."

She insisted on his having a small currant tart, because he
liked sweets.

"I don't want it, mother," he pleaded.

"Yes," she insisted; "you'll have it."

And she looked round for the waitress. But the waitress was
busy, and Mrs. Morel did not like to bother her then. So the
mother and son waited for the girl's pleasure, whilst she flirted
among the men.

"Brazen hussy!" said Mrs. Morel to Paul. "Look now, she's
taking that man *his* pudding, and he came long after us."

"It doesn't matter, mother," said Paul.

Mrs. Morel was angry. But she was too poor, and her orders
were too meagre, so that she had not the courage to insist on
her rights just then. They waited and waited.

"Should we go, mother?" he said.

Then Mrs. Morel stood up. The girl was passing near.

"Will you bring one currant tart?" said Mrs. Morel clearly.

The girl looked round insolently.

"Directly," she said.

"We have waited quite long enough," said Mrs. Morel.

In a moment the girl came back with the tart. Mrs. Morel
asked coldly for the bill. Paul wanted to sink through the floor.
He marvelled at his mother's hardness. He knew that only
years of battling had taught her to insist even so little on her
rights. She shrank as much as he.

"It's the last time I go *there* for anything!" she declared,
when they were outside the place, thankful to be clear.

"We'll go," she said, "and look at Keep's and Boot's, and one
or two places, shall we?"

They had discussions over the pictures, and Mrs. Morel
wanted to buy him a little sable brush that he hankered after.
But this indulgence he refused. He stood in front of milliners'
shops and drapers' shops almost bored, but content for her to
be interested. They wandered on.

"Now, just look at those black grapes!" she said. "They make your mouth water. I've wanted some of those for years, but I s'll have to wait a bit before I get them."

Then she rejoiced in the florists, standing in the doorway sniffing.

"Oh! oh! Isn't it simply lovely!"

Paul saw, in the darkness of the shop, an elegant young lady in black peering over the counter curiously.

"They're looking at you," he said, trying to draw his mother away.

"But what is it?" she exclaimed, refusing to be moved.

"Stocks!" he answered, sniffing hastily. "Look, there's a tubful."

"So there is—red and white. But really, I never knew stocks to smell like it!" And, to his great relief, she moved out of the doorway, but only to stand in front of the window.

"Paul!" she cried to him, who was trying to get out of sight of the elegant young lady in black—the shop-girl. "Paul! Just look here!"

He came reluctantly back.

"Now, just look at that fuchsia!" she exclaimed, pointing.

"H'm!" He made a curious, interested sound. "You'd think every second as the flowers was going to fall off, they hang so big an' heavy."

"And such an abundance!" she cried.

"And the way they drop downwards with their threads and knots!"

"Yes!" she exclaimed. "Lovely!"

"I wonder who'll buy it!" he said.

"I wonder!" she answered. "Not us."

"It would die in our parlour."

"Yes, beastly cold, sunless hole; it kills every bit of a plant you put in, and the kitchen chokes them to death."

They bought a few things, and set off towards the station. Looking up the canal, through the dark pass of the buildings, they saw the Castle on its bluff of brown, green-bushed rock, in a positive miracle of delicate sunshine.

"Won't it be nice for me to come out at dinner-times?" said Paul. "I can go all round here and see everything. I s'll love it."

"You will," assented his mother.

He had spent a perfect afternoon with his mother. They

arrived home in the mellow evening, happy, and glowing, and tired.

In the morning he filled in the form for his season-ticket and took it to the station. When he got back, his mother was just beginning to wash the floor. He sat crouched up on the sofa.

"He says it'll be here on Saturday," he said.

"And how much will it be?"

"About one pound eleven," he said.

She went on washing her floor in silence.

"Is it a lot?" he asked.

"It's no more than I thought," she answered.

"An' I s'll earn eight shillings a week," he said.

She did not answer, but went on with her work. At last she said:

"That William promised me, when he went to London, as he'd give me a pound a month. He has given me ten shillings—twice; and now I know he hasn't a farthing if I asked him. Not that I want it. Only just now you'd think he might be able to help with this ticket, which I'd never expected."

"He earns a lot," said Paul.

"He earns a hundred and thirty pounds. But they're all alike. They're large in promises, but it's precious little fulfilment you get."

"He spends over fifty shillings a week on himself," said Paul.

"And I keep this house on less than thirty," she replied; "and am supposed to find money for extras. But they don't care about helping you, once they've gone. He'd rather spend it on that dressed-up creature."

"She should have her own money if she's so grand," said Paul.

"She should, but she hasn't. I asked him. And I know he doesn't buy her a gold bangle for nothing. I wonder whoever bought *me* a gold bangle."

William was succeeding with his "Gipsy", as he called her. He asked the girl—her name was Louisa Lily Denys Western—for a photograph to send to his mother. The photo came—a handsome brunette, taken in profile, smirking slightly—and, it might be, quite naked, for on the photograph not a scrap of clothing was to be seen, only a naked bust.

"Yes," wrote Mrs. Morel to her son, "the photograph of Louie is very striking, and I can see she must be attractive. But do you think, my boy, it was very good taste of a girl to give her young man that photo to send to his mother—the first? Certainly the shoulders are beautiful, as you say. But I hardly expected to see so much of them at the first view."

Morel found the photograph standing on the chiffonier in the parlour. He came out with it between his thick thumb and finger.

"Who dost reckon this is?" he asked of his wife.

"It's the girl our William is going with," replied Mrs. Morel.

"H'm! 'Er's a bright spark, from th' look on 'er, an' one as wunna do him owermuch good neither. Who is she?"

"Her name is Louisa Lily Denys Western."

"An' come again to-morrer!" exclaimed the miner. "An' is 'er an actress?"

"She is not. She's supposed to be a lady."

"I'll bet!" he exclaimed, still staring at the photo. "A lady, is she? An' how much does she reckon ter keep up this sort o' game on?"

"On nothing. She lives with an old aunt, whom she hates, and takes what bit of money's given her."

"H'm!" said Morel, laying down the photograph. "Then he's a fool to ha' ta'en up wi' such a one as that."

"Dear Mater," William replied. "I'm sorry you didn't like the photograph. It never occurred to me when I sent it, that you mightn't think it decent. However, I told Gyp that it didn't quite suit your prim and proper notions, so she's going to send you another, that I hope will please you better. She's always being photographed; in fact, the photographers *ask* her if they may take her for nothing."

Presently the new photograph came, with a little silly note from the girl. This time the young lady was seen in a black satin evening bodice, cut square, with little puff sleeves, and black lace hanging down her beautiful arms.

"I wonder if she ever wears anything except evening clothes," said Mrs. Morel sarcastically. "I'm sure I *ought* to be impressed."

"You are disagreeable, mother," said Paul. "I think the first one with bare shoulders is lovely."

"Do you?" answered his mother. "Well, I don't."

On the Monday morning the boy got up at six to start work. He had the season-ticket, which had cost such bitterness, in his waistcoat pocket. He loved it with its bars of yellow across. His mother packed his dinner in a small, shut-up basket, and he set off at a quarter to seven to catch the 7.15 train. Mrs. Morel came to the entry-end to see him off.

It was a perfect morning. From the ash tree the slender green fruits that the children call "pigeons" were twinkling gaily down on a little breeze, into the front gardens of the houses. The valley was full of a lustrous dark-haze, through which the ripe corn shimmered, and in which the steam from Minton pit melted swiftly. Puffs of wind came. Paul looked over the high woods of Aldersley, where the country gleamed, and home had never pulled at him so powerfully.

"Good-morning, mother," he said, smiling, but feeling very unhappy.

"Good-morning," she replied cheerfully and tenderly.

She stood in her white apron on the open road, watching him as he crossed the field. He had a small, compact body that looked full of life. She felt, as she saw him trudging over the field, that where he determined to go he would get. She thought of William. He would have leaped the fence instead of going round the stile. He was away in London, doing well. Paul would be working in Nottingham. Now she had two sons in the world. She could think of two places, great centres of industry, and feel that she had put a man into each of them, that these men would work out what *she* wanted; they were derived from her, they were of her, and their works also would be hers. All the morning long she thought of Paul.

At eight o'clock he climbed the dismal stairs of Jordan's Surgical Appliance Factory, and stood helplessly against the first great parcel-rack, waiting for somebody to pick him up. The place was still not awake. Over the counters were great dust sheets. Two men only had arrived, and were heard talking in a corner, as they took off their coats and rolled up their shirt-sleeves. It was ten past eight. Evidently there was no rush of punctuality. Paul listened to the voices of the two clerks. Then he heard someone cough, and saw in the office at the end of the room an old, decaying clerk, in a round smoking-cap of black velvet embroidered with red and green, opening letters. He waited and waited. One of the junior clerks went to the old man, greeted him cheerily and loudly. Evidently the old "chief" was deaf. Then the young fellow came striding importantly down to his counter. He spied Paul.

"Hello!" he said. "You the new lad?"

"Yes," said Paul.

"H'm! What's your name?"

"Paul Morel."

"Paul Morel? All right, you come on round here."

Paul followed him round the rectangle of counters. The room was second storey. It had a great hole in the middle of the floor, fenced as with a wall of counters, and down this wide shaft the lifts went, and the light for the bottom storey. Also there was a corresponding big, oblong hole in the ceiling, and one could see above, over the fence of the top floor, some machinery; and right away overhead was the glass roof, and all light for the three storeys came downwards, getting dimmer, so that it was always night on the ground floor and rather gloomy on the second floor. The factory was the top floor, the warehouse the second, the storehouse the ground floor. It was an insanitary, ancient place.

Paul was led round to a very dark corner.

"This is the 'Spiral' corner," said the clerk. "You're Spiral, with Pappleworth. He's your boss, but he's not come yet. He doesn't get here till half-past eight. So you can fetch the letters, if you like, from Mr. Melling down there."

The young man pointed to the old clerk in the office.

"All right," said Paul.

"Here's a peg to hang your cap on. Here are your entry ledgers. Mr. Pappleworth won't be long."

And the thin young man stalked away with long, busy strides over the hollow wooden floor.

After a minute or two Paul went down and stood in the door of the glass office. The old clerk in the smoking-cap looked down over the rim of his spectacles.

"Good-morning," he said, kindly and impressively. "You want the letters for the Spiral department, Thomas?"

Paul resented being called "Thomas". But he took the letters and returned to his dark place, where the counter made an angle, where the great parcel-rack came to an end, and where there were three doors in the corner. He sat on a high stool and read the letters—those whose handwriting was not too difficult. They ran as follows:

"Will you please send me at once a pair of lady's silk spiral thigh-hose, without feet, such as I had from you last year; length, thigh to knee, etc." Or, "Major Chamberlain wishes to repeat his previous order for a silk non-elastic suspensory bandage."

Many of these letters, some of them in French or Norwegian, were a great puzzle to the boy. He sat on his stool nervously awaiting the arrival of his "boss". He suffered tortures of shyness when, at half-past eight, the factory girls for upstairs trooped past him.

Mr. Pappleworth arrived, chewing a chlorodyne gum, at about twenty to nine, when all the other men were at work. He was a thin, sallow man with a red nose, quick, staccato, and smartly but stiffly dressed. He was about thirty-six years old. There was something rather "doggy", rather smart, rather 'cute and shrewd, and something warm, and something slightly contemptible about him.

"You my new lad?" he said.

Paul stood up and said he was.

"Fetched the letters?"

Mr. Pappleworth gave a chew to his gum.

"Yes."

"Copied 'em?"

"No."

"Well, come on then, let's look slippy. Changed your coat?"

"No."

"You want to bring an old coat and leave it here." He pronounced the last words with the chlorodyne gum between his side teeth. He vanished into the darkness behind the great parcel-rack, reappeared coatless, turning up a smart striped shirt-cuff over a thin and hairy arm. Then he slipped into his coat. Paul noticed how thin he was, and that his trousers were in folds behind. He seized a stool, dragged it beside the boy's, and sat down.

"Sit down," he said.

Paul took a seat.

Mr. Pappleworth was very close to him. The man seized the letters, snatched a long entry-book out of a rack in front of him, flung it open, seized a pen, and said:

"Now look here. You want to copy these letters in here." He sniffed twice, gave a quick chew at his gum, stared fixedly at a letter, then went very still and absorbed, and wrote the entry rapidly, in a beautiful flourishing hand. He glanced quickly at Paul.

"See that?"

"Yes."

"Think you can do it all right?"

"Yes."

"All right then, let's see you."

He sprang off his stool. Paul took a pen. Mr. Pappleworth disappeared. Paul rather liked copying the letters, but he wrote slowly, laboriously, and exceedingly badly. He was doing the fourth letter, and feeling quite busy and happy, when Mr Pappleworth reappeared.

"Now then, how'r' yer getting on? Done 'em?"

He leaned over the boy's shoulder, chewing, and smelling of chlorodyne.

"Strike my bob, lad, but you're a beautiful writer!" he exclaimed satirically. "Ne'er mind, how many h'yer done? Only three! I'd 'a eaten 'em. Get on, my lad, an' put numbers on 'em. Here, look! Get on!"

Paul ground away at the letters, whilst Mr. Pappleworth fussed over various jobs. Suddenly the boy started as a shrill whistle sounded near his ear. Mr. Pappleworth came, took a plug out of a pipe, and said, in an amazingly cross and bossy voice :

"Yes?"

Paul heard a faint voice, like a woman's, out of the mouth of the tube. He gazed in wonder, never having seen a speaking-tube before.

"Well," said Mr. Pappleworth disagreeably into the tube, "you'd better get some of your back work done, then."

Again the woman's tiny voice was heard, sounding pretty and cross.

"I've not time to stand here while you talk," said Mr. Papple-worth, and he pushed the plug into the tube.

"Come, my lad," he said imploringly to Paul, "there's Polly crying out for them orders. Can't you buck up a bit? Here, come out!"

He took the book, to Paul's immense chagrin, and began the copying himself. He worked quickly and well. This done, he seized some strips of long yellow paper, about three inches wide, and made out the day's orders for the work-girls.

"You'd better watch me," he said to Paul, working all the while rapidly. Paul watched the weird little drawings of legs, and thighs, and ankles, with the strokes across and the numbers, and the few brief directions which his chief made upon the yellow paper. Then Mr. Pappleworth finished and jumped up.

"Come on with me," he said, and the yellow papers flying

in his hands, he dashed through a door and down some stairs, into the basement where the gas was burning. They crossed the cold, damp storeroom, then a long, dreary room with a long table on trestles, into a smaller, cosy apartment, not very high, which had been built on to the main building. In this room a small woman with a red serge blouse, and her black hair done on top of her head, was waiting like a proud little bantam.

"Here y'are!" said Pappleworth.

"I think it is 'here you are'!" exclaimed Polly. "The girls have been here nearly half an hour waiting. Just think of the time wasted!"

"*You* think of getting your work done and not talking so much," said Mr. Pappleworth. "You could ha' been finishing off."

"You know quite well we finished everything off on Saturday!" cried Polly, flying at him, her dark eyes flashing.

"Tu-tu-tu-tu-terterter!" he mocked. "Here's your new lad. Don't ruin him as you did the last."

"As we did the last!" repeated Polly. "Yes, *we* do a lot of ruining, we do. My word, a lad would *take* some ruining after he'd been with you."

"It's time for work now, not for talk," said Mr. Pappleworth severely and coldly.

"It was time for work some time back," said Polly, marching away with her head in the air. She was an erect little body of forty.

In that room were two round spiral machines on the bench under the window. Through the inner doorway was another longer room, with six more machines. A little group of girls, nicely dressed in white aprons, stood talking together.

"Have you nothing else to do but talk?" said Mr. Pappleworth.

"Only wait for you," said one handsome girl, laughing.

"Well, get on, get on," he said. "Come on, my lad. You'll know your road down here again."

And Paul ran upstairs after his chief. He was given some checking and invoicing to do. He stood at the desk, labouring in his execrable handwriting. Presently Mr. Jordan came strutting down from the glass office and stood behind him, to the boy's great discomfort. Suddenly a red and fat finger was thrust on the form he was filling in.

"*Mr.* J. A. Bates, Esquire!" exclaimed the cross voice just behind his ear.

Paul looked at "Mr. J. A. Bates, Esquire" in his own vile writing, and wondered what was the matter now.

"Didn't they teach you any better than *that* while they were at it? If you put 'Mr.' you don't put Esquire'—a man can't be both at once."

The boy regretted his too-much generosity in disposing of honours, hesitated, and with trembling fingers, scratched out the "Mr." Then all at once Mr. Jordan snatched away the invoice.

"Make another! Are you going to send *that* to a gentleman?" And he tore up the blue form irritably.

Paul, his ears red with shame, began again. Still Mr. Jordan watched.

"I don't know what they *do* teach in schools. You'll have to write better than that. Lads learn nothing nowadays, but how to recite poetry and play the fiddle. Have you seen his writing?" he asked of Mr. Pappleworth.

"Yes; prime, isn't it?" replied Mr. Pappleworth indifferently.

Mr. Jordan gave a little grunt, not unamiable. Paul divined that his master's bark was worse than his bite. Indeed, the little manufacturer, although he spoke bad English, was quite gentleman enough to leave his men alone and to take no notice of trifles. But he knew he did not look like the boss and owner of the show, so he had to play his rôle of proprietor at first, to put things on a right footing.

"Let's see, *what's* your name?" asked Mr. Pappleworth of the boy.

"Paul Morel."

It is curious that children suffer so much at having to pronounce their own names.

"Paul Morel, is it? All right, you Paul-Morel through them things there, and then——"

Mr. Pappleworth subsided on to a stool, and began writing. A girl came up from out of a door just behind, put some newly-pressed elastic web appliances on the counter, and returned. Mr. Pappleworth picked up the whitey-blue knee-band, examined it, and its yellow order-paper quickly, and put it on one side. Next was a flesh-pink "leg". He went through the few things, wrote out a couple of orders, and called to Paul to accompany him. This time they went through the door whence the girl had emerged. There Paul found himself at the top of a little wooden flight of steps, and below him saw a room with windows round two sides, and at the farther end half a dozen girls sitting bending over the benches in the light from the window, sewing. They were singing together "Two Little Girls in Blue". Hearing the door opened, they all turned round, to see Mr. Pappleworth and Paul looking down on them from the far end of the room. They stopped singing.

"Can't you make a bit less row?" said Mr. Pappleworth. "Folk'll think we keep cats."

A hunchback woman on a high stool turned her long, rather heavy face towards Mr. Pappleworth, and said, in a contralto voice:

"They're all tom-cats then."

In vain Mr. Pappleworth tried to be impressive for Paul's benefit. He descended the steps into the finishing-off room, and went to the hunchback Fanny. She had such a short body on her high stool that her head, with its great bands of bright brown hair, seemed over large, as did her pale, heavy face. She wore a dress of green-black cashmere, and her wrists, coming out of the narrow cuffs, were thin and flat, as she put down her work nervously. He showed her something that was wrong with a knee-cap.

"Well," she said, "you needn't come blaming it on to me. It's not my fault." Her colour mounted to her cheek.

"I never said it *was* your fault. Will you do as I tell you?" replied Mr. Pappleworth shortly.

"You don't say it's my fault, but you'd like to make out as it was," the hunchback woman cried, almost in tears. Then she snatched the knee-cap from her "boss", saying: "Yes, I'll do it for you, but you needn't be snappy."

"Here's your new lad," said Mr. Pappleworth.

Fanny turned, smiling very gently on Paul.

"Oh!" she said.

"Yes; don't make a softy of him between you."

"It's not us as 'ud make a softy of him," she said indignantly.

"Come on then, Paul," said Mr. Pappleworth.

"*Au revoy*, Paul," said one of the girls.

There was a titter of laughter. Paul went out, blushing deeply, not having spoken a word.

The day was very long. All morning the work-people were coming to speak to Mr. Pappleworth. Paul was writing or learning to make up parcels, ready for the midday post. At one o'clock, or, rather, at a quarter to one, Mr. Pappleworth disappeared to catch his train: he lived in the suburbs. At one o'clock, Paul, feeling very lost, took his dinner-basket down into the stockroom in the basement, that had the long table on trestles, and ate his meal hurriedly, alone in that cellar of gloom and desolation. Then he went out of doors. The brightness and the freedom of the streets made him feel adventurous and happy. But at two o'clock he was back in the corner of the big room. Soon the work-girls went trooping past, making remarks. It was the commoner girls who worked upstairs at the heavy tasks of truss-making and the finishing of artificial limbs. He waited for Mr. Pappleworth, not knowing what to do, sitting scribbling on the yellow order-paper. Mr. Pappleworth came at twenty minutes to three. Then he sat and gossiped with Paul, treating the boy entirely as an equal, even in age.

In the afternoon there was never very much to do, unless it were near the week-end, and the accounts had to be made up. At five o'clock all the men went down into the dungeon with the table on trestles, and there they had tea, eating bread-and-butter on the bare, dirty boards, talking with the same kind of ugly haste and slovenliness with which they ate their meal. And yet upstairs the atmosphere among them was always jolly and clear. The cellar and the trestles affected them.

After tea, when all the gases were lighted, *work* went more briskly. There was the big evening post to get off. The hose came up warm and newly pressed from the workrooms. Paul had made out the invoices. Now he had the packing up and addressing to do, then he had to weigh his stock of parcels on the scales. Everywhere voices were calling weights, there was the chink of metal, the rapid snapping of string, the hurrying to old Mr. Melling for stamps. And at last the postman came with his sack, laughing and jolly. Then everything slacked off, and Paul took his dinner-basket and ran to the station to catch the eight-twenty train. The day in the factory was just twelve hours long.

His mother sat waiting for him rather anxiously. He had to walk from Keston, so was not home until about twenty past nine. And he left the house before seven in the morning. Mrs. Morel was rather anxious about his health. But she herself had had to put up with so much that she expected her children to take the same odds. They must go through with what came. And Paul stayed at Jordan's, although all the time he was there his health suffered from the darkness and lack of air and the long hours.

He came in pale and tired. His mother looked at him. She saw he was rather pleased, and her anxiety all went.

"Well, and how was it?" she asked.

"Ever so funny, mother," he replied. "You don't have to work a bit hard, and they're nice with you."

"And did you get on all right?"

"Yes: they only say my writing's bad. But Mr. Papple-worth—he's my man—said to Mr. Jordan I should be all right. I'm Spiral, mother; you must come and see. It's ever so nice."

Soon he liked Jordan's. Mr. Pappleworth, who had a certain "saloon bar" flavour about him, was always natural, and treated him as if he had been a comrade. Sometimes the "Spiral boss" was irritable, and chewed more lozenges than ever. Even then, however, he was not offensive, but one of those people who hurt themselves by their own irritability more than they hurt other people.

"Haven't you done that *yet*?" he would cry. "Go on, be a month of Sundays."

Again, and Paul could understand him least then, he was jocular and in high spirits.

"I'm going to bring my little Yorkshire terrier bitch to-morrow," he said jubilantly to Paul.

"What's a Yorkshire terrier?"

"*Don't* know what a Yorkshire terrier is? *Don't know a Yorkshire*——" Mr. Pappleworth was aghast.

"Is it a little silky one—colours of iron and rusty silver?"

"*That's* it, my lad. She's a gem. She's had five pounds' worth of pups already, and she's worth over seven pounds herself; and she doesn't weigh twenty ounces."

The next day the bitch came. She was a shivering, miserable morsel. Paul did not care for her; she seemed so like a wet rag that would never dry. Then a man called for her, and began to make coarse jokes. But Mr. Pappleworth nodded his head in the direction of the boy, and the talk went on *sotto voce.*

Mr. Jordan only made one more excursion to watch Paul, and then the only fault he found was seeing the boy lay his pen on the counter.

"Put your pen in your ear, if you're going to be a clerk. Pen

in your ear!" And one day he said to the lad: "Why don't you
hold your shoulders straighter? Come down here," when he
took him into the glass office and fitted him with special braces
for keeping the shoulders square.

But Paul liked the girls best. The men seemed common and
rather dull. He liked them all, but they were uninteresting.
Polly, the little brisk overseer downstairs, finding Paul eating
in the cellar, asked him if she could cook him anything on her
little stove. Next day his mother gave him a dish that could
be heated up. He took it into the pleasant, clean room to Polly.
And very soon it grew to be an established custom that he
should have dinner with her. When he came in at eight in
the morning he took his basket to her, and when he came
down at one o'clock she had his dinner ready.

He was not very tall, and pale, with thick chestnut hair,
irregular features, and a wide, full mouth. She was like a
small bird. He often called her a "robinet". Though naturally
rather quiet, he would sit and chatter with her for hours telling her about his home. The girls all liked to hear him talk.
They often gathered in a little circle while he sat on a bench,
and held forth to them, laughing. Some of them regarded him
as a curious little creature, so serious, yet so bright and jolly,
and always so delicate in his way with them. They all liked
him, and he adored them. Polly he felt he belonged to. Then
Connie, with her mane of red hair, her face of apple-blossom,
her murmuring voice, such a lady in her shabby black frock,
appealed to his romantic side.

"When you sit winding," he said, "it looks as if you were
spinning at a spinning-wheel—it looks ever so nice. You remind me of Elaine in the 'Idylls of the King'. I'd draw you if
I could."

And she glanced at him blushing shyly. And later on he
had a sketch he prized very much: Connie sitting on the stool
before the wheel, her flowing mane of red hair on her rusty
black frock, her red mouth shut and serious, running the
scarlet thread off the hank on to the reel.

With Louie, handsome and brazen, who always seemed to
thrust her hip at him, he usually joked.

Emma was rather plain, rather old, and condescending. But
to condescend to him made her happy, and he did not mind.

"How do you put needles in?" he asked.

"Go away and don't bother."

"But I ought to know how to put needles in."

She ground at her machine all the while steadily.

"There are many things you ought to know," she replied.

"Tell me, then, how to stick needles in the machine."

"Oh, the boy, what a nuisance he is! Why, *this* is how you do it."

He watched her attentively. Suddenly a whistle piped. Then Polly appeared, and said in a clear voice:

"Mr. Pappleworth wants to know how much longer you're going to be down here playing with the girls, Paul."

Paul flew upstairs, calling "Good-bye!" and Emma drew herself up.

"It wasn't *me* who wanted him to play with the machine," she said.

As a rule, when all the girls came back at two o'clock, he ran upstairs to Fanny, the hunchback, in the finishing-off room. Mr. Pappleworth did not appear till twenty to three, and he often found his boy sitting beside Fanny, talking, or drawing, or singing with the girls.

Often, after a minute's hesitation, Fanny would begin to sing. She had a fine contralto voice. Everybody joined in the chorus, and it went well. Paul was not at all embarrassed, after a while, sitting in the room with the half a dozen work-girls.

At the end of the song Fanny would say:

"I know you've been laughing at me."

"Don't be so soft, Fanny!" cried one of the girls.

Once there was mention of Connie's red hair.

"Fanny's is better, to my fancy," said Emma.

"You needn't try to make a fool of me," said Fanny, flushing deeply.

"No, but she has, Paul; she's got beautiful hair."

"It's a treat of a colour," said he. "That coldish colour like earth, and yet shiny. It's like bog-water."

"Goodness me!" exclaimed one girl, laughing.

"How I do but get criticised," said Fanny.

"But you should see it down, Paul," cried Emma earnestly. "It's simply beautiful. Put it down for him, Fanny, if he wants something to paint."

Fanny would not, and yet she wanted to.

"Then I'll take it down myself," said the lad.

"Well, you can if you like," said Fanny.

And he carefully took the pins out of the knot, and the rush of hair, of uniform dark brown, slid over the humped back.

"What a lovely lot!" he exclaimed.

The girls watched. There was silence. The youth shook the hair loose from the coil.

"It's splendid!" he said, smelling its perfume. "I'll bet it's worth pounds."

"I'll leave it you when I die, Paul," said Fanny, half joking.

"You look just like anybody else, sitting drying their hair," said one of the girls to the long-legged hunchback.

Poor Fanny was morbidly sensitive, always imagining insults. Polly was curt and business-like. The two departments were for ever at war, and Paul was always finding Fanny in tears. Then he was made the recipient of all her woes, and he had to plead her case with Polly.

So the time went along happily enough. The factory had a homely feel. No one was rushed or driven. Paul always enjoyed it when the work got faster, towards post-time, and all the men united in labour. He liked to watch his fellow-clerks at work. The man was the work and the work was the man, one thing, for the time being. It was different with the girls. The real woman never seemed to be there at the task, but as if left out, waiting.

From the train going home at night he used to watch the lights of the town, sprinkled thick on the hills, fusing together in a blaze in the valleys. He felt rich in life and happy. Drawing farther off, there was a patch of lights at Bulwell like myriad petals shaken to the ground from the shed stars; and beyond was the red glare of the furnaces, playing like hot breath on the clouds.

He had to walk two and more miles from Keston home, up two long hills, down two short hills. He was often tired, and he counted the lamps climbing the hill above him, how many more to pass. And from the hill-top, on pitch-dark nights, he looked round on the villages five or six miles away, that shone like swarms of glittering living things, almost a heaven against his feet. Marlpool and Heanor scattered the far-off darkness with brilliance. And occasionally the black valley space between was traced, violated by a great train rushing south to London or north to Scotland. The trains roared by like projectiles level on the darkness, fuming and burning, making the valley clang with their passage. They were gone, and the lights of the towns and villages glittered in silence.

And then he came to the corner at home, which faced the other side of the night. The ash-tree seemed a friend now. His mother rose with gladness as he entered. He put his eight shillings proudly on the table.

"It'll help, mother?" he asked wistfully.

"There's precious little left," she answered, "after your ticket and dinners and such are taken off."

Then he told her the budget of the day. His life-story, like an Arabian Nights, was told night after night to his mother. It was almost as if it were her own life.

CHAPTER VI

DEATH IN THE FAMILY

ARTHUR MOREL was growing up. He was a quick, careless, impulsive boy, a good deal like his father. He hated study, made a great moan if he had to work, and escaped as soon as possible to his sport again.

In appearance he remained the flower of the family, being well made, graceful, and full of life. His dark brown hair and fresh colouring, and his exquisite dark blue eyes shaded with long lashes, together with his generous manner and fiery temper, made him a favourite. But as he grew older his temper became uncertain. He flew into rages over nothing, seemed unbearably raw and irritable.

His mother, whom he loved, wearied of him sometimes. He thought only of himself. When he wanted amusement, all that stood in his way he hated, even if it were she. When he was in trouble he moaned to her ceaselessly.

"Goodness, boy!" she said, when he groaned about a master who, he said, hated him, "if you don't like it, alter it, and if you can't alter it, put up with it."

And his father, whom he had loved and who had worshipped him, he came to detest. As he grew older Morel fell into a slow ruin. His body, which had been beautiful in movement and in being, shrank, did not seem to ripen with the years, but to get mean and rather despicable. There came over him a look of meanness and of paltriness. And when the mean-looking elderly man bullied or ordered the boy about, Arthur was furious. Moreover, Morel's manners got worse and worse, his habits

somewhat disgusting. When the children were growing up
and in the crucial stage of adolescence, the father was like
some ugly irritant to their souls. His manners in the house
were the same as he used among the colliers down pit.

"Dirty nuisance!" Arthur would cry, jumping up and going
straight out of the house when his father disgusted him. And
Morel persisted the more because his children hated it. He
seemed to take a kind of satisfaction in disgusting them, and
driving them nearly mad, while they were so irritably sensitive
at the age of fourteen or fifteen. So that Arthur, who was
growing up when his father was degenerate and elderly, hated
him worst of all.

Then, sometimes, the father would seem to feel the contemptuous hatred of his children.

"There's not a man tries harder for his family!" he would
shout. "He does his best for them, and then gets treated like
a dog. But I'm not going to stand it, I tell you!"

But for the threat and the fact that he did not try so hard as
he imagined, they would have felt sorry. As it was, the battle
now went on nearly all between father and children, he persisting in his dirty and disgusting ways, just to assert his independence. They loathed him.

Arthur was so inflamed and irritable at last, that when he
won a scholarship for the Grammar School in Nottingham, his
mother decided to let him live in town, with one of her sisters,
and only come home at week-ends.

Annie was still a junior teacher in the Board-school, earning
about four shillings a week. But soon she would have fifteen
shillings, since she had passed her examination, and there
would be financial peace in the house.

Mrs. Morel clung now to Paul. He was quiet and not brilliant. But still he stuck to his painting, and still he stuck to his
mother. Everything he did was for her. She waited for his
coming home in the evening, and then she unburdened herself
of all she had pondered, or of all that had occurred to her
during the day. He sat and listened with his earnestness. The
two shared lives.

William was engaged now to his brunette, and had bought
her an engagement ring that cost eight guineas. The children
gasped at such a fabulous price.

"Eight guineas!" said Morel. "More fool him! If he'd gen
me some on't, it 'ud ha' looked better on 'im."

"Given *you* some of it!" cried Mrs. Morel. "Why give *you* some of it!"

She remembered *he* had bought no engagement ring at all, and she preferred William, who was not mean, if he were foolish. But now the young man talked only of the dances to which he went with his betrothed, and the different resplendent clothes she wore; or he told his mother with glee how they went to the theatre like great swells.

He wanted to bring the girl home. Mrs. Morel said she should come at the Christmas. This time William arrived with a lady, but with no presents. Mrs. Morel had prepared supper. Hearing footsteps, she rose and went to the door. William entered.

"Hello, mother!" He kissed her hastily, then stood aside to present a tall, handsome girl, who was wearing a costume of fine black-and-white check, and furs.

"Here's Gyp!"

Miss Western held out her hand and showed her teeth in a small smile.

"Oh, how do you do, Mrs. Morel!" she exclaimed.

"I am afraid you will be hungry," said Mrs. Morel.

"Oh no, we had dinner in the train. Have you got my gloves, Chubby?"

William Morel, big and raw-boned, looked at her quickly.

"How should I?" he said.

"Then I've lost them. Don't be cross with me."

A frown went over his face, but he said nothing. She glanced round the kitchen. It was small and curious to her, with its glittering kissing-bunch, its evergreens behind the pictures, its wooden chairs and little deal table. At that moment Morel came in.

"Hello, dad!"

"Hello, my son! Tha's let on me!"

The two shook hands, and William presented the lady. She gave the same smile that showed her teeth.

"How do you do, Mr. Morel?"

Morel bowed obsequiously.

"I'm very well, and I hope so are you. You must make yourself very welcome."

"Oh, thank you," she replied, rather amused.

"You will like to go upstairs," said Mrs. Morel.

"If you don't mind; but not if it is any trouble to you."

"It is no trouble. Annie will take you. Walter, carry up this box."

"And don't be an hour dressing yourself up," said William to his betrothed.

Annie took a brass candlestick, and, too shy almost to speak, preceded the young lady to the front bedroom, which Mr. and Mrs. Morel had vacated for her. It, too, was small and cold by candle-light. The colliers' wives only lit fires in bedrooms in case of extreme illness.

"Shall I unstrap the box?" asked Annie.

"Oh, thank you very much!"

Annie played the part of maid, then went downstairs for hot water.

"I think she's rather tired, mother," said William. "It's a beastly journey, and we had such a rush."

"Is there anything I can give her?" asked Mrs. Morel.

"Oh no, she'll be all right."

But there was a chill in the atmosphere. After half an hour Miss Western came down, having put on a purplish-coloured dress, very fine for the collier's kitchen.

"I told you you'd no need to change," said William to her.

"Oh, Chubby!" Then she turned with that sweetish smile to Mrs. Morel. "Don't you think he's always grumbling, Mrs. Morel?"

"Is he?" said Mrs. Morel. "That's not very nice of him."

"It isn't, really!"

"You are cold," said the mother. "Won't you come near the fire?"

Morel jumped out of his arm-chair.

"Come and sit you here!" he cried. "Come and sit you here!"

"No, dad, keep your own chair. Sit on the sofa, Gyp," said William.

"No, no!" cried Morel. "This cheer's warmest. Come and sit here, Miss Wesson."

"Thank you so much," said the girl, seating herself in the collier's arm-chair, the place of honour. She shivered, feeling the warmth of the kitchen penetrate her.

"Fetch me a hanky, Chubby dear!" she said, putting up her mouth to him, and using the same intimate tone as if they were alone; which made the rest of the family feel as if they

ought not to be present. The young lady evidently did not
realise them as people: they were creatures to her for the
present. William winced.

In such a household, in Streatham, Miss Western would have
been a lady condescending to her inferiors. These people were
to her, certainly clownish—in short, the working classes. How
was she to adjust herself?

"I'll go," said Annie.

Miss Western took no notice, as if a servant had spoken.
But when the girl came downstairs again with the handkerchief, she said: "Oh, thank you!" in a gracious way.

She sat and talked about the dinner on the train, which had
been so poor; about London, about dances. She was really very
nervous, and chattered from fear. Morel sat all the time
smoking his thick twist tobacco, watching her, and listening
to her glib London speech, as he puffed. Mrs. Morel, dressed
up in her best black silk blouse, answered quietly and rather
briefly. The three children sat round in silence and admiration.
Miss Western was the princess. Everything of the best was got
out for her: the best cups, the best spoons, the best table cloth,
the best coffee-jug. The children thought she must find it quite
grand. She felt strange, not able to realize the people, not
knowing how to treat them. William joked, and was slightly
uncomfortable.

At about ten o'clock he said to her:

"Aren't you tired, Gyp?"

"Rather, Chubby," she answered, at once in the intimate
tones and putting her head slightly on one side.

"I'll light her the candle, mother," he said.

"Very well," replied the mother.

Miss Western stood up, held out her hand to Mrs. Morel.

"Good-night, Mrs. Morel," she said.

Paul sat at the boiler, letting the water run from the tap
into a stone beer-bottle. Annie swathed the bottle in an old
flannel pit-singlet, and kissed her mother good-night. She was
to share the room with the lady, because the house was full.

"You wait a minute," said Mrs. Morel to Annie. And Annie
sat nursing the hot-water bottle. Miss Western shook hands all
round, to everybody's discomfort, and took her departure, preceded by William. In five minutes he was downstairs again.
His heart was rather sore; he did not know why. He talked
very little till everybody had gone to bed, but himself and his

mother. Then he stood with his legs apart, in his old attitude on the hearth-rug, and said hesitatingly:

"Well, mother?"

"Well, my son?"

She sat in the rocking-chair, feeling somehow hurt and humiliated, for his sake.

"Do you like her?"

"Yes," came the slow answer.

"She's shy yet, mother. She's not used to it. It's different from her aunt's house, you know."

"Of course it is, my boy; and she must find it difficult."

"She does." Then he frowned swiftly. "If only she wouldn't put on her blessed airs!"

"It's only her first awkwardness, my boy. She'll be all right."

"That's it, mother," he replied gratefully. But his brow was gloomy. "You know, she's not like you, mother. She's not serious, and she can't think."

"She's young, my boy."

"Yes; and she's had no sort of show. Her mother died when she was a child. Since then she's lived with her aunt, whom she can't bear. And her father was a rake. She's had no love."

"No! Well, you must make up to her."

"And so—you have to forgive her a lot of things."

"What do you have to forgive her, my boy?"

"I dunno. When she seems shallow, you have to remember she's never had anybody to bring her deeper side out. And she's fearfully fond of me."

"Anybody can see that."

"But you know, mother—she's—she's different from us. Those sort of people, like those she lives amongst, they don't seem to have the same principles."

"You mustn't judge too hastily," said Mrs. Morel.

But he seemed uneasy within himself.

In the morning, however, he was up singing and larking round the house.

"Hello!" he called, sitting on the stairs. "Are you getting up?"

"Yes," her voice called faintly.

"Merry Christmas!" he shouted to her.

Her laugh, pretty and tinkling, was heard in the bedroom. She did not come down in half an hour.

"Was she *really* getting up when she said she was?" he asked of Annie.

"Yes, she was," replied Annie.

He waited a while, then went to the stairs again.

"Happy New Year," he called.

"Thank you, Chubby dear!" came the laughing voice, far away.

"Buck up!" he implored.

It was nearly an hour, and still he was waiting for her. Morel, who always rose before six, looked at the clock.

"Well, it's a winder!" he exclaimed.

The family had breakfasted, all but William. He went to the foot of the stairs.

"Shall I have to send you an Easter egg up there?" he called, rather crossly. She only laughed. The family expected, after that time of preparation, something like magic. At last she came, looking very nice in a blouse and skirt.

"Have you *really* been all this time getting ready?" he asked.

"Chubby dear! That question is not permitted, is it, Mrs. Morel?"

She played the grand lady at first. When she went with William to chapel, he in his frock-coat and silk hat, she in her furs and London-made costume, Paul and Arthur and Annie expected everybody to bow to the ground in admiration. And Morel, standing in his Sunday suit at the end of the road, watching the gallant pair go, felt he was the father of princes and princesses.

And yet she was not so grand. For a year now she had been a sort of secretary or clerk in a London office. But while she was with the Morels she queened it. She sat and let Annie or Paul wait on her as if they were her servants. She treated Mrs. Morel with a certain glibness and Morel with patronage. But after a day or so she began to change her tune.

William always wanted Paul or Annie to go along with them on their walks. It was so much more interesting. And Paul really *did* admire "Gipsy" whole-heartedly; in fact, his mother scarcely forgave the boy for the adulation with which he treated the girl.

On the second day, when Lily said: "Oh, Annie, do you know where I left my muff?" William replied:

"You know it is in your bedroom. Why do you ask Annie?"

And Lily went upstairs with a cross, shut mouth. But it

angered the young man that she made a servant of his sister.

On the third evening William and Lily were sitting together in the parlour by the fire in the dark. At a quarter to eleven Mrs. Morel was heard raking the fire. William came out to the kitchen, followed by his beloved.

"Is it as late as that, mother?" he said. She had been sitting alone.

"It is not *late*, my boy, but it is as late as I usually sit up."

"Won't you go to bed, then?" he asked.

"And leave you two? No, my boy, I don't believe in it."

"Can't you trust us, mother?"

"Whether I can or not, I won't do it. You can stay till eleven if you like, and I can read."

"Go to bed, Gyp," he said to his girl. "We won't keep mater waiting."

"Annie has left the candle burning, Lily," said Mrs. Morel; "I think you will see."

"Yes, thank you. Good-night, Mrs. Morel."

William kissed his sweetheart at the foot of the stairs, and she went. He returned to the kitchen.

"Can't you trust us, mother?" he repeated, rather offended.

"My boy, I tell you I don't *believe* in leaving two young things like you alone downstairs when everyone else is in bed."

And he was forced to take this answer. He kissed his mother good-night.

At Easter he came over alone. And then he discussed his sweetheart endlessly with his mother.

"You know, mother, when I'm away from her I don't care for her a bit. I shouldn't care if I never saw her again. But, then, when I'm with her in the evenings I am awfully fond of her."

"It's a queer sort of love to marry on," said Mrs. Morel, "if she holds you no more than that!"

"It *is* funny!" he exclaimed. It worried and perplexed him. "But yet—there's so much between us now I couldn't give her up."

"You know best," said Mrs. Morel. "But if it is as you say, I wouldn't call it *love*—at any rate, it doesn't look much like it."

"Oh, I don't know, mother. She's an orphan, and——"

They never came to any sort of conclusion. He seemed

puzzled and rather fretted. She was rather reserved. All his strength and money went in keeping this girl. He could scarcely afford to take his mother to Nottingham when he came over.

Paul's wages had been raised at Christmas to ten shillings, to his great joy. He was quite happy at Jordan's, but his health suffered from the long hours and the confinement. His mother, to whom he became more and more significant, thought how to help.

His half-day holiday was on Monday afternoon. On a Monday morning in May, as the two sat alone at breakfast, she said:

"I think it will be a fine day."

He looked up in surprise. This meant something.

"You know Mr. Leivers has gone to live on a new farm. Well, he asked me last week if I wouldn't go and see Mrs. Leivers, and I promised to bring you on Monday if it's fine. Shall we go?"

"I say, little woman, how lovely!" he cried. "And we'll go this afternoon?"

Paul hurried off to the station jubilant. Down Derby Road was a cherry-tree that glistened. The old brick wall by the Statutes ground burned scarlet, spring was a very flame of green. And the steep swoop of highroad lay, in its cool morning dust, splendid with patterns of sunshine and shadow, perfectly still. The trees sloped their great green shoulders proudly; and inside the warehouse all the morning, the boy had a vision of spring outside.

When he came home at dinner-time his mother was rather excited.

"Are we going?" he asked.

"When I'm ready," she replied.

Presently he got up.

"Go and get dressed while I wash up," he said.

She did so. He washed the pots, straightened, and then took her boots. They were quite clean. Mrs. Morel was one of those naturally exquisite people who can walk in mud without dirtying their shoes. But Paul had to clean them for her. They were kid boots at eight shillings a pair. He, however, thought them the most dainty boots in the world, and he cleaned them with as much reverence as if they had been flowers.

Suddenly she appeared in the inner doorway rather shyly.

She had got a new cotton blouse on. Paul jumped up and went forward.

"Oh, my stars!" he exclaimed. "What a bobby-dazzler!"

She sniffed in a little haughty way, and put her head up.

"It's not a bobby-dazzler at all!" she replied. "It's very quiet."

She walked forward, whilst he hovered round her.

"Well," she asked, quite shy, but pretending to be high and mighty, "do you like it?"

"Awfully! You *are* a fine little woman to go jaunting out with!"

He went and surveyed her from the back.

"Well," he said, "if I was walking down the street behind you, I should say: 'Doesn't *that* little person fancy herself!'"

"Well, she doesn't," replied Mrs. Morel. "She's not sure it suits her."

"Oh no! she wants to be in dirty black, looking as if she was wrapped in burnt paper. It *does* suit you, and *I* say you look nice."

She sniffed in her little way, pleased, but pretending to know better.

"Well," she said, "it's cost me just three shillings. You couldn't have got it ready-made for that price, could you?"

"I should think you couldn't," he replied.

"And, you know, it's good stuff."

"Awfully pretty," he said.

The blouse was white, with a little sprig of heliotrope and black.

"Too young for me, though, I'm afraid," she said.

"Too young for you!" he exclaimed in disgust. "Why don't you buy some false white hair and stick it on your head."

"I s'll soon have no need," she replied. "I'm going white fast enough."

"Well, you've no business to," he said. "What do I want with a white-haired mother?"

"I'm afraid you'll have to put up with one, my lad," she said rather strangely.

They set off in great style, she carrying the umbrella William had given her, because of the sun. Paul was considerably taller than she, though he was not big. He fancied himself.

On the fallow land the young wheat shone silkily. Minton

pit waved its plumes of white steam, coughed, and rattled
hoarsely.

"Now look at that!" said Mrs. Morel. Mother and son stood
on the road to watch. Along the ridge of the great pit-hill
crawled a little group in silhouette against the sky, a horse, a
small truck, and a man. They climbed the incline against the
heavens. At the end the man tipped the wagon. There was an
undue rattle as the waste fell down the sheer slope of the
enormous bank.

"You sit a minute, mother," he said, and she took a seat on
a bank, whilst he sketched rapidly. She was silent whilst he
worked, looking round at the afternoon, the red cottages
shining among their greenness.

"The world is a wonderful place," she said, "and wonderfully beautiful."

"And so's the pit," he said. "Look how it heaps together, like
something alive almost—a big creature that you don't know."

"Yes," she said. "Perhaps!"

"And all the trucks standing waiting, like a string of beasts
to be fed," he said.

"And very thankful I am they *are* standing," she said, "for
that means they'll turn middling time this week."

"But I like the feel of *men* on things, while they're alive.
There's a feel of men about trucks, because they've been
handled with men's hands, all of them."

"Yes," said Mrs. Morel.

They went along under the trees of the highroad. He was
constantly informing her, but she was interested. They passed
the end of Nethermere, that was tossing its sunshine like petals
lightly in its lap. Then they turned on a private road, and
in some trepidation approached a big farm. A dog barked
furiously. A woman came out to see.

"Is this the way to Willey Farm?" Mrs. Morel asked.

Paul hung behind in terror of being sent back. But the
woman was amiable, and directed them. The mother and
son went through the wheat and oats, over a little bridge into
a wild meadow. Peewits, with their white breasts glistening,
wheeled and screamed about them. The lake was still and
blue. High overhead a heron floated. Opposite, the wood
heaped on the hill, green and still.

"It's a wild road, mother," said Paul. "Just like Canada."

"Isn't it beautiful!" said Mrs. Morel, looking round.

"See that heron—see—see her legs?"

He directed his mother, what she must see and what not.
And she was quite content.

"But now," she said, "which way? He told me through the
wood."

The wood, fenced and dark, lay on their left.

"I can feel a bit of a path this road," said Paul. "You've got
town feet, somehow or other, you have."

They found a little gate, and soon were in a broad green alley
of the wood, with a new thicket of fir and pine on one hand,
an old oak glade dipping down on the other. And among the
oaks the bluebells stood in pools of azure, under the new green
hazels, upon a pale fawn floor of oak-leaves. He found flowers
for her.

"Here's a bit of new-mown hay," he said; then, again, he
brought her forget-me-nots. And, again, his heart hurt with
love, seeing her hand, used with work, holding the little bunch
of flowers he gave her. She was perfectly happy.

But at the end of the riding was a fence to climb. Paul was
over in a second.

"Come," he said, "let me help you."

"No, go away. I will do it in my own way."

He stood below with his hands up ready to help her. She
climbed cautiously.

"What a way to climb!" he exclaimed scornfully, when she
was safely to earth again.

"Hateful stiles!" she cried.

"Duffer of a little woman," he replied, "who can't get over
'em."

In front, along the edge of the wood, was a cluster of low
red farm buildings. The two hastened forward. Flush with
the wood was the apple orchard, where blossom was falling
on the grindstone. The pond was deep under a hedge and over-
hanging oak trees. Some cows stood in the shade. The farm
and buildings, three sides of a quadrangle, embraced the sunshine towards the wood. It was very still.

Mother and son went into the small railed garden, where was
a scent of red gillivers. By the open door were some floury
loaves, put out to cool. A hen was just coming to peck them.
Then, in the doorway suddenly appeared a girl in a dirty apron.
She was about fourteen years old, had a rosy dark face, a bunch
of short black curls, very fine and free, and dark eyes; shy,

questioning, a little resentful of the strangers, she disappeared. In a minute another figure appeared, a small, frail woman, rosy, with great dark brown eyes.

"Oh!" she exclaimed, smiling with a little glow, "you've come, then. I *am* glad to see you." Her voice was intimate and rather sad.

The two women shook hands.

"Now are you sure we're not a bother to you?" said Mrs. Morel. "I know what a farming life is."

"Oh no! We're only too thankful to see a new face, it's so lost up here."

"I suppose so," said Mrs. Morel.

They were taken through into the parlour—a long, low room, with a great bunch of guelder-roses in the fireplace. There the women talked, whilst Paul went out to survey the land. He was in the garden smelling the gillivers and looking at the plants, when the girl came out quickly to the heap of coal which stood by the fence.

"I suppose these are cabbage-roses?" he said to her, pointing to the bushes along the fence.

She looked at him with startled, big brown eyes.

"I suppose they are cabbage-roses when they come out?" he said.

"I don't know," she faltered. "They're white with pink middles."

"Then they're maiden-blush."

Miriam flushed. She had a beautiful warm colouring.

"I don't know," she said.

"You don't have *much* in your garden," he said.

"This is our first year here," she answered, in a distant, rather superior way, drawing back and going indoors. He did not notice, but went his round of exploration. Presently his mother came out, and they went through the buildings. Paul was hugely delighted.

"And I suppose you have the fowls and calves and pigs to look after?" said Mrs. Morel to Mrs. Leivers.

"No," replied the little woman. "I can't find time to look after cattle, and I'm not used to it. It's as much as I can do to keep going in the house."

"Well, I suppose it is," said Mrs. Morel

Presently the girl came out.

"Tea is ready, mother," she said in a musical, quiet voice.

"Oh, thank you, Miriam, then we'll come," replied her mother, almost ingratiatingly. "Would you *care* to have tea now, Mrs. Morel?"

"Of course," said Mrs. Morel. "Whenever it's ready."

Paul and his mother and Mrs. Leivers had tea together. Then they went out into the wood that was flooded with bluebells, while fumy forget-me-nots were in the paths. The mother and son were in ecstasy together.

When they got back to the house, Mr. Leivers and Edgar, the eldest son, were in the kitchen. Edgar was about eighteen. Then Geoffrey and Maurice, big lads of twelve and thirteen, were in from school. Mr. Leivers was a good-looking man in the prime of life, with a golden-brown moustache, and blue eyes screwed up against the weather.

The boys were condescending, but Paul scarcely observed it. They went round for eggs, scrambling into all sorts of places. As they were feeding the fowls Miriam came out. The boys took no notice of her. One hen, with her yellow chickens, was in a coop. Maurice took his hand full of corn and let the hen peck from it.

"Durst you do it?" he asked of Paul.

"Let's see," said Paul.

He had a small hand, warm, and rather capable-looking. Miriam watched. He held the corn to the hen. The bird eyed it with her hard, bright eye, and suddenly made a peck into his hand. He started, and laughed. "Rap, rap, rap!" went the bird's beak in his palm. He laughed again, and the other boys joined.

"She knocks you, and nips you, but she never hurts," said Paul, when the last corn had gone.

"Now, Miriam," said Maurice, "you come an' 'ave a go."

"No," she cried, shrinking back.

"Ha! baby. The mardy-kid!" said her brothers.

"It doesn't hurt a bit," said Paul. "It only just nips rather nicely."

"No," she still cried, shaking her black curls and shrinking.

"She dursn't," said Geoffrey. "She niver durst do anything except recite poitry."

"Dursn't jump off a gate, dursn't tweedle, dursn't go on a slide, dursn't stop a girl hittin' her. She can do nowt but go about thinkin' herself somebody. 'The Lady of the Lake.' Yah!" cried Maurice.

Miriam was crimson with shame and misery.

"I dare do more than you," she cried. "You're never anything but cowards and bullies."

"Oh, cowards and bullies!" they repeated mincingly, mocking her speech.

> "Not such a clown shall anger me,
> A boor is answered silently,"

he quoted against her, shouting with laughter.

She went indoors. Paul went with the boys into the orchard, where they had rigged up a parallel bar. They did feats of strength. He was more agile than strong, but it served. He fingered a piece of apple-blossom that hung low on a swinging bough.

"I wouldn't get the apple-blossom," said Edgar, the eldest brother. "There'll be no apples next year."

"I wasn't going to get it," replied Paul, going away.

The boys felt hostile to him; they were more interested in their own pursuits. He wandered back to the house to look for his mother. As he went round the back, he saw Miriam kneeling in front of the hen-coop, some maize in her hand, biting her lip, and crouching in an intense attitude. The hen was eyeing her wickedly. Very gingerly she put forward her hand. The hen bobbed for her. She drew back quickly with a cry, half of fear, half of chagrin.

"It won't hurt you," said Paul.

She flushed crimson and started up.

"I only wanted to try," she said in a low voice.

"See, it doesn't hurt," he said, and, putting only two corns in his palm, he let the hen peck, peck, peck at his bare hand. "It only makes you laugh," he said.

She put her hand forward and dragged it away, tried again, and started back with a cry. He frowned.

"Why, I'd let her take corn from my face," said Paul, "only she bumps a bit. She's ever so neat. If she wasn't, look how much ground she'd peck up every day."

He waited grimly, and watched. At last Miriam let the bird peck from her hand. She gave a little cry—fear, and pain because of fear—rather pathetic. But she had done it, and she did it again.

"There, you see," said the boy. "It doesn't hurt, does it?"

She looked at him with dilated dark eyes.

"No," she laughed, trembling.

Then she rose and went indoors. She seemed to be in some way resentful of the boy.

"He thinks I'm only a common girl," she thought, and she wanted to prove she was a grand person like the "Lady of the Lake".

Paul found his mother ready to go home. She smiled on her son. He took the great bunch of flowers. Mr. and Mrs. Leivers walked down the fields with them. The hills were golden with evening; deep in the woods showed the darkening purple of bluebells. It was everywhere perfectly still, save for the rustling of leaves and birds.

"But it is a beautiful place," said Mrs. Morel.

"Yes," answered Mr. Leivers; "it's a nice little place, if only it weren't for the rabbits. The pasture's bitten down to nothing. I dunno if ever I s'll get the rent off it."

He clapped his hands, and the field broke into motion near the woods, brown rabbits hopping everywhere.

"Would you believe it!" exclaimed Mrs. Morel.

She and Paul went on alone together.

"Wasn't it lovely, mother?" he said quietly.

A thin moon was coming out. His heart was full of happiness till it hurt. His mother had to chatter, because she, too, wanted to cry with happiness.

"Now *wouldn't* I help that man!" she said. "*Wouldn't* I see to the fowls and the young stock! And *I'd* learn to milk, and *I'd* talk with him, and *I'd* plan with him. My word, if I were his wife, the farm would be run, I know! But there, she hasn't the strength—she simply hasn't the strength. She ought never to have been burdened like it, you know. I'm sorry for her, and I'm sorry for him too. My word, if *I'd* had him, I shouldn't have thought him a bad husband! Not that she does either; and she's very lovable."

William came home again with his sweetheart at the Whitsuntide. He had one week of his holidays then. It was beautiful weather. As a rule, William and Lily and Paul went out in the morning together for a walk. William did not talk to his beloved much, except to tell her things from his boyhood. Paul talked endlessly to both of them. They lay down, all three, in a meadow by Minton Church. On one side, by the Castle Farm, was a beautiful quivering screen of poplars. Haw-

thorn was dropping from the hedges; penny daisies and ragged
robin were in the field, like laughter. William, a big fellow of
twenty-three, thinner now and even a bit gaunt, lay back in
the sunshine and dreamed, while she fingered with his hair.
Paul went gathering the big daisies. She had taken off her hat;
her hair was black as a horse's mane. Paul came back and
threaded daisies in her jet-black hair—big spangles of white
and yellow, and just a pink touch of ragged robin.

"Now you look like a young witch-woman," the boy said to
her. "Doesn't she, William?"

Lily laughed. William opened his eyes and looked at her.
In his gaze was a certain baffled look of misery and fierce
appreciation.

"Has he made a sight of me?" she asked, laughing down on
her lover.

"That he has!" said William, smiling.

He looked at her. Her beauty seemed to hurt him. He glanced
at her flower-decked head and frowned.

"You look nice enough, if that's what you want to know,"
he said.

And she walked without her hat. In a little while William
recovered, and was rather tender to her. Coming to a bridge,
he carved her initials and his in a heart.

          L. L. W. — *3 letters - More formal*
          W. M.

She watched his strong, nervous hand, with its glistening
hairs and freckles, as he carved, and she seemed fascinated
by it.

All the time there was a feeling of sadness and warmth, and
a certain tenderness in the house, whilst William and Lily were
at home. But often he got irritable. She had brought, for an
eight-days' stay, five dresses and six blouses.

"Oh, would you mind," she said to Annie, "washing me these
two blouses, and these things?"

And Annie stood washing when William and Lily went out
the next morning. Mrs. Morel was furious. And sometimes the
young man, catching a glimpse of his sweetheart's attitude *class*
towards his sister, hated her.

On Sunday morning she looked very beautiful in a dress of
foulard, silky and sweeping, and blue as a jay-bird's feather, and

in a large cream hat covered with many roses, mostly crimson. Nobody could admire her enough. But in the evening, when she was going out, she asked again:

"Chubby, have you got my gloves?"

"Which?" asked William

"My new black *suède*."

"No."

There was a hunt. She had lost them.

"Look here, mother," said William, "that's the fourth pair she's lost since Christmas—at five shillings a pair!"

"You only gave me *two* of them," she remonstrated.

And in the evening, after supper, he stood on the hearth-rug whilst she sat on the sofa, and he seemed to hate her. In the afternoon he had left her whilst he went to see some old friend. She had sat looking at a book. After supper William wanted to write a letter.

"Here is your book, Lily," said Mrs. Morel. "Would you care to go on with it for a few minutes?"

"No, thank you," said the girl. "I will sit still."

"But it is so dull."

William scribbled irritably at a great rate. As he sealed the envelope he said:

"Read a book! Why, she's never read a book in her life."

"Oh, go along!" said Mrs. Morel, cross with the exaggeration.

"It's true, mother—she hasn't," he cried, jumping up and taking his old position on the hearth-rug. "She's never read a book in her life."

"'Er's like me," chimed in Morel. "'Er canna see what there is i' books, ter sit borin' your nose in 'em for, nor more can I."

"But you shouldn't say these things," said Mrs. Morel to her son.

"But it's true, mother—she *can't* read. What did you give her?"

"Well, I gave her a little thing of Annie Swan's. Nobody wants to read dry stuff on Sunday afternoon."

"Well, I'll bet she didn't read ten lines of it."

"You are mistaken," said his mother.

All the time Lily sat miserably on the sofa. He turned to her swiftly.

"*Did* you read any?" he asked.

"Yes, I did," she replied.

"How much?"

"I don't know how many pages."

"Tell me *one thing* you read."

She could not.

She never got beyond the second page. He read a great deal, and had a quick, active intelligence. She could understand nothing but love-making and chatter. He was accustomed to having all his thoughts sifted through his mother's mind; so, when he wanted companionship, and was asked in reply to be the billing and twittering lover, he hated his betrothed.

"You know, mother," he said, when he was alone with her at night, "she's no idea of money, she's so wessel-brained. When she's paid, she'll suddenly buy such rot as *marrons glacés*, and then I have to buy her season ticket, and her extras, even her underclothing. And she wants to get married, and I think myself we might as well get married next year. But at this rate——"

"A fine mess of a marriage it would be," replied his mother. "I should consider it again, my boy."

"Oh, well, I've gone too far to break off now," he said, "and so I shall get married as soon as I can."

"Very well, my boy. If you will, you will, and there's no stopping you; but I tell you, *I* can't sleep when I think about it."

"Oh, she'll be all right, mother. We shall manage."

"And she lets you buy her underclothing?" asked the mother.

"Well," he began apologetically, "she didn't ask me; but one morning—and it *was* cold—I found her on the station shivering, not able to keep still; so I asked her if she was well wrapped up. She said: 'I think so.' So I said: 'Have you got warm underthings on?' And she said: 'No, they were cotton.' I asked her why on earth she hadn't got something thicker on in weather like that, and she said because she *had* nothing. And there she is—a bronchial subject! I *had* to take her and get some warm things. Well, mother, I shouldn't mind the money if we had any. And, you know, she *ought* to keep enough to pay for her season-ticket; but no, she comes to me about that, and I have to find the money."

"It's a poor lookout," said Mrs. Morel bitterly.

He was pale, and his rugged face, that used to be so perfectly careless and laughing, was stamped with conflict and despair.

"But I can't give her up now; it's gone too far," he said. "And, besides, for *some* things I couldn't do without her."

"My boy, remember you're taking your life in your hands,"

said Mrs. Morel. "*Nothing* is as bad as a marriage that's a hopeless failure. Mine was bad enough, God knows, and ought to teach you something; but it might have been worse by a long chalk."

He leaned with his back against the side of the chimney-piece, his hands in his pockets. He was a big, raw-boned man, who looked as if he would go to the world's end if he wanted to. But she saw the despair on his face.

"I couldn't give her up now," he said.

"Well," she said, "remember there are worse wrongs than breaking off an engagement."

"I can't give her up *now*," he said.

The clock ticked on; mother and son remained in silence, a conflict between them; but he would say no more. At last she said:

"Well, go to bed, my son. You'll feel better in the morning, and perhaps you'll know better."

He kissed her, and went. She raked the fire. Her heart was heavy now as it had never been. Before, with her husband, things had seemed to be breaking down in her, but they did not destroy her power to live. Now her soul felt lamed in itself. It was her hope that was struck.

And so often William manifested the same hatred towards his betrothed. On the last evening at home he was railing against her.

"Well," he said, "if you don't believe me, what she's like, would you believe she has been confirmed three times?"

"Nonsense!" laughed Mrs. Morel.

"Nonsense or not, she *has*! That's what confirmation means for her—a bit of a theatrical show where she can cut a figure."

"I haven't, Mrs. Morel!" cried the girl—"I haven't! it is not true!"

"What!" he cried, flashing round on her. "Once in Bromley, once in Beckenham, and once somewhere else."

"Nowhere else!" she said, in tears—"nowhere else!"

"It *was*! And if it wasn't why were you confirmed *twice*?"

"Once I was only fourteen, Mrs. Morel," she pleaded, tears in her eyes.

"Yes," said Mrs. Morel; "I can quite understand it, child. Take no notice of him. You ought to be ashamed, William, saying such things."

"But it's true. She's religious—she had blue velvet Prayer-

Lily needs to be shown off — photos all she has, [handwritten annotation]

Books—and she's not as much religion, or anything else, in her than that table-leg. Gets confirmed three times for show, to show herself off, and that's how she is in *everything—everything*!"

The girl sat on the sofa, crying. She was not strong.

"As for *love*!" he cried, "you might as well ask a fly to love you! It'll love settling on you——"

"Now, say no more," commanded Mrs. Morel. "If you want to say these things, you must find another place than this. I am ashamed of you, William! Why don't you be more manly. To do nothing but find fault with a girl, and then pretend you're engaged to her!"

Mrs. Morel subsided in wrath and indignation.

William was silent, and later he repented, kissed and comforted the girl. Yet it was true, what he had said. He hated her. *Lily* [handwritten annotation]

When they were going away, Mrs. Morel accompanied them as far as Nottingham. It was a long way to Keston station.

"You know, mother," he said to her, "Gyp's shallow. Nothing goes deep with her."

"William, I *wish* you wouldn't say these things," said Mrs. Morel, very uncomfortable for the girl who walked beside her.

"But it doesn't, mother. She's very much in love with me now, but if I died she'd have forgotten me in three months."

Mrs. Morel was afraid. Her heart beat furiously, hearing the quiet bitterness of her son's last speech.

"How do you know?" she replied. "You *don't* know, and therefore you've no right to say such a thing."

"He's always saying these things!" cried the girl.

"In three months after I was buried you'd have somebody else, and I should be forgotten," he said. "And that's your love!"

Mrs. Morel saw them into the train in Nottingham, then she returned home.

"There's one comfort," she said to Paul—"he'll never have any money to marry on, that I *am* sure of. And so she'll save him that way."

So she took cheer. Matters were not yet very desperate. She firmly believed William would never marry his Gipsy. She waited, and she kept Paul near to her.

All summer long William's letters had a feverish tone; he seemed unnatural and intense. Sometimes he was exaggeratedly jolly, usually he was flat and bitter in his letter.

"Ah," his mother said, "I'm afraid he's ruining himself against that creature, who isn't worthy of his love—no, no more than a rag doll."

He wanted to come home. The midsummer holiday was gone; it was a long while to Christmas. He wrote in wild excitement, saying he could come for Saturday and Sunday at Goose Fair, the first week in October.

"You are not well, my boy," said his mother, when she saw him.

She was almost in tears at having him to herself again.

"No, I've not been well," he said. "I've seemed to have a dragging cold all the last month, but it's going, I think."

It was sunny October weather. He seemed wild with joy, like a schoolboy escaped; then again he was silent and reserved. He was more gaunt than ever, and there was a haggard look in his eyes.

"You are doing too much," said his mother to him.

He was doing extra work, trying to make some money to marry on, he said. He only talked to his mother once on the Saturday night; then he was sad and tender about his beloved.

"And yet, you know, mother, for all that, if I died she'd be broken-hearted for two months, and then she'd start to forget me. You'd see, she'd never come home here to look at my grave, not even once."

"Why, William," said his mother, "you're not going to die, so why talk about it?"

"But whether or not——" he replied.

"And she can't help it. She is like that, and if you choose her—well, you can't grumble," said his mother.

On the Sunday morning, as he was putting his collar on:

"Look," he said to his mother, holding up his chin, "what a rash my collar's made under my chin!"

Just at the junction of chin and throat was a big red inflamation.

"It ought not to do that," said his mother. "Here, put a bit of this soothing ointment on. You should wear different collars."

He went away on Sunday midnight, seeming better and more solid for his two days at home.

On Tuesday morning came a telegram from London that he was ill. Mrs. Morel got off her knees from washing the floor, read the telegram, called a neighbour, went to her landlady and borrowed a sovereign, put on her things, and set off. She hurried to Keston, caught an express for London in Nottingham. She had to wait in Nottingham nearly an hour. A small figure in her black bonnet, she was anxiously asking the porters if they knew how to get to Elmers End. The journey was three hours. She sat in her corner in a kind of stupor, never moving. At King's Cross still no one could tell her how to get to Elmers End. Carrying her string bag, that contained her nightdress, a comb and brush, she went from person to person. At last they sent her underground to Cannon Street.

It was six o'clock when she arrived at William's lodging. The blinds were not down.

"How is he?" she asked.

"No better," said the landlady.

She followed the woman upstairs. William lay on the bed, with bloodshot eyes, his face rather discoloured. The clothes were tossed about, there was no fire in the room, a glass of milk stood on the stand at his bedside. No one had been with him.

"Why, my son!" said the mother bravely.

He did not answer. He looked at her, but did not see her. Then he began to say, in a dull voice, as if repeating a letter from dictation: "Owing to a leakage in the hold of this vessel, the sugar had set, and become converted into rock. It needed hacking——"

He was quite unconscious. It had been his business to examine some such cargo of sugar in the Port of London.

"How long has he been like this?" the mother asked the landlady.

"He got home at six o'clock on Monday morning, and he seemed to sleep all day; then in the night we heard him talking, and this morning he asked for you. So I wired, and we fetched the doctor."

"Will you have a fire made?"

Mrs. Morel tried to soothe her son, to keep him still.

The doctor came. It was pneumonia, and, he said, a peculiar erysipelas, which had started under the chin where the collar chafed, and was spreading over the face. He hoped it would not get to the brain.

Mrs. Morel settled down to nurse. She prayed for William, prayed that he would recognise her. But the young man's face grew more discoloured. In the night she struggled with him. He raved, and raved, and would not come to consciousness. At two o'clock, in a dreadful paroxysm, he died.

Mrs. Morel sat perfectly still for an hour in the lodging bedroom; then she roused the household.

At six o'clock, with the aid of the charwoman, she laid him out; then she went round the dreary London village to the registrar and the doctor.

At nine o'clock to the cottage on Scargill Street came another wire:

"William died last night. Let father come, bring money."

Annie, Paul, and Arthur were at home; Mr. Morel was gone to work. The three children said not a word. Annie began to whimper with fear; Paul set off for his father.

It was a beautiful day. At Brinsley pit the white steam melted slowly in the sunshine of a soft blue sky; the wheels of the headstocks twinkled high up; the screen, shuffling its coal into the trucks, made a busy noise.

"I want my father; he's got to go to London," said the boy to the first man he met on the bank.

"Tha wants Walter Morel? Go in theer an' tell Joe Ward."

Paul went into the little top office.

"I want my father; he's got to go to London."

"Thy feyther? Is he down? What's his name?"

"Mr. Morel."

"What, Walter? Is owt amiss?"

"He's got to go to London."

The man went to the telephone and rang up the bottom office.

"Walter Morel's wanted, number 42, Hard. Summat's amiss; there's his lad here."

Then he turned round to Paul.

"He'll be up in a few minutes," he said.

Paul wandered out to the pit-top. He watched the chair come up, with its wagon of coal. The great iron cage sank back on its rest, a full carfle was hauled off, an empty tram run on to the chair, a bell ting'ed somewhere, the chair heaved, then dropped like a stone.

Paul did not realise William was dead; it was impossible, with such a bustle going on. The puller-off swung the small truck on to the turn-table, another man ran with it along the bank down the curving lines.

"And William is dead, and my mother's in London, and what will she be doing?" the boy asked himself, as if it were a conundrum.

He watched chair after chair come up, and still no father. At last, standing beside a wagon, a man's form! the chair sank on its rests, Morel stepped off. He was slightly lame from an accident.

"Is it thee, Paul? Is 'e worse?"

"You've got to go to London."

The two walked off the pit-bank, where men were watching curiously. As they came out and went along the railway, with the sunny autumn field on one side and a wall of trucks on the other, Morel said in a frightened voice:

" 'E's niver gone, child?"

"Yes."

"When wor't?"

"Last night. We had a telegram from my mother."

Morel walked on a few strides, then leaned up against a truck-side, his hand over his eyes. He was not crying. Paul stood looking round, waiting. On the weighing machine a truck trundled slowly. Paul saw everything, except his father leaning against the truck as if he were tired.

Morel had only once before been to London. He set off, scared and peaked, to help his wife. That was on Tuesday. The children were left alone in the house. Paul went to work, Arthur went to school, and Annie had in a friend to be with her.

On Saturday night, as Paul was turning the corner, coming home from Keston, he saw his mother and father, who had come to Sethley Bridge Station. They were walking in silence in the dark, tired, straggling apart. The boy waited.

"Mother!" he said, in the darkness.

Mrs. Morel's small figure seemed not to observe. He spoke again.

"Paul!" she said, uninterestedly.

She let him kiss her, but she seemed unaware of him.

In the house she was the same—small, white, and mute. She noticed nothing, she said nothing, only:

"The coffin will be here to-night, Walter. You'd better see about some help." Then, turning to the children: "We're bringing him home."

Then she relapsed into the same mute looking into space,

her hands folded on her lap. Paul, looking at her, felt he could not breathe. The house was dead silent.

"I went to work, mother," he said plaintively.

"Did you?" she answered, dully.

After half an hour Morel, troubled and bewildered, came in again.

"Wheer s'll we ha'e him when he *does* come?" he asked his wife.

"In the front-room."

"Then I'd better shift th' table?"

"Yes."

"An' ha'e him across th' chairs?"

"You know there—— Yes, I suppose so."

Morel and Paul went, with a candle, into the parlour. There was no gas there. The father unscrewed the top of the big mahogany oval table, and cleared the middle of the room; then he arranged six chairs opposite each other, so that the coffin could stand on their beds.

"You niver seed such a length as he is!" said the miner, and watching anxiously as he worked.

Paul went to the bay window and looked out. The ash-tree stood monstrous and black in front of the wide darkness. It was a faintly luminous night. Paul went back to his mother.

At ten o'clock Morel called:

"He's here!"

Everyone started. There was a noise of unbarring and unlocking the front door, which opened straight from the night into the room.

"Bring another candle," called Morel.

Annie and Arthur went. Paul followed with his mother. He stood with his arm round her waist in the inner doorway. Down the middle of the cleared room waited six chairs, face to face. In the window, against the lace curtains, Arthur held up one candle, and by the open door, against the night, Annie stood leaning forward, her brass candlestick glittering.

There was the noise of wheels. Outside in the darkness of the street below Paul could see horses and a black vehicle, one lamp, and a few pale faces; then some men, miners, all in their shirt-sleeves, seemed to struggle in the obscurity. Presently two men appeared, bowed beneath a great weight. It was Morel and his neighbour.

"Steady!" called Morel, out of breath.

He and his fellow mounted the steep garden step, heaved into the candlelight with their gleaming coffin-end. Limbs of other men were seen struggling behind. Morel and Burns, in front, staggered; the great dark weight swayed.

"Steady, steady!" cried Morel, as if in pain.

All the six bearers were up in the small garden, holding the great coffin aloft. There were three more steps to the door. The yellow lamp of the carriage shone alone down the black road.

"Now then!" said Morel.

The coffin swayed, the men began to mount the three steps with their load. Annie's candle flickered, and she whimpered as the first men appeared, and the limbs and bowed heads of six men struggled to climb into the room, bearing the coffin that rode like sorrow on their living flesh.

"Oh, my son—my son!" Mrs. Morel sang softly, and each time the coffin swung to the unequal climbing of the men: "Oh, my son—my son—my son!"

"Mother!" Paul whimpered, his hand round her waist. She did not hear.

"Oh, my son—my son!" she repeated.

Paul saw drops of sweat fall from his father's brow. Six men were in the room—six coatless men, with yielding, struggling limbs, filling the room and knocking against the furniture. The coffin veered, and was gently lowered on to the chairs. The sweat fell from Morel's face on its boards.

"My word, he's a weight!" said a man, and the five miners sighed, bowed, and, trembling with the struggle, descended the steps again, closing the door behind them.

The family was alone in the parlour with the great polished box. William, when laid out, was six feet four inches long. Like a monument lay the bright brown, ponderous coffin. Paul thought it would never be got out of the room again. His mother was stroking the polished wood.

They buried him on the Monday in the little cemetery on the hillside that looks over the fields at the big church and the houses. It was sunny, and the white chrysanthemums frilled themselves in the warmth.

Mrs. Morel could not be persuaded, after this, to talk and take her old bright interest in life. She remained shut off. All the way home in the train she had said to herself: "If only it could have been me!"

typical of her

When Paul came home at night he found his mother sitting, her day's work done, with hands folded in her lap upon her coarse apron. She always used to have changed her dress and put on a black apron, before. Now Annie set his supper, and his mother sat looking blankly in front of her, her mouth shut tight. Then he beat his brains for news to tell her.

"Mother, Miss Jordan was down to-day, and she said my sketch of a colliery at work was beautiful."

But Mrs. Morel took no notice. Night after night he forced himself to tell her things, although she did not listen. It drove him almost insane to have her thus. At last:

"What's a-matter, mother?" he asked.

She did not hear.

"What's a-matter?" he persisted. "Mother, what's a-matter?"

"You know what's the matter," she said irritably, turning away.

The lad—he was sixteen years old—went to bed drearily. He was cut off and wretched through October, November and December. His mother tried, but she could not rouse herself. She could only brood on her dead son; he had been let to die so cruelly.

At last, on December 23, with his five shillings Christmas-box in his pocket, Paul wandered blindly home. His mother looked at him, and her heart stood still.

"What's the matter?" she asked.

"I'm badly, mother!" he replied. "Mr. Jordan gave me five shillings for a Christmas-box!"

He handed it to her with trembling hands. She put it on the table.

"You aren't glad!" he reproached her; but he trembled violently.

"Where hurts you?" she said, unbuttoning his overcoat.

It was the old question.

"I feel badly, mother."

She undressed him and put him to bed. He had pneumonia dangerously, the doctor said.

"Might he never have had it if I'd kept him at home, not let him go to Nottingham?" was one of the first things she asked.

"He might not have been so bad," said the doctor.

Mrs. Morel stood condemned on her own ground.

"I should have watched the living, not the dead," she told herself.

Paul was very ill. His mother lay in bed at nights with him; they could not afford a nurse. He grew worse, and the crisis approached. One night he tossed into consciousness in the ghastly, sickly feeling of dissolution, when all the cells in the body seem in intense irritability to be breaking down, and consciousness makes a last flare of struggle, like madness.

"I s'll die, mother!" he cried, heaving for breath on the pillow.

She lifted him up, crying in a small voice:

"Oh, my son—my son!"

That brought him to. He realised her. His whole will rose up and arrested him. He put his head on her breast, and took ease of her for love.

"For some things," said his aunt, "it was a good thing Paul was ill that Christmas. I believe it saved his mother."

Paul was in bed for seven weeks. He got up white and fragile. His father had bought him a pot of scarlet and gold tulips. They used to flame in the window in the March sunshine as he sat on the sofa chattering to his mother. The two knitted together in perfect intimacy. Mrs. Morel's life now rooted itself in Paul.

William had been a prophet. Mrs. Morel had a little present and a letter from Lily at Christmas. Mrs. Morel's sister had a letter at the New Year.

"I was at a ball last night. Some delightful people were there, and I enjoyed myself thoroughly," said the letter. "I had every dance—did not sit out one."

Mrs. Morel never heard any more of her.

Morel and his wife were gentle with each other for some time after the death of their son. He would go into a kind of daze, staring wide-eyed and blank across the room. Then he got up suddenly and hurried out to the Three Spots, returning in his normal state. But never in his life would he go for a walk up Shepstone, past the office where his son had worked, and he always avoided the cemetery.

PART TWO

CHAPTER VII

LAD-AND-GIRL LOVE

PAUL had been many times up to Willey Farm during the autumn. He was friends with the two youngest boys. Edgar the eldest, would not condescend at first. And Miriam also refused to be approached. She was afraid of being set at nought, as by her own brothers. The girl was romantic in her soul. Everywhere was a Walter Scott heroine being loved by men with helmets or with plumes in their caps. She herself was something of a princess turned into a swine-girl in her own imagination. And she was afraid lest this boy, who, nevertheless, looked something like a Walter Scott hero, who could paint and speak French, and knew what algebra meant, and who went by train to Nottingham every day, might consider her simply as the swine-girl, unable to perceive the princess beneath; so she held aloof.

Her great companion was her mother. They were both brown-eyed, and inclined to be mystical, such women as treasure religion inside them, breathe it in their nostrils, and see the whole of life in a mist thereof. So to Miriam, Christ and God made one great figure, which she loved tremblingly and passionately when a tremendous sunset burned out the western sky, and Ediths, and Lucys, and Rowenas, Brian de Bois Guilberts, Rob Roys, and Guy Mannerings, rustled the sunny leaves in the morning, or sat in her bedroom aloft, alone, when it snowed. That was life to her. For the rest, she drudged in the house, which work she would not have minded had not her clean red floor been mucked up immediately by the trampling farm-boots of her brothers. She madly wanted her little brother of four to let her swathe him and stifle him in her love; she went to church reverently, with bowed head, and quivered in anguish from the vulgarity of the other choir-girls and from the common-sounding voice of the curate; she fought with her brothers, whom she considered brutal louts; and she held not her father in too high esteem because he did not carry any mystical ideals cherished in his heart, but only wanted to have as easy a time as he could, and his meals when he was ready for them.

She hated her position as swine-girl. She wanted to be considered. She wanted to learn, thinking that if she could read, as Paul said he could read, "Colomba", or the "Voyage autour de ma Chambre", the world would have a different face for her and a deepened respect. She could not be princess by wealth or standing. So she was mad to have learning whereon to pride herself. For she was different from other folk, and must not be scooped up among the common fry. Learning was the only distinction to which she thought to aspire.

Her beauty—that of a shy, wild, quiveringly sensitive thing —seemed nothing to her. Even her soul, so strong for rhapsody, was not enough. She must have something to reinforce her pride, because she felt different from other people. Paul she eyed rather wistfully. On the whole, she scorned the male sex. But here was a new specimen, quick, light, graceful, who could be gentle and who could be sad, and who was clever, and who knew a lot, and who had a death in the family. The boy's poor morsel of learning exalted him almost sky-high in her esteem. Yet she tried hard to scorn him, because he would not see in her the princess but only the swine-girl. And he scarcely observed her.

Then he was so ill, and she felt he would be weak. Then she would be stronger than he. Then she could love him. If she could be mistress of him in his weakness, take care of him, if he could depend on her, if she could, as it were, have him in her arms, how she would love him!

As soon as the skies brightened and plum-blossom was out, Paul drove off in the milkman's heavy float up to Willey Farm. Mr. Leivers shouted in a kindly fashion at the boy, then clicked to the horse as they climbed the hill slowly, in the freshness of the morning. White clouds went on their way, crowding to the back of the hills that were rousing in the spring-time. The water of Nethermere lay below, very blue against the seared meadows and the thorn-trees.

It was four and a half miles' drive. Tiny buds on the hedges, vivid as copper-green, were opening into rosettes; and thrushes called, and blackbirds shrieked and scolded. It was a new, glamorous world.

Miriam, peeping through the kitchen window, saw the horse walk through the big white gate into the farmyard that was backed by the oak-wood, still bare. Then a youth in a heavy overcoat climbed down. He put up his hands for the whip and the rug that the good-looking, ruddy farmer handed down to him.

Miriam appeared in the doorway. She was nearly sixteen, very beautiful, with her warm colouring, her gravity, her eyes dilating suddenly like an ecstasy.

"I say," said Paul, turning shyly aside, "your daffodils are nearly out. Isn't it early? But don't they look cold?"

"Cold!" said Miriam, in her musical, caressing voice.

"The green on their buds——" and he faltered into silence timidly.

"Let me take the rug," said Miriam over-gently.

"I can carry it," he answered, rather injured. But he yielded it to her.

Then Mrs. Leivers appeared.

"I'm sure you're tired and cold," she said. "Let me take your coat. It *is* heavy. You mustn't walk far in it."

She helped him off with his coat. He was quite unused to such attention. She was almost smothered under its weight.

"Why, mother," laughed the farmer as he passed through the kitchen, swinging the great milk-churns, "you've got almost more than you can manage there."

She beat up the sofa cushions for the youth.

The kitchen was very small and irregular. The farm had been originally a labourer's cottage. And the furniture was old and battered. But Paul loved it—loved the sack-bag that formed the hearthrug, and the funny little corner under the stairs, and the small window deep in the corner, through which, bending a little, he could see the plum trees in the back garden and the lovely round hills beyond.

"Won't you lie down?" said Mrs. Leivers.

"Oh no; I'm not tired," he said. "Isn't it lovely coming out, don't you think? I saw a sloe-bush in blossom and a lot of celandines. I'm glad it's sunny."

"Can I give you anything to eat or to drink?"

"No, thank you."

"How's your mother?"

"I think she's tired now. I think she's had too much to do. Perhaps in a little while she'll go to Skegness with me. Then she'll be able to rest. I s'll be glad if she can."

"Yes," replied Mrs. Leivers. "It's a wonder she isn't ill herself."

Miriam was moving about preparing dinner. Paul watched everything that happened. His face was pale and thin, but his eyes were quick and bright with life as ever. He watched the strange, almost rhapsodic way in which the girl moved about, carrying a great stew-jar to the oven, or looking in the saucepan. The atmosphere was different from that of his own home, where everything seemed so ordinary. When Mr. Leivers called loudly outside to the horse, that was reaching over to feed on the rose-bushes in the garden, the girl started, looked round with dark eyes, as if something had come breaking in on her world. There was a sense of silence inside the house and out. Miriam seemed as in some dreamy tale, a maiden in bondage, her spirit dreaming in a land far away and magical. And her discoloured, old blue frock and her broken boots seemed only like the romantic rags of King Cophetua's beggar-maid.

She suddenly became aware of his keen blue eyes upon her, taking her all in. Instantly her broken boots and her frayed old frock hurt her. She resented his seeing everything. Even he knew that her stocking was not pulled up. She went into the scullery, blushing deeply. And afterwards her hands trembled slightly at her work. She nearly dropped all she handled. When her inside dream was shaken, her body quivered with trepidation. She resented that he saw so much.

Mrs. Leivers sat for some time talking to the boy, although she was needed at her work. She was too polite to leave him. Presently she excused herself and rose. After a while she looked into the tin saucepan.

"Oh *dear*, Miriam," she cried, "these potatoes have boiled dry!"

Miriam started as if she had been stung.

"*Have* they, mother?" she cried.

"I shouldn't care, Miriam," said the mother, "if I hadn't trusted them to you." She peered into the pan.

The girl stiffened as if from a blow. Her dark eyes dilated; she remained standing in the same spot.

"Well," she answered, gripped tight in self-conscious shame, "I'm sure I looked at them five minutes since."

"Yes," said the mother, "I know it's easily done."

"They're not much burned," said Paul. "It doesn't matter, does it?"

Mrs. Leivers looked at the youth with her brown, hurt eyes.

"It wouldn't matter but for the boys," she said to him. "Only Miriam knows what a trouble they make if the potatoes are 'caught'."

"Then," thought Paul to himself, "you shouldn't let them make a trouble."

After a while Edgar came in. He wore leggings, and his boots were covered with earth. He was rather small, rather formal, for a farmer. He glanced at Paul, nodded to him distantly, and said:

"Dinner ready?"

"Nearly, Edgar," replied the mother apologetically.

"I'm ready for mine," said the young man, taking up the newspaper and reading. Presently the rest of the family trooped in. Dinner was served. The meal went rather brutally. The over-gentleness and apologetic tone of the mother brought out all the brutality of manners in the sons. Edgar tasted the potatoes, moved his mouth quickly like a rabbit, looked indignantly at his mother, and said:

"These potatoes are burnt, mother."

"Yes, Edgar. I forgot them for a minute. Perhaps you'll have bread if you can't eat them."

Edgar looked in anger across at Miriam.

"What was Miriam doing that she couldn't attend to them?" he said.

Miriam looked up. Her mouth opened, her dark eyes blazed and winced, but she said nothing. She swallowed her anger and her shame, bowing her dark head.

"I'm sure she was trying hard," said the mother.

"She hasn't got sense even to boil the potatoes," said Edgar. "What is she kept at home for?"

"On'y for eating everything that's left in th' pantry," said Maurice.

"They don't forget that potato-pie against our Miriam," laughed the father.

She was utterly humiliated. The mother sat in silence, suffering, like some saint out of place at the brutal board.

It puzzled Paul. He wondered vaguely why all this intense feeling went running because of a few burnt potatoes. The mother exalted everything—even a bit of housework—to the plane of a religious trust. The sons resented this; they felt

themselves cut away underneath, and they answered with
brutality and also with a sneering superciliousness.

Paul was just opening out from childhood into manhood.
This atmosphere, where everything took a religious value,
came with a subtle fascination to him. There was something
in the air. His own mother was logical. Here there was something different, something he loved, something that at times
he hated.

*Paul
+
Mother*

Miriam quarrelled with her brothers fiercely. Later in the
afternoon, when they had gone away again, her mother said:
"You disappointed me at dinner-time, Miriam."

The girl dropped her head.

"They are such *brutes*!" she suddenly cried, looking up
with flashing eyes.

"But hadn't you promised not to answer them?" said the
mother. "And I believed in you. I *can't* stand it when you
wrangle."

"But they're so hateful!" cried Miriam, "and—and *low*."

"Yes, dear. But how often have I asked you not to answer
Edgar back? Can't you let him say what he likes?"

"But why should he say what he likes?"

"Aren't you strong enough to bear it, Miriam, if even for
my sake? Are you so weak that you must wrangle with
them?"

Mrs. Leivers stuck unflinchingly to this doctrine of "the
other cheek". She could not instil it at all into the boys. With
the girls she succeeded better, and Miriam was the child of
her heart. The boys loathed the other cheek when it was presented to them. Miriam was often sufficiently lofty to turn it.
Then they spat on her and hated her. But she walked in her
proud humility, living within herself.

Miriam

There was always this feeling of jangle and discord in the
Leivers family. Although the boys resented so bitterly this
eternal appeal to their deeper feelings of resignation and
proud humility, yet it had its effect on them. They could not
establish between themselves and an outsider just the ordinary
human feeling and unexaggerated friendship; they were
always restless for the something deeper. Ordinary folk
seemed shallow to them, trivial and inconsiderable. And
so they were unaccustomed, painfully uncouth in the
simplest social intercourse, suffering, and yet insolent in their
superiority. Then beneath was the yearning for the soul-

intimacy to which they could not attain because they were too dumb, and every approach to close connection was blocked by their clumsy contempt of other people. They wanted genuine intimacy, but they could not get even normally near to anyone, because they scorned to take the first steps, they scorned the triviality which forms common human intercourse.

Paul fell under Mrs. Leivers's spell. Everything had a religious and intensified meaning when he was with her. His soul, hurt, highly developed, sought her as if for nourishment. Together they seemed to sift the vital fact from an experience.

Miriam was her mother's daughter. In the sunshine of the afternoon mother and daughter went down the fields with him. They looked for nests. There was a jenny wren's in the hedge by the orchard.

"I *do* want you to see this," said Mrs. Leivers.

He crouched down and carefully put his finger through the thorns into the round door of the nest.

"It's almost as if you were feeling inside the live body of the bird," he said, "it's so warm. They say a bird makes its nest round like a cup with pressing its breast on it. Then how did it make the ceiling round, I wonder?"

The nest seemed to start into life for the two women. After that, Miriam came to see it every day. It seemed so close to her. Again, going down the hedgeside with the girl, he noticed the celandines, scalloped splashes of gold, on the side of the ditch.

"I like them," he said, "when their petals go flat back with the sunshine. They seemed to be pressing themselves at the sun."

And then the celandines ever after drew her with a little spell. Anthropomorphic as she was, she stimulated him into appreciating things thus, and then they lived for her. She seemed to need things kindling in her imagination or in her soul before she felt she had them. And she was cut off from ordinary life by her religious intensity which made the world for her either a nunnery garden or a paradise, where sin and knowledge were not, or else an ugly, cruel thing.

So it was in this atmosphere of subtle intimacy, this meeting in their common feeling for something in Nature, that their love started.

Personally, he was a long time before he realized her. For ten months he had to stay at home after his illness. For a while he went to Skegness with his mother, and was perfectly happy. But even from the seaside he wrote long letters to Mrs. Leivers about the shore and the sea. And he brought back his beloved sketches of the flat Lincoln coast, anxious for them to see. Almost they would interest the Leivers more than they interested his mother. It was not his art Mrs. Morel cared about; it was himself and his achievement. But Mrs. Leivers and her children were almost his disciples. They kindled him and made him glow to his work, whereas his mother's influence was to make him quietly determined, patient, dogged, unwearied.

He soon was friends with the boys, whose rudeness was only superficial. They had all, when they could trust themselves, a strange gentleness and lovableness.

"Will you come with me on to the fallow?" asked Edgar, rather hesitatingly.

Paul went joyfully, and spent the afternoon helping to hoe or to single turnips with his friend. He used to lie with the three brothers in the hay piled up in the barn and tell them about Nottingham and about Jordan's. In return, they taught him to milk, and let him do little jobs—chopping hay or pulping turnips—just as much as he liked. At midsummer he worked all through hay-harvest with them, and then he loved them. The family was so cut off from the world actually. They seemed, somehow, like *"les derniers fils d'une race épuisée"*. Though the lads were strong and healthy, yet they had all that over-sensitiveness and hanging-back which made them so lonely, yet also such close, delicate friends once their intimacy was won. Paul loved them dearly, and they him.

Miriam came later. But he had come into her life before she made any mark on his. One dull afternoon, when the men were on the land and the rest at school, only Miriam and her mother at home, the girl said to him, after having hesitated for some time:

"Have you seen the swing?"

"No," he answered. "Where?"

"In the cowshed," she replied.

She always hesitated to offer or to show him anything. Men have such different standards of worth from women, and her dear things—the valuable things to her—her brothers had so often mocked or flouted.

"Come on, then," he replied, jumping up.

There were two cowsheds, one on either side of the barn. In the lower, darker shed there was standing for four cows. Hens flew scolding over the manger-wall as the youth and girl went forward for the great thick rope which hung from the beam in the darkness overhead, and was pushed back over a peg in the wall.

"It's something like a rope!" he exclaimed appreciatively; and he sat down on it, anxious to try it. Then immediately he rose.

"Come on, then, and have first go," he said to the girl.

"See," she answered, going into the barn, "we put some bags on the seat"; and she made the swing comfortable for him. That gave her pleasure. He held the rope.

"Come on, then," he said to her.

"No, I won't go first," she answered.

She stood aside in her still, aloof fashion.

"Why?"

"You go," she pleaded.

Almost for the first time in her life she had the pleasure of giving up to a man, of spoiling him. Paul looked at her.

"All right," he said, sitting down. "Mind out!"

He set off with a spring, and in a moment was flying through the air, almost out of the door of the shed, the upper half of which was open, showing outside the drizzling rain, the filthy yard, the cattle standing disconsolate against the black cart-shed, and at the back of all the grey-green wall of the wood. She stood below in her crimson tam-o'-shanter and watched. He looked down at her, and she saw his blue eyes sparkling.

"It's a treat of a swing," he said.

"Yes."

He was swinging through the air, every bit of him swinging, like a bird that swoops for joy of movement. And he looked down at her. Her crimson cap hung over her dark curls, her beautiful warm face, so still in a kind of brooding, was lifted towards him. It was dark and rather cold in the shed. Suddenly a swallow came down from the high roof and darted out of the door.

"I didn't know a bird was watching," he called.

He swung negligently. She could feel him falling and lifting through the air, as if he were lying on some force.

"Now I'll die," he said, in a detached, dreamy voice, as though he were the dying motion of the swing. She watched

him, fascinated. Suddenly he put on the brake and jumped
out.

"I've had a long turn," he said. "But it's a treat of a swing—
it's a real treat of a swing!"

Miriam was amused that he took a swing so seriously and
felt so warmly over it.

"No; you go on," she said.

"Why, don't you want one?" he asked, astonished.

"Well, not much. I'll have just a little."

She sat down, whilst he kept the bags in place for her.

"It's so ripping!" he said, setting her in motion. "Keep your
heels up, or they'll bang the manger wall."

She felt the accuracy with which he caught her, exactly at
the right moment, and the exactly proportionate strength of
his thrust, and she was afraid. Down to her bowels went the
hot wave of fear. She was in his hands. Again, firm and inevitable came the thrust at the right moment. She gripped the
rope, almost swooning.

"Ha!" she laughed in fear. "No higher!"

"But you're not a *bit* high," he remonstrated.

"But no higher."

He heard the fear in her voice, and desisted. Her heart
melted in hot pain when the moment came for him to thrust
her forward again. But he left her alone. She began to breathe.

"Won't you really go any farther?" he asked. "Should I
keep you there?"

"No; let me go by myself," she answered.

He moved aside and watched her.

"Why, you're scarcely moving," he said.

She laughed slightly with shame, and in a moment got down.

"They say if you can swing you won't be sea-sick," he said,
as he mounted again. "I don't believe I should ever be sea-
sick."

Away he went. There was something fascinating to her in
him. For the moment he was nothing but a piece of swinging
stuff; not a particle of him that did not swing. She could never
lose herself so, nor could her brothers. It roused a warmth in
her. It were almost as if he were a flame that had lit a warmth
in her whilst he swung in the middle air.

And gradually the intimacy with the family concentrated
for Paul on three persons—the mother, Edgar, and Miriam. To
the mother he went for that sympathy and that appeal which

seemed to draw him out. Edgar was his very close friend. And to Miriam he more or less condescended, because she seemed so humble.

But the girl gradually sought him out. If he brought up his sketch-book, it was she who pondered longest over the last picture. Then she would look up at him. Suddenly, her dark eyes alight like water that shakes with a stream of gold in the dark, she would ask:

"Why do I like this so?"

Always something in his breast shrank from these close, intimate, dazzled looks of hers.

"Why *do* you?" he asked.

"I don't know. It seems so true."

"It's because—it's because there is scarcely any shadow in it; it's more shimmery, as if I'd painted the shimmering protoplasm in the leaves and everywhere, and not the stiffness of the shape. That seems dead to me. Only this shimmeriness is the real living. The shape is a dead crust. The shimmer is inside really."

And she, with her little finger in her mouth, would ponder these sayings. They gave her a feeling of life again, and vivified things which had meant nothing to her. She managed to find some meaning in his struggling, abstract speeches. And they were the medium through which she came distinctly at her beloved objects.

Another day she sat at sunset whilst he was painting some pine-trees which caught the red glare from the west. He had been quiet.

"There you are!" he said suddenly. "I wanted that. Now, look at them and tell me, are they pine trunks or are they red coals, standing-up pieces of fire in that darkness? There's God's burning bush for you, that burned not away."

Miriam looked, and was frightened. But the pine trunks were wonderful to her, and distinct. He packed his box and rose. Suddenly he looked at her.

"Why are you always sad?" he asked her.

"Sad!" she exclaimed, looking up at him with startled, wonderful brown eyes.

"Yes," he replied. "You are always sad."

"I am not—oh, not a bit!" she cried.

"But even your joy is like a flame coming off of sadness," he persisted. "You're never jolly, or even just all right."

"No," she pondered. "I wonder—why?"

"Because you're not; because you're different inside, like a pine-tree, and then you flare up; but you're not just like an ordinary tree, with fidgety leaves and jolly——"

He got tangled up in his own speech; but she brooded on it, and he had a strange, roused sensation, as if his feelings were new. She got so near him. It was a strange stimulant.

Then sometimes he hated her. Her youngest brother was only five. He was a frail lad, with immense brown eyes in his quaint fragile face—one of Reynolds's "Choir of Angels", with a touch of elf. Often Miriam kneeled to the child and drew him to her.

"Eh, my Hubert!" she sang, in a voice heavy and surcharged with love. "Eh, my Hubert!"

And, folding him in her arms, she swayed slightly from side to side with love, her face half lifted, her eyes half closed, her voice drenched with love.

"Don't!" said the child, uneasy—"don't, Miriam!"

"Yes; you love me, don't you?" she murmured deep in her throat, almost as if she were in a trance, and swaying also as if she were swooned in an ecstasy of love.

"Don't!" repeated the child, a frown on his clear brow.

"You love me, don't you?" she murmured.

"What do you make such a *fuss* for?" cried Paul, all in suffering because of her extreme emotion. "Why can't you be ordinary with him?"

She let the child go, and rose, and said nothing. Her intensity, which would leave no emotion on a normal plane, irritated the youth into a frenzy. And this fearful, naked contact of her on small occasions shocked him. He was used to his mother's reserve. And on such occasions he was thankful in his heart and soul that he had his mother, so sane and wholesome.

All the life of Miriam's body was in her eyes, which were usually dark as a dark church, but could flame with light like a conflagration. Her face scarcely ever altered from its look of brooding. She might have been one of the women who went with Mary when Jesus was dead. Her body was not flexible and living. She walked with a swing, rather heavily, her head bowed forward, pondering. She was not clumsy, and yet none of her movements seemed quite *the* movement. Often, when wiping the dishes, she would stand in bewilderment and chagrin because she had pulled in two halves a cup or a tumbler. It was as if, in her fear and self-mistrust, she put too much strength into the effort. There was no looseness or abandon about her. Everything was gripped stiff with intensity, and her effort, overcharged, closed in on itself.

She rarely varied from her swinging, forward, intense walk. Occasionally she ran with Paul down the fields. Then her eyes blazed naked in a kind of ecstasy that frightened him. But she was physically afraid. If she were getting over a stile, she gripped his hands in a little hard anguish, and began to lose her presence of mind. And he could not persuade her to jump from even a small height. Her eyes dilated, became exposed and palpitating.

"No!" she cried, half laughing in terror—"no!"

"You shall!" he cried once, and, jerking her forward, he brought her falling from the fence. But her wild "Ah!" of pain, as if she were losing consciousness, cut him. She landed on her feet safely, and afterwards had courage in this respect.

She was very much dissatisfied with her lot.

"Don't you like being at home?" Paul asked her, surprised.

"Who would?" she answered, low and intense. "What is it? I'm all day cleaning what the boys make just as bad in five minutes. I don't *want* to be at home."

"What do you want, then?"

"I want to do something. I want a chance like anybody else. Why should I, because I'm a girl, be kept at home and not allowed to be anything? What chance *have* I?"

"Chance of what?"

"Of knowing anything—of learning, of doing anything. It's not fair, because I'm a woman."

She seemed very bitter. Paul wondered. In his own home Annie was almost glad to be a girl. She had not so much responsibility; things were lighter for her. She never wanted to be other than a girl. But Miriam almost fiercely wished she were a man. And yet she hated men at the same time.

"But it's as well to be a woman as a man," he said, frowning.

"Ha! Is it? Men have everything."

"I should think women ought to be as glad to be women as men are to be men," he answered.

"No!"—she shook her head—"no! Everything the men have."

"But what do you want?" he asked.

"I want to learn. Why *should* it be that I know nothing?"

"What! such as mathematics and French?"

"Why *shouldn't* I know mathematics? Yes!" she cried, her eye expanding in a kind of defiance.

"Well, you can learn as much as I know," he said. "I'll teach you, if you like."

Her eyes dilated. She mistrusted him as teacher.

"Would you?" he asked.

Her head had dropped, and she was sucking her finger broodingly.

"Yes," she said hesitatingly.

He used to tell his mother all these things.

"I'm going to teach Miriam algebra," he said.

"Well," replied Mrs. Morel, "I hope she'll get fat on it."

Practical mother

When he went up to the farm on the Monday evening, it was drawing twilight. Miriam was just sweeping up the kitchen, and was kneeling at the hearth when he entered. Everyone was out but her. She looked round at him, flushed, her dark eyes shining, her fine hair falling about her face.

"Hello!" she said, soft and musical. "I knew it was you."

"How?"

"I knew your step. Nobody treads so quick and firm."

He sat down, sighing.

"Ready to do some algebra?" he asked, drawing a little book from his pocket.

"But——"

He could feel her backing away.

"You said you wanted," he insisted.

"To-night, though?" she faltered.

"But I came on purpose. And if you want to learn it, you must begin."

She took up her ashes in the dustpan and looked at him, half tremulously, laughing.

"Yes, but to-night! You see, I haven't thought of it."

"Well, my goodness! Take the ashes and come."

He went and sat on the stone bench in the back-yard, where the big milk-cans were standing, tipped up, to air. The men were in the cowsheds. He could hear the little sing-song of the milk spurting into the pails. Presently she came, bringing some big greenish apples.

"You know you like them," she said.

He took a bite.

"Sit down," he said, with his mouth full.

She was short-sighted, and peered over his shoulder. It irritated him. He gave her the book quickly.

"Here," he said. "It's only letters for figures. You put down '*a*' instead of '2' or '6'."

They worked, he talking, she with her head down on the book. He was quick and hasty. She never answered. Occasionally, when he demanded of her, "Do you see?" she looked up at him, her eyes wide with the half-laugh that comes of fear. "Don't you?" he cried.

He had been too fast. But she said nothing. He questioned her more, then got hot. It made his blood rouse to see her there, as it were, at his mercy, her mouth open, her eyes dilated with laughter that was afraid, apologetic, ashamed. Then Edgar came along with two buckets of milk.

"Hello!" he said. "What are you doing?"

"Algebra," replied Paul.

"Algebra!" repeated Edgar curiously. Then he passed on with a laugh. Paul took a bite at his forgotten apple, looked at the miserable cabbages in the garden, pecked into lace by the fowls, and he wanted to pull them up. Then he glanced at Miriam. She was poring over the book, seemed absorbed in it, yet trembling lest she could not get at it. It made him cross. She was ruddy and beautiful. Yet her soul seemed to be intensely supplicating. The algebra-book she closed, shrinking, knowing he was angered; and at the same instant he grew gentle, seeing her hurt because she did not understand.

But things came slowly to her. And when she held herself in a grip, seemed so utterly humble before the lesson, it made his blood rouse. He stormed at her, got ashamed, continued the lesson, and grew furious again, abusing her. She listened in silence. Occasionally, very rarely, she defended herself. Her liquid dark eyes blazed at him.

"You don't give me time to learn it," she said.

"All right," he answered, throwing the book on the table and lighting a cigarette. Then, after a while, he went back to her repentant. So the lessons went. He was always either in a rage or very gentle.

"What do you tremble your *soul* before it for?" he cried. "You don't learn algebra with your blessed soul. Can't you look at it with your clear simple wits?"

Often, when he went again into the kitchen, Mrs. Leivers would look at him reproachfully, saying:

"Paul, don't be so hard on Miriam. She may not be quick, but I'm sure she tries."

"I can't help it," he said rather pitiably. "I go off like it."

"You don't mind me, Miriam, do you?" he asked of the girl later.

"No," she reassured him in her beautiful deep tones—"no, I don't mind."

"Don't mind me; it's my fault."

But, in spite of himself, his blood began to boil with her. It was strange that no one else made him in such fury. He flared against her. Once he threw the pencil in her face. There was a silence. She turned her face slightly aside.

"I didn't——" he began, but got no farther, feeling weak in all his bones. She never reproached him or was angry with him. He was often cruelly ashamed. But still again his anger burst like a bubble surcharged; and still, when he saw her eager, silent, as it were, blind face, he felt he wanted to throw the pencil in it; and still, when he saw her hand trembling and her mouth parted with suffering, his heart was scalded with pain for her. And because of the intensity to which she roused him, he sought her.

Then he often avoided her and went with Edgar. Miriam and her brother were naturally antagonistic. Edgar was a rationalist, who was curious, and had a sort of scientific interest in life. It was a great bitterness to Miriam to see herself deserted by Paul for Edgar, who seemed so much lower. But the youth was very happy with her elder brother. The two men spent afternoons together on the land or in the loft doing carpentry, when it rained. And they talked together, or Paul taught Edgar the songs he himself had learned from Annie at the piano. And often all the men, Mr. Leivers as well, had bitter debates on the nationalizing of the land and similar problems. Paul had already heard his mother's views, and as these were as yet his own, he argued for her. Miriam attended and took part, but was all the time waiting until it should be over and a personal communication might begin.

"After all," she said within herself, "if the land were nationalized, Edgar and Paul and I would be just the same." So she waited for the youth to come back to her.

He was studying for his painting. He loved to sit at home,

alone with his mother, at night, working and working. She sewed or read. Then, looking up from his task, he would rest his eyes for a moment on her face, that was bright with living warmth, and he returned gladly to his work.

"I can do my best things when you sit there in your rocking-chair, mother," he said.

"I'm sure!" she exclaimed, sniffing with mock scepticism. But she felt it was so, and her heart quivered with brightness. For many hours she sat still, slightly conscious of him labouring away, whilst she worked or read her book. And he, with all his soul's intensity directing his pencil, could feel her warmth inside him like strength. They were both very happy so, and both unconscious of it. These times, that meant so much, and which were real living, they almost ignored.

He was conscious only when stimulated. A sketch finished, he always wanted to take it to Miriam. Then he was stimulated into knowledge of the work he had produced unconsciously. In contact with Miriam he gained insight; his vision went deeper. From his mother he drew the life-warmth, the strength to produce; Miriam urged this warmth into intensity like a white light.

When he returned to the factory the conditions of work were better. He had Wednesday afternoon off to go to the Art School—Miss Jordan's provision—returning in the evening. Then the factory closed at six instead of eight on Thursday and Friday evenings.

One evening in the summer Miriam and he went over the fields by Herod's Farm on their way from the library home. So it was only three miles to Willey Farm. There was a yellow glow over the mowing-grass, and the sorrel-heads burned crimson. Gradually, as they walked along the high land, the gold in the west sank down to red, the red to crimson, and then the chill blue crept up against the glow.

They came out upon the high road to Alfreton, which ran white between the darkening fields. There Paul hesitated. It was two miles home for him, one mile forward for Miriam. They both looked up the road that ran in shadow right under the glow of the north-west sky. On the crest of the hill, Selby, with its stark houses and the up-pricked headstocks of the pit, stood in black silhouette small against the sky.

He looked at his watch.

"Nine o'clock!" he said.

The pair stood, loth to part, hugging their books.

"The wood is so lovely now," she said. "I wanted you to see it."

He followed her slowly across the road to the white gate.

"They grumble so if I'm late," he said.

"But you're not doing anything wrong," she answered impatiently.

He followed her across the nibbled pasture in the dusk. There was a coolness in the wood, a scent of leaves, of honeysuckle, and a twilight. The two walked in silence. Night came wonderfully there, among the throng of dark tree-trunks. He looked round, expectant.

She wanted to show him a certain wild-rose bush she had discovered. She knew it was wonderful. And yet, till he had seen it, she felt it had not come into her soul. Only he could make it her own, immortal. She was dissatisfied.

Dew was already on the paths. In the old oak-wood a mist was rising, and he hesitated, wondering whether one whiteness were a strand of fog or only campion-flowers pallid in a cloud.

By the time they came to the pine-trees Miriam was getting very eager and very tense. Her bush might be gone. She might not be able to find it; and she wanted it so much. Almost passionately she wanted to be with him when he stood before the flowers. They were going to have a communion together— something that thrilled her, something holy. He was walking beside her in silence. They were very near to each other. She trembled, and he listened, vaguely anxious.

Coming to the edge of the wood, they saw the sky in front, like mother-of-pearl, and the earth growing dark. Somewhere on the outermost branches of the pine-wood the honeysuckle was streaming scent.

"Where?" he asked.

"Down the middle path," she murmured, quivering.

When they turned the corner of the path she stood still. In the wide walk between the pines, gazing rather frightened, she could distinguish nothing for some moments; the greying light robbed things of their colour. Then she saw her bush.

"Ah!" she cried, hastening forward.

It was very still. The tree was tall and straggling. It had thrown its briers over a hawthorn-bush, and its long streamers trailed thick, right down to the grass, splashing the darkness everywhere with great spilt stars, pure white. In bosses of ivory and in large splashed stars the roses gleamed on the darkness of foliage and stems and grass. Paul and Miriam stood close together, silent, and watched. Point after point the steady roses shone out to them, seeming to kindle something in their souls. The dusk came like smoke around and still did not put out the roses.

Paul looked into Miriam's eyes. She was pale and expectant with wonder, her lips were parted, and her dark eyes lay open to him. His look seemed to travel down into her. Her soul quivered. It was the communion she wanted. He turned aside, as if pained. He turned to the bush.

"They seem as if they walk like butterflies, and shake themselves," he said.

She looked at her roses. They were white, some incurved and holy, others expanded in an ecstasy. The tree was dark as a shadow. She lifted her hand impulsively to the flowers; she went forward and touched them in worship.

"Let us go," he said.

There was a cool scent of ivory roses—a white, virgin scent. Something made him feel anxious and imprisoned. The two walked in silence.

"Till Sunday," he said quietly, and left her; and she walked home slowly, feeling her soul satisfied with the holiness of the night. He stumbled down the path. And as soon as he was out of the wood, in the free open meadow, where he could breathe, he started to run as fast as he could. It was like a delicious delirium in his veins.

Always when he went with Miriam, and it grew rather late, he knew his mother was fretting and getting angry about him— why, he could not understand. As he went into the house, flinging down his cap, his mother looked up at the clock. She had been sitting thinking, because a chill to her eyes prevented her reading. She could feel Paul being drawn away by this girl. And she did not care for Miriam. "She is one of those who will want to suck a man's soul out till he has none of his own left," she said to herself; "and he is just such a gaby as to let himself be absorbed. She will never let him become a man; she never will." So, while he was away with Miriam, Mrs. Morel grew more and more worked up.

She glanced at the clock and said, coldly and rather tired:

"You have been far enough to-night."

His soul, warm and exposed from contact with the girl, shrank.

"You must have been right home with her," his mother continued.

He would not answer. Mrs. Morel, looking at him quickly, saw his hair was damp on his forehead with haste, saw him frowning in his heavy fashion, resentfully. *— Paul of Mother*

"She must be wonderfully fascinating, that you can't get away from her, but must go trailing eight miles at this time of night."

He was hurt between the past glamour with Miriam and the knowledge that his mother fretted. He had meant not to say anything, to refuse to answer. But he could not harden his heart to ignore his mother.

"I *do* like to talk to her," he answered irritably.

"Is there nobody else to talk to?"

"You wouldn't say anything if I went with Edgar."

"You know I should. You know, whoever you went with, I should say it was too far for you to go trailing, late at night, when you've been to Nottingham. Besides"—her voice suddenly flashed into anger and contempt—"it is disgusting—bits of lads and girls courting."

"It is *not* courting," he cried.

"I don't know what else you call it."

"It's not! Do you think we *spoon* and do? We only talk."

"Till goodness knows what time and distance," was the sarcastic rejoinder.

Paul snapped at the laces of his boots angrily.

"What are you so mad about?" he asked. "Because you don't like her."

"I don't say I don't like her. But I don't hold with children keeping company, and never did."

"But you don't mind our Annie going out with Jim Inger."

"They've more sense than you two." *— True but they feel*

"Why?"

"Our Annie's not one of the deep sort."

He failed to see the meaning of this remark. But his mother looked tired. She was never so strong after William's death; and her eyes hurt her.

"Well," he said, "it's so pretty in the country. Mr. Sleath asked about you. He said he'd missed you. Are you a bit better?"

Mother Paul disharmony

"I ought to have been in bed a long time ago," she replied.

"Why, mother, you know you wouldn't have gone before quarter-past ten."

"Oh, yes, I should!"

"Oh, little woman, you'd say anything now you're disagreeable with me, wouldn't you?"

He kissed her forehead that he knew so well: the deep marks between the brows, the rising of the fine hair, greying now, and the proud setting of the temples. His hand lingered on her shoulder after his kiss. Then he went slowly to bed. He had forgotten Miriam; he only saw how his mother's hair was lifted back from her warm, broad brow. And somehow, she was hurt.

Then the next time he saw Miriam he said to her:

"Don't let me be late to-night—not later than ten o'clock. My mother gets so upset."

Miriam dropped her head, brooding.

"Why does she get upset?" she asked.

"Because she says I oughtn't to be out late when I have to get up early."

"Very well!" said Miriam, rather quietly, with just a touch of a sneer.

He resented that. And he was usually late again.

That there was any love growing between him and Miriam neither of them would have acknowledged. He thought he was too sane for such sentimentality, and she thought herself too lofty. They both were late in coming to maturity, and psychical ripeness was much behind even the physical. Miriam was exceedingly sensitive, as her mother had always been. The slightest grossness made her recoil almost in anguish. Her brothers were brutal, but never coarse in speech. The men did all the discussing of farm matters outside. But, perhaps, because of the continual business of birth and of begetting which goes on upon every farm, Miriam was the more hypersensitive to the matter, and her blood was chastened almost to disgust of the faintest suggestion of such intercourse. Paul took his pitch from her, and their intimacy went on in an utterly blanched and chaste fashion. It could never be mentioned that the mare was in foal.

When he was nineteen, he was earning only twenty shillings a week, but he was happy. His painting went well, and life went well enough. On the Good Friday he organised a walk to the Hemlock Stone. There were three lads of his own age, then

Annie and Arthur, Miriam and Geoffrey. Arthur, apprenticed as an electrician in Nottingham, was home for the holiday. Morel, as usual, was up early, whistling and sawing in the yard. At seven o'clock the family heard him buy threepennyworth of hot-cross buns; he talked with gusto to the little girl who brought them, calling her "my darling". He turned away several boys who came with more buns, telling them they had been "kested" by a little lass. Then Mrs. Morel got up, and the family straggled down. It was an immense luxury to everybody, this lying in bed just beyond the ordinary time on a weekday. And Paul and Arthur read before breakfast, and had the meal unwashed, sitting in their shirt-sleeves. This was another holiday luxury. The room was warm. Everything felt free of care and anxiety. There was a sense of plenty in the house.

While the boys were reading, Mrs. Morel went into the garden. They were now in another house, an old one, near the Scargill Street home, which had been left soon after William had died. Directly came an excited cry from the garden:

"Paul! Paul! come and look!"

It was his mother's voice. He threw down his book and went out. There was a long garden that ran to a field. It was a grey, cold day, with a sharp wind blowing out of Derbyshire. Two fields away Bestwood began, with a jumble of roofs and red house-ends, out of which rose the church tower and the spire of the Congregational Chapel. And beyond went woods and hills, right away to the pale grey heights of the Pennine Chain.

Paul looked down the garden for his mother. Her head appeared among the young currant-bushes.

"Come here!" she cried.

"What for?" he answered.

"Come and see."

She had been looking at the buds on the currant trees. Paul went up.

"To think," she said, "that here I might never have seen them!"

Her son went to her side. Under the fence, in a little bed, was a ravel of poor grassy leaves, such as come from very immature bulbs, and three scyllas in bloom. Mrs. Morel pointed to the deep blue flowers.

"Now, just see those!" she exclaimed. "I was looking at the currant bushes, when, thinks I to myself, 'There's something

very blue; is it a bit of sugar-bag?' and there, behold you!
Sugar-bag! Three glories of the snow, and *such* beauties! But
where on earth did they come from?"

"I don't know," said Paul.

"Well, that's a marvel, now! I *thought* I knew every weed
and blade in this garden. But *haven't* they done well? You see,
that gooseberry-bush just shelters them. Not nipped, not
touched!"

He crouched down and turned up the bells of the little blue
flowers.

"They're a glorious colour!" he said.

"Aren't they!" she cried. "I guess they come from Switzerland, where they say they have such lovely things. Fancy them
against the snow! But where have they come from? They can't
have *blown* here, can they?"

Then he remembered having set here a lot of little trash of
bulbs to mature.

"And you never told me," she said.

"No! I thought I'd leave it till they might flower."

"And now, you see! I might have missed them. And I've
never had a glory of the snow in my garden in my life."

She was full of excitement and elation. The garden was an
endless joy to her. Paul was thankful for her sake at last to be
in a house with a long garden that went down to a field. Every
morning after breakfast she went out and was happy pottering
about in it. And it was true, she knew every weed and
blade.

Everybody turned up for the walk. Food was packed, and
they set off, a merry, delighted party. They hung over the wall
of the mill-race, dropped paper in the water on one side of the
tunnel and watched it shoot out on the other. They stood on
the footbridge over Boathouse Station and looked at the metals
gleaming coldly.

"You should see the Flying Scotsman come through at half-
past six!" said Leonard, whose father was a signalman. "Lad,
but she doesn't half buzz!" and the little party looked up the
lines one way, to London, and the other way, to Scotland, and
they felt the touch of these two magical places.

In Ilkeston the colliers were waiting in gangs for the public-
houses to open. It was a town of idleness and lounging. At
Stanton Gate the iron foundry blazed. Over everything there
were great discussions. At Trowell they crossed again from

Derbyshire into Nottinghamshire. They came to the Hemlock Stone at dinner-time. Its field was crowded with folk from Nottingham and Ilkeston.

They had expected a venerable and dignified monument. They found a little, gnarled, twisted stump of rock, something like a decayed mushroom, standing out pathetically on the side of a field. Leonard and Dick immediately proceeded to carve their initials, "L. W." and "R. P.", in the old red sandstone; but Paul desisted, because he had read in the newspaper satirical remarks about initial-carvers, who could find no other road to immortality. Then all the lads climbed to the top of the rock to look round.

Everywhere in the field below, factory girls and lads were eating lunch or sporting about. Beyond was the garden of an old manor. It had yew-hedges and thick clumps and borders of yellow crocuses round the lawn.

"See," said Paul to Miriam, "what a quiet garden!"

She saw the dark yews and the golden crocuses, then she looked gratefully. He had not seemed to belong to her among all these others; he was different then—not her Paul, who understood the slightest quiver of her innermost soul, but something else, speaking another language than hers. How it hurt her, and deadened her very perceptions. Only when he came right back to her, leaving his other, his lesser self, as she thought, would she feel alive again. And now he asked her to look at this garden, wanting the contact with her again. Impatient of the set in the field, she turned to the quiet lawn, surrounded by sheaves of shut-up crocuses. A feeling of stillness, almost of ecstasy, came over her. It felt almost as if she were alone with him in this garden.

Then he left her again and joined the others. Soon they started home. Miriam loitered behind, alone. She did not fit in with the others; she could very rarely get into human relations with anyone: so her friend, her companion, her lover, was Nature. She saw the sun declining wanly. In the dusky, cold hedgerows were some red leaves. She lingered to gather them, tenderly, passionately. The love in her finger-tips caressed the leaves; the passion in her heart came to a glow upon the leaves.

Suddenly she realised she was alone in a strange road, and she hurried forward. Turning a corner in the lane, she came upon Paul, who stood bent over something, his mind fixed on it, working away steadily, patiently, a little hopelessly. She hesitated in her approach, to watch.

He remained concentrated in the middle of the road. Beyond, one rift of rich gold in that colourless grey evening seemed to make him stand out in dark relief. She saw him, slender and firm, as if the setting sun had given him to her. A deep pain took hold of her, and she knew she must love him. And she had discovered him, discovered in him a rare potentiality, discovered his loneliness. Quivering as at some "annunciation", she went slowly forward.

At last he looked up.

"Why," he exclaimed gratefully, "have you waited for me!"

She saw a deep shadow in his eyes.

"What is it?" she asked.

"The spring broken here;" and he showed her where his umbrella was injured.

Instantly, with some shame, she knew he had not done the damage himself, but that Geoffrey was responsible.

"It is only an old umbrella, isn't it?" she asked.

She wondered why he, who did not usually trouble over trifles, made such a mountain of this molehill.

"But it was William's an' my mother can't help but know," he said quietly, still patiently working at the umbrella.

The words went through Miriam like a blade. This, then, was the confirmation of her vision of him! She looked at him. But there was about him a certain reserve, and she dared not comfort him, not even speak softly to him.

"Come on," he said. "I can't do it;" and they went in silence along the road.

That same evening they were walking along under the trees by Nether Green. He was talking to her fretfully, seemed to be struggling to convince himself.

"You know," he said, with an effort, "if one person loves, the other does."

"Ah!" she answered. "Like mother said to me when I was little, 'Love begets love.'"

"Yes, something like that, I think it *must* be."

"I hope so, because, if it were not, love might be a very terrible thing," she said.

"Yes, but it *is*—at least with most people," he answered.

And Miriam, thinking he had assured himself, felt strong in herself. She always regarded that sudden coming upon him in the lane as a revelation. And this conversation remained graven in her mind as one of the letters of the law.

Now she stood with him and for him. When, about this time, he outraged the family feeling at Willey Farm by some overbearing insult, she stuck to him, and believed he was right. *subconscious* And at this time she dreamed dreams of him, vivid, unforgettable. These dreams came again later on, developed to a more subtle psychological stage.

On the Easter Monday the same party took an excursion to Wingfield Manor. It was great excitement to Miriam to catch a train at Sethley Bridge, amid all the bustle of the Bank Holiday crowd. They left the train at Alfreton. Paul was interested in the street and in the colliers with their dogs. Here was a new race of miners. Miriam did not live till they came to the church. They were all rather timid of entering, with their bags of food, for fear of being turned out. Leonard, a comic, thin fellow, went first; Paul, who would have died rather than be sent back, went last. The place was decorated for Easter. In the font hundreds of white narcissi seemed to be growing. The air was dim and coloured from the windows and thrilled with a subtle scent of lilies and narcissi. In that atmosphere Miriam's soul came into a glow. Paul was afraid of the things he mustn't do; and he was sensitive to the feel of the place. Miriam turned to him. He answered. They were together. He would not go beyond the Communion-rail She loved him for that. Her soul expanded into prayer beside him. He felt the strange fascination of shadowy religious places. All his latent mysticism quivered into life. She was drawn to him. He was a prayer along with her.

Miriam very rarely talked to the other lads. They at once became awkward in conversation with her. So usually she was silent.

It was past midday when they climbed the steep path to the manor. All things shone softly in the sun, which was wonderfully warm and enlivening. Celandines and violets were out. Everybody was tip-top full with happiness. The glitter of the ivy, the soft, atmospheric grey of the castle walls, the gentleness of everything near the ruin, was perfect.

The manor is of hard, pale grey stone, and the other walls are blank and calm. The young folk were in raptures. They went in trepidation, almost afraid that the delight of exploring this ruin might be denied them. In the first courtyard, within the high broken walls, were farm-carts, with their shafts lying idle on the ground, the tyres of the wheels brilliant with gold-red rust. It was very still.

All eagerly paid their sixpences, and went timidly through the fine clean arch of the inner courtyard. They were shy. Here on the pavement, where the hall had been, an old thorn tree was budding. All kinds of strange openings and broken rooms were in the shadow around them.

After lunch they set off once more to explore the ruin. This time the girls went with the boys, who could act as guides and expositors. There was one tall tower in a corner, rather tottering, where they say Mary Queen of Scots was imprisoned.

"Think of the Queen going up here!" said Miriam in a low voice, as she climbed the hollow stairs.

"If she could get up," said Paul, "for she had rheumatism like anything. I reckon they treated her rottenly."

"You don't think she deserved it?" asked Miriam.

"No, I don't. She was only lively."

They continued to mount the winding staircase. A high wind, blowing through the loopholes, went rushing up the shaft, and filled the girl's skirts like a balloon, so that she was ashamed, until he took the hem of her dress and held it down for her. He did it perfectly simply, as he would have picked up her glove. She remembered this always.

Round the broken top of the tower the ivy bushed out, old and handsome. Also, there were a few chill gilivers, in pale cold bud. Miriam wanted to lean over for some ivy, but he would not let her. Instead, she had to wait behind him, and take from him each spray as he gathered it and held it to her, each one separately, in the purest manner of chivalry. The tower seemed to rock in the wind. They looked over miles and miles of wooded country, and country with gleams of pasture.

The crypt underneath the manor was beautiful, and in perfect preservation. Paul made a drawing: Miriam stayed with him. She was thinking of Mary Queen of Scots looking with her strained, hopeless eyes, that could not understand misery, over the hills whence no help came, or sitting in this crypt, being told of a God as cold as the place she sat in.

They set off again gaily, looking round on their beloved manor that stood so clean and big on its hill.

"Supposing you could have *that* farm," said Paul to Miriam.

"Yes!"

"Wouldn't it be lovely to come and see you!"

They were now in the bare country of stone walls, which he loved, and which, though only ten miles from home, seemed so foreign to Miriam. The party was straggling. As they were crossing a large meadow that sloped away from the sun, along a path embedded with innumerable tiny glittering points, Paul, walking alongside, laced his fingers in the strings of the bag Miriam was carrying, and instantly she felt Annie behind, watchful and jealous. But the meadow was bathed in a glory of sunshine, and the path was jewelled, and it was seldom that he gave her any sign. She held her fingers very still among the strings of the bag, his fingers touching; and the place was golden as a vision.

At last they came into the straggling grey village of Crich, that lies high. Beyond the village was the famous Crich Stand that Paul could see from the garden at home. The party pushed on. Great expanse of country spread around and below. The lads were eager to get to the top of the hill. It was capped by a round knoll, half of which was by now cut away, and on the top of which stood an ancient monument, sturdy and squat, for signalling in old days far down into the level lands of Nottinghamshire and Leicestershire.

It was blowing so hard, high up there in the exposed place, that the only way to be safe was to stand nailed by the wind to the wall of the tower. At their feet fell the precipice where the limestone was quarried away. Below was a jumble of hills and tiny villages—Matlock, Ambergate, Stoney Middleton. The lads were eager to spy out the church of Bestwood, far away among the rather crowded country on the left. They were disgusted that it seemed to stand on a plain. They saw the hills of Derbyshire fall into the monotony of the Midlands that swept away South.

Miriam was somewhat scared by the wind, but the lads enjoyed it. They went on, miles and miles, to Whatstandwell. All the food was eaten, everybody was hungry, and there was very little money to get home with. But they managed to procure a loaf and a currant-loaf, which they hacked to pieces with shut-knives, and ate sitting on the wall near the bridge, watching the bright Derwent rushing by, and the brakes from Matlock pulling up at the inn.

Paul was now pale with weariness. He had been responsible for the party all day, and now he was done. Miriam understood, and kept close to him, and he left himself in her hands.

They had an hour to wait at Ambergate Station. Trains came, crowded with excursionists returning to Manchester, Birmingham, and London.

"We might be going there—folk easily might think we're going that far," said Paul.

They got back rather late. Miriam, walking home with Geoffrey, watched the moon rise big and red and misty. She felt something was fulfilled in her.

She had an elder sister, Agatha, who was a school-teacher. Between the two girls was a feud. Miriam considered Agatha worldly. And she wanted herself to be a school-teacher.

One Saturday afternoon Agatha and Miriam were upstairs dressing. Their bedroom was over the stable. It was a low room, not very large, and bare. Miriam had nailed on the wall a reproduction of Veronese's "St. Catherine". She loved the woman who sat in the window, dreaming. Her own windows were too small to sit in. But the front one was dripped over with honeysuckle and virginia creeper, and looked upon the tree-tops of the oak-wood across the yard, while the little back window, no bigger than a handkerchief, was a loophole to the east, to the dawn beating up against the beloved round hills.

The two sisters did not talk much to each other. Agatha, who was fair and small and determined, had rebelled against the home atmosphere, against the doctrine of "the other cheek". She was out in the world now, in a fair way to be independent. And she insisted on worldly values, on appearance, on manners, on position, which Miriam would fain have ignored.

Both girls liked to be upstairs, out of the way, when Paul came. They preferred to come running down, open the stair-foot door, and see him watching, expectant of them. Miriam stood painfully pulling over her head a rosary he had given her. It caught in the fine mesh of her hair. But at last she had it on, and the red-brown wooden beads looked well against her cool brown neck. She was a well-developed girl, and very handsome. But in the little looking-glass nailed against the whitewashed wall she could only see a fragment of herself at a time. Agatha had bought a little mirror of her own, which she propped up to suit herself. Miriam was near the window. Suddenly she heard the well-known click of the chain, and she saw Paul fling open the gate, push his bicycle into the yard. She saw him look at the house, and she shrank away. He walked in a nonchalant fashion, and his bicycle went with him as if it were a live thing.

"Paul's come!" she exclaimed.

"Aren't you glad?" said Agatha cuttingly.

Miriam stood still in amazement and bewilderment.

"Well, aren't you?" she asked.

"Yes, but I'm not going to let him see it, and think I wanted him."

Miriam was startled. She heard him putting his bicycle in the stable underneath, and talking to Jimmy, who had been a pit-horse, and who was seedy.

"Well, Jimmy my lad, how are ter? Nobbut sick an' sadly, like? Why, then, it's a shame, my owd lad."

She heard the rope run through the hole as the horse lifted its head from the lad's caress. How she loved to listen when he thought only the horse could hear. But there was a serpent in her Eden. She searched earnestly in herself to see if she wanted Paul Morel. She felt there would be some disgrace in it. Full of twisted feeling, she was afraid she did want him. She stood self-convicted. Then came an agony of new shame. She shrank within herself in a coil of torture. Did she want Paul Morel, and did he know she wanted him? What a subtle infamy upon her. She felt as if her whole soul coiled into knots of shame.

Agatha was dressed first, and ran downstairs. Miriam heard her greet the lad gaily, knew exactly how brilliant her grey eyes became with that tone. She herself would have felt it bold to have greeted him in such wise. Yet there she stood under the self-accusation of wanting him, tied to that stake of torture. In bitter perplexity she kneeled down and prayed:

"O Lord, let me not love Paul Morel. Keep me from loving him, if I ought not to love him."

Something anomalous in the prayer arrested her. She lifted her head and pondered. How could it be wrong to love him? Love was God's gift. And yet it caused her shame. That was because of him, Paul Morel. But, then, it was not his affair, it was her own, between herself and God. She was to be a sacrifice. But it was God's sacrifice, not Paul Morel's or her own. After a few minutes she hid her face in the pillow again, and said:

"But, Lord, if it is Thy will that I should love him, make

me love him—as Christ would, who died for the souls of men.
Make me love him splendidly, because he is Thy son.'

She remained kneeling for some time, quite still, and deeply
moved, her black hair against the red squares and the lavender-
sprigged squares of the patchwork quilt. Prayer was almost
essential to her. Then she fell into that rapture of self-sacrifice,
identifying herself with a God who was sacrificed, which gives
to so many human souls their deepest bliss.

When she went downstairs Paul was lying back in an arm-
chair, holding forth with much vehemence to Agatha, who was
scorning a little painting he had brought to show her. Miriam
glanced at the two, and avoided their levity. She went into
the parlour to be alone.

It was tea-time before she was able to speak to Paul, and
then her manner was so distant he thought he had offended
her.

Miriam discontinued her practice of going each Thursday
evening to the library in Bestwood. After calling for Paul
regularly during the whole spring, a number of trifling incidents
and tiny insults from his family awakened her to their attitude
towards her, and she decided to go no more. So she announced
to Paul one evening she would not call at his house again for
him on Thursday nights.

"Why?" he asked, very short.

"Nothing. Only I'd rather not."

"Very well."

"But," she faltered, "if you'd care to meet me, we could
still go together."

"Meet you where?"

"Somewhere—where you like."

"I shan't meet you anywhere. I don't see why you shouldn't
keep calling for me. But if you won't, I don't want to meet
you."

So the Thursday evenings which had been so precious to her,
and to him, were dropped. He worked instead. Mrs. Morel
sniffed with satisfaction at this arrangement.

He would not have it that they were lovers. The intimacy
between them had been kept so abstract, such a matter of the
soul, all thought and weary struggle into consciousness, that he
saw it only as a platonic friendship. He stoutly denied there
was anything else between them. Miriam was silent, or else
she very quietly agreed. He was a fool who did not know what

was happening to himself. By tacit agreement they ignored
the remarks and insinuations of their acquaintances.

"We aren't lovers, we are friends," he said to her. *"We*
know it. Let them talk. What does it matter what they say."

Sometimes, as they were walking together, she slipped her
arm timidly into his. But he always resented it, and she knew
it. It caused a violent conflict in him. With Miriam he was
always on the high plane of abstraction, when his natural fire
of love was transmitted into the fine stream of thought. She
would have it so. If he were jolly and, as she put it, flippant,
she waited till he came back to her, till the change had taken
place in him again, and he was wrestling with his own soul,
frowning, passionate in his desire for understanding. And in
this passion for understanding her soul lay close to his; she
had him all to herself. But he must be made abstract first.

Then, if she put her arm in his, it caused him almost torture.
His consciousness seemed to split. The place where she was
touching him ran hot with friction. He was one internecine
battle, and he became cruel to her because of it.

One evening in midsummer Miriam called at the house, warm
from climbing. Paul was alone in the kitchen; his mother could
be heard moving about upstairs.

"Come and look at the sweet-peas," he said to the girl.

They went into the garden. The sky behind the townlet and
the church was orange-red; the flower-garden was flooded with
a strange warm light that lifted every leaf into significance.
Paul passed along a fine row of sweet-peas, gathering a blossom
here and there, all cream and pale blue. Miriam followed,
breathing the fragrance. To her, flowers appealed with such
strength she felt she must make them part of herself. When
she bent and breathed a flower, it was as if she and the flower
were loving each other. Paul hated her for it. There seemed
a sort of exposure about the action, something too intimate.

When he had got a fair bunch, they returned to the house.
He listened for a moment to his mother's quiet movement upstairs, then he said:

"Come here, and let me pin them in for you." He arranged
them two or three at a time in the bosom of her dress, step-
ping back now and then to see the effect. "You know," he said,
taking the pin out of his mouth, "a woman ought always to
arrange her flowers before her glass."

Miriam laughed. She thought flowers ought to be pinned in

one's dress without any care. That Paul should take pains to fix her flowers for her was his whim.

He was rather offended at her laughter.

"Some women do—those who look decent," he said.

Miriam laughed again, but mirthlessly, to hear him thus mix her up with women in a general way. From most men she would have ignored it. But from him it hurt her.

He had nearly finished arranging the flowers when he heard his mother's footstep on the stairs. Hurriedly he pushed in the last pin and turned away.

"Don't let mater know," he said.

Miriam picked up her books and stood in the doorway looking with chagrin at the beautiful sunset. She would call for Paul no more, she said.

"Good-evening, Mrs. Morel," she said, in a deferential way. She sounded as if she felt she had no right to be there.

"Oh, is it you, Miriam?" replied Mrs. Morel coolly.

But Paul insisted on everybody's accepting his friendship with the girl, and Mrs. Morel was too wise to have any open rupture.

It was not till he was twenty years old that the family could ever afford to go away for a holiday. Mrs. Morel had never been away for a holiday, except to see her sister, since she had been married. Now at last Paul had saved enough money, and they were all going. There was to be a party: some of Annie's friends, one friend of Paul's, a young man in the same office where William had previously been, and Miriam.

It was great excitement writing for rooms. Paul and his mother debated it endlessly between them. They wanted a furnished cottage for two weeks. She thought one week would be enough, but he insisted on two.

At last they got an answer from Mablethorpe, a cottage such as they wished for thirty shillings a week. There was immense jubilation. Paul was wild with joy for his mother's sake. She would have a real holiday now. He and she sat at evening picturing what it would be like. Annie came in, and Leonard, and Alice, and Kitty. There was wild rejoicing and anticipation. Paul told Miriam. She seemed to brood with joy over it. But the Morel's house rang with excitement.

They were to go on Saturday morning by the seven train. Paul suggested that Miriam should sleep at his house, because it was so far for her to walk. She came down for supper. Every-

body was so excited that even Miriam was accepted with
warmth. But almost as soon as she entered the feeling in the
family became close and tight. He had discovered a poem by
Jean Ingelow which mentioned Mablethorpe, and so he must
read it to Miriam. He would never have got so far in the direction of sentimentality as to read poetry to his own family.
But now they condescended to listen. Miriam sat on the sofa
absorbed in him. She always seemed absorbed in him, and by
him, when he was present. Mrs. Morel sat jealously in her
own chair. She was going to hear also. And even Annie and
the father attended, Morel with his head cocked on one side,
like somebody listening to a sermon and feeling conscious of
the fact. Paul ducked his head over the book. He had got
now all the audience he cared for. And Mrs. Morel and Annie
almost contested with Miriam who should listen best and win
his favour. He was in very high feather.

"But," interrupted Mrs. Morel, "what *is* the 'Bride of Enderby'
that the bells are supposed to ring?"

"It's an old tune they used to play on the bells for a warning
against water. I suppose the Bride of Enderby was drowned in
a flood," he replied. He had not the faintest knowledge what
it really was, but he would never have sunk so low as to confess that to his womenfolk. They listened and believed him.
He believed himself.

"And the people knew what that tune meant?" said his
mother.

"Yes—just like the Scotch when they heard 'The Flowers o'
the Forest'—and when they used to ring the bells backward
for alarm."

"How?" said Annie. "A bell sounds the same whether it's
rung backwards or forwards."

"But," he said, "if you start with the deep bell and ring up
to the high one—der—der—der—der—der—der—der—der!"

He ran up the scale. Everybody thought it clever. He
thought so too. Then, waiting a minute, he continued the
poem.

"Hm!" said Mrs. Morel curiously, when he finished. "But I
wish everything that's written weren't so sad."

"*I* canna see what they want drownin' theirselves for," said
Morel.

There was a pause. Annie got up to clear the table.
Miriam rose to help with the pots.

"Let *me* help to wash up," she said.

"Certainly not," cried Annie. "You sit down again. There aren't many."

And Miriam, who could not be familiar and insist, sat down again to look at the book with Paul.

He was master of the party; his father was no good. And great tortures he suffered lest the tin box should be put out at Firsby instead of at Mablethorpe. And he wasn't equal to getting a carriage. His bold little mother did that.

"Here!" she cried to a man. "Here!"

Paul and Annie got behind the rest, convulsed with shamed laughter.

"How much will it be to drive to Brook Cottage?" said Mrs. Morel.

"Two shillings."

"Why, how far is it?"

"A good way."

"I don't believe it," she said.

But she scrambled in. There were eight crowded in one old seaside carriage.

"You see," said Mrs. Morel, "it's only threepence each, and if it were a tram-car——"

They drove along. Each cottage they came to, Mrs. Morel cried:

"Is it this? Now, this is it!"

Everybody sat breathless. They drove past. There was a universal sigh.

"I'm thankful it wasn't that brute," said Mrs. Morel. "I *was* frightened." They drove on and on.

At last they descended at a house that stood alone over the dyke by the highroad. There was wild excitement because they had to cross a little bridge to get into the front garden. But they loved the house that lay so solitary, with a sea-meadow on one side, and immense expanse of land patched in white barley, yellow oats, red wheat, and green root-crops, flat and stretching level to the sky.

Paul kept accounts. He and his mother ran the show. The total expenses—lodging, food, everything—was sixteen shillings a week per person. He and Leonard went bathing in the morning. Morel was wandering abroad quite early.

"You, Paul," his mother called from the bedroom, "eat a piece of bread-and-butter."

"All right," he answered.

And when he got back he saw his mother presiding in state at the breakfast-table. The woman of the house was young. Her husband was blind, and she did laundry work. So Mrs. Morel always washed the pots in the kitchen and made the beds.

"But you said you'd have a real holiday," said Paul, "and now you work."

"Work!" she exclaimed. "What are you talking about!"

He loved to go with her across the fields to the village and the sea. She was afraid of the plank bridge, and he abused her for being a baby. On the whole he stuck to her as if he were *her* man.

Miriam did not get much of him, except, perhaps, when all the others went to the "Coons". Coons were insufferably stupid to Miriam, so he thought they were to himself also, and he preached priggishly to Annie about the fatuity of listening to them. Yet he, too, knew all their songs, and sang them along the roads roisterously. And if he found himself listening, the stupidity pleased him very much. Yet to Annie he said:

"Such rot! there isn't a grain of intelligence in it. Nobody with more gumption than a grasshopper could go and sit and listen." And to Miriam he said, with much scorn of Annie and the others: "I suppose they're at the 'Coons'."

It was queer to see Miriam singing coon songs. She had a straight chin that went in a perpendicular line from the lower lip to the turn. She always reminded Paul of some sad Botticelli angel when she sang, even when it was:

> "Come down lover's lane
> For a walk with me, talk with me."

Only when he sketched, or at evening when the others were at the "Coons", she had him to herself. He talked to her endlessly about his love of horizontals: how they, the great levels of sky and land in Lincolnshire, meant to him the eternality of the will, just as the bowed Norman arches of the church, repeating themselves, meant the dogged leaping forward of the persistent human soul, on and on, nobody knows where; in contradiction to the perpendicular lines and to the Gothic arch, which, he said, leapt up at heaven and touched the ecstasy and lost itself in the divine. Himself, he said, was Norman, Miriam was Gothic. She bowed in consent even to that.

One evening he and she went up the great sweeping shore of sand towards Theddlethorpe. The long breakers plunged and ran in a hiss of foam along the coast. It was a warm evening. There was not a figure but themselves on the far reaches of sand, no noise but the sound of the sea. Paul loved to see it clanging at the land. He loved to feel himself between the noise of it and the silence of the sandy shore. Miriam was with him. Everything grew very intense. It was quite dark when they turned again. The way home was through a gap in the sandhills, and then along a raised grass road between two dykes. The country was black and still. From behind the sandhills came the whisper of the sea. Paul and Miriam walked in silence. Suddenly he started. The whole of his blood seemed to burst into flame, and he could scarcely breathe. An enormous orange moon was staring at them from the rim of the sandhills. He stood still, looking at it.

"Ah!" cried Miriam, when she saw it.

He remained perfectly still, staring at the immense and ruddy moon, the only thing in the far-reaching darkness of the level. His heart beat heavily, the muscles of his arms contracted.

"What is it?" murmured Miriam, waiting for him.

He turned and looked at her. She stood beside him, for ever in shadow. Her face, covered with the darkness of her hat, was watching him unseen. But she was brooding. She was slightly afraid—deeply moved and religious. That was her best state. He was impotent against it. His blood was concentrated like a flame in his chest. But he could not get across to her. There were flashes in his blood. But somehow she ignored them. She was expecting some religious state in him. Still yearning, she was half aware of his passion, and gazed at him, troubled.

"What is it?" she murmured again.

"It's the moon," he answered, frowning.

"Yes," she assented. "Isn't it wonderful?" She was curious about him. The crisis was past.

He did not know himself what was the matter. He was naturally so young, and their intimacy was so abstract, he did not know he wanted to crush her on to his breast to ease the ache there. He was afraid of her. The fact that he might want her as a man wants a woman had in him been suppressed into a shame. When she shrank in her convulsed, coiled torture from the thought of such a thing, he had winced to the depths of his soul. And now this "purity" prevented even their first love-kiss. It was as if she could scarcely stand the shock of physical love, even a passionate kiss, and then he was too shrinking and sensitive to give it.

As they walked along the dark fen-meadow he watched the moon and did not speak. She plodded beside him. He hated her, for she seemed in some way to make him despise himself. Looking ahead—he saw the one light in the darkness, the window of their lamp-lit cottage.

He loved to think of his mother, and the other jolly people.

"Well, everybody else has been in long ago!" said his mother as they entered.

"What does that matter!" he cried irritably. "I can go a walk if I like, can't I?"

"And I should have thought you could get in to supper with the rest," said Mrs. Morel.

"I shall please myself," he retorted. "It's not *late*. I shall do as I like."

"Very well," said his mother cuttingly, "then *do* as you like." And she took no further notice of him that evening. Which he pretended neither to notice nor to care about, but sat reading. Miriam read also, obliterating herself. Mrs. Morel hated her for making her son like this. She watched Paul growing irritable, priggish, and melancholic. For this she put the blame on Miriam. Annie and all her friends joined against the girl. Miriam had no friend of her own, only Paul. But she did not suffer so much, because she despised the triviality of these other people.

And Paul hated her because, somehow, she spoilt his ease and naturalness. And he writhed himself with a feeling of humiliation.

CHAPTER VIII

STRIFE IN LOVE

ARTHUR finished his apprenticeship, and got a job on the electrical plant at Minton Pit. He earned very little, but had a good chance of getting on. But he was wild and restless. He did not drink nor gamble. Yet he somehow contrived to get into endless scrapes, always through some hot-headed thought-lessness. Either he went rabbiting in the woods, like a poacher, or he stayed in Nottingham all night instead of coming home, or he miscalculated his dive into the canal at Bestwood, and scored his chest into one mass of wounds on the raw stones and tins at the bottom.

He had not been at his work many months when again he did not come home one night.

"Do you know where Arthur is?" asked Paul at breakfast.

"I do not," replied his mother.

"He is a fool," said Paul. "And if he *did* anything I shouldn't mind. But no, he simply can't come away from a game of whist, or else he must see a girl home from the skating-rink—quite proprietously—and so can't get home. He's a fool."

"I don't know that it would make it any better if he did something to make us all ashamed," said Mrs. Morel.

"Well, *I* should respect him more," said Paul.

"I very much doubt it," said his mother coldly.

They went on with breakfast.

"Are you fearfully fond of him?" Paul asked his mother.

"What do you ask that for?"

"Because they say a woman always like the youngest best."

"She may do—but I don't. No, he wearies me."

"And you'd actually rather he was good?"

"I'd rather he showed some of a man's common sense."

Paul was raw and irritable. He also wearied his mother very often. She saw the sunshine going out of him, and she resented it.

As they were finishing breakfast came the postman with a letter from Derby. Mrs. Morel screwed up her eyes to look at the address.

"Give it here, blind eye!" exclaimed her son, snatching it away from her.

She started, and almost boxed his ears.

"It's from your son, Arthur," he said.

"What now——!" cried Mrs. Morel.

" 'My dearest Mother,' " Paul read, " 'I don't know what made me such a fool. I want you to come and fetch me back from here. I came with Jack Bredon yesterday, instead of going to work, and enlisted. He said he was sick of wearing the seat of a stool out, and, like the idiot you know I am, I came away with him.

" 'I have taken the King's shilling, but perhaps if you came for me they would let me go back with you. I was a fool when I did it. I don't want to be in the army. My dear mother, I am nothing but a trouble to you. But if you get me out of this, I promise I will have more sense and consideration. . . .' "

Mrs. Morel sat down in her rocking-chair.

"Well, *now*," she cried, "let him stop!"

"Yes," said Paul, "let him stop."

There was silence. The mother sat with her hands folded in her apron, her face set, thinking.

"If I'm not *sick*!" she cried suddenly. "Sick!"

"Now," said Paul, beginning to frown, "you're not going to worry your soul out about this, do you hear."

"I suppose I'm to take it as a blessing," she flashed, turning on her son.

"You're not going to mount it up to a tragedy, so there," he retorted.

"The *fool*!—the young fool!" she cried.

"He'll look well in uniform," said Paul irritatingly.

His mother turned on him like a fury.

"Oh, will he!" she cried. "Not in my eyes!"

"He should get in a cavalry regiment; he'll have the time of his life, and will look an awful swell."

"Swell!—*swell*!—a mighty swell idea indeed!—a common soldier!"

"Well," said Paul, "what am I but a common clerk?"

"A good deal, my boy!" cried his mother, stung.

"What?"

"At any rate, a *man*, and not a thing in a red coat."

"I shouldn't mind being in a red coat—or dark blue, that would suit me better—if they didn't boss me about too much."

But his mother had ceased to listen.

"Just as he was getting on, or might have been getting on, at his job—a young nuisance—here he goes and ruins himself for life. What good will he be, do you think, after *this*?"

"It may lick him into shape beautifully," said Paul.

"Lick him into shape!—lick what marrow there *was* out of his bones. A *soldier*!—a common *soldier*!—nothing but a body that makes movements when it hears a shout! It's a fine thing!"

"I can't understand why it upsets you," said Paul.

"No, perhaps you can't. But *I* understand"; and she sat

back in her chair, her chin in one hand, holding her elbow with the other, brimmed up with wrath and chagrin.

"And shall you go to Derby?" asked Paul.

"Yes."

"It's no good."

"I'll see for myself."

"And why on earth don't you let him stop. It's just what he wants."

"Of course," cried the mother, "*you* know what he wants!"

She got ready and went by the first train to Derby, where she saw her son and the sergeant. It was, however, no good.

When Morel was having his dinner in the evening, she said suddenly:

"I've had to go to Derby to-day."

The miner turned up his eyes, showing the whites in his black face.

"Has ter, lass. What took thee there?"

"That Arthur!"

"Oh—an' what's agate now?"

"He's only enlisted."

Morel put down his knife and leaned back in his chair.

"Nay," he said, "that he niver 'as!"

"And is going down to Aldershot to-morrow."

"Well!" exclaimed the miner. "That's a winder." He considered it a moment, said "H'm!" and proceeded with his dinner. Suddenly his face contracted with wrath. "I hope he may never set foot i' my house again," he said.

"The idea!" cried Mrs. Morel. "Saying such a thing!"

"I do," repeated Morel. "A fool as runs away for a soldier, let 'im look after 'issen; I s'll do no more for 'im."

"A fat sight you have done as it is," she said.

And Morel was almost ashamed to go to his public-house that evening.

"Well, did you go?" said Paul to his mother when he came home.

"I did."

"And could you see him?"

"Yes."

"And what did he say?"

"He blubbered when I came away."

"H'm!"

"And so did I, so you needn't 'h'm'!"

Mrs. Morel fretted after her son. She knew he would not like the army. He did not. The discipline was intolerable to him.

"But the doctor," she said with some pride to Paul, "said he was perfectly proportioned—almost exactly; all his measurements were correct. He *is* good-looking, you know."

"He's awfully nice-looking. But he doesn't fetch the girls like William, does he?"

"No; it's a different character. He's a good deal like his father, irresponsible."

To console his mother, Paul did not go much to Willey Farm at this time. And in the autumn exhibition of students' work in the Castle he had two studies, a landscape in water-colour and a still life in oil, both of which had first-prize awards. He was highly excited.

"What do you think I've got for my pictures, mother?" he asked, coming home one evening. She saw by his eyes he was glad. Her face flushed.

"Now, how should I know, my boy!"

"A first prize for those glass jars——"

"H'm!"

"And a first prize for that sketch up at Willey Farm."

"Both first?"

"Yes."

"H'm!"

There was a rosy, bright look about her, though she said nothing.

"It's nice," he said, "isn't it?"

"It is."

"Why don't you praise me up to the skies?"

She laughed.

"I should have the trouble of dragging you down again," she said.

But she was full of joy, nevertheless. William had brought her his sporting trophies. She kept them still, and she did not forgive his death. Arthur was handsome—at least, a good specimen—and warm and generous, and probably would do well in the end. But Paul was going to distinguish himself. She had a great belief in him, the more because he was unaware of his own powers. There was so much to come out of him. Life for her was rich with promise. She was to see herself fulfilled. Not for nothing had been her struggle.

Several times during the exhibition Mrs. Morel went to the

Castle unknown to Paul. She wandered down the long room looking at the other exhibits. Yes, they were good. But they had not in them a certain something which she demanded for her satisfaction. Some made her jealous, they were so good. She looked at them a long time trying to find fault with them. Then suddenly she had a shock that made her heart beat. There hung Paul's picture! She knew it as if it were printed on her heart.

"Name—Paul Morel—First Prize."

It looked so strange, there in public, on the walls of the Castle gallery, where in her lifetime she had seen so many pictures. And she glanced round to see if anyone had noticed her again in front of the same sketch.

But she felt a proud woman. When she met well-dressed ladies going home to the Park, she thought to herself:

"Yes, you look very well—but I wonder if *your* son has two first prizes in the Castle."

And she walked on, as proud a little woman as any in Nottingham. And Paul felt he had done something for her, if only a trifle. All his work was hers.

One day, as he was going up Castle Gate, he met Miriam. He had seen her on the Sunday, and had not expected to meet her in town. She was walking with a rather striking woman, blonde, with a sullen expression, and a defiant carriage. It was strange how Miriam, in her bowed, meditative bearing, looked dwarfed beside this woman with the handsome shoulders. Miriam watched Paul searchingly. His gaze was on the stranger, who ignored him. The girl saw his masculine spirit rear its head.

"Hello!" he said, "you didn't tell me you were coming to town."

"No," replied Miriam, half apologetically. "I drove in to Cattle Market with father."

He looked at her companion.

"I've told you about Mrs. Dawes," said Miriam huskily; she was nervous. "Clara, do you know Paul?"

"I think I've seen him before," replied Mrs. Dawes indifferently, as she shook hands with him. She had scornful grey eyes, a skin like white honey, and a full mouth, with a slightly lifted upper lip that did not know whether it was raised in scorn of all men or out of eagerness to be kissed, but which believed the former. She carried her head back, as if she had drawn away in contempt, perhaps from men also. She wore a large, dowdy hat of black beaver, and a sort of slightly affected simple dress that made her look rather sack-like. She was evidently poor, and had not much taste. Miriam usually looked nice.

"Where have you seen me?" Paul asked of the woman.

She looked at him as if she would not trouble to answer. Then:

"Walking with Louie Travers," she said.

Louie was one of the "Spiral" girls.

"Why, do you know her?" he asked.

She did not answer. He turned to Miriam.

"Where are you going?" he asked.

"To the Castle."

"What train are you going home by?"

"I am driving with father. I wish you could come too. What time are you free?"

"You know not till eight to-night, damn it!"

And directly the two women moved on.

Paul remembered that Clara Dawes was the daughter of an old friend of Mrs. Leivers. Miriam had sought her out because she had once been Spiral overseer at Jordan's, and because her husband, Baxter Dawes, was smith for the factory, making the irons for cripple instruments, and so on. Through her Miriam felt she got into direct contact with Jordan's, and could estimate better Paul's position. But Mrs. Dawes was separated from her husband, and had taken up Women's Rights. She was supposed to be clever. It interested Paul.

Baxter Dawes he knew and disliked. The smith was a man of thirty-one or thirty-two. He came occasionally through Paul's corner—a big, well-set man, also striking to look at, and handsome. There was a peculiar similarity between himself and his wife. He had the same white skin, with a clear, golden tinge. His hair was of soft brown, his moustache was golden. And he had a similar defiance in his bearing and manner. But then came the difference. His eyes, dark brown and quick-shifting, were dissolute. They protruded very slightly, and his eyelids hung over them in a way that was half hate. His mouth, too, was sensual. His whole manner was of cowed defiance, as if he were ready to knock anybody down who disapproved of him—perhaps because he really disapproved of himself.

From the first day he had hated Paul. Finding the lad's impersonal, deliberate gaze of an artist on his face, he got into a fury.

"What are yer lookin' at?" he sneered, bullying.

The boy glanced away. But the smith used to stand behind the counter and talk to Mr. Pappleworth. His speech was dirty, with a kind of rottenness. Again he found the youth with his cool, critical gaze fixed on his face. The smith started round as if he had been stung.

"What'r yer lookin' at, three hap'orth o' pap?" he snarled.

The boy shrugged his shoulders slightly.

"Why yer——!" shouted Dawes.

"Leave him alone," said Mr. Pappleworth, in that insinuating voice which means, "He's only one of your good little sops who can't help it."

Since that time the boy used to look at the man every time he came through with the same curious criticism, glancing away before he met the smith's eye. It made Dawes furious. They hated each other in silence.

Clara Dawes had no children. When she had left her husband the home had been broken up, and she had gone to live with her mother. Dawes lodged with his sister. In the same house was a sister-in-law, and somehow Paul knew that this girl, Louie Travers, was now Dawes's woman. She was a handsome, insolent hussy, who mocked at the youth, and yet flushed if he walked along to the station with her as she went home.

The next time he went to see Miriam it was Saturday evening. She had a fire in the parlour, and was waiting for him. The others, except her father and mother and the young children, had gone out, so the two had the parlour together. It was a long, low, warm room. There were three of Paul's small sketches on the wall, and his photo was on the mantelpiece. On the table and on the high old rosewood piano were bowls of coloured leaves. He sat in the arm-chair, she crouched on the hearthrug near his feet. The glow was warm on her handsome, pensive face as she kneeled there like a devotee.

"What did you think of Mrs. Dawes?" she asked quietly.

"She doesn't look very amiable," he replied.

"No, but don't you think she's a fine woman?" she said, in a deep tone.

"Yes—in stature. But without a grain of taste. I like her for some things. *Is* she disagreeable?"

"I don't think so. I think she's dissatisfied."

"What with?"

"Well—how would *you* like to be tied for life to a man like that?"

"Why did she marry him, then, if she was to have revulsions so soon?"

"Ay, why did she!" repeated Miriam bitterly.

"And I should have thought she had enough fight in her to match him," he said.

Miriam bowed her head.

"Ay?" she queried satirically. "What makes you think so?"

"Look at her mouth—made for passion—and the very set-back of her throat——" He threw his head back in Clara's defiant manner.

Miriam bowed a little lower.

"Yes," she said.

There was a silence for some moments, while he thought of Clara.

"And what were the things you liked about her?" she asked.

"I don't know—her skin and the texture of her—and her—I don't know—there's a sort of fierceness somewhere in her. I appreciate her as an artist, that's all."

"Yes."

He wondered why Miriam crouched there brooding in that strange way. It irritated him.

"You don't really like her, do you?" he asked the girl.

She looked at him with her great, dazzled dark eyes.

"I do," she said.

"You don't—you can't—not really."

"Then what?" she asked slowly.

"Eh, I don't know—perhaps you like her because she's got a grudge against men."

That was more probably one of his own reasons for liking Mrs. Dawes, but this did not occur to him. They were silent. There had come into his forehead a knitting of the brows which was becoming habitual with him, particularly when he was with Miriam. She longed to smooth it away, and she was afraid of it. It seemed the stamp of a man who was not her man in Paul Morel.

There were some crimson berries among the leaves in the bowl. He reached over and pulled out a bunch.

"If you put red berries in your hair," he said, "why would you look like some witch or priestess, and never like a reveller?"

She laughed with a naked, painful sound.

"I don't know," she said.

His vigorous warm hands were playing excitedly with the berries.

"Why can't you laugh?" he said. "You never laugh laughter. You only laugh when something is odd or incongruous, and then it almost seems to hurt you."

She bowed her head as if he were scolding her.

"I wish you could laugh at me just for one minute—just for one minute. I feel as if it would set something free."

"But"—and she looked up at him with eyes frightened and struggling—"I do laugh at you—I *do*."

"Never! There's always a kind of intensity. When you laugh I could always cry; it seems as if it shows up your suffering. Oh, you make me knit the brows of my very soul and cogitate."

Slowly she shook her head despairingly.

"I'm sure I don't want to," she said.

"I'm so damned spiritual with *you* always!" he cried.

She remained silent, thinking, "Then why don't you be otherwise." But he saw her crouching, brooding figure, and it seemed to tear him in two.

"But, there, it's autumn," he said, "and everybody feels like a disembodied spirit then."

There was still another silence. This peculiar sadness between them thrilled her soul. He seemed so beautiful with his eyes gone dark, and looking as if they were deep as the deepest well.

"You make me so spiritual!" he lamented. "And I don't want to be spiritual."

She took her finger from her mouth with a little pop, and looked up at him almost challenging. But still her soul was naked in her great dark eyes, and there was the same yearning appeal upon her. If he could have kissed her in abstract purity he would have done so. But he could not kiss her thus—and she seemed to leave no other way. And she yearned to him.

He gave a brief laugh.

"Well," he said, "get that French and we'll do some—some Verlaine."

"Yes," she said in a deep tone, almost of resignation. And she rose and got the books. And her rather red, nervous hands looked so pitiful, he was mad to comfort her and kiss her. But then he dared not—or could not. There was something prevented him. His kisses were wrong for her. They continued the reading till ten o'clock, when they went into the kitchen, and Paul was natural and jolly again with the father and mother. His eyes were dark and shining; there was a kind of fascination about him.

When he went into the barn for his bicycle he found the front wheel punctured.

"Fetch me a drop of water in a bowl," he said to her. "I shall be late, and then I s'll catch it."

He lighted the hurricane lamp, took off his coat, turned up the bicycle, and set speedily to work. Miriam came with the bowl of water and stood close to him, watching. She loved to see his hands doing things. He was slim and vigorous, with a kind of easiness even in his most hasty movements. And busy at his work he seemed to forget her. She loved him absorbedly. She wanted to run her hands down his sides. She always wanted to embrace him, so long as he did not want her.

"There!" he said, rising suddenly. "Now, could you have done it quicker?"

"No!" she laughed.

He straightened himself. His back was towards her. She put her two hands on his sides, and ran them quickly down.

"You are so *fine!*" she said.

He laughed, hating her voice, but his blood roused to a wave of flame by her hands. She did not seem to realise *him* in all this. He might have been an object. She never realised the male he was.

He lighted his bicycle-lamp, bounced the machine on the barn floor to see that the tyres were sound, and buttoned his coat.

"That's all right!" he said.

She was trying the brakes, that she knew were broken.

"Did you have them mended?" she asked.

"No!"

"But why didn't you?"

"The back one goes on a bit."

"But it's not safe."

"I can use my toe."

"I wish you'd had them mended," she murmured.

"Don't worry—come to tea to-morrow, with Edgar."

"Shall we?"

"Do—about four. I'll come to meet you."

"Very well."

She was pleased. They went across the dark yard to the gate. Looking across, he saw through the uncurtained window of the kitchen the heads of Mr. and Mrs. Leivers in the warm glow. It looked very cosy. The road, with pine trees, was quite black in front.

"Till to-morrow," he said, jumping on his bicycle.

"You'll take care, won't you?" she pleaded.

"Yes."

His voice already came out of the darkness. She stood a moment watching the light from his lamp race into obscurity along the ground. She turned very slowly indoors. Orion was wheeling up over the wood, his dog twinkling after him, half smothered. For the rest the world was full of darkness, and silent, save for the breathing of cattle in their stalls. She prayed earnestly for his safety that night. When he left her, she often lay in anxiety, wondering if he had got home safely.

He dropped down the hills on his bicycle. The roads were greasy, so he had to let it go. He felt a pleasure as the machine plunged over the second, steeper drop in the hill. "Here goes!" he said. It was risky, because of the curve in the darkness at the bottom, and because of the brewers' waggons with drunken waggoners asleep. His bicycle seemed to fall beneath him, and he loved it. Recklessness is almost a man's revenge on his woman. He feels he is not valued, so he will risk destroying himself to deprive her altogether.

The stars on the lake seemed to leap like grasshoppers, silver upon the blackness, as he spun past. Then there was the long climb home.

"See, mother!" he said, as he threw her the berries and leaves on to the table.

"H'm!" she said, glancing at them, then away again. She sat reading, alone, as she always did.

"Aren't they pretty?"

"Yes."

He knew she was cross with him. After a few minutes he said:

"Edgar and Miriam are coming to tea to-morrow."

She did not answer.

"You don't mind?"

Still she did not answer.

"Do you?" he asked.

"You know whether I mind or not."

"I don't see why you should. I have plenty of meals there."

"You do."

"Then why do you begrudge them tea?"

"I begrudge whom tea?"

"What are you so horrid for?"

"Oh, say no more! You've asked her to tea, it's quite sufficient. She'll come."

He was very angry with his mother. He knew it was merely Miriam she objected to. He flung off his boots and went to bed.

Paul went to meet his friends the next afternoon. He was glad to see them coming. They arrived home at about four o'clock. Everywhere was clean and still for Sunday afternoon. Mrs. Morel sat in her black dress and black apron. She rose to meet the visitors. With Edgar she was cordial, but with Miriam cold and rather grudging. Yet Paul thought the girl looked so nice in her brown cashmere frock.

He helped his mother to get the tea ready. Miriam would have gladly proffered, but was afraid. He was rather proud of his home. There was about it now, he thought, a certain distinction. The chairs were only wooden, and the sofa was old. But the hearthrug and cushions were cosy; the pictures were prints in good taste; there was a simplicity in everything, and plenty of books. He was never ashamed in the least of his home, nor was Miriam of hers, because both were what they should be, and warm. And then he was proud of the table; the china was pretty, the cloth was fine. It did not matter that the spoons were not silver nor the knives ivory-handled; everything looked nice. Mrs. Morel had managed wonderfully while her children were growing up, so that nothing was out of place.

Miriam talked books a little. That was her unfailing topic. But Mrs. Morel was not cordial, and turned soon to Edgar.

At first Edgar and Miriam used to go into Mrs. Morel's pew. Morel never went to chapel, preferring the public-house. Mrs. Morel, like a little champion, sat at the head of her pew, Paul at the other end; and at first Miriam sat next to him. Then the chapel was like home. It was a pretty place, with dark pews and slim, elegant pillars, and flowers. And the same people had sat in the same places ever since he was a boy. It was wonderfully sweet and soothing to sit there for an hour and a half, next to Miriam, and near to his mother, uniting his two loves under the spell of the place of worship. Then he felt warm and happy and religious at once. And after chapel he walked home with Miriam, whilst Mrs. Morel spent the rest of the evening with her old friend, Mrs. Burns. He was keenly alive on his walks on Sunday nights with Edgar and Miriam. He never went past the pits at night, by the lighted lamp-house, the tall black head-stocks and lines of trucks, past the fans spinning slowly like shadows, without the feeling of Miriam returning to him, keen and almost unbearable.

She did not very long occupy the Morels' pew. Her father took one for themselves once more. It was under the little gallery, opposite the Morels'. When Paul and his mother came in the chapel the Leivers's pew was always empty. He was anxious for fear she would not come: it was so far, and there were so many rainy Sundays. Then, often very late indeed, she came in, with her long stride, her head bowed, her face hidden under her hat of dark green velvet. Her face, as she sat opposite, was always in shadow. But it gave him a very keen feeling, as if all his soul stirred within him, to see her there. It was not the same glow, happiness, and pride, that he felt in having his mother in charge: something more wonderful, less human, and tinged to intensity by a pain, as if there were something he could not get to.

At this time he was beginning to question the orthodox creed. He was twenty-one, and she was twenty. She was beginning to dread the spring: he became so wild, and hurt her so much. All the way he went cruelly smashing her beliefs. Edgar enjoyed it. He was by nature critical and rather dispassionate. But Miriam suffered exquisite pain, as, with an intellect like a knife, the man she loved examined her religion in which she lived and moved and had her being. But he did not spare her. He was cruel. And when they went alone he was even more fierce, as if he would kill her soul. He bled her beliefs till she almost lost consciousness.

"She exults—she exults as she carries him off from me," Mrs. Morel cried in her heart when Paul had gone. "She's not like an ordinary woman, who can leave me my share in him. She wants to absorb him. She wants to draw him out and absorb him till there is nothing left of him, even for himself. He will never be a man on his own feet—she will suck him up." So the mother sat, and battled and brooded bitterly.

And he, coming home from his walks with Miriam, was wild with torture. He walked biting his lips and with clenched fists, going at a great rate. Then, brought up against a stile, he stood for some minutes, and did not move. There was a great hollow of darkness fronting him, and on the black up-slopes patches of tiny lights, and in the lowest trough of the night, a flare of the pit. It was all weird and dreadful. Why was he torn so, almost bewildered, and unable to move? Why did his mother sit at home and suffer? He knew she suffered badly. But why should she? And why did he hate Miriam, and feel so cruel towards her, at the thought of his mother. If Miriam caused his mother suffering, then he hated her—and he easily hated her. Why did she make him feel as if he were un-certain of himself, insecure, an indefinite thing, as if he had not sufficient sheathing to prevent the night and the space breaking into him? How he hated her! And then, what a rush of tenderness and humility!

Suddenly he plunged on again, running home. His mother saw on him the marks of some agony, and she said nothing. But he had to make her talk to him. Then she was angry with him for going so far with Miriam.

"Why don't you like her, mother?" he cried in despair.

"I don't know, my boy," she replied piteously. "I'm sure I've tried to like her. I've tried and tried, but I can't—I can't!"

And he felt dreary and hopeless between the two.

Spring was the worst time. He was changeable, and intense and cruel. So he decided to stay away from her. Then came the hours when he knew Miriam was expecting him. His mother watched him growing restless. He could not go on with his work. He could do nothing. It was as if something were drawing his soul out towards Willey Farm. Then he put on his hat and went, saying nothing. And his mother knew he was gone. And as soon as he was on the way he sighed with relief. And when he was with her he was cruel again.

One day in March he lay on the bank of Nethermere, with Miriam sitting beside him. It was a glistening, white-and-blue day. Big clouds, so brilliant, went by overhead, while shadows *he is uncomfortable with himself with both Mother & Miriam*

stole along on the water. The clear spaces in the sky were of clean, cold blue. Paul lay on his back in the old grass, looking up. He could not bear to look at Miriam. She seemed to want him, and he resisted. He resisted all the time. He wanted now to give her passion and tenderness, and he could not. He felt that she wanted the soul out of his body, and not him. All his strength and energy she drew into herself through some channel which united them. She did not want to meet him, so that there were two of them, man and woman together. She wanted to draw all of him into her. It urged him to an intensity like madness, which fascinated him, as drug-taking might.

He was discussing Michael Angelo. It felt to her as if she were fingering the very quivering tissue, the very protoplasm of life, as she heard him. It gave her deepest satisfaction. And in the end it frightened her. There he lay in the white intensity of his search, and his voice gradually filled her with fear, so level it was, almost inhuman, as if in a trance.

"Don't talk any more," she pleaded softly, laying her hand on his forehead.

He lay quite still, almost unable to move. His body was somewhere discarded.

"Why not? Are you tired?"

"Yes, and it wears you out."

He laughed shortly, realising.

"Yet you always make me like it," he said.

"I don't wish to," she said, very low.

"Not when you've gone too far, and you feel you can't bear it. But your unconscious self always asks it of me. And I suppose I want it."

He went on, in his dead fashion:

"If only you could want *me*, and not want what I can reel off for you!"

"I!" she cried bitterly—"I! Why, when would you let me take you?"

"Then it's my fault," he said, and, gathering himself together, he got up and began to talk trivialities. He felt insubstantial. In a vague way he hated her for it. And he knew he was as much to blame himself. This, however, did not prevent his hating her.

hates himself

One evening about this time he had walked along the home road with her. They stood by the pasture leading down to the

like modern psychotherapy

wood, unable to part. As the stars came out the clouds closed.
They had glimpses of their own constellation, Orion, towards
the west. His jewels glimmered for a moment, his dog ran
low, struggling with difficulty through the spume of cloud.

Orion was for them chief in significance among the con-
stellations. They had gazed at him in their strange, surcharged
hours of feeling, until they seemed themselves to live in every
one of his stars. This evening Paul had been moody and perverse. Orion had seemed just an ordinary constellation to him.
He had fought against his glamour and fascination. Miriam
was watching her lover's mood carefully. But he said nothing
that gave him away, till the moment came to part, when he
stood frowning gloomily at the gathered clouds, behind which
the great constellation must be striding still.

There was to be a little party at his house the next day, at
which she was to attend.

"I shan't come and meet you," he said.

"Oh, very well; it's not very nice out," she replied slowly.

"It's not that—only they don't like me to. They say I care
more for you than for them. And you understand, don't you?
You know it's only friendship."

Miriam was astonished and hurt for him. It had cost him
an effort. She left him, wanting to spare him any further
humiliation. A fine rain blew in her face as she walked along
the road. She was hurt deep down; and she despised him for
being blown about by any wind of authority. And in her
heart of hearts, unconsciously, she felt that he was trying to
get away from her. This she would never have acknowledged.
She pitied him.

At this time Paul became an important factor in Jordan's
warehouse. Mr. Pappleworth left to set up a business of his
own, and Paul remained with Mr. Jordan as Spiral overseer.
His wages were to be raised to thirty shillings at the year-end,
if things went well.

Still on Friday night Miriam often came down for her French
lesson. Paul did not go so frequently to Willey Farm, and she
grieved at the thought of her education's coming to end; moreover, they both loved to be together, in spite of discords.
So they read Balzac, and did compositions, and felt highly
cultured.

Friday night was reckoning night for the miners. Morel
"reckoned"—shared up the money of the stall—either in the

New Inn at Bretty or in his own house, according as his fellow-butties wished. Barker had turned a non-drinker, so now the men reckoned at Morel's house.

Annie, who had been teaching away, was at home again. She was still a tomboy; and she was engaged to be married. Paul was studying design.

Morel was always in good spirits on Friday evening, unless the week's earnings were small. He bustled immediately after his dinner, prepared to get washed. It was decorum for the women to absent themselves while the men reckoned. Women were not supposed to spy into such a masculine privacy as the butties' reckoning, nor were they to know the exact amount of the week's earnings. So, whilst her father was spluttering in the scullery, Annie went out to spend an hour with a neighbour. Mrs. Morel attended to her baking.

"Shut that doo-er!" bawled Morel furiously.

Annie banged it behind her, and was gone.

"If tha oppens it again while I'm weshin' me, I'll ma'e thy jaw rattle," he threatened from the midst of his soap-suds. Paul and the mother frowned to hear him.

Presently he came running out of the scullery, with the soapy water dripping from him, dithering with cold.

"Oh, my sirs!" he said. "Wheer's my towel?"

It was hung on a chair to warm before the fire, otherwise he would have bullied and blustered. He squatted on his heels before the hot baking-fire to dry himself.

"F-ff-f!" he went, pretending to shudder with cold .

"Goodness, man, don't be such a kid!" said Mrs. Morel. "It's *not* cold."

"Thee strip thysen stark nak'd to wesh thy flesh i' that scullery," said the miner, as he rubbed his hair; "nowt b'r a ice-'ouse!"

"And I shouldn't make that fuss," replied his wife.

"No, tha'd drop down stiff, as dead as a door-knob, wi' thy nesh sides."

"Why is a door-knob deader than anything else?" asked Paul, curious.

"Eh, I dunno; that's what they say," replied his father. "But there's that much draught i' yon scullery, as it blows through your ribs like through a five-barred gate."

"It would have some difficulty in blowing through yours," said Mrs. Morel.

Morel looked down ruefully at his sides.

"Me!" he exclaimed. "I'm nowt b'r a skinned rabbit. My bones fair juts out on me."

"I should like to know where," retorted his wife.

"Iv'ry-wheer! I'm nobbut a sack o' faggots."

Mrs. Morel laughed. He had still a wonderfully young body, muscular, without any fat. His skin was smooth and clear. It might have been the body of a man of twenty-eight, except that there were, perhaps, too many blue scars, like tattoo-marks, where the coal-dust remained under the skin, and that his chest was too hairy. But he put his hand on his side ruefully. It was his fixed belief that, because he did not get fat, he was as thin as a starved rat.

Paul looked at his father's thick, brownish hands all scarred, with broken nails, rubbing the fine smoothness of his sides, and the incongruity struck him. It seemed strange they were the same flesh.

"I suppose," he said to his father, "you had a good figure once."

"Eh!" exclaimed the miner, glancing round, startled and timid, like a child.

"He had," exclaimed Mrs. Morel, "if he didn't hurtle himself up as if he was trying to get in the smallest space he could."

"Me!" exclaimed Morel—"me a good figure! I wor niver much more n'r a skeleton."

"Man!" cried his wife, "don't be such a pulamiter!"

"'Strewth!" he said. "Tha's niver knowed me but what I looked as if I wor goin' off in a rapid decline."

She sat and laughed.

"You've had a constitution like iron," she said; "and never a man had a better start, if it was body that counted. You should have seen him as a young man," she cried suddenly to Paul, drawing herself up to imitate her husband's once handsome bearing.

Morel watched her shyly. He saw again the passion she had had for him. It blazed upon her for a moment. He was shy, rather scared, and humble. Yet again he felt his old glow. And then immediately he felt the ruin he had made during these years. He wanted to bustle about, to run away from it.

"Gi'e my back a bit of a wesh," he asked her.

His wife brought a well-soaped flannel and clapped it on his shoulders. He gave a jump.

"Eh, tha mucky little 'ussy!" he cried. "Cowd as death!"

"You ought to have been a salamander," she laughed, washing his back. It was very rarely she would do anything so personal for him. The children did those things.

"The next world won't be half hot enough for you," she added.

"No," he said; "tha'lt see as it's draughty for me."

But she had finished. She wiped him in a desultory fashion, and went upstairs, returning immediately with his shifting-trousers. When he was dried he struggled into his shirt. Then, ruddy and shiny, with hair on end, and his flannelette shirt hanging over his pit-trousers, he stood warming the garments he was going to put on. He turned them, he pulled them inside out, he scorched them.

"Goodness, man!" cried Mrs. Morel, "get dressed!"

"Should thee like to clap thysen into britches as cowd as a tub o' water?" he said.

At last he took off his pit-trousers and donned decent black. He did all this on the hearth-rug, as he would have done if Annie and her familiar friends had been present.

Mrs. Morel turned the bread in the oven. Then from the red earthenware panchion of dough that stood in a corner she took another handful of paste, worked it to the proper shape, and dropped it into a tin. As she was doing so Barker knocked and entered. He was a quiet, compact little man, who looked as if he would go through a stone wall. His black hair was cropped short, his head was bony. Like most miners, he was pale, but healthy and taut.

"Evenin', missis," he nodded to Mrs. Morel, and he seated himself with a sigh.

"Good-evening," she replied cordially.

"Tha's made thy heels crack," said Morel.

"I dunno as I have," said Barker.

He sat, as the men always did in Morel's kitchen, effacing himself rather.

"How's missis?" she asked of him.

He had told her some time back:

"We're expectin' us third just now, you see."

"Well," he answered, rubbing his head, "she keeps pretty middlin', I think."

"Let's see—when?" asked Mrs. Morel.

"Well, I shouldn't be surprised any time now."

"Ah! And she's kept fairly?"

"Yes, tidy."

"That's a blessing, for she's none too strong."

"No. An' I've done another silly trick."

"What's that?"

Mrs. Morel knew Barker wouldn't do anything very silly.

"I'm come be-out th' market-bag."

"You can have mine."

"Nay, you'll be wantin' that yourself."

"I shan't. I take a string bag always."

She saw the determined little collier buying in the week's groceries and meat on the Friday nights, and she admired him. "Barker's little, but he's ten times the man you are," she said to her husband.

Just then Wesson entered. He was thin, rather frail-looking, with a boyish ingenuousness and a slightly foolish smile, despite his seven children. But his wife was a passionate woman.

"I see you've kested me," he said, smiling rather vapidly.

"Yes," replied Barker.

The newcomer took off his cap and his big woollen muffler. His nose was pointed and red.

"I'm afraid you're cold, Mr. Wesson," said Mrs. Morel.

"It's a bit nippy," he replied.

"Then come to the fire."

"Nay, I s'll do where I am."

Both colliers sat away back. They could not be induced to come on to the hearth. The hearth is sacred to the family.

"Go thy ways i' th' arm-chair," cried Morel cheerily.

"Nay, thank yer; I'm very nicely here."

"Yes, come, of course," insisted Mrs. Morel.

He rose and went awkwardly. He sat in Morel's arm-chair awkwardly. It was too great a familiarity. But the fire made him blissfully happy.

"And how's that chest of yours?" demanded Mrs. Morel.

He smiled again, with his blue eyes rather sunny.

"Oh, it's very middlin'," he said.

"Wi' a rattle in it like a kettle-drum," said Barker shortly.

"T-t-t-t!" went Mrs. Morel rapidly with her tongue. "Did you have that flannel singlet made?"

"Not yet," he smiled.

"Then, why didn't you?" she cried.

"It'll come," he smiled.

"Ah, an' Doomsday!" exclaimed Barker.

Barker and Morel were both impatient of Wesson. But, then, they were both as hard as nails, physically.

When Morel was nearly ready he pushed the bag of money to Paul.

"Count it, boy," he asked humbly.

Paul impatiently turned from his books and pencil, tipped the bag upside down on the table. There was a five-pound bag of silver, sovereigns and loose money. He counted quickly, referred to the checks—the written papers giving amount of coal—put the money in order. Then Barker glanced at the checks.

Mrs. Morel went upstairs, and the three men came to table. Morel, as master of the house, sat in his arm-chair, with his back to the hot fire. The two butties had cooler seats. None of them counted the money.

"What did we say Simpson's was?" asked Morel; and the butties cavilled for a minute over the dayman's earnings. Then the amount was put aside.

"An' Bill Naylor's?"

This money also was taken from the pack.

Then, because Wesson lived in one of the company's houses, and his rent had been deducted, Morel and Barker took four-and-six each. And because Morel's coals had come, and the leading was stopped, Barker and Wesson took four shillings each. Then it was plain sailing. Morel gave each of them a sovereign till there were no more sovereigns; each half a crown till there were no more half-crowns; each a shilling till there were no more shillings. If there was anything at the end that wouldn't split, Morel took it and stood drinks.

Then the three men rose and went. Morel scuttled out of the house before his wife came down. She heard the door close, and descended. She looked hastily at the bread in the oven. Then, glancing on the table, she saw her money lying. Paul had been working all the time. But now he felt his mother counting the week's money, and her wrath rising.

"T-t-t-t!" went her tongue.

He frowned. He could not work when she was cross. She counted again.

"A measly twenty-five shillings!" she exclaimed. "How much was the cheque?"

"Ten pounds eleven," said Paul irritably. He dreaded what
was coming.

"And he gives me a scrattlin' twenty-five, an' his club this
week! But I know him. He thinks because *you're* earning he
needn't keep the house any longer. No, all he has to do with
his money is to guttle it. But I'll show him!"

"Oh, mother, don't!" cried Paul. — Paul is a good guy

"Don't what, I should like to know?" she exclaimed.

"Don't carry on again. I can't work."

She went very quiet.

"Yes, it's all very well," she said; "but how do you think
I'm going to manage?"

"Well, it won't make it any better to whittle about it."

"I should like to know what you'd do if you had it to put
up with."

"It won't be long. You can have my money. Let him go
to hell."

He went back to his work, and she tied her bonnet-strings
grimly. When she was fretted he could not bear it. But now
he began to insist on her recognizing him.

"The two loaves at the top," she said, "will be done in twenty
minutes. Don't forget them."

"All right," he answered; and she went to market.

He remained alone working. But his usual intense concentration became unsettled. He listened for the yard-gate. At a
quarter-past seven came a low knock, and Miriam entered.

"All alone?" she said.

"Yes."

As if at home, she took off her tam-o'-shanter and her long
coat, hanging them up. It gave him a thrill. This might be
their own house, his and hers. Then she came back and peered
over his work.

"What is it?" she asked.

"Still design, for decorating stuffs, and for embroidery."

She bent short-sightedly over the drawings.

It irritated him that she peered so into everything that was
his, searching him out. He went into the parlour and returned
with a bundle of brownish linen. Carefully unfolding it, he
spread it on the floor. It proved to be a curtain or *portière*,
beautifully stencilled with a design on roses.

"Ah, how beautiful!" she cried.

The spread cloth, with its wonderful reddish roses and dark

green stems, all so simple, and somehow so wicked-looking, lay
at her feet. She went on her knees before it, her dark curls
dropping. He saw her crouched voluptuously before his work,
and his heart beat quickly. Suddenly she looked up at him.

"Why does it seem cruel?" she asked.

"What?"

"There seems a feeling of cruelty about it," she said.

"It's jolly good, whether or not," he replied, folding up his
work with a lover's hands.

She rose slowly, pondering.

"And what will you do with it?" she asked.

"Send it to Liberty's. I did it for my mother, but I think
she'd rather have the money."

"Yes," said Miriam. He had spoken with a touch of bitterness, and Miriam sympathised. Money would have been
nothing to *her*.

He took the cloth back into the parlour. When he returned
he threw to Miriam a smaller piece. It was a cushion-cover
with the same design.

"I did that for you," he said.

She fingered the work with trembling hands, and did not
speak. He became embarrassed.

"By Jove, the bread!" he cried.

He took the top loaves out, tapped them vigorously. They
were done. He put them on the hearth to cool. Then he went
to the scullery, wetted his hands, scooped the last white dough
out of the punchion, and dropped it in a baking-tin. Miriam
was still bent over her painted cloth. He stood rubbing the bits
of dough from his hands.

"You do like it?" he asked.

She looked up at him, with her dark eyes one flame of love.
He laughed uncomfortably. Then he began to talk about the
design. There was for him the most intense pleasure in talking
about his work to Miriam. All his passion, all his wild blood,
went into this intercourse with her, when he talked and conceived his work. She brought forth to him his imaginations.
She did not understand, any more than a woman understands
when she conceives a child in her womb. But this was life for
her and for him.

While they were talking, a young woman of about twenty-
two, small and pale, hollow-eyed, yet with a relentless look
about her, entered the room. She was a friend at the Morel's.

"Take your things off," said Paul.

"No, I'm not stopping."

She sat down in the arm-chair opposite Paul and Miriam, who were on the sofa. Miriam moved a little farther from him. The room was hot, with a scent of new bread. Brown, crisp loaves stood on the hearth.

"I shouldn't have expected to see you here to-night, Miriam Leivers," said Beatrice wickedly.

"Why not?" murmured Miriam huskily.

"Why, let's look at your shoes."

Miriam remained uncomfortably still.

"If tha doesna tha durs'na," laughed Beatrice.

Miriam put her feet from under her dress. Her boots had that queer, irresolute, rather pathetic look about them, which showed how self-conscious and self-mistrustful she was. And they were covered with mud.

"Glory! You're a positive muck-heap," exclaimed Beatrice. "Who cleans your boots?"

"I clean them myself."

"Then you wanted a job," said Beatrice. "It would ha' taken a lot of men to ha' brought me down here to-night. But love laughs at sludge, doesn't it, 'Postle my duck?"

"*Inter alia*," he said.

"Oh, Lord! are you going to spout foreign languages? What does it mean, Miriam?"

There was a fine sarcasm in the last question, but Miriam did not see it.

" 'Among other things,' I believe," she said humbly.

Beatrice put her tongue between her teeth and laughed wickedly.

" 'Among other things,' 'Postle?" she repeated. "Do you mean love laughs at mothers, and fathers, and sisters, and brothers, and men friends, and lady friends, and even at the b'loved himself?"

She affected a great innocence.

"In fact, it's one big smile," he replied.

"Up its sleeve, 'Postle Morel—you believe me," she said; and she went off into another burst of wicked, silent laughter.

Miriam sat silent, withdrawn into herself. Every one of Paul's friends delighted in taking sides against her, and he left her in the lurch—seemed almost to have a sort of revenge upon her then.

"Are you still at school?" asked Miriam of Beatrice.

"Yes."

"You've not had your notice, then?"

"I expect it at Easter."

"Isn't it an awful shame, to turn you off merely because you didn't pass the exam.?"

"I don't know," said Beatrice coldly.

"Agatha says you're as good as any teacher anywhere. It seems to me ridiculous. I wonder why you didn't pass."

"Short of brains, eh, 'Postle?" said Beatrice briefly.

"Only brains to bite with," replied Paul, laughing.

"Nuisance!" she cried; and, springing from her seat, she rushed and boxed his ears. She had beautiful small hands. He held her wrists while she wrestled with him. At last she broke free, and seized two handfuls of his thick, dark brown hair, which she shook.

"Beat!" he said, as he pulled his hair straight with his fingers. "I hate you!"

She laughed with glee.

"Mind!" she said. "I want to sit next to you."

"I'd as lief be neighbours with a vixen," he said, nevertheless making place for her between him and Miriam.

"Did it ruffle his pretty hair, then!" she cried; and, with her hair-comb, she combed him straight. "And his nice little moustache!" she exclaimed. She tilted his head back and combed his young moustache. "It's a wicked moustache, 'Postle," she said. "It's a red for danger. Have you got any of those cigarettes?"

He pulled his cigarette-case from his pocket. Beatrice looked inside it.

"And fancy me having Connie's last cig.," said Beatrice, putting the thing between her teeth. He held a lit match to her, and she puffed daintily.

"Thanks so much, darling," she said mockingly.

It gave her a wicked delight.

"Don't you think he does it nicely, Miriam?" she asked.

"Oh, very!" said Miriam.

He took a cigarette for himself.

"Light, old boy?" said Beatrice, tilting her cigarette at him.

He bent forward to her to light his cigarette at hers. She was winking at him as he did so. Miriam saw his eyes trembling with mischief, and his full, almost sensual, mouth quivering.

He was not himself, and she could not bear it. As he was
now, she had no connection with him; she might as well not
have existed. She saw the cigarette dancing on his full red
lips. She hated his thick hair for being tumbled loose on his
forehead.

"Sweet boy!" said Beatrice, tipping up his chin and giving
him a little kiss on the cheek.

"I s'll kiss thee back, Beat," he said.

"Tha wunna!" she giggled, jumping up and going away.
"Isn't he shameless, Miriam?"

"Quite," said Miriam. "By the way, aren't you forgetting
the bread?"

"By Jove!" he cried, flinging open the oven door.

Out puffed the bluish smoke and a smell of burned
bread.

"Oh, golly!" cried Beatrice, coming to his side. He crouched
before the oven, she peered over his shoulder. "This is what
comes of the oblivion of love, my boy."

Paul was ruefully removing the loaves. One was burnt black
on the hot side; another was hard as a brick.

"Poor mater!" said Paul.

"You want to grate it," said Beatrice. "Fetch me the nutmeg-
grater."

She arranged the bread in the oven. He brought the grater,
and she grated the bread on to a newspaper on the table. He
set the doors open to blow away the smell of burned bread.
Beatrice grated away, puffing her cigarette, knocking the char-
coal off the poor loaf.

"My word, Miriam! you're in for it this time," said Beatrice.

"I!" exclaimed Miriam in amazement.

"You'd better be gone when his mother comes in. I know
why King Alfred burned the cakes. Now I see it! 'Postle
would fix up a tale about his work making him forget, if he
thought it would wash. If that old woman had come in a bit
sooner, she'd have boxed the brazen thing's ears who made
the oblivion, instead of poor Alfred's."

She giggled as she scraped the loaf. Even Miriam laughed in
spite of herself. Paul mended the fire ruefully.

The garden gate was heard to bang.

"Quick!" cried Beatrice, giving Paul the scraped loaf. "Wrap
it up in a damp towel."

Paul disappeared into the scullery. Beatrice hastily blew her scrapings into the fire, and sat down innocently. Annie came bursting in. She was an abrupt, quite smart young woman. She blinked in the strong light.

"Smell of burning!" she exclaimed.

"It's the cigarettes," replied Beatrice demurely.

"Where's Paul?"

Leonard had followed Annie. He had a long comic face and blue eyes, very sad.

"I suppose he's left you to settle it between you," he said. He nodded sympathetically to Miriam, and became gently sarcastic to Beatrice.

"No," said Beatrice, "he's gone off with number nine."

"I just met number five inquiring for him," said Leonard.

"Yes—we're going to share him up like Solomon's baby," said Beatrice.

Annie laughed.

"Oh, ay," said Leonard. "And which bit should you have?"

"I don't know," said Beatrice. "I'll let all the others pick first."

"An' you'd have the leavings, like?" said Leonard, twisting up a comic face.

Annie was looking in the oven. Miriam sat ignored. Paul entered.

"This bread's a fine sight, our Paul," said Annie.

"Then you should stop an' look after it," said Paul.

"You mean *you* should do what you're reckoning to do," replied Annie.

"He should, shouldn't he!" cried Beatrice.

"I s'd think he'd got plenty on hand," said Leonard.

"You had a nasty walk, didn't you, Miriam?" said Annie.

"Yes—but I'd been in all week——"

"And you wanted a bit of a change, like," insinuated Leonard kindly.

"Well, you can't be stuck in the house for ever," Annie agreed. She was quite amiable. Beatrice pulled on her coat, and went out with Leonard and Annie. She would meet her own boy.

"Don't forget that bread, our Paul," cried Annie. "Good-night, Miriam. I don't think it will rain."

When they had all gone, Paul fetched the swathed loaf, unwrapped it, and surveyed it sadly.

"It's a mess!" he said.

"But," answered Miriam impatiently, "what is it, after all—twopence ha'penny."

"Yes, but—it's the mater's precious baking, and she'll take it to heart. However, it's no good bothering."

He took the loaf back into the scullery. There was a little distance between him and Miriam. He stood balanced opposite her for some moments considering, thinking of his behaviour with Beatrice. He felt guilty inside himself, and yet glad. For some inscrutable reason it served Miriam right. He was not going to repent. She wondered what he was thinking of as he stood suspended. His thick hair was tumbled over his forehead. Why might she not push it back for him, and remove the marks of Beatrice's comb? Why might she not press his body with her two hands. It looked so firm, and every whit living. And he would let other girls, why not her?

Suddenly he started into life. It made her quiver almost with terror as he quickly pushed the hair off his forehead and came towards her.

"Half-past eight!" he said. "We'd better buck up. Where's your French?"

Miriam shyly and rather bitterly produced her exercise-book. Every week she wrote for him a sort of diary of her inner life, in her own French. He had found this was the only way to get her to do compositions. And her diary was mostly a love-letter. He would read it now; she felt as if her soul's history were going to be desecrated by him in his present mood. He sat beside her. She watched his hand, firm and warm, rigorously scoring her work. He was reading only the French, ignoring her soul that was there. But gradually his hand forgot its work. He read in silence, motionless. She quivered.

" 'Ce matin les oiseaux m'ont éveillé,' " he read. " 'Il faisait encore un crépuscule. Mais la petite fenêtre de ma chambre était blême, et puis, jaûne, et tous les oiseaux du bois éclatèrent dans un chanson vif et résonnant. Toute l'aûbe tressaillit. J'avais rêvé de vous. Est-ce que vous voyez aussi l'aûbe? Les oiseaux m'éveillent presque tous les matins, et toujours il y a quelque chose de terreur dans le cri des grives. Il est si clair——' "

Miriam sat tremulous, half ashamed. He remained quite still, trying to understand. He only knew she loved him. He was afraid of her love for him. It was too good for him, and he

Paul

was inadequate. His own love was at fault, not hers. Ashamed,
he corrected her work, humbly writing above her words.

"Look," he said quietly, "the past participle conjugated with
avoir agrees with the direct object when it precedes."

She bent forward, trying to see and to understand. Her free,
fine curls tickled his face. He started as if they had been red
hot, shuddering. He saw her peering forward at the page, her
red lips parted piteously, the black hair springing in fine
strands across her tawny, ruddy cheek. She was coloured
like a pomegranate for richness. His breath came short as he
watched her. Suddenly she looked up at him. Her dark eyes
were naked with their love, afraid, and yearning. His eyes,
too, were dark, and they hurt her. They seemed to master
her. She lost all her self-control, was exposed in fear. And
he knew, before he could kiss her, he must drive something
out of himself. And a touch of hate for her crept back again
into his heart. He returned to her exercise.

Suddenly he flung down the pencil, and was at the oven in
a leap, turning the bread. For Miriam he was too quick. She
started violently, and it hurt her with real pain. Even the way
he crouched before the oven hurt her. There seemed to be
something cruel in it, something cruel in the swift way he
pitched the bread out of the tins, caught it up again. If only
he had been gentle in his movements she would have felt so
rich and warm. As it was, she was hurt.

He returned and finished the exercise.

"You've done well this week," he said.

She saw he was flattered by her diary. It did not repay her
entirely.

"You really do blossom out sometimes," he said. "You ought
to write poetry."

She lifted her head with joy, then she shook it mistrustfully.

"I don't trust myself," she said.

"You should try!"

Again she shook her head.

"Shall we read, or is it too late?" he asked.

"It is late—but we can read just a little," she pleaded.

She was really getting now the food for her life during the
next week. He made her copy Baudelaire's "Le Balcon". Then
he read it for her. His voice was soft and caressing, but growing almost brutal. He had a way of lifting his lips and showing his teeth, passionately and bitterly, when he was much

moved. This he did now. It made Miriam feel as if he were
trampling on her. She dared not look at him, but sat with her
head bowed. She could not understand why he got into such
a tumult and fury. It made her wretched. She did not like
Baudelaire, on the whole—nor Verlaine.

"Behold her singing in the field
Yon solitary highland lass."

That nourished her heart. So did "Fair Ines". And—

"It was a beauteous evening, calm and pure,
And breathing holy quiet like a nun."

These were like herself. And there was he, saying in his
throat bitterly:

"Tu te rappelleras la beauté des caresses."

The poem was finished; he took the bread out of the oven,
arranging the burnt loaves at the bottom of the panchion, the
good ones at the top. The desiccated loaf remained swathed
up in the scullery.

"Mater needn't know till morning," he said. "It won't upset
her so much then as at night."

Miriam looked in the bookcase, saw what postcards and
letters he had received, saw what books were there. She took
one that had interested him. Then he turned down the gas and
they set off. He did not trouble to lock the door.

He was not home again until a quarter to eleven. His mother
was seated in the rocking-chair. Annie, with a rope of hair
hanging down her back, remained sitting on a low stool before
the fire, her elbows on her knees, gloomily. On the table stood
the offending loaf unswathed. Paul entered rather breathless.
No one spoke. His mother was reading the little local newspaper. He took off his coat, and went to sit down on the sofa.
His mother moved curtly aside to let him pass. No one spoke.
He was very uncomfortable. For some minutes he sat pretending to read a piece of paper he found on the table. Then——

"I forgot that bread, mother," he said.

There was no answer from either woman.

"Well," he said, "it's only twopence ha'penny. I can pay
you for that."

Being angry, he put three pennies on the table and slid them towards his mother. She turned away her head. Her mouth was shut tightly.

Poor Mama

"Yes," said Annie, "you don't know how badly my mother is!"

The girl sat staring glumly into the fire.

"Why is she badly?" asked Paul, in his overbearing way.

"Well!" said Annie. "She could scarcely get home."

He looked closely at his mother. She looked ill.

"*Why* could you scarcely get home?" he asked her, still sharply. She would not answer.

"I found her as white as a sheet sitting here," said Annie, with a suggestion of tears in her voice.

"Well, *why*?" insisted Paul. His brows were knitting, his eyes dilating passionately.

"It was enough to upset anybody," said Mrs. Morel, "hugging those parcels—meat, and green-groceries, and a pair of curtains——"

"Well, why *did* you hug them; you needn't have done."

"Then who would?"

"Let Annie fetch the meat."

"Yes, and I *would* fetch the meat, but how was I to know. You were off with Miriam, instead of being in when my mother came."

"And what was the matter with you?" asked Paul of his mother.

"I suppose it's my heart," she replied. Certainly she looked bluish round the mouth.

"And have you felt it before?"

"Yes—often enough."

"Then why haven't you told me?—and why haven't you seen a doctor?"

Mrs. Morel shifted in her chair, angry with him for his hectoring.

"You'd never notice anything," said Annie. "You're too eager to be off with Miriam."

"Oh, am I—and any worse than you with Leonard?"

"*I* was in at a quarter to ten."

There was silence in the room for a time.

"I should have thought," said Mrs. Morel bitterly, "that she wouldn't have occupied you so entirely as to burn a whole ovenful of bread."

She is very possesive

"Beatrice was here as well as she."

"Very likely. But we know why the bread is spoilt."

"Why?" he flashed.

"Because you were engrossed with Miriam," replied Mrs. Morel hotly.

"Oh, very well—then it was *not*!" he replied angrily.

He was distressed and wretched. Seizing a paper, he began to read. Annie, her blouse unfastened, her long ropes of hair twisted into a plait, went up to bed, bidding him a very curt good-night.

Paul sat pretending to read. He knew his mother wanted to upbraid him. He also wanted to know what had made her ill, for he was troubled. So, instead of running away to bed, as he would have liked to do, he sat and waited. There was a tense silence. The clock ticked loudly.

"You'd better go to bed before your father comes in," said the mother harshly. "And if you're going to have anything to eat, you'd better get it."

"I don't want anything."

It was his mother's custom to bring him some trifle for supper on Friday night, the night of luxury for the colliers. He was too angry to go and find it in the pantry this night. This insulted her.

"If I *wanted* you to go to Selby on Friday night, I can imagine the scene," said Mrs. Morel. "But you're never too tired to go if *she* will come for you. Nay, you neither want to eat nor drink then."

"I can't let her go alone."

"Can't you? And why does she come?"

"Not because I ask her."

"She doesn't come without you want her——"

"Well, what if I *do* want her——" he replied.

"Why, nothing, if it was sensible or reasonable. But to go trapseing up there miles and miles in the mud, coming home at midnight, and got to go to Nottingham in the morning——"

"If I hadn't, you'd be just the same."

"Yes, I should, because there's no sense in it. Is she *so* fascinating that you must follow her all that way?" Mrs. Morel was bitterly sarcastic. She sat still, with averted face, stroking with a rhythmic, jerked movement, the black sateen of her apron. It was a movement that hurt Paul to see.

"I do like her," he said, "but——"

"*Like* her!" said Mrs. Morel, in the same biting tones. "It seems to me you like nothing and nobody else. There's neither Annie, nor me, nor anyone now for you."

"What nonsense, mother—you know I don't love her—I—I tell you I *don't* love her—she doesn't even walk with my arm, because I don't want her to."

"Then why do you fly to her so often?"

"I *do* like to talk to her—I never said I didn't. But I *don't* love her."

"Is there nobody else to talk to?"

"Not about the things we talk of. There's a lot of things that you're not interested in, that——"

"What things?"

Mrs. Morel was so intense that Paul began to pant.

"Why—painting—and books. *You* don't care about Herbert Spencer."

"No," was the sad reply. "And *you* won't at my age."

"Well, but I do now—and Miriam does——"

"And how do you know," Mrs. Morel flashed defiantly, "that *I* shouldn't. Do you ever try me!"

"But you don't, mother, you know you don't care whether a picture's decorative or not; you don't care what *manner* it is in."

"How do you know I don't care? Do you ever try me? Do you ever talk to me about these things, to try?"

"But it's not that that matters to you, mother, you know t's not."

"What is it, then—what is it, then, that matters to me?" she flashed. He knitted his brows with pain.

"You're old, mother, and we're young."

He only meant that the interests of *her* age were not the interests of his. But he realised the moment he had spoken that he had said the wrong thing.

"Yes, I know it well—I am old. And therefore I may stand aside; I have nothing more to do with you. You only want me to wait on you—the rest is for Miriam."

He could not bear it. Instinctively he realised that he was life to her. And, after all, she was the chief thing to him, the only supreme thing.

"You know it isn't, mother, you know it isn't!"

She was moved to pity by his cry.

"It looks a great deal like it," she said, half putting aside her despair.

"No, mother—I really *don't* love her. I talk to her, but I want to come home to you."

He had taken off his collar and tie, and rose, bare-throated, to go to bed. As he stooped to kiss his mother, she threw her arms round his neck, hid her face on his shoulder, and cried, in a whimpering voice, so unlike her own that he writhed in agony:

"I can't bear it. I could let another woman—but not her. She'd leave me no room, not a bit of room——"

And immediately he hated Miriam bitterly.

"And I've never—you know, Paul—I've never had a husband —not really——"

He stroked his mother's hair, and his mouth was on her throat.

"And she exults so in taking you from me—she's not like ordinary girls."

"Well, I don't love her, mother," he murmured, bowing his head and hiding his eyes on her shoulder in misery. His mother kissed him a long, fervent kiss.

"My boy!" she said, in a voice trembling with passionate love.

Without knowing, he gently stroked her face.

"There," said his mother, "now go to bed. You'll be *so* tired in the morning." As she was speaking she heard her husband coming. "There's your father—now go." Suddenly she looked at him almost as if in fear. "Perhaps I'm selfish. If you want her, take her, my boy."

His mother looked so strange, Paul kissed her, trembling.

"Ha—mother!" he said softly.

Morel came in, walking unevenly. His hat was over one corner of his eye. He balanced in the doorway.

"At your mischief again?" he said venomously.

Mrs. Morel's emotion turned into sudden hate of the drunkard who had come in thus upon her.

"At any rate, it is sober," she said.

"H'm—h'm! h'm—h'm!" he sneered. He went into the passage, hung up his hat and coat. Then they heard him go down three steps to the pantry. He returned with a piece of pork-pie in his fist. It was what Mrs. Morel had bought for her son.

"Nor was that bought for you. If you can give me no more than twenty-five shillings, I'm sure I'm not going to buy you pork-pie to stuff, after you've swilled a bellyful of beer."

"Wha-at—wha-at!" snarled Morel, toppling in his balance. "Wha-at—not for me?" He looked at the piece of meat and crust, and suddenly, in a vicious spurt of temper, flung it into the fire.

Hate for father

Paul started to his feet.

"Waste your own stuff!" he cried.

"What—what!" suddenly shouted Morel, jumping up and clenching his fist. "I'll show yer, yer young jockey!"

"All right!" said Paul viciously, putting his head on one side. "Show me!"

He would at that moment dearly have loved to have a smack at something. Morel was half crouching, fists up, ready to spring. The young man stood, smiling with his lips.

"Ussha!" hissed the father, swiping round with a great stroke just past his son's face. He dared not, even though so close, really touch the young man, but swerved an inch away.

"Right!" said Paul, his eyes upon the side of his father's mouth, where in another instant his fist would have hit. He ached for that stroke. But he heard a faint moan from behind. His mother was deadly pale and dark at the mouth. Morel was dancing up to deliver another blow.

"Father!" said Paul, so that the word rang.

Morel started, and stood at attention.

"Mother!" moaned the boy. "Mother!"

She began to struggle with herself. Her open eyes watched him, although she could not move. Gradually she was coming to herself. He laid her down on the sofa, and ran upstairs for a little whisky, which at last she could sip. The tears were hopping down his face. As he kneeled in front of her he did not cry, but the tears ran down his face quickly. Morel, on the opposite side of the room, sat with his elbows on his knees glaring across.

"What's a-matter with 'er?" he asked.

"Faint!" replied Paul.

"H'm!"

The elderly man began to unlace his boots. He stumbled off to bed. His last fight was fought in that home.

Paul kneeled there, stroking his mother's hand.

"Don't be poorly, mother—don't be poorly!" he said time after time.

"It's nothing, my boy," she murmured.

At last he rose, fetched in a large piece of coal, and raked the fire. Then he cleared the room, put everything straight, laid the things for breakfast, and brought his mother's candle.

"Can you go to bed, mother?"

"Yes, I'll come."

"Sleep with Annie, mother, not with him."

"No. I'll sleep in my own bed."

"Don't sleep with him, mother."

"I'll sleep in my own bed."

She rose, and he turned out the gas, then followed her closely upstairs, carrying her candle. On the landing he kissed her close.

"Good-night, mother."

"Good-night!" she said.

He pressed his face upon the pillow in a fury of misery. And yet, somewhere in his soul, he was at peace because he still loved his mother best. It was the bitter peace of resignation.

The efforts of his father to conciliate him next day were a great humiliation to him.

Everybody tried to forget the scene. — It was too really

CHAPTER IX

DEFEAT OF MIRIAM

PAUL was dissatisfied with himself and with everything. The deepest of his love belonged to his mother. When he felt he had hurt her, or wounded his love for her, he could not bear it. Now it was spring, and there was battle between him and Miriam. This year he had a good deal against her. She was vaguely aware of it. The old feeling that she was to be a sacrifice to this love, which she had had when she prayed, was mingled in all her emotions. She did not at the bottom believe she ever would have him. She did not believe in herself primarily: doubted whether she could ever be what he would demand of her. Certainly she never saw herself living happily through a lifetime with him. She saw tragedy, sorrow, and sacrifice ahead. And in sacrifice she was proud, in renunciation she was strong, for she did not trust herself to support everyday life. She was prepared for the big things and the deep things, like tragedy. It was the sufficiency of the small day-life she could not trust.

The Easter holidays began happily. Paul was his own frank self. Yet she felt it would go wrong. On the Sunday afternoon she stood at her bedroom window, looking across at the oak-trees of the wood, in whose branches a twilight was tangled, below the bright sky of the afternoon. Grey-green rosettes of honeysuckle leaves hung before the window, some already, she fancied, showing bud. It was spring, which she loved and dreaded.

Hearing the clack of the gate she stood in suspense. It was a bright grey day. Paul came into the yard with his bicycle, which glittered as he walked. Usually he rang his bell and laughed towards the house. To-day he walked with shut lips and cold, cruel bearing, that had something of a slouch and a sneer in it. She knew him well by now, and could tell from that keen-looking, aloof young body of his what was happening inside him. There was a cold correctness in the way he put his bicycle in its place, that made her heart sink.

She came downstairs nervously. She was wearing a new net blouse that she thought became her. It had a high collar with a tiny ruff, reminding her of Mary, Queen of Scots, and making her, she thought, look wonderfully a woman, and dignified. At twenty she was full-breasted and luxuriously formed. Her face was still like a soft rich mask, unchangeable. But her eyes, once lifted, were wonderful. She was afraid of him. He would notice her new blouse.

He, being in a hard, ironical mood, was entertaining the family to a description of a service given in the Primitive Methodist Chapel, conducted by one of the well-known preachers of the sect. He sat at the head of the table, his mobile face, with the eyes that could be so beautiful, shining with tenderness or dancing with laughter, now taking on one expression and then another, in imitation of various people he was mocking. His mockery always hurt her; it was too near the reality. He was too clever and cruel. She felt that when his eyes were like this, hard with mocking hate, he would spare neither himself nor anybody else. But Mrs. Leivers was wiping her eyes with laughter, and Mr. Leivers, just awake from his Sunday nap, was rubbing his head in amusement. The three brothers sat with ruffled, sleepy appearance in their shirt-sleeves, giving a guffaw from time to time. The whole family loved a "take-off" more than anything.

He took no notice of Miriam. Later, she saw him remark her new blouse, saw that the artist approved, but it won from him not a spark of warmth. She was nervous, could hardly reach the teacups from the shelves.

When the men went out to milk, she ventured to address him personally.

"You were late," she said.

"Was I?" he answered.

There was silence for a while.

"Was it rough riding?" she asked.

"I didn't notice it."

She continued quickly to lay the table. When she had finished——

"Tea won't be for a few minutes. Will you come and look at the daffodils?" she said.

He rose without answering. They went out into the back garden under the budding damson-trees. The hills and the sky were clean and cold. Everything looked washed, rather hard. Miriam glanced at Paul. He was pale and impassive. It seemed cruel to her that his eyes and brows, which she loved, could look so hurting.

"Has the wind made you tired?" she asked. She detected an underneath feeling of weariness about him.

"No, I think not," he answered.

"It must be rough on the road—the wood moans so."

"You can see by the clouds it's a south-west wind; that helps me here."

"You see, I don't cycle, so I don't understand," she murmured.

"Is there need to cycle to know that!" he said.

She thought his sarcasms were unnecessary. They went forward in silence. Round the wild, tussocky lawn at the back of the house was a thorn hedge, under which daffodils were craning forward from among their sheaves of grey-green blades. The cheeks of the flowers were greenish with cold. But still some had burst, and their gold ruffled and glowed. Miriam went on her knees before one cluster, took a wild-looking daffodil between her hands, turned up its face of gold to her, and bowed down, caressing it with her mouth and cheeks and brow. He stood aside, with his hands in his pockets, watching her. One after another she turned up to him the faces of the yellow, bursten flowers appealingly, fondling them lavishly all the while.

"Aren't they magnificent?" she murmured.

"Magnificent! It's a bit thick—they're pretty!"

She bowed again to her flowers at his censure of her praise. He watched her crouching, sipping the flowers with fervid kisses.

"Why must you always be fondling things?" he said irritably.

"But I love to touch them," she replied, hurt.

"Can you never like things without clutching them as if you wanted to pull the heart out of them? Why don't you have a bit more restraint, or reserve, or something?"

She looked up at him full of pain, then continued slowly to stroke her lips against a ruffled flower. Their scent, as she smelled it, was so much kinder than he; it almost made her cry.

"You wheedle the soul out of things," he said. "I would never wheedle—at any rate, I'd go straight."

He scarcely knew what he was saying. These things came from him mechanically. She looked at him. His body seemed one weapon, firm and hard against her.

"You're always begging things to love you," he said, "as if you were a beggar for love. Even the flowers, you have to fawn on them——"

Rhythmically, Miriam was swaying and stroking the flower with her mouth, inhaling the scent which ever after made her shudder as it came to her nostrils.

"You don't want to love—your eternal and abnormal craving is to be loved. You aren't positive, you're negative. You absorb, absorb, as if you must fill yourself up with love, because you've got a shortage somewhere."

She was stunned by his cruelty, and did not hear. He had not the faintest notion of what he was saying. It was as if his fretted, tortured soul, run hot by thwarted passion, jetted off these sayings like sparks from electricity. She did not grasp anything he said. She only sat crouched beneath his cruelty and his hatred of her. She never realised in a flash. Over everything she brooded and brooded.

After tea he stayed with Edgar and the brothers, taking no notice of Miriam. She, extremely unhappy on this looked-for holiday, waited for him. And at last he yielded and came to her. She was determined to track this mood of his to its origin. She counted it not much more than a mood.

"Shall we go through the wood a little way?" she asked him, knowing he never refused a direct request.

They went down to the warren. On the middle path they passed a trap, a narrow horseshoe hedge of small fir-boughs, baited with the guts of a rabbit. Paul glanced at it frowning. She caught his eye.

"Isn't it dreadful?" she asked.

"I don't know! Is it worse than a weasel with its teeth in a rabbit's throat? One weasel or many rabbits? One or the other must go!"

He was taking the bitterness of life badly. She was rather sorry for him.

"We will go back to the house," he said. "I don't want to walk out."

They went past the lilac-tree, whose bronze leaf-buds were coming unfastened. Just a fragment remained of the haystack, a monument squared and brown, like a pillar of stone. There was a little bed of hay from the last cutting.

"Let us sit here a minute," said Miriam.

He sat down against his will, resting his back against the hard wall of hay. They faced the amphitheatre of round hills that glowed with sunset, tiny white farms standing out, the meadows golden, the woods dark and yet luminous, tree-tops folded over tree-tops, distinct in the distance. The evening had cleared, and the east was tender with a magenta flush under which the land lay still and rich.

"Isn't it beautiful?" she pleaded.

But he only scowled. He would rather have had it ugly just then.

At that moment a big bull-terrier came rushing up, open-mouthed, pranced his two paws on the youth's shoulders, licking his face. Paul drew back, laughing. Bill was a great relief to him. He pushed the dog aside, but it came leaping back.

"Get out," said the lad, "or I'll dot thee one."

But the dog was not to be pushed away. So Paul had a little battle with the creature, pitching poor Bill away from him, who, however, only floundered tumultously back again, wild with joy. The two fought together, the man laughing grudgingly, the dog grinning all over. Miriam watched them. There was something pathetic about the man. He wanted so badly to love, to be tender. The rough way he bowled the dog over was really loving. Bill got up, panting with happiness, his brown eyes rolling in his white face, and lumbered back again. He adored Paul. The lad frowned.

"Bill, I've had enough o' thee," he said.

But the dog only stood with two heavy paws, that quivered with love, upon his thigh, and flickered a red tongue at him. He drew back.

"No," he said—"no—I've had enough."

And in a minute the dog trotted off happily, to vary the fun.

He remained staring miserably across at the hills, whose still beauty he begrudged. He wanted to go and cycle with Edgar. Yet he had not the courage to leave Miriam.

"Why are you sad?" she asked humbly.

"I'm not sad; why should I be," he answered. "I'm only normal."

She wondered why he always claimed to be normal when he was disagreeable.

"But what is the matter?" she pleaded, coaxing him soothingly.

"Nothing!"

"Nay!" she murmured.

He picked up a stick and began to stab the earth with it.

"You'd far better not talk," he said.

"But I wish to know——" she replied.

He laughed resentfully.

"You always do," he said.

"It's not fair to me," she murmured.

He thrust, thrust, thrust at the ground with the pointed stick, digging up little clods of earth as if he were in a fever of irritation. She gently and firmly laid her hand on his wrist.

"Don't!" she said. "Put it away."

He flung the stick into the currant-bushes, and leaned back. Now he was bottled up.

"What is it?" she pleaded softly.

He lay perfectly still, only his eyes alive, and they full of torment.

"You know," he said at length, rather wearily—"you know —we'd better break off."

It was what she dreaded. Swiftly everything seemed to darken before her eyes.

"Why!" she murmured. "What has happened?"

"Nothing has happened. We only realise where we are. It's no good——"

She waited in silence, sadly, patiently. It was no good being impatient with him. At any rate, he would tell her now what ailed him.

"We agreed on friendship," he went on in a dull, monotonous voice. "How often *have* we agreed for friendship! And yet— it neither stops there, nor gets anywhere else."

He was silent again. She brooded. What did he mean? He was so wearying. There was something he would not yield. Yet she must be patient with him.

"I can only give friendship—it's all I'm capable of—it's a flaw in my make-up. The thing overbalances to one side—I hate a toppling balance. Let us have done."

There was warmth of fury in his last phrases. He meant she loved him more than he her. Perhaps he could not love her. Perhaps she had not in herself that which he wanted. It was the deepest motive of her soul, this self-mistrust. It was so deep she dared neither realise nor acknowledge. Perhaps she was deficient. Like an infinitely subtle shame, it kept her always back. If it were so, she would do without him. She would never let herself want him. She would merely see.

"But what has happened?" she said.

"Nothing—it's all in myself—it only comes out just now. We're always like this towards Easter-time."

He grovelled so helplessly, she pitied him. At least she never floundered in such a pitiable way. After all, it was he who was chiefly humiliated.

"What do you want?" she asked him.

"Why—I mustn't come often—that's all. Why should I monopolise you when I'm not—— You see, I'm deficient in something with regard to you——"

He was telling her he did not love her, and so ought to leave her a chance with another man. How foolish and blind and shamefully clumsy he was! What were other men to her! What were men to her at all! But he, ah! she loved his soul. Was *he* deficient in something? Perhaps he was.

"But I don't understand," she said huskily. "Yesterday——"

The night was turning jangled and hateful to him as the twilight faded. And she bowed under her suffering.

"I know," he cried, "you never will! You'll never believe

that I can't—can't physically, any more than I can fly up like a skylark——"

"What?" she murmured. Now she dreaded.

"Love you."

He hated her bitterly at that moment because he made her suffer. Love her! She knew he loved her. He really belonged to her. This about not loving her, physically, bodily, was a mere perversity on his part, because he knew she loved him. He was stupid like a child. He belonged to her. His soul wanted her. She guessed somebody had been influencing him. She felt upon him the hardness, the foreignness of another influence.

"What have they been saying at home?" she asked.

"It's not that," he answered.

And then she knew it was. She despised them for their commonness, his people. They did not know what things were really worth.

He and she talked very little more that night. After all he left her to cycle with Edgar.

He had come back to his mother. Hers was the strongest tie in his life. When he thought round, Miriam shrank away. There was a vague, unreal feel about her. And nobody else mattered. There was one place in the world that stood solid and did not melt into unreality: the place where his mother was. Everybody else could grow shadowy, almost non-existent to him, but she could not. It was as if the pivot and pole of his life, from which he could not escape, was his mother.

And in the same way she waited for him. In him was established her life now. After all, the life beyond offered very little to Mrs. Morel. She saw that our chance for *doing* is here, and doing counted with her. Paul was going to prove that she had been right; he was going to make a man whom nothing should shift off his feet; he was going to alter the face of the earth in some way which mattered. Wherever he went she felt her soul went with him. Whatever he did she felt her soul stood by him, ready, as it were, to hand him his tools. She could not bear it when he was with Miriam. William was dead. She would fight to keep Paul.

And he came back to her. And in his soul was a feeling of the satisfaction of self-sacrifice because he was faithful to her. She loved him first; he loved her first. And yet it was not enough. His new young life, so strong and imperious, was urged towards something else It made him mad with restlessness. She saw this, and wished bitterly that Miriam had been a woman who could take this new life of his, and leave her the roots. He fought against his mother almost as he fought against Miriam.

It was a week before he went again to Willey Farm. Miriam had suffered a great deal, and was afraid to see him again. Was she now to endure the ignominy of his abandoning her? That would only be superficial and temporary. He would come back. She held the keys to his soul. But meanwhile, how he would torture her with his battle against her. She shrank from it.

Paul to Miriam

However, the Sunday after Easter he came to tea. Mrs. Leivers was glad to see him. She gathered something was fretting him, that he found things hard. He seemed to drift to her for comfort. And she was good to him. She did him that great kindness of treating him almost with reverence.

He met her with the young children in the front garden.

"I'm glad you've come," said the mother, looking at him with her great appealing brown eyes. "It is such a sunny day. I was just going down the fields for the first time this year."

He felt she would like him to come. That soothed him. They went, talking simply, he gentle and humble. He could have wept with gratitude that she was deferential to him. He was feeling humiliated.

At the bottom of the Mow Close they found a thrush's nest.

"Shall I show you the eggs?" he said.

"Do!" replied Mrs. Leivers. "They seem *such* a sign of spring, and so hopeful."

He put aside the thorns, and took out the eggs, holding them in the palm of his hand.

"They are quite hot—I think we frightened her off them," he said.

"Ay, poor thing!" said Mrs. Leivers.

Miriam could not help touching the eggs, and his hand which, it seemed to her, cradled them so well.

"Isn't it a strange warmth!" she murmured, to get near him.

"Blood heat," he answered.

She watched him putting them back, his body pressed against the hedge, his arm reaching slowly through the thorns, his hand folded carefully over the eggs. He was concentrated on the act. Seeing him so, she loved him; he seemed so simple and sufficient to himself. And she could not get to him.

After tea she stood hesitating at the bookshelf. He took "Tartarin de Tarascon". Again they sat on the bank of hay at the foot of the stack. He read a couple of pages, but without any heart for it. Again the dog came racing up to repeat the fun of the other day. He shoved his muzzle in the man's chest. Paul fingered his ear for a moment. Then he pushed him away.

"Go away, Bill," he said. "I don't want you."

Bill slunk off, and Miriam wondered and dreaded what was coming. There was a silence about the youth that made her still with apprehension. It was not his furies, but his quiet resolutions that she feared.

Turning his face a little to one side, so that she could not see him, he began, speaking slowly and painfully:

"Do you think—if I didn't come up so much—you might get to like somebody else—another man?"

So this was what he was still harping on.

"But I don't know any other men. Why do you ask?" she replied, in a low tone that should have been a reproach to him.

"Why," he blurted, "because they say I've no right to come up like this—without we mean to marry——"

Miriam was indignant at anybody's forcing the issues between them. She had been furious with her own father for suggesting to Paul, laughingly, that he knew why he came so much.

"Who says?" she asked, wondering if her people had anything to do with it. They had not.

"Mother—and the others. They say at this rate everybody will consider me engaged, and I ought to consider myself so, because it's not fair to you. And I've tried to find out—and I don't think I love you as a man ought to love his wife. What do *you* think about it?"

Miriam bowed her head moodily. She was angry at having this struggle. People should leave him and her alone.

"I don't know," she murmured.

"Do you think we love each other enough to marry?" he asked definitely. It made her tremble.

"No," she answered truthfully. "I don't think so—we're too young."

"I thought perhaps," he went on miserably, "that you, with your intensity in things, might have given me more—than I could ever make up to you. And even now—if you think it better—we'll be engaged."

Now Miriam wanted to cry. And she was angry, too. He was always such a child for people to do as they liked with.

"No, I don't think so," she said firmly.

He pondered a minute.

"You see," he said, "with me—I don't think one person would ever monopolize me—be everything to me—I think never."

This she did not consider.

"No," she murmured. Then, after a pause, she looked at him, and her dark eyes flashed.

"This is your mother," she said. "I know she never liked me."

"No, no, it isn't," he said hastily. "It was for your sake she spoke this time. She only said, if I was going on, I ought to consider myself engaged." There was a silence. "And if I ask you to come down any time, you won't stop away, will you?"

She did not answer. By this time she was very angry.

"Well, what shall we do?" she said shortly. "I suppose I'd better drop French. I was just beginning to get on with it. But I suppose I can go on alone."

"I don't see that we need," he said. "I can give you a French lesson, surely."

"Well—and there are Sunday nights. I shan't stop coming to chapel, because I enjoy it, and it's all the social life I get. But you've no need to come home with me. I can go alone."

"All right," he answered, rather taken aback. "But if I ask Edgar, he'll always come with us, and then they can say nothing."

There was silence. After all, then, she would not lose much. For all their talk down at his home there would not be much difference. She wished they would mind their own business.

"And you won't think about it, and let it trouble you, will you?" he asked.

"Oh no," replied Miriam, without looking at him.

He was silent. She thought him unstable. He had no fixity of purpose, no anchor of righteousness that held him.

"Because," he continued, "a man gets across his bicycle—and goes to work—and does all sorts of things. But a woman broods."

"No, I shan't bother," said Miriam. And she meant it.

It had gone rather chilly. They went indoors.

"How white Paul looks!" Mrs. Leivers exclaimed. "Miriam,

you shouldn't have let him sit out of doors. Do you think you've taken cold, Paul?"

"Oh, no!" he laughed.

But he felt done up. It wore him out, the conflict in himself. Miriam pitied him now. But quite early, before nine o'clock, he rose to go.

"You're not going home, are you?" asked Mrs. Leivers anxiously.

"Yes," he replied. "I said I'd be early." He was very awkward.

"But this *is* early," said Mrs. Leivers.

Miriam sat in the rocking-chair, and did not speak. He hesitated, expecting her to rise and go with him to the barn as usual for his bicycle. She remained as she was. He was at a loss.

"Well—good-night, all!" he faltered.

She spoke her good-night along with all the others. But as he went past the window he looked in. She saw him pale, his brows knit slightly in a way that had become constant with him, his eyes dark with pain.

She rose and went to the doorway to wave good-bye to him as he passed through the gate. He rode slowly under the pine-trees, feeling a cur and a miserable wretch. His bicycle went tilting down the hills at random. He thought it would be a relief to break one's neck.

Two days later he sent her up a book and a little note, urging her to read and be busy.

At this time he gave all his friendship to Edgar. He loved the family so much, he loved the farm so much; it was the dearest place on earth to him. His home was not so lovable. It was his mother. But then he would have been just as happy with his mother anywhere. Whereas Willey Farm he loved passionately. He loved the little pokey kitchen, where men's boots tramped, and the dog slept with one eye open for fear of being trodden on; where the lamp hung over the table at night, and everything was so silent. He loved Miriam's long, low parlour, with its atmosphere of romance, its flowers, its books, its high rosewood piano. He loved the gardens and the buildings that stood with their scarlet roofs on the naked edges of the fields, crept towards the wood as if for cosiness, the wild country scooping down a valley and up the uncultured hills of the other side. Only to be there was an exhilaration and a joy to him. He loved Mrs. Leivers, with her unworldliness and her quaint cynicism; he loved Mr. Leivers, so warm and young and lovable; he loved Edgar, who lit up when he came, and the boys and the children and Bill—even the sow Circe and the Indian game-cock called Tippoo. All this besides Miriam. He could not give it up.

So he went as often, but he was usually with Edgar. Only all the family, including the father, joined in charades and games at evening. And later, Miriam drew them together, and they read "Macbeth" out of penny books, taking parts. It was great excitement. Miriam was glad, and Mrs. Leivers was glad, and Mr. Leivers enjoyed it. Then they all learned songs together from tonic sol-fa, singing in a circle round the fire. But now Paul was very rarely alone with Miriam. She waited. When she and Edgar and he walked home together from chapel or from the literary society in Bestwood, she knew his talk, so passionate and so unorthodox nowadays, was for her. She did envy Edgar, however, his cycling with Paul, his Friday nights, his days working in the fields. For her Friday nights and her French lessons were gone. She was nearly always alone, walking, pondering in the wood, reading, studying, dreaming, waiting. And he wrote to her frequently.

One Sunday evening they attained to their old rare harmony. Edgar had stayed to Communion—he wondered what it was like—with Mrs. Morel. So Paul came on alone with Miriam to his home. He was more or less under her spell again. As usual, they were discussing the sermon. He was setting now full sail towards Agnosticism, but such a religious Agnosticism that Miriam did not suffer so badly. They were at the Renan "Vie de Jésus" stage. Miriam was the threshing-floor on which he threshed out all his beliefs. While he trampled his ideas upon her soul, the truth came out for him. She alone was his threshing-floor. She alone helped him towards realization. Almost impassive, she submitted to his argument and expounding. And somehow, because of her, he gradually realized where he was wrong. And what he realized, she realized. She felt he could not do without her.

They came to the silent house. He took the key out of the scullery window, and they entered. All the time he went on with his discussion. He lit the gas, mended the fire, and brought her some cakes from the pantry. She sat on the sofa, quietly, with a plate on her knee. She wore a large white hat with some pinkish flowers. It was a cheap hat, but he liked it. Her face beneath was still and pensive, golden-brown and ruddy. Always her ears were hid in her short curls. She watched him.

She liked him on Sundays. Then he wore a dark suit that showed the lithe movement of his body. There was a clean, clear-cut look about him. He went on with his thinking to her. Suddenly he reached for a Bible. Miriam liked the way he reached up—so sharp, straight to the mark. He turned the pages quickly, and read her a chapter of St. John. As he sat in the arm-chair reading, intent, his voice only thinking, she felt as if he were using her unconsciously as a man uses his tools at some work he is bent on. She loved it. And the wistfulness of his voice was like a reaching to something, and it was as if she were what he reached with. She sat back on the sofa away from him, and yet feeling herself the very instrument his hand grasped. It gave her great pleasure.

Then he began to falter and to get self-conscious. And when he came to the verse, "A woman, when she is in travail, hath sorrow because her hour is come", he missed it out. Miriam had felt him growing uncomfortable. She shrank when the well-known words did not follow. He went on reading, but she did not hear. A grief and shame made her bend her head. Six months ago he would have read it simply. Now there was a scotch in his running with her. Now she felt there was really something hostile between them, something of which they were ashamed.

She ate her cake mechanically. He tried to go on with his argument, but could not get back the right note. Soon Edgar came in. Mrs. Morel had gone to her friends'. The three set off to Willey Farm.

Miriam brooded over his split with her. There was something else he wanted. He could not be satisfied; he could give her no peace. There was between them now always a ground for strife. She wanted to prove him. She believed that his chief need in life was herself. If she could prove it, both to herself and to him, the rest might go; she could simply trust to the future.

So in May she asked him to come to Willey Farm and meet Mrs. Dawes. There was something he hankered after. She saw him, whenever they spoke of Clara Dawes, rouse and get slightly angry. He said he did not like her. Yet he was keen to know about her. Well, he should put himself to the test.

She believed that there were in him desires for higher things, and desires for lower, and that the desire for the higher would conquer. At any rate, he should try. She forgot that her "higher" and "lower" were arbitrary.

He was rather excited at the idea of meeting Clara at Willey Farm. Mrs. Dawes came for the day. Her heavy, dun-coloured hair was coiled on top of her head. She wore a white blouse and navy skirt, and somehow, wherever she was, seemed to make things look paltry and insignificant. When she was in the room, the kitchen seemed too small and mean altogether. Miriam's beautiful twilighty parlour looked stiff and stupid. All the Leivers were eclipsed like candles. They found her rather hard to put up with. Yet she was perfectly amiable, but indifferent, and rather hard.

Paul did not come till afternoon. He was early. As he swung off his bicycle, Miriam saw him look round at the house eagerly. He would be disappointed if the visitor had not come. Miriam went out to meet him, bowing her head because of the sunshine. Nasturtiums were coming out crimson under the cool green shadow of their leaves. The girl stood, dark-haired, glad to see him.

"Hasn't Clara come?" he asked.

"Yes," replied Miriam in her musical tone. "She's reading."

He wheeled his bicycle into the barn. He had put on a handsome tie, of which he was rather proud, and socks to match.

"She came this morning?" he asked.

"Yes," replied Miriam, as she walked at his side. "You said you'd bring me that letter from the man at Liberty's. Have you remembered?"

"Oh, dash, no!" he said. "But nag at me till you get it."

"I don't like to nag at you."

"Do it whether or not. And is she any more agreeable?" he continued.

"You know I always think she is quite agreeable."

He was silent. Evidently his eagerness to be early to-day had been the newcomer. Miriam already began to suffer. They went together towards the house. He took the clips off his trousers, but was too lazy to brush the dust from his shoes, in spite of the socks and tie.

Clara sat in the cool parlour reading. He saw the nape of her white neck, and the fine hair lifted from it. She rose, looking at him indifferently. To shake hands she lifted her arm straight, in a manner that seemed at once to keep him at a distance, and yet to fling something to him. He noticed how her breasts swelled inside her blouse, and how her shoulder curved handsomely under the thin muslin at the top of her arm.

"You have chosen a fine day," he said.

"It happens so," she said.

"Yes," he said; "I am glad."

She sat down, not thanking him for his politeness.

"What have you been doing all morning?" asked Paul of Miriam.

"Well, you see," said Miriam, coughing huskily, "Clara only came with father—and so—she's not been here very long."

Clara sat leaning on the table, holding aloof. He noticed her hands were large, but well kept. And the skin on them seemed almost coarse, opaque, and white, with fine golden hairs. She did not mind if he observed her hands. She intended to scorn him. Her heavy arm lay negligently on the table. Her mouth was closed as if she were offended, and she kept her face slightly averted.

"You were at Margaret Bonford's meeting the other evening," he said to her.

Miriam did not know this courteous Paul. Clara glanced at him.

"Yes," she said.

"Why," asked Miriam, "how do you know?"

"I went in for a few minutes before the train came," he answered.

Clara turned away again rather disdainfully.

"I think she's a lovable little woman," said Paul.

"Margaret Bonford!" exclaimed Clara. "She's a great deal cleverer than most men."

"Well, I didn't say she wasn't," he said, deprecating. "She's lovable for all that."

"And, of course, that is all that matters," said Clara witheringly.

He rubbed his head, rather perplexed, rather annoyed.

"I suppose it matters more than her cleverness," he said; "which, after all, would never get her to heaven."

"It's not heaven she wants to get—it's her fair share on earth," retorted Clara. She spoke as if he were responsible for some deprivation which Miss Bonford suffered.

"Well," he said, "I thought she was warm, and awfully nice—only too frail. I wished she was sitting comfortably in peace——"

" 'Darning her husband's stockings,' " said Clara scathingly.

"I'm sure she wouldn't mind darning even my stockings," he said. "And I'm sure she'd do them well. Just as I wouldn't mind blacking her boots if she wanted me to."

But Clara refused to answer this sally of his. He talked to Miriam for a little while. The other woman held aloof.

"Well," he said, "I think I'll go and see Edgar. Is he on the land?"

"I believe," said Miriam, "he's gone for a load of coal. He should be back directly."

"Then," he said, "I'll go and meet him."

Miriam dared not propose anything for the three of them. He rose and left them.

On the top road, where the gorse was out, he saw Edgar walking lazily beside the mare, who nodded her white-starred forehead as she dragged the clanking load of coal. The young farmer's face lighted up as he saw his friend. Edgar was good-looking, with dark, warm eyes. His clothes were old and rather disreputable, and he walked with considerable pride.

"Hello!" he said, seeing Paul bareheaded. "Where are you going?"

"Came to meet you. Can't stand 'Nevermore'."

Edgar's teeth flashed in a laugh of amusement.

"Who is 'Nevermore'?" he asked.

"The lady—Mrs. Dawes—it ought to be Mrs. The Raven that quothed 'Nevermore'."

Edgar laughed with glee.

"Don't you like her?" he asked.

"Not a fat lot," said Paul. "Why, do you?"

"No!" The answer came with a deep ring of conviction. "No!" Edgar pursed up his lips. "I can't say she's much in my line." He mused a little. Then: "But why do you call her 'Nevermore'?" he asked.

"Well," said Paul, "if she looks at a man she says haughtily 'Nevermore', and if she looks at herself in the looking-glass she says disdainfully 'Nevermore', and if she thinks back she says it in disgust, and if she looks forward she says it cynically."

gorse

Edgar considered this speech, failed to make much out of it, and said, laughing:

"You think she's a man-hater?"

"*She* thinks she is," replied Paul.

"But you don't think so?"

"No," replied Paul.

"Wasn't she nice with you, then?"

"Could you imagine her *nice* with anybody?" asked the young man.

Edgar laughed. Together they unloaded the coal in the yard. Paul was rather self-conscious, because he knew Clara could see if she looked out of the window. She didn't look.

On Saturday afternoons the horses were brushed down and groomed. Paul and Edgar worked together, sneezing with the dust that came from the pelts of Jimmy and Flower.

"Do you know a new song to teach me?" said Edgar.

He continued to work all the time. The back of his neck was sun-red when he bent down, and his fingers that held the brush were thick. Paul watched him sometimes.

" 'Mary Morrison'?" suggested the younger.

Edgar agreed. He had a good tenor voice, and he loved to learn all the songs his friend could teach him, so that he could sing whilst he was carting. Paul had a very indifferent baritone voice, but a good ear. However, he sang softly, for fear of Clara. Edgar repeated the line in a clear tenor. At times they both broke off to sneeze, and first one, then the other, abused his horse.

Miriam was impatient of men. It took so little to amuse them—even Paul. She thought it anomalous in him that he could be so thoroughly absorbed in a triviality.

It was tea-time when they had finished.

"What song was that?" asked Miriam.

Edgar told her. The conversation turned to singing.

"We have such jolly times," Miriam said to Clara.

Mrs. Dawes ate her meal in a slow, dignified way. Whenever the men were present she grew distant.

"Do you like singing?" Miriam asked her.

"If it is good," she said.

Paul, of course, coloured.

"You mean if it is high-class and trained?" he said.

"I think a voice needs training before the singing is anything," she said.

"You might as well insist on having people's voices trained before you allowed them to talk," he replied. "Really, people sing for their own pleasure, as a rule."

"And it may be for other people's discomfort."

"Then the other people should have flaps to their ears," he replied.

The boys laughed. There was a silence. He flushed deeply, and ate in silence.

After tea, when all the men had gone but Paul, Mrs. Leivers said to Clara:

"And you find life happier now?"

"Infinitely."

"And you are satisfied?"

"So long as I can be free and independent." — Clara

"And you don't *miss* anything in your life?" asked Mrs. Leivers gently.

"I've put all that behind me."

Paul had been feeling uncomfortable during this discourse. He got up.

"You'll find you're always tumbling over the things you've put behind you," he said. Then he took his departure to the cow-sheds. He felt he had been witty, and his manly pride was high. He whistled as he went down the brick track.

Miriam came for him a little later to know if he would go with Clara and her for a walk. They set off down to Strelley Mill Farm. As they were going beside the brook, on the Willey Water side, looking through the brake at the edge of the wood, where pink campions glowed under a few sunbeams, they saw, beyond the tree-trunks and the thin hazel bushes, a man leading a great bay horse through the gullies. The big red beast seemed to dance romantically through that dimness of green hazel drift, away there where the air was shadowy, as if it were in the past, among the fading bluebells that might have bloomed for Deidre or Iseult.

The three stood charmed.

"What a treat to be a knight," he said, "and to have a pavilion here."

"And to have us shut up safely?" replied Clara.

"Yes," he answered, "singing with your maids at your broidery. I would carry your banner of white and green and heliotrope. I would have 'W.S.P.U.' emblazoned on my shield, beneath a woman rampant."

There are shifts of mood in the book. Warmth verse discord

"I have no doubt," said Clara, "that you would much rather fight for a woman than let her fight for herself."

"I would. When she fights for herself she seems like a dog before a looking-glass, gone into a mad fury with its own shadow."

"And *you* are the looking-glass?" she asked, with a curl of the lip.

"Or the shadow," he replied.

"I am afraid," she said, "that you are too clever."

"Well, I leave it to you to be *good*," he retorted, laughing. "Be good, sweet maid, and just let *me* be clever."

But Clara wearied of his flippancy. Suddenly, looking at her, he saw that the upward lifting of her face was misery and not scorn. His heart grew tender for everybody. He turned and was gentle with Miriam, whom he had neglected till then.

At the wood's edge they met Limb, a thin, swarthy man of forty, tenant of Strelley Mill, which he ran as a cattle-raising farm. He held the halter of the powerful stallion indifferently, as if he were tired. The three stood to let him pass over the stepping-stones of the first brook. Paul admired that so large an animal should walk on such springy toes, with an endless excess of vigour. Limb pulled up before them.

"Tell your father, Miss Leivers," he said, in a peculiar piping voice, "that his young beas'es 'as broke that bottom fence three days an' runnin'."

"Which?" asked Miriam, tremulous.

The great horse breathed heavily, shifting round its red flanks, and looking suspiciously with its wonderful big eyes upwards from under its lowered head and falling mane.

"Come along a bit," replied Limb, "an' I'll show you."

The man and the stallion went forward. It danced sideways, shaking its white fetlocks and looking frightened, as it felt itself in the brook.

"No hanky-pankyin'," said the man affectionately to the beast.

It went up the bank in little leaps, then splashed finely through the second brook. Clara, walking with a kind of sulky abandon, watched it half-fascinated, half-contemptuous. Limb stopped and pointed to the fence under some willows.

"There, you see where they got through," he said. "My man's druv 'em back three times."

swarthy

"Yes," answered Miriam, colouring as if she were at fault.

"Are you comin' in?" asked the man.

"No, thanks; but we should like to go by the pond."

"Well, just as you've a mind," he said.

The horse gave little whinneys of pleasure at being so near home.

"He is glad to be back," said Clara, who was interested in the creature.

"Yes—'e's been a tidy step to-day."

They went through the gate, and saw approaching them from the big farm-house a smallish, dark, excitable-looking woman of about thirty-five. Her hair was touched with grey, her dark eyes looked wild. She walked with her hands behind her back. Her brother went forward. As it saw her, the big bay stallion whinneyed again. She came up excitedly.

"Are you home again, my boy!" she said tenderly to the horse, not to the man. The great beast shifted round to her, ducking his head. She smuggled into his mouth the wrinkled yellow apple she had been hiding behind her back, then she kissed him near the eyes. He gave a big sigh of pleasure. She held his head in her arms against her breast.

"Isn't he splendid!" said Miriam to her.

Miss Limb looked up. Her dark eyes glanced straight at Paul.

"Oh, good-evening, Miss Leivers," she said. "It's ages since you've been down."

Miriam introduced her friends.

"Your horse *is* a fine fellow!" said Clara.

"Isn't he!" Again she kissed him. "As loving as any man!"

"More loving than most men, I should think," replied Clara. — *of the horse*

"He's a nice boy!" cried the woman, again embracing the horse.

Clara, fascinated by the big beast, went up to stroke his neck.

"He's quite gentle," said Miss Limb. "Don't you think big fellows are?"

"He's a beauty!" replied Clara.

She wanted to look in his eyes. She wanted him to look at her.

"It's a pity he can't talk," she said.

"Oh, but he can—all but," replied the other woman.

Then her brother moved on with the horse.

"Are you coming in? *Do* come in, Mr.—I didn't catch it."

"Morel," said Miriam. "No, we won't come in, but we should like to go by the mill-pond."

"Yes—yes, do. Do you fish, Mr. Morel?"

"No," said Paul.

"Because if you do you might come and fish any time," said Miss Limb. "We scarcely see a soul from week's end to week's end. I should be thankful."

"What fish are there in the pond?" he asked.

They went through the front garden, over the sluice, and up the steep bank to the pond, which lay in shadow, with its two wooded islets. Paul walked with Miss Limb.

"I shouldn't mind swimming here," he said.

"Do," she replied. "Come when you like. My brother will be awfully pleased to talk with you. He is so quiet, because there is no one to talk to. Do come and swim."

Clara came up.

"It's a fine depth," she said, "and so clear."

"Yes," said Miss Limb.

"Do you swim?" said Paul. "Miss Limb was just saying we could come when we liked."

"Of course there's the farm-hands," said Miss Limb.

They talked a few moments, then went on up the wild hill, leaving the lonely, haggard-eyed woman on the bank.

The hillside was all ripe with sunshine. It was wild and tussocky, given over to rabbits. The three walked in silence. Then:

"She makes me feel uncomfortable," said Paul.

"You mean Miss Limb?" asked Miriam. "Yes."

"What's a matter with her? Is she going dotty with being too lonely?"

"Yes," said Miriam. "It's not the right sort of life for her. I think it's cruel to bury her there. I really ought to go and see her more. But—she upsets me."

"She makes me feel sorry for her—yes, and she bothers me," he said.

"I suppose," blurted Clara suddenly, "she wants a man."

The other two were silent for a few moments.

"But it's the loneliness sends her cracked," said Paul.

Clara did not answer, but strode on uphill. She was walking with her hand hanging, her legs swinging as she kicked through the dead thistles and the tussocky grass, her arms hanging loose. Rather than walking, her handsome body seemed to be blundering up the hill. A hot wave went over Paul. He was curious about her. Perhaps life had been cruel to her. He forgot Miriam, who was walking beside him talking to him. She glanced at him, finding he did not answer her. His eyes were fixed ahead on Clara.

"Do you still think she is disagreeable?" she asked.

He did not notice that the question was sudden. It ran with his thoughts.

"Something's the matter with her," he said.

"Yes," answered Miriam.

They found at the top of the hill a hidden wild field, two sides of which were backed by the wood, the other sides by high loose hedges of hawthorn and elder bushes. Between these overgrown bushes were gaps that the cattle might have walked through had there been any cattle now. There the turf was smooth as velveteen, padded and holed by the rabbits. The field itself was coarse, and crowded with tall, big cowslips that had never been cut. Clusters of strong flowers rose everywhere above the coarse tussocks of bent. It was like a roadstead crowded with tall, fairy shipping.

"Ah!" cried Miriam, and she looked at Paul, her dark eyes dilating. He smiled. Together they enjoyed the field of flowers. Clara, a little way off, was looking at the cowslips disconsolately. Paul and Miriam stayed close together, talking in subdued tones. He kneeled on one knee, quickly gathering the best blossoms, moving from tuft to tuft restlessly, talking softly all the time. Miriam plucked the flowers lovingly, lingering over them. He always seemed to her too quick and almost scientific. Yet his bunches had a natural beauty more than hers. He loved them, but as if they were his and he had a right to them. She had more reverence for them: they held something she had not.

The flowers were very fresh and sweet. He wanted to drink them. As he gathered them, he ate the little yellow trumpets. Clara was still wandering about disconsolately. Going towards her, he said:

"Why don't you get some?"

"I don't believe in it. They look better growing."

"But you'd like some?"

"They want to be left."

"I don't believe they do."

"I don't want the corpses of flowers about me," she said.

"That's a stiff, artificial notion," he said. "They don't die any quicker in water than on their roots. And besides, they *look* nice in a bowl—they look jolly. And you only call a thing a corpse because it looks corpse-like."

"Whether it is one or not?" she argued.

"It isn't one to me. A dead flower isn't a corpse of a flower."

Clara now ignored him.

"And even so—what right have you to pull them?" she asked.

"Because I like them, and want them—and there's plenty of them."

"And that is sufficient?"

"Yes. Why not? I'm sure they'd smell nice in your room in Nottingham."

"And I should have the pleasure of watching them die."

"But then—it does not matter if they do die."

Whereupon he left her, and went stooping over the clumps of tangled flowers which thickly sprinkled the field like pale, luminous foam-clots. Miriam had come close. Clara was kneeling, breathing some scent from the cowslips.

"I think," said Miriam, "if you treat them with reverence you don't do them any harm. It is the spirit you pluck them in that matters."

"Yes," he said. "But no, you get 'em because you want 'em, and that's all." He held out his bunch.

Miriam was silent. He picked some more.

"Look at these!" he continued; "sturdy and lusty like little trees and like boys with fat legs."

Clara's hat lay on the grass not far off. She was kneeling, bending forward still to smell the flowers. Her neck gave him a sharp pang, such a beautiful thing, yet not proud of itself just now. Her breasts swung slightly in her blouse. The arching curve of her back was beautiful and strong; she wore no stays. Suddenly, without knowing, he was scattering a handful of cowslips over her hair and neck, saying:

"Ashes to ashes, and dust to dust,
If the Lord won't have you the devil must."

The chill flowers fell on her neck. She looked up at him, with almost pitiful, scared grey eyes, wondering what he was doing. Flowers fell on her face, and she shut her eyes.

Suddenly, standing there above her, he felt awkward.

"I thought you wanted a funeral," he said, ill at ease.

Clara laughed strangely, and rose, picking the cowslips from her hair. She took up her hat and pinned it on. One flower had remained tangled in her hair. He saw, but would not tell her. He gathered up the flowers he had sprinkled over her.

At the edge of the wood the bluebells had flowed over into the field and stood there like flood-water. But they were fading now. Clara strayed up to them. He wandered after her. The bluebells pleased him.

"Look how they've come out of the wood!" he said.

Then she turned with a flash of warmth and of gratitude.

"Yes," she smiled.

His blood beat up.

"It makes me think of the wild men of the woods, how terrified they would be when they got breast to breast with the open space."

"Do you think they were?" she asked.

"I wonder which was more frightened among old tribes—those bursting out of their darkness of woods upon all the space of light, or those from the open tiptoeing into the forests."

"I should think the second," she answered.

"Yes, you *do* feel like one of the open space sort, trying to force yourself into the dark, don't you?"

"How should I know?" she answered queerly.

The conversation ended there.

The evening was deepening over the earth. Already the valley was full of shadow. One tiny square of light stood opposite at Crossleigh Bank Farm. Brightness was swimming on the tops of the hills. Miriam came up slowly, her face in her big, loose bunch of flowers, walking ankle-deep through the scattered froth of the cowslips. Beyond her the trees were coming into shape, all shadow.

"Shall we go?" she asked.

And the three turned away. They were all silent. Going down the path they could see the light of home right across, and on the ridge of the hill a thin dark outline with little lights, where the colliery village touched the sky.

"It has been nice, hasn't it?" he asked.

Miriam murmured assent. Clara was silent.

"Don't you think so?" he persisted.

But she walked with her head up, and still did not answer. He could tell by the way she moved, as if she didn't care, that she suffered.

Change in time

At this time Paul took his mother to Lincoln. She was bright and enthusiastic as ever, but as he sat opposite her in the railway carriage, she seemed to look frail. He had a momentary sensation as if she were slipping away from him. Then he wanted to get hold of her, to fasten her, almost to chain her. He felt he must keep hold of her with his hand.

They drew near to the city. Both were at the window looking for the cathedral.

"There she is, mother!" he cried.

They saw the great cathedral lying couchant above the plain.

"Ah!" she exclaimed. "So she is!"

He looked at his mother. Her blue eyes were watching the cathedral quietly. She seemed again to be beyond him. Something in the eternal repose of the uplifted cathedral, blue and noble against the sky, was reflected in her, something of the fatality. What was, *was*. With all his young will he could not alter it. He saw her face, the skin still fresh and pink and downy, but crow's-feet near her eyes, her eyelids steady, sinking a little, her mouth always closed with disillusion; and there was on her the same eternal look, as if she knew fate at last. He beat against it with all the strength of his soul.

"Look, mother, how big she is above the town! Think, there are streets and streets below her! She looks bigger than the city altogether."

"So she does!" exclaimed his mother, breaking bright into life again. But he had seen her sitting, looking steady out of the window at the cathedral, her face and eyes fixed, reflecting the relentlessness of life. And the crow's-feet near her eyes, and her mouth shut so hard, made him feel he would go mad.

They ate a meal that she considered wildly extravagant.

"Don't imagine I like it," she said, as she ate her cutlet. "I *don't* like it, I really don't! Just *think* of your money wasted!"

"You never mind my money," he said. "You forget I'm a fellow taking his girl for an outing."

And he bought her some blue violets.

"Stop it at once, sir!" she commanded. "How can I do it?"

"You've got nothing to do. Stand still!"

couchant

And in the middle of High Street he stuck the flowers in her coat.

"An old thing like me!" she said, sniffing.

"You see," he said, "I want people to think we're awful swells. So look ikey."

"I'll jowl your head," she laughed.

"Strut!" he commanded. "Be a fantail pigeon."

It took him an hour to get her through the street. She stood above Glory Hole, she stood before Stone Bow, she stood everywhere, and exclaimed.

A man came up, took off his hat, and bowed to her.

"Can I show you the town, madam?"

"No, thank you," she answered. "I've got my son."

Then Paul was cross with her for not answering with more dignity.

"You go away with you!" she exclaimed. "Ha! that's the Jew's House. Now, do you remember that lecture, Paul——?"

But she could scarcely climb the cathedral hill. He did not notice. Then suddenly he found her unable to speak. He took her into a little public-house, where she rested.

"It's nothing," she said. "My heart is only a bit old; one must expect it."

He did not answer, but looked at her. Again his heart was crushed in a hot grip. He wanted to cry, he wanted to smash things in fury.

They set off again, pace by pace, so slowly. And every step seemed like a weight on his chest. He felt as if his heart would burst. At last they came to the top. She stood enchanted, looking at the castle gate, looking at the cathedral front. She had quite forgotten herself.

"Now *this* is better than I thought it could be!" she cried.

But he hated it. Everywhere he followed her, brooding. They sat together in the cathedral. They attended a little service in the choir. She was timid.

"I suppose it is open to anybody?" she asked him.

"Yes," he replied. "Do you think they'd have the damned cheek to send us away."

"Well, I'm sure," she exclaimed, "they would if they heard your language."

Her face seemed to shine again with joy and peace during the service. And all the time he was wanting to rage and smash things and cry.

Afterwards, when they were leaning over the wall, looking at the town below, he blurted suddenly:

"Why can't a man have a *young* mother? What is she old for?"

"Well," his mother laughed, "she can scarcely help it."

"And why wasn't I the oldest son? Look—they say the young ones have the advantage—but look, *they* had the young mother. You should have had me for your eldest son."

"*I* didn't arrange it," she remonstrated. "Come to consider, you're as much to blame as me."

He turned on her, white, his eyes furious.

"What are you old for!" he said, mad with his impotence. "Why can't you walk? *Why* can't you come with me to places?"

"At one time," she replied, "I could have run up that hill a good deal better than you."

"What's the good of that to *me*?" he cried, hitting his fist on the wall. Then he became plaintive. "It's too bad of you to be ill, Little, it is——"

"Ill!" she cried. "I'm a bit old, and you'll have to put up with it, that's all."

They were quiet. But it was as much as they could bear. They got jolly again over tea. As they sat by Brayford, watching the boats, he told her about Clara. His mother asked him innumerable questions.

"Then who does she live with?"

"With her mother, on Bluebell Hill."

"And have they enough to keep them?"

"I don't think so. I think they do lace work."

"And wherein lies her charm, my boy?"

"I don't know that she's charming, mother. But she's nice. And she seems straight, you know—not a bit deep, not a bit."

"But she's a good deal older than you."

"She's thirty, I'm going of twenty-three."

"You haven't told me what you like her for."

"Because I don't know—a sort of defiant way she's got—a sort of angry way."

Mrs. Morel considered. She would have been glad now for her son to fall in love with some woman who would—she did not know what. But he fretted so, got so furious suddenly, and again was melancholic. She wished he knew some nice woman—— She did not know what she wished, but left it vague. At any rate, she was not hostile to the idea of Clara.

Annie, too, was getting married. Leonard had gone away to work in Birmingham. One week-end when he was home she had said to him:

"You don't look very well, my lad."

"I dunno," he said. "I feel anyhow or nohow, ma."

He called her "ma" already in his boyish fashion.

"Are you sure they're good lodgings?" she asked.

"Yes—yes. Only—it's a winder when you have to pour your own tea out—an' nobody to grouse if you team it in your saucer and sup it up. It somehow takes a' the taste out of it."

Mrs. Morel laughed.

"And so it knocks you up?" she said.

"I dunno. I want to get married," he blurted, twisting his fingers and looking down at his boots. There was a silence.

"But," she exclaimed, "I thought you said you'd wait another year."

"Yes, I did say so," he replied stubbornly.

Again she considered.

"And you know," she said, "Annie's a bit of a spendthrift. She's saved no more than eleven pounds. And I know, lad, you haven't had much chance."

He coloured up to the ears.

"I've got thirty-three quid," he said.

"It doesn't go far," she answered.

He said nothing, but twisted his fingers.

"And you know," she said, "I've nothing——"

"I didn't want, ma!" he cried, very red, suffering and remonstrating.

"No, my lad, I know. I was only wishing I had. And take away five pounds for the wedding and things—it leaves twenty-nine pounds. You won't do much on that."

He twisted still, impotent, stubborn, not looking up.

"But do you really want to get married?" she asked. "Do you feel as if you ought?"

He gave her one straight look from his blue eyes.

"Yes," he said.

"Then," she replied, "we must all do the best we can for it, lad."

The next time he looked up there were tears in his eyes.

"I don't want Annie to feel handicapped," he said, struggling.

"My lad," she said, "you're steady—you've got a decent place. If a man had *needed* me I'd have married him on his last week's wages. She may find it a bit hard to start humbly. Young girls *are* like that. They look forward to the fine home they think they'll have. But *I* had expensive furniture. It's not everything."

So the wedding took place almost immediately. Arthur came home, and was splendid in uniform. Annie looked nice in a dove-grey dress that she could take for Sundays. Morel called her a fool for getting married, and was cool with his son-in-law. Mrs. Morel had white tips in her bonnet, and some white on her blouse, and was teased by both her sons for fancying herself so grand. Leonard was jolly and cordial, and felt a fearful fool. Paul could not quite see what Annie wanted to get married for. He was fond of her, and she of him. Still, he hoped rather lugubriously that it would turn out all right. Arthur was astonishingly handsome in his scarlet and yellow, and he knew it well, but was secretly ashamed of the uniform. Annie cried her eyes up in the kitchen, on leaving her mother. Mrs. Morel cried a little, then patted her on the back and said:

"But don't cry, child, he'll be good to you."

Morel stamped and said she was a fool to go and tie herself up. Leonard looked white and overwrought. Mrs. Morel said to him:

"I s'll trust her to you, my lad, and hold you responsible for her."

"You can," he said, nearly dead with the ordeal. And it was all over.

When Morel and Arthur were in bed, Paul sat talking, as he often did, with his mother.

"You're not sorry she's married, mother, are you?" he asked.

"I'm not sorry she's married—but—it seems strange that she should go from me. It even seems to me hard that she can prefer to go with her Leonard. That's how mothers are— I know it's silly."

"And shall you be miserable about her?"

"When I think of my own wedding day," his mother answered, "I can only hope her life will be different."

"But you can trust him to be good to her?"

"Yes, yes. They say he's not good enough for her. But I say

if a man is *genuine*, as he is, and a girl is fond of him—then—
it should be all right. He's as good as she."

"So you don't mind?"

"I would *never* have let a daughter of mine marry a man I
didn't *feel* to be genuine through and through. And yet, there's
a gap now she's gone."

They were both miserable, and wanted her back again. It
seemed to Paul his mother looked lonely, in her new black silk
blouse with its bit of white trimming.

"At any rate, mother, I s'll never marry," he said.

"Ay, they all say that, my lad. You've not met the one yet.
Only wait a year or two."

"But I shan't marry, mother. I shall live with you, and we'll
have a servant."

"Ay, my lad, it's easy to talk. We'll see when the time
comes."

"What time? I'm nearly twenty-three."

"Yes, you're not one that would marry young. But in three
years' time——"

"I shall be with you just the same."

"We'll see, my boy, we'll see."

"But you don't want me to marry?"

"I shouldn't like to think of you going through your life
without anybody to care for you and do—no."

"And you think I ought to marry?"

"Sooner or later every man ought."

"But you'd rather it were later."

"It would be hard—and very hard. It's as they say:

> " 'A son's my son till he takes him a wife,
>   But my daughter's my daughter the whole of her life.' "

"And you think I'd let a wife take me from you?"

"Well, you wouldn't ask her to marry your mother as well
as you," Mrs. Morel smiled.

"She could do what she liked; she wouldn't have to
interfere."

"She wouldn't—till she'd got you—and then you'd see."

"I never will see. I'll never marry while I've got you—I
won't."

"But I shouldn't like to leave you with nobody, my boy,"
she cried.

"You're not going to leave me. What are you? Fifty-three! I'll give you till seventy-five. There you are, I'm fat and forty-four. Then I'll marry a staid body. See!"

His mother sat and laughed.

"Go to bed," she said—"go to bed."

"And we'll have a pretty house, you and me, and a servant, and it'll be just all right. I s'll perhaps be rich with my painting."

"Will you go to bed!"

"And then you s'll have a pony-carriage. See yourself—a little Queen Victoria trotting round."

"I tell you to go to bed," she laughed.

He kissed her and went. His plans for the future were always the same.

Mrs. Morel sat brooding—about her daughter, about Paul, about Arthur. She fretted at losing Annie. The family was very closely bound. And she felt she *must* live now, to be with her children. Life was so rich for her. Paul wanted her, and so did Arthur. Arthur never knew how deeply he loved her. He was a creature of the moment. Never yet had he been forced to realise himself. The army had disciplined his body, but not his soul. He was in perfect health and very handsome. His dark, vigorous hair sat close to his smallish head. There was something childish about his nose, something almost girlish about his dark blue eyes. But he had the full red mouth of a man under his brown moustache, and his jaw was strong. It was his father's mouth; it was the nose and eyes of her own mother's people—good-looking, weak-principled folk. Mrs. Morel was anxious about him. Once he had really run the rig he was safe. But how far would he go?

The army had not really done him any good. He resented bitterly the authority of the officers. He hated having to obey as if he were an animal. But he had too much sense to kick. So he turned his attention to getting the best out of it. He could sing, he was a boon-companion. Often he got into scrapes, but they were the manly scrapes that are easily condoned. So he made a good time out of it, whilst his self-respect was in suppression. He trusted to his good looks and handsome figure, his refinement, his decent education to get him most of what he wanted, and he was not disappointed. Yet he was restless. Something seemed to gnaw him inside. He was never still, he was never alone. With his mother he was rather humble. Paul he admired and loved and despised slightly. And Paul admired and loved and despised him slightly.

Mrs. Morel had had a few pounds left to her by her father, and she decided to buy her son out of the army. He was wild with joy. Now he was like a lad taking a holiday.

He had always been fond of Beatrice Wyld, and during his furlough he picked up with her again. She was stronger and better in health. The two often went long walks together, Arthur taking her arm in soldier's fashion, rather stiffly. And she came to play the piano whilst he sang. Then Arthur would unhook his tunic collar. He grew flushed, his eyes were bright, he sang in a manly tenor. Afterwards they sat together on the sofa. He seemed to flaunt his body: she was aware of him so —the strong chest, the sides, the thighs in their close-fitting trousers.

He liked to lapse into the dialect when he talked to her. She would sometimes smoke with him. Occasionally she would only take a few whiffs at his cigarette.

"Nay," he said to her one evening, when she reached for his cigarette. "Nay, tha doesna. I'll gi'e thee a smoke kiss if ter's a mind."

"I wanted a whiff, no kiss at all," she answered.

"Well, an' tha s'lt ha'e a whiff," he said, "along wi' t' kiss."

"I want a draw at thy fag," she cried, snatching for the cigarette between his lips.

He was sitting with his shoulder touching her. She was small and quick as lightning. He just escaped.

"I'll gi'e thee a smoke kiss," he said.

"Tha'rt a knivey nuisance, Arty Morel," she said, sitting back.

"Ha'e a smoke kiss?"

The soldier leaned forward to her, smiling. His face was near hers.

"Shonna!" she replied, turning away her head.

He took a draw at his cigarette, and pursed up his mouth, and put his lips close to her. His dark-brown cropped moustache stood out like a brush. She looked at the puckered crimson lips, then suddenly snatched the cigarette from his fingers and darted away. He, leaping after her, seized the comb from her back hair. She turned, threw the cigarette at him. He picked it up, put it in his mouth, and sat down.

"Nuisance!" she cried. "Give me my comb!"

She was afraid that her hair, specially done for him, would come down. She stood with her hands to her head. He hid the comb between his knees.

"I've non got it," he said.

The cigarette trembled between his lips with laughter as he spoke.

"Liar!" she said.

" 'S true as I'm here!" he laughed, showing his hands.

"You brazen imp!" she exclaimed, rushing and scuffling for the comb, which he had under his knees. As she wrestled with him, pulling at his smooth, tight-covered knees, he laughed till he lay back on the sofa shaking with laughter. The cigarette fell from his mouth almost singeing his throat. Under his delicate tan the blood flushed up, and he laughed till his blue eyes were blinded, his throat swollen almost to choking. Then he sat up. Beatrice was putting in her comb.

"Tha tickled me, Beat," he said thickly.

Like a flash her small white hand went out and smacked his face. He started up, glaring at her. They stared at each other. Slowly the flush mounted her cheek, she dropped her eyes, then her head. He sat down sulkily. She went into the scullery to adjust her hair. In private there she shed a few tears, she did not know what for.

When she returned she was pursed up close. But it was only a film over her fire. He, with ruffled hair, was sulking upon the sofa. She sat down opposite, in the arm-chair, and neither spoke. The clock ticked in the silence like blows.

"You are a little cat, Beat," he said at length, half apologetically.

"Well, you shouldn't be brazen," she replied.

There was again a long silence. He whistled to himself like a man much agitated but defiant. Suddenly she went across to him and kissed him.

"Did it, pore fing!" she mocked.

He lifted his face, smiling curiously.

"Kiss?" he invited her.

"Daren't I?" she asked.

"Go on!" he challenged, his mouth lifted to her.

Deliberately, and with a peculiar quivering smile that seemed to overspread her whole body, she put her mouth on his. Immediately his arms folded round her. As soon as the long kiss was finished she drew back her head from him, put her delicate fingers on his neck, through the open collar. Then she closed her eyes, giving herself up again in a kiss.

She acted of her own free will. What she would do she did, and made nobody responsible.

Paul felt life changing around him. The conditions of youth were gone. Now it was a home of grown-up people. Annie was a married woman, Arthur was following his own pleasure in a way unknown to his folk. For so long they had all lived at home, and gone out to pass their time. But now, for Annie and Arthur, life lay outside their mother's house. They came home for holiday and for rest. So there was that strange, half-empty feeling about the house, as if the birds had flown. Paul became more and more unsettled. Annie and Arthur had gone. He was restless to follow. Yet home was for him beside his mother. And still there was something else, something outside, something he wanted.

He grew more and more restless. Miriam did not satisfy him. His old mad desire to be with her grew weaker. Sometimes he met Clara in Nottingham, sometimes he went to meetings with her, sometimes he saw her at Willey Farm. But on these last occasions the situation became strained. There was a triangle of antagonism between Paul and Clara and Miriam. With Clara he took on a smart, worldly, mocking tone very antagonistic to Miriam. It did not matter what went before. She might be intimate and sad with him. Then as soon as Clara appeared, it all vanished, and he played to the newcomer.

Miriam had one beautiful evening with him in the hay. He had been on the horse-rake, and having finished, came to help her to put the hay in cocks. Then he talked to her of his hopes and despairs, and his whole soul seemed to lie bare before her. She felt as if she watched the very quivering stuff of life in him. The moon came out: they walked home together: he seemed to have come to her because he needed her so badly, and she listened to him, gave him all her love and her faith. It seemed to her he brought her the best of himself to keep, and that she would guard it all her life. Nay, the sky did not cherish the stars more surely and eternally than she would guard the good in the soul of Paul Morel. She went on home alone, feeling exalted, glad in her faith.

And then, the next day, Clara came. They were to have tea in the hayfield. Miriam watched the evening drawing to gold and shadow. And all the time Paul was sporting with Clara. He made higher and higher heaps of hay that they were jumping over. Miriam did not care for the game, and stood aside. Edgar and Geoffrey and Maurice and Clara and Paul jumped. Paul won, because he was light. Clara's blood was roused. She could run like an Amazon. Paul loved the determined way she rushed at the haycock and leaped, landed on the other side, her breasts shaken, her thick hair come undone.

"You touched!" he cried. "You touched!"

"No!" she flashed, turning to Edgar. "I didn't touch, did I? Wasn't I clear?"

"I couldn't say," laughed Edgar.

None of them could say.

"But you touched," said Paul. "You're beaten."

"I did *not* touch!" she cried.

"As plain as anything," said Paul.

"Box his ears for me!" she cried to Edgar.

"Nay," Edgar laughed. "I daren't. You must do it yourself."

"And nothing can alter the fact that you touched," laughed Paul.

She was furious with him. Her little triumph before these lads and men was gone. She had forgotten herself in the game. Now he was to humble her.

"I think you are despicable!" she said.

And again he laughed, in a way that tortured Miriam.

"And I *knew* you couldn't jump that heap," he teased.

She turned her back on him. Yet everybody could see that the only person she listened to, or was conscious of, was he, and he of her. It pleased the men to see this battle between them. But Miriam was tortured.

Paul could choose the lesser in place of the higher, she saw. He could be unfaithful to himself, unfaithful to the real, deep Paul Morel. There was a danger of his becoming frivolous, of his running after his satisfaction like any Arthur, or like his father. It made Miriam bitter to think that he should throw away his soul for this flippant traffic of triviality with Clara. She walked in bitterness and silence, while the other two rallied each other, and Paul sported.

And afterwards, he would not own it, but he was rather ashamed of himself, and prostrated himself before Miriam. Then again he rebelled.

"It's not religious to be religious," he said. "I reckon a crow is religious when it sails across the sky. But it only does it because it feels itself carried to where it's going, not because it thinks it is being eternal."

But Miriam knew that one should be religious in everything, have God, whatever God might be, present in everything.

"I don't believe God knows such a lot about Himself," he cried. "God doesn't *know* things, He *is* things. And I'm sure He's not soulful."

And then it seemed to her that Paul was arguing God on to his own side, because he wanted his own way and his own pleasure. There was a long battle between him and her. He was utterly unfaithful to her even in her own presence; then he was ashamed, then repentant; then he hated her, and went off again. Those were the ever-recurring conditions.

She fretted him to the bottom of his soul. There she remained —sad, pensive, a worshipper. And he caused her sorrow. Half the time he grieved for her, half the time he hated her. She was his conscience; and he felt, somehow, he had got a conscience that was too much for him. He could not leave her, because in one way she did hold the best of him. He could not stay with her because she did not take the rest of him, which was three-quarters. So he chafed himself into rawness over her.

When she was twenty-one he wrote her a letter which could only have been written to her.

"May I speak of our old, worn love, this last time. It, too, is changing, is it not? Say, has not the body of that love died, and left you its invulnerable soul? You see, I can give you a spirit love, I have given it you this long, long time; but not embodied passion. See, you are a nun. I have given you what I would give a holy nun—as a mystic monk to a mystic nun. Surely you esteem it best. Yet you regret—no, have regretted— the other. In all our relations no body enters. I do not talk to you through the senses—rather through the spirit. That is why we cannot love in the common sense. Ours is not an everyday affection. As yet we are mortal, and to live side by side with one another would be dreadful, for somehow with you I cannot long be trivial, and, you know, to be always beyond this mortal state would be to lose it. If people marry, they must live together as affectionate humans, who may be commonplace with each other without feeling awkward—not as two souls. So I feel it.

"Ought I to send this letter?—I doubt it. But there—it is best to understand. *Au revoir*."

Miriam read this letter twice, after which she sealed it up. A year later she broke the seal to show her mother the letter.

"You are a nun—you are a nun." The words went into her heart again and again. Nothing he ever had said had gone into her so deeply, fixedly, like a mortal wound.

She answered him two days after the party.

" 'Our intimacy would have been all-beautiful but for one little mistake,' " she quoted. "Was the mistake mine?"

Almost immediately he replied to her from Nottingham, sending her at the same time a little "Omar Khayyám".

"I am glad you answered; you are so calm and natural you put me to shame. What a ranter I am! We are often out of sympathy. But in fundamentals we may always be together I think.

"I must thank you for your sympathy with my painting and drawing. Many a sketch is dedicated to you. I do look forward to your criticisms, which, to my shame and glory, are always grand appreciations. It is a lovely joke, that. *Au revoir*."

This was the end of the first phase of Paul's love affair. He was now about twenty-three years old, and, though still virgin, the sex instinct that Miriam had over-refined for so long now grew particularly strong. Often, as he talked to Clara Dawes, came that thickening and quickening of his blood, that peculiar concentration in the breast, as if something were alive there, a new self or a new centre of consciousness, warning him that sooner or later he would have to ask one woman or another. But he belonged to Miriam. Of that she was so fixedly sure that he allowed her right.

CHAPTER X

CLARA

WHEN he was twenty-three years old, Paul sent in a landscape to the winter exhibition at Nottingham Castle. Miss Jordan had taken a good deal of interest in him, and invited him to her house, where he met other artists. He was beginning to grow ambitious.

One morning the postman came just as he was washing in the scullery. Suddenly he heard a wild noise from his mother. Rushing into the kitchen, he found her standing on the hearth-rug wildly waving a letter and crying "Hurrah!" as if she had gone mad. He was shocked and frightened.

"Why, mother!" he exclaimed.

She flew to him, flung her arms round him for a moment, then waved the letter, crying:

"Hurrah, my boy! I knew we should do it!"

He was afraid of her—the small, severe woman with greying hair suddenly bursting out in such frenzy. The postman came running back, afraid something had happened. They saw his tipped cap over the short curtains. Mrs. Morel rushed to the door.

"His picture's got first prize, Fred," she cried, "and is sold for twenty guineas."

"My word, that's something like!" said the young postman, whom they had known all his life.

"And Major Moreton has bought it!" she cried.

"It looks like meanin' something, that does, Mrs. Morel," said the postman, his blue eyes bright. He was glad to have brought such a lucky letter. Mrs. Morel went indoors and sat down, trembling. Paul was afraid lest she might have misread the letter, and might be disappointed after all. He scrutinised it once, twice. Yes, he became convinced it was true. Then he sat down, his heart beating with joy.

"Mother!" he exclaimed.

"Didn't I *say* we should do it!" she said, pretending she was not crying.

He took the kettle off the fire and mashed the tea.

"You didn't think, mother——" he began tentatively.

"No, my son—not so much—but I expected a good deal."

"But not so much," he said.

"No—no—but I knew we should do it."

And then she recovered her composure, apparently at least. He sat with his shirt turned back, showing his young throat almost like a girl's, and the towel in his hand, his hair sticking up wet.

"Twenty guineas, mother! That's just what you wanted to buy Arthur out. Now you needn't borrow any. It'll just do."

"Indeed, I shan't take it all," she said.

"But why?"

"Because I shan't."

"Well—you have twelve pounds, I'll have nine."

They cavilled about sharing the twenty guineas. She wanted to take only the five pounds she needed. He would not hear of it. So they got over the stress of emotion by quarrelling.

Morel came home at night from the pit, saying:

"They tell me Paul's got first prize for his picture, and sold it to Lord Henry Bentley for fifty pound."

"Oh, what stories people do tell!" she cried.

"Ha!" he answered. "I said I wor sure it wor a lie. But they said tha'd told Fred Hodgkisson."

"As if I would tell him such stuff!"

"Ha!" assented the miner.

But he was disappointed nevertheless.

"It's true he has got the first prize," said Mrs Morel.

The miner sat heavily in his chair.

"Has he, beguy!" he exclaimed.

He stared across the room fixedly.

"But as for fifty pounds—such nonsense!" She was silent awhile. "Major Moreton bought it for twenty guineas, that's true."

"Twenty guineas! Tha niver says!" exclaimed Morel.

"Yes, and it was worth it."

"Ay!" he said. "I don't misdoubt it. But twenty guineas for a bit of a paintin' as he knocked off in an hour or two!"

He was silent with conceit of his son. Mrs. Morel sniffed, as if it were nothing.

"And when does he handle th' money?" asked the collier.

"That I couldn't tell you. When the picture is sent home, I suppose."

There was silence. Morel stared at the sugar-basin instead of eating his dinner. His black arm, with the hand all gnarled with work lay on the table. His wife pretended not to see him rub the back of his hand across his eyes, nor the smear in the coal-dust on his black face.

"Yes, an' that other lad 'ud 'a done as much if they hadna ha' killed 'im," he said quietly.

The thought of William went through Mrs. Morel like a cold blade. It left her feeling she was tired, and wanted rest.

Paul was invited to dinner at Mr. Jordan's. Afterwards he said:

cavilled

"Mother, I want an evening suit."

"Yes, I was afraid you would," she said. She was glad. There was a moment or two of silence. "There's that one of William's," she continued, "that I know cost four pounds ten and which he'd only worn three times."

"Should you like me to wear it, mother?" he asked.

"Yes. I think it would fit you—at least the coat. The trousers would want shortening."

He went upstairs and put on the coat and vest. Coming down, he looked strange in a flannel collar and a flannel shirt-front, with an evening coat and vest. It was rather large.

"The tailor can make it right," she said, smoothing her hand over his shoulder. "It's beautiful stuff. I never could find in my heart to let your father wear the trousers, and very glad I am now."

And as she smoothed her hand over the silk collar she thought of her eldest son. But this son was living enough inside the clothes. She passed her hand down his back to feel him. He was alive and hers. The other was dead.

He went out to dinner several times in his evening suit that had been William's. Each time his mother's heart was firm with pride and joy. He was started now. The studs she and the children had bought for William were in his shirt-front; he wore one of William's dress shirts. But he had an elegant figure. His face was rough, but warm-looking and rather pleasing. He did not look particularly a gentleman, but she thought he looked quite a man.

He told her everything that took place, everything that was said. It was as if she had been there. And he was dying to introduce her to these new friends who had dinner at seven-thirty in the evening.

"Go along with you!" she said. "What do they want to know me for?"

"They do!" he cried indignantly. "If they want to know me —and they say they do—then they want to know you, because you are quite as clever as I am."

"Go along with you, child!" she laughed.

But she began to spare her hands. They, too, were work-gnarled now. The skin was shiny with so much hot water, the knuckles rather swollen. But she began to be careful to keep them out of soda. She regretted what they had been—so small and exquisite. And when Annie insisted on her having more stylish blouses to suit her age, she submitted. She even went so far as to allow a black velvet bow to be placed on her hair. Then she sniffed in her sarcastic manner, and was sure she looked a sight. But she looked a lady, Paul declared, as much as Mrs. Major Moreton, and far, far nicer. The family was coming on. Only Morel remained unchanged, or rather, lapsed slowly.

Paul and his mother now had long discussions about life. Religion was fading into the background. He had shovelled away all the beliefs that would hamper him, had cleared the ground, and come more or less to the bedrock of belief that one should feel inside oneself for right and wrong, and should have the patience to gradually realise one's God. Now life interested him more.

"You know," he said to his mother, "I don't want to belong to the well-to-do middle class. I like my common people best. I belong to the common people."

"But if anyone else said so, my son, wouldn't you be in a tear. *You* know you consider yourself equal to any gentleman."

"In myself," he answered, "not in my class or my education or my manners. But in myself I am."

"Very well, then. Then why talk about the common people?"

"Because—the difference between people isn't in their class, but in themselves. Only from the middle classes one gets ideas, and from the common people—life itself, warmth. You feel their hates and loves."

"It's all very well, my boy. But, then, why don't you go and talk to your father's pals?"

"But they're rather different."

"Not at all. They're the common people. After all, whom do you mix with now—among the common people? Those that exchange ideas, like the middle classes. The rest don't interest you."

"But—there's the life——"

"I don't believe there's a jot more life from Miriam than you could get from any educated girl—say Miss Moreton. It is *you* who are snobbish about class."

She frankly *wanted* him to climb into the middle classes, a thing not very difficult, she knew. And she wanted him in the end to marry a lady.

Now she began to combat him in his restless fretting. He

still kept up his connection with Miriam, could neither break free nor go the whole length of engagement. And this indecision seemed to bleed him of his energy. Moreover, his mother suspected him of an unrecognised leaning towards Clara, and, since the latter was a married woman, she wished he would fall in love with one of the girls in a better station of life. But he was stupid, and would refuse to love or even to admire a girl much, just because she was his social superior.

"My boy," said his mother to him, "all your cleverness, your breaking away from old things, and taking life in your own hands, doesn't seem to bring you much happiness."

"What is happiness!" he cried. "It's nothing to me! How *am* I to be happy?"

The plump question disturbed her.

"That's for you to judge, my lad. But if you could meet some *good* woman who would *make* you happy—and you began to think of settling your life—when you have the means—so that you could work without all this fretting—it would be much better for you."

[margin note: She doesn't want him to decide unless it agrees with her judgement]

He frowned. His mother caught him on the raw of his wound of Miriam. He pushed the tumbled hair off his forehead, his eyes full of pain and fire.

"You mean easy, mother," he cried. "That's a woman's whole doctrine for life—ease of soul and physical comfort. And I do despise it."

"Oh, do you!" replied his mother. "And do you call yours a divine discontent?"

"Yes. I don't care about its divinity. But damn your happiness! So long as life's full, it doesn't matter whether it's happy or not. I'm afraid your happiness would bore me."

[margin note: Paul to Mother]

"You never give it a chance," she said. Then suddenly all her passion of grief over him broke out. "But it does matter!" she cried. "And you *ought* to be happy, you ought to try to be happy, to live to be happy. How could I bear to think your life wouldn't be a happy one!"

"Your own's been bad enough, mater, but it hasn't left you so much worse off than the folk who've been happier. I reckon you've done well. And I am the same. Aren't I well enough off?"

."You're not, my son. Battle—battle—and suffer. It's about all you do, as far as I can see."

"But why not, my dear? I tell you it's the best——"

"It isn't. And one *ought* to be happy, one *ought*."

By this time Mrs. Morel was trembling violently. Struggles of this kind often took place between her and her son, when she seemed to fight for his very life against his own will to die. He took her in his arms. She was ill and pitiful.

"Never mind, Little," he murmured. "So long as you don't feel life's paltry and a miserable business, the rest doesn't matter, happiness or unhappiness."

She pressed him to her.

"But I want you to be happy," she said pathetically.

"Eh, my dear—say rather you want me to live."

Mrs. Morel felt as if her heart would break for him. At this rate she knew he would not live. He had that poignant carelessness about himself, his own suffering, his own life, which is a form of slow suicide. It almost broke her heart. With all the passion of her strong nature she hated Miriam for having in this subtle way undermined his joy. It did not matter to her that Miriam could not help it. Miriam did it, and she hated her.

She wished so much he would fall in love with a girl equal to be his mate—educated and strong. But he would not look at anybody above him in station. He seemed to like Mrs. Dawes. At any rate that feeling was wholesome. His mother prayed and prayed for him, that he might not be wasted. That was all her prayer—not for his soul or his righteousness, but that he might not be wasted. And while he slept, for hours and hours she thought and prayed for him.

He drifted away from Miriam imperceptibly, without knowing he was going. Arthur only left the army to be married. The baby was born six months after his wedding. Mrs. Morel got him a job under the firm again, at twenty-one shillings a week. She furnished for him, with the help of Beatrice's mother, a little cottage of two rooms. He was caught now. It did not matter how he kicked and struggled, he was fast. For a time he chafed, was irritable with his young wife, who loved him; he went almost distracted when the baby, which was delicate, cried or gave trouble. He grumbled for hours to his mother. She only said: "Well, my lad, you did it yourself, now you must make the best of it." And then the grit came out in him. He buckled to work, undertook his responsibilities, acknowledged that he belonged to his wife and child, and did make a good best of it. He had never been very closely inbound into the family. Now he was gone altogether.

The months went slowly along. Paul had more or less got into connection with the Socialist, Suffragette, Unitarian people in Nottingham, owing to his acquaintance with Clara. One day a friend of his and of Clara's, in Bestwood, asked him to take a message to Mrs. Dawes. He went in the evening across Sneinton Market to Bluebell Hill. He found the house in a mean little street paved with granite cobbles and having causeways of dark blue, grooved bricks. The front door went up a step from off this rough pavement, where the feet of the passers-by rasped and clattered. The brown paint on the door was so old that the naked wood showed between the rents. He stood on the street below and knocked. There came a heavy footstep; a large, stout woman of about sixty towered above him. He looked up at her from the pavement. She had a rather severe face.

She admitted him into the parlour, which opened on to the street. It was a small, stuffy, defunct room, of mahogany, and deathly enlargements of photographs of departed people done in carbon. Mrs. Radford left him. She was stately, almost martial. In a moment Clara appeared. She flushed deeply, and he was covered with confusion. It seemed as if she did not like being discovered in her home circumstances.

"I thought it couldn't be your voice," she said.

But she might as well be hung for a sheep as for a lamb. She invited him out of the mausoleum of a parlour into the kitchen.

That was a little, darkish room too, but it was smothered in white lace. The mother had seated herself again by the cupboard, and was drawing thread from a vast web of lace. A clump of fluff and ravelled cotton was at her right hand, a heap of three-quarter-inch lace lay on her left, whilst in front of her was the mountain of lace web, piling the hearthrug. Threads of curly cotton, pulled out from between the lengths of lace, strewed over the fender and the fireplace. Paul dared not go forward, for fear of treading on piles of white stuff.

On the table was a jenny for carding the lace. There was a pack of brown cardboard squares, a pack of cards of lace, a little box of pins, and on the sofa lay a heap of drawn lace.

The room was all lace, and it was so dark and warm that the white, snowy stuff seemed the more distinct.

"If you're coming in you won't have to mind the work," said Mrs. Radford. "I know we're about blocked up. But sit you down."

Clara, much embarrassed, gave him a chair against the wall opposite the white heaps. Then she herself took her place on the sofa, shamedly.

"Will you drink a bottle of stout?" Mrs. Radford asked. "Clara, get him a bottle of stout."

He protested, but Mrs. Radford insisted.

"You look as if you could do with it," she said. "Haven't you never any more colour than that?"

"It's only a thick skin I've got that doesn't show the blood through," he answered.

Clara, ashamed and chagrined, brought him a bottle of stout and a glass. He poured out some of the black stuff.

"Well," he said, lifting the glass, "here's health!"

"And thank you," said Mrs. Radford.

He took a drink of stout.

"And light yourself a cigarette, so long as you don't set the house on fire," said Mrs. Radford.

"Thank you," he replied.

"Nay, you needn't thank me," she answered. "I s'll be glad to smell a bit of smoke in th' 'ouse again. A house o' women is as dead as a house wi' no fire, to my thinkin'. I'm not a spider as likes a corner to myself. I like a man about, if he's only something to snap at."

Clara began to work. Her jenny spun with a subdued buzz; the white lace hopped from between her fingers on to the card. It was filled; she snipped off the length, and pinned the end down to the banded lace. Then she put a new card in her jenny. Paul watched her. She sat square and magnificent. Her throat and arms were bare. The blood still mantled below her ears; she bent her head in shame of her humility. Her face was set on her work. Her arms were creamy and full of life beside the white lace; her large, well-kept hands worked with a balanced movement, as if nothing would hurry them. He, not knowing, watched her all the time. He saw the arch of her neck from the shoulder, as she bent her head; he saw the coil of dun hair; he watched her moving, gleaming arms.

"I've heard a bit about you from Clara," continued the mother. "You're in Jordan's, aren't you?" She drew her lace unceasing.

"Yes."

"Ay, well, and I can remember when Thomas Jordan used to ask *me* for one of my toffies."

"Did he?" laughed Paul. "And did he get it?"

"Sometimes he did, sometimes he didn't—which was latterly. For he's the sort that takes all and gives naught, he is—or used to be."

"I think he's very decent," said Paul.

"Yes; well, I'm glad to hear it."

Mrs. Radford looked across at him steadily. There was something determined about her that he liked. Her face was falling loose, but her eyes were calm, and there was something strong in her that made it seem she was not old; merely her wrinkles and loose cheeks were an anachronism. She had the strength and sang-froid of a woman in the prime of life. She continued drawing the lace with slow, dignified movements. The big web came up inevitably over her apron; the length of lace fell away at her side. Her arms were finely shapen, but glossy and yellow as old ivory. They had not the peculiar dull gleam that made Clara's so fascinating to him.

"And you've been going with Miriam Leivers?" the mother asked him.

"Well——" he answered.

"Yes, she's a nice girl," she continued. "She's very nice, but she's a bit too much above this world to suit my fancy."

"She is a bit like that," he agreed.

"She'll never be satisfied till she's got wings and can fly over everybody's head, she won't," she said.

Clara broke in, and he told her his message. She spoke humbly to him. He had surprised her in her drudgery. To have her humble made him feel as if he were lifting his head in expectation.

"Do you like jennying?" he asked.

"What can a woman do!" she replied bitterly.

"Is it sweated?"

"More or less. Isn't *all* woman's work? That's another trick the men have played, since we force ourselves into the labour market."

"Now then, you shut up about the men," said her mother. "If the women wasn't fools, the men wouldn't be bad uns, that's what I say. No man was ever that bad wi' me but what he got it back again. Not but what they're a lousy lot, there's no denying it."

"But they're all right really, aren't they?" he asked.

"Well, they're a bit different from women," she answered.

"Would you care to be back at Jordan's?" he asked Clara.

"I don't think so," she replied.

"Yes, she would!" cried her mother; "thank her stars if she could get back. Don't you listen to her. She's for ever on that 'igh horse of hers, an' it's back's that thin an' starved it'll cut her i' two one of these days."

Clara suffered badly from her mother. Paul felt as if his eyes were coming very wide open. Wasn't he to take Clara's fulminations so seriously, after all? She spun steadily at her work. He experienced a thrill of joy, thinking she might need his help. She seemed denied and deprived of so much. And her arm moved mechanically, that should never have been subdued to a mechanism, and her head was bowed to the lace, that never should have been bowed. She seemed to be stranded there among the refuse that life has thrown away, doing her jennying. It was a bitter thing to her to be put aside by life, as if it had no use for her. No wonder she protested.

She came with him to the door. He stood below in the mean street, looking up at her. So fine she was in her stature and her bearing, she reminded him of Juno dethroned. As she stood in the doorway, she winced from the street, from her surroundings.

"And you will go with Mrs. Hodgkisson to Hucknall?"

He was talking quite meaninglessly, only watching her. Her grey eyes at last met his. They looked dumb with humiliation, pleading with a kind of captive misery. He was shaken and at a loss. He had thought her high and mighty.

When he left her, he wanted to run. He went to the station in a sort of dream, and was at home without realising he had moved out of her street.

He had an idea that Susan, the overseer of the Spiral girls, was about to be married. He asked her the next day.

"I say, Susan, I heard a whisper of your getting married. What about it?"

Susan flushed red.

"Who's been talking to you?" she replied.

"Nobody. I merely heard a whisper that you *were* thinking——"

"Well, I am, though you needn't tell anybody. What's more, I wish I wasn't!"

"Nay, Susan, you won't make me believe that."

"Shan't I? You *can* believe it, though. I'd rather stop here a thousand times."

Paul was perturbed.

"Why, Susan?"

The girl's colour was high, and her eyes flashed.

"That's why!"

"And must you?"

For answer, she looked at him. There was about him a candour and gentleness which made the women trust him. He understood.

"Ah, I'm sorry," he said.

Tears came to her eyes.

"But you'll see it'll turn out all right. You'll make the best of it," he continued rather wistfully.

"There's nothing else for it."

"Yea, there's making the worst of it. Try and make it all right."

He soon made occasion to call again on Clara.

"Would you," he said, "care to come back to Jordan's?"

She put down her work, laid her beautiful arms on the table, and looked at him for some moments without answering. Gradually the flush mounted her cheek.

"Why?" she asked.

Paul felt rather awkward.

"Well, because Susan is thinking of leaving," he said.

Clara went on with her jennying. The white lace leaped in little jumps and bounds on to the card. He waited for her. Without raising her head, she said at last, in a peculiar low voice:

"Have you said anything about it?"

"Except to you, not a word."

There was again a long silence.

"I will apply when the advertisement is out," she said.

"You will apply before that. I will let you know exactly when."

She went on spinning her little machine, and did not contradict him.

Clara came to Jordan's. Some of the older hands, Fanny among them, remembered her earlier rule, and cordially disliked the memory. Clara had always been "ikey", reserved, and superior. She had never mixed with the girls as one of themselves. If she had occasion to find fault, she did it coolly and with perfect politeness, which the defaulter felt to be a bigger insult than crossness. Towards Fanny, the poor, over-strung hunchback, Clara was unfailingly compassionate and gentle, as a result of which Fanny shed more bitter tears than ever the rough tongues of the other overseers had caused her.

There was something in Clara that Paul disliked, and much that piqued him. If she were about, he always watched her strong throat or her neck, upon which the blonde hair grew low and fluffy. There was a fine down, almost invisible, upon the skin of her face and arms, and when once he had perceived it, he saw it always.

When he was at his work, painting in the afternoon, she would come and stand near to him, perfectly motionless. Then he felt her, though she neither spoke nor touched him. Although she stood a yard away he felt as if he were in contact with her. Then he could paint no more. He flung down the brushes, and turned to talk to her.

Sometimes she praised his work; sometimes she was critical and cold.

"You are affected in that piece," she would say; and, as there was an element of truth in her condemnation, his blood boiled with anger.

Again: "What of this?" he would ask enthusiastically.

"H'm!" She made a small doubtful sound. "It doesn't interest me much."

"Because you don't understand it," he retorted.

"Then why ask me about it?"

"Because I thought you would understand."

She would shrug her shoulders in scorn of his work. She maddened him. He was furious. Then he abused her, and went into passionate exposition of his stuff. This amused and stimulated her. But she never owned that she had been wrong.

During the ten years that she had belonged to the women's movement she had acquired a fair amount of education, and, having had some of Miriam's passion to be instructed, had taught herself French, and could read in that language with a struggle. She considered herself as a woman apart, and particularly apart, from her class. The girls in the Spiral department were all of good homes. It was a small, special industry, and had a certain distinction. There was an air of refinement in both rooms. But Clara was aloof also from her fellow-workers.

None of these things, however, did she reveal to Paul. She

Paul
was

was not the one to give herself away. There was a sense of
mystery about her. She was so reserved, he felt she had much
to reserve. Her history was open on the surface, but its inner
meaning was hidden from everybody. It was exciting. And
then sometimes he caught her looking at him from under her
brows with an almost furtive, sullen scrutiny, which made
him move quickly. Often she met his eyes. But then her own
were, as it were, covered over, revealing nothing. She gave
him a little, lenient smile. She was to him extraordinarily
provocative, because of the knowledge she seemed to possess,
and gathered fruit of experience he could not attain.

One day he picked up a copy of *Lettres de mon Moulin*
from her work-bench.

"You read French, do you?" he cried.

Clara glanced round negligently. She was making an elastic
stocking of heliotrope silk, turning the Spiral machine with
slow, balanced regularity, occasionally bending down to see
her work or to adjust the needles; then her magnificent neck,
with its down and fine pencils of hair, shone white against
the lavender, lustrous silk. She turned a few more rounds,
and stopped.

"What did you say?" she asked, smiling sweetly.

Paul's eyes glittered at her insolent indifference to him.

"I did not know you read French," he said, very polite.

"Did you not?" she replied, with a faint, sarcastic smile.

"Rotten swank!" he said, but scarcely loud enough to be
heard.

He shut his mouth angrily as he watched her. She seemed to
scorn the work she mechanically produced; yet the hose she
made were as nearly perfect as possible.

"You don't like Spiral work," he said.

"Oh, well, all work is work," she answered, as if she knew
all about it.

He marvelled at her coldness. He had to do everything hotly.
She must be something special.

opposite
Miriam

"What would you prefer to do?" he asked.

She laughed at him indulgently, as she said:

"There is so little likelihood of my ever being given a choice,
that I haven't wasted time considering."

"Pah!" he said, contemptuous on his side now. "You only
say that because you're too proud to own up what you want
and can't get."

"You know me very well," she replied coldly.

"I know you think you're terrific great shakes, and that you live under the eternal insult of working in a factory."

He was very angry and very rude. She merely turned away from him in disdain. He walked whistling down the room, flirted and laughed with Hilda.

Later on he said to himself:

"What was I so impudent to Clara for?" He was rather annoyed with himself, at the same time glad. "Serve her right; she stinks with silent pride," he said to himself angrily.

In the afternoon he came down. There was a certain weight on his heart which he wanted to remove. He thought to do it by offering her chocolates.

"Have one?" he said. "I bought a handful to sweeten me up."

To his great relief, she accepted. He sat on the work-bench beside her machine, twisting a piece of silk round his finger. She loved him for his quick, unexpected movements, like a young animal. His feet swung as he pondered. The sweets lay strewn on the bench. She bent over her machine, grinding rhythmically, then stooping to see the stocking that hung beneath, pulled down by the weight. He watched the handsome crouching of her back, and the apron-strings curling on the floor.

"There is always about you," he said, "a sort of waiting. Whatever I see you doing, you're not really there: you are waiting—like Penelope when she did her weaving." He could not help a spurt of wickedness. "I'll call you Penelope," he said.

"Would it make any difference?" she said, carefully removing one of her needles.

"That doesn't matter, so long as it pleases me. Here, I say, you seem to forget I'm your boss. It just occurs to me."

"And what does that mean?" she asked coolly.

"It means I've got a right to boss you.'

"Is there anything you want to complain about?"

"Oh, I say, you needn't be nasty," he said angrily.

"I don't know what you want." she said, continuing her task.

"I want you to treat me nicely and respectfully."

"Call you 'sir', perhaps?" she asked quietly.

"Yes, call me 'sir'. I should love it."

"Then I wish you would go upstairs, sir."

His mouth closed, and a frown came on his face. He jumped suddenly down.

"You're too blessed superior for anything," he said.

And he went away to the other girls. He felt he was being angrier than he had any need to be. In fact, he doubted slightly that he was showing off. But if he were, then he would. Clara heard him laughing, in a way she hated, with the girls down the next room.

When at evening he went through the department after the girls had gone, he saw his chocolates lying untouched in front of Clara's machine. He left them. In the morning they were still there, and Clara was at work. Later on Minnie, a little brunette they called Pussy, called to him:

"Hey, haven't you got a chocolate for anybody?"

"Sorry, Pussy," he replied. "I meant to have offered them; then I went and forgot 'em."

"I think you did," she answered.

"I'll bring you some this afternoon. You don't want them after they've been lying about, do you?"

"Oh, I'm not particular," smiled Pussy.

"Oh no," he said. "They'll be dusty."

He went up to Clara's bench.

"Sorry I left these things littering about," he said.

She flushed scarlet. He gathered them together in his fist.

"They'll be dirty now," he said. "You should have taken them. I wonder why you didn't. I meant to have told you I wanted you to."

He flung them out of the window into the yard below. He just glanced at her. She winced from his eyes.

In the afternoon he brought another packet.

"Will you take some?" he said, offering them first to Clara. "These are fresh."

She accepted one, and put it on to the bench.

"Oh, take several—for luck," he said.

She took a couple more, and put them on the bench also. Then she turned in confusion to her work. He went on up the room.

"Here you are, Pussy," he said. "Don't be greedy!"

"Are they all for her?" cried the others, rushing up.

"Of course they're not," he said.

The girls clamoured round. Pussy drew back from her mates.

"Come out!" she cried. "I can have first pick, can't I, Paul?"

"Be nice with 'em," he said, and went away.

"You *are* a dear," the girls cried.

"Tenpence," he answered.

He went past Clara without speaking. She felt the three chocolate creams would burn her if she touched them. It needed all her courage to slip them into the pocket of her apron.

The girls loved him and were afraid of him. He was so nice while he was nice, but if he were offended, so distant, treating them as if they scarcely existed, or not more than the bobbins of thread. And then, if they were impudent, he said quietly: "Do you mind going on with your work," and stood and watched.

When he celebrated his twenty-third birthday, the house was in trouble. Arthur was just going to be married. His mother was not well. His father, getting an old man, and lame from his accidents, was given a paltry, poor job. Miriam was an eternal reproach. He felt he owed himself to her, yet could not give himself. The house, moreover, needed his support. He was pulled in all directions. He was not glad it was his birthday. It made him bitter.

He got to work at eight o'clock. Most of the clerks had not turned up. The girls were not due till 8.30. As he was changing his coat, he heard a voice behind him say:

"Paul, Paul, I want you."

It was Fanny, the hunchback, standing at the top of her stairs, her face radiant with a secret. Paul looked at her in astonishment.

"I want you," she said.

He stood, at a loss.

"Come on," she coaxed. "Come before you begin on the letters."

He went down the half-dozen steps into her dry, narrow, "finishing-off" room. Fanny walked before him: her black bodice was short—the waist was under her armpits—and her green-black cashmere skirt seemed very long, as she strode with big strides before the young man, himself so graceful. She went to her seat at the narrow end of the room, where the window opened on to chimney-pots. Paul watched her thin hands and her flat red wrists as she excitedly twitched her white apron, which was spread on the bench in front of her. She hesitated.

"You didn't think we'd forgot you?" she asked, reproachful.

"Why?" he asked. He had forgotten his birthday himself.

" 'Why,' he says! 'Why!' Why, look here!" She pointed to the calendar, and he saw, surrounding the big black number "21", hundreds of little crosses in black-lead.

"Oh, kisses for my birthday," he laughed. "How did you know?"

"Yes, you want to know, don't you?" Fanny mocked, hugely delighted. "There's one from everybody—except Lady Clara—and two from some. But I shan't tell you how many *I* put."

"Oh, I know, you're spooney," he said.

"There you *are* mistaken!" she cried, indignant. "I could never be so soft." Her voice was strong and contralto.

"You always pretend to be such a hard-hearted hussy," he laughed. "And you know you're as sentimental——"

"I'd rather be called sentimental than frozen meat," Fanny blurted. Paul knew she referred to Clara, and he smiled.

"Do you say such nasty things about me?" he laughed.

"No, my duck," the hunchback woman answered, lavishly tender. She was thirty-nine. "No, my duck, because you don't think yourself a fine figure in marble and us nothing but dirt. I'm as good as you, aren't I, Paul?" and the question delighted her.

"Why, we're not better than one another, are we?" he replied.

"But I'm as good as you, aren't I, Paul?" she persisted daringly.

"Of course you are. If it comes to goodness, you're better."

She was rather afraid of the situation. She might get hysterical.

"I thought I'd get here before the others—won't they say I'm deep! Now shut your eyes——" she said.

"And open your mouth, and see what God sends you," he continued, suiting action to words, and expecting a piece of chocolate. He heard the rustle of the apron, and a faint clink of metal. "I'm going to look," he said.

He opened his eyes. Fanny, her long cheeks flushed, her blue eyes shining, was gazing at him. There was a little bundle of paint-tubes on the bench before him. He turned pale.

"No, Fanny," he said quickly.

"From us all," she answered hastily.

"No, but——"

"Are they the right sort?" she asked, rocking herself with delight.

"Jove! they're the best in the catalogue."

"But they're the right sorts?" she cried.

"They're off the little list I'd made to get when my ship came in." He bit his lip.

Fanny was overcome with emotion. She must turn the conversation.

"They was all on thorns to do it; they all paid their shares, all except the Queen of Sheba."

The Queen of Sheba was Clara.

"And wouldn't she join?" Paul asked.

"She didn't get the chance; we never told her; we wasn't going to have *her* bossing *this* show. We didn't *want* her to join."

Paul laughed at the woman. He was much moved. At last he must go. She was very close to him. Suddenly she flung her arms round his neck and kissed him vehemently.

"I can give you a kiss to-day," she said apologetically. "You've looked so white, it's made my heart ache."

Paul kissed her, and left her. Her arms were so pitifully thin that his heart ached also.

That day he met Clara as he ran downstairs to wash his hands at dinner-time.

"You have stayed to dinner!" he exclaimed. It was unusual for her.

"Yes; and I seem to have dined on old surgical-appliance stock. I *must* go out now, or I shall feel stale india-rubber right through."

She lingered. He instantly caught at her wish.

"You are going anywhere?" he asked.

They went together up to the Castle. Outdoors she dressed very plainly, down to ugliness; indoors she always looked nice. She walked with hesitating steps alongside Paul, bowing and turning away from him. Dowdy in dress, and drooping, she showed to great disadvantage. He could scarcely recognise her strong form, that seemed to slumber with power. She appeared almost insignificant, drowning her stature in her stoop, as she shrank from the public gaze.

The Castle grounds were very green and fresh. Climbing the precipitous ascent, he laughed and chattered, but she was silent, seeming to brood over something. There was scarcely time to go inside the squat, square building that crowns the bluff of rock. They leaned upon the wall where the cliff runs sheer down to the Park. Below them, in their holes in the sandstone, pigeons preened themselves and cooed softly. Away down upon the boulevard at the foot of the rock, tiny trees stood in their own pools of shadow, and tiny people went scurrying about in almost ludicrous importance.

"You feel as if you could scoop up the folk like tadpoles. and have a handful of them," he said.

She laughed, answering:

"Yes; it is not necessary to get far off in order to see us proportionately. The trees are much more significant."

"Bulk only," he said.

She laughed cynically.

Away beyond the boulevard the thin stripes of the metals showed upon the railway-track, whose margin was crowded with little stacks of timber, beside which smoking toy engines fussed. Then the silver string of the canal lay at random among the black heaps. Beyond, the dwellings, very dense on the river flat, looked like black, poisonous herbage, in thick rows and crowded beds, stretching right away, broken now and then by taller plants, right to where the river glistened in a hieroglyph across the country. The steep scarp cliffs across the river looked puny. Great stretches of country darkened with trees and faintly brightened with corn-land, spread towards the haze, where the hills rose blue beyond grey.

"It is comforting," said Mrs. Dawes, "to think the town goes no farther. It is only a *little* sore upon the country yet."

"A little scab," Paul said.

She shivered. She loathed the town. Looking drearily across at the country which was forbidden her, her impassive face, pale and hostile, she reminded Paul of one of the bitter, remorseful angels.

"But the town's all right," he said; "it's only temporary. This is the crude, clumsy make-shift we've practised on, till we find out what the idea is. The town will come all right."

The pigeons in the pockets of rock, among the perched bushes, cooed comfortably. To the left the large church of St. Mary rose into space, to keep close company with the Castle, above the heaped rubble of the town. Mrs. Dawes smiled brightly as she looked across the country.

"I feel better," she said.

"Thank you," he replied. "Great compliment!"

"Oh, my brother!" she laughed.

"H'm! that's snatching back with the left hand what you gave with the right, and no mistake," he said.

She laughed in amusement at him.

"But what was the matter with you?" he asked. "I know you were brooding something special. I can see the stamp of it on your face yet."

"I think I will not tell you," she said.

"All right, hug it," he answered.

She flushed and bit her lip.

"No," she said, "it was the girls."

"What about 'em?" Paul asked.

"They have been plotting something for a week now, and to-day they seem particularly full of it. All alike; they insult me with their secrecy."

"Do they?" he asked in concern.

"I should not mind," she went on, in the metallic, angry tone, "if they did not thrust it into my face—the fact that they have a secret."

"Just like women," said he.

"It is hateful, their mean gloating," she said intensely.

Paul was silent. He knew what the girls gloated over. He was sorry to be the cause of this new dissension.

"They can have all the secrets in the world," she went on, brooding bitterly; "but they might refrain from glorying in them, and making me feel more out of it than ever. It is— it is almost unbearable."

Paul thought for a few minutes. He was much perturbed.

"I will tell you what it's all about," he said, pale and nervous. "It's my birthday, and they've bought me a fine lot of paints, all the girls. They're jealous of you"—he felt her stiffen coldly at the word 'jealous'—"merely because I sometimes bring you a book," he added slowly. "But, you see, it's only a trifle. Don't bother about it, will you—because"—he laughed quickly —"well, what would they say if they saw us here now, in spite of their victory?"

She was angry with him for his clumsy reference to their present intimacy. It was almost insolent of him. Yet he was so quiet, she forgave him, although it cost her an effort.

Their two hands lay on the rough stone parapet of the Castle wall. He had inherited from his mother a fineness of mould, so that his hands were small and vigorous. Hers were large, to match her large limbs, but white and powerful looking. As Paul looked at them he knew her. "She is wanting somebody to take her hands—for all she is so contemptuous of us," he said to himself. And she saw nothing but his two hands, so warm and alive, which seemed to live for her. He was brooding now, staring out over the country from under sullen brows. The little, interesting diversity of shapes had vanished from the scene; all that remained was a vast, dark matrix of sorrow and tragedy, the same in all the houses and the river-flats and the people and the birds; they were only shapen differently. And now that the forms seemed to have melted away, there remained the mass from which all the landscape was composed, a dark mass of struggle and pain. The factory, the girls, his mother, the large, uplifted church, the thicket of the town, merged into one atmosphere—dark, brooding, and sorrowful, every bit.

"Is that two o'clock striking?" Mrs. Dawes said in surprise.

Paul started, and everything sprang into form, regained its individuality, its forgetfulness, and its cheerfulness.

They hurried back to work.

When he was in the rush of preparing for the night's post, examining the work up from Fanny's room, which smelt of ironing, the evening postman came in.

" 'Mr. Paul Morel,' " he said, smiling, handing Paul a package. "A lady's handwriting! Don't let the girls see it."

The postman, himself a favourite, was pleased to make fun of the girls' affection for Paul.

It was a volume of verse with a brief note : "You will allow me to send you this, and so spare me my isolation. I also sympathise and wish you well.—C.D." Paul flushed hot.

"Good Lord! Mrs. Dawes. She can't afford it. Good Lord, who ever'd have thought it!"

He was suddenly intensely moved. He was filled with the warmth of her. In the glow he could almost feel her as if she were present—her arms, her shoulders, her bosom, see them, feel them, almost contain them.

This move on the part of Clara brought them into closer intimacy. The other girls noticed that when Paul met Mrs. Dawes his eyes lifted and gave that peculiar bright greeting which they could interpret. Knowing he was unaware, Clara made no sign, save that occasionally she turned aside her face from him when he came upon her.

They walked out together very often at dinner-time; it was quite open, quite frank. Everybody seemed to feel that he was quite unaware of the state of his own feeling, and that nothing was wrong. He talked to her now with some of the old fervour with which he had talked to Miriam, but he cared less about the talk; he did not bother about his conclusions.

One day in October they went out to Lambley for tea. Suddenly they came to a halt on top of the hill. He climbed and sat on a gate, she sat on the stile. The afternoon was perfectly still, with a dim haze, and yellow sheaves glowing through. They were quiet.

"How old were you when you married?" he asked quietly.

"Twenty-two."

Her voice was subdued, almost submissive. She would tell him now.

"It is eight years ago?"

"Yes."

"And when did you leave him?"

"Three years ago."

"Five years! Did you love him when you married him?"

She was silent for some time; then she said slowly:

"I thought I did—more or less. I didn't think much about it. And he wanted me. I was very prudish then."

"And you sort of walked into it without thinking?"

"Yes. I seemed to have been asleep nearly all my life."

"Somnambule? But—when did you wake up?"

"I don't know that I ever did, or ever have—since I was a child."

"You went to sleep as you grew to be a woman? How queer! And he didn't wake you?"

"No; he never got there," she replied, in a monotone.

The brown birds dashed over the hedges where the rose-hips stood naked and scarlet.

"Got where?" he asked.

"At me. He never really mattered to me."

The afternoon was so gently warm and dim. Red roofs of the cottages burned among the blue haze. He loved the day. He could feel, but he could not understand, what Clara was saying.

"But why did you leave him? Was he horrid to you?"

She shuddered lightly.

"He—he sort of degraded me. He wanted to bully me because he hadn't got me. And then I felt as if I wanted to run, as if I was fastened and bound up. And he seemed dirty."

"I see."

He did not at all see.

"And was he always dirty?" he asked.

"A bit," she replied slowly. "And then he seemed as if he couldn't get *at* me, really. And then he got brutal—he *was* brutal!"

"And why did you leave him finally?"

"Because—because he was unfaithful to me——"

They were both silent for some time. Her hand lay on the gate-post as she balanced. He put his own over it. His heart beat quickly.

"But did you—were you ever—did you ever give him a chance?"

"Chance? How?"

"To come near to you."

"I married him—and I was willing——"

They both strove to keep their voices steady.

"I believe he loves you," he said.

"It looks like it," she replied.

He wanted to take his hand away, and could not. She saved him by removing her own. After a silence, he began again:

"Did you leave him out of count all along?"

"He left me," she said.

"And I suppose he couldn't *make* himself mean everything to you?"

"He tried to bully me into it."

But the conversation had got them both out of their depth. Suddenly Paul jumped down.

"Come on," he said. "Let's go and get some tea."

They found a cottage, where they sat in the cold parlour. She poured out his tea. She was very quiet. He felt she had withdrawn again from him. After tea, she stared broodingly into her tea-cup, twisting her wedding ring all the time. In her abstraction she took the ring off her finger, stood it up, and spun it upon the table. The gold became a diaphanous, glittering globe. It fell, and the ring was quivering upon the table. She spun it again and again. Paul watched, fascinated.

But she was a married woman, and he believed in simple

friendship. And he considered that he was perfectly honourable with regard to her. It was only a friendship between man and woman, such as any civilised persons might have.

He was like so many young men of his own age. Sex had become so complicated in him that he would have denied that he ever could want Clara or Miriam or any woman whom he *knew*. Sex desire was a sort of detached thing, that did not belong to a woman. He loved Miriam with his soul. He grew warm at the thought of Clara, he battled with her, he knew the curves of her breast and shoulders as if they had been moulded inside him; and yet he did not positively desire her. He would have denied it for ever. He believed himself really bound to Miriam. If ever he should marry, some time in the far future, it would be his duty to marry Miriam. That he gave Clara to understand, and she said nothing, but left him to his courses. He came to her, Mrs. Dawes, whenever he could. Then he wrote frequently to Miriam, and visited the girl occasionally. So he went on through the winter; but he seemed not so fretted. His mother was easier about him. She thought he was getting away from Miriam.

Miriam knew now how strong was the attraction of Clara for him; but still she was certain that the best in him would triumph. His feeling for Mrs. Dawes—who, moreover, was a married woman—was shallow and temporal, compared with his love for herself. He would come back to her, she was sure; with some of his young freshness gone, perhaps, but cured of his desire for the lesser things which other women than herself could give him. She could bear all if he were inwardly true to her and must come back.

He saw none of the anomaly of his position. Miriam was his old friend, lover, and she belonged to Bestwood and home and his youth. Clara was a newer friend, and she belonged to Nottingham, to life, to the world. It seemed to him quite plain.

Mrs. Dawes and he had many periods of coolness, when they saw little of each other; but they always came together again.

"Were you horrid with Baxter Dawes?" he asked her. It was a thing that seemed to trouble him.

"In what way?"

"Oh, I don't know. But weren't you horrid with him? Didn't you do something that knocked him to pieces?"

"What, pray?"

"Making him feel as if he were nothing—*I* know," Paul declared.

"You are so clever, my friend," she said coolly.

The conversation broke off there. But it made her cool with him for some time.

She very rarely saw Miriam now. The friendship between the two women was not broken off, but considerably weakened.

"Will you come in to the concert on Sunday afternoon?" Clara asked him just after Christmas.

"I promised to go up to Willey Farm," he replied.

"Oh, very well."

"You don't mind, do you?" he asked.

"Why should I?" she answered.

Which almost annoyed him.

"You know," he said, "Miriam and I have been a lot to each other ever since I was sixteen—that's seven years now."

"It's a long time," Clara replied.

"Yes; but somehow she—it doesn't go right——"

"How?" asked Clara.

"She seems to draw me and draw me, and she wouldn't leave a single hair of me free to fall out and blow away—she'd keep it."

"But you like to be kept."

"No," he said, "I don't. I wish it could be normal, give and take—like me and you. I want a woman to keep me, but not in her pocket."

"But if you love her, it couldn't be normal, like me and you."

"Yes; I should love her better then. She sort of wants me so much that I can't give myself."

"Wants you how?"

"Wants the soul out of my body. I can't help shrinking back from her."

"And yet you love her!"

"No, I don't love her. I never even kiss her."

"Why not?" Clara asked.

"I don't know."

"I suppose you're afraid," she said.

"I'm not. Something in me shrinks from her like hell—she so good, when I'm not good."

"How do you know what she is?"

"I do! I know she wants a sort of soul union."

"But how do you know what she wants?"

"I've been with her for seven years."

"And you haven't found out the very first thing about her."

"What's that?"

"That she doesn't want any of your soul communion. That's your own imagination. She wants you."

He pondered over this. Perhaps he was wrong.

"But she seems——" he began.

"You've never tried," she answered.

CHAPTER XI

THE TEST ON MIRIAM

WITH the spring came again the old madness and battle. Now he knew he would have to go to Miriam. But what was his reluctance? He told himself it was only a sort of overstrong virginity in her and him which neither could break through. He might have married her; but his circumstances at home made it difficult, and, moreover, he did not want to marry. Marriage was for life, and because they had become close companions, he and she, he did not see that it should inevitably follow they should be man and wife. He did not feel that he wanted marriage with Miriam. He wished he did. He would have given his head to have felt a joyous desire to marry her and to have her. Then why couldn't he bring it off? There was some obstacle; and what was the obstacle? It lay in the physical bondage. He shrank from the physical contact. But why? With her he felt bound up inside himself. He could not go out to her. Something struggled in him, but he could not get to her. Why? She loved him. Clara said she even wanted him; then why couldn't he go to her, make love to her, kiss her? Why, when she put her arm in his, timidly, as they walked, did he feel he would burst forth in brutality and recoil? He owed himself to her; he wanted to belong to her. Perhaps the recoil and the shrinking from her was love in its first fierce modesty. He had no aversion for her. No, it was the opposite; it was a strong desire battling with a still stronger shyness and virginity. It seemed as if virginity were a positive force, which fought and won in both of them. And with her he felt it so hard to overcome; yet he was nearest to her, and with her alone could he deliberately break through. And he owed himself to her. Then, if they could get things right, they could marry; but he would not marry unless he could feel strong in the joy of it—never. He could not have faced his mother. It seemed to him that to sacrifice himself in a marriage he did not want would be degrading, and would undo all his life, make it a nullity. He would try what he *could* do.

And he had a great tenderness for Miriam. Always, she was sad, dreaming her religion; and he was nearly a religion to her. He could not bear to fail her. It would all come right if they tried.

He looked round. A good many of the nicest men he knew were like himself, bound in by their own virginity, which they could not break out of. They were so sensitive to their women that they would go without them for ever rather than do them a hurt, an injustice. Being the sons of mothers whose husbands had blundered rather brutally through their feminine sanctities, they were themselves too diffident and shy. They could easier deny themselves than incur any reproach from a woman; for a woman was like their mother, and they were full of the sense of their mother. They preferred themselves to suffer the misery of celibacy, rather than risk the other person.

He went back to her. Something in her, when he looked at her, brought the tears almost to his eyes. One day he stood behind her as she sang. Annie was playing a song on the piano. As Miriam sang her mouth seemed hopeless. She sang like a nun singing to heaven. It reminded him so much of the mouth and eyes of one who sings beside a Botticelli Madonna, so spiritual. Again, hot as steel, came up the pain in him. Why must he ask her for the other thing? Why was there his blood battling with her? If only he could have been always gentle, tender with her, breathing with her the atmosphere of reverie and religious dreams, he would give his right hand. It was not fair to hurt her. There seemed an eternal maidenhood about her; and when he thought of her mother, he saw the great brown eyes of a maiden who was nearly scared and shocked out of her virgin maidenhood, but not quite, in spite of her seven children. They had been born almost leaving her out of count, not of her, but upon her. So she could never let them go, because she never had possessed them.

Mrs. Morel saw him going again frequently to Miriam, and

was astonished. He said nothing to his mother. He did not
explain nor excuse himself. If he came home late, and she
reproached him, he frowned and turned on her in an overbearing way:

"I shall come home when I like," he said; "I am old enough."

"Must she keep you till this time?"

"It is I who stay," he answered.

"And she lets you? But very well," she said.

And she went to bed, leaving the door unlocked for him; but
she lay listening until he came, often long after. It was a great
bitterness to her that he had gone back to Miriam. She recognised, however, the uselessness of any further interference.
He went to Willey Farm as a man now, not as a youth. She
had no right over him. There was a coldness between him
and her. He hardly told her anything. Discarded, she waited
on him, cooked for him still, and loved to slave for him; but
her face closed again like a mask. There was nothing for her
to do now but the housework; for all the rest he had gone to
Miriam. She could not forgive him. Miriam killed the joy and
the warmth in him. He had been such a jolly lad, and full of
the warmest affection; now he grew colder, more and more
irritable and gloomy. It reminded her of William; but Paul
was worse. He did things with more intensity, and more
realisation of what he was about. His mother knew how he
was suffering for want of a woman, and she saw him going to
Miriam. If he had made up his mind, nothing on earth would
alter him. Mrs. Morel was tired. She began to give up at last;
she had finished. She was in the way.

He went on determinedly. He realised more or less what
his mother felt. It only hardened his soul. He made himself
callous towards her; but it was like being callous to his own
health. It undermined him quickly; yet he persisted.

He lay back in the rocking-chair at Willey Farm one evening.
He had been talking to Miriam for some weeks, but had not
come to the point. Now he said suddenly:

"I am twenty-four, almost."

She had been brooding. She looked up at him suddenly in
surprise.

"Yes. What makes you say it?"

There was something in the charged atmosphere that she
dreaded.

"Sir Thomas More says one can marry at twenty-four."

She laughed quaintly, saying:

"Does it need Sir Thomas More's sanction?"

"No; but one ought to marry about then."

"Ay," she answered broodingly; and she waited.

"I can't marry you," he continued slowly, "not now, because we've no money, and they depend on me at home."

She sat half-guessing what was coming.

"But I want to marry now——"

"You want to marry?" she repeated.

"A woman—you know what I mean."

She was silent.

"Now, at last, I must," he said.

"Ay," she answered.

"And you love me?"

She laughed bitterly.

"Why are you ashamed of it," he answered. "You wouldn't be ashamed before your God, why are you before people?"

"Nay," she answered deeply, "I am not ashamed."

"You are," he replied bitterly; "and it's my fault. But you know I can't help being—as I am—don't you?"

"I know you can't help it," she replied.

"I love you an awful lot—then there is something short."

"Where?" she answered, looking at him.

"Oh, in me! It is I who ought to be ashamed—like a spiritual cripple. And I am ashamed. It is misery. Why is it?"

"I don't know," replied Miriam.

"And I don't know," he repeated. "Don't you think we have been too fierce in our what they call purity? Don't you think that to be so much afraid and averse is a sort of dirtiness?"

She looked at him with startled dark eyes.

"You recoiled away from anything of the sort, and I took the motion from you, and recoiled also, perhaps worse."

There was silence in the room for some time.

"Yes," she said, "it is so."

"There is between us," he said, "all these years of intimacy. I feel naked enough before you. Do you understand?"

"I think so," she answered.

"And you love me?"

She laughed.

"Don't be bitter," he pleaded.

She looked at him and was sorry for him; his eyes were dark with torture. She was sorry for him; it was worse for him to have this deflated love than for herself, who could never be properly mated. He was restless, for ever urging forward and trying to find a way out. He might do as he liked, and have what he liked of her.

"Nay," she said softly, "I am not bitter."

She felt she could bear anything for him; she would suffer for him. She put her hand on his knee as he leaned forward in his chair. He took it and kissed it; but it hurt to do so. He felt he was putting himself aside. He sat there sacrificed to her purity, which felt more like nullity. How could he kiss her hand passionately, when it would drive her away, and leave nothing but pain? Yet slowly he drew her to him and kissed her.

They knew each other too well to pretend anything. As she kissed him, she watched his eyes; they were staring across the room, with a peculiar dark blaze in them that fascinated her. He was perfectly still. She could feel his heart throbbing heavily in his breast.

"What are you thinking about?" she asked.

The blaze in his eyes shuddered, became uncertain.

"I was thinking, all the while, I love you. I have been obstinate."

She sank her head on his breast.

"Yes," she answered.

"That's all," he said, and his voice seemed sure, and his mouth was kissing her throat.

Then she raised her head and looked into his eyes with her full gaze of love. The blaze struggled, seemed to try to get away from her, and then was quenched. He turned his head quickly aside. It was a moment of anguish.

"Kiss me," she whispered.

He shut his eyes, and kissed her, and his arms folded her closer and closer.

When she walked home with him over the fields, he said:

"I am glad I came back to you. I feel so simple with you— as if there was nothing to hide. We will be happy?"

"Yes," she murmured, and the tears came to her eyes.

"Some sort of perversity in our souls," he said, "makes us not want, get away from, the very thing we want. We have to fight against that."

"Yes," she said, and she felt stunned.

As she stood under the drooping-thorn tree, in the darkness

by the roadside, he kissed her, and his fingers wandered over
her face. In the darkness, where he could not see her but only
feel her, his passion flooded him. He clasped her very close.

"Sometime you will have me?" he murmured, hiding his face
on her shoulder. It was so difficult.

"Not now," she said.

His hopes and his heart sunk. A dreariness came over him.

"No," he said.

His clasp of her slackened.

"I love to feel your arm *there*!" she said, pressing his arm
against her back, where it went round her waist. "It rests
me so."

He tightened the pressure of his arm upon the small of her
back to rest her.

"We belong to each other," he said.

"Yes."

"Then why shouldn't we belong to each other altogether?"

"But——" she faltered.

"I know it's a lot to ask," he said; "but there's not much risk
for you really—not in the Gretchen way. You can trust me
there?"

"Oh, I can trust you." The answer came quick and strong.
"It's not that—it's not that at all—but——"

"What?"

She hid her face in his neck with a little cry of misery.

"I don't know!" she cried.

She seemed slightly hysterical, but with a sort of horror. His
heart died in him.

"You don't think it ugly?" he asked.

"No, not now. You have *taught* me it isn't."

"You are afraid?"

She calmed herself hastily.

"Yes, I am only afraid," she said.

He kissed her tenderly.

"Never mind," he said. "You should please yourself."

Suddenly she gripped his arms round her, and clenched her
body stiff.

"You *shall* have me," she said, through her shut teeth.

His heart beat up again like fire. He folded her close, and
his mouth was on her throat. She could not bear it. She drew
away. He disengaged her.

"Won't you be late?" she asked gently.

He sighed, scarcely hearing what she said. She waited, wishing he would go. At last he kissed her quickly and climbed the fence. Looking round he saw the pale blotch of her face down in the darkness under the hanging tree. There was no more of her but this pale blotch.

"Good-bye!" she called softly. She had no body, only a voice and a dim face. He turned away and ran down the road, his fists clenched; and when he came to the wall over the lake he leaned there, almost stunned, looking up the black water.

Miriam plunged home over the meadows. She was not afraid of people, what they might say; but she dreaded the issue with him. Yes, she would let him have her if he insisted; and then, when she thought of it afterwards, her heart went down. He would be disappointed, he would find no satisfaction, and then he would go away. Yet he was so insistent; and over this, which did not seem so all-important to her, was their love to break down. After all, he was only like other men, seeking his satisfaction. Oh, but there was something more in him, something deeper! She could trust to it, in spite of all desires. He said that possession was a great moment in life. All strong emotions concentrated there. Perhaps it was so. There was something divine in it; then she would submit, religiously, to the sacrifice. He should have her. And at the thought her whole body clenched itself involuntarily, hard, as if against something; but Life forced her through this gate of suffering, too, and she would submit. At any rate, it would give him what he wanted, which was her deepest wish. She brooded and brooded and brooded herself towards accepting him.

He courted her now like a lover. Often, when he grew hot, she put his face from her, held it between her hands, and looked in his eyes. He could not meet her gaze. Her dark eyes, full of love, earnest and searching, made him turn away. Not for an instant would she let him forget. Back again he had to torture himself into a sense of his responsibility and hers. Never any relaxing, never any leaving himself to the great hunger and impersonality of passion; he must be brought back to a deliberate, reflective creature. As if from a swoon of passion she called him back to the littleness, the personal relationship. He could not bear it. "Leave me alone—leave me alone!" he wanted to cry; but she wanted him to look at her with eyes full of love. His eyes, full of the dark, impersonal fire of desire, did not belong to her.

There was a great crop of cherries at the farm. The trees at
the back of the house, very large and tall, hung thick with
scarlet and crimson drops, under the dark leaves. Paul and
Edgar were gathering the fruit one evening. It had been a hot
day, and now the clouds were rolling in the sky, dark and
warm. Paul climbed high in the tree, above the scarlet roofs
of the buildings. The wind, moaning steadily, made the whole
tree rock with a subtle, thrilling motion that stirred the blood.
The young man, perched insecurely in the slender branches,
rocked till he felt slightly drunk, reached down the boughs,
where the scarlet beady cherries hung thick underneath, and
tore off handful after handful of the sleek, cool-fleshed fruit.
Cherries touched his ears and his neck as he stretched forward,
their chill finger-tips sending a flash down his blood. All shades
of red, from a golden vermilion to a rich crimson, glowed and
met his eyes under a darkness of leaves.

The sun, going down, suddenly caught the broken clouds.
Immense piles of gold flared out in the south-east, heaped in
soft, glowing yellow right up the sky. The world, till now
dusk and grey, reflected the gold glow, astonished. Everywhere
the trees, and the grass, and the far-off water, seemed roused
from the twilight and shining.

Miriam came out wondering.

"Oh!" Paul heard her mellow voice call, "isn't it wonderful?"

He looked down. There was a faint gold glimmer on her
face, that looked very soft, turned up to him.

"How high you are!" she said.

Beside her, on the rhubarb leaves, were four dead birds,
thieves that had been shot. Paul saw some cherry stones hanging quite bleached, like skeletons, picked clear of flesh. He
looked down again to Miriam.

"Clouds are on fire," he said.

"Beautiful!" she cried.

She seemed so small, so soft, so tender, down there. He threw
a handful of cherries at her. She was startled and frightened.
He laughed with a low, chuckling sound, and pelted her. She
ran for shelter, picking up some cherries. Two fine red pairs
she hung over her ears; then she looked up again.

"Haven't you got enough?" she asked.

"Nearly. It is like being on a ship up here."

"And how long will you stay?"

"While the sunset lasts."

She went to the fence and sat there, watching the gold clouds fall to pieces, and go in immense, rose-coloured ruin towards the darkness. Gold flamed to scarlet, like pain in its intense brightness. Then the scarlet sank to rose, and rose to crimson, and quickly the passion went out of the sky. All the world was dark grey. Paul scrambled quickly down with his basket, tearing his shirt-sleeve as he did so.

"They are lovely," said Miriam, fingering the cherries.

"I've torn my sleeve," he answered.

She took the three-cornered rip, saying:

"I shall have to mend it." It was near the shoulder. She put her fingers through the tear. "How warm!" she said.

He laughed. There was a new, strange note in his voice, one that made her pant.

"Shall we stay out?" he said.

"Won't it rain?" she asked.

"No, let us walk a little way."

They went down the fields and into the thick plantation of fir-trees and pines.

"Shall we go in among the trees?" he asked.

"Do you want to?"

"Yes."

It was very dark among the firs, and the sharp spines pricked her face. She was afraid. Paul was silent and strange.

"I like the darkness," he said. "I wish it were thicker—good, thick darkness."

He seemed to be almost unaware of her as a person: she was only to him then a woman. She was afraid.

He stood against a pine-tree trunk and took her in his arms. She relinquished herself to him, but it was a sacrifice in which she felt something of horror. This thick-voiced, oblivious man was a stranger to her.

Later it began to rain. The pine-trees smelled very strong. Paul lay with his head on the ground, on the dead pine needles, listening to the sharp hiss of the rain—a steady, keen noise. His heart was down, very heavy. Now he realised that she had not been with him all the time, that her soul had stood apart, in a sort of horror. He was physically at rest, but no more. Very dreary at heart, very sad, and very tender, his fingers wandered over her face pitifully. Now again she loved him deeply. He was tender and beautiful.

"The rain!" he said.

"Yes—is it coming on you?"

She put her hands over him, on his hair, on his shoulders, to feel if the raindrops fell on him. She loved him dearly. He, as he lay with his face on the dead pine-leaves, felt extraordinarily quiet. He did not mind if the raindrops came on him: he would have lain and got wet through: he felt as if nothing mattered, as if his living were smeared away into the beyond, near and quite lovable. This strange, gentle reaching-out to death was new to him.

"We must go," said Miriam.

"Yes," he answered, but did not move.

To him now, life seemed a shadow, day a white shadow; night, and death, and stillness, and inaction, this seemed like *being*. To be alive, to be urgent and insistent—that was *not-to-be*. The highest of all was to melt out into the darkness and sway there, identified with the great Being.

"The rain is coming in on us," said Miriam.

He rose, and assisted her.

"It is a pity," he said.

"What?"

"To have to go. I feel so still."

"Still!" she repeated.

"Stiller than I have ever been in my life."

He was walking with his hand in hers. She pressed his fingers, feeling a slight fear. Now he seemed beyond her; she had a fear lest she should lose him.

"The fir-trees are like presences on the darkness: each one only a presence."

She was afraid, and said nothing.

"A sort of hush: the whole night wondering and asleep: I suppose that's what we do in death—sleep in wonder."

She had been afraid before of the brute in him: now of the mystic. She trod beside him in silence. The rain fell with a heavy "Hush!" on the trees. At last they gained the cart-shed.

"Let us stay here awhile," he said.

There was a sound of rain everywhere, smothering everything.

"I feel so strange and still," he said; "along with everything."

"Ay," she answered patiently.

He seemed again unaware of her, though he held her hand close.

"To be rid of our individuality, which is our will, which is our effort—to live effortless, a kind of curious sleep—that is very beautiful, I think; that is our after-life—our immortality."

"Yes?"

"Yes—and very beautiful to have."

"You don't usually say that."

"No."

In a while they went indoors. Everybody looked at them curiously. He still kept the quiet, heavy look in his eyes, the stillness in his voice. Instinctively, they all left him alone.

About this time Miriam's grandmother, who lived in a tiny cottage in Woodlinton, fell ill, and the girl was sent to keep house. It was a beautiful little place. The cottage had a big garden in front, with red brick walls, against which the plum trees were nailed. At the back another garden was separated from the fields by a tall old hedge. It was very pretty. Miriam had not much to do, so she found time for her beloved reading, and for writing little introspective pieces which interested her.

At the holiday-time her grandmother, being better, was driven to Derby to stay with her daughter for a day or two. She was a crotchety old lady, and might return the second day or the third; so Miriam stayed alone in the cottage, which also pleased her.

Paul used often to cycle over, and they had as a rule peaceful and happy times. He did not embarrass her much; but then on the Monday of the holiday he was to spend a whole day with her.

It was perfect weather. He left his mother, telling her where he was going. She would be alone all the day. It cast a shadow over him; but he had three days that were all his own, when he was going to do as he liked. It was sweet to rush through the morning lanes on his bicycle.

He got to the cottage at about eleven o'clock. Miriam was busy preparing dinner. She looked so perfectly in keeping with the little kitchen, ruddy and busy. He kissed her and sat down to watch. The room was small and cosy. The sofa was covered all over with a sort of linen in squares of red and pale blue, old, much washed, but pretty. There was a stuffed owl in a case over a corner cupboard. The sunlight came through the leaves of the scented geraniums in the window. She was cooking a chicken in his honour. It was their cottage for the day, and they were man and wife. He beat the eggs for her and peeled the potatoes. He thought she gave a feeling of home almost like his mother; and no one could look more beautiful, with her tumbled curls, when she was flushed from the fire.

The dinner was a great success. Like a young husband, he carved. They talked all the time with unflagging zest. Then he wiped the dishes she had washed, and they went out down the fields. There was a bright little brook that ran into a bog at the foot of a very steep bank. Here they wandered, picking still a few marsh-marigolds and many big blue forget-me-nots. Then she sat on the bank with her hands full of flowers, mostly golden water-blobs. As she put her face down into the marigolds, it was all overcast with a yellow shine.

"Your face is bright," he said, "like a transfiguration."

She looked at him, questioning. He laughed pleadingly to her, laying his hands on hers. Then he kissed her fingers, then her face.

The world was all steeped in sunshine, and quite still, yet not asleep, but quivering with a kind of expectancy.

"I have never seen anything more beautiful than this," he said. He held her hand fast all the time.

"And the water singing to itself as it runs—do you love it?" She looked at him full of love. His eyes were very dark, very bright.

"Don't you think it's a great day?' he asked.

She murmured her assent. She *was* happy, and he saw it.

"And our day—just between us," he said.

They lingered a little while. Then they stood up upon the sweet thyme, and he looked down at her simply.

"Will you come?" he asked.

They went back to the house, hand in hand, in silence. The chickens came scampering down the path to her. He locked the door, and they had the little house to themselves.

He never forgot seeing her as she lay on the bed, when he was unfastening his collar. First he saw only her beauty, and was blind with it. She had the most beautiful body he had ever imagined. He stood unable to move or speak, looking at her, his face half-smiling with wonder. And then he wanted her, but as he went forward to her, her hands lifted in a little pleading movement, and he looked at her face, and stopped. Her big brown eyes were watching him, still and resigned and loving; she lay as if she had given herself up to sacrifice: there was her body for him; but the look at the back of her eyes, like a creature awaiting immolation, arrested him, and all his blood fell back.

"You are sure you want me?" he asked, as if a cold shadow had come over him.

"Yes, quite sure."

She was very quiet, very calm. She only realised that she was doing something for him. He could hardly bear it. She lay to be sacrificed for him because she loved him so much. And he had to sacrifice her. For a second, he wished he were sexless or dead. Then he shut his eyes again to her, and his blood beat back again.

And afterwards he loved her—loved her to the last fibre of his being. He loved her. But he wanted, somehow, to cry. There was something he could not bear for her sake. He stayed with her till quite late at night. As he rode home he felt that he was finally initiated. He was a youth no longer. But why had he the dull pain in his soul? Why did the thought of death, the after-life, seem so sweet and consoling?

He spent the week with Miriam, and wore her out with his passion before it was gone. He had always, almost wilfully, to put her out of count, and act from the brute strength of his own feelings. And he could not do it often, and there remained afterwards always the sense of failure and of death. If he were really with her, he had to put aside himself and his desire. If he would have her, he had to put her aside.

"When I come to you," he asked her, his eyes dark with pain and shame, "you don't really want me, do you?"

"Ah, yes!" she replied quickly.

He looked at her.

"Nay," he said.

She began to tremble.

"You see," she said, taking his face and shutting it out against her shoulder—"you see—as we are—how can I get used to you? It would come all right if we were married."

He lifted her head, and looked at her.

"You mean, now, it is always too much shock?"

"Yes—and——"

"You are always clenched against me."

She was trembling with agitation.

"You see," she said, "I'm not used to the thought——"

"You are lately," he said.

"But all my life. Mother said to me: 'There is one thing in

marriage that is always dreadful, but you have to bear it.' And I believed it."

"And still believe it," he said.

"No!" she cried hastily. "I believe, as you do, that loving, even in *that* way, is the high-water mark of living."

"That doesn't alter the fact that you never *want* it."

"No," she said, taking his head in her arms and rocking in despair. "Don't say so! You don't understand." She rocked with pain. "Don't I want your children?"

"But not me."

"How can you say so? But we must be married to have children——"

"Shall we be married, then? *I* want you to have my children."

He kissed her hand reverently. She pondered sadly, watching him.

"We are too young," she said at length.

"Twenty-four and twenty-three——"

"Not yet," she pleaded, as she rocked herself in distress.

"When you will," he said.

She bowed her head gravely. The tone of hopelessness in which he said these things grieved her deeply. It had always been a failure between them. Tacitly, she acquiesced in what he felt.

And after a week of love he said to his mother suddenly one Sunday night, just as they were going to bed:

"I shan't go so much to Miriam's, mother."

She was surprised, but she would not ask him anything.

"You please yourself,' she said.

So he went to bed. But there was a new quietness about him which she had wondered at. She almost guessed. She would leave him alone, however. Precipitation might spoil things. She watched him in his loneliness, wondering where he would end. He was sick, and much too quiet for him. There was a perpetual little knitting of his brows, such as she had seen when he was a small baby, and which had been gone for many years. Now it was the same again. And she could do nothing for him. He had to go on alone, make his own way.

He continued faithful to Miriam. For one day he had loved her utterly. But it never came again. The sense of failure grew stronger. At first it was only a sadness. Then he began to feel he could not go on. He wanted to run, to go abroad, anything. Gradually he ceased to ask her to have him. Instead of drawing them together, it put them apart. And then he realised, consciously, that it was no good. It was useless trying: it would never be a success between them.

For some months he had seen very little of Clara. They had occasionally walked out for half an hour at dinner-time. But he always reserved himself for Miriam. With Clara, however, his brow cleared, and he was gay again. She treated him indulgently, as if he were a child. He thought he did not mind. But deep below the surface it piqued him.

Sometimes Miriam said:

"What about Clara? I hear nothing of her lately."

"I walked with her about twenty minutes yesterday," he replied.

"And what did she talk about?"

"I don't know. I suppose I did all the jawing—I usually do. I think I was telling her about the strike, and how the women took it."

"Yes."

So he gave the account of himself.

But insidiously, without his knowing it, the warmth he felt for Clara drew him away from Miriam, for whom he felt responsible, and to whom he felt he belonged. He thought he was being quite faithful to her. It was not easy to estimate exactly the strength and warmth of one's feelings for a woman till they have run away with one.

He began to give more time to his men friends. There was Jessop, at the art school; Swain, who was chemistry demonstrator at the university; Newton, who was a teacher; besides Edgar and Miriam's younger brothers. Pleading work, he sketched and studied with Jessop. He called in the University for Swain, and the two went "down town" together. Having come home in the train with Newton, he called and had a game of billiards with him in the Moon and Stars. If he gave to Miriam the excuse of his men friends, he felt quite justified. His mother began to be relieved. He always told her where he had been.

During the summer Clara wore sometimes a dress of soft cotton stuff with loose sleeves. When she lifted her hands, her sleeves fell back, and her beautiful strong arms shone out.

"Half a minute," he cried. "Hold your arm still."

He made sketches of her hand and arm, and the drawings

contained some of the fascination the real thing had for him.
Miriam, who always went scrupulously through his books and
papers, saw the drawings.

"I think Clara has such beautiful arms," he said.

"Yes! When did you draw them?"

"On Tuesday, in the work-room. You know, I've got a
corner where I can work. Often I can do every single thing
they need in the department, before dinner. Then I work for
myself in the afternoon, and just see to things at night."

"Yes," she said, turning the leaves of his sketch-book.

Frequently he hated Miriam. He hated her as she bent
forward and pored over his things. He hated her way of
patiently casting him up, as if he were an endless psychological
account. When he was with her, he hated her for having got
him, and yet not got him, and he tortured her. She took all and
gave nothing, he said. At least, she gave no living warmth. She
was never alive, and giving off life. Looking for her was like
looking for something which did not exist. She was only his
conscience, not his mate. He hated her violently, and was more
cruel to her. They dragged on till the next summer. He saw
more and more of Clara.

At last he spoke. He had been sitting working at home one
evening. There was between him and his mother a peculiar
condition of people frankly finding fault with each other. Mrs.
Morel was strong on her feet again. He was not going to stick
to Miriam. Very well; then she would stand aloof till he said
something. It had been coming a long time, this bursting of the
storm in him, when he would come back to her. This evening
there was between them a peculiar condition of suspense. He
worked feverishly and mechanically, so that he could escape
from himself. It grew late. Through the open door, stealthily,
came the scent of madonna lilies, almost as if it were prowling
abroad. Suddenly he got up and went out of doors.

The beauty of the night made him want to shout. A half-
moon, dusky gold, was sinking behind the black sycamore at
the end of the garden, making the sky dull purple with its
glow. Nearer, a dim white fence of lilies went across the
garden, and the air all round seemed to stir with scent, as if
it were alive. He went across the bed of pinks, whose keen
perfume came sharply across the rocking, heavy scent of the
lilies, and stood alongside the white barrier of flowers. They
flagged all loose, as if they were panting. The scent made him

drunk. He went down to the field to watch the moon sink under.

A corncrake in the hay-close called insistently. The moon slid quite quickly downwards, growing more flushed. Behind him the great flowers leaned as if they were calling. And then, like a shock, he caught another perfume, something raw and coarse. Hunting round, he found the purple iris, touched their fleshy throats and their dark, grasping hands. At any rate, he had found something. They stood stiff in the darkness. Their scent was brutal. The moon was melting down upon the crest of the hill. It was gone; all was dark. The corncrake called still.

Breaking off a pink, he suddenly went indoors.

"Come, my boy," said his mother. "I'm sure it s time you went to bed."

He stood with the pink against his lips.

"I shall break off with Miriam, mother," he answered calmly.

She looked up at him over her spectacles. He was staring back at her, unswerving. She met his eyes for a moment, then took off her glasses. He was white. The male was up in him, dominant. She did not want to see him too clearly.

"But I thought——" she began.

"Well," he answered, "I don't love her. I don't want to marry her—so I shall have done."

"But," exclaimed his mother, amazed, "I thought lately you had made up your mind to have her, and so I said nothing."

"I had—I wanted to—but now I don't want. It's no good. I shall break off on Sunday. I ought to, oughtn't I?"

"You know best. You know I said so long ago."

"I can't help that now. I shall break off on Sunday."

"Well," said his mother, "I think it will be best. But lately I decided you had made up your mind to have her, so I said nothing, and should have said nothing. But I say as I have always said, I *don't* think she is suited to you."

"On Sunday I break off," he said, smelling the pink. He put the flower in his mouth. Unthinking, he bared his teeth, closed them on the blossom slowly, and had a mouthful of petals. These he spat into the fire, kissed his mother, and went to bed.

On Sunday he went up to the farm in the early afternoon. He had written Miriam that they would walk over the fields to Hucknall. His mother was very tender with him. He said nothing. But she saw the effort it was costing. The peculiar set look on his face stilled her.

"Never mind, my son," she said. "You will be so much better when it is all over."

Paul glanced swiftly at his mother in surprise and resentment. He did not want sympathy.

Miriam met him at the lane-end. She was wearing a new dress of figured muslin that had short sleeves. Those short sleeves, and Miriam's brown-skinned arms beneath them—such pitiful, resigned arms—gave him so much pain that they helped to make him cruel. She had made herself look so beautiful and fresh for him. She seemed to blossom for him alone. Every time he looked at her—a mature young woman now, and beautiful in her new dress—it hurt so much that his heart seemed almost to be bursting with the restraint he put on it. But he had decided, and it was irrevocable.

On the hills they sat down, and he lay with his head in her lap, whilst she fingered his hair. She knew that "he was not there," as she put it. Often, when she had him with her, she looked for him, and could not find him. But this afternoon she was not prepared.

It was nearly five o'clock when he told her. They were sitting on the bank of a stream, where the lip of turf hung over a hollow bank of yellow earth, and he was hacking away with a stick, as he did when he was perturbed and cruel.

"I have been thinking," he said, "we ought to break off."

"Why?" she cried in surprise.

"Because it's no good going on."

"Why is it no good?"

"It isn't. I don't want to marry. I don't want ever to marry. And if we're not going to marry, it's no good going on."

"But why do you say this now?"

"Because I've made up my mind."

"And what about these last months, and the things you told me then?"

"I can't help it! I don't want to go on."

"You don't want any more of me?"

"I want us to break off—you be free of me, I free of you."

"And what about these last months?"

"I don't know. I've not told you anything but what I thought was true."

"Then why are you different now?"

"I'm not—I'm the same—only I know it's no good going on."

"You haven't told me why it's no good."

"Because I don't want to go on—and I don't want to marry."

"How many times have you offered to marry me, and I wouldn't?"

"I know; but I want us to break off."

There was silence for a moment or two, while he dug viciously at the earth. She bent her head, pondering. He was an unreasonable child. He was like an infant which, when it has drunk its fill, throws away and smashes the cup. She looked at him, feeling she could get hold of him and *wring* some consistency out of him. But she was helpless. Then she cried:

"I have said you were only fourteen—you are only *four*!"

He still dug at the earth viciously. He heard.

"You are a child of four," she repeated in her anger.

He did not answer, but said in his heart: "All right; if I'm a child of four, what do you want me for? *I* don't want another mother." But he said nothing to her, and there was silence.

"And have you told your people?" she asked.

"I have told my mother."

There was another long interval of silence.

"Then what do you *want*?" she asked.

"Why, I want us to separate. We have lived on each other all these years; now let us stop. I will go my own way without you, and you will go your way without me. You will have an independent life of your own then."

There was in it some truth that, in spite of her bitterness, she could not help registering. She knew she felt in a sort of bondage to him, which she hated because she could not control it. She hated her love for him from the moment it grew too strong for her. And, deep down, she had hated him because she loved him and he dominated her. She had resisted his domination. She had fought to keep herself free of him in the last issue. And she *was* free of him, even more than he of her.

"And," he continued, "we shall always be more or less each other's work. You have done a lot for me, I for you. Now let us start and live by ourselves."

"What do you want to do?" she asked.

"Nothing—only to be free," he answered.

She, however, knew in her heart that Clara's influence was over him to liberate him. But she said nothing.

"And what have I to tell my mother?" she asked.

"I told my mother," he answered, "that I was breaking off—clean and altogether."

"I shall not tell them at home," she said.

Frowning, "You please yourself," he said.

He knew he had landed her in a nasty hole, and was leaving her in the lurch. It angered him. *he feels*

"Tell them you wouldn't and won't marry me, and have broken off," he said. "It's true enough."

She bit her finger moodily. She thought over their whole affair. She had known it would come to this; she had seen it all along. It chimed with her bitter expectation.

"Always—it has always been so!" she cried. "It has been one long battle between us—you fighting away from me."

It came from her unawares, like a flash of lightning. The man's heart stood still. Was this how she saw it?

"But we've had *some* perfect hours, *some* perfect times, when we were together!" he pleaded

"Never!" she cried; "never! It has always been you fighting me off." *discord*

"Not always—not at first!" he pleaded.

"Always, from the very beginning—always the same!"

She had finished, but she had done enough. He sat aghast. He had wanted to say: "It has been good, but it is at an end." *oh yes!!* *oh no—*
And she—she whose love he had believed in when he had despised himself—denied that their love had ever been love. "He had always fought away from her?" Then it had been monstrous. There had never been anything really between them; all the time he had been imagining something where there was nothing. And she had known. She had known so much, and had told him so little. She had known all the time. All the time this was at the bottom of her!

He sat silent in bitterness. At last the whole affair appeared in a cynical aspect to him. She had really played with him, not he with her. She had hidden all her condemnation from him, had flattered him, and despised him. She despised him now. He grew intellectual and cruel.

"You ought to marry a man who worships you," he said; "then you could do as you liked with him. Plenty of men will worship you, if you get on the private side of their natures. You ought to marry one such. They would never fight you off."

"Thank you!" she said. "But don't advise me to marry someone else any more. You've done it before."

"Very well," he said; "I will say no more."

He sat still, feeling as if he had had a blow, instead of giving one. Their eight years of friendship and love, *the* eight years of his life, were nullified.

"When did you think of this?" she asked.

"I thought definitely on Thursday night."

"I knew it was coming," she said.

That pleased him bitterly. "Oh, very well! If she knew then it doesn't come as a surprise to her," he thought.

"And have you said anything to Clara?" she asked.

"No; but I shall tell her now."

There was a silence.

"Do you remember the things you said this time last year, in my grandmother's house—nay last month even?"

"Yes," he said; "I do! And I meant them! I can't help that it's failed."

"It has failed because you want something else."

"It would have failed whether or not. *You* never believed in me."

She laughed strangely.

He sat in silence. He was full of a feeling that she had deceived him. She had despised him when he thought she worshipped him. She had let him say wrong things, and had not contradicted him. She had let him fight alone. But it stuck in his throat that she had despised him whilst he thought she worshipped him. She should have told him when she found fault with him. She had not played fair. He hated her. All these years she had treated him as if he were a hero, and thought of him secretly as an infant, a foolish child. Then why had she left the foolish child to his folly? His heart was hard against her.

She sat full of bitterness. She had known—oh, well she had known! All the time he was away from her she had summed him up, seen his littleness, his meanness, and his folly. Even she had guarded her soul against him. She was not overthrown, not prostrated, not even much hurt. She had known. Only why, as he sat there, had he still this strange dominance over her? His very movements fascinated her as if she were hypnotised by him. Yet he was despicable, false, inconsistent, and mean. Why this bondage for her? Why was it the movement of his arm stirred her as nothing else in the world could? Why was she fastened to him? Why, even now, if he looked at her and commanded her, would she have to obey? She would obey him in his trifling commands. But once he was obeyed, then she had him in her power, she knew, to lead him where she would. She was sure of herself. Only, this new influence! Ah, he was not a man! He was a baby that cries for the newest toy. And all the attachment of his soul would not keep him. Very well, he would have to go. But he would come back when he had tired of his new sensation.

He hacked at the earth till she was fretted to death. She rose. He sat flinging lumps of earth in the stream.

"We will go and have tea here?" he asked.

"Yes," she answered.

They chattered over irrelevant subjects during tea. He held forth on the love of ornament—the cottage parlour moved him thereto—and its connection with æsthetics. She was cold and quiet. As they walked home, she asked:

"And we shall not see each other?"

"No—or rarely," he answered.

"Nor write?" she asked, almost sarcastically.

"As you will," he answered. "We're not strangers—never should be, whatever happened. I will write to you now and again. You please yourself."

"I see!" she answered cuttingly.

But he was at that stage at which nothing else hurts. He had made a great cleavage in his life. He had had a great shock when she had told him their love had been always a conflict. Nothing more mattered. If it never had been much, there was no need to make a fuss that it was ended.

He left her at the lane-end. As she went home, solitary, in her new frock, having her people to face at the other end, he stood still with shame and pain in the highroad, thinking of the suffering he caused her.

In the reaction towards restoring his self-esteem, he went into the Willow Tree for a drink. There were four girls who had been out for the day, drinking a modest glass of port. They had some chocolates on the table. Paul sat near with his whisky. He noticed the girls whispering and nudging. Presently one, a bonny dark hussy, leaned to him and said:

"Have a chocolate?"

The others laughed loudly at her impudence.

"All right," said Paul. "Give me a hard one—nut. I don't like creams."

"Here you are, then," said the girl; "here's an almond for you."

She held the sweet between her fingers. He opened his mouth. She popped it in, and blushed.

"You *are* nice!" he said.

"Well," she answered, "we thought you looked overcast, and they dared me offer you a chocolate."

"I don't mind if I have another—another sort," he said.

And presently they were all laughing together.

It was nine o'clock when he got home, falling dark. He entered the house in silence. His mother, who had been waiting, rose anxiously.

"I told her," he said.

"I'm glad," replied the mother, with great relief.

He hung up his cap wearily.

"I said we'd have done altogether," he said.

"That's right, my son," said the mother. "It's hard for her now, but best in the long run. I know. You weren't suited for her."

He laughed shakily as he sat down.

"I've had such a lark with some girls in a pub," he said.

His mother looked at him. He had forgotten Miriam now. He told her about the girls in the Willow Tree. Mrs. Morel looked at him. It seemed unreal, his gaiety. At the back of it was too much horror and misery.

"Now have some supper," she said very gently.

Afterwards he said wistfully:

"She never thought she'd have me, mother, not from the first, and so she's not disappointed."

"I'm afraid," said his mother, "she doesn't give up hopes of you yet."

"No," he said, "perhaps not."

"You'll find it's better to have done," she said.

"I don't know," he said desperately.

"Well, leave her alone," replied his mother.

So he left her, and she was alone. Very few people cared for her, and she for very few people. She remained alone with herself, waiting.

CHAPTER XII

PASSION

HE was gradually making it possible to earn a livelihood by his art. Liberty's had taken several of his painted designs on various stuffs, and he could sell designs for embroideries, for altar-cloths, and similar things, in one or two places. It was not very much he made at present, but he might extend it. He had also made friends with the designer for a pottery firm, and was gaining some knowledge of his new acquaintance's art. The applied arts interested him very much. At the same time he laboured slowly at his pictures. He loved to paint large figures, full of light, but not merely made up of lights and cast shadows, like the impressionists; rather definite figures that had a certain luminous quality, like some of Michael Angelo's people. And these he fitted into a landscape, in what he thought true proportion. He worked a great deal from memory, using everybody he knew. He believed firmly in his work, that it was good and valuable. In spite of fits of depression, shrinking, everything, he believed in his work.

He was twenty-four when he said his first confident thing to his mother.

"Mother," he said, "I s'll make a painter that they'll attend to."

She sniffed in her quaint fashion. It was like a half-pleased shrug of the shoulders.

"Very well, my boy, we'll see," she said.

"You shall see, my pigeon! You see if you're not swanky one of these days!"

"I'm quite content, my boy," she smiled.

"But you'll have to alter. Look at you with Minnie!"

Minnie was the small servant, a girl of fourteen.

"And what about Minnie?" asked Mrs. Morel, with dignity.

"I heard her this morning: 'Eh, Mrs. Morel! I was going to do that,' when you went out in the rain for some coal," he said. "That looks a lot like your being able to manage servants!"

"Well, it was only the child's niceness," said Mrs. Morel.

"And you apologising to her: 'You can't do two things at once, can you?'"

"She *was* busy washing up," replied Mrs. Morel.

"And what did she say? 'It could easy have waited a bit. Now look how your feet paddle!'"

"Yes—brazen young baggage!" said Mrs. Morel, smiling.

He looked at his mother, laughing. She was quite warm and rosy again with love of him. It seemed as if all the sunshine were on her for a moment. He continued his work gladly. She seemed so well when she was happy that he forgot her grey hair.

And that year she went with him to the Isle of Wight for a holiday. It was too exciting for them both, and too beautiful. Mrs. Morel was full of joy and wonder. But he would have her walk with him more than she was able. She had a bad fainting bout. So grey her face was, so blue her mouth! It was agony to him. He felt as if someone were pushing a knife in his chest. Then she was better again, and he forgot. But the anxiety remained inside him, like a wound that did not close.

After leaving Miriam he went almost straight to Clara. On the Monday following the day of the rupture he went down to the work-room. She looked up at him and smiled. They had grown very intimate unawares. She saw a new brightness about him.

"Well, Queen of Sheba!" he said, laughing.

"But why?" she asked.

"I think it suits you. You've got a new frock on."

She flushed, asking:

"And what of it?"

"Suits you—awfully! *I* could design you a dress."

"How would it be?"

He stood in front of her, his eyes glittering as he expounded. He kept her eyes fixed with his. Then suddenly he took hold of her. She half-started back. He drew the stuff of her blouse tighter, smoothed it over her breast.

"More *so*!" he explained.

But they were both of them flaming with blushes, and immediately he ran away. He had touched her. His whole body was quivering with the sensation.

There was already a sort of secret understanding between them. The next evening he went to the cinematograph with her for a few minutes before train-time. As they sat, he saw her hand lying near him. For some moments he dared not touch it. The pictures danced and dithered. Then he took her hand in his. It was large and firm; it filled his grasp. He held

it fast. She neither moved nor made any sign. When they
came out his train was due. He hesitated.

"Good-night," she said. He darted away across the road.

The next day he came again, talking to her. She was rather
superior with him.

"Shall we go a walk on Monday?" he asked.

She turned her face aside.

"Shall you tell Miriam?" she replied sarcastically.

"I have broken off with her," he said.

"When?"

"Last Sunday."

"You quarrelled?"

"No! I had made up my mind. I told her quite definitely I
should consider myself free."

Clara did not answer, and he returned to his work. She was
so quiet and so superb!

On the Saturday evening he asked her to come and drink
coffee with him in a restaurant, meeting him after work was
over. She came, looking very reserved and very distant. He
had three-quarters of an hour to train-time.

"We will walk a little while," he said.

She agreed, and they went past the Castle into the Park.
He was afraid of her. She walked moodily at his side, with a
kind of resentful, reluctant, angry walk. He was afraid to take
her hand.

"Which way shall we go?" he asked as they walked in
darkness.

"I don't mind."

"Then we'll go up the steps."

He suddenly turned round. They had passed the Park steps.
She stood still in resentment at his suddenly abandoning her.
He looked for her. She stood aloof. He caught her suddenly in
his arms, held her strained for a moment, kissed her. Then he
let her go.

"Come along," he said, penitent.

She followed him. He took her hand and kissed her finger-
tips. They went in silence. When they came to the light, he
let go her hand. Neither spoke till they reached the station.
Then they looked each other in the eyes.

"Good-night," she said.

And he went for his train. His body acted mechanically.
People talked to him. He heard faint echoes answering them.

He was in a delirium. He felt that he would go mad if Monday
did not come at once. On Monday he would see her again.
All himself was pitched there, ahead. Sunday intervened. He
could not bear it. He could not see her till Monday. And Sunday intervened—hour after hour of tension. He wanted to
beat his head against the door of the carriage. But he sat still.
He drank some whisky on the way home, but it only made it
worse. His mother must not be upset, that was all. He dis-
sembled, and got quickly to bed. There he sat, dressed, with
his chin on his knees, staring out of the window at the far
hill, with its few lights. He neither thought nor slept, but sat
perfectly still, staring. And when at last he was so cold that
he came to himself, he found his watch had stopped at half-
past two. It was after three o'clock. He was exhausted, but
still there was the torment of knowing it was only Sunday
morning. He went to bed and slept. Then he cycled all day
long, till he was fagged out. And he scarcely knew where he
had been. But the day after was Monday. He slept till four
o'clock. Then he lay and thought. He was coming nearer to
himself—he could see himself, real, somewhere in front. She
would go a walk with him in the afternoon. Afternoon! It
seemed years ahead.

Slowly the hours crawled. His father got up; he heard him
pottering about. Then the miner set off to the pit, his heavy
boots scraping the yard. Cocks were still crowing. A cart went
down the road. His mother got up. She knocked the fire.
Presently she called him softly. He answered as if he were
asleep. This shell of himself did well.

He was walking to the station—another mile! The train was
near Nottingham. Would it stop before the tunnels? But it
did not matter; it would get there before dinner-time. He was
at Jordan's. She would come in half an hour. At any rate, she
would be near. He had done the letters. She would be
there. Perhaps she had not come. He ran downstairs. Ah!
he saw her through the glass door. Her shoulders stooping a little to her work made him feel he could not go forward;
he could not stand. He went in. He was pale, nervous,
awkward, and quite cold. Would she misunderstand him? He
could not write his real self with this shell.

"And this afternoon," he struggled to say. "You will come?"

"I think so," she replied, murmuring.

He stood before her, unable to say a word. She hid her face

from him. Again came over him the feeling that he would lose
consciousness. He set his teeth and went upstairs. He had done
everything correctly yet, and he would do so. All the morning
things seemed a long way off, as they do to a man under chloroform. He himself seemed under a tight band of constraint.
Then there was his other self, in the distance, doing things,
entering stuff in a ledger, and he watched that far-off him carefully to see he made no mistake.

But the ache and strain of it could not go on much longer.
He worked incessantly. Still it was only twelve o'clock. As
if he had nailed his clothing against the desk, he stood there
and worked, forcing every stroke out of himself. It was a
quarter to one; he could clear away. Then he ran downstairs.

"You will meet me at the Fountain at two o'clock," he said.

"I can't be there till half-past."

"Yes!" he said.

She saw his dark, mad eyes.

"I will try at a quarter past."

And he had to be content. He went and got some dinner.
All the time he was still under chloroform, and every minute
was stretched out indefinitely. He walked miles of streets.
Then he thought he would be late at the meeting-place. He
was at the Fountain at five past two. The torture of the next
quarter of an hour was refined beyond expression. It was the
anguish of combining the living self with the shell. Then he
saw her. She came! And he was there.

"You are late," he said.

"Only five minutes," she answered.

"I'd never have done it to you," he laughed.

She was in a dark blue costume. He looked at her beautiful
figure.

"You want some flowers," he said, going to the nearest
florist's.

She followed him in silence. He bought her a bunch of
scarlet, brick-red carnations. She put them in her coat, flushing.

"That's a fine colour!" he said.

"I'd rather have had something softer," she said.

He laughed.

"Do you feel like a blot of vermilion walking down the
street?" he said.

She hung her head, afraid of the people they met. He looked
sideways at her as they walked. There was a wonderful close

down on her face near the ear that he wanted to touch. And a certain heaviness, the heaviness of a very full ear of corn that dips slightly in the wind, that there was about her, made his brain spin. He seemed to be spinning down the street, everything going round.

As they sat in the tramcar, she leaned her heavy shoulder against him, and he took her hand. He felt himself coming round from the anæsthetic, beginning to breathe. Her ear, half-hidden among her blonde hair, was near to him. The temptation to kiss it was almost too great. But there were other people on top of the car. It still remained to him to kiss it. After all, he was not himself, he was some attribute of hers, like the sunshine that fell on her.

He looked quickly away. It had been raining. The big bluff of the Castle rock was streaked with rain, as it reared above the flat of the town. They crossed the wide, black space of the Midland Railway, and passed the cattle enclosure that stood out white. Then they ran down sordid Wilford Road.

She rocked slightly to the tram's motion, and as she leaned against him, rocked upon him. He was a vigorous, slender man, with exhaustless energy. His face was rough, with rough-hewn features, like the common people's; but his eyes under the deep brows were so full of life that they fascinated her. They seemed to dance, and yet they were still trembling on the finest balance of laughter. His mouth the same was just going to spring into a laugh of triumph, yet did not. There was a sharp suspense about him. She bit her lip moodily. His hand was hard clenched over hers.

They paid their two halfpennies at the turnstile and crossed the bridge. The Trent was very full. It swept silent and insidious under the bridge, travelling in a soft body. There had been a great deal of rain. On the river levels were flat gleams of flood water. The sky was grey, with glisten of silver here and there. In Wilford churchyard the dahlias were sodden with rain— wet black-crimson balls. No one was on the path that went along the green river meadow, along the elm-tree colonnade.

There was the faintest haze over the silvery-dark water and the green meadow-bank, and the elm-trees that were spangled with gold. The river slid by in a body, utterly silent and swift, intertwining among itself like some subtle, complex creature. Clara walked moodily beside him.

"Why," she asked at length, in rather a jarring tone, "did you leave Miriam?"

He frowned.

"Because I *wanted* to leave her," he said

"Why?"

"Because I didn't want to go on with her. And I didn't want to marry."

She was silent for a moment. They picked their way down the muddy path. Drops of water fell from the elm-trees.

"You didn't want to marry Miriam, or you didn't want to marry at all?" she asked.

"Both," he answered—"both!"

They had to manœuvre to get to the stile, because of the pools of water.

"And what did she say?" Clara asked.

"Miriam? She said I was a baby of four, and that I always *had* battled her off."

Clara pondered over this for a time.

"But you have really been going with her for some time?" she asked.

"Yes."

"And now you don't want any more of her?"

"No. I know it's no good."

She pondered again

"Don't you think you've treated her rather badly?" she asked.

"Yes; I ought to have dropped it years back. But it would have been no good going on. Two wrongs don't make a right."

"How old *are* you?" Clara asked.

"Twenty-five."

"And I am thirty," she said.

"I know you are."

"I shall be thirty-one—or *am* I thirty-one?"

"I neither know nor care. What does it matter!"

They were at the entrance to the Grove. The wet, red track, already sticky with fallen leaves, went up the steep bank between the grass. On either side stood the elm-trees like pillars along a great aisle, arching over and making high up a roof from which the dead leaves fell. All was empty and silent and wet. She stood on top of the stile, and he held both her hands. Laughing, she looked down into his eyes. Then she leaped. Her breast came against his; he held her, and covered her face with kisses.

They went on up the slippery, steep red path. Presently she released his hand and put it round her waist.

"You press the vein in my arm, holding it so tightly," she said.

They walked along. His finger-tips felt the rocking of her breast. All was silent and deserted. On the left the red wet plough-land showed through the doorways between the elm-boles and their branches. On the right, looking down, they could see the tree-tops of elms growing far beneath them, hear occasionally the gurgle of the river. Sometimes there below they caught glimpses of the full, soft-sliding Trent, and of water-meadows dotted with small cattle.

"It has scarcely altered since little Kirke White used to come," he said.

But he was watching her throat below the ear, where the flush was fusing into the honey-white, and her mouth that pouted disconsolate. She stirred against him as she walked, and his body was like a taut string.

Half-way up the big colonnade of elms, where the Grove rose highest above the river, their forward movement faltered to an end. He led her across to the grass, under the trees at the edge of the path. The cliff of red earth sloped swiftly down, through trees and bushes, to the river that glimmered and was dark between the foliage. The far-below water-meadows were very green. He and she stood leaning against one another, silent, afraid, their bodies touching all along. There came a quick gurgle from the river below.

"Why," he asked at length, "did you hate Baxter Dawes?"

She turned to him with a splendid movement. Her mouth was offered him, and her throat; her eyes were half-shut; her breast was tilted as if it asked for him. He flashed with a small laugh, shut his eyes, and met her in a long, whole kiss. Her mouth fused with his; their bodies were sealed and annealed. It was some minutes before they withdrew. They were standing beside the public path.

"Will you go down to the river?" he asked.

She looked at him, leaving herself in his hands. He went over the brim of the declivity and began to climb down.

"It is slippery," he said.

"Never mind," she replied.

The red clay went down almost sheer. He slid, went from one tuft of grass to the next, hanging on to the bushes, making for a little platform at the foot of a tree. There he waited for her, laughing with excitement. Her shoes were clogged with red earth. It was hard for her. He frowned. At last he caught her hand, and she stood beside him. The cliff rose above them and fell away below. Her colour was up, her eyes flashed. He looked at the big drop below them.

"It's risky," he said; "or messy, at any rate. Shall we go back?"

"Not for my sake," she said quickly.

"All right. You see, I can't help you; I should only hinder. Give me that little parcel and your gloves. Your poor shoes!"

They stood perched on the face of the declivity, under the trees.

"Well, I'll go again," he said.

Away he went, slipping. staggering, sliding to the next tree, into which he fell with a slam that nearly shook the breath out of him. She came after cautiously, hanging on to the twigs and grasses. So they descended, stage by stage, to the river's brink. There, to his disgust, the flood had eaten away the path, and the red decline ran straight into the water. He dug in his heels and brought himself up violently. The string of the parcel broke with a snap; the brown parcel bounded down, leaped into the water, and sailed smoothly away. He hung on to his tree.

"Well, I'll be damned!" he cried crossly. Then he laughed. She was coming perilously down.

"Mind!" he warned her. He stood with his back to the tree, waiting. "Come now," he called, opening his arms.

She let herself run. He caught her, and together they stood watching the dark water scoop at the raw edge of the bank. The parcel had sailed out of sight.

"It doesn't matter," she said.

He held her close and kissed her. There was only room for their four feet.

"It's a swindle!" he said. "But there's a rut where a man has been, so if we go on I guess we shall find the path again."

The river slid and twined its great volume. On the other bank cattle were feeding on the desolate flats. The cliff rose high above Paul and Clara on their right hand. They stood against the tree in the watery silence.

"Let us try going forward," he said; and they struggled in

the red clay along the groove a man's nailed boots had made. They were hot and flushed. Their barkled shoes hung heavy on their steps. At last they found the broken path. It was littered with rubble from the water, but at any rate it was easier. They cleaned their boots with twigs. His heart was beating thick and fast.

Suddenly, coming on to the little level, he saw two figures of men standing silent at the water's edge. His heart leaped. They were fishing. He turned and put his hand up warningly to Clara. She hesitated, buttoned her coat. The two went on together.

The fishermen turned curiously to watch the two intruders on their privacy and solitude. They had had a fire, but it was nearly out. All kept perfectly still. The men turned again to their fishing, stood over the grey glinting river like statues. Clara went with bowed head, flushing; he was laughing to himself. Directly they passed out of sight behind the willows.

"Now they ought to be drowned," said Paul softly.

Clare did not answer. They toiled forward along a tiny path on the river's lip. Suddenly it vanished. The bank was sheer red solid clay in front of them, sloping straight into the river. He stood and cursed beneath his breath, setting his teeth.

"It's impossible!" said Clara.

He stood erect, looking round. Just ahead were two islets in the stream, covered with osiers. But they were unattainable. The cliff came down like a sloping wall from far above their heads. Behind, not far back, were the fishermen. Across the river the distant cattle fed silently in the desolate afternoon. He cursed again deeply under his breath. He gazed up the great steep bank. Was there no hope but to scale back to the public path?

"Stop a minute," he said, and, digging his heels sideways into the steep bank of red clay, he began nimbly to mount. He looked across at every tree-foot. At last he found what he wanted. Two beech-trees side by side on the hill held a little level on the upper face between their roots. It was littered with damp leaves, but it would do. The fishermen were perhaps sufficiently out of sight. He threw down his rainproof and waved to her to come.

She toiled to his side. Arriving there, she looked at him heavily, dumbly, and laid her head on his shoulder. He held her fast as he looked round. They were safe enough from all but the small, lonely cows over the river. He sunk his mouth on her throat, where he felt her heavy pulse beat under his lips. Everything was perfectly still. There was nothing in the afternoon but themselves.

When she arose, he, looking on the ground all the time, saw suddenly sprinkled on the black wet beech-roots many scarlet carnation petals, like splashed drops of blood; and red, small splashes fell from her bosom, streaming down her dress to her feet.

"Your flowers are smashed," he said.

She looked at him heavily as she put back her hair. Suddenly he put his finger-tips on her cheek.

"Why dost look so heavy?" he reproached her.

She smiled sadly, as if she felt alone in herself. He caressed her cheek with his fingers, and kissed her.

"Nay!" he said. "Never thee bother!"

She gripped his fingers tight, and laughed shakily. Then she dropped her hand. He put the hair back from her brows, stroking her temples, kissing them lightly.

"But tha shouldna worrit!" he said softly, pleading.

"No, I don't worry!" she laughed tenderly and resigned.

"Yea, tha does! Dunna thee worrit," he implored, caressing.

"No!" she consoled him, kissing him.

They had a stiff climb to get to the top again. It took them a quarter of an hour. When he got on to the level grass, he threw off his cap, wiped the sweat from his forehead, and sighed.

"Now we're back at the ordinary level," he said.

She sat down, panting, on the tussocky grass. Her cheeks were flushed pink. He kissed her, and she gave way to joy.

"And now I'll clean thy boots and make thee fit for respectable folk," he said.

He kneeled at her feet, worked away with a stick and tufts of grass. She put her fingers in his hair, drew his head to her, and kissed it.

"What am I supposed to be doing," he said, looking at her laughing; "cleaning shoes or dibbling with love? Answer me that!"

"Just whichever I please," she replied.

"I'm your boot-boy for the time being, and nothing else!"

But they remained looking into each other's eyes and laughing. Then they kissed with little nibbling kisses.

"T-t-t-t!" he went with his tongue, like his mother. "I tell you, nothing gets done when there's a woman about."

And he returned to his boot-cleaning, singing softly. She touched his thick hair, and he kissed her fingers. He worked away at her shoes. At last they were quite presentable.

"There you are, you see!" he said. "Aren't I a great hand at restoring you to respectability? Stand up! There, you look as irreproachable as Britannia herself!"

He cleaned his own boots a little, washed his hands in a puddle, and sang. They went on into Clifton village. He was madly in love with her; every movement she made, every crease in her garments, sent a hot flash through him and seemed adorable.

The old lady at whose house they had tea was roused into gaiety by them.

"I could wish you'd had something of a better day," she said, hovering round.

"Nay!" he laughed. "We've been saying how nice it is."

The old lady looked at him curiously. There was a peculiar glow and charm about him. His eyes were dark and laughing. He rubbed his moustache with a glad movement.

"Have you been saying *so*!" she exclaimed, a light rousing in her old eyes.

"Truly!" he laughed.

"Then I'm sure the day's good enough," said the old lady. She fussed about, and did not want to leave them.

"I don't know whether you'd like some radishes as well," she said to Clara; "but I've got some in the garden—*and* a cucumber."

Clara flushed. She looked very handsome.

"I should like some radishes," she answered.

And the old lady pottered off gleefully.

"If she knew!" said Clara quietly to him.

"Well, she doesn't know; and it shows we're nice in ourselves, at any rate. You look quite enough to satisfy an archangel, and I'm sure I feel harmless—so—if it makes you look nice, and makes folk happy when they have us, and makes us happy—why, we're not cheating them out of much!"

They went on with the meal. When they were going away, the old lady came timidly with three tiny dahlias in full blow, neat as bees, and speckled scarlet and white. She stood before Clara, pleased with herself, saying:

"I don't know whether——" and holding the flowers forward in her old hand.

"Oh, how pretty!" cried Clara, accepting the flowers.

"Shall she have them all?" asked Paul reproachfully of the old woman.

"Yes, she shall have them all," she replied, beaming with joy. "You have got enough for your share."

"Ah, but I shall ask her to give me one!" he teased.

"Then she does as she pleases," said the old lady, smiling. And she bobbed a little curtsey of delight.

Clara was rather quiet and uncomfortable. As they walked along, he said:

"You don't feel criminal, do you?"

She looked at him with startled grey eyes.

"Criminal!" she said. "No."

"But you seem to feel you have done a wrong?"

"No," she said. "I only think, 'If they knew!'"

"If they knew, they'd cease to understand. As it is, they do understand, and they like it. What do they matter? Here, with only the trees and me, you don't feel not the least bit wrong, do you?"

He took her by the arm, held her facing him, holding her eyes with his. Something fretted him.

"Not sinners, are we?" he said, with an uneasy little frown.

"No," she replied.

He kissed her, laughing.

"You like your little bit of guiltiness, I believe," he said. "I believe Eve enjoyed it, when she went cowering out of Paradise."

But there was a certain glow and quietness about her that made him glad. When he was alone in the railway-carriage, he found himself tumultuously happy, and the people exceedingly nice, and the night lovely, and everything good.

Mrs. Morel was sitting reading when he got home. Her health was not good now, and there had come that ivory pallor into her face which he never noticed, and which afterwards he never forgot. She did not mention her own ill-health to him. After all, she thought, it was not much.

"You are late!" she said, looking at him.

His eyes were shining; his face seemed to glow. He smiled to her.

"Yes; I've been down Clifton Grove with Clara."

His mother looked at him again.

"But won't people talk?" she said.

"Why? They know she's a suffragette, and so on. And what if they do talk!"

"Of course, there may be nothing wrong in it," said his mother. "But you know what folks are, and if once she gets talked about——"

"Well, I can't help it. Their jaw isn't so almighty important, after all."

"I think you ought to consider *her*."

"So I *do*! What can people say?—that we take a walk together. I believe you're jealous."

"You know I should be *glad* if she weren't a married woman."

"Well, my dear, she lives separate from her husband, and talks on platforms; so she's already singled out from the sheep, and, as far as I can see, hasn't much to lose. No; her life's nothing to her, so what's the worth of nothing? She goes with me—it becomes something. Then she must pay—we both must pay! Folk are so frightened of paying; they'd rather starve and die."

"Very well, my son. We'll see how it will end."

"Very well, my mother. I'll abide by the end."

"We'll see!"

"And she's—she's *awfully* nice, mother; she is really! You don't know!"

"That's not the same as marrying her."

"It's perhaps better."

There was silence for a while. He wanted to ask his mother something, but was afraid.

"Should you like to know her?" He hesitated.

"Yes," said Mrs. Morel coolly. "I should like to know what she's like."

"But she's nice, mother, she is! And not a bit common!"

"I never suggested she was."

"But you seem to think she's—not as good as—— She's better than ninety-nine folk out of a hundred, I tell you! She's *better*, she is! She's fair, she's honest, she straight! There isn't anything underhand or superior about her. Don't be mean about her!"

Mrs. Morel flushed.

"I am sure I am not mean about her. She may be quite as you say, but——"

"You don't approve," he finished.

"And do you expect me to?" she answered coldly.

"Yes!—yes!—if you'd anything about you, you'd be glad! Do you *want* to see her?"

"I said I did."

"Then I'll bring her—shall I bring her here?"

"You please yourself."

"Then I *will* bring her here—one Sunday—to tea. If you think a horrid thing about her, I shan't forgive you."

His mother laughed.

"As if it would make any difference!" she said. He knew he had won.

"Oh, but it feels so fine, when she's there! She's such a queen in her way."

Occasionally he still walked a little way from chapel with Miriam and Edgar. He did not go up to the farm. She, however, was very much the same with him, and he did not feel embarrassed in her presence. One evening she was alone when he accompanied her. They began by talking books: it was their unfailing topic. Mrs. Morel had said that his and Miriam's affair was like a fire fed on books—if there were no more volumes it would die out. Miriam, for her part, boasted that she could read him like a book, could place her finger any minute on the chapter and the line. He, easily taken in, believed that Miriam knew more about him than anyone else. So it pleased him to talk to her about himself, like the simplest egoist. Very soon the conversation drifted to his own doings. It flattered him immensely that he was of such supreme interest.

"And what have you been doing lately?"

"I—oh, not much! I made a sketch of Bestwood from the garden, that is nearly right at last. It's the hundredth try."

So they went on. Then she said:

"You've not been out, then, lately?"

"Yes; I went up Clifton Grove on Monday afternoon with Clara."

"It was not very nice weather," said Miriam, "was it?"

"But I wanted to go out, and it was all right. The Trent *is* full."

"And did you go to Barton?" she asked.

"No; we had tea in Clifton."

"*Did* you! That would be nice."

"It was! The jolliest old woman! She gave us several pom-pom dahlias, as pretty as you like."

Miriam bowed her head and brooded. He was quite unconscious of concealing anything from her.

"What made her give them you?" she asked.

He laughed.

"Because she liked us—because we were jolly, I should think."

Miriam put her finger in her mouth.

"Were you late home?" she asked.

At last he resented her tone.

"I caught the seven-thirty."

"Ha!"

They walked on in silence, and he was angry.

"And how *is* Clara?" asked Miriam.

"Quite all right, I think."

"That's good!" she said, with a tinge of irony. "By the way, what of her husband? One never hears anything of him."

"He's got some other woman, and is also quite all right," he replied. "At least, so I think."

"I see—you don't know for certain. Don't you think a position like that is hard on a woman?"

"Rottenly hard!"

"It's so unjust!" said Miriam. "The man does as he likes——"

"Then let the woman also," he said.

"How can she? And if she does, look at her position!"

"What of it?"

"Why, it's impossible! You don't understand what a woman forfeits——"

"No, I don't. But if a woman's got nothing but her fair fame to feed on, why, it's thin tack, and a donkey would die of it!"

So she understood his moral attitude, at least, and she knew he would act accordingly.

She never asked him anything direct, but she got to know enough.

Another day, when he saw Miriam, the conversation turned to marriage, then to Clara's marriage with Dawes.

"You see," he said, "she never knew the fearful importance of marriage. She thought it was all in the day's march—it would have to come—and Dawes—well, a good many women would have given their souls to get him; so why not him? Then she developed into the *femme incomprise*, and treated him badly, I'll bet my boots."

"And she left him because he didn't understand her?"

"I suppose so. I suppose she had to. It isn't altogether a question of understanding; it's a question of living. With him, she was only half-alive; the rest was dormant, deadened. And the dormant woman was the *femme incomprise*, and she *had* to be awakened."

"And what about him."

"I don't know. I rather think he loves her as much as he can, but he's a fool."

"It was something like your mother and father," said Miriam.

'Yes; but my mother, I believe, got real joy and satisfaction out of my father at first. I believe she had a passion for him; that's why she stayed with him. After all, they were bound to each other."

"Yes," said Miriam.

"That's what one *must have*, I think," he continued—"the real, real flame of feeling through another person—once, only once, if it only lasts three months. See, my mother looks as if she'd *had* everything that was necessary for her living and developing. There's not a tiny bit of feeling of sterility about her."

"No," said Miriam.

"And with my father, at first, I'm sure she had the real thing. She knows; she has been there. You can feel it about her, and about him, and about hundreds of people you meet every day; and, once it has happened to you, you can go on with anything and ripen."

"What happened, exactly?" asked Miriam.

"It's so hard to say, but the something big and intense that changes you when you really come together with somebody else. It almost seems to fertilise your soul and make it that you can go on and mature."

"And you think your mother had it with your father?"

"Yes; and at the bottom she feels grateful to him for giving it her, even now, though they are miles apart."

"And you think Clara never had it?"

"I'm sure."

Miriam pondered this. She saw what he was seeking—a sort of baptism of fire in passion, it seemed to her. She realised that he would never be satisfied till he had it. Perhaps it was essential to him, as to some men, to sow wild oats; and afterwards, when he was satisfied, he would not rage with restlessness any more, but could settle down and give her his life into her hands. Well, then, if he must go, let him go and have his fill—something big and intense, he called it. At any rate, when he had got it, he would not want it—that he said himself; he would want the other thing that she could give him. He would want to be owned, so that he could work. It seemed to her a bitter thing that he must go, but she could let him go into an inn for a glass of whisky, so she could let him go to Clara, so long as it was something that would satisfy a need in him, and leave him free for herself to possess.

"Have you told your mother about Clara?" she asked.

She knew this would be a test of the seriousness of his feeling for the other woman: she knew he was going to Clara for something vital, not as a man goes for pleasure to a prostitute, if he told his mother.

"Yes," he said, "and she is coming to tea on Sunday."

"To your house?"

"Yes; I want mater to see her."

"Ah!"

There was a silence. Things had gone quicker than she thought. She felt a sudden bitterness that he could leave her so soon and so entirely. And was Clara to be accepted by his people, who had been so hostile to herself?

"I may call in as I go to chapel," she said. "It is a long time since I saw Clara."

"Very well," he said, astonished, and unconsciously angry.

On the Sunday afternoon he went to Keston to meet Clara at the station. As he stood on the platform he was trying to examine in himself if he had a premonition.

"Do I *feel* as if she'd come?" he said to himself, and he tried to find out. His heart felt queer and contracted. That seemed like foreboding. Then he *had* a foreboding she would not come! Then she would not come, and instead of taking her over the fields home, as he had imagined, he would have to go alone. The train was late; the afternoon would be wasted, and the evening. He hated her for not coming. Why had she promised, then, if she could not keep her promise? Perhaps she had missed her train—he himself was always missing trains—but that was no reason why she should miss this particular one. He was angry with her; he was furious.

Suddenly he saw the train crawling, sneaking round the corner. Here, then, was the train, but of course she had not come. The green engine hissed along the platform, the row of brown carriages drew up, several doors opened. No; she had not come! No! Yes; ah, there she was! She had a big black hat on! He was at her side in a moment.

"I thought you weren't coming," he said.

She was laughing rather breathlessly as she put out her hand to him; their eyes met. He took her quickly along the platform, talking at a great rate to hide his feeling. She looked beautiful. In her hat were large silk roses, coloured like tarnished gold. Her costume of dark cloth fitted so beautifully over her breast and shoulders. His pride went up as he walked with her. He felt the station people, who knew him, eyed her with awe and admiration.

"I was sure you weren't coming," he laughed shakily.

She laughed in answer, almost with a little cry.

"And I wondered, when I was in the train, what*ever* I should do if you weren't there!" she said.

He caught her hand impulsively, and they went along the narrow twitchel. They took the road into Nuttall and over the Reckoning House Farm. It was a blue, mild day. Everywhere the brown leaves lay scattered; many scarlet hips stood upon the hedge beside the wood. He gathered a few for her to wear.

"Though, really," he said, as he fitted them into the breast of her coat, "you ought to object to my getting them, because of the birds. But they don't care much for rose-hips in this part, where they can get plenty of stuff. You often find the berries going rotten in the springtime."

So he chattered, scarcely aware of what he said, only knowing he was putting berries in the bosom of her coat, while she stood patiently for him. And she watched his quick hands, so full of life, and it seemed to her she had never *seen* anything before. Till now, everything had been indistinct.

They came near to the colliery. It stood quite still and black among the corn-fields, its immense heap of slag seen rising almost from the oats.

"What a pity there is a coal-pit here where it is so pretty!" said Clara.

"Do you think so?" he answered. "You see, I am so used to it I should miss it. No; and I like the pits here and there. I like the rows of trucks, and the headstocks, and the steam in the daytime, and the lights at night. When I was a boy, I always thought a pillar of cloud by day and a pillar of fire by night was a pit, with its steam, and its lights, and the burning bank,—and I thought the Lord was always at the pit-top."

As they drew near home she walked in silence, and seemed to hang back. He pressed her fingers in his own. She flushed, but gave no response.

"Don't you want to come home?" he asked.

"Yes, I want to come," she replied.

It did not occur to him that her position in his home would be rather a peculiar and difficult one. To him it seemed just as if one of his men friends were going to be introduced to his mother, only nicer.

The Morels lived in a house in an ugly street that ran down a steep hill. The street itself was hideous. The house was rather superior to most. It was old, grimy, with a big bay window, and it was semi-detached; but it looked gloomy. Then Paul opened the door to the garden, and all was different. The sunny afternoon was there, like another land. By the path grew tansy and little trees. In front of the window was a plot of sunny grass, with old lilacs round it. And away went the garden, with heaps of dishevelled chrysanthemums in the sunshine, down to the sycamore-tree, and the field, and beyond one looked over a few red-roofed cottages to the hills with all the glow of the autumn afternoon.

Mrs. Morel sat in her rocking-chair, wearing her black silk blouse. Her grey-brown hair was taken smooth back from her brow and her high temples; her face was rather pale. Clara, suffering, followed Paul into the kitchen. Mrs. Morel rose. Clara thought her a lady, even rather stiff. The young woman was very nervous. She had almost a wistful look, almost resigned.

"Mother—Clara," said Paul.

Mrs. Morel held out her hand and smiled.

"He has told me a good deal about you," she said.

The blood flamed in Clara's cheek.

"I hope you don't mind my coming," she faltered.

"I was pleased when he said he would bring you," replied Mrs. Morel.

Paul, watching, felt his heart contract with pain. His mother looked so small, and sallow, and done-for beside the luxuriant Clara.

"It's such a pretty day, mother!" he said. "And we saw a jay."

His mother looked at him; he had turned to her. She thought what a man he seemed, in his dark, well-made clothes. He was pale and detached-looking; it would be hard for any woman to keep him. Her heart glowed; then she was sorry for Clara.

"Perhaps you'll leave your things in the parlour," said Mrs. Morel nicely to the young woman.

"Oh, thank you," she replied.

"Come on," said Paul, and he led the way into the little front room, with its old piano, its mahogany furniture, its yellowing marble mantelpiece. A fire was burning; the place was littered with books and drawing-boards. "I leave my things lying about," he said. "It's so much easier."

rebellion

She loved his artist's paraphernalia, and the books, and the photos of people. Soon he was telling her: this was William, this was William's young lady in the evening dress, this was Annie and her husband, this was Arthur and his wife and the baby. She felt as if she were being taken into the family. He showed her photos, books, sketches, and they talked a little while. Then they returned to the kitchen. Mrs. Morel put aside her book. Clara wore a blouse of fine silk chiffon, with narrow black-and-white stripes; her hair was done simply, coiled on top of her head. She looked rather stately and reserved.

"You have gone to live down Sneinton Boulevard?" said Mrs. Morel. "When I was a girl—girl, I say!—when l was a young woman we lived in Minerva Terrace."

"Oh, did you!" said Clara. "I have a friend in number 6."

And the conversation had started. They talked Nottingham and Nottingham people; it interested them both. Clara was still rather nervous; Mrs. Morel was still somewhat on her dignity. She clipped her language very clear and precise. But they were going to get on well together, Paul saw.

Mrs. Morel measured herself against the younger woman, and found herself easily stronger. Clara was deferential. She knew Paul's surprising regard for his mother, and she had dreaded the meeting, expecting someone rather hard and cold.

She was surprised to find this little interested woman chatting
with such readiness; and then she felt, as she felt with Paul,
that she would not care to stand in Mrs. Morel's way. There
was something so hard and certain in his mother, as if she
never had a misgiving in her life.

Presently Morel came down, ruffled and yawning, from his
afternoon sleep. He scratched his grizzled head, he podded in
his stocking feet, his waistcoat hung open over his shirt. He
seemed incongruous.

"This is Mrs. Dawes, father," said Paul.

Then Morel pulled himself together. Clara saw Paul's manner
of bowing and shaking hands.

"Oh, indeed!" exclaimed Morel. "I am very glad to see you
—I am, I assure you. But don't disturb yourself. No, no make
yourself quite comfortable, and be very welcome."

Clara was astonished at this flood of hospitality from the old
collier. He was so courteous, so gallant! She thought him most
delightful.

"And may you have come far?" he asked.

"Only from Nottingham," she said.

"From Nottingham! Then you have had a beautiful day for
your journey."

Then he strayed into the scullery to wash his hands and face,
and from force of habit came on to the hearth with the towel
to dry himself.

At tea Clara felt the refinement and sang-froid of the household. Mrs. Morel was perfectly at her ease. The pouring out
the tea and attending to the people went on unconsciously,
without interrupting her in her talk. There was a lot of room
at the oval table: the china of dark blue willow-pattern looked
pretty on the glossy cloth. There was a little bowl of small,
yellow chrysanthemums. Clara felt she completed the circle,
and it was a pleasure to her. But she was rather afraid of the
self-possession of the Morels, father and all. She took their
tone; there was a feeling of balance. It was a cool, clear atmosphere, where everyone was himself, and in harmony. Clara
enjoyed it, but there was a fear deep at the bottom of her.

Paul cleared the table whilst his mother and Clara talked.
Clara was conscious of his quick, vigorous body as it came and
went, seeming blown quickly by a wind at its work. It was
almost like the hither and thither of a leaf that comes unexpected. Most of herself went with him. By the way she

leaned forward, as if listening, Mrs. Morel could see she was possessed elsewhere as she talked, and again the elder woman was sorry for her.

Having finished, he strolled down the garden, leaving the two women to talk. It was a hazy, sunny afternoon, mild and soft. Clara glanced through the window after him as he loitered among the chrysanthemums. She felt as if something almost tangible fastened her to him; yet he seemed so easy in his grace-ful, indolent movement, so detached as he tied up the too-heavy flower branches to their stakes, that she wanted to shriek in her helplessness.

Mrs. Morel rose.

"You will let me help you wash up," said Clara.

"Eh, there are so few, it will only take a minute," said the other.

Clara, however, dried the tea-things, and was glad to be on such good terms with his mother; but it was torture not to be able to follow him down the garden. At last she allowed her-self to go; she felt as if a rope were taken off her ankle.

The afternoon was golden over the hills of Derbyshire. He stood across in the other garden, beside a bush of pale Michael-mas daisies, watching the last bees crawl into the hive. Hearing her coming, he turned to her with an easy motion, saying:

"It's the end of the run with these chaps."

Clara stood near him. Over the low red wall in front was the country and the far-off hills, all golden dim.

At that moment Miriam was entering through the garden-door. She saw Clara go up to him, saw him turn, and saw them come to rest together. Something in their perfect isolation together made her know that it was accomplished between them, that they were, as she put it, married. She walked very slowly down the cinder-track of the long garden.

Clara had pulled a button from a hollyhock spire, and was breaking it to get the seeds. Above her bowed head the pink flowers stared, as if defending her. The last bees were falling down to the hive.

"Count your money," laughed Paul, as she broke the flat seeds one by one from the roll of coin. She looked at him.

"I'm well off," she said, smiling.

"How much? Pf!" He snapped his fingers. "Can I turn them into gold?"

"I'm afraid not," she laughed.

They looked into each other's eyes, laughing. At that moment they became aware of Miriam. There was a click, and everything had altered.

"Hello, Miriam!" he exclaimed. "You said you'd come!"

"Yes. Had you forgotten?"

She shook hands with Clara, saying:

"It seems strange to see you here."

"Yes," replied the other; "it seems strange to be here."

There was a hesitation.

"This is pretty, isn't it?" said Miriam.

"I like it very much," replied Clara.

Then Miriam realised that Clara was accepted as she had never been.

"Have you come down alone?" asked Paul.

"Yes; I went to Agatha's to tea. We are going to chapel. I only called in for a moment to see Clara."

"You should have come in here to tea," he said.

Miriam laughed shortly, and Clara turned impatiently aside.

"Do you like the chrysanthemums?" he asked.

"Yes; they are very fine," replied Miriam.

"Which sort do you like best?" he asked.

"I don't know. The bronze, I think."

"I don't think you've seen all the sorts. Come and look. Come and see which are *your* favourites, Clara."

He led the two women back to his own garden, where the towsled bushes of flowers of all colours stood raggedly along the path down to the field. The situation did not embarrass him, to his knowledge.

"Look, Miriam; these are the white ones that came from your garden. They aren't so fine here, are they?"

"No," said Miriam.

"But they're hardier. You're so sheltered; things grow big and tender, and then die. These little yellow ones I like. Will you have some?"

While they were out there the bells began to ring in the church, sounding loud across the town and the field. Miriam looked at the tower, proud among the clustering roofs, and remembered the sketches he had brought her. It had been different then, but he had not left her even yet. She asked him for a book to read. He ran indoors.

"What! is that Miriam?" asked his mother coldly.

"Yes; she said she'd call and see Clara."

contradiction

"You told her, then?" came the sarcastic answer.
"Yes; why shouldn't I?"

"There's certainly no reason why you shouldn't," said Mrs. Morel, and she returned to her book. He winced from his mother's irony, frowned irritably, thinking: "Why can't I do as I like?"

"You've not seen Mrs. Morel before?" Miriam was saying to Clara.

"No; but she's *so* nice!"

"Yes," said Miriam, dropping her head; "in some ways she's very fine."

"I should think so."

"Had Paul told you much about her?"

"He had talked a good deal."

"Ha!"

There was silence until he returned with the book.

"When will you want it back?" Miriam asked.

"When you like," he answered.

Clara turned to go indoors, whilst he accompanied Miriam to the gate.

"When will you come up to Willey Farm?" the latter asked.

"I couldn't say," replied Clara.

"Mother asked me to say she'd be pleased to see you any time, if you cared to come."

"Thank you; I should like to, but I can't say when."

"Oh, very well!" exclaimed Miriam rather bitterly, turning away.

She went down the path with her mouth to the flowers he had given her.

"You're sure you won't come in?" he said.

"No, thanks."

"We are going to chapel."

"Ah, I shall see you, then!" Miriam was very bitter.

"Yes."

They parted. He felt guilty towards her. She was bitter, and she scorned him. He still belonged to herself, she believed; yet he could have Clara, take her home, sit with her next his mother in chapel, give her the same hymn-book he had given herself years before. She heard him running quickly indoors.

But he did not go straight in. Halting on the plot of grass, he heard his mother's voice, then Clara's answer:

"What I hate is the bloodhound quality in Miriam."

"Yes," said his mother quickly, "yes; *doesn't* it make you hate her, now!"

His heart went hot, and he was angry with them for talking about the girl. What right had they to say that? Something in the speech itself stung him into a flame of hate against Miriam. Then his own heart rebelled furiously at Clara's taking the liberty of speaking so about Miriam. After all, the girl was the better woman of the two, he thought, if it came to goodness. He went indoors. His mother looked excited. She was beating with her hand rhythmically on the sofa-arm, as women do who are wearing out. He could never bear to see the movement. There was a silence; then he began to talk.

In chapel Miriam saw him find the place in the hymn-book for Clara, in exactly the same way as he used for herself. And during the sermon he could see the girl across the chapel, her hat throwing a dark shadow over her face. What did she think, seeing Clara with him? He did not stop to consider. He felt himself cruel towards Miriam.

After chapel he went over Pentrich with Clara. It was a dark autumn night. They had said good-bye to Miriam, and his heart had smitten him as he left the girl alone. "But it serves her right," he said inside himself, and it almost gave him pleasure to go off under her eyes with this other handsome woman.

There was a scent of damp leaves in the darkness. Clara's hand lay warm and inert in his own as they walked. He was full of conflict. The battle that raged inside him made him feel desperate.

Up Pentrich Hill Clara leaned against him as he went. He slid his arm round her waist. Feeling the strong motion of her body under his arm as she walked, the tightness in his chest because of Miriam relaxed, and the hot blood bathed him. He held her closer and closer.

Then: "You still keep on with Miriam," she said quietly.

"Only talk. There never *was* a great deal more than talk between us," he said bitterly.

"Your mother doesn't care for her," said Clara.

"No, or I might have married her. But it's all up really!"

Suddenly his voice went passionate with hate.

"If I was with her now, we should be jawing about the 'Christian Mystery', or some such tack. Thank God, I'm not!"

They walked on in silence for some time.

"But you can't really give her up," said Clara.

"I don't give her up, because there's nothing to give," he said.

"There is for her."

"I don't know why she and I shouldn't be friends as long as we live," he said. "But it'll only be friends."

Clara drew away from him, leaning away from contact with him.

"What are you drawing away for?" he asked.

She did not answer, but drew farther from him.

"Why do you want to walk alone?" he asked.

Still there was no answer. She walked resentfully, hanging her head.

"Because I said I would be friends with Miriam!" he exclaimed.

She would not answer him anything.

"I tell you it's only words that go between us," he persisted, trying to take her again.

She resisted. Suddenly he strode across in front of her, barring her way.

"Damn it!" he said. "What do you want now?"

"You'd better run after Miriam," mocked Clara.

The blood flamed up in him. He stood showing his teeth. She drooped sulkily. The lane was dark, quite lonely. He suddenly caught her in his arms, stretched forward, and put his mouth on her face in a kiss of rage. She turned frantically to avoid him. He held her fast. Hard and relentless his mouth came for her. Her breasts hurt against the wall of his chest. Helpless, she went loose in his arms, and he kissed her, and kissed her.

He heard people coming down the hill.

"Stand up! stand up!" he said thickly, gripping her arm till it hurt. If he had let go, she would have sunk to the ground.

She sighed and walked dizzily beside him. They went on in silence.

"We will go over the fields," he said; and then she woke up.

But she let herself be helped over the stile, and she walked in silence with him over the first dark field. It was the way to Nottingham and to the station, she knew. He seemed to be looking about. They came out on a bare hilltop where stood the dark figure of the ruined windmill. There he halted. They stood together high up in the darkness, looking at the lights scattered on the night before them, handfuls of glittering points, villages lying high and low on the dark, here and there.

"Like treading among the stars," he said, with a quaky laugh.

Then he took her in his arms, and held her fast. She moved aside her mouth to ask, dogged and low:

"What time is it?"

"It doesn't matter," he pleaded thickly.

"Yes it does—yes! I must go!"

"It's early yet," he said.

"What time is it?" she insisted.

All round lay the black night, speckled and spangled with lights.

"I don't know."

She put her hand on his chest, feeling for his watch. He felt the joints fuse into fire. She groped in his waistcoat pocket, while he stood panting. In the darkness she could see the round, pale face of the watch, but not the figures. She stooped over it. He was panting till he could take her in his arms again.

"I can't see," she said.

"Then don't bother."

"Yes; I'm going!" she said, turning away.

"Wait! I'll look!" But he could not see. "I'll strike a match." He secretly hoped it was too late to catch the train. She saw the glowing lantern of his hands as he cradled the light: then his face lit up, his eyes fixed on the watch. Instantly all was dark again. All was black before her eyes; only a glowing match was red near her feet. Where was he?

"What is it?" she asked, afraid.

"You can't do it," his voice answered out of the darkness.

There was a pause. She felt in his power. She had heard the ring in his voice. It frightened her.

"What time is it?" she asked, quiet, definite, hopeless.

"Two minutes to nine," he replied, telling the truth with a struggle.

"And can I get from here to the station in fourteen minutes?"

"No. At any rate——"

She could distinguish his dark form again a yard or so away. She wanted to escape.

"But can't I do it?" she pleaded.

"If you hurry," he said brusquely. "But you could easily walk it, Clara; it's only seven miles to the tram. I'll come with you."

"No; I want to catch the train."

"But why?"

"I do—I want to catch the train."

Suddenly his voice altered.

"Very well," he said, dry and hard. "Come along, then."

And he plunged ahead into the darkness. She ran after him, wanting to cry. Now he was hard and cruel to her. She ran over the rough, dark fields behind him, out of breath, ready to drop. But the double row of lights at the station drew nearer. Suddenly:

"There she is!" he cried, breaking into a run.

There was a faint rattling noise. Away to the right the train, like a luminous caterpillar, was threading across the night. The rattling ceased.

"She's over the viaduct. You'll just do it."

Clara ran, quite out of breath, and fell at last into the train. The whistle blew. He was gone. Gone!—and she was in a carriage full of people. She felt the cruelty of it.

He turned round and plunged home. Before he knew where he was he was in the kitchen at home. He was very pale. His eyes were dark and dangerous-looking, as if he were drunk. His mother looked at him.

"Well, I must say your boots are in a nice state!" she said.

He looked at his feet. Then he took off his overcoat. His mother wondered if he were drunk.

"She caught the train then?" she said.

"Yes."

"I hope *her* feet weren't so filthy. Where on earth you dragged her I don't know!"

He was silent and motionless for some time.

"Did you like her?" he asked grudgingly at last.

"Yes, I liked her. But you'll tire of her, my son; you know you will."

He did not answer. She noticed how he laboured in his breathing.

"Have you been running?" she asked.

"We had to run for the train."

"You'll go and knock yourself up. You'd better drink hot milk."

It was as good a stimulant as he could have, but he refused and went to bed. There he lay face down on the counterpane, and shed tears of rage and pain. There was a physical pain that made him bite his lips till they bled, and the chaos inside him left him unable to think, almost to feel.

"This is how she serves me, is it?" he said in his heart, over and over, pressing his face in the quilt. And he hated her. Again he went over the scene, and again he hated her.

The next day there was a new aloofness about him. Clara was very gentle, almost loving. But he treated her distantly, with a touch of contempt. She sighed, continuing to be gentle. He came round.

One evening of that week Sarah Bernhardt was at the Theatre Royal in Nottingham, giving *"La Dame aux Camélias"*. Paul wanted to see this old and famous actress, and he asked Clara to accompany him. He told his mother to leave the key in the window for him.

"Shall I book seats?" he asked of Clara.

"Yes. And put on an evening suit, will you? I've never seen you in it."

"But, good Lord, Clara! Think of *me* in evening suit at the theatre!" he remonstrated.

"Would you rather not?" she asked.

"I will if you *want* me to; but I s'll feel a fool."

She laughed at him.

"Then feel a fool for my sake, once, won't you?"

The request made his blood flush up.

"I suppose I s'll have to."

"What are you taking a suitcase for?" his mother asked.

He blushed furiously.

"Clara asked me," he said.

"And what seats are you going in?"

"Circle—three-and-six each!"

"Well, I'm sure!" exclaimed his mother sarcastically.

"It's only once in the bluest of blue moons," he said.

He dressed at Jordan's, put on an overcoat and a cap, and met Clara in a café. She was with one of her suffragette friends. She wore an old long coat, which did not suit her, and had a little wrap over her head, which he hated. The three went to the theatre together.

Clara took off her coat on the stairs, and he discovered she was in a sort of semi-evening dress, that left her arms and neck and part of her breast bare. Her hair was done fashionably. The dress, a simple thing of green crape, suited her. She looked quite grand, he thought. He could see her figure inside the frock, as if that were wrapped closely round her. The firmness and the softness of her upright body could almost be felt as he looked at her. He clenched his fists.

And he was to sit all the evening beside her beautiful naked arm, watching the strong throat rise from the strong chest, watching the breasts under the green stuff, the curve of her limbs in the tight dress. Something in him hated her again for submitting him to this torture of nearness. And he loved her as she balanced her head and stared straight in front of her, pouting, wistful, immobile, as if she yielded herself to her fate because it was too strong for her. She could not help herself; she was in the grip of something bigger than herself. A kind of eternal look about her, as if she were a wistful sphinx, made it necessary for him to kiss her. He dropped his programme, and crouched down on the floor to get it, so that he could kiss her hand and wrist. Her beauty was a torture to him. She sat immobile. Only, when the lights went down, she sank a little against him, and he caressed her hand and arm with his fingers. He could smell her faint perfume. All the time his blood kept sweeping up in great white-hot waves that killed his consciousness momentarily.

The drama continued. He saw it all in the distance, going on somewhere; he did not know where, but it seemed far away inside him. He was Clara's white heavy arms, her throat, her moving bosom. That seemed to be himself. Then away somewhere the play went on, and he was identified with that also. There was no himself. The grey and black eyes of Clara, her bosom coming down on him, her arm that he held gripped between his hands, were all that existed. Then he felt himself small and helpless, her towering in her force above him.

Only the intervals, when the lights came up, hurt him expressibly. He wanted to run anywhere, so long at it would be dark again. In a maze, he wandered out for a drink. Then the lights were out, and the strange, insane reality of Clara and the drama took hold of him again.

The play went on. But he was obsessed by the desire to kiss the tiny blue vein that nestled in the bend of her arm. He could feel it. His whole face seemed suspended till he had put his lips there. It must be done. And the other people! At last he bent quickly forward and touched it with his lips. His moustache brushed the sensitive flesh. Clara shivered, drew away her arm.

When all was over, the lights up, the people clapping, he came to himself and looked at his watch. His train was gone.

"I s'll have to walk home!" he said.

Clara looked at him.

"It is too late?" she asked.

He nodded. Then he helped her on with her coat.

"I love you! You look beautiful in that dress," he murmured over her shoulder, among the throng of bustling people.

She remained quiet. Together they went out of the theatre. He saw the cabs waiting, the people passing. It seemed he met a pair of brown eyes which hated him. But he did not know. He and Clara turned away, mechanically taking the direction to the station.

The train had gone. He would have to walk the ten miles home.

"It doesn't matter," he said. "I shall enjoy it."

"Won't you," she said, flushing, "come home for the night? I can sleep with mother."

He looked at her. Their eyes met.

"What will your mother say?" he asked.

"She won't mind."

"You're sure?"

"Quite!"

"*Shall* I come?"

"If you will."

"Very well."

And they turned away. At the first stopping-place they took the car. The wind blew fresh in their faces. The town was dark; the tram tipped in its haste. He sat with her hand fast in his.

"Will your mother be gone to bed?" he asked.

"She may be. I hope not."

They hurried along the silent, dark little street, the only people out of doors. Clara quickly entered the house. He hesitated.

He leaped up the step and was in the room. Her mother appeared in the inner doorway, large and hostile.

"Who have you got there?" she asked.

"It's Mr. Morel; he has missed his train. I thought we might put him up for the night, and save him a ten-mile walk."

"H'm" exclaimed Mrs. Radford. "That's your look-out! If you've invited him, he's very welcome as far as I'm concerned. *You* keep the house!"

"If you don't like me, I'll go away again," he said.

"Nay, nay, you needn't! Come along in! I dunno what you'll think of the supper I'd got her."

It was a little dish of chip potatoes and a piece of bacon. The table was roughly laid for one.

"You can have some more bacon," continued Mrs. Radford. "More chips you can't have."

"It's a shame to bother you," he said.

"Oh, don't you be apologetic! It doesn't *do* wi' me! You treated her to the theatre, didn't you?" There was a sarcasm in the last question.

"Well?" laughed Paul uncomfortably.

"Well, and what's an inch of bacon! Take your coat off."

The big, straight-standing woman was trying to estimate the situation. She moved about the cupboard. Clara took his coat. The room was very warm and cosy in the lamplight.

"My sirs!" exclaimed Mrs. Radford; "but you two's a pair of bright beauties, I must say! What's all that get-up for?"

"I believe we don't know," he said, feeling a victim.

"There isn't room in *this* house for two such bobby-dazzlers, if you fly your kites *that* high!" she rallied them. It was a nasty thrust.

He in his dinner jacket, and Clara in her green dress and bare arms, were confused. They felt they must shelter each other in that little kitchen.

"And look at *that* blossom!" continued Mrs. Radford, pointing to Clara. "What does she reckon she did it for?"

Paul looked at Clara. She was rosy; her neck was warm with blushes. There was a moment of silence.

"You like to see it, don't you?" he asked.

The mother had them in her power. All the time his heart was beating hard, and he was tight with anxiety. But he would fight her.

"Me like to see it!" exclaimed the old woman. "What should I like to see her make a fool of herself for?"

"I've seen people look bigger fools," he said. Clara was under his protection now.

"Oh, ay! and when was that?" came the sarcastic rejoinder.

"When they made frights of themselves," he answered.

Mrs. Radford, large and threatening, stood suspended on the hearthrug, holding her fork.

"They're fools either road," she answered at length, turning to the Dutch oven.

"No," he said, fighting stoutly. "Folk ought to look as well as they can."

"And do you call *that* looking nice!" cried the mother, pointing a scornful fork at Clara. "That—that looks as if it wasn't properly dressed!"

"I believe you're jealous that you can't swank as well," he said laughing.

"Me! I could have worn evening dress with anybody, if I'd wanted to!" came the scornful answer.

"And why didn't you want to?" he asked pertinently. "Or *did* you wear it?"

There was a long pause. Mrs. Radford readjusted the bacon in the Dutch oven. His heart beat fast, for fear he had offended her.

"Me!" she exclaimed at last. "No, I didn't! And when I was in service, I knew as soon as one of the maids came out in bare shoulders what sort *she* was, going to her sixpenny hop!"

"Were you too good to go to a sixpenny hop?" he said.

Clara sat with bowed head. His eyes were dark and glittering. Mrs. Radford took the Dutch oven from the fire, and stood near him, putting bits of bacon on his plate.

"*There's* a nice crozzly bit!" she said.

"Don't give me the best!" he said.

"*She's* got what *she* wants," was the answer.

There was a sort of scornful forbearance in the woman's tone that made Paul know she was mollified.

"But *do* have some!" he said to Clara.

She looked up at him with her grey eyes, humiliated and lonely.

"No thanks!" she said.

"Why won't you?" he answered carelessly.

The blood was beating up like fire in his veins. Mrs. Radford sat down again, large and impressive and aloof. He left Clara altogether to attend to the mother.

"They say Sarah Bernhardt's fifty," he said.

"Fifty! She's turned sixty!" came the scornful answer.

"Well," he said, "you'd never think it! She made me want to howl even now."

"I should like to see myself howling at *that* bad old baggage!"

said Mrs. Radford. "It's time she began to think herself a grand-mother, not a shrieking catamaran——"

He laughed.

"A catamaran is a boat the Malays use," he said.

"And it's a word as *I* use," she retorted.

"My mother does sometimes, and it's no good my telling her," he said.

"I s'd think she boxes your ears," said Mrs. Radford, good-humouredly.

"She'd like to, and she says she will, so I give her a little stool to stand on."

"That's the worst of my mother," said Clara. "She never wants a stool for anything."

"But she often can't touch *that* lady with a long prop," retorted Mrs. Radford to Paul.

"I s'd think she doesn't want touching with a prop," he laughed. "*I* shouldn't."

"It might do the pair of you good to give you a crack on the head with one," said the mother, laughing suddenly.

"Why are you so vindictive towards me?" he said. "I've not stolen anything from you."

"No; I'll watch that," laughed the older woman.

Soon the supper was finished. Mrs. Radford sat guard in her chair. Paul lit a cigarette. Clara went upstairs, returning with a sleeping-suit, which she spread on the fender to air.

"Why, I'd forgot all about *them*!" said Mrs. Radford. "Where have they sprung from?"

"Out of my drawer."

"H'm! You bought 'em for Baxter, an' he wouldn't wear 'em, would he?"—laughing. "Said he reckoned to do wi'out trousers i' bed." She turned confidentially to Paul, saying: "He couldn't *bear* 'em, them pyjama things."

The young man sat making rings of smoke.

"Well, it's everyone to his taste," he laughed.

Then followed a little discussion of the merits of pyjamas.

"My mother loves me in them," he said. "She says I'm a pierrot."

"I can imagine they'd suit you," said Mrs. Radford.

After a while he glanced at the little clock that was ticking on the mantelpiece. It was half-past twelve.

"It is funny," he said, "but it takes hours to settle down to sleep after the theatre."

"It's about time you did," said Mrs. Radford, clearing the table.

"Are *you* tired?" he asked of Clara.

"Not the least bit," she answered, avoiding his eyes.

"Shall we have a game at cribbage?" he said.

"I've forgotten it."

"Well, I'll teach you again. May we play crib, Mrs Radford?" he asked.

"You'll please yourselves," she said; "but it's pretty late."

"A game or so will make us sleepy," he answered.

Clara brought the cards, and sat spinning her wedding-ring whilst he shuffled them. Mrs. Radford was washing up in the scullery. As it grew later Paul felt the situation getting more and more tense.

"Fifteen two, fifteen four, fifteen six, and two's eight——!"

The clock struck one. Still the game continued. Mrs. Radford had done all the little jobs preparatory to going to bed, had locked the door and filled the kettle. Still Paul went on dealing and counting. He was obsessed by Clara's arms and throat. He believed he could see where the division was just beginning for her breasts. He could not leave her. She watched his hands, and felt her joints melt as they moved quickly. She was so near; it was almost as if he touched her, and yet not quite. His mettle was roused. He hated Mrs. Radford. She sat on, nearly dropping asleep, but determined and obstinate in her chair. Paul glanced at her, then at Clara. She met his eyes, that were angry, mocking, and hard as steel. Her own answered him in shame. He knew *she*, at any rate, was of his mind. He played on.

At last Mrs. Radford roused herself stiffly, and said:

"Isn't it nigh on time you two was thinking o' bed?"

Paul played on without answering. He hated her sufficiently to murder her.

"Half a minute," he said.

The elder woman rose and sailed stubbornly into the scullery, returning with his candle, which she put on the mantelpiece. Then she sat down again. The hatred of her went so hot down his veins, he dropped his cards.

"We'll stop, then," he said, but his voice was still a challenge.

Clara saw his mouth shut hard. Again he glanced at her. It seemed like an agreement. She bent over the cards, coughing, to clear her throat.

"Well, I'm glad you've finished," said Mrs. Radford. "Here,

take your things"—she thrust the warm suit in his hand—"and this is your candle. Your room's over this; there's only two, so you can't go far wrong. Well, good-night. I hope you'll rest well."

"I'm sure I shall; I always do," he said.

"Yes; and so you ought at your age," she replied.

He bade good-night to Clara, and went. The twisting stairs of white, scrubbed wood creaked and clanged at every step. He went doggedly. The two doors faced each other. He went in his room, pushed the door to, without fastening the latch.

It was a small room with a large bed. Some of Clara's hairpins were on the dressing-table—her hair-brush. Her clothes and some skirts hung under a cloth in a corner. There was actually a pair of stockings over a chair. He explored the room. Two books of his own were there on the shelf. He undressed, folded his suit, and sat on the bed, listening. Then he blew out the candle, lay down, and in two minutes was almost asleep. Then click!—he was wide awake and writhing in torment. It was as if, when he had nearly got to sleep, something had bitten him suddenly and sent him mad. He sat up and looked at the room in the darkness, his feet doubled under him, perfectly motionless, listening. He heard a cat somewhere away outside; then the heavy, poised tread of the mother; then Clara's distinct voice:

"Will you unfasten my dress?"

There was silence for some time. At last the mother said:

"Now then! aren't you coming up?"

"No, not yet," replied the daughter calmly.

"Oh, very well then! If it's not late enough, stop a bit longer. Only you needn't come waking me up when I've got to sleep."

"I shan't be long," said Clara.

Immediately afterwards Paul heard the mother slowly mounting the stairs. The candlelight flashed through the cracks in his door. Her dress brushed the door, and his heart jumped. Then it was dark, and he heard the clatter of her latch. She was very leisurely indeed in her preparations for sleep. After a long time it was quite still. He sat strung up on the bed, shivering slightly. His door was an inch open. As Clara came upstairs, he would intercept her. He waited. All was dead silence. The clock struck two. Then he heard a slight scrape of the fender downstairs. Now he could not help himself. His shivering was uncontrollable. He felt he must go or die.

He stepped off the bed, and stood a moment, shuddering. Then he went straight to the door. He tried to step lightly. The first stair cracked like a shot. He listened. The old woman stirred in her bed. The staircase was dark. There was a slit of light under the stair-foot door, which opened into the kitchen. He stood a moment. Then he went on, mechanically. Every step creaked, and his back was creeping, lest the old woman's door should open behind him up above. He fumbled with the door at the bottom. The latch opened with a loud clack. He went through into the kitchen, and shut the door noisily behind him. The old woman daren't come now.

Then he stood, arrested. Clara was kneeling on a pile of white underclothing on the hearth-rug, her back towards him, warming herself. She did not look round, but sat crouching on her heels, and her rounded beautiful back was towards him, and her face was hidden. She was warming her body at the fire for consolation. The glow was rosy on one side, the shadow was dark and warm on the other. Her arms hung slack.

He shuddered violently, clenching his teeth and fists hard to keep control. Then he went forward to her. He put one hand on her shoulder, the fingers of the other hand under her chin to raise her face. A convulsed shiver ran through her, once, twice, at his touch. She kept her head bent.

"Sorry!" he murmured, realising that his hands were very cold.

Then she looked up at him, frightened, like a thing that is afraid of death.

"My hands are so cold," he murmured.

"I like it," she whispered, closing her eyes.

The breath of her words were on his mouth. Her arms clasped his knees. The cord of his sleeping-suit dangled against her and made her shiver. As the warmth went into him, his shuddering became less.

At length, unable to stand so any more, he raised her, and she buried her head on his shoulder. His hands went over her slowly with an infinite tenderness of caress. She clung close to him, trying to hide herself against him. He clasped her very fast. Then at last she looked at him, mute, imploring, looking to see if she must be ashamed.

His eyes were dark, very deep, and very quiet. It was as if her beauty and his taking it hurt him, made him sorrowful. He looked at her with a little pain, and was afraid. He was so humble before her. She kissed him fervently on the eyes, first one, then the other, and she folded herself to him. She gave herself. He held her fast. It was a moment intense almost to agony.

She stood letting him adore her and tremble with joy of her. It healed her hurt pride. It healed her; it made her glad. It made her feel erect and proud again. Her pride had been wounded inside her. She had been cheapened. Now she radiated with joy and pride again. It was her restoration and her recognition.

Then he looked at her, his face radiant. They laughed to each other, and he strained her to his chest. The seconds ticked off, the minutes passed, and still the two stood clasped rigid together, mouth to mouth, like a statue in one block.

But again his fingers went seeking over her, restless, wandering, dissatisfied. The hot blood came up wave upon wave. She laid her head on his shoulder.

"Come you to my room," he murmured.

She looked at him and shook her head, her mouth pouting disconsolately, her eyes heavy with passion. He watched her fixedly.

"Yes!" he said.

Again she shook her head.

"Why not?" he asked.

She looked at him still heavily, sorrowfully, and again she shook her head. His eyes hardened, and he gave way.

When, later on, he was back in bed, he wondered why she had refused to come to him openly, so that her mother would know. At any rate, then things would have been definite. And she could have stayed with him the night, without having to go, as she was, to her mother's bed. It was strange, and he could not understand it. And then almost immediately he fell asleep.

He awoke in the morning with someone speaking to him. Opening his eyes, he saw Mrs. Radford, big and stately, looking down on him. She held a cup of tea in her hand.

"Do you think you're going to sleep till Doomsday?" she said.

He laughed at once.

"It ought only to be about five o'clock," he said.

"Well," she answered, "it's half-past seven, whether or not. Here, I've brought you a cup of tea."

He rubbed his face, pushed the tumbled hair off his forehead, and roused himself.

"What's it so late for!" he grumbled.

He resented being wakened. It amused her. She saw his neck in the flannel sleeping-jacket, as white and round as a girl's. He rubbed his hair crossly.

"It's no good your scratching your head," she said. "It won't make it no earlier. Here, an' how long d'you think I'm going to stand waiting wi' this here cup?"

"Oh, dash the cup!" he said.

"You should go to bed earlier," said the woman.

He looked up at her, laughing with impudence.

"I went to bed before *you* did," he said.

"Yes, my Guyney, you did!" she exclaimed.

"Fancy," he said, stirring his tea, "having tea brought to bed to me! My mother'll think I'm ruined for life."

"Don't she never do it?" asked Mrs. Radford.

"She'd as leave think of flying."

"Ah, I always spoilt my lot! That's why they've turned out such bad uns," said the elderly woman.

"You'd only Clara," he said. "And Mr. Radford's in heaven. So I suppose there's only you left to be the bad un."

"I'm not bad; I'm only soft," she said, as she went out of the bedroom. "I'm only a fool, I am!"

Clara was very quiet at breakfast, but she had a sort of air of proprietorship over him that pleased him infinitely. Mrs. Radford was evidently fond of him. He began to talk of his painting.

"What's the good," exclaimed the mother, "of your whittling and worrying and twistin' and too-in' at that painting of yours? What *good* does it do you, I should like to know? You'd better be enjoyin' yourself."

"Oh, but," exclaimed Paul, "I made over thirty guineas last year."

"Did you! Well, that's a consideration, but it's nothing to the time you put in."

"And I've got four pounds owing. A man said he'd give me five pounds if I'd paint him and his missis and the dog and the cottage. And I went and put the fowls in instead of the dog, and he was waxy, so I had to knock a quid off. I was sick of it, and I didn't like the dog. I made a picture of it. What shall I do when he pays me the four pounds?"

"Nay! you know your own uses for your money," said Mrs. Radford.

"But I'm going to bust this four pounds. Should we go to the seaside for a day or two?"

"Who?"

"You and Clara and me."

"What, on your money!" she exclaimed, half-wrathful.

"Why not?"

"*You* wouldn't be long in breaking your neck at a hurdle race!" she said.

"So long as I get a good run for my money! Will you?"

"Nay; you may settle that atween you."

"And you're willing?" he asked, amazed and rejoicing.

"You'll do as you like," said Mrs. Radford, "whether I'm willing or not."

CHAPTER XIII

BAXTER DAWES

Soon after Paul had been to the theatre with Clara, he was drinking in the Punch Bowl with some friends of his when Dawes came in. Clara's husband was growing stout; his eyelids were getting slack over his brown eyes; he was losing his healthy firmness of flesh. He was very evidently on the downward track. Having quarrelled with his sister, he had gone into cheap lodgings. His mistress had left him for a man who would marry her. He had been in prison one night for fighting when he was drunk, and there was a shady betting episode in which he was concerned.

Paul and he were confirmed enemies, and yet there was between them that peculiar feeling of intimacy, as if they were secretly near to each other, which sometimes exists between two people, although they never speak to one another. Paul often thought of Baxter Dawes, often wanted to get at him and be friends with him. He knew that Dawes often thought about him, and that the man was drawn to him by some bond or other. And yet the two never looked at each other save in hostility.

Since he was a superior employee at Jordan's, it was the thing for Paul to offer Dawes a drink.

"What'll you have?" he asked of him.

"Nowt wi' a bleeder like you!" replied the man.

Paul turned away with a slight disdainful movement of the shoulders, very irritating.

"The aristocracy," he continued, "is really a military institution. Take Germany, now. She's got thousands of aristocrats whose only means of existence is the army. They're deadly poor, and life's deadly slow. So they hope for a war. They look for war as a chance of getting on. Till there's a war they are idle good-for-nothings. When there's a war, they are leaders and commanders. There you are, then—they *want* war!"

He was not a favourite debater in the public-house, being too quick and overbearing. He irritated the older men by his assertive manner, and his cocksureness. They listened in silence, and were not sorry when he finished.

Dawes interrupted the young man's flow of eloquence by asking, in a loud sneer:

"Did you learn all that at th' theatre th' other night?"

Paul looked at him; their eyes met. Then he knew Dawes had seen him coming out of the theatre with Clara.

"Why, what about th' theatre?" asked one of Paul's associates, glad to get a dig at the young fellow, and sniffing something tasty.

"Oh, him in a bob-tailed evening suit, on the lardy-da!" sneered Dawes, jerking his head contemptuously at Paul.

"That's comin' it strong," said the mutual friend. "Tart an' all?"

"Tart, begod!" said Dawes.

"Go on; let's have it!" cried the mutual friend.

"You've got it," said Dawes, "an' I reckon Morelly had it an' all."

"Well, I'll be jiggered!" said the mutual friend. "An' was it a proper tart?"

"Tart, God blimey—yes!"

"How do you know?"

"Oh," said Dawes, "I reckon he spent th' night——"

There was a good deal of laughter at Paul's expense.

"But who *was* she? D'you know her?" asked the mutual friend.

"I should *shay sho*," said Dawes.

This brought another burst of laughter.

"Then spit it out," said the mutual friend.

Dawes shook his head, and took a gulp of beer.

"It's a wonder he hasn't let on himself," he said. "He'll be braggin' of it in a bit."

"Come on, Paul," said the friend; "it's no good. You might just as well own up."

"Own up what? That I happened to take a friend to the theatre?"

"Oh well, if it was all right, tell us who she was, lad," said the friend.

"She *was* all right," said Dawes.

Paul was furious. Dawes wiped his golden moustache with his fingers, sneering.

"Strike me——! One o' that sort?" said the mutual friend. "Paul, boy, I'm surprised at you. And do you know her, Baxter?"

"Just a bit, like!"

He winked at the other men.

"Oh well," said Paul, "I'll be going!"

The mutual friend laid a detaining hand on his shoulder.

"Nay," he said, "you don't get off as easy as that, my lad. We've got to have a full account of this business."

"Then get it from Dawes!" he said.

"You shouldn't funk your own deeds, man," remonstrated the friend.

Then Dawes made a remark which caused Paul to throw half a glass of beer in his face.

"Oh, Mr. Morel!" cried the barmaid, and she rang the bell for the "chucker-out".

Dawes spat and rushed for the young man. At that minute a brawny fellow with his shirt-sleeves rolled up and his trousers tight over his haunches intervened.

"Now, then!" he said, pushing his chest in front of Dawes.

"Come out!" cried Dawes.

Paul was leaning, white and quivering, against the brass rail of the bar. He hated Dawes, wished something could exterminate him at that minute; and at the same time, seeing the wet hair on the man's forehead, he thought he looked pathetic. He did not move.

"Come out, you ——," said Dawes.

"That's enough, Dawes," cried the barmaid.

"Come on," said the "chucker-out", with kindly insistence, "you'd better be getting on."

And, by making Dawes edge away from his own close proximity, he worked him to the door.

"*That's* the little sod as started it!" cried Dawes, half-cowed. pointing to Paul Morel.

"Why, what a story, Mr. Dawes!" said the barmaid. "You know it was you all the time."

Still the "chucker-out" kept thrusting his chest forward at him, still he kept edging back, until he was in the doorway and on the steps outside; then he turned round.

"All right," he said, nodding straight at his rival.

Paul had a curious sensation of pity, almost of affection, mingled with violent hate, for the man. The coloured door swung to; there was silence in the bar.

"Serve him jolly well right!" said the barmaid.

"But it's a nasty thing to get a glass of beer in your eyes," said the mutual friend.

"I tell you *I* was glad he did," said the barmaid. "Will you have another, Mr. Morel?"

She held up Paul's glass questioningly. He nodded.

"He's a man as doesn't care for anything, is Baxter Dawes," said one.

"Pooh! is he?" said the barmaid. "He's a loud-mouthed one, he is, and they're never much good. Give me a pleasant-spoken chap, if you want a devil!"

"Well, Paul, my lad," said the friend, "you'll have to take care of yourself now for a while."

"You won't have to give him a chance over you, that's all," said the barmaid.

"Can you box?" asked a friend.

"Not a bit," he answered, still very white.

"I might give you a turn or two," said the friend.

"Thanks, I haven't time."

And presently he took his departure.

"Go along with him, Mr. Jenkinson," whispered the barmaid, tipping Mr. Jenkinson the wink.

The man nodded, took his hat, said: "Good-night all!" very heartily, and followed Paul, calling:

"Half a minute, old man. You an' me's going the same road, I believe."

"Mr. Morel doesn't like it," said the barmaid. "You'll see, we shan't have him in much more. I'm sorry; he's good company. And Baxter Dawes wants locking up, that's what he wants."

Paul would have died rather than his mother should get to know of this affair. He suffered tortures of humiliation and self-consciousness. There was now a good deal of his life of which necessarily he could not speak to his mother. He had a life apart from her—his sexual life. The rest she still kept. But he felt he had to conceal something from her, and it irked him. There was a certain silence between them, and he felt he had, in that silence, to defend himself against her; he felt condemned by her. Then sometimes he hated her, and pulled at her bondage. His life wanted to free itself of her. It was like a circle where life turned back on itself, and got no farther. She bore him, loved him, kept him, and his love turned back into her, so that he could not be free to go forward with his own life, really love another woman. At this period, unknowingly, he resisted his mother's influence. He did not tell her things; there was a distance between them.

Clara was happy, almost sure of him. She felt she had at last got him for herself; and then again came the uncertainty. He told her jestingly of the affair with her husband. Her colour came up, her grey eyes flashed.

"That's him to a 'T'," she cried—"like a navvy! He's not fit for mixing with decent folk."

"Yet you married him," he said.

It made her furious that he reminded her.

"I did!" she cried. "But how was I to know?"

"I think he might have been rather nice," he said.

"You think I made him what he is!" she exclaimed.

"Oh no! he made himself. But there's something about him——"

Clara looked at her lover closely. There was something in him she hated, a sort of detached criticism of herself, a cold ness which made her woman's soul harden against him.

"And what are you going to do?" she asked.

"How?"

"About Baxter."

"There's nothing to do, is there?" he replied.

"You can fight him if you have to, I suppose?" she said.

"No; I haven't the least sense of the 'fist'. It's funny. With most men there's the instinct to clench the fist and hit. It's not so with me. I should want a knife or a pistol or something to fight with."

"Then you'd better carry something," she said.

"Nay," he laughed; "I'm not daggeroso."

"But he'll do something to you. You don't know him."

"All right," he said, "we'll see."

"And you'll let him?"

"Perhaps, if I can't help it."

"And if he kills you?" she said.

"I should be sorry, for his sake and mine."

Clara was silent for a moment.

"You *do* make me angry!" she exclaimed.

"That's nothing afresh," he laughed.

"But why are you so silly? You don't know him."

"And don't want."

"Yes, but you're not going to let a man do as he likes with you?"

"What must I do?" he replied, laughing.

"*I* should carry a revolver," she said. "I'm sure he's dangerous."

"I might blow my fingers off," he said.

"No; but won't you?" she pleaded.

"No."

"Not anything?"

"No."

"And you'll leave him to——?"

"Yes."

"You are a fool!"

"Fact!"

She set her teeth with anger.

"I could *shake* you!" she cried, trembling with passion.

"Why?"

"Let a man like *him* do as he likes with you."

"You can go back to him if he triumphs," he said.

"Do you want me to hate you?" she asked.

"Well, I only tell you," he said.

"And *you* say you *love* me!" she exclaimed, low and indignant.

"Ought I to slay him to please you?" he said. "But if I did, see what a hold he'd have over me."

"Do you think I'm a fool!" she exclaimed.

"Not at all. But you don't understand me, my dear."

There was a pause between them.

"But you ought *not* to expose yourself," she pleaded.

He shrugged his shoulders.

" 'The man in righteousness arrayed,
    The pure and blameless liver,
    Needs not the keen Toledo blade,
    Nor venom-freighted quiver,' "

he quoted.

She looked at him searchingly.

"I wish I could understand you," she said.

"There's simply nothing to understand," he laughed.

She bowed her head, brooding.

He did not see Dawes for several days; then one morning as he ran upstairs from the Spiral room he almost collided with the burly metal-worker.

"What the——!" cried the smith.

"Sorry!" said Paul, and passed on.

"*Sorry!*" sneered Dawes.

Paul whistled lightly, "Put Me among the Girls".

"I'll stop your whistle, my jockey!" he said.

The other took no notice.

"You're goin' to answer for that job of the other night."

Paul went to his desk in his corner, and turned over the leaves of the ledger.

"Go and tell Fanny I want order 097, quick!" he said to his boy.

Dawes stood in the doorway, tall and threatening, looking at the top of the young man's head.

"Six and five's eleven and seven's one-and-six," Paul added aloud.

"An' you hear, do you!" said Dawes.

"*Five and ninepence!*" He wrote a figure. "What's that?" he said.

"I'm going to show you what it is," said the smith.

The other went on adding the figures aloud.

"Yer crawlin' little ——, yer daresn't face me proper!"

Paul quickly snatched the heavy ruler. Dawes started. The young man ruled some lines in his ledger. The elder man was infuriated.

"But wait till I light on you, no matter where it is, I'll settle your hash for a bit, yer little swine!"

"All right," said Paul.

At that the smith started heavily from the doorway. Just then a whistle piped shrilly. Paul went to the speaking-tube.

"Yes!" he said, and he listened. "Er—yes!" He listened, then he laughed. "I'll come down directly. I've got a visitor just now."

Dawes knew from his tone that he had been speaking to Clara. He stepped forward.

"Yer little devil!" he said. "I'll visitor you, inside of two minutes! Think I'm goin' to have *you* whipperty-snappin' round?"

The other clerks in the warehouse looked up. Paul's office-boy appeared, holding some white article.

"Fanny says you could have had it last night if you'd let her know," he said.

"All right," answered Paul, looking at the stocking. "Get it off."

Dawes stood frustrated, helpless with rage. Morel turned round.

"Excuse me a minute," he said to Dawes, and he would have run downstairs.

"By God, I'll stop your gallop!" shouted the smith, seizing him by the arm. He turned quickly.

"Hey! Hey!" cried the office-boy, alarmed.

Thomas Jordan started out of his little glass office, and came running down the room.

"What's a-matter, what's a-matter?" he said, in his old man's sharp voice.

"I'm just goin' ter settle this little ——, that's all," said Dawes desperately.

"What do you mean?" snapped Thomas Jordan.

"What I say," said Dawes, but he hung fire.

Morel was leaning against the counter, ashamed, half-grinning.

"What's it all about?" snapped Thomas Jordan.

"Couldn't say," said Paul, shaking his head and shrugging his shoulders.

"Couldn't yer, couldn't yer!" cried Dawes, thrusting forward his handsome, furious face, and squaring his fist.

"Have you finished?" cried the old man, strutting. "Get off about your business, and don't come here tipsy in the morning."

Dawes turned his big frame slowly upon him.

"Tipsy!" he said. "Who's tipsy? I'm no more tipsy than *you* are!"

"We've heard that song before," snapped the old man. "Now

you get off, and don't be long about it. Comin' *here* with your rowdying."

The smith looked down contemptuously on his employer. His hands, large, and grimy, and yet well shaped for his labour, worked restlessly. Paul remembered they were the hands of Clara's husband, and a flash of hate went through him.

"Get out before you're turned out!" snapped Thomas Jordan.

"Why, who'll turn me out?" said Dawes, beginning to sneer.

Mr. Jordan started, marched up to the smith, waving him off, thrusting his stout little figure at the man, saying:

"Get off my premises—get off!"

He seized and twitched Dawes's arm.

"Come off!" said the smith, and with a jerk of the elbow he sent the little manufacturer staggering backwards.

Before anyone could help him, Thomas Jordan had collided with the flimsy spring-door. It had given way, and let him crash down the half-dozen steps into Fanny's room. There was a second of amazement; then men and girls were running. Dawes stood a moment looking bitterly on the scene, then he took his departure.

Thomas Jordan was shaken and bruised, not otherwise hurt. He was, however, beside himself with rage. He dismissed Dawes from his employment, and summoned him for assault.

At the trial Paul Morel had to give evidence. Asked how the trouble began, he said:

"Dawes took occasion to insult Mrs. Dawes and me because I accompanied her to the theatre one evening; then I threw some beer at him, and he wanted his revenge."

"*Cherchez la femme!*" smiled the magistrate.

The case was dismissed after the magistrate had told Dawes he thought him a skunk.

"You gave the case away," snapped Mr. Jordan to Paul.

"I don't think I did," replied the latter. "Besides, you didn't really want a conviction, did you?"

"What do you think I took the case up for?"

"Well," said Paul, "I'm sorry if I said the wrong thing." Clara was also very angry.

"Why need *my* name have been dragged in?" she said.

"Better speak it openly than leave it to be whispered."

"There was no need for anything at all," she declared.

"We are none the poorer," he said indifferently.

"*You* may not be," she said.

"And you?" he asked.

"I need never have been mentioned."

"I'm sorry," he said; but he did not sound sorry.

He told himself easily: "She will come round." And she did.

He told his mother about the fall of Mr. Jordan and the trial of Dawes. Mrs. Morel watched him closely.

"And what do you think of it all?" she asked him.

"I think he's a fool," he said.

But he was very uncomfortable, nevertheless.

"Have you ever considered where it will end?" his mother said.

"No," he answered; "things work out of themselves."

"They do, in a way one doesn't like, as a rule," said his mother.

"And then one has to put up with them," he said.

"You'll find you're not as good at 'putting up' as you imagine," she said.

He went on working rapidly at his design.

"Do you ever ask *her* opinion?" she said at length.

"What of?"

"Of you, and the whole thing."

"I don't care what her opinion of me is. She's fearfully in love with me, but it's not very deep."

"But quite as deep as your feeling for her."

He looked up at his mother curiously.

"Yes," he said. "You know, mother, I think there must be something the matter with me, that I *can't* love. When she's there, as a rule, I *do* love her. Sometimes, when I see her just as *the woman*, I love her, mother; but then, when she talks and criticises, I often don't listen to her."

"Yet she's as much sense as Miriam."

"Perhaps; and I love her better than Miriam. But *why* don't they hold me?"

The last question was almost a lamentation. His mother turned away her face, sat looking across the room, very quiet, grave, with something of renunciation.

"But you wouldn't want to marry Clara?" she said.

"No; at first perhaps I would. But why—why don't I want to marry her or anybody? I feel sometimes as if I wronged my women, mother."

"How wronged them, my son?"

"I don't know."

He went on painting rather despairingly; he had touched the quick of the trouble.

"And as for wanting to marry," said his mother, "there's plenty of time yet."

"But no, mother. I even love Clara, and I did Miriam; but to *give* myself to them in marriage I couldn't. I couldn't belong to them. They seem to want *me*, and I can't ever give it them."

"You haven't met the right woman."

"And I never shall meet the right woman while you live," he said.

She was very quiet. Now she began to feel again tired, as if she were done.

"We'll see, my son," she answered.

The feeling that things were going in a circle made him mad.

Clara was, indeed, passionately in love with him, and he with her, as far as passion went. In the daytime he forgot her a good deal. She was working in the same building, but he was not aware of it. He was busy, and her existence was of no matter to him. But all the time she was in her Spiral room she had a sense that he was upstairs, a physical sense of his person in the same building. Every second she expected him to come through the door, and when he came it was a shock to her. But he was often short and offhand with her. He gave her his directions in an official manner, keeping her at bay. With what wits she had left she listened to him. She dared not misunderstand or fail to remember, but it was a cruelty to her. She wanted to touch his chest. She knew exactly how his breast was shapen under the waistcoat, and she wanted to touch it. It maddened her to hear his mechanical voice giving orders about the work. She wanted to break through the sham of it, smash the trivial coating of business which covered him with hardness, get at the man again; but she was afraid, and before she could feel one touch of his warmth he was gone, and she ached again.

He knew that she was dreary every evening she did not see him, so he gave her a good deal of his time. The days were often a misery to her, but the evenings and the nights were usually a bliss to them both. Then they were silent. For hours they sat together, or walked together in the dark, and talked only a few, almost meaningless words. But he had her hand in his, and her bosom left its warmth in his chest, making him feel whole.

One evening they were walking down by the canal, and something was troubling him. She knew she had not got him. All the time he whistled softly and persistently to himself. She listened, feeling she could learn more from his whistling than from his speech. It was a sad dissatisfied tune—a tune that made her feel he would not stay with her. She walked on in silence. When they came to the swing bridge he sat down on the great pole, looking at the stars in the water. He was a long way from her. She had been thinking.

"Will you always stay at Jordan's?" she asked.

"No," he answered without reflecting. "No; I s'll leave Nottingham and go abroad—soon."

"Go abroad! What for?"

"I dunno! I feel restless."

"But what shall you do?"

"I shall have to get some steady designing work, and some sort of sale for my pictures first," he said. "I am gradually making my way. I know I am."

"And when do you think you'll go?"

"I don't know. I shall hardly go for long, while there's my mother."

"You couldn't leave her?"

"Not for long."

She looked at the stars in the black water. They lay very white and staring. It was an agony to know he would leave her, but it was almost an agony to have him near her.

"And if you made a nice lot of money, what would you do?" she asked.

"Go somewhere in a pretty house near London with my mother."

"I see."

There was a long pause.

"I could still come and see you," he said. "I don't know. Don't ask me what I should do; I don't know."

There was a silence. The stars shuddered and broke upon the water. There came a breath of wind. He went suddenly to her, and put his hand on her shoulder.

"Don't ask me anything about the future," he said miserably. "I don't know anything. Be with me now, will you, no matter what it is?"

And she took him in her arms. After all, she was a married woman, and she had no right even to what he gave her. He needed her badly. She had him in her arms, and he was miserable. With her warmth she folded him over, consoled him, loved him. She would let the moment stand for itself.

After a moment he lifted his head as if he wanted to speak.

"Clara," he said, struggling.

She caught him passionately to her, pressed his head down on her breast with her hand. She could not bear the suffering in his voice. She was afraid in her soul. He might have anything of her—anything; but she did not want to *know*. She felt she could not bear it. She wanted him to be soothed upon her—soothed. She stood clasping him and caressing him, and he was something unknown to her—something almost uncanny. She wanted to soothe him into forgetfulness.

And soon the struggle went down in his soul, and he forgot. But then Clara was not there for him, only a woman, warm, something he loved and almost worshipped, there in the dark. But it was not Clara, and she submitted to him. The naked hunger and inevitability of his loving her, something strong and blind and ruthless in its primitiveness, made the hour almost terrible to her. She knew how stark and alone he was, and she felt it was great that he came to her; and she took him simply because his need was bigger either than her or him, and her soul was still within her. She did this for him in his need, even if he left her, for she loved him.

All the while the peewits were screaming in the field. When he came to, he wondered what was near his eyes, curving and strong with life in the dark, and what voice it was speaking. Then he realised it was the grass, and the peewit was calling. The warmth was Clara's breathing heaving. He lifted his head, and looked into her eyes. They were dark and shining and strange, life wild at the source staring into his life, stranger to him, yet meeting him; and he put his face down on her throat, afraid. What was she? A strong, strange, wild life, that breathed with his in the darkness through this hour. It was all so much bigger than themselves that he was hushed. They had met, and included in their meeting the thrust of the manifold grass stems, the cry of the peewit, the wheel of the stars.

When they stood up they saw other lovers stealing down the opposite hedge. It seemed natural they were there; the night contained them.

And after such an evening they both were very still, having known the immensity of passion. They felt small, half-afraid, childish and wondering, like Adam and Eve when they lost their innocence and realised the magnificence of the power which drove them out of Paradise and across the great night and the great day of humanity. It was for each of them an initiation and a satisfaction. To know their own nothingness, to know the tremendous living flood which carried them always, gave them rest within themselves. If so great a magnificent power could overwhelm them, identify them altogether with itself, so that they knew they were only grains in the tremendous heave that lifted every grass blade its little height, and every tree, and living thing, then why fret about themselves? They could let themselves be carried by life, and they felt a sort of peace each in the other. There was a verification which they had had together. Nothing could nullify it, nothing could take it away; it was almost their belief in life.

But Clara was not satisfied. Something great was there, she knew; something great enveloped her. But it did not keep her. In the morning it was not the same. They had *known*, but she could not keep the moment. She wanted it again; she wanted something permanent. She had not realised fully. She thought it was he whom she wanted. He was not safe to her. This that had been between them might never be again; he might leave her. She had not got him; she was not satisfied. She had been there, but she had not gripped the—the something—she knew not what—which she was mad to have.

In the morning he had considerable peace, and was happy in himself. It seemed almost as if he had known the baptism of fire in passion, and it left him at rest. But it was not Clara. It was something that happened because of her, but it was not her. They were scarcely any nearer each other. It was as if they had been blind agents of a great force.

When she saw him that day at the factory her heart melted like a drop of fire. It was his body, his brows. The drop of fire grew more intense in her breast; she must hold him. But he, very quiet, very subdued this morning, went on giving his instruction. She followed him into the dark, ugly basement, and lifted her arms to him. He kissed her, and the intensity of passion began to burn him again. Somebody was at the door. He ran upstairs; she returned to her room, moving as if in a trance.

After that the fire slowly went down. He felt more and more that his experience had been impersonal, and not Clara. He loved her. There was a big tenderness, as after a strong emotion they had known together; but it was not she who could keep his soul steady. He had wanted her to be something she could not be.

And she was mad with desire of him. She could not see him without touching him. In the factory, as he talked to her about Spiral hose, she ran her hand secretly along his side. She followed him out into the basement for a quick kiss; her eyes, always mute and yearning, full of unrestrained passion, she kept fixed on his. He was afraid of her, lest she should too flagrantly give herself away before the other girls. She invariably waited for him at dinner-time for him to embrace her before she went. He felt as if she were helpless, almost a burden to him, and it irritated him.

"But what do you always want to be kissing and embracing for?" he said. "Surely there's a time for everything."

She looked up at him, and the hate came into her eyes.

"*Do* I always want to be kissing you?" she said.

"Always, even if I come to ask you about the work. I don't want anything to do with love when I'm at work. Work's work——"

"And what is love?" she asked. "Has it to have special hours?"

"Yes; out of work hours."

"And you'll regulate it according to Mr. Jordan's closing time?"

"Yes; and according to the freedom from business of any sort."

"It is only to exist in spare time?"

"That's all, and not always then—not the kissing sort of love."

"And that's all you think of it?"

"It's quite enough."

"I'm glad you think so."

And she was cold to him for some time—she hated him; and while she was cold and contemptuous, he was uneasy till she had forgiven him again. But when they started afresh they were not any nearer. He kept her because he never satisfied her.

In the spring they went together to the seaside. They had rooms at a little cottage near Theddlethorpe, and lived as man and wife. Mrs. Radford sometimes went with them.

It was known in Nottingham that Paul Morel and Mrs. Dawes

were going together, but as nothing was very obvious, and Clara always a solitary person, and he seemed so simple and innocent, it did not make much difference.

He loved the Lincolnshire coast, and she loved the sea. In the early morning they often went out together to bathe. The grey of the dawn, the far, desolate reaches of the fenland smitten with winter, the sea-meadows rank with herbage, were stark enough to rejoice his soul. As they stepped on to the high-road from their plank bridge, and looked round at the endless monotony of levels, the land a little darker than the sky, the sea sounding small beyond the sandhills, his heart filled strong with the sweeping relentlessness of life. She loved him then. He was solitary and strong, and his eyes had a beautiful light.

They shuddered with cold; then he raced her down the road to the green turf bridge. She could run well. Her colour soon came, her throat was bare, her eyes shone. He loved her for being so luxuriously heavy, and yet so quick. Himself was light; she went with a beautiful rush. They grew warm, and walked hand in hand.

A flush came into the sky, the wan moon, half-way down the west, sank into insignificance. On the shadowy land things began to take life, plants with great leaves became distinct. They came through a pass in the big, cold sandhills on to the beach. The long waste of foreshore lay moaning under the dawn and the sea; the ocean was a flat dark strip with a white edge. Over the gloomy sea the sky grew red. Quickly the fire spread among the clouds and scattered them. Crimson burned to orange, orange to dull gold, and in a golden glitter the sun came up, dribbling fierily over the waves in little splashes, as if someone had gone along and the light had spilled from her pail as she walked.

The breakers ran down the shore in long, hoarse strokes. Tiny seagulls, like specks of spray, wheeled above the line of surf. Their crying seemed larger than they. Far away the coast reached out, and melted into the morning, the tussocky sandhills seemed to sink to a level with the beach. Mablethorpe was tiny on their right. They had alone the space of all this level shore, the sea, and the upcoming sun, the faint noise of the waters, the sharp crying of the gulls.

They had a warm hollow in the sandhills where the wind did not come. He stood looking out to sea.

"It's very fine," he said.

"Now don't get sentimental," she said.

It irritated her to see him standing gazing at the sea, like a solitary and poetic person. He laughed. She quickly undressed.

"There are some fine waves this morning," she said triumphantly.

She was a better swimmer than he; he stood idly watching her.

"Aren't you coming?" she said.

"In a minute," he answered.

She was white and velvet skinned, with heavy shoulders. A little wind, coming from the sea, blew across her body and ruffled her hair.

The morning was of a lovely limpid gold colour. Veils of shadow seemed to be drifting away on the north and the south. Clara stood shrinking slightly from the touch of the wind, twisting her hair. The sea-grass rose behind the white stripped woman. She glanced at the sea, then looked at him. He was watching her with dark eyes which she loved and could not understand. She hugged her breasts between her arms, cringing, laughing:

"Oo, it will be so cold!" she said.

He bent forward and kissed her, held her suddenly close, and kissed her again. She stood waiting. He looked into her eyes, then away at the pale sands.

"Go, then!" he said quietly.

She flung her arms round his neck, drew him against her, kissed him passionately, and went, saying:

"But you'll come in?"

"In a minute."

She went plodding heavily over the sand that was soft as velvet. He, on the sandhills, watched the great pale coast envelop her. She grew smaller, lost proportion, seemed only like a large white bird toiling forward.

"Not much more than a big white pebble on the beach, not much more than a clot of foam being blown and rolled over the sand," he said to himself.

She seemed to move very slowly across the vast sounding shore. As he watched, he lost her. She was dazzled out of sight by the sunshine. Again he saw her, the merest white speck moving against the white, muttering sea-edge.

"Look how little she is!" he said to himself. "She's lost like a grain of sand in the beach—just a concentrated speck blown along, a tiny white foam-bubble, almost nothing among the morning. Why does she absorb me?"

The morning was altogether uninterrupted: she was gone in the water. Far and wide the beach, the sandhills with their blue marram, the shining water, glowed together in immense, unbroken solitude.

"What is she, after all?" he said to himself. "Here's the sea-coast morning, big and permanent and beautiful; there is she, fretting, always unsatisfied, and temporary as a bubble of foam. What does she mean to me, after all? She represents something, like a bubble of foam represents the sea. But what is she? It's not her I care for."

Then, startled by his own unconscious thoughts, that seemed to speak so distinctly that all the morning could hear, he undressed and ran quickly down the sands. She was watching for him. Her arm flashed up to him, she heaved on a wave, subsided, her shoulders in a pool of liquid silver. He jumped through the breakers, and in a moment her hand was on his shoulder.

He was a poor swimmer, and could not stay long in the water. She played round him in triumph, sporting with her superiority, which he begrudged her. The sunshine stood deep and fine on the water. They laughed in the sea for a minute or two, then raced each other back to the sandhills.

When they were drying themselves, panting heavily, he watched her laughing, breathless face, her bright shoulders, her breasts that swayed and made him frightened as she rubbed them, and he thought again:

"But she is magnificent, and even bigger than the morning and the sea. Is she——? Is she——"

She, seeing his dark eyes fixed on her, broke off from her drying with a laugh.

"What are you looking at?" she said.

"You," he answered, laughing.

Her eyes met his, and in a moment he was kissing her white "goose-fleshed" shoulder, and thinking:

"What is she? What is she?"

She loved him in the morning. There was something detached, hard, and elemental about his kisses then, as if he were only conscious of his own will, not in the least of her and her wanting him.

Later in the day he went out sketching.

"You," he said to her, "go with your mother to Sutton. I am so dull."

She stood and looked at him. He knew she wanted to come with him, but he preferred to be alone. She made him feel imprisoned when she was there, as if he could not get a free deep breath, as if there were something on top of him. She felt his desire to be free of her.

In the evening he came back to her. They walked down the shore in the darkness, then sat for awhile in the shelter of the sandhills.

"It seems," she said, as they stared over the darkness of the sea, where no light was to be seen—"it seemed as if you only loved me at night—as if you didn't love me in the daytime."

He ran the cold sand through his fingers, feeling guilty under the accusation.

"The night is free to you," he replied. "In the daytime I want to be by myself."

"But why?" she said. "Why, even now, when we are on this short holiday?"

"I don't know. Love-making stifles me in the daytime."

"But it needn't be always love-making," she said.

"It always is," he answered, "when you and I are together."

She sat feeling very bitter.

"Do you ever want to marry me?" he asked curiously.

"Do you me?" she replied.

"Yes, yes; I should like us to have children," he answered slowly.

She sat with her head bent, fingering the sand.

"But you don't really want a divorce from Baxter, do you?" he said.

It was some minute before she replied.

"No," she said, very deliberately; "I don't think I do."

"Why?"

"I don't know."

"Do you feel as if you belonged to him?"

"No; I don't think so."

"What, then?"

"I think he belongs to me," she replied.

He was silent for some minutes, listening to the wind blowing over the hoarse, dark sea.

"And you never really intended to belong to *me*?" he said.

"Yes, I do belong to you," she answered.

"No," he said; "because you don't want to be divorced."

It was a knot they could not untie, so they left it, took what they could get, and what they could not attain they ignored.

"I consider you treated Baxter rottenly," he said another time.

He half-expected Clara to answer him, as his mother would: "You consider your own affairs, and don't know so much about other people's." But she took him seriously, almost to his own surprise.

"Why?" she said.

"I suppose you thought he was a lily of the valley, and so you put him in an appropriate pot, and tended him according. You made up your mind he was a lily of the valley and it was no good his being a cow-parsnip. You wouldn't have it."

"I certainly never imagined him a lily of the valley."

"You imagined him something he wasn't. That's just what a woman is. She thinks she knows what's good for a man, and she's going to see he gets it; and no matter if he's starving, he may sit and whistle for what he needs, while she's got him, and is giving him what's good for him."

"And what are you doing?" she asked.

"I'm thinking what tune I shall whistle," he laughed.

And instead of boxing his ears, she considered him in earnest.

"You think I want to give you what's good for you?" she asked.

"I hope so; but love should give a sense of freedom, not of prison. Miriam made me feel tied up like a donkey to a stake. I must feed on her patch, and nowhere else. It's sickening!"

"And would *you* let a *woman* do as she likes?"

"Yes; I'll see that she *likes* to love me. If she doesn't—well, I don't hold her."

"If you were as wonderful as you say——," replied Clara.

"I should be the marvel I am," he laughed.

There was a silence in which they hated each other, though they laughed.

"Love's a dog in a manger," he said.

"And which of us is the dog?" she asked.

"Oh well, you, of course."

So there went on a battle between them. She knew she never fully had him. Some part, big and vital in him, she had no hold over; nor did she ever try to get it, or even to realise what it was. And he knew in some way that she held herself still as

Mrs. Dawes. She did not love Dawes, never had loved him; but she believed he loved her, at least depended on her. She felt a certain surety about him that she never felt with Paul Morel. Her passion for the young man had filled her soul, given her a certain satisfaction, eased her of her self-mistrust, her doubt. Whatever else she was, she was inwardly assured. It was almost as if she had gained *herself*, and stood now distinct and complete. She had received her confirmation; but she never believed that her life belonged to Paul Morel, nor his to her. They would separate in the end, and the rest of her life would be an ache after him. But at any rate, she *knew* now, she was sure of herself. And the same could almost be said of him. Together they had received the baptism of life, each through the other; but now their missions were separate. Where he wanted to go she could not come with him. They would have to part sooner or later. Even if they married, and were faithful to each other, still he would have to leave her, go on alone, and she would only have to attend to him when he came home. But it was not possible. Each wanted a mate to go side by side with.

Clara had gone to live with her mother upon Mapperley Plains. One evening, as Paul and she were walking along Woodborough Road, they met Dawes. Morel knew something about the bearing of the man approaching, but he was absorbed in his thinking at the moment, so that only his artist's eye watched the form of the stranger. Then he suddenly turned to Clara with a laugh, and put his hand on her shoulder, saying, laughing:

"But we walk side by side, and yet I'm in London arguing with an imaginary Orpen; and where are you?"

At that instant Dawes passed, almost touching Morel. The young man glanced, saw the dark brown eyes burning, full of hate and yet tired.

"Who was that?" he asked of Clara.

"It was Baxter," she replied.

Paul took his hand from her shoulder and glanced round; then he saw again distinctly the man's form as it approached him. Dawes still walked erect, with his fine shoulders flung back, and his face lifted; but there was a furtive look in his eyes that gave one the impression he was trying to get unnoticed past every person he met, glancing suspiciously to see what they thought of him. And his hands seemed to be wanting to hide. He wore old clothes, the trousers were torn at the

knee, and the handkerchief tied round his throat was dirty;
but his cap was still defiantly over one eye. As she saw him,
Clara felt guilty. There was a tiredness and despair on his face
that made her hate him, because it hurt her.

"He looks shady," said Paul.

But the note of pity in his voice reproached her, and made
her feel hard.

"His true commonness comes out," she answered.

"Do you hate him?" he asked.

"You talk," she said, "about the cruelty of women; I wish
you knew the cruelty of men in their brute force. They simply
don't know that the woman exists."

"Don't *I*?" he said.

"No," she answered.

"Don't I know you exist?"

"About *me* you know nothing," she said bitterly—"about
me!"

"No more than Baxter knew?" he asked.

"Perhaps not as much."

He felt puzzled, and helpless, and angry. There she walked
unknown to him, though they had been through such experience together.

"But you know *me* pretty well," he said.

She did not answer.

"Did you know Baxter as well as you know me?" he asked.

"He wouldn't let me," she said.

"And I have let you know me?"

"It's what men *won't* let you do. They won't let you get
really near to them," she said.

"And haven't I let you?"

"Yes," she answered slowly; "but you've never come near to
me. You can't come out of yourself, you can't. Baxter could
do that better than you."

He walked on pondering. He was angry with her for prefer-
ing Baxter to him.

"You begin to value Baxter now you've not got him," he said.

"No; I can only see where he was different from you."

But he felt she had a grudge against him.

One evening, as they were coming home over the fields, she
startled him by asking:

"Do you think it's worth it—the—the sex part?"

"The act of loving, itself?"

[handwritten margin note: It can, but it doesn't have to.]

"Yes; is it worth anything to you?"

"But how can you separate it?" he said. "It's the culmination of everything. All our intimacy culminates then."

"Not for me," she said.

He was silent. A flash of hate for her came up. After all, she was dissatisfied with him, even there, where he thought they fulfilled each other. But he believed her too implicitly.

"I feel," she continued slowly, "as if I hadn't got you, as if all of you weren't there, and as if it weren't *me* you were taking——"

"Who, then?"

"Something just for yourself. It has been fine, so that I daren't think of it. But is it *me* you want, or is it *It*?"

He again felt guilty. Did he leave Clara out of count, and take simply women? But he thought that was splitting a hair.

"When I had Baxter, actually had him, then I *did* feel as if I had all of him," she said.

"And it was better?" he asked.

"Yes, yes; it was more whole. I don't say you haven't given me more than he ever gave me."

"Or could give you."

"Yes, perhaps; but you've never given me yourself."

He knitted his brows angrily.

"If I start to make love to you," he said, "I just go like a leaf down the wind."

"And leave me out of count," she said.

"And then is it nothing to you?" he asked, almost rigid with chagrin.

"It's something; and sometimes you have carried me away—right away—I know—and—I reverence you for it—but——"

"Don't 'but' me," he said, kissing her quickly, as a fire ran through him.

She submitted, and was silent.

[handwritten margin note: Sex makes him un-controlled]

It was true as he said. As a rule, when he started love-making, the emotion was strong enough to carry with it everything—reason, soul, blood—in a great sweep, like the Trent carries bodily its back-swirls and intertwinings, noiselessly. Gradually the little criticisms, the little sensations, were lost, thought also went, everything borne along in one flood. He became, not a man with a mind, but a great instinct. His hands were like creatures, living; his limbs, his body, were all life and consciousness, subject to no will of his, but living in themselves. Just as he was, so it seemed the vigorous, wintry stars were strong also with life. He and they struck with the same pulse of fire, and the same joy of strength which held the bracken-frond stiff near his eyes held his own body firm. It was as if he, and the stars, and the dark herbage, and Clara were licked up in an immense tongue of flame, which tore onwards and upwards. Everything rushed along in living beside him; everything was still, perfect in itself, along with him. This wonderful stillness in each thing in itself, while it was being borne along in a very ecstasy of living, seemed the highest point of bliss.

And Clara knew this held him to her, so she trusted altogether to the passion. It, however, failed her very often. They did not often reach again the height of that once when the peewits had called. Gradually, some mechanical effort spoilt their loving, or, when they had splendid moments, they had them separately, and not so satisfactorily. So often he seemed merely to be running on alone; often they realised it had been a failure, not what they had wanted. He left her, knowing *that* evening had only made a little split between them. Their loving grew more mechanical, without the marvellous glamour. Gradually they began to introduce novelties, to get back some of the feeling of satisfaction. They would be very near, almost dangerously near to the river, so that the black water ran not far from his face, and it gave a little thrill; or they loved sometimes in a little hollow below the fence of the path where people were passing occasionally, on the edge of the town, and they heard footsteps coming, almost felt the vibration of the tread, and they heard what the passers-by said—strange little things that were never intended to be heard. And afterwards each of them was rather ashamed, and these things caused a distance between the two of them. He began to despise her a little, as if she had merited it!

One night he left her to go to Daybrook Station over the fields. It was very dark, with an attempt at snow, although the spring was so far advanced. Morel had not much time; he plunged forward. The town ceases almost abruptly on the edge of a steep hollow; there the houses with their yellow lights stand up against the darkness. He went over the stile, and dropped quickly into the hollow of the fields. Under the orchard one warm window shone in Swineshead Farm. Paul glanced round. Behind, the houses stood on the brim of the dip, black against the sky, like wild beasts glaring curiously with yellow eyes down into the darkness. It was the town that seemed savage and uncouth, glaring on the clouds at the back of him. Some creature stirred under the willows of the farm pond. It was too dark to distinguish anything.

He was close up to the next stile before he saw a dark shape leaning against it. The man moved aside.

"Good-evening!" he said.

"Good-evening!" Morel answered, not noticing.

"Paul Morel?" said the man.

Then he knew it was Dawes. The man stopped his way.

"I've got yer, have I?" he said awkwardly.

"I shall miss my train," said Paul.

He could see nothing of Dawes's face. The man's teeth seemed to chatter as he talked.

"You're going to get it from me now," said Dawes.

Morel attempted to move forward; the other man stepped in front of him.

"Are yer goin' to take that top-coat off," he said, "or are you goin' to lie down to it?"

Paul was afraid the man was mad.

"But," he said, "I don't know how to fight."

"All right, then," answered Dawes, and before the younger man knew where he was, he was staggering backwards from a blow across the face.

The whole night went black. He tore off his overcoat and coat, dodging a blow, and flung the garments over Dawes. The latter swore savagely. Morel, in his shirt-sleeves, was now alert and furious. He felt his whole body unsheath itself like a claw. He could not fight, so he would use his wits. The other man became more distinct to him; he could see particularly the shirt-breast. Dawes stumbled over Paul's coats, then came rushing forward. The young man's mouth was bleeding. It was the other man's mouth he was dying to get at, and the desire was anguish in its strength. He stepped quickly through the stile, and as Dawes was coming through after him, like a flash he got a blow in over the other's mouth. He shivered with pleasure. Dawes advanced slowly, spitting. Paul was afraid; he moved round to get to the stile again. Suddenly, from out of nowhere, came a great blow against his ear, that sent him falling helpless backwards. He heard Dawes's heavy panting, like a wild beast's, then came a kick on the knee, giving him such agony that he got up and, quite blind, leapt clean under his enemy's guard. He felt blows and kicks, but they did not hurt. He hung on to the bigger man like a wild cat, till at last Dawes fell with a crash, losing his presence of mind. Paul went down with him. Pure instinct brought his hands to the man's neck, and before Dawes, in frenzy and agony, could wrench him free, he had got his fists twisted in the scarf and his knuckles dug in the throat of the other man. He was a pure instinct, without reason or feeling. His body, hard and wonderful in itself, cleaved against the struggling body of the other man; not a muscle in him relaxed. He was quite unconscious, only his body had taken upon itself to kill this other man. For himself, he had neither feeling nor reason. He lay pressed hard against his adversary, his body adjusting itself to its one pure purpose of choking the other man, resisting exactly at the right moment, with exactly the right amount of strength, the struggles of the other, silent, intent, unchanging, gradually pressing its knuckles deeper, feeling the struggles of the other body become wilder and more frenzied. Tighter and tighter grew his body, like a screw that is gradually increasing in pressure, till something breaks.

Then suddenly he relaxed, full of wonder and misgiving. Dawes had been yielding. Morel felt his body flame with pain, as he realised what he was doing; he was all bewildered. Dawes's struggles suddenly renewed themselves in a furious spasm. Paul's hands were wrenched, torn out of the scarf in which they were knotted, and he was flung away, helpless. He heard the horrid sound of the other's gasping, but he lay stunned; then, still dazed, he felt the blows of the other's feet, and lost consciousness.

Dawes, grunting with pain like a beast, was kicking the prostrate body of his rival. Suddenly the whistle of the train shrieked two fields away. He turned round and glared suspiciously. What was coming? He saw the lights of the train draw across his vision. It seemed to him people were approaching. He made off across the field into Nottingham, and dimly in his consciousness as he went, he felt on his foot the place where his boot had knocked against one of the lad's bones. The knock seemed to re-echo inside him; he hurried to get away from it.

Morel gradually came to himself. He knew where he was and what had happened, but he did not want to move. He lay still, with tiny bits of snow tickling his face. It was pleasant to lie quite, quite still. The time passed. It was the bits of snow that kept rousing him when he did not want to be roused. A last his will clicked into action.

"I mustn't lie here," he said; "it's silly."

But still he did not move.

"I said I was going to get up," he repeated. "Why don't I?"

And still it was some time before he had sufficiently pulled himself together to stir; then gradually he got up. Pain made him sick and dazed, but his brain was clear. Reeling, he groped for his coats and got them on, buttoning his overcoat up to his ears. It was some time before he found his cap. He did not know whether his face was still bleeding. Walking blindly, every step making him sick with pain, he went back to the pond and washed his face and hands. The icy water hurt, but helped to bring him back to himself. He crawled back up the hill to the tram. He wanted to get to his mother—he must get to his mother—that was his blind intention. He covered his face as much as he could, and struggled sickly along. Continually the ground seemed to fall away from him as he walked, and he felt himself dropping with a sickening feeling into space; so, like a nightmare, he got through with the journey home.

Everybody was in bed. He looked at himself. His face was discoloured and smeared with blood, almost like a dead man's face. He washed it, and went to bed. The night went by in delirium. In the morning he found his mother looking at him. Her blue eyes—they were all he wanted to see. She was there; he was in her hands.

"It's not much, mother," he said. "It was Baxter Dawes."

"Tell me where it hurts you," she said quietly.

"I don't know—my shoulder. Say it was a bicycle accident, mother."

He could not move his arm. Presently Minnie, the little servant, came upstairs with some tea.

"Your mother's nearly frightened me out of my wits—fainted away," she said.

He felt he could not bear it. His mother nursed him; he told her about it.

"And now I should have done with them all," she said quietly.

"I will, mother."

She covered him up.

"And don't think about it," she said—"only try to go to sleep. The doctor won't be here till eleven."

He had a dislocated shoulder, and the second day acute bronchitis set in. His mother was pale as death now, and very thin. She would sit and look at him, then away into space. There was something between them that neither dared mention. Clara came to see him. Afterwards he said to his mother:

"She makes me tired, mother."

"Yes; I wish she wouldn't come," Mrs. Morel replied.

Another day Miriam came, but she seemed almost like a stranger to him.

"You know, I don't care about them, mother," he said.

"I'm afraid you don't, my son," she replied sadly.

It was given out everywhere that it was a bicycle accident. Soon he was able to go to work again, but now there was a constant sickness and gnawing at his heart. He went to Clara, but there seemed, as it were, nobody there. He could not work. He and his mother seemed almost to avoid each other. There was some secret between them which they could not bear. He was not aware of it. He only knew that his life seemed unbalanced, as if it were going to smash into pieces.

Clara did not know what was the matter with him. She realised that he seemed unaware of her. Even when he came to her he seemed unaware of her; always he was somewhere else. She felt she was clutching for him, and he was somewhere else. It tortured her, and so she tortured him. For a month at a time she kept him at arm's length. He almost hated her, and was driven to her in spite of himself. He went mostly into the company of men, was always at the George or the White Horse. His mother was ill, distant, quiet, shadowy. He was terrified of something; he dared not look at her. Her eyes seemed to grow darker, her face more waxen; still she dragged about at her work.

At Whitsuntide he said he would go to Blackpool for four days with his friend Newton. The latter was a big, jolly fellow, with a touch of the bounder about him. Paul said his mother must go to Sheffield to stay a week with Annie, who lived there. Perhaps the change would do her good. Mrs. Morel was attending a woman's doctor in Nottingham. He said her heart and her digestion were wrong. She consented to go to Sheffield, though she did not want to; but now she would do everything her son wished of her. Paul said he would come for her on the fifth day, and stay also in Sheffield till the holiday was up. It was agreed.

The two young men set off gaily for Blackpool. Mrs. Morel was quite lively as Paul kissed her and left her. Once at the station, he forgot everything. Four days were clear—not an anxiety, not a thought. The two young men simply enjoyed themselves. Paul was like another man. None of himself remained—no Clara, no Miriam, no mother that fretted him. He wrote to them all, and long letters to his mother; but they were jolly letters that made her laugh. He was having a good time, as young fellows will in a place like Blackpool. And underneath it all was a shadow for her.

Paul was very gay, excited at the thought of staying with his mother in Sheffield. Newton was to spend the day with them. Their train was late. Joking, laughing, with their pipes between their teeth, the young men swung their bags on to the tram-car. Paul had bought his mother a little collar of real lace that he wanted to see her wear, so that he could tease her about it.

Annie lived in a nice house, and had a little maid. Paul ran gaily up the steps. He expected his mother laughing in the hall, but it was Annie who opened to him. She seemed distant to him. He stood a second in dismay. Annie let him kiss her cheek.

"Is my mother ill?" he said.

"Yes; she's not very well. Don't upset her."

"Is she in bed?"

"Yes."

And then the queer feeling went over him, as if all the sunshine had gone out of him, and it was all shadow. He dropped the bag and ran upstairs. Hesitating, he opened the door. His mother sat up in bed, wearing a dressing-gown of old-rose colour. She looked at him almost as if she were ashamed of herself, pleading to him, humble. He saw the ashy look about her.

"Mother!" he said.

"I thought you were never coming," she answered gaily.

But he only fell on his knees at the bedside, and buried his face in the bedclothes, crying in agony, and saying:

"Mother—mother—mother!"

She stroked his hair slowly with her thin hand.

"Don't cry," she said. "Don't cry—it's nothing."

But he felt as if his blood was melting into tears, and he cried in terror and pain.

"Don't—don't cry," his mother faltered.

Slowly she stroked his hair. Shocked out of himself, he cried, and the tears hurt in every fibre of his body. Suddenly he stopped, but he dared not lift his face out of the bedclothes.

"You *are* late. Where have you been?" his mother asked.

"The train was late," he replied, muffled in the sheet.

"Yes; that miserable Central! Is Newton come?"

"Yes."

"I'm sure you must be hungry, and they've kept dinner waiting."

With a wrench he looked up at her.

"What is it, mother?" he asked brutally.

She averted her eyes as she answered:

"Only a bit of a tumour, my boy. You needn't trouble. It's been there—the lump has—a long time."

Up came the tears again. His mind was clear and hard, but his body was crying.

"Where?" he said.

She put her hand on her side.

"Here. But you know they can sweal a tumour away."

He stood feeling dazed and helpless, like a child. He thought perhaps it was as she said. Yes; he reassured himself it was so. But all the while his blood and his body knew definitely what it was. He sat down on the bed, and took her hand. She had never had but the one ring—her wedding-ring.

"When were you poorly?" he asked.

"It was yesterday it began," she answered submissively.

"Pains?"

"Yes; but not more than I've often had at home. I believe Dr. Ansell is an alarmist."

"You ought not to have travelled alone," he said, to himself more than to her.

"As if that had anything to do with it!" she answered quickly.

They were silent for a while.

"Now go and have your dinner," she said. "You *must* be hungry."

"Have you had yours?"

"Yes; a beautiful sole I had. Annie *is* good to me."

They talked a little while, then he went downstairs. He was

very white and strained. Newton sat in miserable sympathy.

After dinner he went into the scullery to help Annie to wash up. The little maid had gone on an errand.

"Is it really a tumour?" he asked

Annie began to cry again.

"The pain she had yesterday—I never saw anybody suffer like it!" she cried. "Leonard ran like a madman for Dr. Ansell, and when she'd got to bed she said to me: 'Annie, look at this lump on my side. I wonder what it is?' And there I looked, and I thought I should have dropped. Paul, as true as I'm here, it's a lump as big as my double fist. I said: 'Good gracious, mother, whenever did that come?' 'Why, child,' she said, 'it's been there a long time.' I thought I should have died, our Paul, I did. She's been having these pains for months at home, and nobody looking after her."

The tears came to his eyes, then dried suddenly.

"But she's been attending the doctor in Nottingham—and she never told me," he said.

"If I'd have been at home," said Annie, "I should have seen for myself."

He felt like a man walking in unrealities. In the afternoon he went to see the doctor. The latter was a shrewd, lovable man.

"But what is it?" he said.

The doctor looked at the young man, then knitted his fingers.

"It may be a large tumour which has formed in the membrane," he said slowly, "and which we *may* be able to make go away."

"Can't you operate?" asked Paul.

"Not there," replied the doctor.

"Are you sure?"

"*Quite!*"

Paul meditated a while.

"Are you sure it's a tumour?" he asked. "Why did Dr. Jameson in Nottingham never find out anything about it? She's been going to him for weeks, and he's treated her for heart and indigestion."

"Mrs. Morel never told Dr. Jameson about the lump," said the doctor.

"And do you *know* it's a tumour?"

"No, I am not sure."

"What else *might* it be? You asked my sister if there was cancer in the family. Might it be cancer?"

"I don't know."

"And what shall you do?"

"I should like an examination, with Dr. Jameson."

"Then have one."

"You must arrange about that. His fee wouldn't be less than ten guineas to come here from Nottingham."

"When would you like him to come?"

"I will call in this evening, and we will talk it over."

Paul went away, biting his lip.

His mother could come downstairs for tea, the doctor said. Her son went upstairs to help her. She wore the old-rose dressing-gown that Leonard had given Annie, and, with a little colour in her face, was quite young again.

"But you look quite pretty in that," he said.

"Yes; they make me so fine, I hardly know myself," she answered.

But when she stood up to walk, the colour went. Paul helped her, half-carrying her. At the top of the stairs she was gone. He lifted her up and carried her quickly downstairs; laid her on the couch. She was light and frail. Her face looked as if she were dead, with blue lips shut tight. Her eyes opened— her blue, unfailing eyes—and she looked at him pleadingly, almost wanting him to forgive her. He held brandy to her lips, but her mouth would not open. All the time she watched him lovingly. She was only sorry for him. The tears ran down his face without ceasing, but not a muscle moved. He was intent on getting a little brandy between her lips. Soon she was able to swallow a teaspoonful. She lay back, so tired. The tears continued to run down his face.

"But," she panted, "it'll go off. Don't cry!"

"I'm not doing," he said.

After a while she was better again. He was kneeling beside the couch. They looked into each other's eyes.

"I don't want you to make a trouble of it," she said.

"No, mother. You'll have to be quite still, and then you'll get better soon."

But he was white to the lips, and their eyes as they looked at each other understood. Her eyes were so blue—such a wonderful forget-me-not blue! He felt if only they had been of a different colour he could have borne it better. His heart seemed to be ripping slowly in his breast. He kneeled there, holding her hand, and neither said anything. Then Annie came in.

"Are you all right?" she murmured timidly to her mother.

"Of course," said Mrs. Morel.

Paul sat down and told her about Blackpool. She was curious.

A day or two after, he went to see Dr. Jameson in Nottingham, to arrange for a consulation. Paul had practically no money in the world. But he could borrow.

His mother had been used to go to the public consultation on Saturday morning, when she could see the doctor for only a nominal sum. Her son went on the same day. The waiting-room was full of poor women, who sat patiently on a bench around the wall. Paul thought of his mother, in her little black costume, sitting waiting likewise. The doctor was late. The women all looked rather frightened. Paul asked the nurse in attendance if he could see the doctor immediately he came. It was arranged so. The women sitting patiently round the walls of the room eyed the young man curiously.

At last the doctor came. He was about forty, good-looking, brown-skinned. His wife had died, and he, who had loved her, had specialised on women's ailments. Paul told his name and his mother's. The doctor did not remember.

"Number forty-six M.," said the nurse; and the doctor looked up the case in his book.

"There is a big lump that may be a tumour," said Paul. "But Dr. Ansell was going to write you a letter."

"Ah, yes!" replied the doctor, drawing the letter from his pocket. He was very friendly, affable, busy, kind. He would come to Sheffield the next day.

"What is your father?" he asked.

"He is a coal-miner," replied Paul.

"Not very well off, I suppose?"

"This—I see after this," said Paul.

"And you?" smiled the doctor.

"I am a clerk in Jordan's Appliance Factory."

The doctor smiled at him.

"Er—to go to Sheffield!" he said, putting the tips of his fingers together, and smiling with his eyes. "Eight guineas?"

"Thank you!" said Paul, flushing and rising. "And you'll come to-morrow?"

"To-morrow—Sunday? Yes! Can you tell me about what time there is a train in the afternoon?"

"There is a Central gets in at four-fifteen."

"And will there be any way of getting up to the house? Shall I have to walk?" The doctor smiled.

"There is the tram," said Paul; "the Western Park tram."

The doctor made a note of it.

"Thank you!" he said, and shook hands.

Then Paul went on home to see his father, who was left in the charge of Minnie. Walter Morel was getting very grey now. Paul found him digging in the garden. He had written him a letter. He shook hands with his father.

"Hello, son! Tha has landed, then?" said the father.

"Yes," replied the son. "But I'm going back to-night."

"Are ter, beguy!" exclaimed the collier. "An' has ter eaten owt?"

"No."

"That's just like thee," said Morel. "Come thy ways in."

The father was afraid of the mention of his wife. The two went indoors. Paul ate in silence; his father, with earthy hands, and sleeves rolled up, sat in the arm-chair opposite and looked at him.

"Well, an' how is she?" asked the miner at length, in a little voice.

"She can sit up; she can be carried down for tea," said paul.

"That's a blessin'!" exclaimed Morel. "I hope we s'll soon be havin' her whoam, then. An' what's that Nottingham doctor say?"

"He's going to-morrow to have an examination of her."

"Is he beguy! That's a tidy penny, I'm thinkin'!"

"Eight guineas."

"Eight guineas!" the miner spoke breathlessly. "Well, we mun find it from somewhere."

"I can pay that," said Paul.

There was silence between them for some time.

"She says she hopes you're getting on all right with Minnie," Paul said.

"Yes, I'm all right, an' I wish as she was," answered Morel.

"But Minnie's a good little wench, bless 'er heart!" He sat looking dismal.

"I s'll have to be going at half-past three," said Paul.

"It's a trapse for thee, lad! Eight guineas! An' when dost think she'll be able to get as far as this?"

"We must see what the doctors say to-morrow," Paul said.

Morel sighed deeply. The house seemed strangely empty, and Paul thought his father looked lost, forlorn, and old.

"You'll have to go and see her next week, father," he said.

"I hope she'll be a-whoam by that time," said Morel.

"If she's not," said Paul, "then you must come."

"I dunno wheer I s'll find th' money," said Morel.

"And I'll write to you what the doctor says," said Paul.

"But tha writes i' such a fashion, I canna ma'e it out," said Morel.

"Well, I'll write plain."

It was no good asking Morel to answer, for he could scarcely do more than write his own name.

The doctor came. Leonard felt it his duty to meet him with a cab. The examination did not take long. Annie, Arthur, Paul, and Leonard were waiting in the parlour anxiously. The doctors came down. Paul glanced at them. He had never had any hope, except when he had deceived himself.

"It *may* be a tumour; we must wait and see," said Dr. Jameson.

"And if it is," said Annie, "can you sweal it away?"

"Probably," said the doctor.

Paul put eight sovereigns and half a sovereign on the table. The doctor counted them, took a florin out of his purse, and put that down.

"Thank you!" he said. "I'm sorry Mrs. Morel is so ill. But we must see what we can do."

"There can't be an operation?" said Paul.

The doctor shook his head.

"No," he said; "and even if there could, her heart wouldn't stand it."

"Is her heart risky?" asked Paul.

"Yes; you must be careful with her."

"Very risky?"

"No—er—no, no! Just take care."

And the doctor was gone.

Then Paul carried his mother downstairs. She lay simply, like a child. But when he was on the stairs, she put her arms round his neck, clinging.

"I'm so frightened of these beastly stairs," she said.

And he was frightened, too. He would let Leonard do it another time. He felt he could not carry her.

"He thinks it's only a tumour!" cried Annie to her mother. "And he can swear it away."

"I *knew* he could," protested Mrs. Morel scornfully.

She pretended not to notice that Paul had gone out of the room. He sat in the kitchen, smoking. Then he tried to brush some grey ash off his coat. He looked again. It was one of his mother's grey hairs. It was so long! He held it up, and it drifted into the chimney. He let go. The long grey hair floated and was gone in the blackness of the chimney.

The next day he kissed her before going back to work. It was very early in the morning, and they were alone.

"You won't fret, my boy!" she said.

"No, mother."

"No; it would be silly. And take care of yourself."

"Yes," he answered. Then, after a while: "And I shall come next Saturday, and shall bring my father?"

"I suppose he wants to come," she replied. "At any rate, if he does you'll have to let him."

He kissed her again, and stroked the hair from her temples, gently, tenderly, as if she were a lover.

"Shan't you be late?" she murmured.

"I'm going," he said, very low.

Still he sat a few minutes, stroking the brown and grey hair from her temples.

"And you won't be any worse, mother?"

"No, my son."

"You promise me?"

"Yes; I won't be any worse."

He kissed her, held her in his arms for a moment, and was gone. In the early sunny morning he ran to the station, crying all the way; he did not know what for. And her blue eyes were wide and staring as she thought of him.

In the afternoon he went a walk with Clara. They sat in the little wood where bluebells were standing. He took her hand.

"You'll see," he said to Clara, "she'll never be better."

"Oh, you don't know!" replied the other.

"I do," he said.

She caught him impulsively to her breast.

"Try and forget it, dear," she said; "try and forget it."

"I will," he answered.

Her breast was there, warm for him; her hands were in his hair. It was comforting, and he held his arms round her. But he did not forget. He only talked to Clara of something else. And it was always so. When she felt it coming, the agony, she cried to him:

"Don't think of it, Paul! Don't think of it, my darling!"

And she pressed him to her breast, rocked him, soothed him like a child. So he put the trouble aside for her sake, to take it up again immediately he was alone. All the time, as he went about, he cried mechanically. His mind and hands were busy. He cried, he did not know why. It was his blood weeping. He was just as much alone whether he was with Clara or with the men in the White Horse. Just himself and this pressure inside him, that was all that existed. He read sometimes. He had to keep his mind occupied. And Clara was a way of occupying his mind.

On the Saturday Walter Morel went to Sheffield. He was a forlorn figure, looking rather as if nobody owned him. Paul ran upstairs.

"My father's come," he said, kissing his mother.

"Has he?" she answered weariedly.

The old collier came rather frightened into the bedroom.

"How dun I find thee, lass?" he said, going forward and kissing her in a hasty, timid fashion.

"Well, I'm middlin'," she replied.

"I see tha art," he said. He stood looking down on her. Then he wiped his eyes with his handkerchief. Helpless, and as if nobody owned him, he looked.

"Have you gone on all right?" asked the wife, rather wearily, as if it were an effort to talk to him.

"Yis," he answered. " 'Er's a bit behint-hand now and again, as yer might expect."

"Does she have your dinner ready?" asked Mrs. Morel.

"Well, I've 'ad to shout at 'er once or twice," he said.

"And you *must* shout at her if she's not ready. She *will* leave things to the last minute."

She gave him a few instructions. He sat looking at her as if she were almost a stranger to him, before whom he was awkward and humble, and also as if he had lost his presence of mind, and wanted to run. This feeling that he wanted to run away, that he was on thorns to be gone from so trying a situation, and yet must linger because it looked better, made his presence so trying. He put up his eyebrows for misery, and clenched his fists on his knees, feeling so awkward in presence of big trouble.

Mrs. Morel did not change much. She stayed in Sheffield for two months. If anything, at the end she was rather worse. But she wanted to go home. Annie had her children. Mrs. Morel wanted to go home. So they got a motor-car from Nottingham —for she was too ill to go by train—and she was driven through the sunshine. It was just August; everything was bright and warm. Under the blue sky they could all see she was dying. Yet she was jollier than she had been for weeks. They all laughed and talked.

"Annie," she exclaimed, "I saw a lizard dart on that rock!"

Her eyes were so quick; she was still so full of life.

Morel knew she was coming. He had the front door open. Everybody was on tiptoe. Half the street turned out. They heard the sound of the great motor-car. Mrs. Morel, smiling, drove home down the street.

"And just look at them all come out to see me!" she said. "But there, I suppose I should have done the same. How do you do, Mrs. Mathews? How are you, Mrs. Harrison?"

They none of them could hear, but they saw her smile and nod. And they all saw death on her face, they said. It was a great event in the street.

Morel wanted to carry her indoors, but he was too old. Arthur took her as if she were a child. They had set her a big, deep chair by the hearth where her rocking-chair used to stand. When she was unwrapped and seated, and had drunk a little brandy, she looked round the room.

"Don't think I don't like your house, Annie," she said; "but it's nice to be in my own home again."

And Morel answered huskily:

"It is, lass, it is."

And Minnie, the little quaint maid, said:

"An' we glad t' 'ave yer."

There was a lovely yellow ravel of sunflowers in the garden. She looked out of the window.

"There are my sunflowers!" she said.

CHAPTER XIV

THE RELEASE

"By the way," said Dr. Ansell one evening when Morel was in Sheffield, "we've got a man in the fever hospital here who comes from Nottingham—Dawes. He doesn't seem to have many belongings in this world."

"Baxter Dawes!" Paul exclaimed.

"That's the man—has been a fine fellow, physically, I should think. Been in a bit of a mess lately. You know him?"

"He used to work at the place where I am."

"Did he? Do you know anything about him? He's just sulking, or he'd be a lot better than he is by now."

"I don't know anything of his home circumstances, except that he's separated from his wife and has been a bit down, I believe. But tell him about me, will you? Tell him I'll come and see him"

The next time Morel saw the doctor he said:

"And what about Dawes?"

"I said to him," answered the other, " 'Do you know a man from Nottingham named Morel?' and he looked at me as if he'd jump at my throat. So I said: 'I see you know the name; it's Paul Morel.' Then I told him about your saying you would go and see him. 'What does he want?' he said, as if you were a policeman."

"And did he say he would see me?" asked Paul.

"He wouldn't say anything—good, bad or indifferent," replied the doctor.

"Why not?"

"That's what I want to know. There he lies and sulks, day in, day out. Can't get a word of information out of him."

"Do you think I might go?" asked Paul.

"You might."

There was a feeling of connection between the rival men, more than ever since they had fought. In a way Morel felt guilty towards the other, and more or less responsible. And being in such a state of soul himself, he felt an almost painful nearness to Dawes, who was suffering and despairing, too. Besides, they had met in a naked extremity of hate, and it was a bond. At any rate, the elemental man in each had met.

He went down to the isolation hospital, with Dr. Ansell's card. This sister, a healthy young Irishwoman, led him down the ward.

"A visitor to see you, Jim Crow," she said.

Dawes turned over suddenly with a startled grunt.

"Eh?"

"Caw!" she mocked. "He can only say 'Caw!' I have brought you a gentleman to see you. Now say 'Thank you,' and show some manners."

Dawes looked swiftly with his dark, startled eyes beyond the sister at Paul. His look was full of fear, mistrust, hate, and misery. Morel met the swift, dark eyes, and hesitated. The two men were afraid of the naked selves they had been.

"Dr. Ansell told me you were here," said Morel, holding out his hand.

Dawes mechanically shook hands.

"So I thought I'd come in," continued Paul.

There was no answer. Dawes lay staring at the opposite wall.

"Say 'Caw!' " mocked the nurse. "Say 'Caw!' Jim Crow."

"He is getting on all right?" said Paul to her.

"Oh yes! He lies and imagines he's going to die," said the nurse, "and it frightens every word out of his mouth."

"And you *must* have somebody to talk to," laughed Morel.

"That's it!" laughed the nurse. "Only two old men and a boy who always cries. It *is* hard lines! Here am I dying to hear Jim Crow's voice, and nothing but an odd 'Caw!' will he give!"

"So rough on you!" said Morel.

"Isn't it?" said the nurse.

"I suppose I am a godsend," he laughed.

"Oh, dropped straight from heaven!" laughed the nurse.

Presently she left the two men alone. Dawes was thinner, and handsome again, but life seemed low in him. As the doctor said, he was lying sulking, and would not move forward towards convalescence. He seemed to grudge every beat of his heart.

"Have you had a bad time?" asked Paul.

Suddenly again Dawes looked at him.

"What are you doing in Sheffield?" he asked.

"My mother was taken ill at my sister's in Thurston Street. What are you doing here?"

There was no answer.

"How long have you been in?" Morel asked.

"I couldn't say for sure," Dawes answered grudgingly.

He lay staring across at the wall opposite, as if trying to believe Morel was not there. Paul felt his heart go hard and angry.

"Dr. Ansell told me you were here," he said coldly.

The other man did not answer.

"Typhoid's pretty bad, I know," Morel persisted.

Suddenly Dawes said:

"What did you come for?"

"Because Dr. Ansell said you didn't know anybody here. Do you?"

"I know nobody nowhere," said Dawes.

"Well," said Paul, "it's because you don't choose to, then."

There was another silence.

"We s'll be taking my mother home as soon as we can," said Paul.

"What's a-matter with her?" asked Dawes, with a sick man's interest in illness.

"She's got a cancer."

There was another silence.

"But we want to get her home," said Paul. "We s'll have to get a motor-car."

Dawes lay thinking.

"Why don't you ask Thomas Jordan to lend you his?" said Dawes.

"It's not big enough," Morel answered.

Dawes blinked his dark eyes as he lay thinking.

"Then ask Jack Pilkington; he'd lend it you. You know him."

"I think I s'll hire one," said Paul.

"You're a fool if you do," said Dawes.

The sick man was gaunt and handsome again. Paul was sorry for him because his eyes looked so tired.

"Did you get a job here?" he asked.

"I was only here a day or two before I was taken bad," Dawes replied.

"You want to get in a convalescent home," said Paul.

The other's face clouded again.

"I'm goin' in no convalescent home," he said.

"My father's been in the one at Seathorpe, an' he liked it. Dr. Ansell would get you a recommend."

Dawes lay thinking. It was evident he dared not face the world again.

"The seaside would be all right just now," Morel said. "Sun on those sandhills, and the waves not far out."

The other did not answer.

"By Gad!" Paul concluded, too miserable to bother much; "it's all right when you know you're going to walk again, and swim!"

Dawes glanced at him quickly. The man's dark eyes were afraid to meet any other eyes in the world. But the real misery and helplessness in Paul's tone gave him a feeling of relief.

"Is she far gone?" he asked.

"She's going like wax," Paul answered; "but cheerful— lively!"

He bit his lip. After a minute he rose.

"Well, I'll be going," he said. "I'll leave you this half-crown."

"I don't want it," Dawes muttered.

Morel did not answer, but left the coin on the table.

"Well," he said, "I'll try and run in when I'm back in Sheffield. Happen you might like to see my brother-in-law? He works in Pyecrofts."

"I don't know him," said Dawes.

"He's all right. Should I tell him to come? He might bring you some papers to look at."

The other man did not answer. Paul went. The strong emotion that Dawes aroused in him, repressed, made him shiver.

He did not tell his mother, but next day he spoke to Clara about this interview. It was in the dinner-hour. The two did not often go out together now, but this day he asked her to go with him to the Castle grounds. There they sat while the scarlet geraniums and the yellow calceolarias blazed in the sunlight. She was now always rather protective, and rather resentful towards him.

"Did you know Baxter was in Sheffield Hospital with typhoid?" he asked.

She looked at him with startled grey eyes, and her face went pale.

"No," she said, frightened.

"He's getting better. I went to see him yesterday—the doctor told me."

Clara seemed stricken by the news.

"Is he very bad?" she asked guiltily.

"He has been. He's mending now."

"What did he say to you?"

"Oh, nothing! He seems to be sulking."

There was a distance between the two of them. He gave her more information.

She went about shut up and silent. The next time they took a walk together, she disengaged herself from his arm, and walked at a distance from him. He was wanting her comfort badly.

"Won't you be nice with me?" he asked.

She did not answer.

"What's the matter?" he said, putting his arm across her shoulder.

"Don't!" she said, disengaging herself.

He left her alone, and returned to his own brooding.

"Is it Baxter that upsets you?" he asked at length.

"I *have* been *vile* to him!" she said.

"I've said many a time you haven't treated him well," he replied.

And there was a hostility between them. Each pursued his own train of thought.

"I've treated him—no, I've treated him badly," she said. "And now you treat *me* badly. It serves me right."

"How do I treat you badly?" he said.

"It serves me right," she repeated. "I never considered him worth having, and now you don't consider *me*. But it serves me right. He loved me a thousand times better than you ever did."

"He didn't!" protested Paul.

"He did! At any rate, he did respect me, and that's what you don't do."

"It looked as if he respected you!" he said.

"He did! And I *made* him horrid—I know I did! You've taught me that. And he loved me a thousand times better than ever you do."

"All right," said Paul.

He only wanted to be left alone now. He had his own trouble, which was almost too much to bear. Clara only tormented him and made him tired. He was not sorry when he left her.

She went on the first opportunity to Sheffield to see her

husband. The meeting was not a success. But she left him roses and fruit and money. She wanted to make restitution. It was not that she loved him. As she looked at him lying there her heart did not warm with love. Only she wanted to humble herself to him, to kneel before him. She wanted now to be self-sacrificial. After all, she had failed to make Morel really love her. She was morally frightened.She wanted to do penance.

So she kneeled to Dawes, and it gave him a subtle pleasure. But the distance between them was still very great—too great. It frightened the man. It almost pleased the woman. She liked to feel she was serving him across an insuperable distance. She was proud now.

Morel went to see Dawes once or twice. There was a sort of friendship between the two men, who were all the while deadly rivals. But they never mentioned the woman who was between them.

Mrs. Morel got gradually worse. At first they used to carry her downstairs, sometimes even into the garden. She sat propped in her chair, smiling, and so pretty. The gold wedding-ring shone on her white hand; her hair was carefully brushed. And she watched the tangled sunflowers dying, the chrysanthemums coming out, and the dahlias.

Paul and she were afraid of each other. He knew, and she knew, that she was dying. But they kept up a pretence of cheerfulness. Every morning, when he got up, he went into her room in his pyjamas.

"Did you sleep, my dear?" he asked.

"Yes," she answered.

"Not very well?"

"Well, yes!"

Then he knew she had lain awake. He saw her hand under the bedclothes, pressing the place on her side where the pain was.

"Has it been bad?" he asked.

"No. It hurt a bit, but nothing to mention."

And she sniffed in her old scornful way. As she lay she looked like a girl. And all the while her blue eyes watched him. But there were the dark pain-circles beneath that made him ache again.

"It's a sunny day," he said.

"It's a beautiful day."

"Do you think you'll be carried down?"

"I shall see."

Then he went away to get her breakfast. All day long he was conscious of nothing but her. It was a long ache that made him feverish. Then, when he got home in the early evening, he glanced through the kitchen window. She was not there; she had not got up.

He ran straight upstairs and kissed her. He was almost afraid to ask:

"Didn't you get up, pigeon?"

"No," she said. "It was that morphia; it made me tired."

"I think he gives you too much," he said.

"I think he does," she answered.

He sat down by the bed, miserably. She had a way of curling and lying on her side, like a child. The grey and brown hair was loose over her ear.

"Doesn't it tickle you?" he said, gently putting it back.

"It does," she replied.

His face was near hers. Her blue eyes smiled straight into his, like a girl's—warm, laughing with tender love. It made him pant with terror, agony, and love.

"You want your hair doing in a plait," he said. "Lie still."

And going behind her, he carefully loosened her hair, brushed it out. It was like fine long silk of brown and grey. Her head was snuggled between her shoulders. As he lightly brushed and plaited her hair, he bit his lip and felt dazed. It all seemed unreal, he could not understand it.

At night he often worked in her room, looking up from time to time. And so often he found her blue eyes fixed on him. And when their eyes met, she smiled. He worked away again mechanically, producing good stuff without knowing what he was doing.

Sometimes he came in, very pale and still, with watchful, sudden eyes, like a man who is drunk almost to death. They were both afraid of the veils that were ripping between them.

Then she pretended to be better, chattered to him gaily, made a great fuss over some scraps of news. For they had both come to the condition when they had to make much of the trifles, lest they should give in to the big thing, and their human independence would go smash. They were afraid, so they made light of things and were gay.

Sometimes as she lay he knew she was thinking of the past. Her mouth gradually shut hard in a line. She was holding herself rigid, so that she might die without ever uttering the great cry that was tearing from her. He never forgot that hard, utterly lonely and stubborn clenching of her mouth, which persisted for weeks. Sometimes, when it was lighter, she talked about her husband. Now she hated him. She did not forgive him. She could not bear him to be in the room. And a few things, the things that had been most bitter to her, came up again so strongly that they broke from her, and she told her son.

He felt as if his life were being destroyed, piece by piece, within him. Often the tears came suddenly. He ran to the station, the tear-drops falling on the pavement. Often he could not go on with his work. The pen stopped writing. He sat staring, quite unconscious. And when he came round again he felt sick, and trembled in his limbs. He never questioned what it was. His mind did not try to analyse or understand. He merely submitted, and kept his eyes shut; let the thing go over him.

His mother did the same. She thought of the pain, of the morphia, of the next day; hardly ever of the death. That was coming, she knew. She had to submit to it. But she would never entreat it or make friends with it. Blind, with her face shut hard and blind, she was pushed towards the door. The days passed, the weeks, the months.

Sometimes, in the sunny afternoons, she seemed almost happy.

"I try to think of the nice times—when we went to Mablethorpe, and Robin Hood's Bay, and Shanklin," she said. "After all, not everybody has seen those beautiful places. And wasn't it beautiful! I try to think of that, not of the other things."

Then, again, for a whole evening she spoke not a word; neither did he. They were together, rigid, stubborn, silent. He went into his room at last to go to bed, and leaned against the doorway as if paralysed, unable to go any farther. His consciousness went. A furious storm, he knew not what, seemed to ravage inside him. He stood leaning there, submitting, never questioning.

In the morning they were both normal again, though her face was grey with the morphia, and her body felt like ash. But they were bright again, nevertheless. Often, especially if Annie or Arthur were at home, he neglected her. He did not see much of Clara. Usually he was with men. He was quick and active and lively; but when his friends saw him go white to the gills, his eyes dark and glittering, they had a certain mistrust of him. Sometimes he went to Clara, but she was almost cold to him.

"Take me!" he said simply.

Occasionally she would. But she was afraid. When he had her then, there was something in it that made her shrink away from him—something unnatural. She grew to dread him. He was so quiet, yet so strange. She was afraid of the man who was not there with her, whom she could feel behind this make-believe lover; somebody sinister, that filled her with horror. She began to have a kind of horror of him. It was almost as if he were a criminal. He wanted her—he had her—and it made her feel as if death itself had her in its grip. She lay in horror. There was no man there loving her. She almost hated him. Then came little bouts of tenderness. But she dared not pity him.

Dawes had come to Colonel Seely's Home near Nottingham. There Paul visited him sometimes, Clara very occasionally. Between the two men the friendship developed peculiarly. Dawes, who mended very slowly and seemed very feeble, seemed to leave himself in the hands of Morel.

In the beginning of November Clara reminded Paul that it was her birthday.

"I'd nearly forgotten," he said.

"I'd thought quite," she replied.

"No. Shall we go to the seaside for the week-end?"

They went. It was cold and rather dismal. She waited for him to be warm and tender with her, instead of which he seemed hardly aware of her. He sat in the railway-carriage, looking out, and was startled when she spoke to him. He was not definitely thinking. Things seemed as if they did not exist. She went across to him.

"What is it dear?" she asked.

"Nothing!" he said. "Don't those windmill sails look monotonous?"

He sat holding her hand. He could not talk nor think. It was a comfort, however, to sit holding her hand. She was dissatisfied and miserable. He was not with her; she was nothing.

And in the evening they sat among the sandhills, looking at the black, heavy sea.

"She will never give in," he said quietly.

Clara's heart sank.

"No," she replied.

"There are different ways of dying. My father's people are frightened, and have to be hauled out of life into death like cattle into a slaughter-house, pulled by the neck; but my mother's people are pushed from behind, inch by inch. They are stubborn people, and won't die."

"Yes," said Clara.

"And she won't die. She can't. Mr. Renshaw, the parson, was in the other day. 'Think!' he said to her; 'you will have your mother and father, and your sisters, and your son, in the Other Land.' And she said: 'I have done without them for a long time, and *can* do without them now. It is the living I want, not the dead.' She wants to live even now."

"Oh, how horrible!" said Clara, too frightened to speak.

"And she looks at me, and she wants to stay with me," he went on monotonously. "She's got such a will, it seems as if she would never go—never!"

"Don't think of it!" cried Clara.

"And she was religious—she is religious now—but it is no good. She simply won't give in. And do you know, I said to her on Thursday: 'Mother, if I had to die, I'd die. I'd *will* to die.' And she said to me, sharp: 'Do you think I haven't? Do you think you can die when you like?' "

His voice ceased. He did not cry, only went on speaking monotonously. Clara wanted to run. She looked round. There was the black, re-echoing shore, the dark sky down on her. She got up terrified. She wanted to be where there was light, where there were other people. She wanted to be away from him. He sat with his head dropped, not moving a muscle.

"And I don't want her to eat," he said, "and she knows it. When I ask her: 'Shall you have anything' she's almost afraid to say 'Yes.' 'I'll have a cup of Benger's,' she says. 'It'll only keep your strength up,' I said to her. 'Yes'—and she almost cried—'but there's such a gnawing when I eat nothing, I can't bear it.' So I went and made her the food. It's the cancer that gnaws like that at her. I wish she'd die!"

"Come!" said Clara roughly. "I'm going."

He followed her down the darkness of the sands. He did not come to her. He seemed scarcely aware of her existence. And she was afraid of him, and disliked him.

In the same acute daze they went back to Nottingham. He was always busy, always doing something, always going from one to the other of his friends.

On the Monday he went to see Baxter Dawes. Listless and pale, the man rose to greet the other, clinging to his chair as he held out his hand.

"You shouldn't get up," said Paul.

Dawes sat down heavily, eyeing Morel with a sort of suspicion.

"Don't you waste your time on me," he said, "if you've owt better to do."

"I wanted to come," said Paul. "Here! I brought you some sweets."

The invalid put them aside.

"It's not been much of a week-end," said Morel.

"How's your mother?" asked the other.

"Hardly any different."

"I thought she was perhaps worse, being as you didn't come on Sunday."

"I was at Skegness," said Paul. "I wanted a change."

The other looked at him with dark eyes. He seemed to be waiting, not quite daring to ask, trusting to be told.

"I went with Clara," said Paul.

"I knew as much," said Dawes quietly.

"It was an old promise," said Paul.

"You have it your own way," said Dawes.

This was the first time Clara had been definitely mentioned between them.

"Nay," said Morel slowly; "she's tired of me."

Again Dawes looked at him.

"Since August she's been getting tired of me," Morel repeated.

The two men were very quiet together. Paul suggested a game of draughts. They played in silence.

"I s'll go abroad when my mother's dead," said Paul.

"Abroad!" repeated Dawes.

"Yes; I don't care what I do."

They continued the game. Dawes was winning.

"I s'll have to begin a new start of some sort," said Paul; "and you as well, I suppose."

He took one of Dawes's pieces.

"I dunno where," said the other.

"Things have to happen," Morel said. "It's no good doing anything—at least—no, I don't know. Give me some toffee."

The two men ate sweets, and began another game of draughts.

"What made that scar on your mouth?" asked Dawes.

Paul put his hand hastily to his lips, and looked over the garden.

"I had a bicycle accident," he said.

Dawes's hand trembled as he moved the piece.

"You shouldn't ha' laughed at me," he said, very low.

"When?"

"That night on Woodborough Road, when you and her passed me—you with your hand on her shoulder."

"I never laughed at you," said Paul.

Dawes kept his fingers on the draught-piece.

"I never knew you were there till the very second when you passed," said Morel.

"It was that as did me," Dawes said, very low.

Paul took another sweet.

"I never laughed," he said, "except as I'm always laughing."

They finished the game.

That night Morel walked home from Nottingham, in order to have something to do. The furnaces flared in a red blotch over Bulwell; the black clouds were like a low ceiling. As he went along the ten miles of highroad, he felt as if he were walking out of life, between the black levels of the sky and the earth. But at the end was only the sick-room. If he walked and walked for ever, there was only that place to come to.

He was not tired when he got near home, or he did not know it. Across the field he could see the red firelight leaping in her bedroom window.

"When she's dead," he said to himself, "that fire will go out."

He took off his boots quietly and crept upstairs. His mother's door was wide open, because she slept alone still. The red firelight dashed its glow on the landing. Soft as a shadow, he peeped in her doorway.

"Paul!" she murmured.

His heart seemed to break again. He went in and sat by the bed.

"How late you are!" she murmured.

"Not very," he said.

"Why, what time is it?" The murmur came plaintive and helpless.

"It's only just gone eleven."

That was not true; it was nearly one o'clock.

"Oh!" she said; "I thought it was later."

And he knew the unutterable misery of her nights that would not go.

"Can't you sleep, my pigeon?" he said.

"No, I can't," she wailed.

"Never mind, Little!" he said crooning. "Never mind, my love. I'll stop with you half an hour, my pigeon; then perhaps it will be better."

And he sat by the bedside, slowly, rhythmically stroking her brows with his finger-tips, stroking her eyes shut, soothing her, holding her fingers in his free hand. They could hear the sleepers' breathing in the other rooms.

"Now go to bed," she murmured, lying quite still under his fingers and his love.

"Will you sleep?" he asked.

"Yes, I think so."

"You feel better, my Little, don't you?"

"Yes," she said, like a fretful, half-soothed child.

Still the days and the weeks went by. He hardly ever went to see Clara now. But he wandered restlessly from one person to another for some help, and there was none anywhere. Miriam had written to him tenderly. He went to see her. Her heart was very sore when she saw him, white, gaunt, with his eyes dark and bewildered. Her pity came up, hurting her till she could not bear it.

"How is she?" she asked.

"The same—the same!" he said. "The doctor says she can't last, but I know she will. She'll be here at Christmas."

Miriam shuddered. She drew him to her; she pressed him to her bosom; she kissed him and kissed him. He submitted, but it was torture. She could not kiss his agony. That remained alone and apart. She kissed his face, and roused his blood, while his soul was apart writhing with the agony of death. And she kissed him and fingered his body, till at last, feeling he would go mad, he got away from her. It was not that he wanted just then—not that. And she thought she had soothed him and done him good.

December came, and some snow. He stayed at home all the while now. They could not afford a nurse. Annie came to look after her mother; the parish nurse, whom they loved, came in morning and evening. Paul shared the nursing with Annie.

Often, in the evenings, when friends were in the kitchen with them, they all laughed together and shook with laughter. It was reaction. Paul was so comical, Annie was so quaint. The whole party laughed till they cried, trying to subdue the sound. And Mrs. Morel, lying alone in the darkness heard them, and among her bitterness was a feeling of relief.

Then Paul would go upstairs gingerly, guiltily, to see if she had heard.

"Shall I give you some milk?" he asked.

"A little," she replied plaintively.

And he would put some water with it, so that it should not nourish her. Yet he loved her more than his own life.

She had morphia every night, and her heart got fitful. Annie slept beside her. Paul would go in in the early morning, when his sister got up. His mother was wasted and almost ashen in the morning with the morphia. Darker and darker grew her eyes, all pupil, with the torture. In the mornings the weariness and ache was too much to bear. Yet she could not—would not —weep, or even complain much.

"You slept a bit later this morning, little one," he would say to her.

"Did I?" she answered, with fretful weariness.

"Yes; it's nearly eight o'clock."

He stood looking out of the window. The whole country was bleak and pallid under the snow. Then he felt her pulse. There was a strong stroke and a weak one, like a sound and its echo. That was supposed to betoken the end. She let him feel her wrist, knowing what he wanted.

Sometimes they looked in each other's eyes. Then they almost seemed to make an agreement. It was almost as if he were agreeing to die also. But she did not consent to die; she would not. Her body was wasted to a fragment of ash. Her eyes were dark and full of torture.

"Can't you give her something to put an end to it?" he asked the doctor at last.

But the doctor shook his head.

"She can't last many days now, Mr. Morel," he said.

Paul went indoors.

"I can't bear it much longer; we shall all go mad," said Annie.

The two sat down to breakfast.

"Go and sit with her while we have breakfast, Minnie," said Annie. But the girl was frightened.

Paul went through the country, through the woods, over the snow. He saw the marks of rabbits and birds in the white snow. He wandered miles and miles. A smoky red sunset came on slowly, painfully, lingering. He thought she would die that day. There was a donkey that came up to him over the snow by the wood's edge, and put its head against him, and walked with him alongside. He put his arms round the donkey's neck, and stroked his cheeks against his ears.

His mother, silent, was still alive, with her hard mouth gripped grimly, her eyes of dark torture only living.

It was nearing Christmas; there was more snow. Annie and he felt as if they could go on no more. Still her dark eyes were alive. Morel, silent and frightened, obliterated himself. Sometimes he would go into the sick-room and look at her. Then he backed out, bewildered.

She kept her hold on life still. The miners had been out on strike, and returned a fortnight or so before Christmas. Minnie went upstairs with the feeding-cup. It was two days after the men had been in.

"Have the men been saying their hands are sore, Minnie?" she asked, in the faint, querulous voice that would not give in. Minnie stood surprised.

"Not as I know of, Mrs. Morel," she answered.

"But I'll bet they are sore," said the dying woman, as she moved her head with a sigh of weariness. But, at any rate, there'll be something to buy in with this week."

Not a thing did she let slip.

"Your father's pit things will want well airing, Annie," she said, when the men were going back to work.

"Don't you bother about that, my dear," said Annie.

One night Annie and Paul were alone. Nurse was upstairs.

"She'll live over Christmas," said Annie. They were both full of horror.

"She won't," he replied grimly. "I s'll give her morphia."

"Which?" said Annie.

"All that came from Sheffield," said Paul.

"Ay—do!" said Annie.

The next day he was painting in the bedroom. She seemed to be asleep. He stepped softly backwards and forwards at his painting. Suddenly her small voice wailed:

"Don't walk about, Paul."

He looked round. Her eyes, like dark bubbles in her face, were looking at him.

"No, my dear," he said gently. Another fibre seemed to snap in his heart.

That evening he got all the morphia pills there were, and took them downstairs. Carefully he crushed them to powder.

"What are you doing?" said Annie.

"I s'll put 'em in her night milk."

Then they both laughed together like two conspiring children. On top of all their horror flicked this little sanity.

Nurse did not come that night to settle Mrs. Morel down. Paul went up with the hot milk in a feeding-cup. It was nine o'clock.

She was reared up in bed, and he put the feeding-cup between her lips that he would have died to save from any hurt. She took a sip, then put the spout of the cup away and looked at him with her dark, wondering eyes. He looked at her.

"Oh, it *is* bitter, Paul!" she said, making a little grimace.

"It's a new sleeping draught the doctor gave me for you," he said. "He thought it wouldn't leave you in such a state in the morning."

"And I hope it won't," she said, like a child.

She drank some more of the milk.

"But it *is* horrid!" she said.

He saw her frail fingers over the cup, her lips making a little move.

"I know—I tasted it," he said. "But I'll give you some clean milk afterwards."

"I think so," she said, and she went on with the draught. She was obedient to him like a child. He wondered if she knew. He saw her poor wasted throat moving as she drank with difficulty. Then he ran downstairs for more milk. There were no grains in the bottom of the cup.

"Has she had it?" whispered Annie.

"Yes—and she said it was bitter."

"Oh!" laughed Annie, putting her under lip between her teeth.

"And I told her it was a new draught. Where's that milk?"

They both went upstairs.

"I wonder why nurse didn't come to settle me down?" complained the mother, like a child, wistfully.

"She said she was going to a concert, my love," replied Annie.

"Did she?"

They were silent a minute. Mrs. Morel gulped the little clean milk.

"Annie, that draught *was* horrid!" she said plaintively.

"Was it, my love? Well, never mind."

The mother sighed again with weariness. Her pulse was very irregular.

"Let *us* settle you down," said Annie. "Perhaps nurse will be so late."

"Ay," said the mother—"try."

They turned the clothes back. Paul saw his mother like a girl curled up in her flannel nightdress. Quickly they made one half of the bed, moved her, made the other, straightened her nightgown over her small feet, and covered her up.

"There," said Paul, stroking her softly. "There!—now you'll sleep."

"Yes," she said. "I didn't think you could do the bed so nicely," she added, almost gaily. Then she curled up, with her cheek on her hand, her head snugged between her shoulder. Paul put the long thin plait of grey hair over her shoulder and kissed her.

"You'll sleep, my love," he said.

"Yes," she answered trustfully. "Good-night."

They put out the light, and it was still.

Morel was in bed. Nurse did not come. Annie and Paul came to look at her at about eleven. She seemed to be sleeping as usual after her draught. Her mouth had come a bit open.

"Shall we sit up?" said Paul.

"I s'll lie with her as I always do," said Annie. "She might wake up."

"All right. And call me if you see any difference."

"Yes."

They lingered before the bedroom fire, feeling the night big and black and snowy outside, their two selves alone in the world. At last he went into the next room and went to bed.

He slept almost immediately, but kept waking every now and again. Then he went sound asleep. He started awake at Annie's whispered, "Paul, Paul!" He saw his sister in her white nightdress, with her long plait of hair down her back, standing in the darkness.

"Yes?" he whispered, sitting up.

"Come and look at her."

He slipped out of bed. A bud of gas was burning in the sick chamber. His mother lay with her cheek on her hand, curled up as she had gone to sleep. But her mouth had fallen open, and she breathed with great, hoarse breaths, like snoring, and there were long intervals between.

"She's going!" he whispered.

"Yes," said Annie.

"How long has she been like it?"

"I only just woke up."

Annie huddled into the dressing-gown, Paul wrapped himself in a brown blanket. It was three o'clock. He mended the fire. Then the two sat waiting. The great, snoring breath was taken —held awhile—then given back. There was a space—a long space. Then they started. The great, snoring breath was taken again. He bent close down and looked at her.

"Isn't it awful!" whispered Annie.

He nodded. They sat down again helplessly. Again came the great, snoring breath. Again they hung suspended. Again it was given back, long and harsh. The sound, so irregular, at such wide intervals, sounded through the house. Morel, in his room, slept on. Paul and Annie sat crouched, huddled, motionless. The great snoring sound began again—there was a painful pause while the breath was held—back came the rasping breath. Minute after minute passed. Paul looked at her again, bending low over her.

"She may last like this," he said.

They were both silent. He looked out of the window, and could faintly discern the snow on the garden.

"You go to my bed," he said to Annie. "I'll sit up."

"No," she said, "I'll stop with you."

"I'd rather you didn't," he said.

At last Annie crept out of the room, and he was alone. He hugged himself in his brown blanket, crouched in front of his mother, watching. She looked dreadful, with the bottom jaw fallen back. He watched. Sometimes he thought the great breath would never begin again. He could not bear it—the waiting. Then suddenly, startling him, came the great harsh sound. He mended the fire again, noiselessly. She must not be disturbed. The minutes went by. The night was going, breath by breath. Each time the sound came he felt it wring him, till at last he could not feel so much.

His father got up. Paul heard the miner drawing his stocking on, yawning. Then Morel, in shirt and stockings, entered.

"Hush!" said Paul.

Morel stood watching. Then he looked at his son, helplessly, and in horror.

"Had I better stop a-whoam?" he whispered.

"No. Go to work. She'll last through to-morrow."

"I don't think so."

"Yes. Go to work."

The miner looked at her again, in fear, and went obediently out of the room. Paul saw the tape of his garters swinging against his legs.

After another half-hour Paul went downstairs and drank a cup of tea, then returned. Morel, dressed for the pit, came upstairs again.

"Am I to go?" he said.

"Yes."

And in a few minutes Paul heard his father's heavy steps go thudding over the deadening snow. Miners called in the streets as they tramped in gangs to work. The terrible, long-drawn breaths continued—heave—heave—heave; then a long pause—then—ah-h-h-h-h! as it came back. Far away over the snow sounded the hooters of the ironworks. One after another they crowed and boomed, some small and far away, some near, the blowers of the collieries and the other works. Then there was silence. He mended the fire. The great breaths broke the silence—she looked just the same. He put back the blind and peered out. Still it was dark. Perhaps there was a lighter tinge. Perhaps the snow was bluer. He drew up the blind and got dressed. Then, shuddering, he drank brandy from the bottle on the wash-stand. The snow *was* growing blue. He heard a cart clanking down the street. Yes, it was seven o'clock, and it was coming a little bit light. He heard some people calling. The world was waking. A grey, deathly dawn crept over the snow. Yes, he could see the houses. He put out the gas. It seemed very dark. The breathing came still, but he was almost used to it. He could see her. She was just the same. He wondered if he piled heavy clothes on top of her it would stop. He looked at her. That was not her—not her a bit. If he piled the blanket and heavy coats on her——

Suddenly the door opened, and Annie entered. She looked at him questioningly.

"Just the same," he said calmly.

They whispered together a minute, then went downstairs to get breakfast. It was twenty to eight. Soon Annie came down.

"Isn't it awful! Doesn't she look awful!" she whispered, dazed with horror.

He nodded.

"If she looks like that!" said Annie.

"Drink some tea," he said.

They went upstairs again. Soon the neighbours came with their frightened question:

"How is she?"

It went on just the same. She lay with her cheek in her hand, her mouth fallen open, and the great, ghastly snores came and went.

At ten o'clock nurse came. She looked strange and woebegone.

"Nurse," cried Paul, "she'll last like this for days?"

"She can't, Mr. Morel," said nurse. "She can't."

There was a silence.

"Isn't it dreadful!" wailed the nurse. "Who would have thought she could stand it? Go down now, Mr. Morel, go down."

At last, at about eleven o'clock, he went downstairs and sat in the neighbour's house. Annie was downstairs also. Nurse and Arthur were upstairs. Paul sat with his head in his hand. Suddenly Annie came flying across the yard crying, half mad:

"Paul—Paul—she's gone!"

In a second he was back in his own house and upstairs. She lay curled up and still, with her face on her hand, and nurse was wiping her mouth. They all stood back. He kneeled down, and put his face to hers and his arms round her:

"My love—my love—oh, my love!" he whispered again and again. "My love—oh, my love!"

Then he heard the nurse behind him, crying, saying:

"She's better, Mr. Morel, she's better."

When he took his face up from his warm, dead mother he went straight downstairs and began blacking his boots.

There was a good deal to do, letters to write, and so on. The doctor came and glanced at her, and sighed.

"Ay—poor thing!" he said, then turned away. "Well, call at the surgery about six for the certificate."

The father came home from work at about four o'clock. He dragged silently into the house and sat down. Minnie bustled to give him his dinner. Tired, he laid his black arms on the table. There were swede turnips for his dinner, which he liked. Paul wondered if he knew. It was some time, and nobody had spoken. At last the son said:

"You noticed the blinds were down?"

Morel looked up.

"No," he said. "Why—has she gone?"

"Yes."

"When wor that?"

"About twelve this morning."

"H'm!"

The miner sat still for a moment, then began his dinner. It was as if nothing had happened. He ate his turnips in silence. Afterwards he washed and went upstairs to dress. The door of her room was shut.

"Have you seen her?" Annie asked of him when he came down.

"No," he said.

In a little while he went out. Annie went away, and Paul called on the undertaker, the clergyman, the doctor, the registrar. It was a long business. He got back at nearly eight o'clock. The undertaker was coming soon to measure for the coffin. The house was empty except for her. He took a candle and went upstairs.

The room was cold, that had been warm for so long. Flowers, bottles, plates, all sick-room litter was taken away; everything was harsh and austere. She lay raised on the bed, the sweep of the sheet from the raised feet was like a clean curve of snow, so silent. She lay like a maiden asleep. With his candle in his hand, he bent over her. She lay like a girl asleep and dreaming of her love. The mouth was a little open as if wondering from the suffering, but her face was young, her brow clear and white as if life had never touched it. He looked again at the eyebrows, at the small, winsome nose a bit on one side. She was young again. Only the hair as it arched so beautifully from her temples was mixed with silver, and the two simple plaits that lay on her shoulders were filigree of silver and brown. She would wake up. She would lift her eyelids. She was with him still. He bent and kissed her passionately. But there was coldness against his mouth. He bit his lips with horror. Looking at her, he felt he could never, never let her go. No! He stroked the hair from her temples. That, too, was cold. He saw the mouth so dumb and wondering at the hurt. Then he crouched on the floor, whispering to her:

"Mother, mother!"

He was still with her when the undertakers came, young men who had been to school with him. They touched her reverently, and in a quiet, businesslike fashion. They did not look at her. He watched jealously. He and Annie guarded her fiercely. They would not let anybody come to see her, and the neighbours were offended.

After a while Paul went out of the house, and played cards at a friend's. It was midnight when he got back. His father rose from the couch as he entered, saying in a plaintive way:

"I thought tha wor niver comin', lad."

"I didn't think you'd sit up," said Paul.

His father looked so forlorn. Morel had been a man without fear—simply nothing frightened him. Paul realised with a start that he had been afraid to go to bed, alone in the house with his dead. He was sorry.

"I forgot you'd be alone, father," he said.

"Dost want owt to eat?" asked Morel.

"No."

"Sithee—I made thee a drop o' hot milk. Get it down thee; it's cold enough for owt."

Paul drank it.

After a while Morel went to bed. He hurried past the closed door, and left his own door open. Soon the son came upstairs also. He went in to kiss her good-night, as usual. It was cold and dark. He wished they had kept her fire burning. Still she dreamed her young dream. But she would be cold.

"My dear!" he whispered. "My dear!"

And he did not kiss her, for fear she should be cold and strange to him. It eased him she slept so beautifully. He shut her door softly, not to wake her, and went to bed.

In the morning Morel summoned his courage, hearing Annie downstairs and Paul coughing in the room across the landing. He opened her door, and went into the darkened room. He saw the white uplifted form in the twilight, but her he dared not see. Bewildered, too frightened to possess any of his faculties, he got out of the room again and left her. He never looked at her again. He had not seen her for months, because he had not dared to look. And she looked like his young wife again.

"Have you seen her?" Annie asked of him sharply after breakfast.

"Yes," he said.

"And don't you think she looks nice?"

"Yes."

He went out of the house soon after. And all the time he seemed to be creeping aside to avoid it.

Paul went about from place to place, doing the business of the death. He met Clara in Nottingham, and they had tea together in a café, when they were quite jolly again. She was infinitely relieved to find he did not take it tragically.

Later, when the relatives began to come for the funeral, the affair became public, and the children became social beings. They put themselves aside. They buried her in a furious storm of rain and wind. The wet clay glistened, all the white flowers were soaked. Annie gripped his arm and leaned forward. Down below she saw a dark corner of William's coffin. The oak box sank steadily. She was gone. The rain poured in the grave. The procession of black, with its umbrellas glistening, turned away. The cemetery was deserted under the drenching cold rain.

Paul went home and busied himself supplying the guests with drinks. His father sat in the kitchen with Mrs. Morel's relatives, "superior" people, and wept, and said what a good lass she'd been, and how he'd tried to do everything he could for her—everything. He had striven all his life to do what he could for her, and he'd nothing to reproach himself with. She was gone, but he'd done his best for her. He wiped his eyes with his white handkerchief. He'd nothing to reproach himself for, he repeated. All his life he'd done his best for her.

And that was how he tried to dismiss her. He never thought of her personally. Everything deep in him he denied. Paul hated his father for sitting sentimentalising over her. He knew he would do it in the public-houses. For the real tragedy went on in Morel in spite of himself. Sometimes, later, he came down from his afternoon sleep, white and cowering.

"I *have* been dreaming of thy mother," he said in a small voice.

"Have you, father? When I dream of her it's always just as she was when she was well. I dream of her often, but it seems quite nice and natural, as if nothing had altered."

But Morel crouched in front of the fire in terror.

The weeks passed half-real, not much pain, not much of anything, perhaps a little relief, mostly a *nuit blanche*. Paul went restless from place to place. For some months, since his mother had been worse, he had not made love to Clara. She was, as it were, dumb to him, rather distant. Dawes saw her very occasionally, but the two could not get an inch across the great distance between them. The three of them were drifting forward.

Dawes mended very slowly. He was in the convalescent home at Skegness at Christmas, nearly well again. Paul went to the seaside for a few days. His father was with Annie in Sheffield. Dawes came to Paul's lodgings. His time in the home was up. The two men, between whom was such a big reserve, seemed faithful to each other. Dawes depended on Morel now. He knew Paul and Clara had practically separated.

Two days after Christmas Paul was to go back to Nottingham. The evening before he sat with Dawes smoking before the fire.

"You know Clara's coming down for the day to-morrow?" he said.

The other man glanced at him.

"Yes, you told me," he replied.

Paul drank the remainder of his glass of whisky.

"I told the landlady your wife was coming," he said.

"Did you?" said Dawes, shrinking, but almost leaving himself in the other's hands. He got up rather stiffly, and reached for Morel's glass.

"Let me fill you up," he said.

Paul jumped up.

"You sit still," he said.

But Dawes, with rather shaky hand, continued to mix the drink.

"Say when," he said.

"Thanks!" replied the other. "But you've no business to get up."

"It does me good, lad," replied Dawes. "I begin to think I'm right again, then."

"You are about right, you know."

"I am, certainly I am," said Dawes, nodding to him.

"And Len says he can get you on in Sheffield."

Dawes glanced at him again, with dark eyes that agreed with everything the other would say, perhaps a trifle dominated by him.

"It's funny," said Paul, "starting again. I feel in a lot bigger mess than you."

"In what way, lad?"

"I don't know. I don't know. It's as if I was in a tangled sort of hole, rather dark and dreary, and no road anywhere."

"I know—I understand it," Dawes said, nodding. "But you'll find it'll come all right."

He spoke caressingly.

"I suppose so," said Paul.

Dawes knocked his pipe in a hopeless fashion.

"You've not done for yourself like I have," he said.

Morel saw the wrist and the white hand of the other man gripping the stem of the pipe and knocking out the ash, as if he had given up.

"How old are you?" Paul asked.

"Thirty-nine." replied Dawes, glancing at him.

Those brown eyes, full of the consciousness of failure, almost pleading for reassurance, for someone to re-establish the man in himself, to warm him, to set him up firm again, troubled Paul.

"You'll just be in your prime," said Morel. "You don't look as if much life had gone out of you."

The brown eyes of the other flashed suddenly.

"It hasn't," he said. "The go is there."

Paul looked up and laughed.

"We've both got plenty of life in us yet to make things fly," he said.

The eyes of the two men met. They exchanged one look. Having recognised the stress of passion each in the other, they both drank their whisky.

"Yes, begod!" said Dawes, breathless.

There was a pause.

"And I don't see," said Paul, "why you shouldn't go on where you left off."

"What——" said Dawes, suggestively.

"Yes—fit your old home together again."

Dawes hid his face and shook his head.

"Couldn't be done," he said, and looked up with an ironic smile.

"Why? Because you don't want?"

"Perhaps."

They smoked in silence. Dawes showed his teeth as he bit his pipe stem.

"You mean you don't want her?" asked Paul.

Dawes stared up at the picture with a caustic expression on his face.

"I hardly know," he said.

The smoke floated softly up.

"I believe she wants you," said Paul.

"Do you?" replied the other, soft, satirical, abstract.

"Yes. She never really hitched on to me—you were always there in the background. That's why she wouldn't get a divorce."

Dawes continued to stare in a satirical fashion at the picture over the mantelpiece.

"That's how women are with me," said Paul. "They want me like mad, but they don't want to belong to me. And she *belonged* to you all the time. I knew."

The triumphant male came up in Dawes. He showed his teeth more distinctly.

"Perhaps I was a fool," he said.

"You were a big fool," said Morel.

"But perhaps even *then* you were a bigger fool," said Dawes. There was a touch of triumph and malice in it.

"Do you think so?" said Paul.

They were silent for some time.

"At any rate, I'm clearing out to-morrow," said Morel.

"I see," answered Dawes.

Then they did not talk any more. The instinct to murder each other had returned. They almost avoided each other.

They shared the same bedroom. When they retired Dawes seemed abstract, thinking of something. He sat on the side of the bed in his shirt, looking at his legs.

"Aren't you getting cold?" asked Morel.

"I was lookin' at these legs," replied the other.

"What's up with 'em? They look all right," replied Paul, from his bed.

"They look all right. But there's some water in 'em yet."

"And what about it?"

"Come and look."

Paul reluctantly got out of bed and went to look at the rather handsome legs of the other man that were covered with glistening, dark gold hair.

"Look here," said Dawes, pointing to his shin. "Look at the water under here."

"Where?" said Paul.

The man pressed in his finger-tips. They left little dents that filled up slowly.

"It's nothing," said Paul.

"You feel," said Dawes.

Paul tried with his fingers. It made little dents.

"H'm!" he said.

"Rotten, isn't it?" said Dawes.

"Why? It's nothing much."

"You're not much of a man with water in your legs."

"I can't see as it makes any difference," said Morel. "I've got a weak chest."

He returned to his own bed.

"I suppose the rest of me's all right," said Dawes, and he put out the light.

In the morning it was raining. Morel packed his bag. The sea was grey and shaggy and dismal. He seemed to be cutting himself off from life more and more. It gave him a wicked pleasure to do it.

The two men were at the station. Clara stepped out of the train, and came along the platform, very erect and coldly composed. She wore a long coat and a tweed hat. Both men hated her for her composure. Paul shook hands with her at the barrier. Dawes was leaning against the bookstall, watching. His black overcoat was buttoned up to the chin because of the rain. He was pale, with almost a touch of nobility in his quietness. He came forward, limping slightly.

"You ought to look better than this," she said.

"Oh, I'm all right now."

The three stood at a loss. She kept the two men hesitating near her.

"Shall we go to the lodging straight off," said Paul, "or somewhere else?"

"We may as well go home," said Dawes.

Paul walked on the outside of the pavement, then Dawes, then Clara. They made polite conversation. The sitting-room faced the sea, whose tide, grey and shaggy, hissed not far off.

Morel swung up the big arm-chair.

"Sit down, Jack," he said.

"I don't want that chair," said Dawes.

"Sit down!" Morel repeated.

Clara took off her things and laid them on the couch. She had a slight air of resentment. Lifting her hair with her fingers, she sat down, rather aloof and composed. Paul ran downstairs to speak to the landlady.

"I should think you're cold," said Dawes to his wife. "Come nearer to the fire."

"Thank you, I'm quite warm," she answered.

She looked out of the window at the rain and at the sea.

"When are you going back?" she asked.

"Well, the rooms are taken until to-morrow, so he wants me to stop. He's going back to-night."

"And then you're thinking of going to Sheffield?"

"Yes."

"Are you fit to start work?"

"I'm going to start."

"You've really got a place?"

"Yes—begin on Monday."

"You don't look fit."

"Why don't I?"

She looked again out of the window instead of answering.

"And have you got lodgings in Sheffield?"

"Yes."

Again she looked away out of the window. The panes were blurred with streaming rain.

"And can you manage all right?" she asked.

"I s'd think so. I s'll have to!"

They were silent when Morel returned.

"I shall go by the four-twenty," he said as he entered.

Nobody answered.

"I wish you'd take your boots off," he said to Clara.

"There's a pair of slippers of mine."

"Thank you," she said. "They aren't wet."

He put the slippers near her feet. She left them there.

Morel sat down. Both the men seemed helpless, and each of them had a rather hunted look. But Dawes now carried himself quietly, seemed to yield himself, while Paul seemed to screw himself up. Clara thought she had never seen him look so small and mean. He was as if trying to get himself into the smallest possible compass. And as he went about arranging, and as he sat talking, there seemed something false about him and out of tune. Watching him unknown, she said to herself there was no stability about him. He was fine in his way, passionate, and able to give her drinks of pure life when he was in one mood. And now he looked paltry and insignificant. There was nothing stable about him. Her husband had more manly dignity. At any rate *he* did not waft about with any wind. There was something evanescent about Morel, she thought, something shifting and false. He would never make sure ground for any woman to stand on. She despised him rather for his shrinking together, getting smaller. Her husband at least was manly, and when he was beaten gave in. But this other would never own to being beaten. He would shift round and round, prowl, get smaller. She despised him. And yet she watched him rather than Dawes, and it seemed as if their three fates lay in his hands. She hated him for it.

She seemed to understand better now about men, and what they could or would do. She was less afraid of them, more sure of herself. That they were not the small egoists she had imagined them made her more comfortable. She had learned a good deal—almost as much as she wanted to learn. Her cup had been full. It was still as full as she could carry. On the whole, she would not be sorry when he was gone.

They had dinner, and sat eating nuts and drinking by the fire. Not a serious word had been spoken. Yet Clara realised that Morel was withdrawing from the circle, leaving her the option to stay with her husband. It angered her. He was a mean fellow, after all, to take what he wanted and then give her back. She did not remember that she herself had had what she wanted, and really, at the bottom of her heart, wished to be given back.

Paul felt crumpled up and lonely. His mother had really supported his life. He had loved her; they two had, in fact, faced the world together. Now she was gone, and for ever behind him was the gap in life, the tear in the veil, through which his life seemed to drift slowly, as if he were drawn towards death. He wanted someone of their own free initiative to help him. The lesser things he began to let go from him, for fear of this big thing, the lapse towards death, following in the wake of his beloved. Clara could not stand for him to hold on to. She wanted him, but not to understand him. He felt she wanted the man on top, not the real him that was in trouble. That would be too much trouble to her; he dared not give it her. She could not cope with him. It made him ashamed. So, secretly ashamed because he was in such a mess, because his own hold on life was so unsure, because nobody held him, feeling unsubstantial, shadowy, as if he did not count for much in this concrete world, he drew himself together smaller and smaller. He did not want to die; he would not give in. But he was not afraid of death. If nobody would help, he would go on alone.

Dawes had been driven to the extremity of life, until he was afraid. He could go to the brink of death, he could lie on the edge and look in. Then, cowed, afraid, he had to crawl back, and like a beggar take what offered. There was a certain nobility in it. As Clara saw, he owned himself beaten, and he wanted to be taken back whether or not. That she could do for him.

It was three o'clock.

"I am going by the four-twenty," said Paul again to Clara. "Are you coming then or later?"

"I don't know," she said.

"I'm meeting my father in Nottingham at seven-fifteen," he said.

"Then," she answered, "I'll come later."

Dawes jerked suddenly, as if he had been held on a strain. He looked out over the sea, but he saw nothing.

"There are one or two books in the corner," said Morel. "I've done with 'em."

At about four o'clock he went.

"I shall see you both later," he said, as he shook hands.

"I suppose so," said Dawes. "An' perhaps—one day—I s'll be able to pay you back the money as——"

"I shall come for it, you'll see," laughed Paul. "I s'll be on the rocks before I'm very much older."

"Ay—well——" said Dawes.

"Good-bye," he said to Clara.

"Good-bye," she said, giving him her hand. Then she glanced at him for the last time, dumb and humble.

He was gone. Dawes and his wife sat down again.

"It's a nasty day for travelling," said the man.

"Yes," she answered.

They talked in a desultory fashion until it grew dark. The landlady brought in the tea. Dawes drew up his chair to the table without being invited, like a husband. Then he sat humbly waiting for his cup. She served him as she would, like a wife, not consulting his wish.

After tea, as it drew near to six o'clock, he went to the window. All was dark outside. The sea was roaring.

"It's raining yet," he said.

"Is it?" she answered.

"You won't go to-night, shall you?" he said, hesitating.

She did not answer. He waited.

"I shouldn't go in this rain," he said.

"Do you *want* me to stay?" she asked.

His hand as he held the dark curtain trembled.

"Yes," he said.

He remained with his back to her. She rose and went slowly to him. He let go the curtain, turned, hesitating, towards her. She stood with her hands behind her back, looking up at him in a heavy, inscrutable fashion.

"Do you want me, Baxter?" she asked.

His voice was hoarse as he answered:

"Do you want to come back to me?"

She made a moaning noise, lifted her arms, and put them round his neck, drawing him to her. He hid his face on her shoulder, holding her clasped.

"Take me back!" she whispered, ecstatic. "Take me back, take me back!" And she put her fingers through his fine, thin dark hair, as if she were only semi-conscious. He tightened his grasp on her.

"Do you want me again?" he murmured, broken.

CHAPTER XV

DERELICT

CLARA went with her husband to Sheffield, and Paul scarcely saw her again. Walter Morel seemed to have let all the trouble go over him, and there he was, crawling about on the mud of it, just the same. There was scarcely any bond between father and son, save that each felt he must not let the other go in any actual want. As there was no one to keep on the home, and as they could neither of them bear the emptiness of the house, Paul took lodgings in Nottingham, and Morel went to live with a friendly family in Bestwood.

Everything seemed to have gone smash for the young man. He could not paint. The picture he finished on the day of his mother's death—one that satisfied him—was the last thing he did. At work there was no Clara. When he came home he could not take up his brushes again. There was nothing left.

So he was always in the town at one place or another, drinking, knocking about with the men he knew. It really wearied him. He talked to barmaids, to almost any woman, but there was that dark, strained look in his eyes, as if he were hunting something.

Everything seemed so different, so unreal. There seemed no reason why people should go along the street, and houses pile up in the daylight. There seemed no reason why these things should occupy the space, instead of leaving it empty. His friends talked to him: he heard the sounds, and he answered. But why there should be the noise of speech he could not understand.

He was most himself when he was alone, or working hard and mechanically at the factory. In the latter case there was pure forgetfulness, when he lapsed from consciousness. But it had to come to an end. It hurt him so, that things had lost their reality. The first snowdrops came. He saw the tiny drop-pearls among the grey. They would have given him the liveliest emotion at one time. Now they were there, but they did not seem to mean anything. In a few moments they would cease to occupy that place, and just the space would be, where they had been. Tall, brilliant tram-cars ran along the street at night. It seemed almost a wonder they should trouble to rustle backwards and forwards. "Why trouble to go tilting down to Trent Bridges?" he asked of the big trams. It seemed they just as well might *not* be as be.

The realest thing was the thick darkness at night. That seemed to him whole and comprehensible and restful. He could leave himself to it. Suddenly a piece of paper started near his feet and blew along down the pavement. He stood still, rigid, with clenched fists, a flame of agony going over him. And he saw again the sick-room, his mother, her eyes. Unconsciously he had been with her, in her company. The swift hop of the paper reminded him she was gone. But he had been with her. He wanted everything to stand still, so that he could be with her again.

The days passed, the weeks. But everything seemed to have fused, gone into a conglomerated mass. He could not tell one day from another, one week from another, hardly one place from another. Nothing was distinct or distinguishable. Often he lost himself for an hour at a time, could not remember what he had done.

One evening he came home late to his lodging. The fire was burning low; everybody was in bed. He threw on some more coal, glanced at the table, and decided he wanted no supper. Then he sat down in the arm-chair. It was perfectly still. He did not know anything, yet he saw the dim smoke wavering up the chimney. Presently two mice came out, cautiously, nibbling the fallen crumbs. He watched them as it were from a long way off. The church clock struck two. Far away he could hear the sharp clinking of the trucks on the railway. No, it was not they that were far away. They were there in their places. But where was he himself?

The time passed. The two mice, careering wildly, scampered cheekily over his slippers. He had not moved a muscle. He did not want to move. He was not thinking of anything. It was easier so. There was no wrench of knowing anything. Then, from time to time, some other consciousness, working mechanically, flashed into sharp phrases.

"What am I doing?"

And out of the semi-intoxicated trance came the answer:

"Destroying myself."

Then a dull, live feeling, gone in an instant, told him that it was wrong. After a while, suddenly came the question:

"Why wrong?"

Again there was no answer, but a stroke of hot stubbornness inside his chest resisted his own annihilation.

There was a sound of a heavy cart clanking down the road. Suddenly the electric light went out; there was a bruising thud in the penny-in-the-slot meter. He did not stir, but sat gazing in front of him. Only the mice had scuttled, and the fire glowed red in the dark room.

Then, quite mechanically and more distinctly, the conversation began again inside him.

"She's dead. What was it all for—her struggle?"

That was his despair wanting to go after her.

"You're alive."

"She's not."

"She is—in you."

Suddenly he felt tired with the burden of it.

"You've got to keep alive for her sake," said his will in him.

Something felt sulky, as if it would not rouse.

"You've got to carry forward her living, and what she had done, go on with it."

But he did not want to. He wanted to give up.

"But you can go on with your painting," said the will in him. "Or else you can beget children. They both carry on her effort."

"Painting is not living."

"Then live."

"Marry whom?" came the sulky question.

"As best you can.

"Miriam?"

But he did not trust that.

He rose suddenly, went straight to bed. When he got inside his bedroom and closed the door, he stood with clenched fist.

"Mater, my dear——" he began, with the whole force of his soul. Then he stopped. He would not say it. He would not admit that he wanted to die, to have done. He would not own that life had beaten him, or that death had beaten him. Going straight to bed, he slept at once, abandoning himself to the sleep.

So the weeks went on. Always alone, his soul oscillated, first on the side of death, then on the side of life, doggedly. The real agony was that he had nowhere to go, nothing to do, nothing to say, and *was* nothing himself. Sometimes he ran down the streets as if he were mad: sometimes he was mad; things weren't there, things were there. It made him pant. Sometimes he stood before the bar of the public-house where he called for a drink. Everything suddenly stood back away from him. He saw the face of the barmaid, the gabbling drinkers, his own glass on the slopped, mahogany board, in the distance. There was something between him and them. He could not get into touch. He did not want them; he did not want his drink. Turning abruptly, he went out. On the threshold he stood and looked at the lighted street. But he was not of it or in it. Something separated him. Everything went on there below those lamps, shut away from him. He could not get at them. He felt he couldn't touch the lamp-posts, not if he reached. Where could he go? There was nowhere to go, neither back into the inn, or forward anywhere. He felt stifled. There was nowhere for him. The stress grew inside him; he felt he should smash.

"I mustn't," he said; and, turning blindly, he went in and drank. Sometimes the drink did him good; sometimes it made him worse. He ran down the road. For ever restless, he went here, there, everywhere. He determined to work. But when he had made six strokes, he loathed the pencil violently, got up, and went away, hurried off to a club where he could play cards or billiards, to a place where he could flirt with a bar-maid who was no more to him than the brass pump-handle she drew.

He was very thin and lantern-jawed. He dared not meet his own eyes in the mirror; he never looked at himself. He wanted to get away from himself, but there was nothing to get hold of. In despair he thought of Miriam. Perhaps—perhaps——?

Then, happening to go into the Unitarian Church one Sunday evening, when they stood up to sing the second hymn he saw her before him. The light glistened on her lower lip as she sang. She looked as if she had got something, at any rate: some hope in heaven, if not in earth. Her comfort and her life seemed in the after-world. A warm, strong feeling for her came up. She seemed to yearn, as she sang, for the mystery and comfort. He put his hope in her. He longed for the sermon to be over, to speak to her.

The throng carried her out just before him. He could nearly touch her. She did not know he was there. He saw the brown, humble nape of her neck under its black curls. He would leave himself to her. She was better and bigger than he. He would depend on her.

She went wandering, in her blind way, through the little throngs of people outside the church. She always looked so lost and out of place among people. He went forward and put his hand on her arm. She started violently. Her great brown eyes dilated in fear, then went questioning at the sight of him. He shrank slightly from her.

"I didn't know——" she faltered.

"Nor I," he said.

He looked away. His sudden, flaring hope sank again.

"What are you doing in town?" he asked.

"I'm staying at Cousin Anne's."

"Ha! For long?"

"No; only till to-morrow."

"Must you go straight home?"

She looked at him, then hid her face under her hat-brim.

"No," she said—"no; it's not necessary."

He turned away, and she went with him. They threaded through the throng of church people. The organ was still sounding in St. Mary's. Dark figures came through the lighted doors; people were coming down the steps. The large coloured windows glowed up in the night. The church was like a great lantern suspended. They went down Hollow Stone, and he took the car for the Bridges.

"You will just have supper with me," he said: "then I'll bring you back."

"Very well," she replied, low and husky.

They scarcely spoke while they were on the car. The Trent ran dark and full under the bridge. Away towards Colwick all was black night. He lived down Holme Road, on the naked edge of the town, facing across the river meadows towards Sneinton Hermitage and the steep scrap of Colwick Wood. The floods were out. The silent water and the darkness spread away on their left. Almost afraid, they hurried along by the houses.

Supper was laid. He swung the curtain over the window. There was a bowl of freesias and scarlet anemones on the table. She bent to them. Still touching them with her finger-tips, she looked up at him, saying:

"Aren't they beautiful?"

"Yes," he said. "What will you drink—coffee?"

"I should like it," she said.

"Then excuse me a moment."

He went out to the kitchen.

Miriam took off her things and looked round. It was a bare, severe room. Her photo, Clara's, Annie's, were on the wall. She looked on the drawing-board to see what he was doing. There were only a few meaningless lines. She looked to see what books he was reading. Evidently just an ordinary novel. The letters in the rack she saw were from Annie, Arthur, and from some man or other she did not know. Everything he had touched, everything that was in the least personal to him, she examined with lingering absorption. He had been gone from her for so long, she wanted to rediscover him, his position, what he was now. But there was not much in the room to help her. It only made her feel rather sad, it was so hard and comfortless.

She was curiously examining a sketch-book when he returned with the coffee.

"There's nothing new in it," he said, "and nothing very interesting."

He put down the tray, and went to look over her shoulder. She turned the pages slowly, intent on examining everything.

"H'm!" he said, as she paused at a sketch. "I'd forgotten that. It's not bad, is it?"

"No," she said. "I don't quite understand it."

He took the book from her and went through it. Again he made a curious sound of surprise and pleasure.

"There's some not bad stuff in there," he said.

"Not at all bad," she answered gravely.

He felt again her interest in his work. Or was it for himself? Why was she always most interested in him as he appeared in his work?

They sat down to supper.

"By the way," he said, "didn't I hear something about your earning your own living?"

"Yes," she replied, bowing her dark head over her cup.

"And what of it?"

"I'm merely going to the farming college at Broughton for three months, and I shall probably be kept on as a teacher there."

"I say—that sounds all right for you! You always wanted to be independent."

"Yes."

"Why didn't you tell me?"

"I only knew last week."

"But I heard a month ago," he said.

"Yes; but nothing was settled then."

"I should have thought," he said, "you'd have told me you were trying."

She ate her food in the deliberate, constrained way, almost as if she recoiled a little from doing anything so publicly, that he knew so well.

"I suppose you're glad," he said.

"Very glad."

"Yes—it will be something."

He was rather disappointed.

"I think it will be a great deal," she said, almost haughtily, resentfully.

He laughed shortly.

"Why do you think it won't?" she asked.

"Oh, I don't think it won't be a great deal. Only you'll find earning your own living isn't everything."

"No," she said, swallowing with difficulty; "I don't suppose it is."

"I suppose work *can* be nearly everything to a man," he said, "though it isn't to me. But a woman only works with a part of herself. The real and vital part is covered up."

"But a man can give *all* himself to work?" she asked.

"Yes, practically."

"And a woman only the unimportant part of herself?"

"That's it."

She looked up at him, and her eyes dilated with anger.

"Then," she said, "if it's true, it's a great shame."

"It is. But I don't know everything," he answered.

After supper they drew up to the fire. He swung her a chair facing him, and they sat down. She was wearing a dress of dark claret colour, that suited her dark complexion and her large features. Still, the curls were fine and free, but her face was much older, the brown throat much thinner. She seemed old to him, older than Clara. Her bloom of youth had quickly gone. A sort of stiffness, almost of woodenness, had come upon her. She meditated a little while, then looked at him.

"And how are things with you?" she asked.

"About all right," he answered.

She looked at him, waiting.

"Nay," she said, very low.

Her brown, nervous hands were clasped over her knee. They had still the lack of confidence or repose, the almost hysterical look. He winced as he saw them. Then he laughed mirthlessly. She put her fingers between her lips. His slim, black, tortured body lay quite still in the chair. She suddenly took her finger from her mouth and looked at him.

"And you have broken off with Clara?"

"Yes."

His body lay like an abandoned thing, strewn in the chair.

"You know," she said, "I think we ought to be married."

He opened his eyes for the first time since many months, and attended to her with respect.

"Why?" he said.

"See," she said, "how you waste yourself! You might be ill,

you might die, and I never know—be no more then than if I had never known you."

"And if we married?" he asked.

"At any rate, I could prevent you wasting yourself and being a prey to other women—like—like Clara."

"A prey?" he repeated, smiling.

She bowed her head in silence. He lay feeling his despair come up again.

"I'm not sure," he said slowly, "that marriage would be much good."

"I only think of you," she replied.

"I know you do. But—you love me so much, you want to put me in your pocket. And I should die there smothered."

She bent her head, put her fingers between her lips, while the bitterness surged up in her heart.

"And what will you do otherwise?" she asked.

"I don't know—go on, I suppose. Perhaps I shall soon go abroad."

The despairing doggedness in his tone made her go on her knees on the rug before the fire, very near to him. There she crouched as if she were crushed by something, and could not raise her head. His hands lay quite inert on the arms of his chair. She was aware of them. She felt that now he lay at her mercy. If she could rise, take him, put her arms round him, and say, "You are mine," then he would leave himself to her. But dare she? She could easily sacrifice herself. But dare she assert herself? She was aware of his dark-clothed, slender body, that seemed one stroke of life, sprawled in the chair close to her. But no; she dared not put her arms round it, take it up, and say, "It is mine, this body. Leave it to me." And she wanted to. It called to all her woman's instinct. But she crouched, and dared not. She was afraid he would not let her. She was afraid it was too much. It lay there, his body, abandoned. She knew she ought to take it up and claim it, and claim every right to it. But—could she do it? Her impotence before him, before the strong demand of some unknown thing in him, was her extremity. Her hands fluttered; she half-lifted her head. Her eyes, shuddering, appealing, gone almost distracted, pleaded to him suddenly. His heart caught with pity. He took her hands, drew her to him, and comforted her.

"Will you have me, to marry me?" he said very low.

Oh, why did not he take her? Her very soul belonged to him.

Why would he not take what was his? She had borne so long
the cruelty of belonging to him and not being claimed by him.
Now he was straining her again. It was too much for her. She
drew back her head, held his face between her hands, and
looked him in the eyes. No, he was hard. He wanted something
else. She pleaded to him with all her love not to make it *her*
choice. She could not cope with it, with him, she knew
not with what. But it strained her till she felt she would
break.

"Do you want it?" she asked, very gravely.

"Not much," he replied, with pain.

She turned her face aside; then, raising herself with dignity,
she took his head to her bosom, and rocked him softly. She
was not to have him, then! So she could comfort him. She put
her fingers through his hair. For her, the anguished sweetness
of self-sacrifice. For him, the hate and misery of another
failure. He could not bear it—that breast which was warm and
which cradled him without taking the burden of him. So much
he wanted to rest on her that the feint of rest only tortured
him. He drew away.

"And without marriage we can do nothing?" he asked.

His mouth was lifted from his teeth with pain. She put her
little finger between her lips.

"No," she said, low and like the toll of a bell. "No, I think
not."

It was the end then between them. She could not take him
and relieve him of the responsibility of himself. She could only
sacrifice herself to him—sacrifice herself every day, gladly.
And that he did not want. He wanted her to hold him and
say, with joy and authority: "Stop all this restlessness and
beating against death. You are mine for a mate." She had not
the strength. Or was it a mate she wanted? or did she want a
Christ in him?

He felt, in leaving her, he was defrauding her of life. But
he knew that, in staying, stifling the inner, desperate man, he
was denying his own life. And he did not hope to give life to
her by denying his own.

She sat very quiet. He lit a cigarette. The smoke went up
from it, wavering. He was thinking of his mother, and had
forgotten Miriam. She suddenly looked at him. Her bitterness
came surging up. Her sacrifice, then, was useless. He lay there
aloof, careless about her. Suddenly she saw again his lack of

religion, his restless instability. He would destroy himself like
a perverse child. Well, then, he would!

"I think I must go," she said softly.

By her tone he knew she was despising him. He rose quietly.

"I'll come along with you," he answered.

She stood before the mirror pinning on her hat. How bitter,
how unutterably bitter, it made her that he rejected her sacrifice! Life ahead looked dead, as if the glow were gone out.
She bowed her face over the flowers—the freesias so sweet and
spring-like, the scarlet anemones flaunting over the table. It
was like him to have those flowers.

He moved about the room with a certain sureness of touch,
swift and relentless and quiet. She knew she could not cope
with him. He would escape like a weasel out of her hands.
Yet without him her life would trail on lifeless. Brooding, she
touched the flowers.

"Have them!" he said; and he took them out of the jar,
dripping as they were, and went quickly into the kitchen. She
waited for him, took the flowers, and they went out together,
he talking, she feeling dead.

She was going from him now. In her misery she leaned
against him as they sat on the car. He was unresponsive.
Where would he go? What would be the end of him? She
could not bear it, the vacant feeling where he should be. He
was so foolish, so wasteful, never at peace with himself. And
now where would he go? And what did he care that he wasted
her? He had no religion; it was all for the moment's attraction
that he cared, nothing else, nothing deeper. Well, she would
wait and see how it turned out with him. When he had had
enough he would give in and come to her.

He shook hands and left her at the door of her cousin's
house. When he turned away he felt the last hold for him had
gone. The town, as he sat upon the car, stretched away over
the bay of railway, a level fume of lights. Beyond the town
the country, little smouldering spots for more towns—the sea
—the night—on and on! And he had no place in it! Whatever
spot he stood on, there he stood alone. From his breast, from
his mouth, sprang the endless space, and it was there behind
him, everywhere. The people hurrying along the streets offered
no obstruction to the void in which he found himself. They
were small shadows whose footsteps and voices could be heard,
but in each of them the same night, the same silence. He got off

the car. In the country all was dead still. Little stars shone high up; little stars spread far away in the flood-waters, a firmament below. Everywhere the vastness and terror of the immense night which is roused and stirred for a brief while by the day, but which returns, and will remain at last eternal, holding everything in its silence and its living gloom. There was no Time, only Space. Who could say his mother had lived and did not live? She had been in one place, and was in another; that was all. And his soul could not leave her, wherever she was. Now she was gone abroad into the night, and he was with her still. They were together. But yet there was his body, his chest, that leaned against the stile, his hands on the wooden bar. They seemed something. Where was he?—one tiny upright speck of flesh, less than an ear of wheat lost in the field. He could not bear it. On every side the immense dark silence seemed pressing him, so tiny a spark, into extinction, and yet, almost nothing, he could not be extinct. Night, in which everything was lost, went reaching out, beyond stars and sun. Stars and sun, a few bright grains, went spinning round for terror, and holding each other in embrace, there in a darkness that outpassed them all, and left them tiny and daunted. So much, and himself, infinitesimal, at the core a nothingness, and yet not nothing.

"Mother!" he whispered—"mother!"

She was the only thing that held him up, himself, amid all this. And she was gone, intermingled herself. He wanted her to touch him, have him alongside with her.

But no, he would not give in. Turning sharply, he walked towards the city's gold phosphorescence. His fists were shut, his mouth set fast. He would not take that direction, to the darkness, to follow her. He walked towards the faintly humming, glowing town, quickly.

THE END

II

Sons and Lovers:
Contexts of Response

In the critical section of this volume all footnotes are mine unless they carry the author's initials. Omissions, of course, are indicated by ellipses.

—J.M.

Early Reviews

❖◈❖

The three reviews that follow were probably the most important
early notices on *Sons and Lovers*. *The Athenæum* and *The Saturday
Review* were regarded as the most authoritative English literary
weeklies.

The Athenæum, June 21, 1913

Mr. Lawrence's new novel is a fine, but not altogether a
well-made piece of work. A certain distortion arises from the
fact that, while all the other characters are drawn, as it were,
in the third person, the hero is drawn in the first. The pronoun
"I" is not, indeed, employed for him, but the author has lived
so completely within his creation that the narrative reads like
an autobiography—and, as discerning readers know, autobiographies are less likely than biographies to produce a lifelike
portrait. We are not, at the end of the story, left understanding
the nature of the man about whom it is told. No doubt he
himself would not, in real life, have understood it; but we cannot help thinking that to complete his achievement the novelist
should have made the reader do so.

Nor is the young woman who is the first—and perhaps the
last—love of the hero satisfactorily realized. Many men, and
perhaps most women, will say to themselves as they read: "Yes,
this is how Miriam seemed to Paul, but this is not what Miriam
was." We suspect—and it is a tribute to the strength of the
illusion created—that, if the girl's story had been written, we
should have found her by no means so abnormal a person as
represented, and her wayward lover considerably more comprehensible.

From *The Athenæum*, June 21, 1913, No. 4469, p. 668.

But, although we may rebel, we are held captive from the first page to the last, and certain figures will, we think, remain engraved upon the memory. The story is a "family piece," and all are, with one exception, vividly drawn. The sister's figure is hardly represented at all, and an impression is thus tacitly conveyed that the one girl did not count in the family, and that the mother, whose relation to her sons forms the very kernel of the book, ignored her daughter. Yet the rare glimpses allowed of this daughter indicate a strong and interesting personality, and in real life she would probably have loomed large on the horizon of her slightly younger brother. In the book, she is nothing to him; the two influences in his life are his mother and the girl who understands his artistic work and who craves, as he does, for fuller education. Of these two it is not his contemporary whom he really loves and understands; his mother is far closer to him; she clings to him jealously, fighting against the younger woman's power, and succeeding in holding the pair apart. With his mother's death the son's life loses value and coherence; he is left, indeed, derelict. Her character is a real triumph.

Brilliant, too, is the figure of the hopelessly shallow girl who captured the first-born of the household; and pathetically true is his perception of her nature and his own bondage.

SONS AND LOVERS

When were there written novels so strange as these of Mr.
Lawrence? Now that he has given us three of them we should
be able to make some estimate of his position among writers,
yet there is about him something wilful which eludes judgment.
Passages in *Sons and Lovers* tempt us to place him in a high
class; and it is indeed a good book, even though it has pages
where the author's vision is revealed only behind a dense cloud.
As a story it is the record of the lives of a miner and his family
in the middle counties of England, and from *The White Peacock* we knew how well the Derbyshire and Nottinghamshire
country would be pictured. It can now be added that the scenes
from the towns are little less good. The ruling idea in the book
is the pitiful wastage of the best in men and women, and it is
first shown in the persons of Morel and his wife. The former
is physically a grand specimen of a race which puts its strength
into manual labour, but he is ruined by drink, for his will is
always weak. Mrs. Morel is a good housewife and a decent
woman. Her superior ways mark her to her husband as a lady;
yet she shirks none of the duties which his mate should perform for him, the children, and the home. Unhappily there is
in her something of the shrew, and the association between
the pair serves only to bring out their unpleasant sides. The
young family grows up zealous for the mother; but with the
touch of skill Mr. Lawrence can show the father as the good
fellow whom these others never knew. "He," we read, "always
sang when he mended boots because of the jolly sound of
hammering"; and in that single sentence is revealed the human
creature who should have had pure joy of life and an author
whose inspiration leaves behind the common artifices of the
novelist. There are many other places where the writer quite

From *The Saturday Review* (London), June 21, 1913, pp. 780–781.

surprises us by his power to make the narrative pass from fiction into glowing reality, and as an example we cannot do better than quote from the scene where young Paul and his sweetheart are climbing in the ruined tower: "They continued to mount the winding staircase. A high wind, blowing through the loopholes, went rushing up the shaft and filled the girl's skirts like a balloon, so that she was ashamed, until he took the hem of her dress and held it down for her. He did it perfectly simply, as he would have picked up her glove." No man could have invented this piece of description at the factory of the desk; it is a fragment of life, though we cannot know whether it belongs to the world of fact or had its genesis in some glorious flash of imagination. Origin, however, matters nothing. The passage remains as one which not a novelist in a hundred could produce.

Paul Morel, the miner's second son, is the chief person in the book, and his tragedy is his devotion to his mother, for she absorbs almost everything in him but his passions. Miriam, the girl of the tower episode, does battle for him. Despite her fierce purity she gives herself to his desire, but she cannot hold him even by her sacrifice, and he drifts into a passionate friendship with a second woman. The idea of waste still rules the story. The mother, who has dreaded the influence of Miriam on his affections, almost welcomes the intrigue with Clara, because the latter is less exacting in her demands. Puritan as she is, Mrs. Morel condones the affair with a married woman in order to keep the greater part of her son for herself. The strife between the generations is admirably suggested, and we know of no active English novelist—to-day—who has Mr. Lawrence's power to put in words the rise and fall of passion. The death of the mother and Paul's derelict state are the ends to which the story naturally leads, for the author is too good an artist to allow a conclusion which could stultify the force of all that he has built on the characters of his people. What is wrong in the book is the frequent intrusion of the writer. The men and women use words which are his and not their own; their reading is in the literature for which he cares; often they express thoughts which belong to him and not to them. Mr. Lawrence's inability to efface himself is now his most serious weakness, for the faulty construction of his earlier work is in no way evident in *Sons and Lovers*. After reading most of the more "important" novels of the present year, we can say that we have seen none to excel it in interest and power; the sum of its defects is astonishingly large, but we only note it when they are weighed against the sum of its own qualities.

From *The New York Times*, September 21, 1913. Copyright © 1913 by The New York Times Company. Reprinted by permission.

MOTHER LOVE

There is probably no phrase much more hackneyed than that of "human document," yet it is the only one which at all describes this very unusual book. It is hardly a story; rather the first part of a man's life, from his birth until his 25th year, the conditions surrounding him, his strength and his numerous weaknesses, put before us in a manner which misses no subtlest effect either of emotion or environment. And the heroine of the book is not sweetheart, but mother; the mother with whose marriage the novel begins, with whose pathetic death it reaches its climax. The love for each other of the mother and her son, Paul Morel, is the mainspring of both their lives; it is portrayed tenderly, yet with a truthfulness which slurs nothing even of that friction which is unavoidable between the members of two different generations.

The scene is laid among the collieries of Derbyshire. Paul's father was a miner; his mother, Mrs. Morel, belonged a trifle higher up in the social scale, having made one of those "romantic" marriages with which the old-fashioned sentimental novel used to end, and with which the modern realistic one so frequently begins. The first chapter, which tells of their early married life before the coming of their second son, Paul, is an admirable account of a mismated couple. Walter Morel could never have amounted to very much, but had he possessed a less noble wife he might, by one of those strange contradictions of which life is full, have been a far better man than he actually was. His gradual degeneration is as pitiful as it is inevitable— the change from the joyous, lovable young man to the drunken, ill-tempered father, whose entrance hushed the children's laughter, the mere thought of whom could cast a shadow over all the house. Mrs. Morel was strong enough to remake for herself the life he had so nearly wrecked—he could only drift helplessly upon the rocks. It is wonderfully real, this daily life of the Morel family and the village wherein they lived as reflected in Mr. Lawrence's pages; the more real because he never flaunts his knowledge of the intimate details of existence led by these households whose men toil underground. They slip from his pen so unobtrusively that it is only when we pause and consider that we recognize how full and complete is the background against which he projects his principal characters— Mr. and Mrs. Morel, Paul, Miriam, and Clara.

Paul himself is a person who awakens interest rather than sympathy; it is difficult not to despise him a little for his weakness, his constant need of that strengthening he sought from two other women, but which only his splendid, indomitable little mother could give him—a fact of which he was constantly aware, though he acknowledged it only at the very end. And it is not easy upon any grounds to excuse his treatment of Miriam, even though it was spiritual self-defense which urged him to disloyalty. Mr. Lawrence has small regard for what we term conventional morality; nevertheless, though plain spoken to a degree, his book is not in the least offensive.

It is, in fact, fearless; never coarse, although the relations between Paul, Miriam and Clara are portrayed with absolute frankness. And one must go far to find a better study of an intense woman, so over-spiritualized that she has lost touch with ordinary life and ordinary humanity, than he has given us in the person of Miriam. We pity her for her craving, her self-distrust that forbade her to take the thing she most wanted even when it was almost within her grasp; and yet Paul's final recoil is readily comprehensible, his feeling that she was making his very soul her own—would, as his mother said, leave nothing of him. The long, psychic battle between the two, a battle blindly fought, never really understood, is excellent in its revelation of those motives which lie at the very root of character—motives of which the persons they actuate are so completely ignorant.

Clara is less remarkable than Miriam only because she is necessarily more obvious—a woman in whom the animal predominates, certain after a brief time to weary one like Paul. And better than either, strong of will, rich in love and sympathy, holding her place in her son's heart against even Miriam, who so nearly took him from her, reigning at last supreme over every rival stands the heroic little mother—the best drawn character in a book which contains many admirable portrayals. From the moment when we first meet her taking her elder children to the "wakes" and trying to nerve herself to endure a life which appears to be an endless waiting for something that can never come, until at the last she wages her valiant, losing fight against the cancer that is killing her by inches, she is always real, a fine, true woman, mother to the very core. Mr. Lawrence has mercifully spared us the terrible details of her illness; it is only her "tortured eyes" we see, and her children's grief and horror. Whether or not it was right for Paul to do the thing he did is an open question; only we are sure that in very truth he "loved her better than his own life." His impotent resentment of her growing weakness is an excellent bit of analysis; the effect upon him of her death, which he seemed to take so calmly—the blankness, the unreality and emptiness of all things—strikes home. Without her his life was meaningless; yet live he must and for her sake.

The book is full of short vivid descriptions:

The steep swoop of highroad lay, in its cool morning dust, splendid with patterns of sunshine and shadow, perfectly still. . . . Behind, the houses stood on the brim of the dip, black against the sky, like wild beasts glaring curiously with yellow eyes down into darkness.

Each a picture drawn in a sentence. Although this is a novel of over 500 closely printed pages the style is terse—so terse that at times it produces an effect as of short, sharp hammer strokes.

Yet it is flexible, too, as shown by its success in depicting vary-
ing shades of mood, in expressing those more intimate emotions
which are so very nearly inexpressible. Yet, when all is said,
it is the complex character of Miriam, she who was only Paul's
"conscience, not his mate," and the beautiful bond between
the restless son and the mother whom "his soul could not
leave" even when she slept and "dreamed her young dream"
which makes this book one of rare excellence.

Starting from the Village

✿◈✿

D. H. LAWRENCE

During his last years Lawrence returned in his imagination again
and again to the scene of his origins. *Lady Chatterley's Lover*
(1928) and *The Virgin and the Gypsy* (1930) are set within a
few miles of his birthplace. The following essay, which begins in
recollection and ends in prophecy, shows how deeply Lawrence
cared about the English working-class milieu from which he had
voluntarily banished himself during most of his adult career.

NOTTINGHAM AND THE MINING COUNTRYSIDE [1930]

I was born nearly forty-four years ago, in Eastwood, a mining
village of some three thousand souls, about eight miles from
Nottingham, and one mile from the small stream, the Erewash,
which divides Nottinghamshire from Derbyshire. It is hilly
country, looking west to Crich and towards Matlock, sixteen
miles away, and east and north-east towards Mansfield and the
Sherwood Forest district. To me it seemed, and still seems, an
extremely beautiful countryside, just between the red sandstone
and the oak-trees of Nottingham, and the cold limestone, the
ash-trees, the stone fences of Derbyshire. To me, as a child and
a young man, it was still the old England of the forest and
agricultural past; there were no motor-cars, the mines were, in

---

From *Phoenix: The Posthumous Papers of D. H. Lawrence*, edited by
Edward D. McDonald (New York: The Viking Press, 1936).

a sense, an accident in the landscape, and Robin Hood and his merry men were not very far away.

The string of coal-mines of B.W. & Co. had been opened some sixty years before I was born, and Eastwood had come into being as a consequence. It must have been a tiny village at the beginning of the nineteenth century, a small place of cottages and fragmentary rows of little four-roomed miners' dwellings, the homes of the old colliers of the eighteenth century, who worked in the bits of mines, foot-rill mines with an opening in the hillside into which the miners walked, or wind-lass mines, where the men were wound up one at a time, in a bucket, by a donkey. The windlass mines were still working when my father was a boy—and the shafts of some were still there, when I was a boy.

But somewhere about 1820 the company must have sunk the first big shaft—not very deep—and installed the first machinery of the real industrial colliery. Then came my grandfather, a young man trained to be a tailor, drifting from the south of England, and got the job of company tailor for the Brinsley mine. In those days the company supplied the men with the thick flannel vests, or singlets, and the moleskin trousers lined at the top with flannel, in which the colliers worked. I remember the great rolls of coarse flannel and pit-cloth which stood in the corner of my grandfather's shop when I was a small boy, and the big, strange old sewing-machine, like nothing else on earth, which sewed the massive pit-trousers. But when I was only a child the company discontinued supplying the men with pit-clothes.

My grandfather settled in an old cottage down in a quarry-bed, by the brook at Old Brinsley, near the pit. A mile away, up at Eastwood, the company built the first miners' dwellings— it must be nearly a hundred years ago. Now Eastwood occupies a lovely position on a hilltop, with the steep slope towards Derbyshire and the long slope towards Nottingham. They put up a new church, which stands fine and commanding, even if it has no real form, looking across the awful Erewash Valley at the church of Heanor, similarly commanding, away on a hill beyond. What opportunities, what opportunities! These mining villages *might* have been like the lovely hill-towns of Italy, shapely and fascinating. And what happened?

Most of the little rows of dwellings of the old-style miners were pulled down, and dull little shops began to rise along the Nottingham Road, while on the down-slope of the north side the company erected what is still known as the New Buildings, or the Square. These New Buildings consist of two great hollow squares of dwellings planked down on the rough slope of the hill, little four-room houses with the "front" looking outward into the grim, blank street, and the "back," with a tiny square brick yard, a low wall, and a w.c. and ash-pit, looking into the desert of the square, hard, uneven, jolting black earth tilting rather steeply down, with these little back yards all round, and openings at the corners. The squares were quite big, and absolutely desert, save for the posts for clothes lines, and people passing, children playing on the hard earth. And they were shut in like a barracks enclosure, very strange.

Even fifty years ago the squares were unpopular. It was "common" to live in the Square. It was a little less common to live in the Breach, which consisted of six blocks of rather more pretentious dwellings erected by the company in the valley below, two rows of three blocks, with an alley between. And it was most "common," most degraded of all to live in Dakins Row, two rows of the old dwellings, very old, black, four-roomed little places, that stood on the hill again, not far from the Square.

So the place started. Down the steep street between the squares, Scargill Street, the Wesleyans' chapel was put up, and I was born in the little corner shop just above. Across the other side the Square the miners themselves built the big, barn-like Primitive Methodist chapel. Along the hill-top ran the Nottingham Road, with its scrappy, ugly mid-Victorian shops. The little market-place, with a superb outlook, ended the village on the Derbyshire side, and was just left bare, with the Sun Inn on one side, the chemist across, with the gilt pestle-and-mortar, and a shop at the other corner, the corner of Alfreton Road and Nottingham Road.

In this queer jumble of the old England and the new, I came into consciousness. As I remember, little local speculators already began to straggle dwellings in rows, always in rows, across the fields: nasty red-brick, flat-faced dwellings with dark slate roofs. The bay-window period only began when I was a child. But most of the country was untouched.

There must be three or four hundred company houses in the squares and the streets that surround the squares, like a great barracks wall. There must be sixty or eighty company houses in the Breach. The old Dakins Row will have thirty to forty little holes. Then counting the old cottages and rows left with their old gardens down the lanes and along the twitchells, and even in the midst of Nottingham Road itself, there were houses enough for the population, there was no need for much building. And not much building went on when I was small.

We lived in the Breach, in a corner house. A field-path came under a great hawthorn hedge. On the other side was the brook, with the old sheep-bridge going over into the meadows. The hawthorn hedge by the brook had grown tall as tall trees, and we used to bathe from there in the dipping-hole, where the sheep were dipped, just near the fall from the old mill-dam, where the water rushed. The mill only ceased grinding the local corn when I was a child. And my father, who always worked in Brinsley pit, and who always got up at five o'clock, if not at four, would set off in the dawn across the fields at Coney Grey, and hunt for mushrooms in the long grass, or perhaps pick up a skulking rabbit, which he would bring home at evening inside the lining of his pit-coat.

So that the life was a curious cross between industrialism and the old agricultural England of Shakespeare and Milton and Fielding and George Eliot. The dialect was broad Derbyshire, and always "thee" and "thou." The people lived almost entirely by instinct, men of my father's age could not really read. And the pit did not mechanize men. On the contrary. Under the butty system, the miners worked underground as a sort of intimate community, they knew each other practically naked, and with curious close intimacy, and the darkness and the underground remoteness of the pit "stall," and the continual presence of danger, made the physical, instinctive, and intuitional contact between men very highly developed, a contact almost as close as touch, very real and very powerful. This physical awareness and intimate *togetherness* was at its strongest down pit. When the men came up into the light, they blinked. They had, in a measure, to change their flow. Nevertheless, they brought with them above ground the curious dark intimacy of the mine, the naked sort of contact, and if I think of my childhood, it is always as if there was a lustrous sort of inner darkness, like the gloss of coal, in which we moved and had our real being. My father loved the pit. He was hurt badly, more than once, but he would never stay away. He loved the contact, the intimacy, as men in the war loved the intense male comradeship of the dark days. They did not know what they had lost till they lost it. And I think it is the same with the young colliers of today.

Now the colliers had also an instinct of beauty. The colliers' wives had not. The colliers were deeply alive, instinctively. But they had no daytime ambition, and no daytime intellect. They avoided, really, the rational aspect of life. They preferred to take life instinctively and intuitively. They didn't even care very profoundly about wages. It was the women, naturally, who nagged on this score. There was a big discrepancy, when I was a boy, between the collier who saw, at the best, only a brief few hours of daylight—often no daylight at all during the winter weeks—and the collier's wife, who had all the day to herself when the man was down pit.

The great fallacy is, to pity the man. He didn't dream of pitying himself, till agitators and sentimentalists taught him to. He was happy: or more than happy, he was fulfilled. Or he was fulfilled on the receptive side, not on the expressive. The collier went to the pub and drank in order to continue his intimacy with his mates. They talked endlessly, but it was rather of wonders and marvels, even in politics, than of facts. It was hard facts, in the shape of wife, money, and nagging home necessities, which they fled away from, out of the house to the pub, and out of the house to the pit.

The collier fled out of the house as soon as he could, away from the nagging materialism of the woman. With the women it was always: This is broken, now you've got to mend it! or else: We want this, that and the other, and where is the money coming from? The collier didn't know and didn't care very deeply—his life was otherwise. So he escaped. He roved the countryside with his dog, prowling for a rabbit, for nests, for mushrooms, anything. He loved the countryside, just the indiscriminating feel of it. Or he loved just to sit on his heels and watch—anything or nothing. He was not intellectually interested. Life for him did not consist in facts, but in a flow. Very often, he loved his garden. And very often he had a genuine love of the beauty of flowers. I have known it often and often, in colliers.

Now the love of flowers is a very misleading thing. Most women love flowers as possessions, and as trimmings. They can't look at a flower, and wonder a moment, and pass on. If they see a flower that arrests their attention, they must at once pick it, pluck it. Possession! A possession! Something added on to *me!* And most of the so-called love of flowers today is merely this reaching out of possession and egoism: something I've *got*: something that embellishes *me.* Yet I've seen many a collier stand in his back garden looking down at a flower with that odd, remote sort of contemplation which shows a real awareness of the presence of beauty. It would not even be admiration, or joy, or delight, or any of those things which so often have a root in the possessive instinct. It would be a sort of contemplation: which shows the incipient artist.

The real tragedy of England, as I see it, is the tragedy of ugliness. The country is so lovely: the man-made England is so vile. I know that the ordinary collier, when I was a boy, had a peculiar sense of beauty, coming from his intuitive and instinctive consciousness, which was awakened down pit. And the fact that he met with just cold ugliness and raw materialism when he came up into daylight, and particularly when he came to the Square or the Breach, and to his own table, killed something in him, and in a sense spoiled him as a man. The woman almost invariably nagged about material things. She was taught to do it; she was encouraged to do it. It was a mother's business to see that her sons "got on," and it was the man's business to provide the money. In my father's generation, with the old wild England behind them, and the lack of education, the man was not beaten down. But in my generation, the boys I went to school with, colliers now, have all been beaten down, what with the din-din-dinning of Board Schools, books, cinemas, clergymen, the whole national and human consciousness hammering on the fact of material prosperity above all things.

The men are beaten down, there is prosperity for a time, in their defeat—and then disaster looms ahead. The root of all disaster is disheartenment. And men are disheartened. The men of England, the colliers in particular, are disheartened. They have been betrayed and beaten.

Now though perhaps nobody knew it, it was ugliness which really betrayed the spirit of man, in the nineteenth century. The great crime which the moneyed classes and promoters of industry committed in the palmy Victorian days was the condemning of the workers to ugliness, ugliness, ugliness: meanness and formless and ugly surroundings, ugly ideals, ugly religion, ugly hope, ugly love, ugly clothes, ugly furniture, ugly houses, ugly relationship between workers and employers. The human soul needs actual beauty even more than bread. The middle classes jeer at the colliers for buying pianos—but what is the piano, often as not, but a blind reaching out for beauty. To the woman it is a possession and a piece of furniture and something to feel superior about. But see the elderly colliers trying to learn to play, see them listening with queer alert faces to their daughter's execution of *The Maiden's Prayer*, and you will see a blind, unsatisfied craving for beauty. It is far more deep in the men than the women. The women want show. The men want beauty, and still want it.

If the company, instead of building those sordid and hideous Squares, then, when they had that lovely site to play with, there on the hill top: if they had put a tall column in the middle of the small market-place, and run three parts of a circle of arcade round the pleasant space, where people could stroll or sit, and with handsome houses behind! If they had made big, substantial houses, in apartments of five or six rooms, and with handsome entrances. If above all, they had encouraged song and dancing—for the miners still sang and danced—and provided handsome space for these. If only they had encouraged some form of beauty in dress, some form of beauty in interior life— furniture, decoration. If they had given prizes for the handsomest chair or table, the loveliest scarf, the most charming room that the men or women could make! If only they had done this, there would never have been an industrial problem. The industrial problem arises from the base forcing of all human energy into a competition of mere acquisition.

You may say the working man would not have accepted such a form of life: the Englishman's home is his castle, etc., etc.— "my own little home." But if you can hear every word the next-door people say, there's not much castle. And if you can see everybody in the square if they go to the w.c.! And if your one desire is to get out of your "castle" and your "own little home"! —well, there's not much to be said for it. Anyhow, it's only the woman who idolizes "her own little home"—and it's always the woman at her worst, her most greedy, most possessive, most mean. There's nothing to be said for the "little home" any more: a great scrabble of ugly pettiness over the face of the land.

As a matter of fact, till 1800 the English people were strictly a rural people—very rural. England has had towns for centuries, but they have never been real towns, only clusters of village streets. Never the real *urbs*. The English character has failed to develop the real *urban* side of a man, the civic side. Siena is a bit of a place, but it is a real city, with citizens intimately connected with the city. Nottingham is a vast place sprawling towards a million, and it is nothing more than an amorphous agglomeration. There *is* no Nottingham, in the sense that there is Siena. The Englishman is stupidly undeveloped, as a citizen.

And it is partly due to his "little home" stunt, and partly to his acceptance of hopeless paltriness in his surrounding. The new cities of America are much more genuine cities, in the Roman sense, than is London or Manchester. Even Edinburgh used to be more of a true city than any town England ever produced. That silly little individualism of "the Englishman's home is his castle" and "my own little home" is out of date. It would work almost up to 1800, when every Englishman was still a villager, and a cottager. But the industrial system has brought a great change. The Englishman still likes to think of himself as a "cottager"—"my home, my garden." But it is puerile. Even the farm-labourer today is psychologically a town-bird. The English are town-birds through and through, today, as the inevitable result of their complete industrialization. Yet they don't know how to build a city, how to think of one, or how to live in one. They are all suburban, pseudo-cottagy, and not one of them knows how to be truly urban—the citizen as the Romans were citizens—or the Athenians—or even the Parisians, till the war came.

And this is because we have frustrated that instinct of community which would make us unite in pride and dignity in the bigger gesture of the citizen, not the cottager. The great city means beauty, dignity, and a certain splendour. This is the side of the Englishman that has been thwarted and shockingly betrayed. England is a mean and petty scrabble of paltry dwellings called "homes." I believe in their heart of hearts all Englishmen loathe their little homes—but not the women. What we want is a bigger gesture, a greater scope, a certain splendour, a certain grandeur, and beauty, big beauty. The American does far better than we, in this.

And the promoter of industry, a hundred years ago, dared to perpetrate the ugliness of my native village. And still more monstrous, promoters of industry today are scrabbling over the face of England with miles and square miles of red-brick "homes," like horrible scabs. And the men inside these little red rat-traps get more and more helpless, being more and more humiliated, more and more dissatisfied, like trapped rats. Only the meaner sort of women go on loving the little home which is no more than a rat-trap to her man.

Do away with it all, then. At no matter what cost, start in to alter it. Never mind about wages and industrial squabbling. Turn the attention elsewhere. Pull down my native village to the last brick. Plan a nucleus. Fix the focus. Make a handsome gesture of radiation from the focus. And then put up big buildings, handsome, that sweep to a civic centre. And furnish them with beauty. And make an absolute clean start. Do it place by place. Make a new England. Away with little homes! Away with scrabbling pettiness and paltriness. Look at the contours of the land, and build up from these, with a sufficient nobility. The English may be mentally or spiritually developed. But as citizens of splendid cities they are more ignominious than rabbits. And they nag, nag, nag all the time about politics and wages and all that, like mean narrow housewives.

ADA LAWRENCE CLARKE

An account of the Lawrence family by the novelist's younger sister.

[A REMINISCENCE]

I remember nothing of the house where my brother and I were born, for we left when I was only a few months old and Bert was about two years. The Breach consisted of blocks of houses belonging to Barber, Walker and Co., the pit-owners. Our house was at the end of a row, with a garden on three sides. I remember so well the white currant bushes by the house and the old-fashioned white rose trees in the little front garden. My mother never liked being there, partly because the houses were in a hollow, principally because the backs looked out on to drab patches of garden with ashpits at the bottom.

So about five years later we moved again, to Walker Street, where a row of six bay-windowed houses had just been built. We loved living here. We had a wonderful view of Brinsley, Underwood, Moorgreen, and the High Park woods in the distance. Immediately in front were fields stretching to the Breach which made the best playground one could have. What fun we had round the ancient ash tree which stood just opposite the house—although the moaning wind through its branches scared us as we lay in bed in the winter.

How nice we thought that Walker Street house, with its comfortable kitchen which always looked so homelike. I close my eyes and see again father's wooden armchair on one side of the fireplace, and mother's little rocking-chair on the other; the sofa, with its shake-up bed covered with pretty red chintz and cushions to match, the little painted dresser, and the bookcase with its rows of books of which we were so proud.

From *Early Life of D. H. Lawrence: Together with Hitherto Unpublished Letters and Articles*, by Ada Lawrence and G. Stuart Gelder (London: Martin Secker, 1932), pp. 8–11. Reprinted by permission of W. H. Clarke and G. Stuart Gelder.

The few pictures we possessed consisted chiefly of quite decorative oleographs, and the high mantelpiece was in keeping with the brass candlesticks and father's black carved-iron tobacco jar, side by side with Bert's inkstand shaped like a gnome sitting on a log.

We were proud of our front room or parlour with its well-made mahogany and horse-hair suite of furniture—the little mahogany chiffonier and the oval Spanish mahogany table, which my mother insisted on covering with a fawn and green tapestry table-cloth to match the Brussels carpet. Here again were oleographs, heavily framed in gilt, and the family portrait in the place of honour over the mantelpiece.

Although so unpretentious, there was something about our house which made it different from those of our neighbours. Perhaps this was because mother would have nothing cheap or tawdry, preferring bareness.

I marvel now at the housework she could do, and the wonderful way in which she managed on the little money my father gave her. No wonder we all idolised her. She was small and slight in figure, her brown hair, sprinkled with grey, brushed straight back from a broad brow; clear blue eyes that always looked fearless and unfaltering, and a delicately shaped nose, not quite straight owing to an accident which occurred when she was a girl; tiny hands and feet, and a sure carriage. Some people were ill-natured enough to say that she "put it on" when she spoke, for her English was good and her accent so different from that of the folk round about.

Try as she might, she could never speak the local dialect, and we children were careful about it when we were with her, even though we let fling among our friends. She loved to read, and every week piles of books were fetched from the local library to be enjoyed when we were all in bed. The minister liked to visit her, and they discussed religion and philosophy, for she was an excellent talker, and had a dry, whimsical, fascinating sense of humour. She was never effusive or demonstrative in any way, yet we felt in her a wealth of love and a security past all understanding.

At heart she was deeply religious and a stickler for truth, having great contempt for anything petty, vain or frivolous.

I don't remember seeing her dressed in anything but black and white, or grey, and she never possessed any jewellery. When I was older I persuaded her to have a bodice of mauve, covered with black lace, but she had grave misgivings every time she put it on. How ladylike we thought she looked when dressed for chapel in her black costume, and black silk blouse, little black bonnet decorated with black and white ospreys (she never wore a hat), and an elegant black and white feather boa round her neck.

Before my brother Ernest died we used to listen for her sweet voice singing hymns. After his death I don't remember her singing again.

We used to wonder that mother and father, so utterly unsuitable to each other, should be married. But when I look back I can remember my father as a handsome man of medium height with black wavy hair, dark brown beard and moustache. He boasted that a razor had never touched his face. He had dark flashing eyes and a ruddy complexion. His voice was very melodious, and for some years he was in the choir at Brinsley church. My mother, who had never visited a mining village, met him at a party in Nottingham, and was attracted by his graceful dancing, his musical voice, his gallant manner and his overflowing humour and good spirits. He, on his side, was drawn to the rather quiet, reserved and ladylike girl. Before many months had passed they were married, my mother looking, in the words of her sister, "like an angel" in her dove-coloured silk dress and bonnet. Her brown ringlets were not fastened up until after the birth of her first child.

I wonder if there would have been quite so much misery in our childhood if mother had been just a little more tolerant. Having been brought up in a strict and Puritanical atmosphere, she was a staunch teetotaller, and would have no strong drink in the house. My father, who had received little education, being sent to work when he was seven, felt no desire to read anything but newspapers. Having little in common with mother, he soon began to seek the more congenial society of his friends in the public-house, not solely for the sake of drink, but because in their company he was more sure of himself, and their interests were his interests.

Mother would wait up for [Father] at night, her rage seething, until on his arrival it boiled over in a torrent of biting truths which turned him from his slightly fuddled and pleasantly apologetic mood into a brutal and coarse beast. With palpitating hearts we waited until he came to bed, knowing that not until then could we safely sleep.

He was very clever at his job and handy in the house. When we were all very young he mended our boots and shoes, and was never more happy than when seated tailorwise on the rug, with the hobbing iron, hammering away and singing at the top of his voice. If the pans and kettles leaked he could always mend them, and when the eight-day clock was out of order we loved to watch him take it to pieces, carefully putting the screws and spare parts in saucers, and boiling the works in a big saucepan to clean them thoroughly.

As we grew older we shut him more and more out of our lives, and instinctively turned more to mother, and he, realising this, became more and more distasteful in his habits. He was never really intolerable, and if, instead of wanting the impossible from him, we had tried to interest ourselves in the things for which he really cared, we should have been spared many unhappy and sordid scenes.

He was so proud of us all, and after mother's death when he was asked why he did not marry again he said, "I've had one good woman—the finest woman in the world, and I don't want another." My brother's description of him in *Sons and Lovers*, when mother was dying, seems to me to be writing too deep for tears. He shows a lost man, bewildered by the realisation that she was going from him, and that somehow he had no part in anything.

WILLIAM EDWARD HOPKIN

W. E. Hopkin (1862–1951) was a close friend of Lawrence at
Eastwood and corresponded with him for many years after he had
left England. He was a man of lively intelligence and independent
judgment who held offices as magistrate and member of the County
Council of Nottinghamshire during a long, active life.

[A PERSONAL MEMOIR]

My first meeting with D. H. Lawrence, or rather my first sight
of him, was in 1885 when he was a few weeks old. One day as
I was passing the opening into Victoria Street, Eastwood, Mrs.
Lawrence came out on the main road with her newest baby in
a three-wheeled pram with ironbound wheels. I stopped and
asked how the baby was faring. She uncovered his face and I
saw a puny, fragile little specimen. I could understand the
doubts expressed by Mrs. Lawrence about being able to "rear"
him. Years later Lawrence said to me: "Before I went to school
I was a snuffly-nosed little beggar, seldom without a cold."

Eastwood, Nottinghamshire, where Lawrence was born, is a
busy little town on the Derbyshire border. It depends on coal
mines for its prosperity, but there are none in Eastwood itself.
The nearest are Moorgreen and Brinsley just within a mile. It
was at Brinsley Colliery that John Arthur Lawrence, the writer's
father, spent his working days. He was a good miner, had an
independent spirit and resented interference from the Colliery
officials. In appearance he was a handsome man with a black
beard and fairly high coloured cheeks. He was a very accomplished dancer in his younger days.

Lydia, Lawrence's mother, was a small woman of considerable refinement and culture. In her teens she composed poetry,
some of which appeared in magazines in the district in which

From a B.B.C. talk recorded at Birmingham, England, August 17, 1949.
First published in D. H. Lawrence: A Composite Biography, by Edward
Nehls (Madison, Wisc.: University of Wisconsin Press, 1957–1959), I,
21–25. Reprinted by permission of Mrs. Olive L. Hopkin.

she then lived. As the wife of a miner in a mining community she was out of her element. It was largely, I think, because of her difference from most of the wives about her that she soon became president of the newly founded Co-Operative Women's Guild.

Being a total stranger to mining life and habits she was shocked when Arthur came home from the pit the first day after the honeymoon looking more like a Negro than the man she kissed as he left home for work in the morning. When he insisted on having his dinner after merely washing his hands she was very upset. Arthur told her that coal dust was *clean* dirt, and that it was the habit of all miners to do the same, but she still protested. Then when as the crowning point he insisted on having his bath in the "dolly tub" in front of the kitchen fire and she must wash his back, her cup of anger overflowed, and that was the beginning of the rift. Husband and wife were both determined creatures and neither would give way. It is not for outsiders to judge, but I'm sure that if she had shown tact and patience things might have been very different. Arthur Lawrence was not of the material to mould into his wife's idea of a gentleman. He was one naturally.

The house where Lawrence was born is in a steeply descending street. It has been described by some writers as a sort of mean tenement in a maze of dreary streets. As a matter of fact it is quite a decent house, and from the front door one can see a really beautiful bit of countryside sloping to the north. Mrs. Lawrence had a shop where she sold baby clothes, ribbons, etc. in order to try and augment her husband's earnings. It proved a failure and when Lawrence was two years old the family moved to a house in Breach Bottoms, two long blocks of houses better than those in Victoria Street and in open country. They stayed there for some years and then went to a privately owned house in Walker Street. This house had a bay window which looked out on the fields and woodlands known as High Park, and the young folk felt they had gone up a step in society.

David Herbert, or as he was known locally, "Bert" Lawrence was always a good scholar. He attended Beauvale School until he was 13 when he won a scholarship and went to the High School in Nottingham. Later he attended a training centre at Ilkeston and was first in England and Wales in the Uncertificated Teachers Examination.

Young Lawrence was very sensitive, or as his schoolfellows said, "Mardy," which is a term used to signify a sort of babyish disposition. Never in his life could he bear anything like severe criticism. He either got extremely angry or worried and upset. In his later school and college days he had a few male friends, but in his elementary school days he did not get on with other boys. They despised him because he couldn't take part in their games. I well remember the day when I was passing the school as the scholars were leaving for dinner. He was walking between two girls, and a number of Breach Boys walked behind him monotonously chanting "Dicky Dicky Denches plays with the Wenches." That charge branded any boy as effeminate—the local term is "Mardarse." Bert's chin was in the air as though he cared no jot but his eyes were full of anger and mortification.

In those days things at home were in a bad way. The everlasting quarrels between his father and mother played havoc with his mind, and he used to lie awake in terrible fear that his father would do his mother a mischief. There were periods when peace reigned, and his sister Ada once told me that then the home was a very happy one, for the father did all kinds of things for the youngsters. The greatest single influence in Lawrence's life was his devotion to his mother. As is the wont of mothers, the weakly one of the family received a double share of love and attention, to which Bert responded in full measure, and there grew between them a love stronger and deeper than is usual between parent and child. To see them together sometimes was to imagine them fond lovers. She lavished on him some of the love her husband would have had if all had been well between them, and his passionate love for her made up in some measure for what she lacked from Arthur.

There was no kinship of soul between the father and son. The father was of the earth earthy, and the son, even in early life, was quite often up in the clouds.

Mother and son had a very perfect understanding. Had she taken a tenth part of the trouble, or shall I say pleasure, in trying to understand her husband what a fine family the Lawrences might have been.

As a boy and through his adolescence Lawrence was very fond of indoor games, and especially charades (dances too when the room was suitable). Whatever games were played he must be the leader. If his side failed to win he was very cross. I remember one evening at a party at the house of a friend he pitched into me for what he called "deliberate cheating." We had agreed to act book titles and we entered the room studying a book each and aimlessly wandering about. Lawrence failed to get the title, and when I said it was *The Student's Rome* he went into a temper.

He liked a sing-song, so I bought the *Oxford Song Book*. His favourite was the "Elephant Battery" which he rattled through at a great pace. A few years later he developed a habit I disliked. If any person he took a dislike to was in the room he would not speak but sat silent and sullen. When the person had gone he asked angrily what the devil we had asked him for.

From his early days Lawrence had a great love for nature and the countryside. It was a delight to go rambling with him. How he acquired his knowledge I never knew. He seemed to be one of those rare persons that receive direct revelation from some source. When out with him I occasionally noticed that he would make brief notes on any bit of paper from his pocket. Even as a youth he seemed to see things differently from other folk, and his descriptions were often unusual but illuminating. One sunny June afternoon we came across an old farmhouse with moss-grown tiles near a brook. It was a sleepy sort of day and no breeze stirred the leaves. No person was in sight and the whole place seemed asleep. Lawrence looked at it for a few seconds, and then said, "That house is brooding over its past." In the next field we sat down to rest and Lawrence, with half-closed eyes, told us what incidents the old house was recalling. One of the girls exclaimed, "Why don't you write stories, Bert?" A year or two later I came across the same idea in one of his books. I have been looking it up and it is in *The White Peacock*.

His talents were varied and for a long time I could not make up my mind what he would eventually become. At one time he had a craze for drawing and painting, and I dare say there are still one or two fire-screens and oddments in some of the cottages. He told stories well, and would sometimes recite poetry. His likes and dislikes were decided, and sometimes violent, and especially so later in his career, but it was the same as a boy. He had no use for neuters—he was of the same opinion as the writer of the couplet,

> Neuters in their middle way of steering
> Are neither fish, flesh, fowl, nor good red herring.

From boyhood he always spoke correctly and he was remarkably good in his writing.

Along with that he had an intimate knowledge of the local dialect which is a mixture of border Nottinghamshire and Derbyshire. Sometimes when at my house he and I would speak it for a time, much to the bewilderment of any visitor from elsewhere. These words—"How are you getting on? I hear you have been ill. I do hope it was nothing serious." Spoken in the dialect would be—"How are ter gerrin on surrey? I hear as thou's bin badly. I dow hope its nowt serious."

When Lawrence left Beauvale Elementary School [1898] he was not distinguished for anything, unless it was his tidy habits and his love of study, and a marked difference from the rest. Two things were against him—the teasing and contempt of his schoolfellows, and, what bit deeply into his daily life, the constant and bitter quarrels at home. It was, I think, his weakness and unpopularity with boys that drove him into the arms of girls. He was more in the company of girls than boys, and I used to notice that he had not much use for the Plain Janes. His girl friends were all good-looking and vivacious. In this connection I recall an amusing incident. Later on whenever it was known that Lawrence was staying with us we were invaded by swarms of soulful females—usually schoolteachers. As they came in I gave up my seat. Lawrence said: "For goodness' sake don't be polite. Let 'em find their own. When you get to Heaven you'll get up for every blessed woman who enters until the last seat is gone, and then you'll fall backwards into Hell and serve you jolly well right!"

ANONYMOUS
EASTWOOD MINER, 1955

[A VIEW FROM THE PIT]

The first man I spoke to [in the Breach]—a young-old veteran of the pits properly dressed in flat cap and collarless shirt, 43 years a miner and twice badly injured—was swift off the mark.

"Bert Lawrence? Don't talk to me about him." He gripped my elbow with a hard hand, and gave his judgment.

"I'd put him down as nowt. Given a tip-top education by his father—as fine a man as you'd meet in a day's march. That was on a butty's pay, pound to fifty shilling a week. Then he took all his knowledge away. Didn't give this country a penny back."

He brooded fiercely and then went on. "Spoke to nobody. Never had a pal in his life. Only played ring-o'-roses with young women." At this improbable idyll of memory his spectacles shone in the afternoon sun like signal lamps across half a century.

"But his father, now there was a man. Full of life and friendliness. Big roaring carnation in his coat. They still talk about him in Eastwood." He pointed a hundred yards up the hill, as if to another world. "He could dance, too, till his legs were broke to bits. He got buried." This was announced with professional casualness; then he reverted to the shortcomings of the man whom the rest of the world, outside the Breach, regards as great. "But Bert never acknowledged him properly, not as a father should be. It was the mother. Thought that much of herself. But she was nothing."

Reported by Norman Shrapnel in *The Manchester Guardian*, March 18, 1955, p. 7. Reprinted by permission.

Poems of a Son and Lover

❀◈❀

D. H. LAWRENCE

FROM "FOREWORD TO COLLECTED POEMS"

. . . The poems to Miriam run into the first poems to my mother. Then when I was twenty-three, I went away from home for the first time, to the south of London. From the big new red school where I taught, we could look north and see the Crystal Palace; to me, who saw it then for the first time, in lovely autumn weather, beautiful and softly blue on its hill to the north. And past the school, on an embankment, the trains rushed south to Brighton or to Kent. And round the school the country was still only just being built over, and the elms of Surrey stood tall and noble. It was different from the Midlands.

. . . Then starts the rupture with home, with Miriam, away there in Nottinghamshire. And gradually the long illness, and then the death of my mother; and in the sick year after, the collapse for me of Miriam. . . .

Then, in that year, for me, everything collapsed, save the mystery of death, and the haunting of death in life. I was twenty-five, and from the death of my mother, the world began to dissolve around me, beautiful, iridescent, but passing away

---

The "Foreword" was not published during the author's lifetime. It appears in *The Complete Poems of D. H. Lawrence*, edited by V. De Sola Pinto and F. W. Roberts (New York: The Viking Press, 1964), II, 851, hereafter cited as *Complete Poems*. Copyright 1936 by Frieda Lawrence, © 1964 by the Estate of the late Frieda Lawrence Ravagli.

substanceless. Till I almost dissolved away myself, and was very ill: when I was twenty-six.

Then slowly the world came back: or I myself returned: but to another world. . . .

D. H. LAWRENCE

Mrs. Rachel Annand Taylor, a Scottish poet, became a friend of
Lawrence in 1910.

FROM TWO LETTERS TO
RACHEL ANNAND TAYLOR

From Davidson Rd Boys' School,
South Norwood, S.E., Tuesday [?15 November 1910]

. . . You see, my mother has only a fortnight longer, the
doctor says, and it is true, we have been great lovers. Then my
betrothal of six years' standing I have just broken and rather
disgracefully: I have muddled my love affairs most ridiculously
and most maddeningly. So my times being very much distorted,
I am disagreeable. . . .

From Lynn Croft, Eastwood, Notts,
3 December 1910

. . . I have been at home now ten days. My mother is very
near the end. Today I have been to Leicester. I did not get
home till half past nine. Then I ran upstairs. Oh she was very
bad. The pains had been again.

'Oh my dear' I said, 'is it the pains?'

'Not pain now—Oh the weariness' she moaned, so that I
could hardly hear her. I wish she could die tonight.

My sister and I do all the nursing. My sister is only 22. I sit
upstairs hours and hours till I wonder if ever it were true that
I was at London. I seem to have died since, and that is an old
life, dreamy.

I will tell you. My mother was a clever, ironical delicately

---

moulded woman of good, old burgher descent. She married below her. My father was dark, ruddy, with a fine laugh. He is a coal miner. He was one of the sanguine temperament, warm and hearty, but unstable: he lacked principle, as my mother would have said. He deceived her and lied to her. She despised him—he drank.

Their marriage life has been one carnal, bloody fight. I was born hating my father: as early as ever I can remember, I shivered with horror when he touched me. He was very bad before I was born.

This has been a kind of bond between me and my mother. We have loved each other, almost with a husband and wife love, as well as filial and maternal. We knew each other by instinct. She said to my aunt—about me:

'But it has been different with him. He has seemed to be part of me.'—And that is the real case. We have been like one, so sensitive to each other that we never needed words. It has been rather terrible and has made me, in some respects, abnormal.

I think this peculiar fusion of soul (don't think me high-falutin) never comes twice in a life-time—it doesn't seem natural. When it comes it seems to distribute one's consciousness far abroad from oneself, and one understands! I think no one has got 'Understanding' except through love. Now my mother is nearly dead, and I don't quite know how I am. . . .

Muriel[1] is the girl I have broken with. She loves me to madness, and demands the soul of me. I have been cruel to her, and wronged her, but I did not know.

Nobody can have the soul of me. My mother has had it, and nobody can have it again. Nobody can come into my very self again, and breathe me like an atmosphere. Don't say I am hasty this time—I know. . . .

I look at my father—he is like a cinder. It is very terrible, mis-marriage. . . .

---

[1] *Muriel* and *Miriam* refer to the same real person, that is, to Jessie Chambers. (See headnote, p. 478.)

MAY CHAMBERS HOLBROOK

From a memoir by the sister of Jessie Chambers. (See headnote, p. 478.)

[''MOTHER IS DEAD'']

Bert had come home "to wait—," as he said.

"She doesn't want to die."

"No," I said. "How do you comfort her?"

"I can't, but my sisters do. They say, 'You'll see Ern and Grandmother, and all you have missed so much.' But she says, 'I've learned to do without them. I want to stay with those I have here.' And they tell her again how nice it will be to see them in heaven, and how we shall come to her. They can make believe like that, but I can't, I can't. I've nothing to offer her. No comfort at all."

He sat shaking his head slowly, sorrowfully, looking disconsolate.

"Well, she saw your book," I offered. "It must comfort you to have achieved that while she could have pride in it."

But he was shaking his head.

"No, no," he said sadly.

"No?" I echoed.

"No, she didn't like it."

"Why?" I demanded.

He shook his head sadly.

"I don't know. She didn't like it. Even disliked it."

"Still," I protested, "she must be proud of you, of your ability to write a book. You've given her that. It can't help but be a source of pride."

From *D. H. Lawrence: A Composite Biography*, by Edward Nehls (Madison, Wisc.: University of Wisconsin Press, 1957–1959), III, 618–620. Reprinted by permission of the copyright owners, The Regents of the University of Wisconsin.

"No," he insisted miserably, "she doesn't like what I write. Perhaps if it had been romance. . . . But I couldn't write that."

He had sat with his hands clasped loosely between his knees, his head bent. Now he glanced up at me with a piteous smile.

"Strange, isn't it, that I couldn't please her?"

I shook my head.

"What *did* she want?"

"Me," he said softly. "Just me."

"Death long drawn out is an awful thing," Bert said one day, trying to smile.

"It shouldn't be allowed, really," he said presently, and his voice was rough as if his throat ached. For a long time he sat looking into the fire.

"There Mother lies all day, almost silent."

"And you just watch and wait," I said.

"Just watch and wait," he echoed softly.

After a while he repeated it.

"Just watch and wait, watch and wait. There's nothing more to do. She doesn't talk to us at all now. She hardly speaks. She's hardly conscious and yet," he paused and looked at me, "at the exact right time she says, 'Have they got your father's dinner all ready for when he comes home?'" His eyes and voice were soft and questioning. "Why does she think of that? How does she know the time? If either of the girls is there, she asks, 'Is your father's dinner ready?' It's all she can do to say as much as that, and yet she makes the effort. Why is it? Is it mere habit, the habit of thirty-odd years? Or is it that she regrets, or recalls . . . ?"

His voice trailed off into silence as he looked into the fire.

"She's barely conscious now. I doubt if she knows us."

Bert pressed his back against the high armchair and lifted his head as if bracing himself to say it:

"And Father never goes up to see her."

I said, "But he asks."

"Oh, he asks. Every day as he gets in from the pit, he asks, 'How's your mother today?' and we tell him." His voice fell to a shocked, almost horrified tone. "But he never goes up to see her."

"He knows without seeing," I said.

"But he *ought* to go up," he insisted softly. "He ought to *want* to see her. He should go up."

"He can't," I ventured. "Things have happened between them."

"But he was once her lover," he protested with wide eyes.

"That doesn't matter," I said.

"Then what does matter?" he demanded in a voice that broke as if strangled.

"They're asking when I shall be back at school," Bert said. "They say they must put someone in my place if I'm away much longer."

"How can you tell how long?" I asked indignantly.

"Yes, but they've been very good. It stands to reason they can't manage much longer."

After a long silence, Bert said:

"It isn't Mother lying there now. Really it isn't. It's her body, but she isn't there. I don't care what anybody says, Mother is not there. There's no consciousness at all. She doesn't know any of us. She has no pain because that is killed by morphia. I tell you Mother herself is gone."

A day or two later [9 December 1910], Bert came in with a hurt and tender expression on his face.

"She's gone," I said.

He nodded. "It's all over." He turned as the door opened. "Mother died this morning, Bill."

"Your mother's dead, eh?"

"Mother is dead," he repeated.

We all stood looking, asking with our eyes the questions that were tearing at our hearts. What is death? Where is she now? Oh, where is she now?

Suddenly I said:

"Let us help you. Can we help you? Is there *anything* we can do?"

Then we all sat down to discuss immediate plans. Bill was to drive to the station for the flowers on the day of the funeral.

"I shall write little poems to her," Bert said. "She'd like that."

D. H. LAWRENCE

Except for "Spirits Summoned West," these poems were written between 1910 and 1912, while Lawrence was undergoing the crisis which they describe.

Poems: 1910–1912

END OF ANOTHER HOME HOLIDAY[1]

When shall I see the half-moon sink again
Behind the black sycamore at the end of the garden?
When will the scent of the dim white phlox
Creep up the wall to me, and in at my open window?

Why is it, the long, slow stroke of the midnight bell
    (Will it never finish the twelve?)
Falls again and again on my heart with a heavy reproach?
The moon-mist is over the village, out of the mist speaks the bell,
And all the little roofs of the village bow low, pitiful, beseeching,
    resigned.
—Speak, you my home! what is it I don't do well?

Ah home, suddenly I love you
As I hear the sharp clean trot of a pony down the road,
Succeeding sharp little sounds dropping into silence
Clear upon the long-drawn hoarseness of a train across the valley.

.   .   .

The light has gone out, from under my mother's door.
    That she should love me so!—
    She, so lonely, greying now!
    And I leaving her,
    Bent on my pursuits!

[1] From *Complete Poems*, I, 62–64. Copyright 1920 by B. W. Huebsch, Inc., 1948 by Frieda Lawrence.

Love is the great Asker.
The sun and the rain do not ask the secret
Of the time when the grain struggles down in the dark.
The moon walks her lonely way without anguish,
Because no one grieves over her departure.

Forever, ever by my shoulder pitiful love will linger,
Crouching as little houses crouch under the mist when I turn.
Forever, out of the mist, the church lifts up a reproachful finger,
Pointing my eyes in wretched defiance where love hides her face
    to mourn.

Oh! but the rain creeps down to wet the grain
That struggles alone in the dark,
And asking nothing, patiently steals back again!
The moon sets forth o' nights
To walk the lonely, dusky heights
Serenely, with steps unswerving;
Pursued by no sign of bereavement,
No tears of love unnerving
Her constant tread:
While ever at my side,
Frail and sad, with grey, bowed head,
The beggar-woman, the yearning-eyed
Inexorable love goes lagging.

The wild young heifer, glancing distraught,
With a strange new knocking of life at her side
    Runs seeking a loneliness.
The little grain draws down the earth, to hide.
Nay, even the slumberous egg, as it labours under the shell
    Patiently to divide and self-divide,
Asks to be hidden, and wishes nothing to tell.

But when I draw the scanty cloak of silence over my eyes
Piteous love comes peering under the hood;
Touches the clasp with trembling fingers, and tries
To put her ears to the painful sob of my blood;

While her tears soak through to my breast,
    Where they burn and cauterise.

      .   .   .   .   .   .

    The moon lies back and reddens.
    In the valley a corncrake calls
        Monotonously,
    With a plaintive, unalterable voice, that deadens
        My confident activity;
    With a hoarse, insistent request that falls
        Unweariedly, unweariedly,
           Asking something more of me,
                Yet more of me.

ENDLESS ANXIETY [1]

The hoar-frost crumbles in the sun,
    The crisping steam of a train
Melts in the air, while two black birds
    Sweep past the window again.

Along the vacant road a red
    Telegram-bicycle approaches; I wait
In a thaw of anxiety, for the boy
    To leap down at our gate.

He has passed us by; but is it
    Relief that starts in my breast?
Or a deeper bruise of knowing that still
    She has no rest.

---

[1] *Ibid.*, I, 100.

THE END[1]

If I could have put you in my heart,
If but I could have wrapped you in myself
How glad I should have been!
And now the chart
Of memory unrolls again to me
The course of our journey here, here where we part.

And oh, that you had never, never been
Some of your selves, my love; that some
Of your several faces I had never seen!
And still they come before me, and they go;
And I cry aloud in the moments that intervene.

And oh, my love, as I rock for you tonight
And have not any longer any hope
To heal the suffering, or to make requite
For all your life of asking and despair,
I own that some of me is dead tonight.

THE BRIDE[2]

My love looks like a girl tonight,
        But she is old.
The plaits that lie along her pillow
        Are not gold,
But threaded with filigree silver,
        And uncanny cold.

She looks like a young maiden, since her brow
        Is smooth and fair;

---

[1] *Ibid.*, I, 100.
[2] *Ibid.*, I, 101.

Her cheeks are very smooth, her eyes are closed,
      She sleeps a rare,
Still, winsome sleep, so still, and so composed.

Nay, but she sleeps like a bride, and dreams her dreams
      Of perfect things.
She lies at last, the darling, in the shape of her dream,
      And her dead mouth sings
By its shape, like thrushes in clear evenings.

THE VIRGIN MOTHER [1]

My little love, my darling,
You were a doorway to me;
You let me out of the confines
Into this strange countrie
Where people are crowded like thistles,
Yet are shapely and comely to see.

My little love, my dearest,
Twice you have issued me,
Once from your womb, sweet mother,
Once from your soul, to be
Free of all hearts, my darling,
Of each heart's entrance fee.

And so, my love, my mother,
I shall always be true to you.
Twice I am born, my dearest:
To life, and to death, in you;
And this is the life hereafter
Wherein I am true.

I kiss you good-bye, my darling,
Our ways are different now;
You are a seed in the night-time,

---

[1] *Ibid.*, I, 101–102.

I am a man, to plough
The difficult glebe of the future
For seed to endow.

I kiss you good-bye, my dearest,
It is finished between us here.
Oh, if I were calm as you are,
Sweet and still on your bier!
Oh God, if I had not to leave you
Alone, my dear!

Is the last word now uttered?
Is the farewell said?
Spare me the strength to leave you
Now you are dead.
I must go, but my soul lies helpless
Beside your bed.

SORROW[1]

Why does the thin grey strand
Floating up from the forgotten
Cigarette between my fingers,
Why does it trouble me?

Ah, you will understand;
When I carried my mother downstairs,
A few times only, at the beginning
Of her soft-foot malady.

I should find, for a reprimand
To my gaiety, a few long grey hairs
On the breast of my coat; and one by one
I watched them float up the dark chimney.

[1] *Ibid.*, I, 106–107.

DOLOUR OF AUTUMN[1]

The acrid scents of autumn,
Reminiscent of slinking beasts, make me fear
Everything, tear-trembling stars of autumn
And the snore of the night in my ear.

For suddenly, flush-fallen,
All my life, in a rush
Of shedding away, has left me
Naked exposed on the bush.

I on the bush of the globe
Like a newly-naked berry shrink
Disclosed; but 'tis I who am prowling
As well in the scents that slink

Abroad: I in this naked berry
Of flesh that stands dismayed on the bush!
And I in the stealthy, brindled odours
Prowling about the lush

And acrid night of autumn!
My soul, along with the rout
Rank and treacherous, prowling
Disseminated out.

For the night, with a great breath taken
Has drawn my spirit outside
Me, till I reel with disseminated consciousness
Like a man who has died.

At the same time stand exposed
Here on the bush of the globe,
A newly-naked berry of flesh
For the stars to probe.

---

[1] *Ibid.*, I, 107–108.

THE INHERITANCE[1]

Since you did depart
Out of my reach, my darling,
Into the hidden,
I see each shadow start
With recognition, and I
Am wonder-ridden.

I am dazed with the farewell
But I scarcely feel your loss.
You left me a gift
Of tongues, so the shadows tell
Me things, and the silences toss
Me their drift.

You sent me a cloven fire
Out of death, and it burns in the draught
Of the breathing hosts,
Kindles the darkening pyre
Of the mournful, till people waft
Like candid ghosts.

Form after form, in the streets
Waves like a ghost along
Kindled to me;
The star above the house-tops greets
Me every eve with a long
Song fierily.

And all day long, the town
Glimmers with subtle ghosts

---

[1] *Ibid.*, I, 108–109.

Going up and down
In the common, prison-like dress,
Yet their daunted looking flickers
To me, that I answer Yes!

So I am not lonely nor sad
Although bereaved of you,
My love.
I move among a townfolk clad
With words, but the night shows through
Their words as they move.

SILENCE[1]

Since I lost you, I am silence-haunted;
    Sounds wave their little wings
A moment, then in weariness settle
    On the flood that soundless swings.

Whether the people in the street
    Like pattering ripples go by,
Or whether the theatre sighs and sighs
    With a loud, hoarse sigh:

Or the wind shakes a ravel of light
    Over the dead-black river,
Or last night's echoings
    Make the daybreak shiver:

I feel the silence waiting
    To sip them all up again,
In its last completeness drinking
    Down the noise of men.

[1] *Ibid.*, I, 109.

BROODING GRIEF[1]

A yellow leaf, from the darkness
Hops like a frog before me;
Why should I start and stand still?
I was watching the woman that bore me
Stretched in the brindled darkness
Of the sick-room, rigid with will
To die: and the quick leaf tore me
Back to this rainy swill
Of leaves and lamps and the city street mingled
    before me.

LAST WORDS TO MIRIAM[2]

Yours is the sullen sorrow,
    The disgrace is also mine;
Your love was intense and thorough,
Mine was the love of a growing flower
    For the sunshine.

You had the power to explore me,
    Blossom me stalk by stalk;
You woke my spirit, and bore me
To consciousness, you gave me the dour
    Awareness—then I suffered a balk.

Body to body I could not
    Love you, although I would.
We kissed, we kissed though we should not.
You yielded, we threw the last cast,
    And it was no good.

---

[1] *Ibid.*, I, 110–111.
[2] *Ibid.*, I, 111–112.

You only endured, and it broke
    My craftsman's nerve.
No flesh responded to my stroke;
So I failed to give you the last
    Fine torture you did deserve.

You are shapely, you are adorned
    But opaque and null in the flesh;
Who, had I but pierced with the thorned
Full anguish, perhaps had been cast
    In a lovely illumined mesh

Like a painted window; the best
    Fire passed through your flesh,
Undrossed it, and left it blest
In clean new awareness. But now
    Who shall take you afresh?

Now who will burn you free
    From your body's deadness and dross?
Since the fire has failed in me,
What man will stoop in your flesh to plough
    The shrieking cross?

A mute, nearly beautiful thing
    Is your face, that fills me with shame
As I see it hardening;
I should have been cruel enough to bring
    You through the flame.

SUBMERGENCE[1]

When along the pavement,
Palpitating flames of life,
People flicker round me,

I forget my bereavement,
The gap in my life's constellation,
The place where a star used to be.

Nay, though the pole-star
Is blown out like a candle,
And all the heavens are wandering in disarray,
Yet when pleiads of people are
Deployed around me, and I see
The street's long, outstretched milky-way!

When people flicker down the pavement
I forget my bereavement.

THE SHADOW OF DEATH [1]

The earth again like a ship steams out of the dark sea over
The edge of the blue, and the sun stands up to see us glide
Slowly into another day; slowly the rover
Vessel of darkness takes the rising tide.

I, on the deck, am startled by this dawn confronting
Me who am issued amazed from the darkness, stripped
And quailing here in the sunshine, betrayed from haunting
The soundless night whereon our days are shipped.

Feeling myself undawning, the day's light playing upon me,
I who am substance of shadow, I all compact
Of the stuff of the night, finding myself all wrongly
Among crowds of things in the sunshine jostled and racked.

I with the night on my lips, I sigh with the silence of death;
And what do I care though the very stones should cry me
        unreal, though the clouds

Shine in conceit of substance upon me, who am less than
    the rain!
Do I not know the darkness within them? What are they
    but shrouds?

The clouds go down the sky with a wealthy ease,
Casting a shadow of scorn upon me for my share in death;
    but I
Hold my own in the midst of them, darkling defy
The whole of the day to extinguish the shadow I lift on the
    breeze.

Yea, though the very clouds have vantage over me
Enjoying their glancing flight, though love is dead,
I still am not homeless here, I've a tent by day
Of darkness whereon she sleeps on her perfect bed.

Spirits Summoned West [1]

In "Spirits Summoned West" Lawrence looks back from a certain distance in space and time and tries to make amends for having passed so far out of the orbit of the mother and of "Miriam" in the pursuit of his artist's destiny. Of course, this comment doesn't begin to do justice to the extraordinary suggestiveness of this "haunted" poem.

SPIRITS SUMMONED WEST [1]

England seems full of graves to me,
Full of graves.

Women I loved and cherished, like my mother;
Yet I had to tell them to die.

England seems covered with graves to me,
Women's graves.

Women who were gentle
And who loved me
And whom I loved
And told to die.

Women with the beautiful eyes of the old days,
Belief in love, and sorrow of such belief.
"Hush, my love, then, hush.
Hush, and die, my dear!"

Women of the older generation, who knew
The full doom of loving and not being able to take back.
Who understood at last what it was to be told to die.

Now that the graves are made, and covered;

---

[1] *Ibid.*, I, 410–412.

Now that in England pansies and such-like grow on the
    graves of women;
Now that in England is silence, where before was a moving
    of soft-skirted women,
Women with eyes that were gentle in olden belief in love;
Now then that all their yearning is hushed, and covered
    over with earth.

England seems like one grave to me.

And I, I sit on this high American desert
With dark-wrapped Rocky Mountains motionless squatting
    around in a ring,
Remembering I told them to die, to sink into the grave in
    England,
The gentle-kneed women.

So now I whisper: *Come away,*
Come away from the place of graves, come west,
Women,
Women whom I loved and told to die.

Come back to me now,
Now the divided yearning is over;
Now you are husbandless indeed, no more husband to
    cherish like a child
And wrestle with for the prize of perfect love.
No more children to launch in a world you mistrust.
Now you need know in part
No longer, or carry the burden of a man on your heart,
Or the burden of Man writ large.

Now you are disemburdened of Man and a man
Come back to me.
Now you are free of the toils of a would-be-perfect love
Come to me and be still.

Come back then, you who were wives and mothers

And always virgins
Overlooked.
Come back then, mother, my love, whom I told to die.
It was only I who saw the virgin you
That had no home.

The overlooked virgin,
My love.

You overlooked her too.

Now that the grave is made of mother and wife,
Now that the grave is made and lidded over with turf:

Come, delicate, overlooked virgin, come back to me
And be still,
Be glad.

I didn't tell you to die, for nothing.
I wanted the virgin you to be home at last
In my heart.

Inside my innermost heart,
Where the virgin in woman comes home to a man.

The homeless virgin
Who never in all her life could find the way home
To that difficult innermost place in a man.

Now come west, come home,
Women I've loved for gentleness,
For the virginal you.
Find the way now that you never could find in life,
So I told you to die.

Virginal first and last
Is woman.
Now at this last, my love, my many a love,

You whom I loved for gentleness,
Come home to me.

They are many, and I loved them, shall always love them,
And they know it,
The virgins.
And my heart is glad to have them at last.

Now that the wife and mother and mistress is buried in earth,
In English earth,
Come home to me, my love, my loves, my many loves,
Come west to me.

For virgins are not exclusive of virgins
As wives are of wives;
And motherhood is jealous,
But in virginity jealousy does not enter.

Taos [1923]

Two Women

❖◈❖

JESSIE CHAMBERS

Jessie Chambers (1887–1944) was the constant companion of Lawrence's youth and the person upon whom he based the character of Miriam. She was a partial collaborator on early drafts of *Sons and Lovers*, and it was on her initiative that his earliest poems and stories found a publisher. She became the wife of Mr. John R. Wood of Nottingham in 1915.

Lawrence wrote to Jessie Chambers in the spring of 1911:

    . . . *You say you died a death of me, but the death you died of me I must have died also, or you wouldn't have gone on caring about me. . . . They tore me from you, the love of my life. . . . It was the slaughter of the foetus in the womb. . . . I've got a grinning skull-and-crossbones headache. The amount of energy required to live is—how many volts a second?*[1]

[THE CLARIFICATION THAT TIME BRINGS]

    . . . Lawrence began to write his autobiographical novel during 1911, which was perhaps the most arid year of his life. He did not tell me himself that he was at work upon this theme. I heard of it through 'Helen'. He had been working on it for the greater part of the year, and it was some time after our brief meeting in October that he sent the entire manuscript to me, and asked me to tell him what I thought of it.

He had written about two-thirds of the story, and seemed to have come to a standstill. The whole thing was somehow tied up. The characters were locked together in a frustrating

From Jessie Chambers, *D. H. Lawrence: A Personal Record*, by "E. T.," 2d revised edition (New York: Barnes and Noble, 1965), pp. 190–192, 193, 197–198, 201–202, 203–204, 214–215, 216, 219–220, 222–223. Reprinted by permission of Barnes and Noble, Inc., and Frank Cass and Company.

[1] From *Collected Letters*, I, 78.

bondage, and there seemed no way out. The writing oppressed me with a sense of strain. It was extremely tired writing. I was sure that Lawrence had had to force himself to do it. The spontaneity that I had come to regard as the distinguishing feature of his writing was quite lacking. He was telling the story of his mother's married life, but the telling seemed to be at second hand, and lacked the living touch. I could not help feeling that his treatment of the theme was far behind the reality in vividness and dramatic strength. Now and again he seemed to strike a curious, half-apologetic note, bordering on the sentimental. . . . A nonconformist minister whose sermons the mother helped to compose was the foil to the brutal husband. He gave the boy Paul a box of paints, and the mother's heart glowed with pride as she saw her son's budding power. . . . It was story-bookish. The elder brother Ernest, whose short career had always seemed to me most moving and dramatic, was not there at all. I was amazed to find there was no mention of him. The character Lawrence called Miriam was in the story, but placed in a bourgeois setting, in the same family from which he later took the Alvina of *The Lost Girl*. He had placed Miriam in this household as a sort of foundling, and it was there that Paul Morel made her acquaintance.

The theme developed into the mother's opposition to Paul's love for Miriam. In this connection several remarks in this first draft impressed me particularly. Lawrence had written: 'What was it he (Paul Morel) wanted of her (Miriam)? Did he want her to break his mother down in him? Was that what he wanted?'

And again: 'Mrs. Morel saw that if Miriam could only win her son's sex sympathy there would be nothing left for her.'

In another place he said: 'Miriam looked upon Paul as a young man tied to his mother's apron-strings.' Finally, referring to the people around Miriam, he said: 'How should they understand her—petty tradespeople!' But the issue was left quite unresolved. Lawrence had carried the situation to the point of deadlock and stopped there.

As I read through the manuscript I had before me all the

time the vivid picture of the reality. I felt again the tenseness of the conflict, and the impending spiritual clash. So in my reply I told him I was very surprised that he had kept so far from reality in his story; that I thought what had really happened was much more poignant and interesting than the situations he had invented. In particular I was surprised that he had omitted the story of Ernest, which seemed to me vital enough to be worth telling as it actually happened. Finally I suggested that he should write the whole story again, and keep it true to life.

Two considerations prompted me to make these suggestions. First of all I felt that the theme, if treated adequately, had in it the stuff of a magnificent story. It only wanted setting down, and Lawrence possessed the miraculous power of translating the raw material of life into significant form. That was my first reaction to the problem. My deeper thought was that in the doing of it Lawrence might free himself from his strange obsession with his mother. I thought he might be able to work out the theme in the realm of spiritual reality, where alone it could be worked out, and so resolve the conflict in himself. Since he had elected to deal with the big and difficult subject of his family, and the interactions of the various relationships, I felt he ought to do it faithfully—'with both hands earnestly', as he was fond of quoting. It seemed to me that if he was able to treat the theme with strict integrity he would thereby walk into freedom, and cast off the trammelling past like an old skin. . . .

He fell in absolutely with my suggestion and asked me to write what I could remember of our early days, because, as he truthfully said, my recollection of those days was so much clearer than his. I agreed to do so, and began almost at once, but had not got very far when word came that Lawrence was dangerously ill with pneumonia. I was sure he would get better and went on writing the notes for him. When he was convalescent the first thing he wrote was a tiny pencilled message to me, saying: 'Did I frighten you all? I'm sorry. Never mind, I'm soon going to be all right.' . . .

The writing of the novel (still called *Paul Morel*) now went on apace. Lawrence passed the manuscript on to me as he wrote it, a few sheets at a time, just as he had done with *The White Peacock*, only that this story was written with incomparably greater speed and intensity.

The early pages delighted me. Here was all that spontaneous flow, the seemingly effortless translation of life that filled me with admiration. His descriptions of family life were so vivid, so exact, and so concerned with everyday things we had never even noticed before. There was Mrs. Morel ready for ironing, lightly spitting on the iron to test its heat, invested with a reality and significance hitherto unsuspected. It was his power to transmute the common experiences into significance that I always felt to be Lawrence's greatest gift. He did not distinguish between small and great happenings; the common round was full of mystery, awaiting interpretation. Born and bred of working people, he had the rare gift of seeing them from within, and revealing them on their own plane. An incident that particularly pleased me was where Morel was recovering from an accident at the pit, and his friend Jerry came to see him. The conversation of the two men and their tenderness to one another were a revelation to me. I felt that Lawrence was coming into his true kingdom as a creative artist, and an interpreter of the people to whom he belonged. . . .

The novel was written in this state of spirit, at a white heat of concentration. The writing of it was fundamentally a terrific fight for a bursting of the tension. The break came in the treatment of Miriam. As the sheets of manuscript came rapidly to me I was bewildered and dismayed at that treatment. I began to perceive that I had set Lawrence a task far beyond his strength. In my confidence I had not doubted that he would work out the problem with integrity. But he burked the real issue. It was his old inability to face his problem squarely. His mother had to be supreme, and for the sake of that supremacy every disloyalty was permissible.

The realization of this slowly dawned on me as I read the manuscript. He asked for my opinion, but comment seemed futile—not merely futile, but impossible. I could not appeal to Lawrence for justice as between his treatment of Mrs. Morel and Miriam. He left off coming to see me and sent the manuscript by post. His avoidance of me was significant. I felt it was useless to attempt to argue the matter out with him. Either he was aware of what he was doing and persisted, or he did not know, and in that case no amount of telling would enlighten him. It was one of the things he had to find out for himself. The baffling truth, of course, lay between the two. He was aware, but he was under the spell of the domination that had ruled his life hitherto, and he refused to know. So instead of a release and a deliverance from bondage, the bondage was glorified and made absolute. His mother conquered indeed, but the vanquished one was her son. In *Sons and Lovers* Lawrence handed his mother the laurels of victory.

The Clara of the second half of the story was a clever adaptation of elements from three people, and her creation arose as a complement to Lawrence's mood of failure and defeat. The events related had no foundation in fact, whatever their psychological significance. Having utterly failed to come to grips with his problem in real life, he created the imaginary Clara as a compensation. Even in the novel the compensation is unreal and illusory, for at the end Paul Morel calmly hands her back to her husband, and remains suspended over the abyss of his despair. Many of the incidents struck me as cheap and commonplace, in spite of the hard brilliance of the narration. I realized that I had naively credited Lawrence with superhuman powers of detachment. . . .

Lawrence had said that he never took sides; but his attitude placed him tacitly on the side of those who had mocked at love—except mother-love. He seemed to have identified himself with the prevailing atmosphere of ridicule and innuendo. It was a fatal alignment, for it made me see him as a philistine of the philistines, and not, as I had always believed, inwardly honouring an unspoken bond, and suffering himself from the strange hostility to love. He had sometimes argued—in an effort to convince himself—that morality and art have nothing to do with one another. However that might be, I could not help feeling that integrity and art have a great deal to do with one another. The best I could think of him was that he had run with the hare and hunted with the hounds . . . His significance withered and his dimensions shrank. He ceased to matter supremely. . . .

I saw Lawrence for the next and last time on a Sunday morning some three weeks later when father and I drove to my sister's cottage. I did not know that Lawrence was spending the week-end there, but I was not surprised to see him. We arrived unexpectedly and I could not help seeing that my coming startled him. He looked a different man from the one I had seen momentarily at the barrier of the railway station. The look of despair was gone. He appeared more ordinary and equable. But for once I saw Lawrence tongue-tied. He didn't know what to say to us. He went outside and sat on the low garden wall, leaning forward and looking intently at the ground, in an odd attitude of concentration. Presently he came into the cottage and looked at me curiously as though he would ask whether I had brought him some message. I asked him if he would care to drive home with us. He said he would like to, only my sister was expecting him to stay. So, true to his habit of letting other people make his decisions, he left it with her, and she, having prepared for him, naturally preferred that he should stay. But he drove part of the way with us. He almost winced at my father's casual tone, so different from the warmth of old days.

Lawrence talked to us with a forced brightness about his going to Germany. He expected to go within a few days. I asked about his work, and he spoke of a play that was perhaps going to be produced in London. On the level above Watnall hill he got out of the trap to return by the footpath over the fields. We shook hands and said good-bye like casual acquaintances, and father hoped he would manage to keep in better health. Lawrence thanked him. Before we disappeared round a bend in the road I turned and saw him still standing where he had alighted, looking after us. I waved my hand and he raised his hat with the familiar gesture. I never saw him again. . . .

It was not long before I had a postcard from Lawrence, a beautiful view of Trier Cathedral. In another week or so came a letter in which he said: 'I am going through *Paul Morel*. I'm sorry it turned out as it has. You'll have to go on forgiving me.'

His words aroused no response in me. My forgiveness or non-forgiveness was equally irrelevant. What mattered was something in himself, something he had to find out, which only the inexorable logic of circumstance could show him. As for myself, I felt that I had suffered a terrible inner injury. It required all my effort to avoid a collapse. . . .

Lawrence had not replied to my letter telling him I was glad to feel myself set free, and in the following spring his first book of poems was published. A copy came to me from the publisher—with the author's compliments. These were for the most part the poems that Lawrence had written in the thick little college notebook that I knew so well. Very few of the pieces were new to me. I was glad to receive the book, so I asked my sister for his address, and wrote, thanking him for it, and made a few remarks about the poems. His reply, and also a bulky parcel of proof-sheets, came several days later. I felt that my comments were unwelcome, for Lawrence wrote: 'I think the little poetry book is all right . . . I'm sending you the proofs of the novel, I think you ought to see it before it's published. I heard from A. that you were in digs. again. Send the novel on to her when you've done with it [here he gave her address]. This last year hasn't been all roses for me. I've had my ups and my downs out here with Frieda. But we mean to marry as soon as the divorce is through. We shall settle down quite quietly somewhere, probably in Berkshire. Frieda and I discuss you endlessly. We should like you to come out to us some time, if you would care to. But we are leaving here in about a week, it's getting too hot for us, I mean the weather, not the place. I must leave off now, they're waiting for me. . . .'

I read his letter several times, not knowing whether to laugh or to cry. I felt suffocated. The clumsiness of his approach was plain, but to my mind there was a priggish note as well. It was the tone of the letter that offended me. There was the off-handed attempt to be casual and matter-of-fact, and yet to appeal to my sympathy. I wondered also why he should send his novel to me in this manner, as though I was a stranger to it. I knew it far too well to have any desire to read it again. Indeed, I didn't dare to risk a second reading, for I was by no means sure of my capacity to recover a second time. I did glance through some pages, however, hoping that in the interval his outlook might have mellowed and led him to soften some harshness. But I found both story and mood alike unchanged. . . .

In the days when the cloud of his mother's disapproval first began to loom heavy over our young horizon, Lawrence said to me, 'Of course, it will be *you* who will write my epitaph.'

I was too pained and startled to speak, and answered only with a shake of the head. He smiled at me brilliantly and re-iterated softly, nodding:

'Oh yes, you will. It will fall to you to write my epitaph.'

And from time to time in moments of intense feeling he would repeat his strange forecast. His words had no literal meaning for me then, because in those days Lawrence and death seemed to stand at opposite poles. He was always to me a symbol of overflowing life. He seemed able to enter into other lives, and not only human lives. With wild things, flowers and birds, a rabbit in a snare, the speckled eggs in a hole in the ground he was in primal sympathy—a living vibration passed between him and them, so that I always saw him, in the strict-est sense of the word, immortal. Perhaps it was because these intuitions of hidden things flashed upon us now and again in swift illumination that he laid this task upon me. And with the clarification that time brings and its truer perspective, those of us whose youth was the richer for knowing him see again the dear familiar figure, and we remember how much of our joy came to us through the inspiration of Lawrence's gay and dauntless spirit.

FRIEDA LAWRENCE RAVAGLI

Frieda Lawrence, née von Richthofen (1879–1956), left her English husband, Ernest Weekley, to marry Lawrence, whom she survived by a quarter century. Her last years were spent in northern New Mexico as the wife of Captain Angelo Ravagli. In addition to her autobiography, *Not I But the Wind* . . . , she wrote *The Memoirs and Correspondence of Frieda Lawrence*, issued posthumously in 1961 under the editorship of E. W. Tedlock.

[AS I LOOK BACK]

As I look back now it surprises me that Lawrence could have loved me at first sight as he did. I hardly think I could have been a very lovable woman at the time. I was thirty-one and had three children. My marriage seemed a success. I had all a woman can reasonably ask. Yet there I was, all "smock ravelled," to use one of Lawrence's phrases.

I had just met a remarkable disciple of Freud and was full of undigested theories. This friend did a lot for me. I was living like a somnambulist in a conventional set life and he awakened the consciousness of my own proper self.

Being born and reborn is no joke, and being born into your own intrinsic self, that separates and singles you out from all the rest—it's a painful process.

When people talk about sex, I don't know what they mean—as if sex hopped about by itself like a frog, as if it had no relation to the rest of living, one's growth, one's ripening. What people mean by sex will always remain incomprehensible to me, but I am thankful to say sex is a mystery to me.

Theories applied to life aren't any use. Fanatically I believed that if only sex were "free" the world would straight-away turn into a paradise. I suffered and struggled at outs with society, and felt absolutely isolated. The process left me unbalanced. I felt alone. What could I do, when there were so many mil-

From *Not I But the Wind* . . . (New York: The Viking Press, 1934), pp. 3–6, 55–57. Reprinted by permission of Laurence Pollinger Ltd. and the Estate of the late Mrs. Frieda Lawrence.

lions who thought differently from me? But I couldn't give in, I couldn't submit. It wasn't that I felt hostile, only different. I could not accept society. And then Lawrence came. It was an April day in 1912. He came for lunch, to see my husband about a lectureship at a German University. Lawrence was also at a critical period of his life just then. The death of his mother had shaken the foundations of his health for a second time. He had given up his post as a schoolmaster at Croydon. He had done with his past life.

I see him before me as he entered the house. A long thin figure, quick straight legs, light sure movements. He seemed so obviously simple. Yet he arrested my attention. There was something more than met the eye. What kind of a bird was this?

The half-hour before lunch the two of us talked in my room, French windows open, curtains fluttering in the spring wind, my children playing on the lawn.

He said he had finished with his attempts at knowing women. I was amazed at the way he fiercely denounced them. I had never before heard anything like it. I laughed, yet I could tell he had tried very hard, and had cared. We talked about Œdipus and understanding leaped through our words.

After leaving, that night, he walked all the way to his home. It was a walk of at least five hours. Soon afterwards he wrote to me: "You are the most wonderful woman in all England."

I wrote back: "You don't know many women in England, how do you know?" He told me, the second time we met: "You are quite unaware of your husband, you take no notice of him." I disliked the directness of this criticism.

He came on Easter Sunday [7 April 1912]. It was a bright, sunny day. The children were in the garden hunting for Easter eggs.

The maids were out and I wanted to make some tea. I tried to turn on the gas but didn't know how. Lawrence became cross at such ignorance. Such a direct critic! It was something my High and Mightiness was very little accustomed to.

Yet Lawrence really understood me. From the first he saw through me like glass, saw how hard I was trying to keep up a cheerful front. I thought it was so despicable and unproud and unclean to be miserable, but he saw through my hard and bright shell.

What I cannot understand is how he could have loved me and wanted me at that time. I certainly did have what he called "sex in the head"; a theory of loving men. My real self was frightened and shrank from contact like a wild thing.

So our relationship developed.

One day we met at a station in Derbyshire. My two small girls were with us. We went for a long walk through the early-spring woods and fields. The children were running here and there as young creatures will.

We came to a small brook, a little stone bridge crossed it. Lawrence made the children some paper boats and put matches in them and let them float downstream under the bridge. Then he put daisies in the brook, and they floated down with their upturned faces. Crouched by the brook, playing there with the children, Lawrence forgot about me completely.

Suddenly I knew I loved him. He had touched a new tenderness in me. After that, things happened quickly.

He came to see me one Sunday. My husband was away and I said: "Stay the night with me." "No, I will not stay in your husband's house while he is away, but you must tell him the truth and we will go away together, because I love you."

I was frightened. I knew how terrible such a thing would be for my husband, he had always trusted me. But a force stronger than myself made me deal him the blow. I left the next day. I left my son with his father, my two little girls I took to their grandparents in London. I said good-bye to them on Hampstead Heath, blind and blank with pain, dimly feeling I should never again live with them as I had done.

Lawrence met me at Charing Cross Station, to go away with him, never to leave him again.

He seemed to have lifted me body and soul out of all my past life. This young man of twenty-six had taken all my fate, all my destiny, into his hands. And we had known each other barely for six weeks. There had been nothing else for me to do but submit. . . .

At Gargnano we found Villa Igéa to spend the winter.

Lawrence for the first time had a place of his own. The first floor of a large villa, our windows looking over the lake, the road running underneath, opposite us the Monte Baldo in rosy sunsets. "Green star Sirius dribbling over the lake," as Lawrence says in one of his poems.

Here began my first attempt at housekeeping. It was uphill work, in that big bare kitchen with the "fornelli" and the big copper pans. Often the stews and "fritti" had to be rescued, and he would come nobly from his work, never grumbling, when I called: "Lorenzo, the pigeons are burning, what shall I do?"

The first time I washed sheets was a disaster. They were so large and wet, their wetness was overwhelming. The kitchen floor was flooded, the table drenched, I dripped from hair to feet.

When Lawrence found me all misery he called: "The One and Only" (which name stood for the one and only phoenix, when I was uppish) "is drowning, oh, dear!" I was rescued and dried, the kitchen wiped and soon the sheets were hanging to dry in the garden where the "cachi" were hanging red from the trees. One morning he brought me breakfast in bed and in the Italian bedroom there was a spittoon and to my horror a scorpion was on it. To Lawrence's surprise I said, when he killed it: "Birds of a feather flock together."

"Ungrateful woman . . . here I am the faithful knight killing the dragons and that's all I get."

One of our favourite walks was to Bogliacco, the next village on the Garda, where we drank wine and ate chestnuts with the Bersaglieri who seemed quiet and sad and didn't say much. My window high up over the road was a joy to me. Bersaglieri came past in their running march with a gay spark of a tenente at their head, singing: "Tripoli sara' Italiana." Secretly people did their bargaining under my windows, at night the youths played their guitars; when I peeped Lawrence was cross.

He was then rewriting his *Sons and Lovers*, the first book he wrote with me, and I lived and suffered that book, and wrote bits of it when he would ask me: "What do you think my mother felt like then?" I had to go deeply into the character of Miriam and all the others; when he wrote his mother's death he was ill and his grief made me ill too, and he said: "If my mother had lived I could never have loved you, she wouldn't have let me go." But I think he got over it; only, this fierce and overpowerful love had harmed the boy who was not strong enough to bear it. In after years he said: "I would write a different *Sons and Lovers* now; my mother was wrong, and I thought she was absolutely right."

I think a man is born twice: first his mother bears him, then he has to be reborn from the woman he loves. Once, sitting on the little steamer on the lake he said: "Look, that little woman is like my mother." His mother, though dead, seemed so alive and *there* still to him.

Towards the end of *Sons and Lovers* I got fed up and turned against all this "house of Atreus" feeling, and I wrote a skit called: *Paul Morel, or His Mother's Darling*. He read it and said, coldly: "This kind of thing isn't called a skit."

While we were at Villa Igéa Lawrence wrote also *Twilight in Italy*, and most of the poems from *Look! We Have Come Through!*

His courage in facing the dark recesses of his own soul impressed me always, scared me sometimes.

In his heart of hearts I think he always dreaded women, felt that they were in the end more powerful than men. Woman is so absolute and undeniable. Man moves, his spirit flies here and there, but you can't go beyond a woman. From her man is born and to her he returns for his ultimate need of body and soul. She is like earth and death to which all return.

Lawrence and Psychoanalysis

✿❖✿❖✿❖✿❖✿❖✿❖✿❖✿❖✿❖✿❖✿❖✿❖✿❖✿❖✿❖✿❖✿❖✿❖✿❖✿

D. H. LAWRENCE

TO EDWARD GARNETT

From Villa Igéa, Gargnano, Italy, 14 November 1912

Dear Garnett: Your letter has just come. I hasten to tell you I sent the MS. of the *Paul Morel* novel to Duckworth registered, yesterday. And I want to defend it, quick. I wrote it again, pruning it and shaping it and filling it in. I tell you it has got form—*form*: haven't I made it patiently, out of sweat as well as blood. It follows this idea: a woman of character and refinement goes into the lower class, and has no satisfaction in her own life. She has had a passion for her husband, so the children are born of passion, and have heaps of vitality. But as her sons grow up she selects them as lovers—first the eldest, then the second. These sons are *urged* into life by their reciprocal love of their mother—urged on and on. But when they come to manhood, they can't love, because their mother is the strongest power in their lives, and holds them. It's rather like Goethe and his mother and Frau von Stein and Christiana—As soon as the young men come into contact with women, there's a split. William gives his sex to a fribble, and his mother holds his

---

492 / CONTEXTS OF RESPONSE

soul. But the split kills him, because he doesn't know where he is. The next son gets a woman who fights for his soul—fights his mother. The son loves the mother—all the sons hate and are jealous of the father. The battle goes on between the mother and the girl, with the son as object. The mother gradually proves stronger, because of the tie of blood. The son decides to leave his soul in his mother's hands, and, like his elder brother go for passion. He gets passion. Then the split begins to tell again. But, almost unconsciously, the mother realises what is the matter, and begins to die. The son casts off his mistress, attends to his mother dying. He is left in the end naked of everything, with the drift towards death.

It is a great tragedy, and I tell you I have written a great book. It's the tragedy of thousands of young men in England . . .

SIMON O. LESSER

Simon O. Lesser has been a research associate at University of
Chicago Institute, the New York Psychoanalytic Institute, the
Washington School of Psychiatry, and the Institute for Motiva-
tional Research. He has taught English at New York University and
lectures in English at the University of Massachusetts. His *Fiction
and the Unconscious* applies psychoanalytic principles to problems
of criticism with flexibility and tact and, in the following excerpt,
with direct relevance to *Sons and Lovers*.

[TWO MODES OF INSIGHT]

If certain aspects of the subject matter of fiction tend to
arouse anxiety, others tend to still it. Narrative art begins to
checkmate anxiety at its very source. It offers us gratifications of
buried impulses, gratifications more extreme than we would
be likely to fantasy for ourselves, much less act out, but at the
same time it shows how inexorably such gratifications lead to
punishment, and the punishments are terrible, too, scaled to the
transgressions. Were it otherwise, fiction would indeed increase
inner tension, both by arousing feelings of guilt and by making
the impulses it released more clamorous and more difficult to
control. In fact . . . the cathartic experience we have in reading
fiction strengthens the hand of the ego in controlling repudiated
impulses.

Other safeguards are necessary, however; the unleashing of
warded-off tendencies is a dangerous affair. The additional
safeguards are provided by form.

Form combats anxiety first of all by trying to reduce feelings of guilt—not only the guilt aroused by a particular story,
but the guilt which hounds us always because of our unaccept-
able, and in particular, our destructive, impulses. By its very
nature form is committed to love and creation rather than

From *Fiction and the Unconscious* (Boston: The Beacon Press, 1957),
pp. 173–178. Copyright © 1957 by Simon O. Lesser. Reprinted by
permission.

hatred and destruction. It manifests an almost material determination to protect everything it treats from harm, to emphasize its wholeness, its vitality, its perfection. In responding to form we are protesting that we, too, are dominated by love, and at the same time are atoning for the rage and hatred which we cannot completely eradicate from our hearts even when we take refuge in the realm of art.

The solicitude form displays for everything it touches is only one of the means it employs to inform us that it respects the values of the ego and superego. One attribute of form, mastery or control, could be looked upon as an "objective correlative" of certain functions of the ego, those concerned with regulating the instincts and bringing them into harmony with the demands of conscience. Control is a kind of animal trainer in whose presence we feel safe no matter how great the ferocity of the animals which are brought forth. The analogy is apt, for it suggests the precise feeling a firmly controlled story arouses in us—a feeling not so much of freedom from danger as of security in the face of danger.

Of the already identified resources available to form for combatting anxiety, we need remind ourselves of only one more: its capacity to keep the most frightening implications of its material from the attention of consciousness. Unpalatable matters may be disguised but we shall not pause to consider the various means used to accomplish this. We are already familiar with some of them, and the subject of disguise is discussed elsewhere. Furthermore, if by disguise we mean the deliberate, or even the pre-conscious or unconscious, *alteration* of material so that its real significance will not be perceived, though important it is far less important a device than was originally thought. Fiction seldom has to go this far out of its way to conceal anything. The language in which it is likely to be conceived and cast from the start—a language so natural to fiction that it has been accepted unthinkingly by generations of storytellers and readers alike—tends by its very nature to inhibit the apprehension of anxiety-producing layers of meaning in conceptual terms. Fiction speaks to us in a language which *effortlessly* conceals many things from conscious awareness at the same time that it communicates them to the unconscious with extraordinary vividness.

I am by no means sure that I have succeeded in conveying the nature of this language or the extent to which fiction utilizes it. The concept of non-discursive communication is new in esthetic theory, and may not seem applicable to the literary arts since their medium is words. But anyone can quickly acquire an appreciation of the difference between the language of fiction and ordinary conceptual discourse by undertaking a simple and pleasant experiment. The experiment I propose is to read in quick succession Freud's "The Most Prevalent Form of Degradation in Erotic Life" and D. H. Lawrence's *Sons and Lovers*. By coincidence they were written at about the same time and published within a year of one another—the paper in 1912, the novel in 1913. They have an almost schematic correspondence: they both explore the painful opposition which arises in some men between tender and sensual love—an opposition which may be so extreme that, "Where such men love they have no desire and where they desire they cannot love." Both works show that the primary factor to which this opposition can be traced is the young boy's overattachment to the mother.

Despite the close relationship between the novel and the paper, which could be developed in greater detail, *one could read the former after reading the latter without becoming aware of it.* It is necessary to read the novel in a way quite different from that in which one ordinarily reads fiction—to have advance knowledge of the parallels and to be looking for them—to become aware of them during the act of reading. Is this because Lawrence learned of Freud's ideas, or by coincidence had precisely the same ideas, and then sought to embody them in a work of fiction which would at the same time conceal them from awareness? Almost certainly this is not the explanation. Lawrence may have never been aware of some of

the ideas to be found in his novel;[1] and he was not primarily
concerned with the ideas of which he was aware *as ideas*, as
abstract generalities. He was concerned with telling a story—
a story which grew out of his own experience and needs. He
was concerned with Paul Morel (behind whom it is impossible
not to discern Lawrence) and his mother and Miriam and
Clara. His story represents an attempt to imagine how matters
would have worked out among these people—and to some
extent, of course, to re-experience actual occurrences. Whatever explanations are offered for his characters' conduct are
intuitive, casual and fragmentary; very few generalizations are
drawn.

It happens that the behavior of Lawrence's characters illustrates some of the very mechanisms Freud explains systemati-
cally in "The Most Prevalent Form of Degradation in Erotic
Life." From Lawrence's novel the dissecting intelligence of
the critic can abstract the main ideas Freud develops in his
paper; and it is worthwhile to abstract them—doing so may
help the critic to crystallize certain of his impressions of the
book. But whereas Freud labored to bring his ideas before us
as clearly as possible, it would not be an exaggeration to say
that Lawrence was determined that we should *not* have
"ideas," that we should not think conceptually, as we read his
story. More accurately, he had a different objective: to engage us emotionally, to induce us to share the experiences of
his characters; and he intuitively recognized that he could not
achieve this objective if he spoke to the intellect alone. Lawrence himself, as Aldous Huxley has pointed out, "refused to
know abstractly." As man and as artist, he felt driven to
render his story with as much concreteness, vividness and im-

[1] There is no evidence, for example, that he recognized the extent to
which Paul's tie to his mother determined his very selection of Miriam
and his failure to respond to either Miriam or Clara in a way which did
justice to all their qualities. Lawrence did, however, recognize that Paul
was fettered to his mother and that this made it difficult for him to
establish a good relationship with any other woman. See *The Letters of
D. H. Lawrence*, edited by Aldous Huxley (New York: Viking, 1932),
p. 78. [S.O.L.]

mediacy as he could muster. The scenes and incidents must speak for themselves, and they speak in a language which is vaguer but richer and more stirring than the language of intellectual discourse.

There is no word which will quite do justice to the way the language he employs is apprehended. Consider the scene where Paul, walking in his mother's garden at night, decides finally to give up Miriam. It is apparent enough that we do not formulate the meaning of this scene; how can one formulate the precise significance of the scent of a flower? Nor is it quite accurate to say that we *infer* what is going on in Paul; the word implies a more purposive kind of intellectual activity and a greater gulf between reader and character than actually obtains at this point. Even the word *sense* implies such a gulf. If we are absorbed in the novel, we are emphatically linked with Paul, we feel what he feels, we are affected as he is affected by the sights, smells and sounds which assail him. It would be redundant and, we sense, a profanation to state what we feel in words.

In a sense it is foolish to compare paper and novel, they are incommensurate; but the reading of both in quick succession is likely to give us increased respect for the capacity of fiction to deal with potentially disturbing material without arousing anxiety. Freud's essay may make us squirm at times. There is some evidence that one of the statements his argument demanded caused him to recoil, despite his scientific detachment and long habit of confronting the facts about man's nature, however repugnant they might be. Though the novel gives us an experience of greater immediacy and intensity than the paper, it produces less of that disquiet which is a sign of inner anxiety. Of course, the sensory language of fiction, of which Lawrence was such a master, is only one of the factors responsible for this achievement.

SIGMUND FREUD

Sigmund Freud (1856–1939), the founder of psychoanalysis, is one of the master spirits of the contemporary world. The following essay is one of his studies in "metapsychology," a term Freud used to designate those of his writings which applied the insights derived from clinical practice and scientific research to the largest questions of modern civilization and its discontents.

THE MOST PREVALENT FORM OF DEGRADATION IN EROTIC LIFE (1912)

I

If a practising psychoanalyst asks himself what disorder he is most often called upon to remedy, he is obliged to reply—apart from anxiety in all its many forms—psychical impotence. This strange disorder affects men of a strongly libidinous nature, and is manifested by a refusal on the part of the sexual organs to execute the sexual act, although both before and after the attempt they can show themselves intact and competent to do so, and although a strong mental inclination to carry out the act is present. The man gets his first inkling in the direction of understanding his condition by discovering that he fails in this way only with certain women, whereas it never happens with others. He knows then that the inhibition of his masculine potency is due to some quality in the sexual object, and sometimes he describes having had a sensation of holding back, of having perceived some check within him which interfered successfully with his conscious intention. What this inner opposition is, however, he cannot guess, or what quality in the sexual

From *The Collected Papers of Sigmund Freud*, Chapter XII, Volume 4, edited by Ernest Jones (New York: Basic Books, Inc., 1959), 203–216; also published in *The Complete Psychological Works of Sigmund Freud*, Standard Edition, Volume 11 (London: The Hogarth Press Ltd.). Reprinted by permission of Basic Books, Inc., Sigmund Freud Copyrights Ltd., Mrs. Alix Strachey, and The Hogarth Press Ltd.

object makes it active. If the failure has been repeated several times he probably concludes, by the familiar erroneous line of argument, that a recollection of the first occasion acted as a disturbance by causing anxiety and brought about the subsequent failures; the first occasion itself he refers to some "accidental" occurrence.

Psychoanalytic studies of psychical impotence have already been carried out and published by various writers.[1] Every analyst can, from his own experience, confirm the explanations adduced in them. The disorder is in fact due to the inhibiting influence of certain complexes in the mind that are withdrawn from the knowledge of the person in question. As the most universal feature of this pathogenic material an incestuous fixation on mother and sister which has not been surmounted stands out. In addition to this, the influence of accidental impressions of a painful kind connected with infantile sexuality comes into consideration, together with those factors which in general reduce the amount of libido available for the female sexual object.[2]

When cases of severe psychical impotence are subjected to exhaustive study by means of psychoanalysis, the following psycho-sexual processes are found to be operative. Here again—as very probably in all neurotic disorders—the root of the trouble lies in an arrest occurring during the course of development of the libido to that ultimate form which may be called normal. To ensure a fully normal attitude in love, two currents of feeling have to unite—we may describe them as the tender, affectionate feelings and the sensual feelings—and this confluence of the two currents has in these cases not been achieved.

Of these two currents affection is the older. It springs from the very earliest years of childhood, and was formed on the foundation provided by the interests of the self-preservative instinct; it is directed towards the members of the family and

---

[1] M. Steiner, *Die funktionelle Impotenz des Mannes und ihre Behandlung*; W. Stekel, in *Nervöse Angstzustände und ihre Behandlung*; Ferenczi, "Analytic Interpretation and Treatment of Psychosexual Impotence." [S.F.]

[2] W. Stekel, *loc. cit.*, p. 191 *et seq.* [S.F.]

those who have care of the child. From the very beginning elements from the sexual instincts are taken up into it—component-parts of the erotic interest—which are more or less clearly visible in childhood and are invariably discovered in the neurotic by psychoanalysis in later years. This tender feeling represents the earliest childish choice of object. From this we see that the sexual instincts find their first *objects* along the paths laid down by the ego-instincts and in accordance with the value set by the latter on their objects, in just the same way that the first sexual *satisfactions* are experienced, *i.e.* in connection with the bodily functions necessary for self-preservation. The "affection" shown to the child by its parents and attendants which seldom fails to betray its erotic character ("a child is an erotic plaything") does a great deal to increase the erotic contributions to the cathexes that are put forth by the ego-instincts in the child, and to raise them to a level which is bound to leave its mark on future development, especially when certain other circumstances leading to the same result are present.

These fixations of the child's feelings of affection are maintained through childhood, continually absorbing erotic elements, which are thus deflected from their sexual aims. Then, when the age of puberty is reached, there supervenes upon this state of things a powerful current of "sensual" feeling the aims of which can no longer be disguised. It never fails, apparently, to pursue the earlier paths and to invest the objects of the primary infantile choice with currents of libido that are now far stronger. But in relation to these objects it is confronted by the obstacle of the incest-barrier that has in the meanwhile been erected; consequently it seeks as soon as possible to pass on from these objects unsuited for real satisfaction to others in the world outside, with whom a real sexual life may be carried on. These new objects are still chosen after the pattern (imago) of the infantile ones; in time, however, they attract to themselves the tender feeling that had been anchored to those others. A man shall leave father and mother—according to the Biblical precept—and cleave to his wife; then are tenderness and sensuality united. The greatest intensity of sensual passion will bring with it the highest mental estimation of the object (the normal overestimation of the sexual object characteristic of men).

Two factors will determine whether this advance in the development of the libido is accomplished successfully or otherwise. First, there is the degree of frustration in reality which is opposed to the new object-choice and reduces its value for the person concerned. For there is no sense in entering upon a choice of object if one is not to be allowed to choose at all or has no prospect of being able to choose one fit for the part. The second factor is the degree of attraction that may be exercised by the infantile objects which should be relinquished, and this is proportionate to the erotic cathexis already attaching to them in childhood. If these two factors are sufficiently powerful, the general mechanism leading to the formation of neurosis will come into operation. The libido turns away from reality, and is absorbed into the creation of phantasy (introversion), strengthens the images of the first sexual objects, and becomes fixated to them. The incest-barrier, however, necessarily has the effect that the libido attaching to these objects should remain in the unconscious. The sensual current of feeling is now attached to unconscious ideas of objects, and discharge of it in onanistic acts contributes to a strengthening of this fixation. It constitutes no change in this state of affairs if the step forward to extraneous objects which miscarried in reality is now made in phantasy, if in the phantasied situations leading up to onanistic gratification the extraneous objects are but replacements of the original ones. The phantasies become capable of entering consciousness by this replacement, but in the direction of applying the libido externally in the real world no advance has been made.

In this way it may happen that the whole current of sensual feeling in a young man may remain attached in the unconscious to incestuous objects, or, to put it in another way, may be fixated to incestuous phantasies. The result of this is then total impotence, which is perhaps even reinforced by an actual weakening, developing concurrently, of the organs destined to execute the sexual act.

Less severe conditions will suffice to bring about what is usually called psychical impotence. It is not necessary that the whole amount of sensual feeling should be fated to conceal itself behind the tender feelings; it may remain sufficiently strong and unchecked to secure some outlet for itself in reality. The sexual activity of such people shows unmistakable signs, however, that it has not behind it the whole mental energy belonging to the instinct. It is capricious, easily upset, often clumsily carried out, and not very pleasurable. Above all, however, it avoids all association with feelings of tenderness. A restriction has thus been laid upon the object-choice. The sensual feeling that has remained active seeks only objects evoking no reminder of the incestuous persons forbidden to it; the impression made by someone who seems deserving of high estimation leads, not to a sensual excitation, but to feelings of tenderness which remain erotically ineffectual. The erotic life of such people remains dissociated, divided between two channels, the same two that are personified in art as heavenly and earthly (or animal) love. Where such men love they have no desire and where they desire they cannot love. In order to keep their sensuality out of contact with the objects they love, they seek out objects whom they need not love; and, in accordance with the laws of the "sensitivity of complexes" and the "return of the repressed," the strange refusal implied in psychical impotence is made whenever the objects selected in order to avoid incest possess some trait, often quite inconspicuous, reminiscent of the objects that must be avoided.

The principal means of protection used by men against this complaint consists in *lowering* the sexual object in their own estimation, while reserving for the incestuous object and for those who represent it the overestimation normally felt for the sexual object. As soon as the sexual object fulfils the condition of being degraded, sensual feeling can have free play, considerable sexual capacity and a high degree of pleasure can be developed. Another factor also contributes to this result. There is usually little refinement in the ways of obtaining erotic pleasure habitual to people in whom the tender and the sensual currents of feeling are not properly merged; they have remained addicted to perverse sexual aims which they feel it a considerable deprivation not to gratify, yet to such men this seems possible only with a sexual object who in their estimate is degraded and worth little.

The motives behind the phantasies mentioned in the preceding paper, by which boys degrade the mother to the level of a prostitute, now become intelligible. They represent efforts to bridge the gulf between the two currents of erotic feeling, at least in phantasy: by degrading her, to win the mother as an object for sensual desires.

II

So far we have pursued our inquiry into psychical impotence from a medico-psychological angle which is not justified by the title of this paper.[3] It will prove however, that this introduction was necessary in order to provide an approach to our actual theme.

We have reduced psychical impotence to a disunion between the tender and sensual currents of erotic feeling, and have explained this inhibition in development itself as an effect of strong fixations in childhood and of frustration in reality later, after the incest-barrier has intervened. There is one principal objection to raise against this doctrine: it does too much, it explains why certain persons suffer from psychical impotence, but it makes it seem puzzling that others can escape the affliction. Since all the factors that appear to be involved, the strong fixation in childhood, the incest-barrier, and the frustration in the years of development after puberty, are demonstrably present in practically all civilized persons, one would be justified in expecting that psychical impotence was universally prevalent in civilized countries and not a disease of particular individuals.

---

[3] Cf. *The Collected Papers of Sigmund Freud*, IV, edited by Ernest Jones, New York: Basic Books, Inc., 1959, p. 54.

It would not be difficult to escape from this conclusion by pointing to the quantitative element in the causation of disease, that greater or lesser amount of each single factor which determines whether or not recognizable disease results. But although this argument is in my opinion sound, I do not myself intend to employ it in refuting the objection advanced above. I shall, on the contrary, put forward the proposition that psychical impotence is far more widespread than is generally supposed, and that some degree of this condition does in fact characterize the erotic life of civilized peoples.

If one enlarges the meaning of the term psychical impotence, and ceases to limit it to failure to perform the act of coitus, although an intention to derive pleasure from it is present and the genital apparatus is intact, it would comprise, to begin with, all those men who are described as psychoanaesthetic, *i.e.* who never fail in the act but who perform it without special pleasure—a state of things which is commoner than one might think. Psychoanalytic study of such cases has discovered the same aetiological factors in them as those found in psychical impotence, when employed in the narrower sense, without at first discovering any explanation of the symptomatic difference between the two. By an analogy which is easy to justify, one is led on from these anaesthetic men to consider the enormous number of frigid women, whose attitude to love can in fact not be described or understood better than by equating it with psychical impotence in men, although the latter is more conspicuous.[4]

If, however, instead of attributing a wide significance to the term psychical impotence, we look about for instances of its peculiar symptomatology in less marked forms, we shall not be able to deny that the behaviour in love of the men of present-day civilization bears in general the character of the psychically impotent type. In only very few people of culture are the two

---

[4] At the same time I willingly admit that the frigidity of women is a complicated subject which can also be approached from another angle. [S.F.]

strains of tenderness and sensuality duly fused into one; the man almost always feels his sexual activity hampered by his respect for the woman and only develops full sexual potency when he finds himself in the presence of a lower type of sexual object; and this again is partly conditioned by the circumstance that his sexual aims include those of perverse sexual components, which he does not like to gratify with a woman he respects. Full sexual satisfaction only comes when he can give himself up wholeheartedly to enjoyment, which with his well-brought-up wife, for instance, he does not venture to do. Hence comes his need for a less exalted sexual object, a woman ethically inferior, to whom he need ascribe no aesthetic misgivings, and who does not know the rest of his life and cannot criticize him. It is to such a woman that he prefers to devote his sexual potency, even when all the tenderness in him belongs to one of a higher type. It is possible, too, that the tendency so often observed in men of the highest rank in society to take a woman of a low class as a permanent mistress, or even as a wife, is nothing but a consequence of the need for a lower type of sexual object on which, psychologically, the possibility of complete gratification depends.

I do not hesitate to lay the responsibility also for this very common condition in the erotic life of civilized men on the two factors operative in absolute psychical impotence, namely, the very strong incestuous fixation of childhood and the frustration by reality suffered during adolescence. It has an ugly sound and a paradoxical as well, but nevertheless it must be said that whoever is to be really free and happy in love must have overcome his deference for women and come to terms with the idea of incest with mother or sister. Anyone who in the face of this test subjects himself to serious self-examination will indubitably find that at the bottom of his heart he too regards the sexual act as something degrading, which soils and contaminates not only the body. And he will only be able to look for the origin of this attitude, which he will certainly not willingly acknowledge, in that period of his youth in which his sexual passions were already strongly developed but in which gratification of them with an object outside the family was almost as completely prohibited as with an incestuous one.

The women of our civilized world are similarly affected by their up-bringing and further, too, by the reaction upon them of this attitude in men. Naturally the effect upon a woman is just as unfavourable if the man comes to her without his full potency as if, after overestimating her in the early stages of falling in love, he then, having successfully possessed himself of her, sets her at naught. Women show little need to degrade the sexual object; no doubt this has some connection with the circumstance that as a rule they develop little of the sexual overestimation natural to men. The long abstinence from sexuality to which they are forced and the lingering of their sensuality in phantasy have in them, however, another important consequence. It is often not possible for them later on to undo the connection thus formed in their minds between sensual activities and something forbidden, and they turn out to be psychically impotent, *i.e.* frigid, when at last such activities do become permissible. This is the source of the desire in so many women to keep even legitimate relations secret for a time; and of the appearance of the capacity for normal sensation in others as soon as the condition of prohibition is restored by a secret intrigue—untrue to the husband, they can keep a second order of faith with the lover.

In my opinion the necessary condition of forbiddenness in the erotic life of women holds the same place as the man's need to lower his sexual object. Both are the consequence of the long period of delay between sexual maturity and sexual activity which is demanded by education for social reasons. The aim of both is to overcome the psychical impotence resulting from the lack of union between tenderness and sensuality. That the effect of the same causes differs so greatly in men and in women is perhaps due to another difference in the behaviour of the two sexes. Women belonging to the higher levels of civilization do not usually transgress the prohibition against sexual activities during the period of waiting, and thus they acquire this close association between the forbidden and the sexual. Men usually overstep the prohibition under the condition of lowering the standard of object they require, and so carry this condition on into their subsequent erotic life.

In view of the strenuous efforts being made in the civilized world at the present day to reform sexual life, it is not superfluous to remind the reader that psychoanalytic investigations have no more bias in any direction than has any other scientific research. In tracing back to its concealed sources what is manifest, psychoanalysis has no aim but that of disclosing connections. It can but be satisfied if what it has brought to light is of use in effecting reforms by substituting more advantageous for injurious conditions. It cannot, however, predict whether other, perhaps even greater, sacrifices may not result from other institutions.

III

The fact that the restrictions imposed by cultural education upon erotic life involve a general lowering of the sexual object may prompt us to turn our eyes from the object to the instincts themselves. The injurious results of the deprivation of sexual enjoyment at the beginning manifest themselves in lack of full satisfaction when sexual desire is later given free rein in marriage. But, on the other hand, unrestrained sexual liberty from the beginning leads to no better result. It is easy to show that the value the mind sets on erotic needs instantly sinks as soon as satisfaction becomes readily obtainable. Some obstacle is necessary to swell the tide of the libido to its height; and at all periods of history, wherever natural barriers in the way of satisfaction have not sufficed, mankind has erected conventional ones in order to be able to enjoy love. This is true both of individuals and of nations. In times during which no obstacles to sexual satisfaction existed, such as, may be, during the decline of the civilizations of antiquity, love became worthless, life became empty, and strong reaction-formations were necessary before the indispensable emotional value of love could be recovered. In this context it may be stated that the ascetic tendency of Christianity had the effect of raising the psychical value of love in a way that heathen antiquity could never achieve; it developed greatest significance in the lives of the ascetic monks, which were almost entirely occupied with struggles against libidinous temptation.

One's first inclination undoubtedly is to see in this difficulty a universal characteristic of our organic instincts. It is certainly true in a general way that the importance of an instinctual desire is mentally increased by frustration of it. Suppose one made the experiment of exposing a number of utterly different human beings to hunger under the same conditions. As the imperative need for food rose in them all their individual differences would be effaced and instead the uniform manifestations of one unsatisfied instinct would appear. But is it also true, conversely, that the mental value of an instinct invariably sinks with gratification of it? One thinks, for instance, of the relation of the wine-drinker to wine. Is it not a fact that wine always affords the drinker the same toxic satisfaction—one that in poetry has so often been likened to the erotic and that science as well may regard as comparable? Has one ever heard of a drinker being forced constantly to change his wine because he soon gets tired of always drinking the same? On the contrary, habit binds a man more and more to the particular kind of wine he drinks. Do we ever find a drinker impelled to go to another country where the wine is dearer or where alcohol is prohibited, in order to stimulate his dwindling pleasure in it by these obstacles? Nothing of the sort. If we listen to what our great lovers of alcohol say about their attitude to wine, for instance, B. Böcklin,[5] it sounds like the most perfect harmony, a model of a happy marriage. Why is the relation of the lover to his sexual object so very different?

However strange it may sound, I think the possibility must be considered that something in the nature of the sexual instinct itself is unfavorable to the achievement of absolute gratification. When we think of the long and difficult evolution

[5] G. Floerke, Zehn Jahre mit Böcklin, 2 Aufl., 1902, p. 16. [S.F.]

the instinct goes through, two factors to which this difficulty
might be ascribed at once emerge. First, in consequence of the
two "thrusts" of sexual development impelling towards choice
of an object, together with the intervention of the incest-barrier
between the two, the ultimate object selected is never the
original one but only a surrogate for it. Psychoanalysis has
shown us, however, that when the original object of an instinctual desire becomes lost in consequence of repression, it
is often replaced by an endless series of substitute-objects, none
of which ever give full satisfaction. This may explain the lack of
stability in object-choice, the "craving for stimulus," which is
so often a feature of the love of adults.

Secondly, we know that at its beginning the sexual instinct
is divided into a large number of components—or, rather, it
develops from them—not all of which can be carried on into
its final form; some have to be suppressed or turned to other
uses before the final form results. Above all, the coprophilic
elements in the instinct have proved incompatible with our
aesthetic ideas, probably since the time when man developed
an upright posture and so removed his organ of smell from the
ground; further, a considerable proportion of the sadistic elements belonging to the erotic instinct have to be abandoned.
All such developmental processes, however, relate only to the
upper layers of the complicated structure. The fundamental
processes which promote erotic excitation remain always the
same. Excremental things are all too intimately and inseparably
bound up with sexual things; the position of the genital organs
—*inter urinas et faeces*—remains the decisive and unchangeable
factor. One might say, modifying a well-known saying of the
great Napoleon's, "Anatomy is destiny." The genitals themselves have not undergone the development of the rest of the
human form in the direction of beauty; they have retained
their animal cast; and so even to-day love, too, is in essence as
animal as it ever was. The erotic instincts are hard to mould;
training of them achieves now too much, now too little. What
culture tries to make out of them seems attainable only at the
cost of a sensible loss of pleasure; the persistence of the im-

pulses that are not enrolled in adult sexual activity makes itself felt in an absence of satisfaction.

So perhaps we must make up our minds to the idea that altogether it is not possible for the claims of the sexual instinct to be reconciled with the demands of culture, that in consequence of his cultural development renunciation and suffering, as well as the danger of his extinction at some far future time, are not to be eluded by the race of man. This gloomy prognosis rests, it is true, on the single conjecture that the lack of satisfaction accompanying culture is the necessary consequence of certain peculiarities developed by the sexual instinct under the pressure of culture. This very incapacity in the sexual instinct to yield full satisfaction as soon as it submits to the first demands of culture becomes the source, however, of the grandest cultural achievements, which are brought to birth by ever greater sublimation of the components of the sexual instinct. For what motive would induce man to put his sexual energy to other uses if by any disposal of it he could obtain fully satisfying pleasure? He would never let go of this pleasure and would make no further progress. It seems, therefore, that the irreconcilable antagonism between the demands of the two instincts—the sexual and the egoistic—have made man capable of ever greater achievements, though, it is true, under the continual menace of danger, such as that of the neuroses to which at the present time the weaker are succumbing.

The purpose of science is neither to alarm nor to reassure. But I myself freely admit that such far-reaching conclusions as those drawn here should be built up on a broader foundation, and that perhaps developments in other directions will enable mankind to remedy the effects of these, which we have here been considering in isolation.

J. MIDDLETON MURRY

John Middleton Murry (1889–1957), English editor, critic, and close friend of Lawrence, published over forty books, three of them on Lawrence: *Son of Woman, Reminiscences of D. H. Lawrence,* and his most thoughtful and best balanced appraisal, *Love, Freedom, and Society.*

[GENIUS AND A SYNDROME]

When we seek to understand the cause of that 'disruption in his soul' which preceded the invasion of it by the dark floods of hatred and underlay the imagination of *The Plumed Serpent,* we are driven back to a consideration of Lawrence's childhood conditioning. Certainly, we might be content to regard it as exclusively a spiritual happening: a 'deep death in belief', amounting to a crucifixion of his soul, following upon the realization that the idea of love, on which society purported to be based, was a pitiful illusion. Contemplation of the happening at that level would lead one far and, it may be, far enough. But we are withheld from resting there by two considerations. The first is that, if we are at all responsive to the newness and truth of Lawrence's vision of man, a merely spiritual understanding is not enough. We are required, most peremptorily by himself, to understand him in his unity of body and soul. Once again, it is the body, he says, 'which feels real passion, real hate, real grief'; and the reality of Lawrence's suffering is indubitable. The second is that we are aware, long before the actual disruption in his soul, of the presence in him of conflicting elements which he does his utmost to hold together, but which, if circumstances are adverse, may well produce a psychical disruption. This conflict is no invention of mine. It is acknowledged and exhibited, with a terrifying veracity, by Lawrence himself, in such a document as *Look!*

From *Love, Freedom and Society* by John Middleton Murry (London: Jonathan Cape, 1957), pp. 59–65. Reprinted by permission of Jonathan Cape Ltd. and the John Middleton Murry Estate.

We have come through! It is a conflict in his most intimate being, in his relation with his wife, wherein the struggle between the light and the darkness, between love and hate, reaches an intensity far beyond any known to common experience. We need not doubt that, as Lawrence proclaimed, he (or rather they) had emerged from this conflict, with his personality intact, but deepened. But, on top of this, and at a moment when he may be fairly described as convalescent rather than completely recovered, came the disaster of the war. An apocalypse in the macrocosm followed hard upon an apocalpse in the microcosm. It was the same organic sensibility which had to endure both. But one may, at least for a moment, conceive that Lawrence might have been spared the convulsion in the macrocosm, and that he might have been suffered to reach a resolution of his intimate conflict in peace.

It was not to be; and perhaps, if we examine the nature of his organic sensibility we may dimly discern why it could not be. That investigation we cannot avoid, if we take Lawrence's doctrine seriously.

In 'The Nightmare'[1] Somers says to himself:

Let them label me unfit. I know my own body is fragile in its way, but also it is very strong, and it's the only body that would carry my particular self.

We do not doubt the truth of that. We know probably more of Lawrence's particular self than of anybody's of our time, and we are aware of a correspondence between it and his body. And his assertion that, though his body was fragile, it was also very strong is also true, if we understand by strength something more than the merely physical. It needed strength, of no ordinary kind, to accomplish the astonishing amount of writing he did and to endure the constant travel under difficult conditions.

---

[1] The title of a chapter in Lawrence's *Kangaroo*. It describes in fictional guise Lawrence's own unpleasant experiences with English military and civil authorities during the First World War.

He got the uttermost out of his body, and he went to the uttermost in the exploration and revelation of his self.

He was a man of much more than the usual organic sensibility. He was tubercular. (Whether phthisis is effect or cause of the abnormally responsive psycho-somatic condition, who knows?) When we compare him with other tubercular men of genius, we find him, I think, more acutely conscious than they of his physical frailty as compared to other men, more inclined to compensate for it in the drama of his imagination; and this, I think, is because he passed his impressionable childhood in a compact community where hard physical labour was the test of manhood. On the other side of the account, his origin in the real working-class of seventy years ago gave him a comprehensive knowledge and awareness of society peculiar to himself. He had no need to plunge himself, like Orwell, among down-and-outs, or like Stevenson, into emigrant steerage, to make a willed and partial contact with the proletariat. In this respect he resembles Tchehov more than his English similars: Tchehov whose peasant origins made him immune, as he said, from Tolstoy's temptation to idealize peasant virtues. But Russia in the 1870s was very different from England in the 1890s. Lawrence was a kind of spearhead, an advancing taproot, in that social upsurge of the working-class under industrialism and democracy which has been characteristic of Western society, but most remarkable in England. Sociologically, Lawrence might be regarded as the first commanding genius produced by the English Education Act of 1870, who made his progress upward through the social body, typically, as a teacher trained in the institutions of that Act and teaching in its schools. Significantly, Rupert Birkin, the first of Lawrence's autobiographical presentations of his adult self, is imagined as an Inspector of Schools, the point at which the new educational system met the humane and exclusive education of the pre-democratic era. This process of social transformation was completed in his intimate life, by his marriage to a charmingly natural German aristocrat.

Further, his childhood and adolescence were passed in a place where the discrepancy and conflict between the new industrial order and the old agricultural order were nakedly visible: in a mining village of ugly company-built terrace-houses erupted in the midst of a lovely surrounding landscape. From this crudity, by instinct, he took refuge in the natural beauty of a small farm and its household; refuge, too, from the tension of his own home, where his mother, with all the strength of her indomitable will, strove to extricate herself and him from submersion in the feckless animal existence of his father.

Lawrence surmised that this tension between his parents, existing previous to his own birth, was the origin of his bodily fragility. Without doubt, the strain of his inward division between love and loyalty to his mother, and his unconscious attachment to his father, vastly increased his sensitivity. He became praeternaturally aware, prematurely in love—with his mother. That particular conditioning, it may be said, was abnormal. Abnormal is always a dangerous word, difficult to use meaningfully. Lawrence's conditioning was abnormal in its intensity rather than its essence. The Freudian analysts were to find in *Sons and Lovers*, the great novel in which he portrayed his childhood and adolescence, a classical paradigm of a situation which they believed to be typical. Typical, certainly, was the urge within the family for social advancement, not in the mere materialistic sense, but conceived as the entry to a realm of culture and consciousness, of freedom and responsibility. This, in *The Rainbow*, Lawrence represented as peculiar to the women: but he was generalizing from his own particular experience. In a different kind of working-class family, it might have been the urge of the man, with the woman playing the negative part.

In Lawrence's case the force of this social urge coincided with that of his mother's intense love for him. He was, as he describes in *Fantasia of the Unconscious*, forced towards consciousness and responsibility: into becoming his mother's man, what she dreamed and desired her husband might have been. No wonder he sought refuge from the stress in the placid life and natural piety of Willey Farm; or that he found extreme difficulty in achieving sexual fulfilment, in his own deep sense of the phrase, with his chosen woman. Here, it seems, one must regard Lawrence as abnormal in a positive sense of the word. Most other tubercular men of genius have been sterile and childless, but none of them, to my knowledge, has come near to being so preoccupied by the sexual relation as Lawrence. It is a main theme of nearly all his books; and they are thronged with innumerable descriptions of the sexual struggle which are outside the experience, and beyond the imaginative scope, of ordinary men and women. Here we are faced with something different from the more than usual organic sensibility of tubercular genius. That presents us with a picture of life, or an utterance of thought and emotion arising from experience, which we can receive as a revelation. There is enormous riches of such revelation in Lawrence's books. But there is also a substantial and persistent element in them which is not of this kind at all—a sort of sexual esotericism, occult and mysterious, which we can explain only as the expression of some personal idiosyncrasy. And since Lawrence himself offers an explanation of this kind in *Fantasia of the Unconscious*, which seems entirely convincing, as far as it goes, we cannot but accept it.

In that book, he describes with wonderful vividness the relation of a mother to her son which is indistinguishable from his own relation to his mother. When the father has failed the mother by not accepting 'responsibility for the next purposive step into the future' (as Lawrence's father conspicuously refused it), then, he says:

The unhappy woman beats about for her insatiable satisfaction, seeking whom she may devour. And usually, she turns to her child. Here she provokes what she wants. Here, in her own son who belongs to her, she seems to find the perfect response for which she is craving . . . So she throws herself into a last great love for her son, a final and fatal devotion, that would have been the richness and strength of her husband and is poison to her boy. [*Fantasia of the Unconscious*, New York: The Viking Press, 1960, p. 157.]

Lawrence then describes how the establishment of what he calls the 'upper love-and-cognition circuit inevitably provokes the lower sex-sensual centres',—upper and lower are, of course, not ethical but physiological epithets—and continues:

> And then what? The son gets on swimmingly for a time till he is faced with the actual fact of sex-necessity. He gleefully inherits his adolescence and the world at large, mother-supported, mother-loved. Everything comes to him in glamour, he feels he sees wondrous much, understands a whole heaven, mother-stimulated. Think of the power which a mature woman thus infuses into her boy. He flares up like a flame in oxygen. No wonder they say geniuses mostly have great mothers. They mostly have sad fates.
>
> [*Fantasia of the Unconscious*, p. 159.]

Whether Lawrence himself really believed that this conditioning fully accounted for his genius, I do not know. Certainly he suggests it here. Elsewhere in *Fantasia* he suggests that excessive stimulation of the "upper love-and-cognition circuit" is the cause of a disposition to phthisis. So that, in fact, he offers this conditioning as the prime cause of his genius and his tuberculosis. But literary genius occurs in men and women whose childhood conditioning is quite different from this. Let the fact of literary genius remain the miracle and mystery it is. What we can fairly say is that it is probably true that such conditioning, together with the phthisical disposition that accompanies it, gives a peculiar intensity and glamour to the experience and the creations of literary genius.

But there is no reason at all to doubt or qualify the personal truth of what Lawrence goes on to say:

> And then?—and then, with this glamorous youth? What is he actually to do with his sensual, sexual self? Bury it? Or make an effort with a stranger? For he is taught, even by his mother, that his manhood must not forego sex. Yet he is linked up in ideal love already, the best he will ever know . . . You will not easily get a man to believe that his carnal love for the woman he has made his wife is as high a love as that he felt for his mother.
>
> [*Fantasia of the Unconscious*, pp. 159–160.]

I believe that to be the original clue to the element of perversity which is so inextricably interwoven in Lawrence's writings. Not that his preoccupation with the sexual relation between man and woman is in itself perverse. Quite the contrary. The sexual relation is the one of most fundamental importance to human life, and Lawrence's concentration upon it is absolutely justified: evidence of his strength not of his weakness; of his centrality, not of his eccentricity. But the kind of sexual relation which Lawrence frequently exhibits as crucial in his novels is vitiated by abnormality, in the positive sense: it is without universal validity. When Lawrence says, 'You will not easily get a man to believe that his carnal love for the woman he has made his wife is as high a love as he felt for his mother', he has left out an important word. To be true, it should read: 'You will not easily get *such* a man to believe . . .' He is universalizing a very peculiar experience. As Lawrence exhibits the case in *Fantasia,* it is evident that in his view his genius, and his belief that his carnal love for his wife was not as high a love as he felt for his mother, had the same origin, and were complementary to each other. In the form: the peculiar intensity of Lawrence's genius was complementary to a feeling of guilt in his physical love for his wife, it is almost certainly true. But we must add: complementary also to his tubercular predisposition. We are in the presence of what the doctors call a syndrome: mother-fixation, phthisis, intensity of genius. That psycho-somatic syndrome does not, of course, account for the genius itself: it cannot be reduced to those elements in combination. But it does account for the most disturbing manifestations of that genius.

PHILIP RIEFF

Philip Rieff, cultural historian and historian of ideas, has taught at
the University of Chicago and the University of California and is
Professor of Sociology at the University of Pennsylvania. In 1957–
1958 he was a Fellow of the Center for Advanced Study in the
Behavioral Sciences. He is the author of, among other books, *Freud:
The Mind of the Moralist*, and the editor of Lawrence's *Psychoanalysis and the Unconscious* and *Fantasia of the Unconscious*.

TWO HONEST MEN

One could stock a sizeable library with literature born of the
desire to quarrel with Freud. Of all the books in this library
the most curious by far would be two by D. H. Lawrence, in
which Lawrence begins by accusing Freud of being morally
subversive and then goes on to unpack his own brand of moral
subversion. For Lawrence to accuse Freud would seem a perfect case of the pot calling the kettle black.

In 1921, Lawrence published *Psycho-analysis and the Unconscious*. It aroused little interest, even among the premature
anti-Freudians, those early in the field that Lawrence now
entered. Lawrence's remedy, where understandable, seemed as
dangerous as the disease. Of course, Freud himself did not stir.
He was not a man easily drawn into controversy, especially on
the moral implications of his thought. What scant notice the
book received was good humoured. One moral subversive had
fallen out with another. *Psycho-analysis and the Unconscious*
was treated as a bizarre and often incomprehensible new testament in the religion of sex, written specially to compete with
the then not very old testament according to Freud. In the
first few pages Freud does appear cast in the role of Judas,
putting the finger on the gentle Jesus of the "unconscious" for
the police forces of civilization. Lawrence himself soon appears
as the good disciple, defending the "true unconscious" against

---

From *The Listener*, LXIII (May 5, 1960), 794–796; presented as a
broadcast talk on the B.B.C. Third Programme. Copyright © Philip Rieff
1966. Reprinted by permission of the author.

what he considers to be Freud's misunderstanding of it—as consisting mainly of repressed ideas, too ugly for thinking and too powerful not to dominate our thinking.

What Freud would explore cautiously, as a labyrinth containing monsters, Lawrence would follow hopefully. Psychoanalysis found what it was trained to suspect in the dark corners. Being, as he once remarked, a 'fearfully religious man', Lawrence found in those same dark corners inhabited by 'gagged, bound, maniacal repressions' the dark gods. Being by temper and training an atheist, Freud had missed the beautiful part of the unconscious. In fact, Lawrence believed, the ugly part is actually created by the suppression of the beautiful part, consciousness of which he calls the 'old religious faculty'. The trouble with Freud was that he discovered with scientific probity what he should have greeted with religious ecstasy.

Having failed to make himself clear the first time, Lawrence immediately tried again. *Fantasia of the Unconscious,* published in 1922, was equally neglected. To the evident pleasure of his critics, who treated Lawrence to the same charge of moral subversion that Lawrence made against Freud, Lawrence the artist had strayed too far from his art. Those few critical friends whom Lawrence had at the time kindly ignored both works, preferring to avoid the embarrassment of defending the artist against his urges toward prophecy. The embarrassment lingers; both books are ignored. Yet they tell us something important about Lawrence the moralist: that he was not so different from Freud the moralist as he wanted to believe.

Freud the moralist is a hard man to find. He never preaches at us openly, as Lawrence does. He has no message, in the old sense of something positive and constructive to offer. Nevertheless, as Lawrence was among the first to realize, Freud's apparently strict attention to psycho-analytic therapy contains moral implications that, when drawn, constitute a very powerful message.

That message seemed to Lawrence so fundamentally dangerous as to warrant denunciation. Freud was indeed a scientist; he had carried science where it did not belong but was compelled, by its own vitality, to go: into the inner life. Bad enough that science had gone so far in conquering outer nature, now Freud was bringing up the real possibility of a technology that could reduce feeling. A technology of the heart was more than Lawrence could tolerate. That was carrying science too far. Never mind that Freud himself limited the power of his science to shrink and control the emotions. What Lawrence feared was where Freud led, not merely where he stood. And, as a scientist, Freud did hope that his pessimism was unwarranted, that in time his new psycho-analytical knowledge would pay off, as all science must, in the increase of power—finally, power over the instinctual sources of life itself.

So it is because Freud rightly considered himself a scientist that Lawrence writes of his disagreement with him in the following remarkable challenge: 'First and foremost, the issue is a moral issue. It is not here a matter of reform, new moral values. It is the life and death of all morality'. Knowingly, Lawrence concluded, Freud was 'out, under a therapeutic disguise, to do away entirely with the moral faculty in man'. No more severe charge could be invented. Doing away with the moral faculty was not impossible, Lawrence thought. Tap the unconscious sources, develop techniques of control, and the job could be done, like any other job science chose to undertake. Freud was merely the pioneer, the theoretician of the possibility. After him would come the men with the paraphernalia. Where science went, technology always followed—unless it preceded. Lawrence had to offer alternatives that were thoroughly anti-scientific. No wonder, then, that when he tried to go beyond criticism of Freud to some doctrine of his own, he seemed eccentric to the literary public. That public is educated, however sketchily in detail, to the same assumptions made by our scientific men. The pre-scientific world is the one Lawrence tried to save.

This intention makes both books quixotic. Lawrence argues for the kind of knowledge in which nature is reverenced and trusted rather than studied and manipulated. There is a classicism about Lawrence's desire to hold up nature as a model. In the classical tradition that knowledge is true and good which helps us conform to nature—instead of forcing nature to conform to our instructed desires. When Freud joined a theory of human nature to a therapy for it and declared theory and therapy identical, he was clearly in the scientific tradition first announced as a programme for moderns by Francis Bacon.

Lawrence tried to argue for a cause that literary men had dropped long ago. By the nineteen-twenties, when Lawrence appeared as a polemicist against Freud's science, the two cultures had become one. D. H. Lawrence was the last literary man of major talent seriously to oppose scientific theory, as such, and to try to rehabilitate an anti-scientific theory, which he was forced to call 'religious'. He follows Blake and Baudelaire; he has had no major follower.

Lawrence's anti-scientific position is stated clearly and simply, as the occasion demanded, in the preface of his little history book for young readers which he published in 1926. There we learn that science, like the arts, can only serve the unconscious or comment on it. A historian who ignores the connexion between the unconscious and the events which he must ascertain, order, and verify is engaged in 'hackwork': scientific 'hackwork', but hackwork, none the less—or so Lawrence warns his young readers. First-rate historical writing would have to get 'inside the hearts, or souls, of men'. There, from time to time, takes place 'some strange surging, some welling-up of unknown powers. These powers', Lawrence continues, 'that well up inside the hearts of men, are the fountains and origins of human history. And the welling-up has no ascribable cause. It is naked cause itself'. And so, we learn, the Crusades, the Renaissance, the Reformation should be treated as vicissitudes of instinct, not as expressions of class interest, or new nationalisms. 'They are', Lawrence tells us, 'the sheer utterance of life itself, the logic only appearing afterward'.

This sort of advice will seem odd to those unfamiliar with the imagery of mysticism. But mystics, and Lawrence among them, believe in the continuity of all creation. What Lawrence disliked so about science was that it had crippled our capacity for understanding by dividing things up. On the contrary, says Lawrence, all things are one. An earthquake, Lawrence explains, by way of example, is no merely external event; rather 'the mysterious and untellable motion within the hearts of men' is in some way related to the motion within the earth, so that even earthquakes are unaccountably related to man's psychic being—and not merely related, but also 'dependent upon it'.

With such a theory we have not learned to say very much about events, except that they happen. But Lawrence is no respecter of the lust for explanation. With Blake and Baudelaire, he hates that 'heresy of instruction' by which even art must teach us something. Freud is on the other side of the intellectual universe, where art is interesting only for what it teaches us about its own genesis and functions. Yet Freud shares the fundamental apprehension of mysticism: the continuity of creation. He aimed to do more, however, than watch the instinctual life with 'wonder and reverence'. He did not adopt a prayerful attitude toward nature. What to Lawrence seemed divine symbol, Freud treated as profane symptom. And so the two men would argue—but at least they would be arguing about the same thing, and with less distance between them than Lawrence supposed. That Lawrence took no specific religious statement seriously, except as symbolic, brings him uncomfortably close to his opponent, Freud, who also took no religious statement seriously—except as symptomatic. The difference between symbol and symptom is merely that between advocacy and analysis.

In his passionate opposition to the analytic habit, Lawrence argues as if Freud lacked sympathy for the imagination. Yet Freud's rationalism is very different from that of the eighteenth century, which equated the fantastic with the fraudulent. Moreover, the transition from the chiding of religion by Voltaire or Gibbon to a more sympathetic analysis by Strauss or a Renan, had already taken place before Freud. In his sympathetic handling of therapy, as a learning situation dependent as much, if not more, on the heart than on the head, Freud joined a rationalist aim to a romantic procedure—or, more precisely, the parody of a romantic procedure. I say 'parody' because the Freudian therapeutic pedagogy deliberately reproduces our earlier experiences, and with the intention of reducing rather than renewing their importance. Nevertheless, the 'transference' relation, as Freud called that between the psycho-analyst and his patient, is not one with which the orthodox rationalist can feel at ease; Freud was not really at ease with it himself. Yet he insisted on its fundamental importance: without 'transference' psycho-analytic knowledge was mere intellectualizing, no genuine advance in self-knowledge but only the most foxy kind of 'resistance'. Patients had to be kept close to the analyst. Thus, to mark Freud down as the new leader of the old rationalism demonstrates Lawrence's impatience with fine intellectual distinctions. Lawrence's case for the irrational is weakened by his own rigid rejection of Freud as if he were nothing but a kind of fundamentalist of rationalism.

Of course the fundamentalists of rationalism are still with us. Some of them react violently against injustices lacquered over by spirituality. Many of them place all their faith in changed economic arrangements; they derive some still unanalyzed private pleasure from denying the satisfactions—and sometimes the necessity—of collective make-believe or instinct ritualized. Freud admitted the satisfactions, and would have denied the necessity only for a specially intellectual few, himself among them.

Since, as Freud believed, the impulses cannot be suppressed for long, that morality is more efficient which permits them 'a certain amount of satisfaction'. We are entitled to know something about the impulses that demand, so imperiously, to be satisfied. Neither Lawrence nor Freud recognize an impulse to be good. More important than any disagreement between them is their common assumption that goodness is not, and never was, native. And so, for Lawrence, Christian moral principles are contrary to nature, which amounts to saying that they are wrong. He announced his own 'opposite principle to Christianity: self-fulfilment and social destruction, instead of self-love and self-sacrifice'. At one time Lawrence had hoped that enough new men and women would collect around his opposite principle to form the 'nucleus of a new belief', setting up a 'new centre of attack' on the established culture, far removed from politics or any burning question of the day.

Achieving self-love, as a Christian principle, depends upon accepting the love of God; it is, by divine example, tested by self-sacrifice. Self-fulfilment, on the other hand, is as closely linked with social destruction. Lawrence expressed his own self-fulfilment in what has now become a characteristic way, in 'utter hatred', as he put it, of 'the whole establishment—the whole constitution of England'. In fact, really to fulfill oneself, which should be the aim of life, a genuine social alienation is necessary. 'Entire separation', Lawrence announces, 'that is what must happen to one: not even the nominal shelter left, not even the mere fact of inclusion in the host. One must be entirely cast forth'. This doctrine is now so popular that, lacking a sufficiently authoritarian parental culture, a younger generation casts itself forth, preferring the honesty of otherhood to the hypocrisy of brotherhood. To say 'I hate him like a brother' may, as Dostoevsky and Freud believed, more truly assess the fraternal emotion than to say 'I love him like a brother'.

With this principle of self-fulfilment and social destruction, Lawrence shows himself as the most forthright of modern heresiarchs, chief and father—although only after his death—over all our little heresiarchs: all those professionally angry young father-killers who march along the literary horizon looking for an older generation with some reserves of dignity that might be exposed as class discrimination and coldness; or, what is even more Lawrentian, the Angries, the Beats, and the Espressoists are looking for an older generation with some fixed ideals at which to smile—Christian, socialist, any ideals so long as they are fixed. Certainly contemporary parties of the left will have to face the fact that youth, both in the suburbs and in the espresso bars, suspect them precisely for the fixity of their ideals and

trust the right mainly because they see that the right has no
ideal that it would not willingly and easily exchange tomorrow
for some fresher article.

Lawrence himself found in the fixity of ideals the main cause
of our difficulties as a civilization. He sensed the inevitable
defeat of all genuine moral revolutionaries unless they are educated to accept their own criterion: obsolescence. But this is
nothing more than an ethic of action. To keep moving is the
main Lawrentian principle. We have yet to understand the
restlessness of those who accept that principle.

It was Freud, not Lawrence, who offered a practical programme directed at removing fixations upon ideals to support
the new ethic. Freud had the intellectual courage to see that
there are periods of history in which fixed ideals are salutary—
not in his own or any recent time but, say, in the time of the
Roman Empire, just before the rise of Christianity. What
Freud offers, as an ethic that will not become rigid with pre-
tension, Lawrence could not help but approve. It is the one
moral commitment of which both considered themselves masters—Freud in theory, Lawrence in practice: what I shall call
the ethic of honesty.

Freud reports that he 'once treated a high official who was
bound by oath not to communicate certain state secrets, and
the analysis came to grief as a consequence of this restriction'.
Once established for therapeutic purposes, the ethic of honesty
expands to improve the entire culture. It would hasten the
'change-over to a more realistic and creditable attitude on the
part of society', one in which mental processes could not be
concealed because too many people would be capable of instantly interpreting the consequent symptoms. In a society
in which everyone was analytical, so to say, everyone would be
analyzed.

What recourse, Freud asks, will people have if they cannot
retreat into reticence, and into the privacy of their neurosis?
His answer hints at a civilization different from ours, one that
no longer needs reticence or hypocrisy to keep going. Such
people, he writes, will simply have to 'confess to the instincts

that are at work in them, face the conflict, fight for what they want, or go without'. No more forthright statement of the competitive nature of freedom has ever been made.

The ethic of honesty is by no means so explicit in Lawrence as in Freud. But it is to be found all through the novels and stories, the very basis of the freedom that men and women need in their relations with one another. The ethic has been long recognized. In the eighteenth century, churchmen complained of the new modesty. 'When one wants to eulogize someone', remarked a celebrated French preacher, 'one says: he is an honest man'. Any other claim seemed presumptuous. And what more appropriate virtue can there be for men still so involved in the practice of creating desires and then fulfilling them? One desire alone has become embarrassing: the desire to be good. In some French films—take *The Cousins*—it leads to humiliation and even to death. Mr. V. S. Pritchett has pointed out that George Eliot was the last great novelist to concentrate on the desire to be good. It is plain that even if Freud and Lawrence were mistaken, and we are not really sick from our ideals, nevertheless for a long time and in increasing numbers we have been sick *of* them. These two honest men have helped release us from all the heaped up dishonesties.

The honesty for which both Lawrence and Freud hoped may help toughen us for the hard job of living with ourselves. But are we not, now, tough enough? It is, I think, to Lawrence's credit that if he wanted to clear away dead enthusiasms it was in order to make room for new, live ones. Freud was never enthusiastic, not even for his own science. He possessed that tired wisdom we so admire, a wisdom always sure, beforehand, that every cure breeds its own disease.

Lawrence and Literary Criticism

❖◇

DOROTHY VAN GHENT

Dorothy Van Ghent (1907–1967) taught English at the University of Montana, New York University, Brooklyn College, Bard College, and the University of Kansas, and was Professor of English at the State University of New York at Buffalo. She was the author of, among other books, *The Art of the Novel* and *Willa Cather*, and editor with Willard Maas of *Essential Prose*.

ON SONS AND LOVERS

Novels, like other dramatic art, deal with conflicts of one kind or another—conflicts that are, in the work of the major novelists, drawn from life in the sense that they are representative of real problems in life; and the usual urgency in the novelist is to find the technical means which will afford an ideal resolution of the conflict and solution of the living problem—still "ideal" even if tragic. Technique is his art itself, in its procedural aspect; and the validity of his solution of a problem is dependent upon the adequacy of his technique. The more complex and intransigent the problem, the more subtle his technical strategies will evidently need to be, if they are to be effective. The decade of World War I brought into full and terrible view the collapse of values that had prophetically haunted the minds of novelists as far back as Dostoevsky and Flaubert and Dickens, or even farther back, to Balzac and

From *The English Novel: Form and Function*, by Dorothy Van Ghent (New York: Holt, Rinehart and Winston, 1953), pp. 245–261. Copyright 1953 by Dorothy Van Ghent. Reprinted by permission of Holt, Rinehart, and Winston, Inc.

Stendhal. With that decade, and increasingly since, the problems of modern life have appeared intransigent indeed; and, in general, the growth of that intransigence has been reflected in an increasing concern with technique on the part of the artist. D. H. Lawrence's sensitivity to twentieth century chaos was peculiarly intense, and his passion for order was similarly intense; but this sensitivity and this passion did not lead him to concentrate on refinements and subtleties of novelistic technique in the direction laid out, for instance, by James and Conrad. Hence, as readers first approaching his work, almost inevitably we feel disappointment and even perhaps shock that writing so often "loose" and repetitious and such unrestrained emotionalism over glandular matters should appear in the work of a novelist who is assumed to have an important place in the literary canon. "There is no use," Francis Fergusson says, "trying to appreciate [Lawrence] solely as an artist; he was himself too often impatient of the demands of art, which seemed to him trivial compared with the quest he followed."[1] And Stephen Spender phrases the problem of Lawrence in this way: what interested him "was the tension between art and life, not the complete resolution of the problems of life within the illusion of art. . . . For him literature is a kind of pointer to what is outside literature. . . . This outsideness of reality is for Lawrence the waters of baptism in which man can be reborn."[2] We need to approach Lawrence with a good deal of humility about "art" and a good deal of patience for the disappointments he frequently offers as an artist, for it is only thus that we shall be able to appreciate the innovations he actually made in the novel as well as the importance and profundity of his vision of modern life.

Sons and Lovers appears to have the most conventional chronological organization; it is the kind of organization that a naïve

---

[1] "D. H. Lawrence's Sensibility," in *Critiques and Essays in Modern Fiction*, edited by John W. Aldridge (New York: The Ronald Press Company, 1952), p. 328. [D.V.G.]

[2] "The Life of Literature," in *Partisan Review*, December, 1948. [D.V.G.]

autobiographical novelist would tend to use, with only the thinnest pretense at disguising the personally retrospective nature of the material. We start with the marriage of the parents and the birth of the children. We learn of the daily life of the family while the children are growing up, the work, the small joys, the parental strife. Certain well-defined emotional pressures become apparent: the children are alienated from their father, whose personality degenerates gradually as he feels his exclusion; the mother more and more completely dominates her sons' affections, aspirations, mental habits. Urged by her toward middle-class refinements, they enter white-collar jobs, thus making one more dissociation between themselves and their proletarian father. As they attempt to orient themselves toward biological adulthood, the old split in the family is manifested in a new form, as an internal schism in the characters of the sons; they cannot reconcile sexual choice with the idealism their mother has inculcated. This inner strain leads to the older son's death. The same motif is repeated in the case of Paul, the younger one. Paul's first girl, Miriam, is a cerebral type, and the mother senses in her an obvious rivalry for domination of Paul's sensibility. The mother is the stronger influence, and Paul withdraws from Miriam; but with her own victory Mrs. Morel begins to realize the discord she has produced in his character, and tries to release her hold on him by unconsciously seeking her own death. Paul finds another girl, Clara, but the damage is already too deeply designed, and at the time of his mother's death he voluntarily gives up Clara, knowing that there is but one direction he can take, and that is to go with his mother. At the end he is left emotionally derelict, with only the "drift toward death."

From this slight sketch, it is clear that the book is organized not merely on a chronological plan showing the habits and vicissitudes of a Nottinghamshire miner's family, but that it has a structure rigorously controlled by an idea: an idea of an organic disturbance in the relationships of men and women— a disturbance of sexual polarities that is first seen in the disaffection of mother and father, then in the mother's attempt to substitute her sons for her husband, finally in the sons' unsuccessful struggle to establish natural manhood. Lawrence's development of the idea has certain major implications: it implies that his characters have transgressed against the natural life-directed condition of the human animal—against the elementary biological rhythms he shares with the rest of biological nature; and it implies that this offense against life has been brought about by a failure to respect the complete and terminal individuality of persons—by a twisted desire to "possess" other persons, as the mother tries to "possess" her husband, then her sons, and as Miriam tries to "possess" Paul. Lawrence saw this offense as a disease of modern life in all its manifestations, from sexual relationships to those broad social and political relationships that have changed people from individuals to anonymous economic properties or to military units or to ideological automatons.

The controlling idea is expressed in the various episodes—the narrative logic of the book. It is also expressed in imagery—the book's poetic logic. Perhaps in no other novelist do we find the image so largely replacing episode and discursive analysis, and taking over the expressive functions of these, as it does in Lawrence. The chief reason for the extraordinary predominance of the image as an absolute expressive medium in Lawrence lies in the character of the idea which is his subject. He must make us aware—sensitively aware, not merely conceptually aware—of the profound life force whose rhythms the natural creature obeys; and he must make us aware of the terminal individuality—the absolute "otherness" or "outsideness"—that is the natural form of things and of the uncorrupted person. We must be made aware of these through the *feelings* of his people, for only in feeling have the biological life force and the sense of identity—either the identity of self or of others—any immediacy of reality. He seeks the objective equivalent of feeling in the image. As Francis Fergusson says, Lawrence's imagination was so concrete that he seems not "to distinguish between the reality and the metaphor or symbol which makes

it plain to us."[3] But the most valid symbols are the most concrete realities. Lawrence's great gift for the symbolic image was
a function of his sensitivity to and passion for the meaning of
real things—for the individual expression that real forms have.
In other words, his gift for the image arose directly from his
vision of life as infinitely creative of individual identities, each
whole and separate and to be reverenced as such.

Let us examine the passage with which the first chapter of
Sons and Lovers ends—where Mrs. Morel, pregnant with Paul,
wanders deliriously in the garden, shut out of the house by
Morel in his drunkenness. Mrs. Morel is literally a vessel of the
life force that seems to thrust itself at her in nature from all
sides, but she is also in rebellion against it and the perfume
of the pollen-filled lilies makes her gasp with fear:

The moon was high and magnificent in the August night. Mrs.
Morel, seared with passion, shivered to find herself out there in a
great white light, that fell cold on her, and gave a shock to her
inflamed soul. She stood for a few moments helplessly staring at
the glistening great rhubarb leaves near the door. Then she got the
air into her breast. She walked down the garden path, trembling in
every limb, while the child boiled within her. . . .

She hurried out of the side garden to the front, where she could
stand as if in an immense gulf of white light, the moon streaming
high in face of her, the moonlight standing up from the hills in
front, and filling the valley where the Bottoms crouched, almost
blindingly. There, panting and half weeping in reaction from the
stress, she murmured to herself over and over again: "The nuisance!
the nuisance!"

She became aware of something about her. With an effort she
roused herself to see what it was that penetrated her consciousness.
The tall white lilies were reeling in the moonlight, and the air was
charged with their perfume, as with a presence. Mrs. Morel gasped
slightly in fear. She touched the big, pallid flowers on their petals,
then shivered. They seemed to be stretching in the moonlight. She
put her hand into one white bin: the gold scarcely showed on her

---

[3] Fergusson, *op. cit.*, p. 335. [D.V.G.]

fingers by moonlight. She bent down to look at the binful of yellow pollen; but it only appeared dusky. Then she drank a deep draught of the scent. It almost made her dizzy.

Mrs. Morel leaned on the garden gate, looking out, and she lost herself awhile. She did not know what she thought. Except for a slight feeling of sickness, and her consciousness in the child, herself melted out like a scent into the shiny, pale air.

[pp. 23–24.]

She finally arouses Morel from his drunken sleep and he lets her in. Unfastening her brooch at the bedroom mirror, she sees that her face is smeared with the yellow dust of the lilies.

The imagery of the streaming moonlight is that of a vast torrential force, "magnificent" and inhuman, and it equates not only with that phallic power of which Mrs. Morel is the rebellious vessel but with the greater and universal demiurge that was anciently called Eros—the power springing in plants and hurling the planets, giving the "glistening great rhubarb leaves" their fierce identity, fecundating and stretching the lilies. The smear of yellow pollen on Mrs. Morel's face is a grossly humorous irony. This passage is a typifying instance of the spontaneous identification Lawrence constantly found between image and meaning, between real things and what they symbolize.

Our particular culture has evolved deep prohibitions against the expression, or even the subjective acknowledgment of the kind of phallic reality with which Lawrence was concerned—and with which ancient religions were also concerned. Certainly one factor in the uneasiness that Lawrence frequently causes us is the factor of those cultural prohibitions. But these prohibitions themselves Lawrence saw as disease symptoms, though the disease was far more extensive and radical than a taboo on the phallus. It was a spiritual disease that broke down the sense of identity, of "separate selfhood," while at the same time it broke down the sense of rhythm with universal nature. Paul Morel, working his fairly unconscious, adolescent, sexual way toward Miriam, finds that rhythm and that selfhood in the spatial proportions of a wren's nest in a hedge.

He crouched down and carefully put his finger through the thorns into the round door of the nest.

"It's almost as if you were feeling inside the live body of the bird," he said, "it's so warm. They say a bird makes its nest round like a cup with pressing its breast on it. Then how did it make the ceiling round, I wonder?"

[*p. 148.*]

When Paul takes his first country walk with Clara and Miriam, the appearance of a red stallion in the woods vividly realizes in unforced symbolic dimension the power which will drive Paul from Miriam to Clara, while the image also realizes the great horse itself in its unique and mysterious identity:

As they were going beside the brook, on the Willey Water side, looking through the brake at the edge of the wood, where pink campions glowed under a few sunbeams, they saw, beyond the tree-trunks and the thin hazel bushes, a man leading a great bay horse through the gullies. The big red beast seemed to dance romantically through that dimness of green hazel drift, away there where the air was shadowy, as if it were in the past, among the fading bluebells that might have bloomed for Deirdre. . . .

The great horse breathed heavily, shifting round its red flanks, and looking suspiciously with its wonderful big eyes upwards from under its lowered head and falling mane. . . .

[*pp. 233–234.*]

A simple descriptive passage like the following, showing a hen pecking at a girl's hand, conveys the animal dynamics that is the urgent phase of the phallic power working in the boy and the girl, but its spontaneous symbolism of a larger reality is due to its faithfulness to the way a hen does peck and the feeling of the pecking—due, that is, to the actuality or "identity" of the small, homely circumstance itself:

As he went round the back, he saw Miriam kneeling in front of the hen-coop, some maize in her hand, biting her lip, and crouching in an intense attitude. The hen was eyeing her wickedly. Very gingerly she put forward her hand. The hen bobbed for her. She drew back quickly with a cry, half of fear, half of chagrin.

"It won't hurt you," said Paul.

She flushed crimson and started up.

"I only wanted to try," she said in a low voice.

"See, it doesn't hurt," he said, and, putting only two corns in his palm, he let the hen peck, peck, peck at his bare hand. "It only makes you laugh," he said.

She put her hand forward, and dragged it away, tried again, and started back with a cry. He frowned.

"Why, I'd let her take corn from my face," said Paul, "only she bumps a bit. She's ever so neat. If she wasn't, look how much ground she'd peck up every day."

He waited grimly, and watched. At last Miriam let the bird peck from her hand. She gave a little cry—fear, and pain because of fear—rather pathetic. But she had done it, and she did it again.

"There, you see," said the boy. "It doesn't hurt, does it?"

[p. 127.]

There is more terse and obvious symbolism, of the kind typical in Lawrence, in that sequence where Clara's red carnations splatter their petals over her clothes and on the ground where she and Paul first make love, but we acquire the best and the controlling sense of Lawrence's gift for the image, as dramatic and thematic expression, in those passages where his urgency is to see *things* and to see them clearly and completely in their most individualizing traits, for the character of his vision is such that, in truly seeing them as they are, he sees through them to what they mean.

We frequently notice the differentiating significance of a writer's treatment of nature—that is, of that part of "nature" which is constituted by earth and air and water and the non-human creatures; and we find that attitudes toward nature are deeply associated with attitudes toward human "good," human destiny, human happiness, human salvation, the characteristic problems of being human. One might cite, for instance, in *Tom Jones*, Fielding's highly stylized treatment of outdoor nature (as in the passage in which Tom dreams of Sophia beside the brook, and Mollie Seagrim approaches): here nature has only generalized attributes for whose description and understanding certain epithets in common educated currency are completely adequate—brooks murmur, breezes whisper, birds trill; nature is really a linguistic construction, and this rationalization of nature is appropriate in Fielding's universe since everything there exists ideally as an object of *ratio*, of reasoning intelligence. We notice in Jane Austen's *Pride and Prejudice* (in the description of Darcy's estate, for example) that outdoor nature again has importance only as it serves to express rational and social character—wherefore again the generalized epithet that represents nature as either the servant of intelligence or the space where intelligence operates. In George Eliot's *Adam Bede*, where there is relatively a great deal of "outdoors," nature is man's plowfield, the acre in which he finds social and ethical expression through work; this is only a different variety of the conception of nature as significant by virtue of what man's intelligential and social character makes of it for his ends.

With Emily Brontë, we come nearer to Lawrence, though not very near. In *Wuthering Heights*, nature's importance is due not to its yielding itself up to domestication in man's reason, or offering itself as an instrument by which he expresses his conscience before God or society, but to its fiercely unregenerate difference from all that civilized man is—a difference that it constantly forces on perception by animal-like attacks on and disruptions of human order. In Hardy, nature is also a daemonic entity in its own right, and not only unrationalizable but specifically hostile to the human reason. It is worth noting that, among all English novelists, Hardy and Lawrence have the most faithful touch for the things of nature and the greatest evocative genius in bringing them before the imagination. But there are certain definitive differences of attitude. Both Emily Brontë's and Hardy's worlds are dual, and there is no way of bringing the oppositions of the dualism together: on the one side of the cleavage are those attributes of man that we call "human," his reason, his ethical sensibility; and on the other side is "nature"—the elements and the creatures and man's own instinctive life that he shares with the nonhuman creatures. The opposition is resolved only by destruction of the "human": a destruction that is in Emily Brontë profoundly attractive, in Hardy tragic. But Lawrence's world is multiple rather than dual. Everything in it is a separate and individual "other," every person, every creature, every object (like the madonna lilies, the rhubarb plants, the wren's nest, the stallion); and there is a creative relationship between people and between people and things so long as this "otherness" is acknowledged. When it is denied—and it is denied when man tries to rationalize nature and society, or when he presumptuously assumes the things of nature to be merely instruments for the expression of himself, or when he attempts to exercise personal possessorship over people—then he destroys his own selfhood and exerts a destructive influence all about him.

In *Sons and Lovers*, only in Morel himself, brutalized and spiritually maimed as he is, does the germ of selfhood remain intact; and—this is the correlative proposition in Lawrence—in him only does the biological life force have simple, unequivocal assertion. Morel wants to live, by hook or crook, while his sons want to die. To live is to obey a rhythm involving more than conscious attitudes and involving more than human beings—involving all nature; a rhythm indifferent to the greediness of reason, indifferent to idiosyncrasies of culture and idealism. The image associated with Morel is that of the coalpits, where he descends daily and from which he ascends at night blackened and tired. It is a symbol of rhythmic descent and ascent, like a sexual rhythm, or like the rhythm of sleep and awaking or of death and life. True, the work in the coalpits reverses the natural use of the hours of light and dark and is an economic distortion of that rhythm in nature—and Morel and the other colliers bear the spiritual traumata of that distortion; for Lawrence is dealing with the real environment of modern men, in its complexity and injuriousness. Nevertheless, the work at the pits is still symbolic of the greater rhythm governing life and obedience to which is salvation. Throughout the book, the coalpits are always at the horizon:

On the fallow land the young wheat shone silkily. Minton pit waved its plumes of white steam, coughed, and rattled hoarsely.

"Now look at that!" said Mrs. Morel. Mother and son stood on the road to watch. Along the ridge of the great pit-hill crawled a little group in silhouette against the sky, a horse, a small truck, and a man. They climbed the incline against the heavens. At the end the man tipped the waggon. There was an undue rattle as the waste fell down the sheer slope of the enormous bank. . . .

"Look how it heaps together," [Paul says of the pit] "like something alive almost—a big creature that you don't know. . . . And all the trucks standing waiting, like a string of beasts to be fed. . . . I like the feel of *men* on things, while they're alive. There's a feel of men about trucks, because they've been handled with men's hands, all of them."

[*pp. 122–123.*]

Paul associates the pits not only with virility but with being alive. The trucks themselves become alive because they have been handled by men. The symbolism of the pits is identical with that of Morel, the father, the irrational life principle that is unequally embattled against the death principle in the mother, the rational and idealizing principle working rhythmlessly, greedily, presumptuously, and possessively.

The sons' attitude toward the father is ambivalent, weighted toward hate because the superior cultural equipment of the mother shows his crudeness in relief; but again and again bits of homely characterization of Morel show that the children—and even the mother herself—sense, however uncomfortably, the attractiveness of his simple masculine integrity. He has, uninjurable, what the mother's possessiveness has injured in the sons:

"Shut that doo-er!" bawled Morel furiously.

Annie banged it behind her, and was gone.

"If tha oppens it again while I'm weshin' me, I'll ma'e thy jaw rattle," he threatened from the midst of his soapsuds. Paul and the mother frowned to hear him.

Presently he came running out of the scullery, with the soapy water dripping from him, dithering with cold.

"Oh, my sirs!" he said. "Wheer's my towel?"

It was hung on a chair to warm before the fire, otherwise he would have bullied and blustered. He squatted on his heels before the hot baking-fire to dry himself.

"F-ff-f!" he went, pretending to shudder with cold.

"Goodness, man, don't be such a kid!" said Mrs. Morel. "It's *not* cold."

"Thee strip thysen stark nak'd to wesh thy flesh i' that scullery," said the miner, as he rubbed his hair; "nowt b'r a ice-'ouse!"

"And I shouldn't make that fuss," replied his wife.

"No, tha'd drop down stiff, as dead as a door-knob, wi' thy nesh sides."

"Why is a door-knob deader than anything else?" asked Paul, curious.

"Eh, I dunno; that's what they say," replied his father. "But there's that much draught i' yon scullery, as it blows through your ribs like through a five-barred gate."

"It would have some difficulty in blowing through yours," said Mrs. Morel.

Morel looked down ruefully at his sides.

"Me!" he exclaimed. "I'm nowt b'r a skinned rabbit. My bones fair juts out on me."

"I should like to know where," retorted his wife.

"Iv-ry-wheer! I'm nobbut a sack o' faggots."

Mrs. Morel laughed. He had still a wonderfully young body, muscular, without any fat. His skin was smooth and clear. It might have been the body of a man of twenty-eight, except that there were, perhaps, too many blue scars, like tattoo-marks, where the coal-dust remained under the skin, and that his chest was too hairy. But he put his hands on his sides ruefully. It was his fixed belief that, because he did not get fat, he was as thin as a starved rat.

Paul looked at his father's thick, brownish hands all scarred, with broken nails, rubbing the fine smoothness of his sides, and the incongruity struck him. It seemed strange they were the same flesh.

[*pp. 196–197.*]

Morel talks the dialect that is the speech of physical tenderness in Lawrence's books.[4] It is to the dialect of his father that Paul reverts when he is tussling with Beatrice in adolescent erotic

---

[4] This observation is made by Diana Trilling in her Introduction to *The Portable D. H. Lawrence* (New York: The Viking Press, Inc., 1947). [D.V.G.]

play (letting the mother's bread burn, that he should have been watching), and that Arthur, the only one of the sons whom the mother has not corrupted, uses in his love-making, and that Paul uses again when he makes love to Clara, the uncomplex woman who is able for a while to give him his sexual manhood and his "separate selfhood." The sons never use the dialect with their mother, and Paul never uses it with Miriam. It is the speech used by Mellors in *Lady Chatterley's Lover*; and, significantly perhaps, Mellors' name is an anagram on the name Morel.

Some of the best moments in the children's life are associated with the father, when Morel has his "good" periods and enters again into the intimate activity of the family—and some of the best, most simply objective writing in the book communicates these moments, as for instance the passage in Chapter 4 where Morel is engaged in making fuses:

. . . Morel fetched a sheaf of long sound wheat-straws from the attic. These he cleaned with his hand, till each one gleamed like a stalk of gold, after which he cut the straws into lengths of about six inches, leaving, if he could, a notch at the bottom of each piece. He always had a beautifully sharp knife that could cut a straw clean without hurting it. Then he set in the middle of the table a heap of gun-powder, a little pile of black grains upon the white-scrubbed board. He made and trimmed the straws while Paul and Annie filled and plugged them. Paul loved to see the black grains trickle down a crack in his palm into the mouth of the straw, peppering jollily downwards till the straw was full. Then he bunged up the mouth with a bit of soap—which he got on his thumb-nail from a pat in a saucer—and the straw was finished.

[*p. 64.*]

There is a purity of realization in this very simple kind of exposition that, on the face of it, resists associating itself with any *symbolic* function—if we tend to think of a "symbol" as splitting itself apart into a thing and a meaning, with a mental arrow connecting the two. The best in Lawrence carries the authenticity of a faithfully observed, concrete actuality that refuses to be so split; its symbolism is a radiation that leaves

540 / CONTEXTS OF RESPONSE

it intact in itself. So, in the passage above, the scene is intact as homely realism, but it radiates Lawrence's controlling sense of the characterful integrity of objects—the clean wheat straws, the whitely scrubbed table, the black grains peppering down a crack in the child's palm, the bung of soap on a thumbnail— and that integrity is here associated with the man Morel and his own integrity of warm and absolute maleness. Thus it is another representation of the creative life force witnessed in the independent objectivity of things that are wholly concrete and wholly themselves.

The human attempt to distort and corrupt that selfhood is reflected in Miriam's attitude toward flowers:

Round the wild, tussocky lawn at the back of the house was a thorn hedge, under which daffodils were craning forward from among their sheaves of grey-green blades. The cheeks of the flowers were greenish with cold. But still some had burst, and their gold ruffled and glowed. Miriam went on her knees before one cluster, took a wild-looking daffodil between her hands, turned up its face of gold to her, and bowed down, caressing it with her mouth and cheeks and brow. He stood aside, with his hands in his pockets, watching her. One after another she turned up to him the faces of the yellow, bursten flowers appealingly, fondling them lavishly all the while. . . .

"Why must you always be fondling things!" he said irritably. . . . "Can you never like things without clutching them as if you wanted to pull the heart out of them? . . . You're always begging things to love you. . . . Even the flowers, you have to fawn on them—"

Rhythmically, Miriam was swaying and stroking the flower with her mouth. . . .

"You don't want to love—your eternal and abnormal craving is to be loved. You aren't positive, you're negative. You absorb, absorb, as if you must fill yourself up with love, because you've got a shortage somewhere."

[*pp. 217–218.*]

The relationship of the girl to the flowers is that of a blasphemous possessorship which denies the separateness of living entities—the craving to break down boundaries between thing and thing, that is seen also in Miriam's relationship with Paul, whom she cannot love without trying to absorb him. In contrast, there is the flower imagery in Chapter 11, where Paul goes out into the night and the garden in a moment of emotional struggle:

It grew late. Through the open door, stealthily, came the scent of madonna lilies, almost as if it were prowling abroad. Suddenly he got up and went out of doors.

The beauty of the night made him want to shout. A half-moon, dusky gold, was sinking behind the black sycamore at the end of the garden, making the sky dull purple with its glow. Nearer, a dim white fence of lilies went across the garden, and the air all round seemed to stir with scent, as if it were alive. He went across the bed of pinks, whose keen perfume came sharply across the rocking, heavy scent of the lilies, and stood alongside the white barrier of flowers. They flagged all loose, as if they were panting. The scent made him drunk. He went down to the field to watch the moon sink under.

A corncrake in the hay-close called insistently. The moon slid quite quickly downwards, growing more flushed. Behind him the great flowers leaned as if they were calling. And then, like a shock, he caught another perfume, something raw and coarse. Hunting round, he found the purple iris, touched their fleshy throats and their dark, grasping hands. At any rate, he had found something. They stood stiff in the darkness. Their scent was brutal. The moon was melting down upon the crest of the hill. It was gone; all was dark. The corncrake called still.

[*pp. 293–294.*]

The flowers here have a fierce "thereness" or "otherness" establishing them as existences in their own right—as separate, strange selves—and the demiurgic Eros is rudely insistent in their scent. Paul's perception of that independent life puts him into relation with himself, and the moment of catalytic action is marked by the brief sentence: "At any rate, he had found something." The "something" that he finds is simply the iris, dark, fleshy, mysterious, alien. He goes back into the house and tells his mother that he has decided to break off with Miriam.

Darkness—as the darkness of this night in the garden—has in Lawrence a special symbolic potency. It is a natural and universal symbol, but it offers itself with special richness to Lawrence because of the character of his governing vision. Darkness is half of the rhythm of the day, the darkness of unconsciousness is half of the rhythm of the mind, and the darkness of death is half of the rhythm of life. Denial of this phase of the universal tide is the great sin, the sin committed by modern economy and modern rationalism. In acceptance of the dark, man is renewed to himself—and to light, to consciousness, to reason, to brotherhood. But by refusal to accept that half of the rhythm, he becomes impotent, his reason becomes destructive, and he loses the sense of the independence of others which is essential to brotherhood. In Chapter 13 of *Sons and Lovers* there is a passage that realizes something of what we have been saying. It occurs just after Paul has made love to Clara in a field:

All the while the peewits were screaming in the field. When he came to, he wondered what was near his eyes, curving and strong with life in the dark, and what voice it was speaking. Then he realized it was the grass, and the peewit was calling. The warmth was Clara's breathing heaving. He lifted his head, and looked into her eyes. They were dark and shining and strange, life wild at the source staring into his life, stranger to him, yet meeting him; and he put his face down on her throat, afraid. What was she? A strong, strange, wild life, that breathed with his in the darkness through this hour. It was all so much bigger than themselves that he was hushed. They had met, and included in their meeting the thrust of the manifold grass-stems, the cry of the peewit, the wheel of the stars. . . .

. . . after such an evening they both were very still. . . . They felt small, half afraid, childish, and wondering, like Adam and Eve when they lost their innocence and realized the magnificence of the power which drove them out of Paradise and across the great night and the great day of humanity. It was for each of them an initiation. . . . To know their own nothingness, to know the tremendous living flood which carried them always, gave them rest within themselves. If so great a magnificent power could overwhelm them, identify them altogether with itself, so that they knew they were only grains in the tremendous heave that lifted every grass-blade its little height, and every tree, and living thing, then why fret about themselves? They could let themselves be carried by life, and they felt a sort of peace each in the other. There was a verification which they had had together. Nothing could nullify it, nothing could take it away; it was almost their belief in life.

[*pp.* 353–354.]

But then we are told that "Clara was not satisfied. . . . She thought it was he whom she wanted. . . . She had not got him; she was not satisfied." This is the impulse toward personal possessorship that constantly confuses and distorts human relationships in Lawrence's books; it is a denial of the otherness of people, and a denial, really, of the great inhuman life force, the primal "otherness" through which people have their independent definition as well as their creative community. Paul had felt that "his experience had been impersonal, and not Clara"; and he had wanted the same impersonality in Clara, an impersonality consonant with that of the manifold grass stems and the peewits' calling and the wheel of the stars. André Malraux, in his preface to the French translation of *Lady Chatterley's Lover*, says that this "couple-advocate," Lawrence, is concerned not with his own individuality or that of his mate, but with "being": "Lawrence has no wish to be either happy or great," Malraux says; "he is only concerned with being."[5] The concern with being, with simple being-a-self (as distinguished from imposing the ego or abdicating selfhood in the mass), can be understood only in the context of twentieth century man's resignation to herd ideologies, herd recreations, herd rationalizations. Lawrence's missionary and prophetic impulse, like Dostoevsky's, was to combat the excesses of rationalism and individualism, excesses that have led—paradoxically enough—to the release of monstrously destructive irrationals and to the impotence of the individual. He wanted to bring man's self-definition and creativity back into existence through recognition of and vital relationship with the rhythms that men share with the nonhuman world; for he thought that thus

---

[5] In *Criterion*, XII:xlvii (1932–1933), 217. [D.V.G.]

men could find not only the selves that they had denied, but also the brotherhood they had lost.

The darkness of the phallic consciousness is the correlative of a passionate life assertion, strong as the thrust of the grass stems in the field where Paul and Clara make love, and as the dynamics of the wheeling stars. "In the lowest trough of the night" there is always "a flare of the pit." A pillar of cloud by day, the pit is a pillar of fire by night: and the Lord is at the pit top. As a descent of darkness and an ascent of flame is associated with the secret, essential, scatheless maleness of the father, so also the passionate self-forgetful play of the children is associated with a fiery light in the night—an isolated lamp-post, a blood-red moon, and behind, "the great scoop of darkness, as if all the night were there." It is this understanding of the symbolism of darkness in Lawrence that gives tragic dignity to such a scene as that of the bringing home of William's coffin through the darkness of the night:

Morel and Paul went, with a candle, into the parlour. There was no gas there. The father unscrewed the top of the big mahogany oval table, and cleared the middle of the room; then he arranged six chairs opposite each other, so that the coffin could stand on their beds.

"You niver seed such a length as he is!" said the miner, and watching anxiously as he worked.

Paul went to the bay window and looked out. The ash-tree stood monstrous and black in front of the wide darkness. It was a faintly luminous night. Paul went back to his mother.

At ten o'clock Morel called:

"He's here!"

Everyone started. There was a noise of unbarring and unlocking the front door, which opened straight from the night into the room.

"Bring another candle," called Morel. . . .

There was the noise of wheels. Outside in the darkness of the street below Paul could see horses and a black vehicle, one lamp, and a few pale faces; then some men, miners, all in their shirt-sleeves, seemed to struggle in the obscurity. Presently two men appeared, bowed beneath a great weight. It was Morel and his neighbour.

"Steady!" called Morel, out of breath.

He and his fellow mounted the steep garden step, heaved into the candlelight with their gleaming coffin-end. Limbs of other men were seen struggling behind. Morel and Burns, in front, staggered; the great dark weight swayed.

"Steady, steady!" cried Morel, as if in pain. . . .

The coffin swayed, the men began to mount the three steps with their load. Annie's candle flickered, and she whimpered as the first men appeared, and the limbs and bowed heads of six men struggled to climb into the room, bearing the coffin that rode like sorrow on their living flesh.

[*pp. 138–139.*]

Here the darkness appears in another indivisible aspect of its mystery—as the darkness of death. Perhaps no other modern writer besides Rilke and Mann has tried so sincerely to bring death into relationship with life as Lawrence did, and each under the assumption that life, to know itself creatively, must know its relationship with death; a relationship which the ethos of some hundred and fifty years of rationalism and industrialism and "progress" have striven to exorcise, and by that perversion brought men to an abject worship of death and to holocausts such as that of Hiroshima. *Sons and Lovers* ends with Paul a derelict in the "drift toward death," which Lawrence thought of as the disease syndrome of his time and of Europe. But the death drift, the death worship, is for Lawrence a hideous distortion of the relationship of death to life. In the scene in which William's coffin is brought home, the front door "opened straight from the night into the room." So, in their rhythmic proportions, life and death open straight into each other, as do the light of consciousness and the darkness of the unconscious, and the usurpation of either one is a perversion of the other. Stephen Spender calls Lawrence "the most hopeful modern writer." His "dark gods," Spender says,

. . . are symbols of an inescapable mystery: the point of comprehension where the senses are aware of an otherness in objects which extends beyond the senses, and the possibility of a relationship between the human individual and the forces outside himself, which is capable of creating in him a new state of mind. Lawrence is the most hopeful modern writer, because he looks beyond the human to the nonhuman, which can be discovered within the human.[6]

---

[6] "The Life of Literature," *op. cit.* [D.V.G.]

MARK SPILKA

Mark Spilka has taught at the University of Michigan, teaches English at Brown University, and is the editor of a magazine, *Novel: A Forum on Fiction*. He is the author of *Dickens and Kafka* and the editor of *D. H. Lawrence: A Collection of Critical Essays*.

HOW TO PICK FLOWERS

Father Tiverton has observed, quite shrewdly, that Lawrence had to die as a son before he could become a great artist. That death is chronicled, he thinks, at the end of *Sons and Lovers*, as Paul Morel refuses to follow his mother towards the grave:

> But no, he would not give in. Turning sharply, he walked towards the city's gold phosphorescence. His fists were shut, his mouth set fast. He would not take that direction, to the darkness, to follow her. He walked towards the faintly humming, glowing town, quickly.
>
> [*p. 420.*]

Paul's death as a son implies his birth here as a man, and the potential birth of Lawrence himself as man and artist. It is a tenable theory, and from a biographical point of view, an important one.

But there are a number of other ways, equally important, in which *Sons and Lovers* serves as the matrix for all of Lawrence's future work. The structural rhythms of the book are based, for example, upon poetic rather than narrative logic: the language backs and fills with the struggle between Walter and Gertrude Morel; in the scenes between Paul and Miriam Leivers, the tempo is labored and strained; then it quickens perceptibly when Paul is with Clara Dawes. In each case, the emotional predicament determines the pace of the language, so that the novel surges along, always in key with the inward tensions of the protagonists: and this will prove the general rule in future novels.

From *The Love Ethic of D. H. Lawrence*, by Mark Spilka (Bloomington, Ind.: Indiana University Press, 1955), pp. 39–59. Copyright © 1955 by Indiana University Press. All Rights Reserved. Reprinted by permission.

But Lawrence makes a more crucial connection in this book between language and emotion: for the symbolic scenes are extremely literal, and the symbols seem to function as integral strands in the web of emotional tensions. They are seldom used in the Elizabethan sense, as mere omens of supernatural pleasure or displeasure; instead they seem to express some close relationship between man and nature. Thus Mrs. Morel holds her unwanted baby, Paul, up to the sun, the literal source of life, in a gesture of renunciation; and Morel himself stands fascinated, after a violent quarrel with his wife, as the drops of her blood soak into their baby's scalp—and this literal sealing of the blood-tie breaks his manhood; later on, the young lad Paul stares fixedly at the blood-red moon, which has roused in him his first violent sexual passion—and roused it as a force, not as a symbol. In each case, the relation between man and nature is direct and vital, and sun, blood, and moon are more "integral" than symbolic. This too will prove the general rule in future novels, though almost no one seems to have recognized this rather overwhelming truth about Lawrence's use of symbols.[1]

In *The Later D. H. Lawrence*, for example, Professor William Tindall treats Lawrence as a symbolist, and he tries to align him with the *correspondence* tradition established by Baudelaire. But the French symbolists were searching for the spiritual infinite, and Lawrence was not: his symbols operate at a different level of language than theirs, and for different ends; they are not suggestive evocations of timeless spiritual reality, but material and focal expressions of those vague but powerful forces of nature which occur, quite patently, in time.[2] In the

[1] The outstanding exception here is Dorothy Van Ghent, who speaks of the concrete reality of Lawrence's symbols. [See her essay "On *Sons and Lovers*," earlier in this volume.] See also Frederick Hoffman's view that Lawrence's symbols merely keep affective states alive, *Freudianism and the Literary Mind* (Baton Rouge: Louisiana State University Press, 1945), pp. 178–179. [M.S.]

[2] For a full account of the differences between Lawrence and the symbolists, see Spilka's article, "Was D. H. Lawrence a Symbolist?" *Accent*, XV (Winter, 1955), 49–60. [M.S.]

short story "Sun," for example, a woman moves from the sterile touch of her husband to life-giving contact with the sun.

It was not just taking sun-baths. It was much more than that. Something deep inside her unfolded and relaxed, and she was given. By some mysterious power inside her, deeper than her known consciousness and will, she was put into connection with the sun, and the stream flowed of itself, from her womb. She herself, her conscious self, was secondary, a secondary person, almost an on-looker. The true Juliet was this dark flow from her deep body to the sun. [*The Complete Short Stories of D. H. Lawrence*, Vol. II, New York: The Viking Press, 1961, p. 535.]

A symbolical flow? No, not even a face-saving *correspondence*. Lawrence means what he says here, though embarrassed critics like Tindall will always blithely cancel out his meaning: "the heroine in *Sun*," he writes, "responds with her little blazing consciousness to the 'great blazing consciousness' of heaven. There she lies naked, laughing to herself, with a flower in her navel. Her behavior may seem odd—but only when the symbolic receives a literal interpretation." But there is no other interpretation. The story stands or falls on the woman's living contact with the sun. The connection is organic and dramatic, and what Tindall really finds odd here is the thought that man can live in anything but an alien universe.

Most modern readers will side with Tindall in this respect, but Lawrence felt otherwise, and the only point I want to make is this: that he always wrote otherwise—as if the sun were not merely a gas ball but a source of life, and the moon not merely a satellite but a living force.

II

Strangely enough, he first began to write this way in *Sons and Lovers*, his third and supposedly his most conventional novel. It seems ironic, then, that Mark Schorer should criticise him for failing to use "technique as discovery" in this book—especially when he actually employs here his most characteristic techniques to discover things which Mr. Schorer overlooks, or perhaps ignores, in his justly famous essay.[3] For Lawrence makes his first ambitious attempt, in *Sons and Lovers*, to place his major characters in active relation with a live and responsive universe: and this helps to account, I think, for the strange subjective power of the novel.

We get only a slight hint of this arrangement in the case of Walter Morel. As the book develops, he gradually breaks his own manhood; but this breakdown coincides with an actual shrinkage in physique, and this shrinkage seems to come from the direct contact between Morel and the forces of nature. Thus, instead of facing his problems at home, Morel loves to slip off with his friends for good times; on one of these drunken sprees he falls asleep in an open field, and then wakens, an hour later, feeling queer—and the physical breakdown begins here, with Morel in the act of denying his own manhood. During the bout of illness which follows, his wife begins to cast him off, and she turns to the children, for the first time, "for love and life." Admittedly, the incident is more illusive than real, but the natural contact is there, and it becomes more clearly evident at other points in the novel, when the forces of nature emerge as actual "presences." Before Paul's birth, for example, the drunken Morel shuts his wife out into the garden, and she feels these presences under the "blinding" August moon:

She became aware of something about her. With an effort she roused herself to see what it was that penetrated her consciousness. The tall white lilies were reeling in the moonlight, and the air was charged with their perfume, as with a presence. Mrs. Morel gasped slightly in fear. She touched the big, pallid flowers on their petals, then shivered. They seemed to be stretching in the moonlight. She put her hand into one white bin: the gold scarcely showed on her fingers by moonlight. She bent down to look at the binful of yellow pollen; but it only appeared dusky. Then she drank a deep draught of the scent. It almost made her dizzy.

[*p. 24*.]

Conscious only of the child within her, Mrs. Morel feels herself melting away: "After a time the child, too, melted with

---

[3] "Technique as Discovery," *Hudson Review*, I (1948), 68–87. [M.S.]

her in the mixing-pot of moonlight, and she rested with the hills and lilies and houses, all swum together in a kind of swoon." Later, when Morel lets her back into the house, she smiles faintly upon seeing her face in the bedroom mirror, "all smeared with the yellow dust of lilies." Both mother and unborn child have been enveloped by the powerful dark forces of life (they have not merged with the "infinite"), and the dust becomes a kiss of benediction for them both, the confirmation of their vitality. Later on, in *Aaron's Rod*, Lawrence would see the same flower, the lily, as a symbol of vital individuality— "Flowers with good roots in the mud and muck . . . fearless blossoms in air" and Lilly, the Lawrence-figure in the book, would personify this vitality and aloofness in name and deed.

As these thoughts indicate, flowers are the most important of the "vital forces" in *Sons and Lovers*. The novel is saturated with their presence, and Paul and his three sweethearts are judged, again and again, by their attitude toward them, or more accurately, by their *relations* with them. The "lad-and-girl" affair between Paul and Miriam, for example, is a virtual communion between the two lovers and the flowers they both admire. And this communion begins with Paul's first words to the shy, romantic girl, on their meeting at Willey Farm:

He was in the garden smelling the gillivers and looking at the plants, when the girl came out quickly to the heap of coal which stood by the fence.

"I suppose these are cabbage-roses?" he said to her, pointing to the bushes along the fence. . . .

"I don't know," she faltered. "They're white with pink middles."

"Then they're maiden-blush."

Miriam flushed. . . .

[*p. 125.*]

As the book moves on, the identification of Miriam with maiden-blush is broadened to imply an unhealthy spirituality. Paul grows to hate her worshipful, fawning attitude toward life, an attitude which is consistently revealed by her "relations" with flowers: "When she bent and breathed a flower, it was as if she and the flower were loving each other. Paul hated her for it. There seemed a sort of exposure about the action, something too intimate" (p. 173). This hatred bursts into open resentment as their affair draws toward an end. One day Paul lashes out at the girl, at Willey Farm, for caressing daffodils:

Can you never like things without clutching them as if you wanted to pull the heart out of them? . . .
You wheedle the soul out of things. . . . I would never wheedle—at any rate, I'd go straight. . . .
You're always begging things to love you . . . as if you were a beggar for love. Even the flowers, you have to fawn on them . . .
[p. 218.]

In another context, Lawrence attacks Wordsworth himself for a similar offense—for attempting to melt down a poor primrose "into a Williamish oneness":

He didn't leave it with a soul of its own. It had to have his soul. And nature had to be sweet and pure, Williamish. Sweet-Williamish at that! Anthropomorphized! Anthropomorphism, that allows nothing to call its soul its own, save anthropos. . . . [*The Later D. H. Lawrence*, New York: Alfred Knopf, 1952, p. 209.]

But the primrose was alive in its own right, for Lawrence; it had "its own peculiar primrosy identity . . . its own individuality." And once again his approach to nature is primitive and direct, an affirmation of the "religious dignity" of life "in its humblest and in its highest forms." For if men, animals and plants are all on the same level, at the primitive stage, then none of them can readily usurp the others' souls.

We can safely say, then, that Miriam is Wordsworth, at least in her attitude toward nature, or toward flowers. She is finally damned by Paul as a nun, and certainly this recalls those famous lines by Wordsworth: "It is a beauteous evening, calm and free;/The holy time is quiet as a nun/Breathless with adoration. . . ." Of course, the metaphor is appropriate within context, but Lawrence would never reduce nature to the bloodless spirituality of a nun, with no vitality of its own.

Yet in the early stages of *Sons and Lovers*, Paul Morel, the

Lawrence-figure, has actually joined with Miriam in such blood-less communions over flowers. He has even taken pride in bring-ing them to life in the girl's imagination, and their love has its beginning "in this atmosphere of subtle intimacy, this meeting in their common feeling for something in nature. . . ." But as we know, Miriam's approach to nature is ultimately deadly, and this is the key to the dissembling of their love: she loves Paul as she loves flowers, she worships him as she worships them and Paul feels suffocated by such adoration. This feeling is heavily underscored, for example, in the early "lad-and-girl" courtship scenes: one evening, as the two of them walk through the woods, Miriam leads Paul on, eagerly, to a wild-rose bush she has previously discovered.

> They were going to have a communion together—something that thrilled her, something holy. He was walking beside her in silence. They were very near to each other. She trembled, and he listened, vaguely anxious. . . . Then she saw her bush.
> "Ah!" she cried, hastening forward.
> It was very still. The tree was tall and straggling. It had thrown its briers over a hawthorn-bush, and its long streamers trailed thick, right down to the grass, splashing the darkness everywhere with great spilt stars, pure white. In bosses of ivory and in large splashed stars the roses gleamed on the darkness of foliage and stems and grass. Paul and Miriam stood close together, silent, and watched. Point after point the steady roses shone out to them, seeming to kindle something in their souls. The dusk came like smoke around, and still did not put out the roses.
> Paul looked into Miriam's eyes. She was pale and expectant with wonder, her lips were parted, and her dark eyes lay open to him. His look seemed to travel down into her. Her soul quivered. It was the communion she wanted. . . .
>
> [*pp. 159–160.*]

But once the communion "takes," once Paul has brought the roses into her soul (for their anthropomorphic slaughter), he turns aside, feeling pained, anxious, and imprisoned. They part quickly, and he stumbles away toward home—"as soon as he was out of the wood, in the free open meadow, where he could breathe, he started to run as fast as he could. It was like a delicious delirium in his veins."

A few pages later, Lawrence describes a similar scene between Paul and his mother, and the contrast is brilliantly revealing. Mrs. Morel has just discovered three deep blue scyllas under a bush in the garden. She calls Paul to her side excitedly:

"Now just see those! . . . I was looking at the currant-bushes, when, thinks I to myself, 'There's something very blue; is it a bit of sugar-bag?' and there, behold you! Sugar-bag! Three glories of the snow, and such beauties! But where on earth did they come from?"

"I don't know. . . ."

"Well, that's a marvel, now! I *thought* I knew every weed and blade in this garden. But *haven't* they done well? You see, that gooseberry-bush just shelters them. Not nipped, not touched! . . ."

"They're a glorious color! . . ."

"Aren't they! . . . I guess they come from Switzerland, where they say they have such lovely things. Fancy them against the snow! . . ."

She was full of excitement and elation. The garden was an endless joy to her. . . . Every morning after breakfast she went out and was happy pottering about in it. And it was true, she knew every weed and blade.

[*pp. 163–164.*]

The vitality, the animation, the healthy glow of the life-flame, is typical of Mrs. Morel. Always, when Paul brings her flowers, the scene is gay, lively, warm, or poignant. If the cold family parlor "kills every bit of a plant you put in [it]," outside, in the garden or in the open fields, mother and son are always in bright and vital contact with the nodding heads of surrounding flowers. Indeed, even near death this paradoxically destructive woman fosters sunflowers in her garden [p. 378].

But the most powerful of the floral scenes takes place between Paul and his rival sweethearts, Miriam Leivers and Clara Dawes. And here Richard Aldington makes a terrible (and perhaps typical) blunder, in his *Portrait of a Genius But . . .*:

he attempts to show Lawrence's willfulness and inconsistency (his *but-ness*) by referring to the way Paul and Miriam (i.e., Lawrence and Jessie Chambers) touch flowers: "what was wrong for her was right for him if he happened to want to do it."[4] But this is to miss the whole beauty of the most important revelation scene in *Sons and Lovers*, the scene in which Paul, Miriam, and Clara are together on Lawrence's favorite battleground: an open field in the country. Paul and Clara have just been formally introduced; he is passionately attracted to her, and eventually he will become her lover. But Miriam is aware of this attraction, and she has actually arranged the whole meeting as a test; for she believes that her hold on Paul's "higher" nature, his soul, will prevail over his desires for "lower" things—Clara's body. And her belief seems to be borne out when the three of them come to an open field, with its many "clusters of strong flowers." Ah! cries Miriam, and her eyes meet Paul's. They commune. Clara sulks. Then Paul and Miriam begin to pick flowers:

He kneeled on one knee, quickly gathering the best blossoms, moving from tuft to tuft restlessly, talking softly all the time. Miriam plucked the flowers lovingly, lingering over them. He always seemed to her too quick and almost scientific. Yet his bunches had a natural beauty more than hers. He loved them, but as if they were his and he had a right to them. She had more reverence for them: they held something she had not.

[*p. 237.*]

And there is the crux of the matter: the flowers hold life as Paul himself holds life: his contact with the "God-stuff" is spontaneous and direct—he is alive and organic, and the flowers are his to take. But negative, spiritual, sacrificial Miriam 'wheedle[s] the soul out of things"; she kills life and has no right to it. What is wrong for her is actually right for him,

---

[4] *D. H. Lawrence: Portrait of a Genius But* . . . (New York: Duell, Sloan & Pearce, 1950), pp. 47–48, 60. Dorothy Van Ghent also clarifies some of the passages Aldington misreads in her comments on flower imagery, *The English Novel*, pp. 256–257. [M.S.]

since life kindles life and death kills it—which is the essence of Lawrencean communion.

But the revelation process now extends to Clara Dawes. She has already been sketched out as a disconsolate suffragette, and now she states, militantly, that flowers shouldn't be picked because it kills them. What she means, in effect, is that *she* doesn't want to be "picked" or taken by any man; she has separated from her husband, and for her the flowers become as proud and frigid, in their isolation, as she would like to be in hers. But since Paul believes that life belongs to the living, he begins to argue the point with her; then, as the scene unfolds, he shifts from rational argument to pagan flower dance:

> Clara's hat lay on the grass not far off. She was kneeling, bending forward still to smell the flowers. Her neck gave him a sharp pang, such a beautiful thing, yet not proud of itself just now. Her breasts swung slightly in her blouse. The arching curve of her back was beautiful and strong; she wore no stays. Suddenly, without knowing, he was scattering a handful of cowslips over her hair and neck, saying:
> > "Ashes to ashes, and dust to dust,
> > If the Lord won't have you the devil must."
> The chill flowers fell on her neck. She looked up at him with almost pitiful, scared grey eyes, wondering what he was doing. Flowers fell on her face, and she shut her eyes.
> Suddenly, standing there above her, he felt awkward.
> "I thought you wanted a funeral," he said, ill at ease.
> Clara laughed strangely, and rose, picking the cowslips from her hair. She took up her hat and pinned it on. One flower had remained tangled in her hair. He saw, but would not tell her. He gathered up the flowers he had sprinkled over her.
>
> [*pp.* 238–239.]

Because of this pagan ritual, Paul and Clara now engage in their first warm, spirited conversation—about a patch of blue bells poised in fear at the edge of the wood, like a man about to go outward into life, or like a woman about to enter the dark woods of love. Both images are clearly implied as the scene ends; both reveal character and situation, and on a deeper level, the poised flowers hint at one of Lawrence's favorite major themes—that Western man, living too much in the open spaces of the mind, must sooner or later confront the darker depths of emotion. And the key to all this revelation is how to pick flowers: Miriam, with false reverence; Paul with love, like a lover; and Clara not at all—but at least she respects the life in them, and later, when she is fully "awakened" by Paul, she will pick them, and the flowers, in their turn, will "defend" her—whereas Miriam's sheltered blooms will quickly die [p. 238]. All of which, if it proves nothing else, at least indicates that logic (in this case Mr. Aldington's logic) is not much of a match for the sure intuition of a creative artist.

III

But since flowers are the burden of this argument, the point must be pressed still further: the "picking scene" floods out to the rest of the book, that is, in either direction—backward to the benedictive dust on Mrs. Morel's nose, or forward, to the first love scene between Paul and Clara, and to the final parting of Paul and Miriam in the closing paragraphs of the novel. For Paul, blessed by lily dust, must now claim the flower of life which caught in Clara's hair, and he must also place the flowers of death in Miriam's arms. In the first case, the scarlet carnations which he buys for Clara become an active force when he takes her on a trip to the countryside. Once there, the would-be lovers find a secluded spot near the bank of the Trent river, and for the first time they make love. The flowers give benediction to their union:

> When she arose, he looking on the ground all the time, saw sud-
> denly sprinkled on the black, wet beech-roots many scarlet carnation
> petals, like splashed drops of blood; and red, small splashes fell from
> her bosom, streaming down her dress to her feet.
> "Your flowers are smashed," he said.
>
> [*p. 311.*]

The smashing works both ways, however, for this is the "baptism of fire in passion" which Paul has been seeking. Here

too is the first sign of the vision of love which Lawrence would develop, in time, to full and confident expression as an ethic of renewal. Paul and Clara, because of their affair, will now come into their fullness as man and woman. And this is what Paul seems to be driving at, later on, when he explains to Miriam that Clara had been only half-alive with her husband, and that she needed to be fully awakened:

"That's what one *must have*, I think . . . the real, real flame of feeling through another person—once, only once, if it only lasts three months. See, my mother looks as if she'd *had* everything that was necessary for her living and developing. There's not a tiny bit of a feeling of sterility about her."

"No," said Miriam.

"And with my father, at first I'm sure she had the real thing. She knows; she has been there. You can feel it about her, and about him, and about hundreds of people you meet every day; and, once it has happened to you, you can go on with anything and ripen."

"What has happened exactly?" asked Miriam.

"It's so hard to say, but the something big and intense that changes you when you really come together with somebody else. It almost seems to fertilize your soul and make it that you can go on and mature."

"And you think your mother had it with your father?"

"Yes; and at bottom she feels grateful to him for giving it her, even now, though they are miles apart."

"And you think Clara never had it?"

"I'm sure."

[*pp*. 317–318.]

Paul's convictions are soon borne out: for once this "fertilization" process occurs, Clara is able to take back her husband, and Paul himself becomes man enough to resist the deathward pull from his mother's grave: "Together they had received the baptism of life; but now their missions were separate." The sign of this baptism, the active confirmation of it, was the scattering of red petals across their first bed—for the flowers *participated* in the mystery rite.

As the book ends, Paul makes his final break with Miriam, and even their last meeting, in his Nottingham rooms, is presided over by a bowl of freesias and scarlet anemones, "flaunting over the table." Because of the stifling nature of Miriam's love, Paul refuses to marry her. For her part, Miriam knows that "without him her life would trail on lifeless." But as they leave the rooms, Paul impulsively presents her with the flowers:

"Have them!" he said; and he took them out of the jar, dripping as they were, and went quickly into the kitchen. She waited for him, took the flowers, and they went out together, he talking, she feeling dead.

[p. 419.]

This final contrast between the two is again determined by their active and direct relation to a natural force. For Paul, who is emotionally vital, these are the flowers of life; for Miriam, who feeds wholly on the spirit and on personal affinity, they are the rootless flowers of death. Some fifteen years later, Lawrence would expand upon the general significance of Miriam's failure, using the same powerful floral imagery from this final scene in *Sons and Lovers*:

Oh, what a catastrophe, what a maiming of love when it was made a personal, merely personal feeling, taken away from the rising and the setting of the sun, and cut off from the magic connection of the solstice and the equinox! This is what is the matter with us. We are bleeding at the roots, because [like Miriam] we are cut off from the earth and sun and stars, and love is a grinning mockery, because, poor blossom, we plucked it from its stem on the tree of Life, and expected it to keep on blooming in our civilised vase on the table. ["A Propos of Lady Chatterley's Lover," *Sex, Literature and Censorship*, New York: The Viking Press, 1959, p. 100.]

JULIAN MOYNAHAN

SONS AND LOVERS:
THE SEARCH FOR FORM

Sons and Lovers has always been Lawrence's most popular book and will probably remain so. Stories about poor boys moving upward in life fit readily into the fantasies of self-realization indulged by all readers, especially the young. The novel is full of richly detailed specifications of place and person, it contains two female characters who are beautiful and interesting in very different ways, it is just explicit enough about physical passion to seize the imagination without inflaming it. When I first read it in adolescence I thought it very like a Hardy novel only much more luminous, and for a while I confused in my mind Miriam on her farm with Eustacia Vye beside her signal fire. Despite the claim, or perhaps to confirm the claim, that the Oedipus Complex has a universal appeal when represented in literature, I totally missed the point that Paul Morel was fixated. One knew boys just as responsive to their mothers as Paul was, and it seemed natural for him to feel very sorry when she died. Around 1939, I was probably much more interested that Paul lived in a small crowded house like mine, that when he cycled out to the countryside a pretty, intelligent girl turned up to talk and go hiking with him, that when he took a job in town he had time to paint and get to know another girl who actually slept with him.

Despite its popular appeal, which appears to be quite legitimate, *Sons and Lovers* has sometimes been charged with formlessness and with confusion of form. These two charges are usually presented as one. The first appears quite false, and so far as I know has never been substantiated. The second claim,

From *The Deed of Life: The Novels and Tales of D. H. Lawrence*, by Julian Moynahan (Princeton: Princeton University Press, 1963), pp. 13–31. Copyright © 1963 by Princeton University Press. Reprinted by permission.

that the novel is confused, appears more legitimate but can hardly be considered until the first has been disallowed. That is what I propose to do: to discuss how the novel is organized, and where and how a certain confusion disturbs its essential composure.

Actually, *Sons and Lovers* has three formal orders or matrices, which inhabit the same serial order of narrated words. To a degree, they blend with each other, and enrich one another. The first matrix is autobiographical narrative; the second a scheme taken over from psychoanalytic theory; the third is difficult to name because Lawrence was the first novelist to use it as a context, as opposed to a quality, of human experience, but it might be called the matrix of "life."

Each matrix has its own kind of logical articulation. The autobiographical narrative is articulated in terms of historical sequence (Mrs. Morel gave William his tea *and then* he went to the "Wakes"), and ordinary causality (Paul stopped school at the age of fourteen and went to work at Jordan's Surgical Appliance Co. *because* his family needed the money). The logic of the psychoanalytic scheme depends on a particular explanation of behavior provided by a psychological system that assumes and explains such mechanisms as unconscious motivation and projection. When the narrator says at one point about Paul's attitude toward Miriam, "He wanted now to give her passion and tenderness, and could not," it is a straightforward statement of fact according to the first matrix. But in terms of the psychological scheme it is a diagnostic description of a neurotic symptom belonging to a syndrome precisely defined by Sigmund Freud in a paper first published in 1912.

The logic of the third matrix may be termed, following Lawrence's own usage, "vital" or "passional." It is easier to show in operation than to define a priori. For example: after Mrs. Morel dies of cancer and is laid out in her bedroom, her husband Walter Morel is peculiarly reluctant to enter the room to pay his last respects. When he finally summons courage he stays only long enough to see that the body is there in the darkened room under a sheet. He does not look directly at her and see her, and in fact has not looked directly at her since the beginning of her illness. After the funeral he sits in the kitchen with her "superior" relatives and tearfully explains how he had always done his best by her. Later on, he is troubled during afternoon naps by nightmarish dreams of his dead wife which frighten him badly. According to the first matrix the sequence is ordinary. That is the way Morel is, God help him! It is still ordinary and typical according to the second matrix: the death of a close relative may precipitate an anxiety state in a survivor, and so forth. The same sequence in the vital context, where it actually takes place, leads to a severe judgment on Morel:

> And that was how he tried to dismiss her. He never thought of her personally. Everything deep in him he denied. Paul hated his father for sitting sentimentalising over her. He knew he would do it in the public-houses. For the real tragedy went on in Morel in spite of himself.
>
> [p. 401.]

Passional or vital logic dictates this judgment. The larger indictment against the father in the novel is that he denies the life within him. Here the denial is expressed through his refusal to "see" his dead wife, and his willingness to tell sentimental lies about their relation. In the other contexts these are his experiences. In the vital context the experience violates sanctions that may be mysterious but are also specific and real. The violation is a form of self-violation and is a tragedy, according to the firm, though compassionate, view of the narration.

The three formal orders of *Sons and Lovers* can perhaps best be illustrated by following the hero Paul Morel through the series. As the hero of an autobiographical novel Paul is a youth who grew up in a colliery village, loved and left two women, became a successful commercial artist specializing in designs for textiles, with outlets for his work in such great London stores as Liberty's, and lost a beloved mother in his mid-twenties. According to the psychological scheme, he is a classic instance of oedipal fixation. In the context of what Lawrence was soon to call in his *Study of Thomas Hardy* "the vast un-explored morality of life itself,"[1] Paul is a passionate pilgrim whose every action and impulse is a decision for or against life and accumulates to a body of fate that quite literally spells life or death for him.

The expressive means through which each of these forms is represented can be partially differentiated. The first is represented through a painstaking, richly detailed rendering of the naturalistic surface of ordinary life in both expository and dramatic terms. The psychoanalytic scheme is occasionally pointed up through explicit interpretative commentary, but is largely implicit in the autobiographical narrative as an underlying pattern. The vital context informs the naturalistic narrative, is sometimes pointed up through specific narrative comment ("For the real tragedy went on in Morel in spite of himself"), and is also expressed direct in isolable dramatic scenes of a peculiar kind and in passages of extended description that carry an intensively poetic charge. These scenes and expository passages, in which characters act out their vital destinies, sometimes mislead critics on the prowl for symbolism into supposing they were planted in the narration as "keys" to hidden meaning. But in the sense that symbols always point beyond themselves to something buried, there is little symbolism in *Sons and Lovers*. Early in the novel Miriam is shown afraid to "let herself go" fast and high when she is taking turns with Paul on the barn swing. Later on, she cannot let herself go in her sexual experiences with Paul. The first situation is not meant to adumbrate the second. Both are equally real and final as revelations of Miriam's diminished vitality, her tendency to shrink back from life, whether she is making love, feeding chickens, trying to cope with Mrs. Morel's dislike of her, or merely looking at flowers.

Not every character functions in all three matrices, although all the major characters do. Paul's younger brother Arthur, for

---

[1] See *Phoenix: The Posthumous Papers of D. H. Lawrence*, ed. E. D. McDonald (New York: Viking, 1936), p. 418.

example, has no part in the oedipal pattern, and his vitality, while evident enough, is never at issue. The elder brother William who dies at the end of Part I because he cannot resolve the conflict between his attachments to his mother and to his fiancée belongs mainly to the second matrix, as the first of Mrs. Morel's two fixated son-lovers. Miss Limb, the lonely farm woman in love with the stallion, who appears briefly in Chapter IX: "The Defeat of Miriam," belongs mainly to the third context. Lawrence is interested, not in her psychology or her personal history, but solely in her rapport with the animal as that rapport affects Paul, Miriam, and Clara. Their reactions to her define qualities of being each possesses and clarify the continually modified emotional current passing among the three young people, constituting their relation at that particular time.

Now that the form of *Sons and Lovers* has been defined, it becomes possible to deal with the charge of formal confusion. Confusion arises owing to a final inescapable conflict between the psychoanalytic and the vital contexts. Each approaches experience from a somewhat different angle, interprets it differently, and posits a different sort of hero. Paul is finally caught in a dual focus. As a case study of neurosis he is trapped in a pattern of "repetition compulsion" from which there is no escape this side of the analyst's couch. He therefore seems to be left at the end in the "drift toward death" mentioned in Lawrence's Freudian summary of the novel which he sent in a letter to Edward Garnett.[2] As a "vital" hero Paul, although threatened with death, owing to the sheer difficulty of the human relationships he has thrust upon him in childhood and develops on his own in early manhood, has a better than even chance of maintaining himself whole and alive in the midst of life as the novel ends.

The conflict, with its attendant ambiguities which confuse the presentation of Miriam and Clara as well as Paul, is real but ought not to be exaggerated, as it has been by critics whose

---

[2] See *The Letters of D. H. Lawrence*, ed. A. Huxley (New York: Viking, 1932), pp. 78–79. Hereafter cited as *Letters*.

notions of formal coherence are narrowly based. Psychoanalysis
and Lawrence's kind of vitalism have many points in common
as readings of experience. There is a sense in which the "drift
toward death" means as much in passional as in neurotic terms.
But the two systems of interpretation finally do not coincide.
The Freudian system is weighted toward determinism. Paul,
given his conditioning and the axiom that unconscious processes cannot become conscious and therefore modifiable without
a therapist's aid, is doomed. The vital context is a fluid system
that is fully indeterminate. Short of death there is no occasion
in experience when the individual cannot make the correct, life-
enhancing choice. Even an old wreck like Morel *could* at last
look at his dead wife—the possibility is implied by the very
strictness with which his refusal to do so is judged. The issues
of life and death are fully worked into the very texture of events,
and the road to salvation runs along the edge of the abyss where
Paul stands after his mother's death and his double rejection
of Clara and Miriam.

Although both novels draw upon the same set of remembered facts, *Sons and Lovers* is infinitely superior to *The White
Peacock* as an autobiographical narrative. The latter totally
suppresses the industrial milieu, arbitrarily raises the social
level of the Beardsall family from working class to shabby-
genteel, substitutes preposterous scenes of upper-class "society"
at a manor house called Highclose for the domestic routines
of a miner's household. Cyril, who is quite obviously an early
study for Paul Morel, is also quite obviously in love with his
mother. That is really why he is so half-hearted in his spasmodic
search for adult love and relatedness. But except for a few brief
indications, this crucial relationship is missing from the book.
In Cyril, we get the burden of sick feeling without its referent—
a devouring maternal possessiveness which destroys a son's capacity to move on from childhood attachments into adulthood.

Sons and Lovers not only confronts the mother-son relation
directly but places it at the center of a real world built up
through an astonishingly detailed re-creation of a complex
human environment. In the early chapters the mother's shift

of her affections from her husband to her sons is sketched against a background that includes the social and economic history of the Nottinghamshire-Derbyshire border region going back nearly two centuries, includes two earlier generations of family history, an exhaustive account of the social structure of a colliery village, a description of the patterns of work and recreation of the men who dig the coal and their wives who toil behind the weathered brick façades of the row houses on the valley's southern slope. When Paul begins to visit the Leivers' farm the exposition broadens to include full descriptions of the countryside, which contrasts so finally and suggestively with the grimy village, and of Miriam's entire family, how they came to the farm and how they work it. When he takes a job in Nottingham the exposition broadens again. We come to understand the exact routines of a small Victorian factory, and its human environment as well. And we learn of the surrounding city, with its great grey castle, swift river, hurtling trams, and enormous mills.

This background is deeply relevant to the central conflicts of the book. It conditions the struggle of some of the characters to realize themselves and helps explain the baffled compromise that other characters make with the circumstances into which they were born. I know of no other English novel, with the possible exception of George Eliot's *Middlemarch*, where people are so rooted in concrete social history, and in a region so concretely rendered. It becomes possible to measure the precise degree of freedom or unfreedom enjoyed by each major character in relation to the full human environment.

It is worth spelling some of this out. Gertrude Morel's incompatibility with her husband is conditioned by particular social facts. Her father had been a Nottingham lace manufacturer ruined by an industrial slump. She marries beneath her partly because she has lost her marriage portion, partly because a tentative engagement to a scholarly young man has fallen through. When she comes to the village of Bestwood to live with Morel she leaves a large city in touch with the great world for a narrow, spiritually and economically impoverished mining community dominated by traditional codes affecting all areas of life from child care to the manner in which a collier divides his time, and money, between the pub and the home. She tries to adapt herself, but is soon put off by the uncouth slackness of her husband. Yet his qualities are also conditioned by social facts. His fecklessness is in tune with the community as a whole. The village has changed little in several generations and now faces a diminishing basis of economic support as the long worked coal veins yield an ever narrowing margin of profit. Morel went into the pits at twelve. The warm physical nature which had attracted Gertrude to him is soon ruined by hard work, by serious accidents occurring in the pit at regular intervals, and by drink. The rupture between husband and wife, although inevitable, is never total. In the midst of her contempt she respects what he once was; and Morel's drunken tirades hide an inarticulate admiration for her real refinement and intellectual superiority.

Still, it is equally inevitable that she should turn to her sons as they mature toward manhood. They become the channels into which she pours her long dammed up spiritual energy, and she cannot help using them destructively to break a way through the walls separating her from a larger world. The older son is taken over completely. He wears himself out in ambitious pursuits reflecting an intensity of frustration that is more his mother's than his own. Denied its legitimate satisfactions, Mrs. Morel's will has become inhuman. Paul, with some of the traditional slipperiness of the artist type, evades the full force of the mother's will, but is severely injured by the erotic concomitants of her drive for self-realization through a son's life. At the same time, both sons' choices are closely circumscribed by social facts. They can follow the father into the pit—while fully idiomatic, the expression has a peculiar ring in the context of Bestwood's chapel-going religiosity—or side with their mother in favor of culture, education, and money. The terms in which the choice is posed are preposterously unfair, but they are dictated by prevailing social arrangements, not by the whim of either working-class parent.

The same sort of conditioning operates on characters other than the Morels. Miriam's frigid attitude toward sex and her masochistic, compensatory version of Christian belief comes to her from her mother, a town woman of rather low physical vigor forced to live on a small tenant farm where all must work to the point of exhaustion if the rent is to be cleared each year. Exhausted by her work and childbearing, repelled by the spectacle of farm animals in heat or giving birth, Mrs. Leivers recoils from the sex relation and solaces herself with chapel religion. Clara Dawes's poignant blend of hauteur and humility, as well as her bitter quarrel with Baxter, reflects the conflict between her aspirations and her circumstances. She wants freedom to become someone, but is only free to choose between the factory and a damaged marriage to an ordinary workman. As a suffragette she blames her troubles on the unfranchised status of women, yet the novel makes clear that her lot is the same as her husband's and like poor people's generally.

Lawrence's translation of socioeconomic abstractions into terms of human actuality is thorough. A broken love affair, a family quarrel, Mrs. Morel's anxiety upon entering Lincoln Cathedral lest she be asked to leave because her clothes are not fine enough, are, conversely, events belonging to history. One wonders where there is any margin of freedom left the characters. But the novel insists on this margin of freedom. Mrs. Morel should not have dehumanized her will. Morel should not have hidden his injured feelings behind a shell of brutal cynicism. Miriam should have found the courage to take Paul in the novel's penultimate scene when he was there for the taking. Clara must find the strength and forbearance to re-create her marriage with Dawes. Failure to do these things may fulfill a tragic pattern in history, but it violates the vital sanctions I mentioned earlier. Beyond the close circumscriptions of social fact life goes on. It is the farther context within which human history is placed, as the village, or the city or the lonely farm is set down within wild nature. The individual is rooted in life as well as history and cannot escape his own freedom to make the choices that life will judge by an inscrutable morality.

Paul Morel is the proper hero of *Sons and Lovers* because he holds and uses this freedom in a greater measure than any other character. He imposes himself. In calling the book an autobiographical narrative I do not mean that it is a faithful reproduction of Lawrence's career up to the time his mother died. Recollected material has been reorganized and new material has been added to make a dramatic pattern emphasizing Paul's dominating character. Paul's vitality is stronger, his awareness of vital issues is finer than Lawrence's. The paradox is only apparent and can easily be sustained. In life Lawrence was baffled by Jessie Chambers, whose indignant assertion that they never became lovers compels belief. Lawrence was initiated into sex by a Mrs. Dax. She took him upstairs one afternoon because she thought he needed it. As a boy he worked for a surgical appliance company like Jordan's but left after only a few weeks because the factory girls jeered at him and one day removed his trousers in a dark corner of one of the storerooms.

In *Sons and Lovers* Paul forces his agonized relation with Miriam to the final issue of sexual union and then leaves her only when he is satisfied that they are too much at emotional cross-purposes to marry. He is entirely dominant in the affair with Clara, even to the point of forcing a reconciliation between Baxter and Clara before withdrawing into a *nuit blanche* of grief over his mother's death. He enjoys his work in the factory, develops affectionate ties with the girls who work there, and after several years has so thoroughly shaped the routines of his job to his own needs that he manages to spend only the mornings as a spiral clerk, using his afternoons to paint in a spare room. Finally, he copes with his mother during her illness. After speaking the ghastly sentence, "It is the living I want, not the dead," Mrs. Morel has fixed her will on survival even though she has a metastasized cancer and is in monstrous pain. Paul's decision to perform a mercy killing is simultaneously an act of the purest love, and a victory over the maternal will which guarantees that at the end he will find a way to escape the "drift toward death" which follows her death. It is also a free decision to take a constructive line of action against the destructiveness implicit in Mrs. Morel's will to survive after any real life has left her.

There is no point in saying that Paul's career merely compensates for Lawrence's career, that he is a fantasy dreamed up by Cyril Beardsall during one of his broods on Nethermere shore. Certainly Paul is bigger and freer than the young Lawrence, but he is not freer and bigger than Lawrence's vision of what life can be. Nevertheless it is mainly because Paul is a hero rather than a victim in the context of autobiographical narrative that Lawrence's employment of the psychoanalytic scheme works at cross purposes with the other matrices.

It will be useful here to summarize Lawrence's relation to Freud with particular reference to the period in which he was composing Sons and Lovers.[3] We do not know whether Lawrence had read Freud before he wrote the final draft of Sons and Lovers, but it is definitely known that Frieda had read Freud and discussed psychoanalytic ideas with Lawrence on numerous occasions while he worked on the final draft of the novel. Lawrence's first contact with professional analysts did not come until 1914, when he made the acquaintance of Dr. David Eder and Barbara Low. In Lawrence's later writings he frequently took issue with the Freudians on two points: on the primacy of the sexual impulse in the individual's psychological development; on the value of bringing neurotics to a conscious awareness of repressed instincts and drives. Since one of the principal stresses in his entire career was his attack on the modern tendency to overconceptualize experience, it was in-

---

[3] The most informed discussions of this problem are to be found in Frederick J. Hoffman's *Freudianism and the Literary Mind* (Baton Rouge, Louisiana: Louisiana State University Press, 1945), pp. 149–180, and in the first edition of Harry T. Moore's *The Intelligent Heart* (New York: Farrar Straus & Young, 1954), pp. 131–132.

evitable that he should come to take issue with the Freudian school.

It remains to determine the accuracy of Lawrence's representation of the Oedipus complex from the Freudian standpoint. Without claiming expertness in these matters I should say that Lawrence's construction of a sort of neurotic case history for Paul is both accurate and comprehensive. *Sons and Lovers* presents the mother fixation, the abnormal jealousy of the father, and shows both these tendencies persisting as a disturbing influence in Paul's dealings with men and women outside the family circle; for instance, the affair with Clara, which is broken off as the result of a savage fight between Paul and the jealous husband, represents on one level an acting out of an oedipal fantasy wherein Clara and Baxter Dawes, the estranged and quarrelsome married couple, replace Gertrude and Walter Morel, the hero's own mother and father. Furthermore, the novel dramatizes the conflict in the hero between normal desires and unconscious fixations. It presents his ambivalence—his oscillations between love and hate in the affair with Miriam— and it dramatizes the mechanism of projection whereby Paul transfers his internal conflicts to the outside world.

One further point. The psychological theme of the "split" which Lawrence develops both within the novel and also in the letter to Edward Garnett mentioned earlier is actually the same as that developed by Sigmund Freud in his essay, "The Most Prevalent Form of Degradation in Erotic Life."[4] Here is described a widespread condition of psychical impotence in modern, cultivated men in which individuals, because of an unresolved incestuous attachment for their mothers, combined with an unusually repressed childhood and adolescence, find it impossible to fuse tender and sensual feelings into a wholesome love for a woman of their own age and station in life. These men are sexually attracted by women who are in some way inferior to them, while the tenderness they feel for their femi-

---

[4] *Vide supra*, pp. 498–570. And see pp. 493–497.

nine social equals lacks a sensual quality. They give their souls to women who play the role of mother figures and their bodies to women who for one reason or another can never aspire to represent the overidealized mother.

Thus as Lawrence wrote to Garnett, William Morel "gives his sex to a fribble, and his mother holds his soul." Paul seems to do better by consummating his love for the companionable Miriam. But his constant complaints that she is too soulful and that she is frigid, alike with the death urges he frequently experiences after intercourse with her, show that he cannot heal the split in his affective life through Miriam. Later on he divides his love between the idealized mother and the passionate, shamed, compromised Clara Dawes. In classical neurotic fashion he re-creates again and again the very conditions of unhealth from which he is attempting to escape.

Paul's vitality, his extraordinary capacity to make boldly sensuous responses to his environment, suggest that he is somehow free. The above summary of the facts of his "case" show that he is not. This difference cannot be compromised. It represents a collision between opposed ways of looking at a character, opposed definitions of human instinct and of human fate. One summer evening, after Paul has been sleeping with Miriam for an entire year, he steps suddenly out of doors:

The beauty of the night made him want to shout. A half-moon, dusky gold, was sinking behind the black sycamore at the end of the garden, making the sky dull purple with its glow. Nearer, a dim white fence of lilies went across the garden, and the air all round seemed to stir with scent, as if it were alive. He went across the bed of pinks, whose keen perfume came sharply across the rocking, heavy scent of the lilies, and stood alongside the white barrier of flowers. They flagged all loose, as if they were panting. The scent made him drunk. He went down to the field to watch the moon sink under.

A corncrake in the hay-close called insistently. The moon slid quite quickly downwards, growing more flushed. Behind him the great flowers leaned as if they were calling. And then, like a shock, he caught another perfume, something raw and coarse. Hunting round, he found the purple iris, touched their fleshy throats and their dark, grasping hands. At any rate, he had found something. They stood stiff in the darkness. Their scent was brutal. The moon was melting down upon the crest of the hill. It was gone; all was dark. The corncrake called still.

Breaking off a pink, he suddenly went indoors.

"Come, my boy," said his mother. "I'm sure it's time you went to bed."

He stood with the pink against his lips.

"I shall break off with Miriam, mother," he answered calmly.

[*pp. 293–294.*]

After noting that the raw coarse scent of the iris evokes Clara, as the pinks whose petals he soon spits into the fire evoke Miriam; after noting the presence of the mother and her characteristically domineering mode of address, one must still insist that the decision springs to life out of Paul's fully concrete experience of the night, the garden and the flowers in their nearly overpowering physical actuality. We may find the hero's relation to these a mystery and his decision brutal, but we have to admit that the experience is *sui generis*, not simply another instance of Paul's enslavement to what Freud called, rather abstractedly, an *imago*. Scenes of this type suggest that beneath the layer of disordered instinctual trends constituting Paul's neurosis lie other vital impulses which remain intact and occasionally break through, with a consequent shock of recognition for both the reader and the character. Paul is tied but carries his freedom somewhere inside him, whence it might issue, given the appropriate challenge from the life teeming around him, here represented by a beautiful summer night, to dissolve his bonds and transform his existence.

Thus when Paul goes to Miriam to announce that their love affair is over he is everything despicable that she thinks he is: chiefly, "an infant which, when it has drunk its fill, throws away and smashes the cup" in the name of an illusory freedom. But while she sits there, having seen through him—

His very movements fascinated her as if she were hypnotized by him. Yet he was despicable, false, inconsistent, and mean. . . . Why was it the movement of his arm stirred her as nothing else in the world could?

[p. 298.]

The answer is evident enough. She is stirred by "the movement of active life," by the "quickness" that is imprisoned in him, for which she loves him, yet which neither she nor any other woman, least of all the mother, knows how to release.

The ending of Sons and Lovers shows that Paul Morel's nature does contain an intact core of vitality which is his freedom, that while his responses to his family and mistresses have been "overdetermined" by neuroticism, his fate remains indeterminate au fond. When Mrs. Morel is dead, the hero cries out, "My love—my love—oh, my love!" echoing the cry of the mother—"My son, oh my son"—over the body of William. But for Paul there is no one to turn to, no one to build a new life upon, and he turns away into his white night of spiritual and emotional numbness. He puts his affairs in order by reconciling Clara with Baxter and goes alone to encounter his self-annihilating vision of the voidness of a world which no longer contains his mother. Darkness washes over him in a great flood. It pours from the infinite reaches of space, and wells up from inside, "from his breast, from his mouth." It is a flood of dissolution:

When he turned away he felt the last hold for him had gone. The town, as he sat upon the car, stretched away over the bay of railway, a level fume of lights. Beyond the town the country, little smouldering spots for more towns—the sea—the night—on and on! And he had no place in it! Whatever spot he stood on, there he stood alone. From his breast, from his mouth, sprang the endless space, and it was there behind him, everywhere. The people hurrying along the streets offered no obstruction to the void in which he found himself. They were small shadows whose footsteps and voices could be heard, but in each of them the same night, the same silence. He got off the car. In the country all was dead still. Little stars shone high up; little stars spread far away in the floodwaters, a firmament below. Everywhere the vastness and terror of the immense night which is roused and stirred for a brief while by the day, but which returns, and will remain at last eternal, holding everything in its silence and its living gloom. There was no Time, only Space. Who could say his mother had lived and did not live? She had been in one place, and was in another; that was all. And his soul could not leave her, wherever she was. Now she was gone abroad into the night, and he was with her still. They were together. But yet there was his body, his chest, that leaned against the stile, his hands on the wooden bar. They seemed something. Where was he?—one tiny upright speck of flesh, less than an ear of wheat lost in the field. He could not bear it. On every side the immense dark silence seemed pressing him, so tiny a spark, into extinction, and yet, almost nothing, he could not be extinct. Night, in which everything was lost, went reaching out, beyond stars and sun. Stars and sun, a few bright grains, went spinning round for terror, and holding each other in embrace, there in a darkness that outpassed them all, and left them tiny and daunted. So much, and himself, infinitesimal, at the core a nothingness, and yet not nothing.

[*pp. 419–420.*]

"After such knowledge what forgiveness?" The hero stands on the brink of disintegration, a nothingness, "and yet not nothing." It is clear from the passage that if he is somehow to be saved he has only the stubborn physical fact of his own body and its mysterious life with which to resist the night. The pressure of his body leaning against the stile effectively prevents him from moving toward death and the mother. And in the comparison of the body to an "ear of wheat" there is the faintest suggestion of a germinating potential out of which may spring forth the opportunity of renewal. There is not the slightest indication that escape from self-disintegration will be easy or assured. The movement toward the city's "gold phosphorescence" does not contradict, as some critics have thought, the drift toward death of which Lawrence's thematic summary speaks. A physical body is set in motion toward the "humming, glowing town," but it is clear from the whole tendency of the novel, clear also from Paul's envisionment of stars and sun as "a few bright grains . . . spinning round for terror," that the tiny glow of the town lights up no safe harbor.

Paul Morel at the end is of necessity and by virtue of his own free act released from the maternal bondage which, if long continued, would have destroyed him. But this freedom involves alienation and isolation from the world. As he moves toward the urban settlement which Lawrence describes in his *Study of Thomas Hardy* as "the little fold of law and order, the little walled city within which which man has to defend himself against the waste enormity of nature,"[5] it is possible to see the hero embarking on a quest after health and relatedness. For the dramatization of such a quest, the reader must turn to the later novels.

Here it is enough to attempt some definition of the stance of the vital hero, vis-à-vis the world, since Paul is assuredly the first hero of Lawrence's fiction who can be so called. He faces life with the knowledge that no theological sanctions exist to make its burdens tolerable; that life itself represents the faintest glimmer of warmth within the cold, infinite reaches of dead space; that human life in its various social, economic, and personal orders is filled with destructive forces; that his own integrity is blighted by the conditioning to which he has been exposed. In the face of this knowledge he accepts freely his responsibility for action in conformity with an instinctive morality of life which is largely inscrutable yet by which he will be mercilessly judged. The stance may be considered quixotic, but is not unheroic, especially when compared with the postures of neo-orthodoxy, metaphysical rebellion, or bland indifference which have been assumed by various sorts of gifted people in this century.

[5] See *Phoenix*, p. 419.

G. H. FORD

George H. Ford was born in Canada and served in the Canadian
Army during the Second World War. He has taught at the University of Manitoba and the University of Cincinnati, and is Professor of English and Chairman of the Department at the University
of Rochester. He is the author of, among other books, *Dickens and
His Readers,* and editor with Lauriat Lane, Jr., of *Dickens Critics.*

THE "S" CURVE:
PERSEPHONE TO PLUTO

Autobiographical novels seem to be the easiest kind to write
(most of us have one, or parts of one, in a back drawer of a
desk), but they are very hard to write well. As the thick volumes
of Thomas Wolfe's sprawling novels illustrate, the temptation
to throw in almost any experience which occurred in the author's own life, whether or not it contributes to his hero's
development, is almost irresistible.

Joyce's solution in his *Portrait* was to exclude ruthlessly any
incident or character that did not focus the reader's attention
upon Stephen. The style and organization of *Sons and Lovers*
is much more casual, much less "engineered" (to use a term of
one of Joyce's admirers). Lawrence insisted defensively in a
letter that the novel "*is* a unified whole" even though it may
be "a bit difficult to grip as a whole, at first." And he added
that he hated "the dodge of putting a thick black line round
the figures to throw out the composition." Readers, however,
are entitled to try imposing such thick black lines, and when
they do, it is evident that the structuring of this novel is skillfully devised towards one end, the revelation of "the long
and half-secret process" (as Lawrence calls it in his essay on
Franklin) of a son's development away from his parents. The
organization consists of a sequence of interlocking triangles

---

From *Double Measure: A Study of the Novels and Stories of D. H. Lawrence,* by George H. Ford (New York: Holt, Rinehart and Winston,
1965), pp. 28–47. Copyright © 1965 by George H. Ford. Reprinted by
permission of Holt, Rinehart and Winston, Inc.

such as mother-father-son; mother-elder son-girl; mother-son-spiritual girl; mother-son-physical girl. The attention given to William's affair with Gipsy Western may seem, on first reading, carelessly squandered, yet the linking of this triangle to those triangles in which Paul is more immediately connected is crucial, providing the needed preview, the play within the play, of Paul's doomed relationships with Miriam and Clara. And behind the crippled affairs of both sons, and accounting for both, is the crippled marriage of the Morels.

One must beware of the academic fondness for the blackboard diagram, or the easy reduction of Lawrence's subtle complexities into the simplified formula, the pap for the undergraduate palates, yet the formula is there.

Zola, in his sometimes fatuously cocky manifesto, *Le roman expérimental*, had urged the need for novelists to establish that under such and such conditions of heredity and environment such and such actions and character would inevitably eventuate. It is odd that Lawrence who, like Joyce, was to transform naturalistic techniques beyond recognition, has wittingly or unwittingly followed Zola's prescription in *Sons and Lovers*. The trials and errors of Paul Morel's affairs with Miriam and Clara derived, with the inevitability of cause and effect we expect in naturalistic fiction, from the nature of his parents' marriage.

The married life of the Morels is perhaps the most vivid of Lawrence's many accounts of human conflict. Of their life before marriage we learn little, but there is enough information about their courtship to predict that such a coupling of opposites will result in strenuous tensions. Gertrude Coppard, "a Puritan" and "intellectual" is fascinated by "the dusky, golden softness of this man's sensuous flame of life, that flowed off his flesh like the flame from a candle, not baffled and gripped into incandescence of thought and spirit as her life was." We also learn at the outset, and it is a significant touch, of the miner's proposal at their first meeting, that she should go down with him under the earth. "But tha mun let me ta'e thee down some time, an' tha can see for thysen." Gertrude Morel never did take up the invitation literally, yet the early months of her marriage represent her figurative descent into darkness until she began to fight her way out from it. Later she persuades her children to join her in her ascent and in her repudiation of what her dark mate stood for.

From this matching of opposites derives Paul's crippled love affairs just as from the temptation and fall derived the later events of the Biblical narrative. If we seek such parallels, however, we can in this instance turn not to the Bible, which is usually Lawrence's principal storehouse for analogies, but to a variation of the classical myth of Persephone, to which he makes frequent allusion.

In his version the rape and marriage are the center of interest; the traditional role of the bride's mother, Demeter, is subordinated. It is the tale of a dark man emerging from a cavern in the earth who discovered a fair princess gathering flowers in a field and persuaded her to be carried off to the underworld where he was a king and where she would reign as his queen. For many months the fair woman was happy in the realms of darkness, but after a time she began to feel she had been taken out of one state of trance only to enter another. And she yearned to return to the land of light where there were white-walled temples, and books, and learned priests. Bewildered by the dissatisfaction of his wife the dark king fought hard to prevent her from brooding, but he had to give in and allow her and their children to return to the land above the underground darkness.

The narrative is a variant of a familiar classical myth, and has analogies also to the Danish legend of a merman's marriage to a mortal, a legend on which Matthew Arnold drew for his poem, *The Forsaken Merman*, with its haunting refrain:

> And alone dwell for ever
> The kings of the sea.

In the classical version, the fair woman was called Persephone (the name, according to Robert Graves, signifies "she who brings destruction"), and the dark man was Pluto or Hades. In the Lawrentian version, both in prose and poetry, references to the classical myth are sometimes made directly. In "The Ladybird," for example, the dark Count Dionys Psanek reflects upon his affair with Lady Daphne:

Take her into the underworld. Take her into the dark Hades with him, like Francesca and Paolo. And in hell hold her fast, queen of the underworld, himself master of the underworld.

In one of the poems, *Bavarian Gentians*, the dark blue of these "hellish flowers" stimulated the poet to wish that he could witness the marriage of Persephone and Pluto "as he ravishes her once again/and pierces her once more." More often the analogy is only indirect, and the names are remote enough. In the novels the woman is Gertrude Coppard and the man Walter Morel, or Anna Lensky and Will Brangwen, or Alvina Houghton and an Italian named Cicio, or Kate Leslie and Cipriano, a Mexican general, or the virgin Yvette, a clergyman's daughter, and a gipsy who is finally discovered to be named Joe Boswell.

The contrast of worlds is especially evident in *The Lost Girl*, a novel which Lawrence had originally entitled *Mixed Marriage*. Alvina's relations with Cicio occur first in the "pitch dark," and she tries to fight her way back to light. "Her mind remained distinctly clear. She could criticize him, find fault with him, the things he did." Yet she is "swept away." "Now Alvina felt herself swept . . . into a dusky region where men had dark faces and translucent yellow eyes, where all speech was foreign, and life was not her life. It was as if she had fallen from her own world onto another darker star."

In the short stories are also many instances of the Pluto-Persephone combination as in "The Blind Man," "The Ladybird," and "The Princess." One of the finest of the stories, "Fanny and Annie," pictures the reluctant return to an industrial town of a haughtily beautiful woman who is steeling herself to marry a foundry workman whom she has regarded as alternately attractive and repulsive. From the brilliantly effective opening paragraph describing her arrival in the railway station, one senses that the woman is re-entering Hell itself:

Flame-lurid his face as he turned among the throng of flame-lit and dark faces upon the platform. In the light of the furnace she caught sight of his drifting countenance, like a piece of floating fire. And the nostalgia, the doom of home-coming went through her veins like a drug. His eternal face, flame-lit now! The pulse and darkness of red fire from the furnace towers in the sky, lighting the desultory, industrial crowd on the wayside station, lit him and went out. Of course he did not see her. Flame-lit and unseeing! Always the same.

The possible variations of a classic myth, which Lawrence saw re-enacted daily in his own home in Eastwood, provided him with a seemingly inexhaustible source of inspiration for fiction.

It was suggested earlier that Lawrence's basic narrative consists of an account of his characters' pursuing a search. The situation in the Persephone story is often represented as a crucial stage in such a search, emblematic of the impossibility of a union between opposites and the consequent loneliness of strangers sharing a bed for a lifetime, strangers who remain strangers.

At other times (and the paradox must later be confronted) such a pairing is treated as an ideal, as in the final scenes of a story such as "Daughters of the Vicar." In one of the best of his early essays, *The Spinner and the Monks*, the worlds of light and darkness are contrasted, and Lawrence concludes that the ideal "meeting point" is represented by "Persephone embraced by Pluto." "The two in consummation" he writes, "are perfect, beyond the range of loneliness or solitude." Above all, however, whether such a relationship is presented as a crippling one or as ideal, it provided Lawrence with the kind of dramatic tensions and juxtaposition of opposites which are at the core of his distinctive manner of writing fiction and which affect not only his construction of scenes but his prose style itself. Of *Women in Love* he noted that fault had been found with his style because of "the continual, slightly modified repetition." In reply he argued that "every natural crisis in emotion or passion or understanding comes from this pulsing, frictional to-and-fro which works up to culmination."

How did Lawrence regard the conflict between Walter and Gertrude Morel? And how did he expect us, as readers, to regard them? Was the Persephone figure "right" in her repudiation of her dark mate, or is the subject of right and wrong inappropriate in this instance? So phrased, such questions sound schoolmistressly simple, yet to attempt to answer them can lead into some of the principal problems that confront us in discussing Lawrence's writings.

One such problem is that of heroes and villains. The role of the hero in literature has become almost obsessively topical in recent literary criticism, and it is therefore of interest to have George Orwell's report on what surprised him when he first read Lawrence's fiction.

When I first read D. H. Lawrence's novels, at the age of about twenty, I was puzzled by the fact that there did not seem to be any classification of the characters into 'good' and 'bad.' Lawrence seemed to sympathise with all of them about equally and this was so unusual as to give me the feeling of having lost my bearings. Today no one would think of looking for heroes and villains in a serious novel.

Orwell's statement may appear to be mere nonsense. As a man, Lawrence was as dogmatic and intensely opinionated as his Victorian predecessor, John Ruskin, and his opinions took in as many subjects as Ruskin had embraced. How could such a man create a world without villains and heroes?

When he portrays the managing-engineer, Uncle Tom Brangwen, in *The Rainbow*, it is evident that the writer's loathing of industrialism has produced a hatefully villainous figure. Descriptions such as the following seethe with dislike:

The fine beauty of his skin and his complexion, some almost waxen quality, hid the strange, repellent grossness of him, the slight sense of putrescence, the commonness which revealed itself in his rather fat thighs and loins.

Moreover, if Uncle Tom Brangwen is a villain it is also evident that other characters have been distinctly cast in heroic mold: Don Ramón in *The Plumed Serpent*, for example, or other leaders who bear a resemblance to Lawrence himself. It would be remarkable if the twentieth-century descendent of Carlyle, the author of *Heroes and Hero-Worship*, had written novels in which heroes have been eclipsed.

Yet despite all the qualifying clauses that my objections suggest, Orwell's observation is ultimately a sound one. It provides a helpful corrective against the kind of reader who salivates his way through Lawrence's books as if they were stories of infallible heroes righteously disposing of wicked industrialists or other categories of the unredeemed. Carlyle and Ruskin wrote tracts and essays, and made very few excursions into fiction; Lawrence wrote fiction and occasionally tried his hand at tracts and essays. Especially in his later work, the tracts and essays ("polyanalytics" he called them) do get into the fiction inevitably, for as was suggested earlier Lawrence is certainly not the fastidious aesthetic novelist. A mixture of discourse and image is usually present, and from novels such as *Women in Love* we can distill the discourse to our satisfaction and conclude that we then have the book adequately bottled and labeled. But the distillation process has captured a vapor; the novel that Lawrence wrote is not to be thus confined. For the characteristic rhythm in his fiction is double: thesis thrusting against antithesis, lion against unicorn, darkness against light. Gertrude Morel, that is, is not a good force struggling against a bad force, but simply one kind of force, and her husband another kind. It is this sort of balancing that accounts for Orwell's impression of there being no villains or heroes in the novels.

Arthur Mizener once noted that in "all mediocre fiction which deals with serious moral issues, the author and the reader are Christ harrowing a hell full of all the people who disagree with them." Lawrence's writings can certainly offer adrenal stimulation of this variety. Portraits of inadequate males such as Rico in "St. Mawr" provide especially fine opportunities for such indulgences.[1] Yet most of his work con-

---

[1] Brett's report of Lawrence's reading aloud from "St. Mawr" at the time he was writing the story is revealing. When the horse kicks Rico in the face "You [i.e. Lawrence] read it with such keen joy and pleasure at the

forms, instead, to Mizener's account of the effect of great fiction, which is "the nearest thing we have to the moral effect of experience itself under the ideal conditions which experience never provides, when we can understand it fully and face all its moral implications."

When Walter Morel gets up at dawn to prepare his own breakfast, Lawrence observes that "he preferred to keep the blinds down and the candle lit even when it was daylight." What is meant by associating "darkness" with the father in *Sons and Lovers* and "light" with the mother ought to be generally clear to most readers of Lawrence. The terms are intended to signify contrasting kinds of experience (unconscious or conscious); contrasting ways of acquiring knowledge (through the senses or through reason); contrasting concepts of social structure (static and traditional as in a primitive tribe or dynamic and progressive as in an expanding urban society). Of Lawrence's many attempts to describe these contrasting states, perhaps the most effective is his description of the Marsh Farm in the magnificent opening pages of *The Rainbow*. For generations the Brangwen farmers have lived in a happy state of darkness:

They felt the rush of the sap in spring, they knew the wave which cannot halt, but every year throws forward the seed to begetting, and, falling back, leaves the young-born on the earth. . . . Their life and interrelations were such; feeling the pulse and body of the soil, that opened to their furrow for the grain, and became smooth and supple after their ploughing, and clung to their feet with a weight that pulled like desire.

I select this passage rather than a description of an underground scene to emphasize that darkness is a figurative state which may exist in what is literally bright daylight. The blond-haired

final downfall of Rico and the terrible revenge of the horse, that Frieda is horrified; she says you are cruel . . . with great relish and giggling, you describe Rico's plight. You hate Rico so, that for a moment you are the horse." Dorothy Brett, *Lawrence and Brett, A Friendship* (Philadelphia, 1933), pp. 137-139. [G.H.F.]

Brangwen men move about above the earth's surface, yet they live in a darkness like that of the miners or of the hero of "The Blind Man" who moves in a pitch-dark stable with uncanny confidence.

The wives and daughters of the Brangwens are not always satisfied with such a life of instinct, with men whose "brains were inert." If the Marsh Farm is Eden, the wives and daughters are the Eves who would taste of the Tree of Knowledge. Their eyes lift up from the earth to the spires on the distant hill sides, spires that remind them of a world of culture, "the far-off world of cities and governments and the active scope of man," different from the "blood intimacy" of the farm.

The world of light involves conscious awareness in place of instinctive knowledge. When Ursula Brangwen receives a proposal of marriage from Anthony Schofield, she is attracted physically to the young farmer, but recognizes sadly that his inner world is altogether different from her own:

He was an animal that knows it is subdued. Her heart flamed with sensation of him, of the fascinating thing he offered her, and with sorrow, and with an inconsolable sense of loneliness. Her soul was an infant crying in the night. He had no soul. Oh, and why had she?

In *The White Peacock* the same distinction is made more playfully by Lettie when she teases the farmer, George Saxton: "You are blind; you are only half born; you are gross with good living and heavy sleeping . . . Sunset is nothing to you—it merely happens anywhere."

Furthermore, light may be associated with change of social status. Among the Brangwen women, as with Mrs. Morel, there is a desire not only for intellectual development but for an advancement of their sons from one social class to another. Their sense of time is what the sociologists call "future-oriented" whereas their husbands enjoy instead a relatively "future-ignoring present."

A coal miner may be proud of his work, but as Richard Hoggart emphasizes in his study of working-class attitudes, *The Uses of Literacy*, he has no illusions about the possibility of changing his status and hence very little sense of competitiveness. Light is usually a middle-class attribute, Persephone a middle-class goddess. Finally, light is more often associated with women than with men, but the division is not always so neat. The clergyman, emancipated from the soil and mine, belongs to the world of light as does the industrialist Gerald Crich in *Women in Love*. Most complex of all are men such as Rupert Birkin in the same novel who is related to light but has some intellectual commitment to the values of darkness which at times he seems to be advocating. As stated in the *Last Poems* volume:

> Hell is the home of souls lost in darkness,
> even as heaven is the home of souls lost in light.

And the poet adds: "there are souls that are at home in both homes." Discussion of such complex types can be postponed until later. Also to be postponed is how the values of light and darkness apply to the vexed question of Lawrence's treatment of primitivism and its opposites where again it can be shown, I think, the rhythm is once more a double one.[2]

---

[2] The historian of ideas can demonstrate how Lawrence's awareness of double rhythms may derive from a long tradition evident in such writers as Paracelsus, Schelling, and Hegel, which in England became especially prominent in the 19th century. In Madame H. P. Blavatsky's *Isis Unveiled*, a book which Lawrence encountered early in his career, Paracelsus' principle is cited with approval: "Everything is double in nature; magnetism is positive and negative, active and passive, male and female . . . When the mesmerizer will have learned the grand secret of polarizing the action and endowing his fluid with a bisexual force he will have become the greatest magician living." (Pasadena, 1950, I, p. xxv). And with less of the electrical paraphernalia, Coleridge, in his discussion of Sir Walter Scott's having portrayed the conflict between social groups who value the past and those who value the future, refers to the "two great moving principles of social humanity; religious adherence to the past . . . on the one hand, and the passion for increase of knowledge . . . on the other. In all subjects of deep and lasting interest, you will detect a struggle between the opposites, two polar forces, both of which are alike necessary to human well being." (Quoted by J. H. Raleigh, *Victorian Studies*, VII, 1963, p. 31.) John Stuart Mill, in turn, in his essays on Coleridge and Bentham, developed Coleridge's point at full-length. [G.H.F.]

These preliminaries serve to clear the ground for the question previously raised: how did Lawrence regard the elder Morels? Is *Sons and Lovers* an exposé, like Butler's *The Way of All Flesh* or Aldington's *Death of a Hero*, of a hateful paternal tyranny? In later life Lawrence himself asserted ruefully that he had loaded his dice in *Sons and Lovers* because his portrait of Walter Morel, he then believed, had been harsh and unkind. And from additional evidence concerning his early feelings towards his own father, the model for Walter Morel, we should be led to expect a savage cartoon. "I have to hate him for Mother's sake," the young Bert Lawrence told May Chambers, and the intensity of his hatred astonished her:

Bert seemed to send out jagged waves of hate and loathing that made me shudder. The father was hungry after his day's work in the pit and ate heartily as he talked—evidently so used to the atmosphere of animosity that he did not feel it.

In October, 1910, he assured one correspondent that he had "never had but one parent," and in the following February, three months after the death of his mother, he exclaimed in a letter that he wished his father were in Hell, and added: "I shivered with horror when he touched me." What remains remarkable is that in rewriting *Sons and Lovers* during the following year, Lawrence was able so largely to master his private hatreds and to create, in Walter Morel, not only a vivid portrait (one of the most vividly *presented* characters in all his fiction) but also a portrait of a man with whom the reader can sympathize. "Paul hated his father so," says the novelist, and under the unflinching spotlight we see the father as we might expect to see him:

The collier's small, mean head . . . lay on the bare arms, and the face, dirty and inflamed, with a fleshy nose . . . was turned sideways, asleep with beer and weariness and nasty temper.
[p. 62.]

The spotlight focuses not only upon Walter Morel's physical grossness but upon his ultimate ineffectuality, his blustering

threats to leave home and his ignominious return. Yet the
portrait remains a portrait and not a cartoon because of the
man's vitality and because of his isolation. The picture of his
solitary breakfast is unforgettable, concluding as it does with
these two sentences:

He loved the early morning, and the walk across the fields. So he
appeared at the pit-top, often with a stalk from the hedge between
his teeth, which he chewed all day to keep his mouth moist, down
the mine, feeling quite as happy as when he was in the field.

[*p. 28.*]

That wonderful touch of the hedge stalk, which endows the
collier with the dimensions of an earth spirit, is the kind of
detail that cancels out scenes in which he seems merely "despicable." Most of all, however, to achieve balance, Lawrence
shows Morel as a man to be pitied. He becomes, in his own
home, an "outsider" as Lawrence calls him (an epithet which
gained notoriety through Colin Wilson, author of *The Outsider*, and also, oddly enough, a severe critic of Lawrence).
Morel's isolation is emphasized by his blackness as he roars in
out of the dark night and by his dialect. Like a first-generation
immigrant in the United States, his every sentence puts a gulf
between himself and his children, who speak a different language.[3] His total isolation, at the end, when his wife is dying,
is pictured in scenes that impressed Ada Lawrence as "too deep
for tears." One need not have been a member of the Lawrence
family to endorse her tribute.

The balancing achieved in the presentation of Mrs. Morel is
of a different order. As we close the book, with the death

---

[3] In some of the love scenes Paul uses dialect as it is used by Mellors in
Lady Chatterley's Lover as a kind of lovers' shorthand, a shift into the
language of tenderness. The comic possibilities of dialect are also evident,
although one suspects Lawrence eliminated some of the broader touches, on
Garnett's advice, when he revised *Sons and Lovers*. In his play, *A Collier's
Friday Night*, when the miner's daughter refuses to hang up the father's
wet pit-trousers to dry, he comments: "I wonder how er'd like to clep 'er
arse into wet breeches." In the novel this is toned down to "Should thee
like to clap thysen into britches as cowd as a tub o' water?" [G.H.F.]

scenes in mind, our impression may be that the whole novel has been in the tender elegiac vein of the poems Lawrence wrote after his own mother died. Most readers would agree with Walter Allen when he notes that the novelist is distinctly on the side of the mother. *Sons and Lovers* was written by Persephone's son, yet its portrait of the Persephone figure is much more inclusive than elegiac conventions allow. The spotlight is as unflinchingly turned on Mrs. Morel as it was upon her husband, only in her case, it is the destructiveness of her love in her relationship with others that is exposed.

In recent years, in fact, it has been my experience to encounter readers who argue that Mrs. Morel is a villainous woman, totally incapable of arousing sympathy on the part of any observant reader. She was responsible, they point out, for driving her husband to drink and isolation, for driving one son to death and another to the point of death. The indictment leaves out of account the tenderness of tone—that indefinable quality in drama or fiction—with which Lawrence surrounds his portrait, and with which, in the film version, a distinguished and beautiful actress, Wendy Hiller, was able to endow the role. And yet the indictment is accurate enough. The facts are all there in the novel, but it takes a shift of attitudes, in a later generation, to force the inferences to be made.

Freud is popularly supposed to have changed our attitudes towards sexual restrictions. His more important influence has been to change our attitudes towards the relations of parents and children. Incest itself has always been subject to universal taboo, but it seems that it is only since Freud's theories have filtered into the general consciousness that one can say of a young man: "Poor fellow. He's *sick*. He loves his mother." What Philip Wylie in his *Generation of Vipers* categorized as Momism is by no means extinct, but it is no longer exalted as the highest of virtues. That Lawrence's portrait of the dedicated and energetic Mrs. Morel could be taken by earlier readers (including Jessie Chambers) as an idealization of motherhood and by some later readers as an exposé of motherhood is, in itself, testimony to the balancing which I am suggesting is characteristic of his best work. In 1913 Lawrence wrote to Garnett:

I had a devil of a time getting a bit weaned from my mother, at the age of 22. She suffered, and I suffered, and it seemed all for nothing, just waste cruelty. It's funny. I suppose it's the final breaking away to independence.

Here is the main subject of *Sons and Lovers*, a subject with kinetic potential. That the novel has affected attitudes of readers is probable, but if we are to classify Lawrence as a kinetic writer (as he is usually classified in contrast to Joyce) it should be with the reservation suggested here.

Butler's *The Way of All Flesh*, a typical publication of the post-Victorian era, is a frontal attack on what seemed to its author to be a tyrannical institution, the family. Butler, like Harriet Beecher Stowe in *Uncle Tom's Cabin*, did his work well but not well enough to keep his novel truly fresh.

Sons and Lovers is not an attack against fathers, or mothers, or families. It is a record of a family and of the pathos of its complex interrelationships. Or, to shift the terminology, Karl Menninger's praise of the novel in *Love Against Hate* may be cited. *Sons and Lovers*, says Dr. Menninger, is a classic study of "mother fixation" in which the son's real hostility to the mother has been skillfully concealed.

One reason that Lawrence was able to achieve variety in presenting his basic drama of the dark man and fair woman was that his own attitude towards the protagonists gradually changed.

When Mrs. Lawrence was dying of cancer in 1910, she finally recognized the futility of her long struggle against her husband. As Lawrence says in his essay, "Women Are So Cocksure".

And at fifty, when the best part of life was gone, she realized it. And then what would she not have given to have her life again, her young children, her tipsy husband, and a proper natural insouciance, to get the best out of it all. When woman tries to be too much mistress of fate, particularly of other people's fates what a tragedy!

The significance of Mrs. Lawrence's admission does not seem to have made its full impact on her son in 1910; his own realization of it came later. I suspect that the incident accounts for a curious shift of tone that occurs in *The Lost Girl*. The first part of this novel, written early in 1913,[4] seems to have been infected by his reading of Arnold Bennett, especially the mockingly jocular tone Bennett used to describe life in a small Midlands town. The opening pages of *The Lost Girl* sustain this jocular tone effectively, but in one early scene there is a sudden shift into a different key as Lawrence recalls what his mother had said on her deathbed. When the fifty-two-year-old Miss Frost breaks down into tears before Alvina, her crying is described as "the terrible crying of a woman with a loving heart, whose heart has never been able to relax."

---

[4] The "analytical" novel which Lawrence began writing in January, 1913, is commonly assumed to have been *The Sisters*, but was *The Lost Girl*. *The Sisters*, which he regarded at first as a pot-boiler, was not begun until the spring. Discussions of both novels get off to bad starts when a critic reverses Lawrence's terms and describes *The Lost Girl* as his "pot-boiler" and *Women in Love* as "all analytical—quite unlike *Sons and Lovers*, not a bit visualised." (See *Letters*, I, pp. 183, 193, 197, 200, and, *e.g.*, Eliseo Vivas, *D. H. Lawrence*, p. 21.) By April 5, 1913, he had abandoned *The Lost Girl* temporarily, after completing 200 pages. After the war this batch of manuscript was finally retrieved from Germany where it had been in the keeping of Frieda's family, and by May, 1920, Lawrence was preparing the final version for publication. Not having seen the manuscript I am only guessing when I suggest that the early parts of the published version were not extensively revised. It is significant, however, that during the war and immediately afterwards Lawrence often wished he could resume writing *The Lost Girl* but never attempted to do so until the 1913 manuscript was back in his hands. In January, 1916, he did speak of having written 150 pages of a novel "as blameless as *Cranford*," a phrase which Dr. Leavis tentatively assumed must refer to *The Lost Girl* but which is actually a reference to an early version of *Aaron's Rod*. (See *Letters*, Huxley, p. 427, and F. R. Leavis, *D. H. Lawrence: Novelist*, p. 21n.) In any event, until the tangled chronology of composition is unraveled, it is obviously risky to praise Lawrence, as Middleton Murry did, for the "improvement" displayed in his writing between *Women in Love* and *The Lost Girl*. (See *Son of Woman*, 1931, p. 125.) [G.H.F.]

The terrible sound of "Never now, never now—it is too late," which seemed to ring in the curious, indrawn cries of the elder woman, filled the girl with a deep wisdom. She knew the same would ring in her mother's dying cry. Married or unmarried, it was the same—the same anguish, realised in all its pain after the age of fifty—the loss in never having been able to relax, to submit.

This passage, written after *Sons and Lovers* had been completed, suggests that Lawrence was moving away from the stage of hatred for his father to a stage of understanding his father. In the autumn of 1913 he grew a beard.

The main line of Lawrence's development from this time forward follows what psychoanalysts sometimes describe as an "S" curve. Many of us, in our early years, exhibit a passionate preference for one parent, and his or her standards, and then gradually shift allegiance later. The boy who dotes upon his mother and despises his father can become a man who realizes that his mother's standards were inadequate or stultifying and that what his father had stood for is what the son now recognizes as valid.

The "S" curve may be detected in Mark Twain's jest about reaching the age of twenty-one and being astonished to realize how much his father had learned in the preceding five years. Lawrence had to be much older than twenty-one before the discovery grew upon him.

In 1926 when he was forty-one years old, he told Barbara Weekley that he had "formerly hated his drunken father, but at this time had swung his sympathy towards him, away from his mother." And in a later autobiographical sketch, as yet unpublished, he is even more explicit about his switch of allegiance:

My mother fought with deadly hostility against my father, all her life. He was not hostile, till provoked, then he too was a devil. But my mother began it. She seemed to begrudge his very existence. She begrudged him and hated her own love for him, she fought against his natural charm, vindictively. And by the time she died, at the age of fifty-five, she neither loved nor hated him any more. She had got over her feeling for him, and was 'Free.' So she died of cancer. Her feeling for us, also was divided. We were her own, therefore she loved us. But we were his, so she despised us a little. I was the most delicate . . . She loved me tenderly . . . But now, in the after years, I realize that she had decided I was going to die, and that was a great deal to her.

This realization may have been crystallized in 1924 when Lawrence's father died. The event, which Freudians in particular regard as one of the principal turning points in a man's life, was rarely mentioned by Lawrence. Like James Joyce, whose love for his improvident father was the principal love of his life (according to his brother's testimony), Lawrence had seemingly broken all ties with the man himself.[5] Joyce treated his father to an occasional postcard; Lawrence, whose father could scarcely read, may not have managed even that token of contact. What mattered to both writers was not the actual aging parent but what each had stood for in earlier years. To this image both novelists returned in their writings.

If the "S" curve signifies the main line of Lawrence's development, it should be noted that the line cannot be represented as an unbroken progress. There are many points of turning back. Yet in his characteristic fictional mode of balancing one set of forces against an opposite set of forces, we can readily detect a change of emphasis between his early and late writings. A change of values, implied or explicitly stated, tips the balance from Persephone's side to Pluto's.

In his later years, as was mentioned, Lawrence affirmed that if he could rewrite *Sons and Lovers* he would re-create Walter Morel into a more sympathetic figure than he believed he had originally made him. Actually there was no need for Lawrence

---

[5] See Stanislaus Joyce, *My Brother's Keeper* (New York, 1958), p. 238. When his father died Joyce wrote one of his best known poems, which ends with an appeal: "O, father forsaken, Forgive your son!" The poem is of the same date, 1931, as a short story by Kay Boyle, "Rest Cure," which portrays Lawrence's dying. The story has a perceptive scene of his confronting his father's spirit which is evoked grotesquely by a bewildered red lobster. "I got on very well without you," the son says, but at the end he calls out: "Father, help me." See her *Thirty Stories* (New York, 1946), pp. 23–24. [G.H.F.]

to rewrite the novel, because in other novels and stories he had already provided the corrections. Several instances can be cited of his returning to scenes in *Sons and Lovers* and recasting them in accordance with his later preferences. In *Aaron's Rod* (1922), for example, the hero, a married man who works as a checkweighman at the coal mines, begins to feel suffocated by the chill rigidities of his home in a small mining town. Like the hero of Bunyan's *Pilgrim's Progress*, he resolves to set out on a journey of self-discovery to distant cities, and his first step, like Christian's, involves his cutting himself off from the demands of his wife and children (although he continues to provide them with financial support).

This incident has been severely criticized by M. H. Abrams in a lively essay. According to Mr. Abrams, the incident demonstrates an artist requiring "our consent" to a position which by its eccentricity or perversity arouses "counterbeliefs" in the reader.

Objections to Lawrence on such grounds involve a problem of literary criticism which will often come up in the present study but which must be only circumvented at this point. How do we detect, with certainty, an author's set of values, or, for that matter, a reader's set of values? One can readily say that Mr. Abrams approves of domestic responsibilities, but one cannot affirm, with comparable certainty, that Lawrence is *recommending* the abandoning of wives and children by their restless husbands. What is evident, in this part of *Aaron's Rod*, is that Lawrence was recasting those scenes in *Sons and Lovers* in which Mr. Morel had been shown vowing loudly of his intention to leave home and of his slinking back again, an absurd figure, with domestic responsibilities intact and triumphant.

A similar recasting can be seen in the short story, "Jimmy and the Desperate Woman" (written 1924). An early scene in *Sons and Lovers* had concerned a clergyman who, during a visit with Mrs. Morel, confronts her husband as he comes home from the mines. Morel's irritability and self-pity are stressed in the scene; he appears in his worst light. In the later version, however, Jimmy, an Oxford-trained editor of a literary magazine, confronts the miner-husband of Emily Pinnegar (a woman who writes verses) and on this occasion it is the miner who is endowed with force and dignity. It is the intellectual visitor (one of Lawrence's many later caricatures of Middleton Murry) who this time seems absurd.

But the most striking example of recasting occurs in another short satiric tale, "The Lovely Lady" (published 1927), a late story that illustrates how far along the "S" curve Lawrence's development extended. The lovely lady is a seventy-two-year-old widow who seems thirty in a good light. She is the mother of two sons. The first son, Henry, a handsome young man, had fallen in love with an actress and died "after an awful struggle" because "his mother had humorously despised him for the attachment. So he had. caught some sudden ordinary disease." Her second son, Robert, now thirty-two years old, has been as "fascinated" by his mother as his brother had been. On him the effect of his attachment is that he cannot be a "lover of women." His Miriam-like cousin, who loves him despite his frigidity, recognizes that his mother was "going to kill Robert as she had killed Henry. It was clear murder: a mother murdering her sensitive sons, who were fascinated by her: the Circe!" The story, which involves the mother's exposure and death, is an effective horror story in its own right.

As in "The Rocking-Horse Winner" and in some stories of Henry James, what inspires horror is the spectacle of the perverse imposition of will. But to anyone familiar with Lawrence's life and writings "The Lovely Lady" takes on an additionally hair-raising dimension. Had Mrs. Lawrence lived until 1927, she would have been seventy-four years old (the Lovely Lady was seventy-two). Her son, William Ernest Lawrence, had died at twenty-three under identical circumstances as his counterpart in the story who died at twenty-two. And there is a further parallel, which although purely fanciful and not biographical in this instance, provides a final twist of the knife.

In *Sons and Lovers* the attachment between Mrs. Morel and the Congregational clergyman is of minor significance, not constituting a significant triangle, but in the original version of the novel, *Paul Morel*, the clergyman was a more prominent figure, a serious rival for Mrs. Morel's affections. In "The Lovely Lady," the younger son is the offspring of an affair between the mother and her lover, a Jesuit priest.

In this late story, under the guise of fiction, we are witnessing the spectacle of the mature Lawrence, like Hamlet in the closet, confronting his mother, Gertrude, and reassuring his father's ghost. In the story, Cecilia asks Robert what it was his mother had wanted from life. " 'She didn't even *love* herself,' said Ciss. 'It was something else—what was it?' " And Robert answers: " 'Power to feed on other lives . . . She has fed on me as she fed on Henry.' "

It is startling to put beside this a passage from the recently discovered Chambers papers in which May Chambers records what Lawrence himself had said seventeen years earlier, in 1910, as his own mother was dying:

> "Strange, isn't it, that I couldn't please her?"
> "What *did* she want?" . . .
> "Me," he said softly. "Just me."[6]

And the shift from *Sons and Lovers* is represented not only by a modification of values but by a marked shift of tones and method to which the form of a short story is more readily adapted than is a full-length novel. The tense balancing of forces characteristic of Lawrence's more typical fiction tends to break down when the central character is so incontestably villainous as is the Lovely Lady. When Persephone becomes Circe we can expect that Pluto is apt to become a somewhat righteous hero, a dark Perseus or a St. George, a figure who still carries off maidens to his regions of darkness, but more especially now as their saviour and protector rather than as their mate.

---

[6] Cf. p. 458, this edition.

ALFRED KAZIN

Alfred Kazin taught at Black Mountain College, Smith College, and
Amherst College, and is now Distinguished Professor of English at
the State University of New York at Stony Brook. Among books he
has published are the autobiographical volumes *A Walker in the
City* and *Starting Out in the Thirties*, and two collections of essays:
The Inmost Leaf and *Contemporaries*.

SONS, LOVERS AND MOTHERS

Sons and Lovers was published fifty years ago. In these fifty
years how many autobiographical novels have been written by
young men about the mothers they loved too well, about their
difficulties in "adjusting" to other women, and about themselves as the sensitive writers-to-be who liberated themselves
just in time in order to write their first novel? Such autobiographical novels—psychological devices they usually are, written in order to demonstrate freedom from the all-too-beloved
mother—are one of the great symbols of our time. They are
rooted in the modern emancipation of women. Lawrence
himself, after a return visit in the 1920's to his native Nottinghamshire, lamented that the "wildness" of his father's
generation was gone, that the dutiful sons in his own generation now made "good" husbands. Even working-class mothers
in England, in the last of the Victorian age, had aimed at a
"higher" standard of culture, and despising their husbands and
concentrating on their sons, they had made these sons images
of themselves. These mothers had sought a new dignity and
even a potential freedom for themselves as women, but holding
their sons too close, they robbed them of their necessary "wildness" and masculine force. So the sons grew up in bondage to
their mothers, and the more ambitious culturally these sons
were—Frank O'Connor says that *Sons and Lovers* is the work

Introduction to The Modern Library edition of *Sons and Lovers* (New
York: Random House, 1962); also published as "Sons, Lovers, and
Mothers" in *Partisan Review*, XXIX (Summer 1962), 373–385. Copyright
© 1962 by Random House, Inc. Reprinted by permission of the author.

of "one of the New Men who are largely a creation of the Education Act of 1870"—the more likely they were to try for their emancipation by writing a novel. The cultural aspiration that explains their plight was expected to turn them into novelists.

Sons and Lovers (which is not a first novel) seems easy to imitate. One reason, apart from the relationships involved, is the very directness and surface conventionality of its technique. James Joyce's *A Portrait of the Artist As a Young Man*, published only three years after *Sons and Lovers*, takes us immediately into the "new" novel of the twentieth century. It opens on a bewildering series of images faithful to the unconsciousness of childhood. Proust, who brought out the first volume of his great novel, *A la recherche du temps perdu*, in the same year that Lawrence published *Sons and Lovers*, imposed so highly stylized a unity of mood on the "Ouverture" to *Du côté de chez Swann*, that these impressions of childhood read as if they had been reconstructed to make a dream. But *Sons and Lovers* opens as a nineteenth-century novel with a matter-of-fact description of the setting—the mine, the landscape of "Bestwood," the neighboring streets and houses. This opening could have been written by Arnold Bennett, or any other of the excellent "realists" of the period whose work does not summon up, fifty years later, the ecstasy of imagination that Lawrence's work, along with that of Joyce and Proust, does provide to us. Lawrence is writing close to the actual facts. In his old-fashioned way he is even writing *about* the actual facts. No wonder that a young novelist with nothing but *his* own experiences to start him off may feel that Lawrence's example represents the triumph of experience. Literature has no rites in *Sons and Lovers*; everything follows as if from memory alone. When the struggle begins that makes the novel—the universal modern story of a "refined" and discontented woman who pours out on her sons the love she refuses the husband too "common" for her—the equally universal young novelist to whom all this has happened, the novelist who in our times is likely to have been all too mothered and fatherless, cannot help saying to himself—"Why can't I write this good a novel out of myself? Haven't I suffered as much as D. H. Lawrence and am I not just as sensitive? And isn't this a highly selective age in which 'sensitive' writers count?"

But the most striking thing about Lawrence—as it is about Paul Morel in *Sons and Lovers*—is his sense of his own authority. Though he was certainly not saved from atrocious suffering in relation to his mother, Lawrence's "sensitivity" was in the main concerned with reaching the highest and widest possible consciousness of everything—"nature," family, society, books—that came within his experience as a human being. His sense of his own powers, of himself as a "medium" through which the real life in things could be discovered for other people, was so strong that his personal vividness stayed with his earliest friends as a reminder of the best hopes of their youth; it was instantly recognized by literary people in London when they read his work. You can easily dislike Lawrence for this air of authority, just as many people dislike him for the influence that he exerted during his lifetime and that has grown steadily since his death in 1930. There is already an unmistakable priggish conceit about Paul Morel in his novel. Here is a miner's son who is asked by his mother if his is a "divine discontent" and replies in this style: "Yes, I don't care about its divinity. But damn your happiness! So long as life's full, it doesn't matter whether it's happy or not. I'm afraid your happiness would bore me." But even this contains Lawrence's sense of his own authority. He saw his talent as a sacred possession—he was almost too proud to think of his career as a *literary* one. This sense of having a power that makes for righteousness—this was so strong in Lawrence, and so intimately associated with his mother's influence, that the struggle he describes in *Sons and Lovers*, the struggle to love another woman as he had loved his mother, must be seen as the connection he made between his magic "demon," his gift, and his relationship to his mother.

Freud once wrote that he who is a favorite of the mother becomes a "conqueror." This was certainly Freud's own feeling about himself. The discoverer of the Oedipus complex never doubted that the attachment which, abnormally protracted, makes a son feel that loving any woman but his mother is a "desecration," nevertheless, in its early prime features, gives a particular kind of strength to the son. It is a spiritual strength, not the masculine "wildness" that Lawrence was to miss in contemporary life. Lawrence's own feeling that he was certainly somebody, the pride that was to sustain him despite horribly damaged lungs through so many years of tuberculosis until his death at forty-five; the pride that carried him so far from a miner's cottage; the pride that enabled him, a penniless school-teacher, to run off with a German baroness married to his old teacher and to make her give up her three children; the pride that thirty years after his death still makes him so vivid to us as we read—this pride had not its origin but its *setting*, in the fierce love of Mrs. Arthur Lawrence for "Bert," of Mrs. Morel for her Paul.

Lawrence, who was so full of his own gift, so fully engaged in working it out that he would not acknowledge his gifted contemporaries, certainly did feel that the "essential soul" of him as he would have said, his special demon, his particular gift of vision, his particular claim on immortality, was bound up with his mother. Not "love" in the psychological sense of con-scious consideration, but love in the mythological sense of a sacred connection, was what Lawrence associated with his mother and Paul with Mrs. Morel. Lawrence's power over others is directly traceable to his own sense of the sacredness still possible to life, arising from the powers hidden in ordinary human relationships. The influence he had—if only temporarily —even on a rationalist like Bertrand Russell reminds one of the hold he kept on socialist working-class people he had grown up with and who certainly did not share Lawrence's exalted individualism. Lawrence's "authority," which made him seem unbearably full of himself to those who disliked him, was cer-tainly of a very singular kind. He had an implicit confidence in his views on many questions—on politics as on sex and love; he was able to pontificate in later life about the Etruscans, of whom he knew nothing, as well as to talk dangerous nonsense about "knowing through the blood" and the leader principle. Yet it is Lawrence's struggle to retain all the moral authority that he identified with his mother's love that explains the intensity of *Sons and Lovers,* as it does the particular intensity of Lawrence's style in this book, which he later criticized as too violent. Yet behind this style lies Lawrence's lifelong belief in what he called "quickness," his need to see the "shimmer," the life force in everything, as opposed to the "dead crust" of its external form. Destiny for Lawrence meant his privileged and constant sense of the holiness implicit in this recognition of the life force. Destiny also meant his recognition, as a delicate boy who had already seen his older brother Ernest (the "William" of *Sons and Lovers*) sicken and die of the struggle to attach himself to another woman, that his survival was somehow bound up with fidelity to his mother. Lawrence had absolute faith in his gift, but it was bound up with his physical existence, which was always on trial. He felt that it was in his mother's hands. The gift of life, so particularly precious to him after his near-fatal pneumonia at seventeen (when his brother died), could be easily lost.

With so much at stake, Lawrence put into ultimate terms, life or death, the struggle between Paul Morel's need to hold onto his mother and his desire to love Miriam Leivers as well. The struggle in *Sons and Lovers* is not between love of the mother and love of a young woman; it is the hero's struggle to *keep* the mother as his special strength, never to lose her, not to offend or even to vex her by showing too much partiality to other women. This is why the original of "Miriam Leivers," Jessie Chambers, says in her touching memoir (*D. H. Lawrence: A Personal Record,* by "E.T.") that she had to break with Lawrence after she had seen the final draft of the book, that "the shock of *Sons and Lovers* gave the death-blow to our friendship," for in that book "Lawrence handed his mother the laurels of victory."

That is indeed what Lawrence did; it would not have occurred to him to do anything else. And Jessie Chambers also honestly felt that she minded this for Lawrence's sake, not her own, since by this time there was no longer any question of marriage between them. Jessie, who certainly loved Lawrence for his genius even after she had relinquished all personal claim on him, had launched Lawrence's career by sending out his poems. When Lawrence, after his mother's death, wrote a first draft of Sons and Lovers, he was still unable to work out his situation in a novel. Jessie encouraged him to drop this unsatisfactory version of the later novel and to portray the emotional struggle directly. At his request, she even wrote out narrative sections which Lawrence revised and incorporated into his novel. (Lawrence often had women write out passages for his novels when he wanted to know how a woman would react to a particular situation; Frieda Lawrence was to contribute to his characterization of Mrs. Morel.) Lawrence sent Jessie parts of the manuscript for her comments and further notes. After so much help and even collaboration, Jessie felt betrayed by the book. Lawrence had failed to show, she said, how important a role the girl had played in the development of the young man as an artist. "It was his old inability to face his problem squarely. His mother had to be supreme, and for the sake of that supremacy every disloyalty was permissible."

Lawrence is quoted in Harry T. Moore's biography, The Intelligent Heart, as saying of Miriam-Jessie, she "encouraged my demon. But alas, it was me, not he, whom she loved. So for her too it was a catastrophe. My demon is not easily loved: whereas the ordinary me is. So poor Miriam was let down." Lawrence's tone is exalted, but he certainly justified himself in Sons and Lovers as a novelist, not as a "son." That is the only consideration now. Jessie Chambers herself became an embittered woman. She tried to find her salvation in politics, where the fierce hopes of her generation before 1914 for a new England were certainly not fulfilled. But Lawrence, taking the new draft of Sons and Lovers with him to finish in Germany after he had run off with Frieda, was able, if not to "liberate" himself from his mother in his novel, to write a great novel out of his earliest life and struggles.

That is the triumph Jessie Chambers would not acknowledge

in *Sons and Lovers*, this she could not see—the Lawrence "unable to face his problem squarely" made a great novel out of the "problem," out of his mother, father, brother, the miners, the village, the youthful sweetheart. Whatever Jessie may have thought from being too close to Lawrence himself, whatever Lawrence may have said about his personal struggles during the six-week frenzy in which he launched the new draft, Lawrence felt his "problem" not as something to be solved, but as a subject to be represented. All these early experiences weighed on him with a pressure that he was able to communicate—later he called it "that hard violent style full of sensation and presentation." Jessie Chambers herself described Lawrence's accomplishment when she said, speaking of the new draft of *Sons and Lovers* that she drove Lawrence to write, "It was his power to transmute the common experiences into significance that I always felt to be Lawrence's greatest gift. He did not distinguish between small and great happenings. The common round was full of mystery, awaiting interpretation. Born and bred of working people, he had the rare gift of seeing them from within, and revealing them on their own plane."

Lawrence's particular gift was this ability to represent as valuable anything that came his way. He had the essential religious attribute of *valuing life*, of seeing the most trivial things as a kind of consecration. In part, at least, one can trace this to the poverty, austerity and simplicity of his upbringing. Jessie Chambers once watched Lawrence and his father gathering watercress for tea. "Words cannot convey Lawrence's brimming delight in all these simple things." Delight in simple things is one of the recurring features of the working-class existence described in *Sons and Lovers*. We can understand better the special value that Lawrence identified with his mother's laboriousness and self-denial in the scene where Mrs. Morel, wickedly extravagant, comes home clutching the pot that cost her fivepence and the bunch of pansies and daisies that cost her fourpence. The rapture of the commonest enjoyments and simplest possessions is represented in the mother and father as well as in the young artist Paul, the future D. H. Lawrence. This autobio-

604 / CONTEXTS OF RESPONSE

graphical novel rooted in the writer's early struggles is charged with feeling for his class, his region, his people. Lawrence was not a workingman himself, despite the brief experience in the surgical appliances factory that in the novel becomes Paul Morel's continued job. Chekhov said that the working-class writer purchases with his youth that which a more genteel writer is born with. But Lawrence gained everything, as a writer, from being brought up in the working class, and lost nothing by it. In *Sons and Lovers* he portrays the miners without idealizing them, as a socialist would; he relishes their human qualities (perhaps even a little jealously) and works them up as a subject for his art. He does not identify himself with them; his mother, too, we can be sure from the portrait of Mrs. Morel, tended to be somewhat aloof among the miners' wives. But Lawrence knows *as a writer* that he is related to working people, that he is bound up with them in the same order of physical and intimate existence, that it is workers' lives he has always looked on. Some of the most affecting passages in this novel are based on the force and directness of working-class speech. " 'E's niver gone, child?" Morel says to his son when William dies. Paul answers in "educated" and even prissy English, but the voice of the mines, the fields and the kitchens is rendered straight and unashamed. Lawrence, who knew how much he had lost as a man by siding with his mother in the conflict, describes the miner Morel getting his own breakfast, sitting "down to an hour of joy," with an irresistible appreciation of the physical and human picture involved: "He toasted his bacon on a fork and caught the drops of fat on his bread; then he put the rasher on his thick slice of bread, and cut off chunks with a clasp-knife, poured his tea into his saucer, and was happy."

The writer alone in Lawrence redeemed the weaknesses of being too much his mother's son. We see the common round of life among the miners' families very much as the young Lawrence must have seen it, with the same peculiar directness. His mental world was startlingly without superfluities and wasted motions. What he wrote, he wrote. The striking sense of authority, of inner conviction, that he associated with his mother's love gave him a cutting briskness with things he disapproved. But this same immediacy of response, when it touched what he loved, could reach the greatest emotional depths. The description of William Morel's coffin being carried into the house is a particular example of this. "The coffin swayed, the men began to mount the three steps with their load. Annie's candle flickered, and she whimpered as the first men appeared, and the limbs and bowed heads of six men struggled to climb into the room, bearing the coffin that rode like sorrow on their living flesh." Lawrence's power to move the reader lies in this ability to summon up all the physical attributes associated with an object; he puts you into direct contact with all its properties *as* an object. Rarely has the realistic novelist's need to *present*, to present vividly, continually, and at the highest pitch of pictorial concentration—the gift which has made the novel the supreme literary form of modern times—rarely has this reached such intense clarity of representation as it does in *Sons and Lovers*. There are passages, as in Tolstoy, that make you realize what a loss to directness of vision our increasing self-consciousness in literature represents. Lawrence is still face to face with life, and he can describe the smallest things with the most attentive love and respect.

Lawrence does not describe, he would not attempt to describe, the object as in *itself* it really is. The effect of his prose is always to heighten our consciousness of something, to relate it to ourselves. He is a romantic—and in this book is concerned with the most romantic possible subject for a novelist, the growth of the writer's own consciousness. Yet he succeeded as a novelist, he succeeded brilliantly, because he was convinced that the novel is the great literary form, for no other could reproduce so much of the actual motion or "shimmer" of life, especially as expressed in the relationships between people. Since for Lawrence the great subject of literature was not the writer's own consciousness but consciousness between people, the living felt relationship between them, it was his very concern to represent the "shimmer" of life, the "wholeness"—these could have been mere romantic slogans—that made possible his

brilliance as a novelist. He was to say, in a remarkable essay
called "Why the Novel Matters," that "Only in the novel are
all things given full play, or at least, they may be given full
play, when we realize that life itself, and not inert safety, is the
reason for living. For out of the full play of all things emerges
the only thing that is anything, the wholeness of a man, the
wholeness of a woman, man alive, and live woman." It was
relationship that was sacred to him, as it was the relationships
with his mother, her continuing presence in his mind and life,
that gave him the sense of authority on which all his power
rested. And as a novelist in *Sons and Lovers* he was able to rise
above every conventional pitfall in an autobiographical novel
by centering his whole vision on character as the focus of a
relationship, not as an absolute.

After *Sons and Lovers*, which was his attempt to close up
the past, Lawrence was to move on to novels like *The Rainbow*
(1915) and *Women in Love* (1920), where the "non-human
in humanity" was to be more important to him than "the old-
fashioned human element." The First World War was to make
impossible for Lawrence his belief in the old "stable ego" of
character. Relationships, as the continuing interest of life, became in these more "problematical," less "conventional" novels,
a version of man's general relationship, as an unknown in himself, to his unexplained universe. But the emphasis on growth
and change in *Sons and Lovers*, the great book that closes
Lawrence's first period, is from the known to the unknown; as
Frank O'Connor has said, the book begins as a nineteenth
century novel and turns into a twentieth century one. Where
autobiographical novels with a "sensitive" artist or novelist
as hero tend to emphasize the hero's growth to self-knowledge,
the history of his "development," the striking thing about *Sons
and Lovers*, and an instance of the creative mind behind it,
is that it does not hand the "laurels of victory" to the hero. It
does not allow him any self-sufficient victory over his circumstances. With the greatest possible vividness it shows Paul
Morel engulfed in relationships—with the mother he loves all
too sufficiently, with the "spiritual" Miriam and Clara, neither

of whom he can love whole-heartedly—relationships that are difficult and painful, and that Lawrence leaves arrested in their pain and conflict. When Jessie Chambers said of the first draft of *Sons and Lovers* that "Lawrence had carried the situation to the point of deadlock and had stopped there," she may have been right enough about it as an aborted novel. But Lawrence's primary interest and concern as a novelist, his sense of the continuing *flow* of relationship between people, no matter how unclear and painful, no matter how far away it was from the "solution" that the people themselves may have longed for, is what makes this whole last section of the novel so telling.

But of course it is the opening half of *Sons and Lovers* that makes the book great. The struggle between husband and wife is described with a direct, unflinching power. Lawrence does not try to bring anything to a psychological conclusion. The marriage is a struggle, a continuing friction, a relationship where the wife's old desire for her husband can still flash up through her resentment of his "lowness." That is why everything in the "common round" can be described with such tenderness, for the relationship of husband and wife sweeps into its unconscious passion everything that the young Lawrence loved, and was attached to. Living in a mining village on the edge of old Sherwood Forest, always close to the country, Lawrence was as intimate with nature as any country poet could have been, but he was lucky to see rural England and the industrial Midlands in relation to each other; the country soothed his senses, but a job all day long in a Nottingham factory making out orders for surgical appliances did not encourage nature worship. "On the fallow land the young wheat shone silkily. Minton pit waved its plumes of white steam, coughed, and rattled hoarsely." Lawrence is a great novelist of landscape, for he is concerned with the relationships of people living on farms, or walking out into the country after the week's work in the city. He does not romanticize nature, he describes it in its minute vibrations. In *Sons and Lovers* the emotional effect of the "lyrical" passages depends on Lawrence's extraordinary ability to convey movement and meaning even in non-human things. But in this book nature never provides evasion of human conflict and is not even a projection of human feelings; it is the physical world that Lawrence grew up in, and includes the pit down which a miner must go every day. Paul in convalescence, sitting up in bed, would "see the fluffy horses feeding at the troughs in the field, scattering their hay on the trodden yellow snow; watch the miners troop home—small, black figures trailing slowly in gangs across the white field."

This miniature, exquisite as a Japanese watercolor, is typical of Sons and Lovers—the country lives and seethes, but it has no mystical value. It is the landscape of Nottinghamshire and Derbyshire, and in the book it is still what it was to Lawrence growing up in it, an oasis of refreshment in an industrial world. The countryside arouses young lovers to their buried feelings and it supplies images for the "quickness," the vital current of relationship, that Lawrence valued most in life. It is never sacred in itself. When you consider that this novel came out in 1913, at the height of the "Georgian" period, when so many young poets of Lawrence's generation were mooning over nature, it is striking that his chief interest is always the irreducible ambiguity of human relationships. Lawrence's language, in certain key scenes, certainly recalls the emotional inflation of fiction in the "romantic" heyday preceding the First World War. But the style is actually exalted rather than literary. There is an unmistakably scriptural quality to Lawrence's communication of extreme human feeling. Mr. Morel secretly cut young William's hair, and Mrs. Morel feels that "this act of masculine clumsiness was the spear through the side of her love." The Lawrences were Congregationalist, like American Puritans. They were close to the Lord. The strong sense of himself that Lawrence was always to have, the conviction that what he felt was always terribly important just in the way he felt it, is imparted to Mrs. Morel herself in the great scene in which the insulted husband, dizzy with drink, locks her out of the house. The description of Mrs. Morel's feelings is charged with a kind of frenzy of concern for her; the language sweeps from pole to pole of feeling. Mrs. Morel is pregnant, and her sense of her moral aloneness at this moment is overwhelming. "Mrs. Morel, seared with passion, shivered to find herself out there in a great white light, that fell cold on her, and gave a shock to her inflamed soul." Later we read that "After a time the child, too, melted with her in the mixing-pot of moonlight, and she rested with the hills and lilies and houses, all swum together in a kind of swoon."

In this key scene of the mother's "trouble" (which must have been based on things that Lawrence later heard from his mother), the sense we get of Mrs. Morel, humiliated and enraged but in her innermost being haughtily inviolate, gives us a sense of all the power that Lawrence connected with his mother and of the power in the relationship that flowed between them. In *Sons and Lovers* he was able to re-create, for all time, the moment when the sympathetic bond between them reached its greatest intensity—and the moment when her death broke it. Ever after, Lawrence was to try to re-create this living bond, this magic sympathy, between himself and life. He often succeeded in creating an exciting and fruitful version of it—in relationship to his extraordinary wife Frieda; to a host of friends, disciples, admirers and readers throughout the world; even to his own novels and stories, essays and articles and poems and letters. Unlike Henry James, James Joyce, Marcel Proust, T. S. Eliot, Lawrence always makes you feel that not art but the quality of the lived experience is his greatest concern. That is why it is impossible to pick up anything by him without feeling revivified. Never were a writer's works more truly an allegory of his life, and no other writer of his imaginative standing has in our time written books that are so open to life. Yet one always feels in Lawrence his own vexation and disappointment at not being able to reproduce, in the full consciousness of his genius, the mutual sympathy he had experienced with his mother. One even feels about Lawrence's increasing vexation and disappointment that it tore him apart physically, exhausted and shattered him. Wandering feverishly from continent to continent, increasingly irritable and vulnerable to every human defect and cultural complacency, he seems finally to have died for lack of another place to aim at; for lack, even, of another great fight to wage. His work itself was curiously never enough for him, for he could write so quickly, sitting anywhere under a tree, that the book seemed to fly out of his hand as soon as he had made it; and he was so much the only poet in his imaginative universe that he could not take other writers seriously enough to rejoice in his own greatness. He was searching, one feels, for something infinitely more intangible than fame, or a single person, or a "God"—he was searching for the remembered ecstasy of experience, the quality of feeling, that is even more evanescent than the people we connect with it. Lawrence kept looking for this even after he had reproduced it in *Sons and Lovers*, whose triumph as art was to give him so little lasting satisfaction. Art could not fulfill Lawrence's search, and only death could end it. But the ecstasy of a single human relationship that he tried to reproduce never congealed into a single image or idol or belief. Imaginatively, Lawrence was free; which is why his work could literally rise like a phoenix out of the man who consumed himself in his conflict with himself.

Topics

✿◈✿◈✿◈✿◈✿◈✿◈✿◈✿◈✿◈✿◈✿◈✿◈✿◈✿◈✿◈✿◈✿◈✿◈◈

FOR DISCUSSION AND PAPERS

The many important questions raised in this section are presented as guidance in the preparation of papers. They can be used, equally well, as talking points for class discussion.

I. TONE OF VOICE

In any piece of writing someone is speaking to a listener, present or implied. A book comes to life in a reader's imagination as he begins to pay attention and respond to the stress and intonation of a living voice. This is obvious in a play or a lyric poem: a character talks his way around a stage or a lover complains in a sonnet to his black-browed mistress that she has been two-timing him. The axiom is just as true, although possibly less obvious, when it comes to fiction. *Sons and Lovers* opens, arrestingly, on a curt, informative, yet just possibly dismal note—the succession of a "Bottoms" to a "Hell Row" doesn't sound like much of a net gain—and ends on a note of muted optimism with an account of Paul Morel moving "towards the faintly humming, glowing town, quickly." Why muted? Because of "faintly"—the town might *blaze* with light if the narrator's attitude toward his character were different— and because we are told only that Paul walked in the direction of the town, leaving in abeyance the questions of whether he actually reached it and what he found there.

Of course, the narrator might have ended with "Paul Morel reached the town and lived there happily ever after," except that he is not that sort of narrator. What sort is he? To come back to the main point, he is the sort who uses words in the way in which he uses them and the reader must come to terms with him by paying exact, sensitive attention to the way he speaks. There is no other method of testing *his* sincerity and truth, and, therefore, the truth and value of the story he tells.

The dominant voice of *Sons and Lovers* is the narrator's, but characters also speak for themselves. The father's speech is characteristically slurring, slovenly, inchoate; the mother's sharp, decisive, "superior." Miriam often seems to say less than she intends (her speech is reticent and introverted, is it not?) whereas Clara, who perhaps speaks most expressively in the language of physical gesture and bodily attitude, frequently talks in a challenging tone of argument and indictment. Actually, these summaries are not very satisfactory. Certainly they are no substitute for paying attention to the speech of particular characters, and to the narrator's words, at specific moments and in particular scenes. Only in that way will the reader build up a complex and exact impression of the personages of the book as palpable presences, some growing and struggling in time to become themselves and to find satisfaction with each other, some failing and hardening themselves against the awareness of their own failure.

Exercise on Narrative Tone of Voice (can be done as discussion or as a brief, analytical paper)

Reread the opening paragraphs of *Sons and Lovers*, from "'The Bottoms' succeeded . . ." to "a loop of fine chain, the railway."

1. Point out some ways in which the narrator's tone and selection of details here is that of a good social historian. What is the larger historical process in terms of which the various changes occurring in and around Bestwood over several generations can be understood?

2. Point to some expressions and turns of phrase which you would not expect to find in a historical treatise. Would the historian speak, for example, of gin-pits being "elbowed aside" by

the large mines? What about "the few colliers and the donkeys, burrowing down like ants into the earth, making queer mounds and little black places among the corn-fields . . ."? What sort of talk is this?

3. Where does the narrator situate himself when he describes the railway that ran "from Nuttall, high up on the sandstone among the woods . . . "? What can you say about the rhythm of that whole sentence and how the rhythm affects the reader's response? Would you expect to find this sort of prose rhythm in the work of a professional historian?

4. What, in sum, is the difference between the way this narrator talks in these opening paragraphs and the way a historian would describe the same scene?

Suggestions for longer papers on tone

1. A comparison and contrast between the narrative voice of *Sons and Lovers* and the narrative voice of Lawrence's essay in recollection and prophecy, "Nottingham and the Mining Countryside." (Pp. 432–441.)

2. A study of the social spectrum of *Sons and Lovers* in terms of differences in the way several leading characters use words. Comparisons between Mr. and Mrs. Morel, Clara and Baxter Dawes, Paul and his siblings, Clara and the other girls at the surgical appliance factory should prove particularly illuminating.

3. A comparison of Miriam's tone and attitude in *Sons and Lovers* with that of Jessie Chambers in the section called "Two Women."

II. POINT OF VIEW

This topic follows naturally from a concern with the speaking voice and with the narrator's voice in particular. In speech the narrator of *Sons and Lovers* defines himself and his *attitude* toward the events and characters of his story. At least one critic, Percy Lubbock, has taken the position that point of view—the angle and attitude from which everything narrated is seen and evaluated—is the chief formal problem of prose fiction.

Inasmuch as *Sons and Lovers* has only one narrator, who speaks consistently in the third person and is omniscient, one would not expect any difficult questions about point of view to arise. Yet it is in precisely this area that serious critical questions have been posed, questions bearing on the consistency and sincerity of the narrator's attitude toward several of his characters and their situations.

Suggestions for papers on point of view

1.

"When I first read D. H. Lawrence's novels, at the age of about twenty, I was puzzled by the fact that there did not seem to be any classification of the characters into 'good' and 'bad.' Lawrence seemed to sympathize with all of them about equally and this was so unusual as to give me the feeling of having lost my bearings."

—GEORGE ORWELL (quoted by G. H. Ford, p. 582)

Choose for analysis several episodes in each of which the narrator is following a different character. Is it true that he sympathizes with each character about equally? What are the advantages and what are the risks of the close, empathetic relation that the narrator seems able to establish with nearly every character at some point in the story? Do you agree that the narrator altogether fails to establish any criteria for judging characters and their behavior? If you disagree, how does the narrator establish a basis for such judgment at particular points and for *Sons and Lovers* as a whole?

2. Write a paper on the narrator's presentation of Baxter Dawes. Is his treatment of this character consistent from first to last? How, finally, is Dawes seen and accounted for? With sympathy? With indifference? How is Dawes used in the presentation of other characters? For example, in the presentation of Paul Morel and of Clara.

3. Write a paper based on a careful rereading of the episode in which Paul, Miriam, and Clara spend a Sunday afternoon together walking through the countryside (Chapter IX, pp. 229–240). What is going on among these three characters in this episode and how does the reader come to terms with what

is going on? Is the narrative equally "fair" to each character in this scene? Be sure in considering this last question that you don't mix up the narrator with Paul Morel.

The most serious criticism that has ever been raised against *Sons and Lovers* is that Lawrence does, precisely, confuse the narrative point of view with Paul Morel's attitude. Mark Schorer, in a well-known essay, "Technique as Discovery," (see Bibliography, p. 621), argues that in Part II of *Sons and Lovers* Lawrence fails to separate himself and his emotional problems from Paul and *his* emotional problems, with the result that the narrative point of view in those chapters dealing with the Paul–Miriam–Mrs. Morel triangle wavers, becomes equivocal and ambiguous, falls, if not consciously then unconsciously, into evasiveness and insincerity. This is substantially the same charge that Jessie Chambers made in her memoir, *D. H. Lawrence: A Personal Record*. She felt that Lawrence, because of his own unresolved conflicts, had been less than fair to "Miriam," and had handed "the fruits of victory" to the mother, thereby spoiling the story he had started out to write and crippling his own future development as an artist and as a man. The problem is a fascinating one for treatment in a long paper.

4. Look up the Schorer essay; read the Jessie Chambers excerpt (pp. 478–485) and my own mainly dissenting view in "*Sons and Lovers*: The Search for Form" (pp. 560–576). Then reread Part II of the novel, remembering that the final position you take up must be primarily and concretely based on *your* experience of the language of *Sons and Lovers*, and not on any opinions you may have formed about Lawrence and his problems as a son and lover of women.

5. Toward the end of his life Lawrence remarked that he had not dealt fairly with the character of the father in *Sons and Lovers*; if he had the book to do over again he would have made more of Morel's sensual warmth and capacity for spontaneous enjoyment as against the brittleness and severity of the mother. Write a paper considering the novel's treatment of Walter and Gertrude Morel. Do you agree with Lawrence's

second thoughts on these characters? What evidence is there for maintaining that the narrator's presentation of Walter's character is actually quite balanced and compassionate at bottom? By the same token, is the portrayal of Gertrude marred by idealization and sentimentality? Many readers admire the mother for her fortitude and courage, while others find her cold and domineering. Does this discrepancy necessarily imply a flaw in the narrative presentation of the character?

6. An interesting paper can be written comparing the treatment of the son-lover problem in Lawrence's poems, 1910–1912 (pp. 461–477), with its treatment in the novel. Once again, the question of Lawrence's degree of control over the painful emotions generated by his mother's illness and death and by the decision to break with Jessie Chambers is relevant.

7. Read Simon O. Lesser's "Two Modes of Insight" (pp. 493–497), Freud's "The Most Prevalent Form of Degradation in Erotic Life" (pp. 498–510), and J. Middleton Murry's "Genius and a Syndrome" (pp. 511–517). Write an essay on the uses and limitations of discursive, scientific, and factual (biographical) knowledge in relation to the problem of evaluating and understanding imaginative works of literature such as *Sons and Lovers*, "End of Another Home Holiday," and "Spirits Summoned West."

III. STYLE, FORM AND SYMBOLISM

As a preliminary to this group of suggested papers you are advised to read "On *Sons and Lovers*" by Dorothy Van Ghent (pp. 527–546), "How to Pick Flowers" by Mark Spilka (pp. 547–559), "The S Curve: Persephone to Pluto" by George H. Ford (pp. 577–596), and "*Sons and Lovers*: The Discovery of Form" by the editor (pp. 560–576).

1. Many readers have disagreed about the ending of *Sons and Lovers*. Some have thought that Paul will succeed in making a new life for himself without the mother and others have thought that he is doomed to remain in darkness, neurotically overattached to the mother's memory. Reread the concluding chapters of the novel, paying close attention to Paul's

actions and reactions and to the language in which these are defined. Write a paper interpreting the ending which expresses your own view of Paul's situation when we last see him.

2. The style of *Sons and Lovers* has been called loose and repetitious, yet certain critics have been impressed with Lawrence's verbal resourcefulness in keeping his story moving ahead as a coherent intertwining of expository, dramatic, and "passional" strands of narrative. Centering on a chapter or a substantial episode where, in your view, the question of style is worth raising, give your own view of the book's stylistic resourcefulness *or* confusion.

3. Various critics have pointed to the novel's treatment of landscape; of night, darkness, and the moon; of flowers; and of animals as examples of an essentially poetic symbolism. Other critics have minimized the role of symbolism in *Sons and Lovers*. Lawrence himself spoke approvingly—in connection with his last novel, *Lady Chatterley's Lover*—of symbolism that is "inevitable" rather than contrived. Write a paper exploring this question of symbolism in prose narrative and in *Sons and Lovers* in particular.

IV. OTHER TOPICS

1. A comparison of *Sons and Lovers* and *A Portrait of the Artist as a Young Man*, by James Joyce (a) as imaginative autobiographies; (b) as fictional studies of the growth of an artist. (See Maurice Beebe, "Lawrence's Sacred Fount: The Artist Theme of *Sons and Lovers*," *Texas Studies in Literature and Language*, IV [1962], 539–552.)

2. *Sons and Lovers* as a film. Write a screen "treatment" of the novel. The "treatment" is a detailed synopsis, prepared as a preliminary to the full scenario, and designed to show the producer in summary form the entire sequence of scenes which will make up the finished film. (*Sons and Lovers* has already been made into a film, under the direction of Jack Cardiff. It is generally admired for its sensitive camera work, for Wendy Hiller's performance as Mrs. Morel, and for the large amount of Lawrence's actual dialogue that was retained in the script.)

3. For a long, speculative paper. Looking back at the modern

movement in twentieth-century literature from our present vantage point we can argue, as the English critic A. Alvarez has argued, that "the real impulse behind the modern movement was the desire to attain some degree of psychological realism." Going further, we can say that all genuine discoveries in the sphere of psychological realism will entail the rethinking —not necessarily the abandonment!—of received moral ideas and terms and conventional ideas of the individual's relation to community, class, vocation (work), and to his society as a whole.

Granted that *Sons and Lovers* is a pioneering work of psychological realism in this century, how successful has Lawrence been in dealing with further moral and social questions that rush in on the heels of his discoveries in the psychological sphere? For example, where are freedom, health, vitality to be found and how may they best be preserved? How does the novel encourage us to regard traditional moral imperatives fixed in such expressions as "doing one's duty," "a good son," "contributing to society," "respecting others," "loving one's children"? What does Lawrence's psychological realism show us about the real nature of love and hate, physical aggression, sensuality, ambition, religious experience, feminine submissiveness, the sanctity of the family, the stability and decency of small-town life?

You will be sure to think of many other moral and social problems raised directly or by implication in *Sons and Lovers*. By all means speculate freely but keep your discussion centered and focused on your experience of reading Lawrence's novel.

Bibliography

BOOKS BY D. H. LAWRENCE

The White Peacock. New York: Duffield and Co., 1911.
The Trespasser. London: Duckworth and Co., 1913.
Love Poems and Others. London: Duckworth and Co., 1913.
Sons and Lovers. London: Duckworth and Co., 1913.
The Widowing of Mrs. Holroyd. New York: Mitchell Kennerly, 1914.
The Prussian Officer [and other stories]. London: Duckworth and Co., 1914.
The Rainbow. London: Methuen & Co., 1915.
Twilight in Italy. London: Duckworth and Co., 1916.
Amores. London: Duckworth and Co., 1916.
Look! We Have Come Through! London: Chatto and Windus, 1917.
New Poems. London: Martin Secker, 1918.
Bay. Westminster: The Beaumont Press, 1919.
Touch and Go. London: C. W. Daniel, Ltd., 1920.
Women in Love. New York: Privately printed, 1920.
The Lost Girl. London: Martin Secker, 1920.
Movements in European History [by "Lawrence H. Davison"]. London: Oxford University Press, 1921.
Psychoanalysis and the Unconscious. New York: Thomas Seltzer, 1921.
Tortoises. New York: Thomas Seltzer, 1921.
Sea and Sardinia. New York: Thomas Seltzer, 1921.
Aaron's Rod. New York: Thomas Seltzer, 1922.
Fantasia of the Unconscious. New York: Thomas Seltzer, 1922.
England, My England and Other Stories. New York: Thomas Seltzer, 1922.
The Ladybird, The Fox, The Captain's Doll. London: Martin Secker, 1923.
Studies in Classic American Literature. New York: Thomas Seltzer, 1923.
Kangaroo. London: Martin Secker, 1923.
Birds, Beasts, and Flowers. New York: Thomas Seltzer, 1923.
The Boy in the Bush. By D. H. Lawrence and M. L. Skinner. London: Martin Secker, 1924.
St. Mawr: together with The Princess. London: Martin Secker, 1925.
Reflections on the Death of a Porcupine and Other Essays. Philadelphia: The Centaur Press, 1925.
The Plumed Serpent. London: Martin Secker, 1926.
David. London: Martin Secker, 1926.
Sun. London: E. Archer, 1926.
Glad Ghosts. London: Ernest Benn, Ltd., 1926.
Mornings in Mexico. London: Martin Secker, 1927.
Sun. Unexpurgated edition. Paris: Black Sun Press, 1928.
Rawdon's Roof. London: Elkin Mathews and Marrot, 1928.

The Collected Poems of D. H. Lawrence. Two volumes. London: Martin Secker, 1928.

The Women Who Rode Away and Other Stories. London: Martin Secker, 1928.

Lady Chatterley's Lover. Florence: Privately printed by G. Orioli, 1928.

The Paintings of D. H. Lawrence. London: The Mandrake Press, 1929.

Pansies. London: Martin Secker, 1929.

My Skirmish with Jolly Roger. New York: Random House, 1929.

Pornography and Obscenity. London: Faber and Faber, 1929.

The Escaped Cock [also called *The Man Who Died*]. Paris: Black Sun Press, 1929.

Nettles. London: Faber and Faber, 1930.

The Virgin and the Gypsy. Florence: G. Orioli, 1930.

Love Among the Haystacks and Other Pieces. London: The Nonesuch Press, 1930.

The Triumph of the Machine. London: Faber and Faber, 1930.

A Propos of Lady Chatterley. London: The Mandrake Press, 1930.

Apocalypse. Florence: G. Orioli, 1931.

Etruscan Places. London: Martin Secker, 1932.

Last Poems. Edited by Richard Aldington and G. Orioli. Florence: G. Orioli, 1932.

The Ship of Death and Other Poems. London: Martin Secker, 1933.

The Lovely Lady. London: Martin Secker, 1933.

The Plays of D. H. Lawrence. London: Martin Secker, 1933.

A Collier's Friday Night. London: Martin Secker, 1934.

A Modern Lover. London: Martin Secker, 1934.

The Tales of D. H. Lawrence. London: Martin Secker, 1934.

Foreword to Women in Love. San Francisco: Gelber, Lilienthal, Inc., 1936.

Phoenix: The Posthumous Papers of D. H. Lawrence. Edited by Edward D. McDonald. New York: The Viking Press, 1936.

Poems. 3 vols. London: William Heinemann, Ltd., 1939.

The First Lady Chatterley. New York: The Dial Press, 1944.

The Symbolic Meaning: The Uncollected Versions of Studies in Classic American Literature. Edited by Arnold Armin. Arundel: Centaur Press, Ltd., 1962.

The Collected Letters of D. H. Lawrence. 2 vols. Edited by Harry T. Moore. New York: The Viking Press, 1962.

The Complete Poems of D. H. Lawrence. 2 vols. Edited by Vivian de Sola Pinto and Warren Roberts. New York: The Viking Press, 1964. London: Heinemann, 1964.

The Collected Plays of D. H. Lawrence. New York: The Viking Press, 1965.

Phoenix II: Uncollected, Unpublished, and Other Prose Works. Edited by Warren Roberts and Harry T. Moore. New York: The Viking Press, 1968; London: Heinemann, 1968.

SONS AND LOVERS: SECONDARY SOURCES

Material reprinted in this volume is cited in the respective title notes.

Appleman, Philip. "D. H. Lawrence and the Intrusive Knock." *Modern Fiction Studies*, III (Winter 1957), 330–331.

Beebe, Maurice. "Lawrence's Sacred Fount: The Artist Theme of *Sons and Lovers*." *Texas Studies in Literature and Language*, IV (1962), 539–552.

Brewster, Dorothy, and Burrell, Angus. *Modern Fiction*. New York: Columbia University Press, 1935, pp. 137–47.

Corke, Helen. "D. H. Lawrence as I Saw Him." *Renaissance and Modern Studies*, IV (1960), 5–13.

Craig, G. Armour. "D. H. Lawrence on Thinghood and Selfhood." *Massachusetts Review*, I. (October 1959), 56–60.

Daleski, Herman M. *The Forked Flame: A Study of D. H. Lawrence*. Evanston, Ill. Northwestern University Press, 1965.

Draper, R. P. "D. H. Lawrence on Mother Love." *Essays in Criticism*, VIII (July 1958), 285–289.

Frailberg, Lewis. "The Unattainable Self: D. H. Lawrence's *Sons and Lovers*," in *Twelve Original Essays on Great English Novels*. Detroit: Wayne State University Press, 1960, pp. 175–201.

Greene, Thomas. "Lawrence and the Quixotic Hero." *Sewanee Review*, LIX (October 1951), 559–573.

Gregory, Horace. *D. H. Lawrence: Pilgrim of the Apocalypse*. New York: Grove Press, 1957, pp. 17–28.

Hoffman, Frederick J., and Moore, Harry T., eds. *The Achievement of D. H. Lawrence*. Norman, Okla. University of Oklahoma Press, 1953.

Hough, Graham. *The Dark Sun: A Study of D. H. Lawrence*. New York: Macmillan, 1957, pp. 35–54.

Jeffries, C. "Metaphor in *Sons and Lovers*." *The Personalist*, XXIX (July 1948), 287–292.

Kuttner, Alfred Booth. "*Sons and Lovers*: A Freudian Appreciation." *Psychoanalytic Review*, III (1916), 295–317.

Lawrence, Frieda. *The Memoirs and Correspondence of Frieda Lawrence*, edited by E. W. Tedlock, Jr. New York: The Viking Press, 1961.

Leavis, Frank Raymond. *D. H. Lawrence, Novelist*. New York: A. A. Knopf, 1955.

Moore, Harry T. *The Life and Works of D. H. Lawrence*. New York: Twaine Publishers, 1951, pp. 92–106, 365–387.

Muller, Herbert J. *Modern Fiction: A Study of Values*. New York: Funk and Wagnalls, 1937, pp. 269–272.

Murry, John Middleton. *Son of Woman: The Story of D. H. Lawrence*. London: Jonathan Cape, 1931, pp. 5–22.

Nehls, Edward. *D. H. Lawrence: A Composite Biography*. 3 vols. Madison, Wis.: University of Wisconsin Press, 1957–1959.

O'Connor, Frank. *The Mirror in the Roadway: A Study of the Modern Novel.* New York: A. A. Knopf, 1956, pp. 270–279.

Pritchett, V. S. "*Sons and Lovers*," in *The Living Novel.* New York: Reynal and Hitchcock, 1947, pp. 136–142.

Roberts, Warren F. *D. H. Lawrence.* The Soho Bibliographies. London: Rupert Hart-Davis, 1963.

Schorer, Mark. "Technique as Discovery." *The Hudson Review*, I (Spring 1948), 67–78.

Smith, Grover, Jr. "The Doll-Burners: D. H. Lawrence and Louisa Alcott," *Modern Language Quarterly*, XIX (March, 1958), 28–32.

Spilka, Mark, ed. *D. H. Lawrence: A Collection of Critical Essays.* Englewood Cliffs, N.J.: Prentice-Hall, 1963.

Tedlock, E. W. Jr. *D. H. Lawrence and Sons and Lovers: Sources and Criticism.* New York: New York University Press, 1965.

Weiss, Daniel A. *Oedipus in Nottingham: D. H. Lawrence.* Seattle; University of Washington Press, 1962.

White, William. *D. H. Lawrence, A Checklist: Writings about D. H. Lawrence, 1931–1950.* Detroit: Wayne State University Press, 1950.